# The Inspector Rebus Novels

'Rankin ranks alongside P D James and Michael Dibdin as Britain's finest detective novelist' *Scotland on Sunday*

'Rankin captures, like no one else, that strangeness that is Scotland at the end of the twentieth century. He has always written superb crime fiction ... but what he's also pinning down is instant history' *Literary Review*

'Rankin writes laconic, sophisticated, well-paced thrillers' *The Scotsman*

'One of the fastest-rising contemporary British sleuths is Ian Rankin's Inspector John Rebus, a character who's just begging for the right television treatment. Powerful characterisation and a strong sense of place dominate the Rebus novels ... A talent not to be ignored' *Time Out*

'Rankin strips Edinburgh's polite facade to its gritty skeleton' *The Times*

'The internal police politics and corruption in high places are both portrayed with bone-freezing accuracy. This novel should come with a wind-chill factor warning' *Daily Telegraph*

'A brutal but beautifully written series ... Rankin pushes the procedural form well past conventional genre limits' *New York Times*

## By Ian Rankin

*The Inspector Rebus series*
Knots & Crosses
Hide & Seek
Tooth & Nail
(previously published as *Wolfman*)
A Good Hanging & Other Stories
Strip Jack
The Black Book
Mortal Causes
Let It Bleed
Black & Blue
The Hanging Garden
Death Is Not The End (novella)
Dead Souls
Set in Darkness
Rebus: The Early Years
Rebus: The St Leonard's Years
The Falls
Resurrection Men
A Question of Blood
Fleshmarket Close
Rebus: Capital Crimes
Rebus: The Lost Years

*Other novels*
The Flood
Watchman
Westwind

*Writing as Jack Harvey*
Witch Hunt
Bleeding Hearts
Blood Hunt
The Jack Harvey Novels

*Short Stories*
Beggars Banquet
The Complete Short Stories

# The Black Book

---

# Mortal Causes

## Ian Rankin

ORION

*The Black Book*
First published in Great Britain by Orion in 1993

*Mortal Causes*
First published in Great Britain by Orion in 1994

This omnibus edition published in 2005
by Orion Books Ltd
Orion House, 5 Upper St Martin's Lane
London WC2H 9EA

A CIP catalogue record for this book is available
from the British Library.

ISBN 1 89880 086 3

Printed in Great Britain by
Clays Ltd, St Ives plc

# The Black Book

'To the wicked, all things are wicked; but to the just, all things are just and right.'

James Hogg, *The Private Memoirs and Confessions of a Justified Sinner*

The author wishes to acknowledge the assistance of the Chandler-Fulbright Award in the writing of this book.

# Prologue

There were two of them in the van that early morning, lights on to combat the haar which blew in from the North Sea. It was thick and white like smoke. They drove carefully, being under strict instructions.

'Why does it have to be us?' said the driver, stifling a yawn. 'What's wrong with the other two?'

The passenger was much larger than his companion. Though in his forties, he kept his hair long, cut in the shape of a German military helmet. He kept pulling at the hair on the left side of his head, straightening it out. At the moment, however, he was gripping the sides of his seat. He didn't like the way the driver screwed shut his eyes for the duration of each too-frequent yawn. The passenger was not a conversationalist, but maybe talk would keep the driver awake.

'It's just temporary,' he said. 'Besides, it's not as if it's a daily chore.'

'Thank God for that.' The driver shut his eyes again and yawned. The van glided in towards the grass verge.

'Do you want me to drive?' asked the passenger. Then he smiled. 'You could always kip in the back.'

'Very funny. That's another thing, Jimmy, the *stink*!'

'Meat always smells after a while.'

'Got an answer for everything, eh?'

'Yes.'

'Are we nearly there?'

'I thought you knew the way.'

'On the main roads I do. But with this mist.'

'If we're hugging the coast it can't be far.' The passenger was also thinking: if we're hugging the coast, then two wheels past the verge and we're over a cliff face. It wasn't just this that made him nervous. They'd never used the east coast before, but there was too much attention on the west coast now. So it was an untried run, and *that* made him nervous.

'Here's a road sign.' They braked to peer through the haar. 'Next right.' The driver jolted forwards again. He signalled and pulled in through a low iron gate which was padlocked open. 'What if it had been locked?' he offered.

'I've got cutters in the back.'

'A bloody answer for everything.'

They drove into a small gravelled car park. Though they could not see them, there were wooden tables and benches to one side, where Sunday families could picnic and do battle with the midges. The spot was popular for its view, an uninterrupted spread of sea and sky. When they opened their doors, they could smell and hear the sea. Gulls were already shrieking overhead.

'Must be later than we thought if the birds are up.' They readied themselves for opening the back of the van, then did so. The smell really was foul. Even the stoical passenger wrinkled his nose and tried hard not to breathe.

'Quicker the better,' he said in a rush. The body had been placed in two thick plastic fertiliser sacks, one pulled over the feet and one over the head, so that they over-lapped in the middle. Tape and string had been used to join them. Inside the bags were also a number of breeze blocks, making for a heavy and awkward load. They carried the grotesque parcel low, brushing the wet grass. Their shoes were squelching by the time they passed the sign warning about the cliff face ahead. Even more difficult was the climb over the fence, though it was rickety enough to start with.

'Wouldn't stop a bloody kid,' the driver commented. He was peching, the saliva like glue in his mouth.

'Ca' canny,' said the passenger. They shuffled forwards two inches at a time, until they could all too clearly make out the edge. There was no more land after that, just a vertical fall to the agitated sea. 'Right,' he said. Without ceremony, they heaved the thing out into space, glad immediately to be rid of it. 'Let's go.'

'Man, but that air smells good.' The driver reached into his pocket for a quarter-bottle of whisky. They were halfway back to the van when they heard a car on the road, and the crunch of tyres on gravel.

'Aw, hell's bells.'

The headlights caught them as they reached the van.

'The fuckin' polis!' choked the driver.

'Keep the heid,' warned the passenger. His voice was quiet, but his eyes burned ahead of him. They heard a handbrake being engaged, and the car door opened. A uniformed officer appeared. He was carrying a torch. The headlights and engine had been left on. There was no one else in the car.

The passenger knew the score. This wasn't a set-up. Probably the copper came here towards the end of his night shift. There'd be a flask or a blanket in the car. Coffee or a snooze before signing off for the day.

'Morning,' the uniform said. He wasn't young, and he wasn't used to trouble. A Saturday night punch-up maybe, or disputes between neighbouring farmers. It had been another long boring night for him, another night nearer his pension.

'Morning,' the passenger said. He knew they could bluff this one, if the driver stayed calm. But then he thought, *I'm* the conspicuous one.

'A right pea-souper, eh?' said the policeman.

The passenger nodded.

'That's why we stopped,' explained the driver. 'Thought we'd wait it out.'

'Very sensible.'

The driver watched as the passenger turned to the van and started inspecting its rear driver-side tyre, giving it a kick. He then walked to the rear passenger-side and did the same, before getting down on his knees to peer beneath the vehicle. The policeman watched the performance too.

'Got a bit of trouble?'

'Not really,' the driver said nervously. 'But it's best to be safe.'

'I see you've come a ways.'

The driver nodded. 'Off up to Dundee.'

The policeman frowned. 'From Edinburgh? Why didn't you just stick to the motorway or the A914?'

The driver thought quickly. 'We've a drop-off in Tayport first.'

'Even so,' the policeman started. The driver watched as the passenger rose from his inspection, now sited behind the policeman. He was holding a rock in his hand. The driver kept his eyes glued to the policeman's as the rock rose, then fell. The monologue finished mid-sentence as the body slumped to the ground.

'That's just beautiful.'

'What else could we do?' The passenger was already making for his door. 'Come on, vamoose!'

'Aye,' said the driver, 'another minute and he'd have spotted your ... er ...'

The passenger glowered at him. 'What you mean is, another minute and he'd've smelt the booze on your breath.' He didn't stop glowering until the driver shrugged his agreement.

They turned the van and drove out of the car park. The gulls were still noisy in the distance. The police car's engine was turning over. The headlights picked out the prone unconscious figure. But the torch had broken in the fall.

# 1

It all happened because John Rebus was in his favourite massage parlour reading the Bible.

It all happened because a man walked in through the door in the mistaken belief that any massage parlour sited so close to a brewery and half a dozen good pubs had to be catering to Friday night pay packets and anytime drunks; and therefore had to be bent as a paper-clip.

But the Organ Grinder, God-fearing tenant of the set-up, ran a clean shop, a place where tired muscles were beaten mellow. Rebus was tired: tired of arguments with Patience Aitken, tired of the fact that his brother had turned up seeking shelter in a flat filled to the gunwales with students, and most of all tired of his job.

It had been that kind of week.

On the Monday evening, he'd had a call from his Arden Street flat. The students he'd rented to had Patience's number and knew they could reach him there, but this was the first time they'd ever had reason. The reason was Michael Rebus.

'Hello, John.'

Rebus recognised the voice at once. 'Mickey?'

'How are you, John?'

'Christ, Mickey. Where are you? No, scratch that, I know where you are. I mean –' Michael was laughing softly. 'It's just I heard you'd gone south.'

'Didn't work out.' His voice dropped. 'Thing is, John,

can we talk? I've been dreading this, but I really need to talk to you.'

'Okay.'

'Shall I come round there?'

Rebus thought quickly. Patience was picking up her two nieces from Waverley Station, but all the same ... 'No, stay where you are. I'll come over. The students are a good lot, maybe they'll fix you a cup of tea or a joint while you're waiting.'

There was silence on the line, then Michael's voice: 'I could have done without that.' The line went dead.

Michael Rebus had served three years of a five-year sentence for drug dealing. During that time, John Rebus had visited his brother fewer than half a dozen times. He'd felt relief more than anything when, upon release, Michael had taken a bus to London. That was two years ago, and the brothers had not exchanged a word since. But now Michael was back, bringing with him bad memories of a period in John Rebus's life he'd rather not remember.

The Arden Street flat was suspiciously tidy when he arrived. Only two of the student tenants were around, the couple who slept in what had been Rebus's bedroom. He talked to them in the hallway. They were just going out to the pub, but handed over to him another letter from the Inland Revenue. Really, Rebus would have liked them to stay. When they left, there was silence in the flat. Rebus knew that Michael would be in the living room and he was, crouched in front of the stereo and flipping through stacks of records.

'Look at this lot,' Michael said, his back still to Rebus. 'The Beatles and the Stones, same stuff you used to listen to. Remember how you drove dad daft? What was that record player again ...?'

'A Dansette.'

'That's it. Dad got it saving cigarette coupons.' Michael stood up and turned towards his brother. 'Hello, John.'

'Hello, Michael.'

They didn't hug or shake hands. They just sat down, Rebus on the chair, Michael on the sofa.

'This place has changed,' Michael said.

'I had to buy a few sticks of furniture before I could rent it out.' Already Rebus had noticed a few things – cigarette burns on the carpet, posters (against his explicit instructions) sellotaped to the wallpaper. He opened the taxman's letter.

'You should have seen them leap into action when I told them you were coming round. Hoovering and washing dishes. Who says students are lazy?'

'They're okay.'

'So when did this all happen?'

'A few months ago.'

'They told me you're living with a doctor.'

'Her name's Patience.'

Michael nodded. He looked pale and ill. Rebus tried not to be interested, but he was. The letter from the tax office hinted strongly that they knew he was renting his flat, and didn't he want to declare the income? The back of his head was tingling. It did that when he was fractious, ever since it had been burned in the fire. The doctors said there was nothing he or they could do about it.

Except, of course, not get fractious.

He stuffed the letter into his pocket. 'What do you want, Mickey?'

'Bottom line, John, I need a place to stay. Just for a week or two, till I can get on my feet.' Rebus stared stonily at the posters on the walls as Michael ran on. He wanted to find work ... money was tight ... he'd take any job ... he just needed a chance.

'That's all, John, just one chance.'

Rebus was thinking. Patience had room in her flat, of course. There was space enough there even with the nieces staying. But no way was Rebus going to take his brother back to Oxford Terrace. Things weren't going that well as it was. His late hours and her late hours, his exhaustion and hers, his job involvement and hers. Rebus couldn't see Michael improving things. He thought: I am not my brother's keeper. But all the same.

'We might squeeze you into the box room. I'd have to talk to the students about it.' He couldn't see them saying no, but it seemed polite to ask. How *could* they say no? He was their landlord and flats were hard to find. Especially good flats, especially in Marchmont.

'That would be great.' Michael sounded relieved. He got up from the sofa and walked over to the door of the box room. This was a large ventilated cupboard off the living room. Just big enough for a single bed and a chest of drawers, if you took all the boxes and the rubbish out of it.

'We could probably store all that stuff in the cellar,' said Rebus, standing just behind his brother.

'John,' said Michael, 'the way I feel, I'd be happy enough sleeping in the cellar myself.' And when he turned towards his brother, there were tears in Michael Rebus's eyes.

On Wednesday, Rebus began to realise that his world was a black comedy.

Michael had been moved into the Arden Street flat without any fuss. Rebus had informed Patience of his brother's return, but had said little more than that. She was spending a lot of time with her sister's girls anyway. She'd taken a few days off work to show them Edinburgh. It looked like hard going. Susan at fifteen wanted to do all the things which Jenny, aged eight, didn't or couldn't. Rebus felt almost totally excluded from this female triumvirate, though he would sneak into Jenny's room at night just to re-live the magic and innocence of a child asleep. He also spent time trying to avoid Susan, who seemed only too aware of the differences between women and men.

He was kept busy at work, which meant he didn't think about Michael more than a few dozen times each day. Ah, work, now there was a thing. When Great London Road police station had burnt down, Rebus had been moved to St Leonard's, which was Central District's divisional HQ.

With him had come Detective Sergeant Brian Holmes and, to both their dismays, Chief Superintendent 'Farmer' Watson and Chief Inspector 'Fart' Lauderdale. There had been compensations – newer offices and furniture, better amenities and equipment – but not enough. Rebus was still trying to come to terms with his new workplace. Everything was so tidy, he could never find anything, as a result of which he was always keen to get out of the office and onto the street.

Which was why he ended up at a butcher's shop on South Clerk Street, staring down at a stabbed man.

The man had already been tended to by a local doctor, who'd been standing in line waiting for some pork chops and gammon steaks when the man staggered into the shop. The wound had been dressed initially with a clean butcher's apron, and now everyone was waiting for a stretcher to be unloaded from the ambulance outside.

A constable was filling Rebus in.

'I was only just up the road, so he couldn't have been here more than five minutes when somebody told me, and I came straight here. That's when I radioed in.'

Rebus had picked up the constable's radio message in his car, and had decided to stop by. He kind of wished he hadn't. There was blood smeared across the floor, colouring the sawdust which lay there. Why some butchers still scattered sawdust on their floors he couldn't say. There was also a palm-shaped daub of blood on the white-tiled wall, and another less conclusive splash of the stuff below this.

The wounded man had also left a trail of gleaming drips

outside, all the way along and halfway up Lutton Place (insultingly close to St Leonard's), where they suddenly stopped kerbside.

The man's name was Rory Kintoul, and he had been stabbed in the abdomen. This much they knew. They didn't know much more, because Rory Kintoul was refusing to speak about the incident. This was not an attitude shared by those who had been in the butcher's at the time. They were outside now, passing on news of the excitement to the crowd who had stopped to gawp through the shop window. It reminded Rebus of Saturday afternoon in the St James Centre, when pockets of men would gather outside the TV rental shops, hoping to catch the football scores.

Rebus crouched over Kintoul, just a little intimidatingly.

'And where do you live, Mr Kintoul?'

But the man was not about to answer. A voice came from the other side of the glass display case.

'Duncton Terrace.' The speaker was wearing a bloodied butcher's apron and cleaning a heavy knife on a towel. 'That's in Dalkeith.'

Rebus looked at the butcher. 'And you are . . .?'

'Jim Bone. This is my shop.'

'And you know Mr Kintoul?'

Kintoul had turned his head awkwardly, seeking the butcher's face, as if trying to influence his answer. But, slouched as he was against the display case, he would have required demonic possession to effect such a move.

'I ought to,' said the butcher. 'He's my cousin.'

Rebus was about to say something, but at that moment the stretcher was trolleyed in by two ambulancemen, one of whom almost skited on the slippery floor. It was as they positioned the stretcher in front of Kintoul that Rebus saw something which would stay with him. There were two signs in the display cabinet, one pinned into a side of corned beef, the other into a slab of red sirloin.

12

Cold Cuts, one said. The other stated simply, Fleshing. A large fresh patch of blood was left on the floor as they lifted the butcher's cousin. Cold Cuts and Fleshing. Rebus shivered and made for the door.

On the Friday after work, Rebus decided on a massage. He had promised Patience he'd be in by eight, and it was only six now. Besides, a brutal pummelling always seemed to set him up for the weekend.

But first he wandered into the Broadsword for a pint of the local brew. They didn't come more local than Gibson's Dark, a heavy beer made only six hundred yards away at the Gibson Brewery. A brewery, a pub and a massage parlour: Rebus reckoned if you threw in a good Indian restaurant and a corner shop open till midnight he could live happily here for ever and a day.

Not that he didn't like living with Patience in her Oxford Terrace garden flat. It represented the other side of the tracks, so to speak. Certainly, it seemed a world away from this disreputable corner of Edinburgh, one of many such corners. Rebus wondered why he was so drawn to them.

The air outside was filled with the yeasty smell of beer-making, vying with the even stronger aromas from the city's other much larger breweries. The Broadsword was a popular watering hole, and like most of Edinburgh's popular pubs, it boasted a mixed clientele: students and low lifes with the occasional businessman. The bar had few pretensions; all it had in its favour were good beer and a good cellar. The weekend had already started, and Rebus was squeezed in at the bar, next to a man whose immense alsatian dog was sleeping on the floor behind the barstools. It took up the standing room of at least two adult men, but nobody was asking it to shift. Further along the bar, someone was drinking with one hand and keeping another proprietorial hand on a coatstand which

Rebus assumed they'd just bought at one of the nearby secondhand shops. Everyone at the bar was drinking the same dark brew.

Though there were half a dozen pubs within a five-minute walk of here, only the Broadsword stocked draught Gibson's, the other pubs being tied to one or other of the big breweries. Rebus started to wonder, as the beer slipped down, what effect it would have on his metabolism once the Organ Grinder got to work. He decided against a refill, and instead made for O-Gee's, which was what the Organ Grinder had called his shop. Rebus liked the name; it made the same sound customers made once the Grinder himself got to work – 'Oh Jeez!' But they were always careful not to say anything out loud. The Organ Grinder didn't like to hear blasphemy on the massage table. It upset him, and nobody wanted to be in the hands of an upset Organ Grinder. Nobody wanted to be his monkey.

So, there he was sitting with the Bible in his lap, waiting for his six-thirty appointment. The Bible was the only reading matter on the premises, courtesy of the Organ Grinder himself. Rebus had read it before, but didn't mind reading it again.

Then the front door burst open.

'Where's the girls, eh?' This new client was not only misinformed, but also considerably drunk. There was no way the Grinder would handle drunks.

'Wrong place, pal.' Rebus was about to make mention of a couple of nearby parlours which would be certain to offer the necessary Thai assisted sauna and rub-down, but the man stopped him with a thick pointed finger.

'John bloody Rebus, you son of a shite-breeks!'

Rebus frowned, trying to place the face. His mind flipped through two decades of mug shots. The man saw Rebus's confusion, and spread his hands wide. 'Deek Torrance, you don't remember?'

Rebus shook his head. Torrance was walking determinedly forward. Rebus clenched his fists, ready for anything.

'We went through parachute training together,' said Torrance. 'Christ, you must remember!'

And suddenly Rebus did remember. He remembered everything, the whole black comedy of his past.

They drank in the Broadsword, swopping stories. Deek hadn't lasted in the Parachute Regiment. After a year he'd had enough, and not too long after that he'd bought his way out of the Army altogether.

'Too restless, John, that was my problem. What was yours?'

Rebus shook his head and drank some more beer. 'My problem, Deek? You couldn't put a name to it.' But a name *had* been put to it, first by Mickey's sudden appearance, and now by Deek Torrance. Ghosts, both of them, but Rebus didn't want to be their Scrooge. He bought another round.

'You always said you were going to try for the SAS,' Torrance said.

Rebus shrugged. 'It didn't work out.'

The bar was busier than ever, and at one point Torrance was jostled by a young man trying to manoeuvre a double bass through the mêlée.

'Could you no' leave that outside?'

'Not around here.'

Torrance turned back to Rebus. 'Did you see thon?'

Rebus merely smiled. He felt good after the massage. 'No one brings anything small into a bar around here.' He watched Deek Torrance grunt. Yes, he remembered him now, all right. He'd gotten fatter and balder, his face was roughened and much fleshier than it had been. He didn't even sound the same, not exactly. But there was that one characteristic: the Torrance grunt. A man of few words, Deek Torrance had been. Not now, though, now he had plenty to say.

'So what do you do, Deek?'

Torrance grinned. 'Seeing you're a copper I better not say.' Rebus bided his time. Torrance was drunk to the point of slavering. Sure enough, he couldn't resist. 'I'm in buying and selling, mostly selling.'

'And what do you sell?'

Torrance leaned closer. 'Am I talking to the polis or an old pal?'

'A pal,' said Rebus. 'Strictly off-duty. So what do you sell?'

Torrance grunted. 'Anything you like, John. I'm sort of like Jenners department store ... only I can get things they can't.'

'Such as?' Rebus was looking at the clock above the bar. It couldn't be that late, surely. They always ran the clock ten minutes fast here, but even so.

'Anything at all,' said Torrance. 'Anything from a shag to a shooter. You name it.'

'How about a watch?' Rebus started winding his own. 'Mine only seems to go for a couple of hours at a stretch.'

Torrance looked at it. 'Longines,' he said, pronouncing the word correctly, 'you don't want to chuck that. Get it cleaned, it'll be fine. Mind you, I could probably part-ex it against a Rolex ...?'

'So you sell dodgy watches.'

'Did I say that? I don't recall saying that. *Anything*, John. Whatever the client wants, I'll fetch it for him.' Torrance winked.

'Listen, what time do you make it?'

Torrance shrugged and pulled up the sleeve of his jacket. He wasn't wearing a watch. Rebus was thinking. He'd kept his appointment with the Grinder, Deek happy to wait for him in the anteroom. And afterwards they'd still had time for a pint or two before he had to make his way home. They'd had two ... no, three drinks so far.

16

Maybe he was running a bit late. He caught the barman's attention and tapped at his wrist.

'Twenty past eight,' called the barman.

'I'd better phone Patience,' said Rebus.

But someone was using the public phone to cement some romance. What's more, they'd dragged the receiver into the ladies' toilet so that they could hear above the noise from the bar. The telephone cord was stretched taut, ready to garotte anyone trying to use the toilets. Rebus bided his time, then began staring at the wall-mounted telephone cradle. What the hell. He pushed his finger down on the cradle, released it, then moved back into the throng of drinkers. A young man appeared from inside the ladies' toilet and slammed the receiver hard back into its cradle. He checked for change in his pocket, had none, and started to make for the bar.

Rebus moved in on the phone. He picked it up, but could hear no tone. He tried again, then tried dialling. Nothing. Something had obviously come loose when the man had slammed the receiver home. Shite on a stick. It was nearly half past eight now, and it would take fifteen minutes to drive back to Oxford Terrace. He was going to pay dearly for this.

'You look like you could use a drink,' said Deek Torrance when Rebus joined him at the bar.

'Know what, Deek?' said Rebus. 'My life's a black comedy.'

'Oh well, better than a tragedy, eh?'

Rebus was beginning to wonder what the difference was.

He got back to the flat at twenty past nine. Probably Patience had cooked a meal for the four of them. Probably she'd waited fifteen minutes or so before eating. She'd have kept his meal warm for another fifteen minutes, then dumped it. If it was fish, the cat would have eaten it. Otherwise its destination would be the compost heap in the garden. This had happened before, too many times, really. Yet it kept on happening, and Rebus wasn't sure the excuses of an old friend or a broken watch would work any kind of spell.

The steps down to the garden flat were worn and slippery. Rebus took them carefully, and so was slow to notice the large sports holdall which, illuminated by the orange street-lamp, was sitting on the rattan mat outside the front door of the flat. It was his bag. He unzipped it and looked in. On top of some clothes and a pair of shoes there was a note. He read it through twice.

Don't bother trying the door, I've bolted it. I've also disconnected the doorbell, and the phone is off the hook for the weekend. I'll leave another load of your stuff on the front step Monday morning.

The note needed no signature. Rebus whistled a long breathy note, then tried his key in the lock. It didn't budge. He pressed the doorbell. No sound. As a last resort, he crouched down and peered in through the letterbox. The hall was in darkness, no sign of light from any of the rooms.

'Something came up,' he called. No response. 'I tried phoning, I couldn't get through.' Still nothing. He waited a few more moments, half-expecting Jenny at least to break the silence. Or Susan, she was a right stirrer of trouble. And a heartbreaker too, by the look of her. 'Bye, Patience,' he called. 'Bye, Susan. Bye, Jenny.' Still silence. 'I'm sorry.'

He truly was.

'Just one of those weeks,' he said to himself, picking up the bag.

On Sunday morning, in weak sunshine and a snell wind, Andrew McPhail sneaked back into Edinburgh. He'd been away a long time, and the city had changed. Everywhere and everything had changed. He was still jetlagged from several days ago, and poorer than he should have been due to London's inflated prices. He walked from the bus station to the Broughton area of town, just off Leith Walk. It wasn't a long walk, but every step seemed heavy, though his bags were light. He'd slept badly on the bus, but that was nothing new: he couldn't remember when he'd last had a good night's sleep, sleep without dreams.

The sun looked as though it might disappear at any minute. Thick clouds were pushing in over Leith. McPhail tried to walk faster. He had an address in his pocket, the address of a boarding house. He'd phoned last night, and his landlady was expecting him. She sounded nice on the phone, but it was difficult to tell. He wouldn't mind, no matter what she was like, so long as she kept quiet. He knew that his leaving Canada had been in the Canadian newspapers, and even in some of the American ones, and he supposed that journalists here would be after him for a story. He'd been surprised at slipping so quietly into Heathrow. No one seemed to know who he was, and that was good.

He wanted nothing but a quiet life, though perhaps not as quiet as a few of the past years.

He'd phoned his sister from London and asked her to check directory enquiries for a Mrs MacKenzie in the Bellevue area. (Directory enquiries in London hadn't gone out of their way to help.) Melanie and her mother had lodged with Mrs MacKenzie when he'd first met them, before they moved in together. Alexis was a single parent, a DSS case. Mrs MacKenzie had been a more sympathetic landlady than most. Not that he'd ever visited Melanie and her mum there – Mrs MacKenzie wouldn't have liked it.

She didn't take lodgers much these days, but she was a good Christian and McPhail was persuasive.

19

He stood outside the house. It was a plain two-storey construction finished off in grey pebbledash and ugly double glazing. It looked just the same as the houses either side of it. Mrs MacKenzie answered the door as though she'd been ready for him for some time. She fussed about in the living room and kitchen, then led him upstairs to show him the bathroom, and then finally his own bedroom. It was no larger than a prison cell, but had been nicely decorated (sometime in the mid-1960s, he'd guess). It was fine, he'd no complaints.

'It's lovely,' he told Mrs MacKenzie, who shrugged her shoulders as if to say, of course it is.

'There's tea in the pot,' she said. 'I'll just go make us a cuppy.' Then she remembered something. 'No cooking in the room, mind.'

Andrew McPhail shook his head. 'I don't cook,' he said. She thought of something else and crossed to the window, where the net curtains were still closed.

'Here, I'll open these. You can open a window too, if you want some fresh air.'

'Fresh air would be nice,' he agreed. They both looked out of the window down onto the street.

'It's quiet,' she said. 'Not too much traffic. Of course, there's always a wee bit of noise during the day.'

McPhail could see what she was referring to: there was an old school building across the road with a black iron fence in front of it. It wasn't a large school, probably primary. McPhail's window looked down onto the school gates, just to the right of the main building. Directly behind the gates was the deserted playground.

'I'll get that tea,' said Mrs MacKenzie. When she'd gone, McPhail placed his cases on the springy single bed. Beside the bed was a small writing desk and chair. He lifted the chair and placed it in front of the window, then sat down. He moved a small glass clown further along the sill so that he could rest his chin where it had been. Nothing obscured his view. He sat there in a dream, looking at the playground, until Mrs MacKenzie called to him that the tea was in the living room. 'And a Madeira cake, too.' Andrew McPhail got up with a sigh. He didn't really want the tea now, but he supposed he could always bring it up to his room and leave it untouched till later. He felt tired, bone tired, but he was home and something told him that tonight he would sleep the sleep of the dead.

'Coming, Mrs MacKenzie,' he called, tearing his gaze away from the school.

# 2

On Monday morning word went around St Leonard's police station that Inspector John Rebus was in an impressively worse mood than usual. Some found this hard to believe, and were almost willing to get close enough to Rebus to find out for themselves ... almost.

Others had no choice.

DS Brian Holmes and DC Siobhan Clarke, seated with Rebus in their sectioned-off chunk of the CID room, had the look of people who were resting their backsides on soft-boiled eggs.

'So,' Rebus was saying, 'what about Rory Kintoul?'

'He's out of hospital, sir,' said Siobhan Clarke.

Rebus nodded impatiently. He was waiting for her to put a foot wrong. It wasn't because she was English, or a graduate, or had wealthy parents who'd bought her a flat in the New Town. It wasn't because she was a she. It was just Rebus's way of dealing with young officers.

'And he's still not talking,' said Holmes. 'He won't say what happened, and he's certainly not pressing any charges.'

Brian Holmes looked tired. Rebus noticed this from the corner of his eye. He didn't want to make eye-contact with Holmes, didn't want Holmes to realise that they now had something in common.

Both had been kicked out by their girlfriends.

It had happened to Holmes just over a month ago. As Holmes revealed later, once he'd moved in with an aunt in Barnton, it was all to do with children. He hadn't realised how strongly Nell wanted a baby, and had started to joke about it. Then one day, she'd blown up – an awesome sight – and kicked him out, watched by most of the female neighbours in their mining village south of Edinburgh. Apparently the women neighbours had applauded as Holmes scurried off.

Now, he was working harder than ever. (This also had been a cause of strife between the couple: her hours were fairly regular, his anything but.) He reminded Rebus of a frayed and faded pair of work denims, not far from the end of their life.

'What are you saying?' Rebus asked.

'I'm saying I think we should drop it, sir, with all respect.'

'"With all respect", Brian? That's what people say when they mean "you fucking idiot".' Rebus still wasn't looking at Holmes, but he could feel the young man blushing. Clarke was looking down at her lap.

'Listen,' said Rebus, 'this guy, he staggers a couple of hundred yards with a two-inch gash in his gut. Why?' No answer was forthcoming. 'Why,' Rebus persisted, 'does he walk past a dozen shops, only stopping at his cousin's?'

'Maybe he was making for a doctor's, but had to stop,' Clarke suggested.

'Maybe,' said Rebus dismissively. 'Funny that he can make it into his *cousin's* shop, though.'

'You think it's something to do with the cousin, sir?'

'Let me ask the both of you something else.' Rebus stood up and took a few paces, then retraced his steps, catching Holmes and Clarke exchanging a glance. It set Rebus wondering. At first, there had been sparks between them, sparks of antagonism. But now they were working well together. He just hoped the relationship didn't go further than that. 'Let me ask you this,' he said. 'What do we know about the victim?'

'Not much,' said Holmes.

'He lives in Dalkeith,' Clarke offered. 'Works as a lab technician in the Infirmary. Married, one son.' She shrugged.

'That's it?' asked Rebus.

'That's it, sir.'

'Exactly,' said Rebus. 'He's nobody, a nothing. Not one person we've talked to has had a bad word to say about him. So tell me this: how did he end up getting stabbed? And in the middle of a Wednesday morning? If it had been a mugger, surely he'd tell us about it. As it is, he's clammed up as tight as an Aberdonian's purse at a church collection. He's got something to hide. Christ knows what, but it involves a car.'

'How do you work that out, sir?'

'The blood starts at the kerb, Holmes. Looks to me like he got out of a car and at that point he was already wounded.'

'He drives, sir, but doesn't own a car at present.'

'Smart girl, Clarke.' She prickled at 'girl', but Rebus was talking again. 'And he'd taken a half day off work without telling his wife.' He sat down again. 'Why, why, why? I want the two of you to have another go at him. Tell him we're not happy with his lack of a story. If he can't think of one, we'll pester him till he does. Let him know we mean business.' Rebus paused. 'And after that, do a check on the butcher.'

'Chop chop, sir,' commented Holmes. He was saved by the phone ringing. Rebus picked up the receiver. Maybe it would be Patience.

'DI Rebus.'

'John, can you come to my office?'

It wasn't Patience, it was the Chief Super. 'Two minutes, sir,' said Rebus, putting down the phone. Then, to Holmes and Clarke: 'Get onto it.'

'Yes, sir.'

'You think I'm making too much of this, Brian?'

'Yes, sir.'

'Well, maybe I am. But I don't like a mystery, no matter how small. So bugger off and satisfy my curiosity.'

As they rose, Holmes nodded towards the large suitcase which Rebus had placed behind his desk, supposedly out of view. 'Something I should know about?'

'Yes,' said Rebus. 'It's where I keep all my graft payments. Yours still probably fit in your back pooch.' Holmes didn't look like budging, though Clarke had already retreated to her own desk. Rebus expelled air and lowered his voice. 'I've just joined the ranks of the dispossessed.' Holmes' face became animated. 'Not a bloody word, mind. This is between you and me.'

'Understood.' Holmes thought of something. 'You know, most evenings I eat at the Heartbreak Cafe ...'

'I'll know where to find you then, if I ever need to hear any early Elvis.'

Holmes nodded. 'And Vegas Elvis too. All I mean is, if there's anything I can do ...'

'You could start by disguising yourself as me and trotting along to see Farmer Watson.'

But Holmes was shaking his head. 'I meant anything within reason.'

Within reason. Rebus wondered if it was within reason to be asking the students to put up with him sleeping on the sofa while his brother slept in the box room. Maybe he should offer to lower the rent. When he'd arrived at the flat unannounced on Friday night, three of the students and Michael had been sitting cross-legged on the floor rolling joints and listening to mid-period Rolling Stones. Rebus stared in horror at the cigarette papers in Michael's hand.

'For fuck's sake, Mickey!' So at last Michael Rebus had elicited a reaction from his big brother. The students at least had the grace to look like the criminals they were. 'You're lucky,' Rebus told them all, 'that at this exact second I don't give a shit.'

'Go on, John,' said Michael, offering a half-smoked cigarette. 'It can't do any harm.'

'That's what I mean.' Rebus drew a bottle of whisky out of the carrier-bag he was holding. 'But this can.'

He had proceeded to spend the final hours of the evening sprawled across the sofa supping whisky and singing along to any old record that was put on the turntable. He'd spent much of the weekend in the same spot, too. The students hadn't seemed to mind, though he'd made them put away the drugs for the duration. They cleaned the flat around him, with Michael pitching in, and everyone trooped out to the pub on Saturday night leaving Rebus with the TV and some cans of beer. It didn't look as though Michael had told the students about his prison record; Rebus hoped he'd keep it that way. Michael had offered to move out, or at least give his brother the box room, but Rebus refused. He wasn't sure why.

On Sunday he went to Oxford Terrace, but there didn't seem to be anyone home, and his key still wouldn't open the door. So either the lock had been changed or Patience was hiding in there somewhere, going through her own version of cold turkey with the kids for company.

Now he stood outside Farmer Watson's door and looked down at himself. Sure enough, when he'd gone to Oxford Terrace this morning Patience had left a suitcase of stuff for him outside the door. No note, just the case. He'd changed into the clean suit in the police station toilets. It was a bit crumpled but no more so than anything he usually wore. He hadn't a tie to match, though: Patience had included two horrible brown ties (were they really *his?*) along with the dark blue suit. Brown ties don't make it. He knocked once on the door before opening it.

'Come in, John, come in.' It seemed to Rebus that the

Farmer too was having trouble making St Leonard's fit his ways. The place just didn't feel right. 'Take a seat.' Rebus looked around for a chair. There was one beside the wall, loaded high with files. He lifted these off and tried to find space for them on the floor. If anything, the Chief Super had less space in his office than Rebus himself. 'Still waiting for those bloody filing cabinets,' he admitted. Rebus swung the chair over to the desk and sat down.

'What's up, sir?'

'How are things?'

'Things?'

'Yes.'

'Things are fine, sir.' Rebus wondered if the Farmer knew about Patience. Surely not.

'DC Clarke getting on all right, is she?'

'I've no complaints.'

'Good. We've got a bit of a job coming up, joint operation with Trading Standards.'

'Oh?'

'Chief Inspector Lauderdale will fill in the details, but I wanted to sound you out first, check how things are going.'

'What sort of joint operation?'

'Money lending,' said Watson. 'I forgot to ask, do you want coffee?' Rebus shook his head and watched as Watson bent over in his chair. There being so little space in the room, he'd taken to keeping his coffee-maker on the floor behind his desk, where twice so far to Rebus's knowledge he'd spilt it all across the new beige carpet. When Watson sat up again, he held in his meaty fist a cup of the devil's own drink. The Chief Super's coffee was a minor legend in Edinburgh.

'Money lending with some protection on the side,' Watson corrected. 'But mostly money lending.'

The same old sad story, in other words. People who wouldn't stand a chance in any bank, and with nothing

27

worth pawning, could still borrow money, no matter how bad a risk. The problem was, of course, that the interest ran into the hundreds per cent and arrears could soon mount, bringing more prohibitive interest. It was the most vicious circle of all, vicious because at the end of it all lay intimidation, beatings and worse.

Suddenly, Rebus knew why the Chief Super had wanted this little chat. 'It's not Big Ger, is it?' he asked.

Watson nodded. 'In a way,' he said.

Rebus sprang to his feet. 'This'll be the fourth time in as many years! He always gets off. You know that, I know that!' Normally, he would have recited this on the move, but there was no floorspace worth the name, so he just stood there like a Sunday ranter at the foot of The Mound. 'It's a waste of time trying to pin him on money lending. I thought we'd been through all this a dozen times and decided it was useless going after him without trying another tack.'

'I know, John, I know, but the Trading Standards people are worried. The problem seems bigger than they thought.'

'Bloody Trading Standards.'

'Now, John ...'

'But,' Rebus paused, 'with respect, sir, it's a complete waste of time and manpower. There'll be a surveillance, we'll take a few photos, we'll arrest a couple of the poor saps who act as runners, and nobody'll testify. If the Procurator Fiscal wants Big Ger nailed, then they should give us the resources so we can mount a decent size of operation.'

The problem, of course, was that nobody wanted to nail Morris Gerald Cafferty (known to all as Big Ger) as badly as John Rebus did. He wanted a full scale crucifixion. He wanted to be holding the spear, giving one last poke just to make sure the bastard really was dead. Cafferty was scum, but clever scum. There were always flunkies around to go to jail on his behalf. Because Rebus had failed so often to put the man away, he would rather not think of him at all. Now the Farmer was telling him that there was to be an 'operation'. That would mean long days and nights of surveillance, a lot of paperwork, and the arrests of a few pimply apprentice hardmen at the end of it all.

'John,' said Watson, summoning his powers of character analysis, 'I know how you feel. But let's give it one more shot, eh?'

'I know the kind of shot I'd take at Cafferty given half a chance.' Rebus turned his fist into a gun and mimed the recoil.

Watson smiled. 'Then it's lucky we won't be issuing firearms, isn't it?'

After a moment, Rebus smiled too. He sat down again. 'Go on then, sir,' he said, 'I'm listening.'


At eleven o'clock that evening, Rebus was watching TV in the flat. As usual, there was no one else about. They were either still studying in the University library, or else down at the pub. Since Michael wasn't around either, the pub seemed an odds-on bet. He knew the students were wary, expecting him to kick at least one of them out so he could claim a bedroom. They moved around the flat like eviction notices.

He'd phoned Patience three times, getting the answering machine on each occasion and telling it that he knew she was there and why didn't she pick up the phone?

As a result, the phone was on the floor beside the sofa, and when it rang he dangled an arm, picked up the receiver, and held it to his ear.

'Hello?'

'John?'

Rebus sat up fast. 'Patience, thank Christ you –'

'Listen, this is important.'

'I know it is. I know I was stupid, but you've got to believe –'

'Just listen, will you!' Rebus shut up and listened. He would do whatever she told him, no question. 'They thought you'd be here, so someone from the station just phoned. It's Brian Holmes.'

'What did he want?'

'No, they were phoning *about* him.'

'What about him?'

'He's been in some sort of . . . I don't know. Anyway, he's hurt.'

Still holding the receiver, Rebus stood up, hauling the whole apparatus off the floor with him. 'Where is he?'

'Somewhere in Haymarket, some bar . . .'

'The Heartbreak Cafe?'

'That's it. And listen, John?'

'Yes?'

'We will talk. But not yet. Just give me time.'

'Whatever you say, Patience. Bye.' John Rebus dropped the phone from his hand and grabbed his jacket.

Rebus was parking outside the Heartbreak Cafe barely seven minutes later. That was the beauty of Edinburgh when you could avoid traffic lights. The Heartbreak Cafe had been opened just over a year before by a chef who also happened to be an Elvis Presley fan. He had used some of his extensive memorabilia to decorate the interior, and his cooking skills to come up with a menu which was almost worth a visit even if, like Rebus, you'd never liked Elvis. Holmes had raved about the place since its opening, drooling for hours over the dessert called Blue Suede Choux. The Cafe operated as a bar too, with garish cocktails and 1950s music, plus bottled American beers whose prices would have caused convulsions in the Broadsword pub. Rebus got the idea that Holmes had become friends with the owner; certainly, he'd been spending a lot of time there since the split from Nell, and had put on a fair few pounds as a result.

From the outside, the place looked nothing special: pale cement front wall with a narrow rectangular window in the middle, most of which was filled with neon signs advertising beers. And above this a larger neon sign flashing the name of the restaurant. The action wasn't here, however. Holmes had been set on around the back of the place. A narrow alley, just about able to accommodate the width of a Ford Cortina, led to the patrons' car park. This was small by any restaurant's standards, and was also where the overflowing refuse bins were kept. Most clients, Rebus guessed, would park on the street out front. Holmes only parked back here because he spent so much time in the bar, and because his car had once been scratched when he'd left it out front.

There were two cars in the car park. One was Holmes', and the other almost certainly belonged to the owner of the Heartbreak Cafe. It was an old Ford Capri with a painting of Elvis on its bonnet. Brian Holmes lay between the two cars. So far no one had moved him. He would be moved soon, though, after the doctor had finished his examination. One of the officers present recognised Rebus and came over.

'Nasty blow to the back of the head. He's been out cold for at least twenty minutes. That's how long ago he was found. The owner of the place – that's who found him – recognised him and called in. Could be a fractured skull.'

Rebus nodded, saying nothing, his eyes on the prone figure of his colleague. The other detective was still talking, going on about how Holmes' breathing was regular, the usual reassurances. Rebus walked towards the body, standing over the kneeling doctor. The doctor didn't even glance up, but ordered a uniformed constable, who was holding a flashlight over Brian Holmes, to move it a bit to the left. He then started examining that section of Holmes' skull.

Rebus couldn't see any blood, but that didn't mean much. People died all the time without losing any blood over it. Christ, Brian looked so at peace. It was almost like staring into a casket. He turned to the detective.

'What's the owner's name again?'

'Eddie Ringan.'

'Is he inside?'

The detective nodded. 'Propping up the bar.'

That figured. 'I'll just go have a word,' said Rebus.

Eddie Ringan had nursed what was euphemistically called a drinking problem for several years, long before he'd opened the Heartbreak Cafe. For this reason, people reckoned the venture would fail, as other ventures of his had. But they reckoned wrong, for the sole reason that Eddie managed to find a manager, a manager who not only was some kind of financial guru but was also as straight and as strong as a construction girder. He didn't rip Eddie off, and he kept Eddie where Eddie belonged during working hours – in the kitchen.

Eddie still drank, but he could cook and drink; that wasn't a problem. Especially when there were one or two apprentice chefs around to do the stuff which required focused eyes or rock steady hands. And so, according to Brian Holmes, the Heartbreak Cafe thrived. He still hadn't managed to persuade Rebus to join him there for a meal of King Shrimp Creole or Love Me Tenderloin. Rebus wasn't persuaded to walk through the front door ... until tonight.

The lights were still on. It was like walking into some teenager's shrine to his idol. There were Elvis posters on the walls, Elvis record covers, a life-size cut-out figure of the performer, even an Elvis clock, with the King's arms pointing to the time. The TV was on, an item on the late news. Some oversized charity cheque was being handed over in front of Gibson's Brewery.

There was no one in the place except Eddie Ringan slumped on a barstool, and another man behind the bar, pouring two shots of Jim Beam. Rebus introduced himself and was invited to take a seat. The bartender introduced himself as Pat Calder.

'I'm Mr Ringan's partner.' The way he said it made Rebus wonder if the two young men were more than merely business partners. Holmes hadn't mentioned Eddie was gay. He turned his attention to the chef.

Eddie Ringan was probably in his late twenties, but looked ten years older. He had straight, thinning hair over a large oval-shaped head, all of which sat uneasily above the larger oval of his body. Rebus had seen fat chefs and fatter chefs, and Ringan surely was a living advertisement for *some*body's cooking. His doughy face was showing signs of wear from the drink; not just this evening's scoop, but the weeks and months of steady, heavy consumption. Rebus watched him drain the inch of amber fire in a single savouring swallow.

'Gimme another.'

But Pat Calder shook his head. 'Not if you're driving.' Then, in clear and precise tones: 'This man is a police officer, Eddie. He's come to talk about Brian.'

Eddie Ringan nodded. 'He fell down, hit his head.'

'Is that what you think?' asked Rebus.

'Not really.' For the first time, Ringan looked up from the bartop and into Rebus's eyes. 'Maybe it was a mugger, or maybe it was a warning.'

'What sort of a warning?'

'Eddie's had too many tonight, Inspector,' said Pat Calder. 'He starts imagining –'

'I'm not bloody imagining.' Ringan slapped his palm down on the bartop for emphasis. He was still looking at Rebus. 'You know what it's like. It's either protection

33

money – insurance, they like to call it – or it's the other restaurants ganging up because they don't like the business you're doing and they're not. You make a lot of enemies in this game.'

Rebus was nodding. 'So do you have anyone in mind, Eddie? Anyone in particular?'

But Ringan shook his head in a slow swing. 'Not really. No, not really.'

'But you think maybe *you* were the intended victim?'

Ringan signalled for another drink, and Calder poured. He drank before answering. 'Maybe. I don't know. They could be trying to scare off the customers. Times are hard.'

Rebus turned to Calder, who was staring at Eddie Ringan with a fair amount of revulsion. 'What about you, Mr Calder, any ideas?'

'I think it was just a mugging.'

'Doesn't look like they took anything.'

'Maybe they were interrupted.'

'By someone coming up the alley? Then how did they escape? That car park's a dead end.'

'I don't know.' Rebus kept watching Pat Calder. He was a few years older than Ringan, but looked younger. He'd drawn his dark hair back into what Rebus supposed was a fashionable ponytail, and had kept long straight sideburns reaching down past his ears. He was tall and thin. Indeed, he looked like he could use a good meal. Rebus had seen more meat on a butcher's pencil. 'Maybe,' Calder was saying, 'maybe he did fall after all. It's pretty dark out there. We'll get some lighting put in.'

'Very commendable of you, sir.' Rebus rose from the uncomfortable barstool. 'Meantime, if anything *does* come to mind, and especially if any *names* come to mind, you can always call us.'

'Yes, of course.'

Rebus paused in the doorway. 'Oh, and Mr Calder?'

'Yes?'

'If you let Mr Ringan drive tonight, I'll have him pulled over before he reaches Haymarket. Can't you drive him home?'

'I don't drive.'

'Then I suggest you put your hand in the till for cab fare. Otherwise Mr Ringan's next creation might be Jailhouse Roquefort.'

As Rebus left the restaurant, he could actually hear Eddie Ringan starting to laugh.


He didn't laugh for long. Drink was demanding his attention. 'Gimme another,' he ordered. Pat Calder silently poured to the level of the shot-glass. They'd bought the glasses on a trip to Miami, along with a lot of other stuff. Much of the money had come out of Pat Calder's own pockets, as well as those of his parents. He held the glass in front of Ringan, then toasted him before draining the contents himself. When Ringan started to complain, Calder slapped him across the face.

Ringan looked neither surprised nor hurt. Calder slapped him again.

'You stupid bugger!' he hissed. 'You stupid, stupid bugger!'

'I can't help it,' said Ringan, proffering his empty glass. 'I'm all shook up. Now give me a drink before I do something *really* stupid.'

Pat Calder thought about it for a moment. Then he gave Eddie Ringan the drink.


The ambulance took Brian Holmes to the Royal Infirmary.

Rebus had never been persuaded by this hospital. It seemed full of good intentions and unfilled staff rosters. So he stood close by Brian Holmes' bed, as close as they'd let him stand. And as the night wore on, he didn't flinch; he just slid a little lower down the wall. He was crouching

35

with his head resting against his knees, arms cold against the floor, when he sensed someone towering over him. It was Nell Stapleton. Rebus recognised her by her very height, long before his eyes had reached her tear-stained face.

'Hello there, Nell.'

'Christ, John.' And the tears started again. He pulled himself upright, embracing her quickly. She was throwing words into his ear. 'We talked only this evening. I was horrible. And now this happens ...'

'Hush, Nell. It's not your fault. This sort of thing can happen anytime.'

'Yes, but I can't help remembering, the last time we spoke it was an argument. If we hadn't argued ...'

'Sshh, pet. Calm down now.' He held her tight. Christ, it felt good. He didn't like to think about how good it felt. It felt good all the same. Her perfume, her shape, the way she moulded against him.

'We argued, and he went to that bar, and then ...'

'Sshh, Nell. It's not your fault.'

He believed it, too, though he wasn't sure whose fault it was: protection racketeers? Jealous restaurant owners? Simple neds? A difficult one to call.

'Can I see him?'

'By all means.' Rebus gestured with his arm towards Holmes' bed. He turned away as Nell Stapleton approached it, giving the couple some privacy. Not that the gesture meant anything; Holmes was still unconscious, hooked up to some monitor and with his head heavily bandaged. But he could almost make out the words Nell used when she spoke to her estranged lover. The tone she used made him think of Dr Patience Aitken, made him half-wish *he* were lying unconscious. It was nice to think people were saying nice things about you.

After five minutes, she came tiredly back. 'Hard work?' Rebus offered.

Nell Stapleton nodded. 'You know,' she said quietly, 'I think I've an idea why this happened.'

'Oh?'

She was speaking in a near-whisper, though the ward was quiet. They were the only two souls about on two legs. She sighed loudly. Rebus wondered if she'd ever taken drama classes.

'The black book,' she said. Rebus nodded as though understanding her, then frowned.

'What black book?' he asked.

'I probably shouldn't be telling you, but you're not just someone he works with, are you? You're a friend.' She let out another whistle of air. 'It was Brian's notebook. Nothing official, this was stuff he was looking into on his own.'

Rebus, wary of waking anyone, led her out of the ward. 'A diary?' he asked.

'Not really. It was just that sometimes he used to hear rumours, bits of pub gossip. He'd write them down in the black book. Then he might take things further. It was sort of a hobby with him, but maybe he thought it was also a way to an early promotion. I don't know. We used to argue about that, too. I was hardly seeing him, he was so busy.'

Rebus was staring at the wall of the corridor. The overhead lighting stung his eyes. He'd never heard Holmes mention any kind of notebook.

'What about it?'

Nell was shaking her head. 'It was just something he said, something before we ...' Her hand went to her mouth, as though she were about to cry. 'Before we split up.'

'What was it, Nell?'

'I'm not sure exactly.' Her eyes met Rebus's. 'I just know Brian was scared, and I'd never seen him scared before.'

'Scared of what?'

She shrugged. 'Something in the book.' Then she shook her head again. 'I'm not sure what. I can't help feeling ... feeling I'm somehow responsible. If we'd never ...'

Rebus pulled her to him again. 'There there, pet. It's not your fault.'

'But it *is*! It *is*!'

'No it isn't.' Rebus made his voice sound determined. 'Now, tell me, where did Brian keep this wee black book of his?'

About his person, was the answer. Brian Holmes' clothes and possessions had been removed when the ambulance delivered him to the Infirmary. But Rebus's ID was enough to gain access to the hospital's property department, even at this grim hour. He plucked the notebook out of an A4 envelope's worth of belongings, and had a look at the other contents. Wallet, diary, ID. Watch, keys, small change. Stuff without personality, now that it had been separated from its owner, but strengthening Rebus's conviction that this was no mere mugging.

Nell had gone home still crying, leaving no message to be passed along to Brian. All Rebus knew was that she suspected the beating was something to do with the notebook. And maybe she was right. He sat in the corridor outside Holmes' ward, sipping water and skipping through the cheap leatherette book. Holmes had employed a kind of shorthand, but the code was not nearly complex enough to puzzle another copper. Much of the information had come from a single night and a single action: the night an animal rights group had broken into Fettes HQ's records room. Amongst other things, they'd uncovered evidence of a rent-boy scandal among Edinburgh's most respectable citizens. *This* didn't come as news to John Rebus, but some other entries were intriguing, and especially the one referring to the Central Hotel.

The Central Hotel had been an Edinburgh institution until five years ago, when it had been razed to the ground. An insurance scam was rumoured, and £5,000 had been hoisted by the insurance company involved as a reward for proof that just such a scam had really taken place. But the reward had gone uncollected.

The hotel had once been a traveller's paradise. It was sited on Princes Street, no distance at all from Waverley Station, and so had become a travelling businessman's home-from-home. But in its latter years, the Central had seen business decline. And as genuine business declined, so disingenuous business took over. It was no real secret that the Central's stuffy rooms could be hired by the hour or the afternoon. Room service would provide a bottle of champagne and as much talcum powder as any room's tenants required.

In other words, the Central had become a knocking-shop, and by no means a subtle one. It also catered to the town's shadier elements in all shapes and forms. Wedding parties and stag nights were held for a spread of the city's villains, and underage drinkers could loll in the lounge bar for hours, safe in the knowledge that no honest copper would stray inside the doors. Familiarity bred further contempt, and the lounge bar started to be used for drug deals, and other even less savoury deals too, so that the Central Hotel became something more than a mere knocking-shop. It turned into a swamp.

A swamp with an eviction order over its head.

The police couldn't turn a blind eye forever and a day, especially when complaints from the public were rising by the month. And the more trash was introduced to the Central, the more trash was produced by the place. Until almost no real drinkers went there at all. If you ventured into the Central, you were looking for a woman, cheap drugs, or a fight. And God help you if you weren't.

Then, as had to happen, one night the Central burnt

down. This came as no surprise to anyone; so much so that reporters on the local paper hardly bothered to cover the blaze. The police, of course, were delighted. The fire saved them having to raid the joint.

But the next morning there was a solitary surprise: for though all the hotel's staff and customers had been accounted for, a body turned up amongst the charred ceilings and roofbeams. A body that had been burnt out of all recognition.

A body that had been dead when the fire started.

These scant details Rebus knew. He would not have been a City of Edinburgh detective if he *hadn't* known. Yet here was Holmes' black book, throwing up tantalising clues. Or what looked like tantalising clues. Rebus read the relevant section through again.

Central fire. El was there! Poker game on 1st floor. R. Brothers involved (so maybe Mork too??). Try finding.

He studied Holmes' handwriting, trying to decide whether the journal said El or E1; the letter l or the number 1. And if it was the letter l, did he mean El to stand as the phonetic equivalent of a single letter l? Why the exclamation mark? It seemed that the presence of El (or L or E-One) was some kind of revelation to Brian Holmes. And who the hell were the R. Brothers? Rebus thought at once of Michael and him, the Rebus brothers, but shook the picture from his mind. As for Mork, a bad TV show came to mind, nothing else.

No, he was too tired for this. Tomorrow would be time enough. Maybe by tomorrow Brian would be up and talking. Rebus decided he'd say a little prayer for him before he went to sleep.

# 3

A prayer which went unanswered. Brian Holmes had still not regained consciousness when Rebus phoned the Infirmary at seven o'clock.

'Is he in a coma or something, then?'

The voice on the other end of the phone was cold and factual. 'There will be tests this morning.'

'What sorts of tests?'

'Are you part of Mr Holmes' immediate family?'

'No, I'm bloody not. I'm ...' A police officer? His boss? Just a friend? 'Never mind.' He put down the receiver. One of the students put her head around the living-room door.

'Want some herbal tea?'

'No thanks.'

'A bowl of muesli?'

Rebus shook his head. She smiled at him and disappeared. Herbal tea and muesli, great God almighty. What sort of way was that to start the day? The door of the box room opened from within, and Rebus was startled when a teenage girl dressed only in a man's shirt came out into the daylight, rubbing at her eyes. She smiled at him as she passed, making for the living-room door. She walked on tiptoe, trying not to put too much bare foot on the cold linoleum.

Rebus stared at the living-room door for another ten seconds, then walked over to the box room. Michael was lying naked on the narrow single bed, the bed Rebus had bought secondhand at the weekend. He was rubbing a hand over his chest and staring at the ceiling. The air inside the box room was foetid.

'What the hell do you think you're doing?' Rebus asked.

'She's eighteen, John.'

'That's not what I meant.'

'Oh? What did you mean?'

But Rebus wasn't sure any more. There was just something plain ugly about his brother sharing a box room bed with some student while he slept on the sofa not eight feet away. It was all ugly, all of it. Michael would have to go. Rebus would have to move into a hotel or something. None of it could go on like this much longer. It wasn't fair on the students.

'You should come to the pub more often,' Michael offered. 'That's what's wrong you know.'

'What?'

'You just don't see life, John. It's time you started to live a little.'

Michael was still smiling when his brother slammed the door on him.


'I've just heard about Brian.'

DC Siobhan Clarke looked in some distress. She had lost all colour from her face except for two dots of red high on her cheeks and the paler red of her lips. Rebus nodded for her to sit down. She pulled a chair over to his desk.

'What happened?'

'Somebody hit him over the head.'

'What with?'

Now *that* was a good question, the sort of question a detective would ask. It was also a question Rebus had forgotten to ask last night. 'We don't know,' he said. 'Nor do we have any motive, not yet.'

'It happened outside the Heartbreak Cafe?'

Rebus nodded. 'In the car park out back.'

'He kept saying he was going to take me there for a meal.'

'Brian always keeps his word. Don't worry, Siobhan, he'll be all right.'

She nodded, trying to believe this. 'I'll go see him later.'

'If you like,' said Rebus, not sure quite what his tone was supposed to mean. She looked at him again.

'I like,' she said.

After she'd gone, Rebus read through a message from Chief Inspector Lauderdale. It detailed the initial surveillance plans for the money lending operation. Rebus was asked for questions and 'useful comments'. He smiled at that phrase, knowing Lauderdale had used it hoping to deter Rebus from his usual basic critique of anything put in front of him. Then someone delivered a hefty package, the package he had been waiting for. He lifted the flaps of the cardboard box and started to pull out bulging files. These were the notes referring to the Central Hotel, its history and final sorry end. He knew he had a morning's reading ahead of him, so he found Lauderdale's letter, penned a large OK on it, scrawled his signature beneath, and tossed it into his out tray. Lauderdale wouldn't believe it, wouldn't believe Rebus had accepted the surveillance without so much as a murmur. It was bound to perplex the Chief Inspector.

Not a bad start to the working day.

Rebus sat down with the first file from the box and started to read.

He was filling a second page with his own notes when the telephone rang. It was Nell Stapleton.

'Nell, where are you?' Rebus continued writing, finishing a sentence.

'I'm at work. Just thought I'd call and see if you'd found anything.'

He finished the sentence. 'Such as?'

'Well, what happened to Brian.'

'I'm not sure yet. Maybe he'll tell us when he wakes up. Have you talked to the hospital?'

'First thing.'

'Me too.' Rebus started writing again. There was a nervous silence on the other end of the line.

'What about the black book?'

'Oh, that. Yes, I had a wee read of it.'

'Did you find whatever Brian was afraid of?'

'Maybe and maybe not. Don't worry, Nell, I'm working on it.'

'That's good.' There was genuine relief in her voice. 'Only, when Brian wakes up, don't tell him I told you, will you?'

'Why not? I think it's ... it shows you care about him.'

'Of course I care!'

'That didn't stop you chucking him out.' He wished he hadn't said it, but he had. He could hear her anguish, and imagined her in the University library, trying not to let any of the other staff see her face.

'John,' she said at last, 'you don't know the whole story. You've only heard Brian's side.'

'That's true. Want to tell me yours?'

She thought it over. 'Not like this, on the telephone. Maybe some other time.'

'Any time you like, Nell.'

'I'd better get back to work. Are you going to see Brian today?'

'Maybe tonight. They're running tests all morning. What about you?'

'Oh yes, I'll drop by. It's only two minutes away.'

So it was. Rebus thought of Siobhan Clarke. For some reason, he didn't want the two women to meet at Brian's bedside. 'What time are you thinking of going?'

'Lunchtime, I suppose.'

'One last thing, Nell.'

'Yes?'

'Does Brian have any enemies?'

It took her a little while to answer. 'No.'

Rebus waited to see if she had anything to add. 'Well, take care, Nell.'

'You too, John. Bye.'

After he'd put down the receiver, Rebus started back to his note-taking. But after half a sentence he stopped, tapping his pen thoughtfully against his mouth. He stayed that way for a considerable time, then made some phone calls to his contacts (he didn't like the word 'grasses'), telling them to keep ears open regarding an assault behind the Heartbreak Cafe.

'A colleague of mine, which means it's serious, okay?'

He'd ended up saying 'colleague' but had meant to say 'friend'.

At lunchtime, he walked over to the University and paid his respects at the Department of Pathology. He had called ahead and Dr Curt was ready in his office, wearing a cream-coloured raincoat and humming some piece of classical music which Rebus annoyingly could recognise but not name.

'Ah, Inspector, what a pleasant surprise.'

Rebus blinked. 'Really?'

'Of course. Usually when you're pestering me, it's because of some current and pressing case. But today ...' Curt opened his arms wide. 'No case! And yet you phone me up and invite me to lunch. It can't be very busy along at St Leonard's.'

On the contrary, but Rebus knew the workload was in good hands. Before leaving, he'd loaded enough work onto Siobhan Clarke that she wouldn't have time for a lunch-break, beyond a sandwich and a drink from the cafeteria. When she'd complained, he'd told her she could take time off later in the afternoon to visit Brian Holmes.

'How have you settled in there, by the way?'

Rebus shrugged. 'It doesn't matter to me where they put me. Where do you want to eat?'

'I've taken the liberty of reserving a table at the University Staff Club.'

'What, some sort of canteen?'

Curt laughed, shaking his head. He had ushered Rebus out of his office and was locking the door. 'No,' said Curt. 'There *is* a canteen, of course, but as you're buying I thought we'd opt for something a little bit more refined.'

'Then lead on to the refinery.'

The dining-room was on the ground floor, near the main door of the Staff Club on Chambers Street. They'd walked the short walk, talking about nothing in particular when they could hear one another above the traffic noise. Curt always walked as though he were late for some engagement. Well, he was a busy man: a full teaching load, plus the extra duties heaped on him at one time or another by most of the police forces in Scotland, and most onerously by the City of Edinburgh Police.

The dining-room was small but with plenty of space between the tables. Rebus was pleased to see that the prices were reasonable, though the tally was upped when Curt ordered a bottle of wine.

'My treat,' he said. But Rebus shook his head.

'The Chief Constable's treat,' he corrected. After all, he had every intention of claiming it as a legitimate expense. The wine arrived before the soup. As the waitress poured, Rebus wondered when would be the right moment to open the *real* conversation.

'Slainte!' said Curt, raising his glass. Then: 'So what's this all about? You're not the kind for lunch with a friend, not unless there's something you want, and can't get by buying pints and bridies in some smoky saloon.'

Rebus smiled at this. 'Do you remember the Central Hotel?'

'A dive of a place on Princes Street. It burnt down six or seven years ago.'

'Five years ago actually.'

Curt took another sip of wine. 'There was a smouldering body as I recall. "Crispy batter" we call those.'

'But when you examined the corpse, he hadn't died in the fire, had he?'

'Some new evidence has come to light?'

'Not exactly. I just wanted to ask what you remember about the case.'

'Well, let's see.' Curt broke off as the soup arrived. He took three or four mouthfuls, then wiped a napkin around his lips. 'The body was never identified. I know that we tried dental checks, but to no avail. There was no external evidence, of course, but people stupidly believe that a burned body tells no tales. I cut the deceased open and found, as I'd known I would, that the internal organs were in pretty good shape. Cooked on the outside, raw within, like a good French steak.'

A couple at a nearby table were soundlessly chewing their food, and staring hard at their tabletop. Curt seemed either not to notice or not to mind.

'DNA fingerprinting had been around for four years, but though we got some blood from the heart, we were never given anything to match it against. Of course, the heart was the clincher.'

'Because of the bullet wound.'

'Two wounds, Inspector, entrance and exit. That set you lot scurrying back to the scene, didn't it?'

Rebus nodded. They'd searched the immediate vicinity of the body, then widened the search until a cadet found the bullet. Its calibre was eight millimetre, matching the wound to the heart, but it offered no other clues.

'You also found,' said Rebus, 'that the deceased had suffered a broken arm at some time in the past.'

'Did I?'

'But again it didn't get us any further forward.'

'Especially,' said Curt, mopping his bowl with bread, 'bearing in mind the reputation of the Central. Probably every second person in the place had been in a fight and suffered *some* breakages.'

Rebus was nodding. 'Agreed, yet he was never identified. If he'd been a regular, or one of the staff, surely someone would have come forward. But nobody ever did.'

'Well, it was a long time ago. Are you about to start dusting off some ghosts?'

'There was nothing ghostly about whoever brained Brian Holmes.'

'Sergeant Holmes? What happened?'

Rebus was hoping to spend some of the afternoon reading through more of the case-notes. He'd thought it would take half a day; but this had been optimistic from the start. He was now thinking in terms of half a week, including some evening reading in the flat. There was so much stuff. Lengthy reports from the fire department, the council's building department, news clippings, police reports, interview statements ...

But when he got back to St Leonard's, Lauderdale was waiting. He had received Rebus's hasty comment on the money-lending surveillance, and now wanted to push things on. Which meant that Rebus was trapped in the Chief Inspector's office for the best part of two hours, an hour of it head-to-head stuff. For the other hour, they were joined by Detective Inspector Alister Flower, who had worked out of St Leonard's since its opening day back in September 1989 and bragged continually that when he had shaken hands with the main dignitary at the occasion, they had both turned out to be Masons, with Flower's being the older clan.

Flower resented the incomers from Great London Road. If there were friction and factions within the station, you could be sure Flower was at the back of them somewhere. If anything united Lauderdale and Rebus it was a dislike of Flower, though Lauderdale was slowly being drawn into the Flower camp.

Rebus, however, had contempt even for the funny way the man spelt his first name. He called him 'Little Weed' and thought probably Flower had something to do with the taxman's sudden inquiries.

In the operation against the money lenders, Flower was to lead the other surveillance team. Typically, in an effort to appease the man, Lauderdale offered him the pick of the surveillances. One would be of a pub where the lenders were said to hang out and take payments. The other would be of what looked like the nominal HQ of the gang, an office attached to a mini-cab firm on Gorgie Road.

'I've okayed the Gorgie surveillance with Divisional HQ West,' said Lauderdale, as ever efficient behind a desk. Take him out onto the streets, Rebus knew, and he was about as efficient as pepper on a vindaloo.

'Well,' said Flower, 'if it's okay with Inspector Rebus, I think I'd prefer the watch on the pub. It's a bit closer to home.' And Flower smiled.

'Interesting choice,' said Rebus, his arms folded, legs stretched out in front of him.

Lauderdale was nodding, his eyes flitting between the two men. 'Well, that's settled then. Now, let's get down to details.'

The same details, in fact, that Rebus and he had gone through in the hour prior to Flower's arrival. Rebus tried to concentrate but couldn't. He was desperate to get back to the Central Hotel records. But the more agitated he grew, the slower things moved.

The plan itself was simple. The money lenders worked out of the Firth Pub in Tollcross. They picked up business there, and generally hung around waiting for debtors to come and pay the weekly dues. The money was taken at some point to the office in Gorgie. This office also was used as a drop-off point by debtors, and here the leading visible player could be found.

The men working out of the Firth were bit-parts. They collected cash, and maybe even used some verbal persuasion when payment was late. But when it came to the crunch, everyone paid dues to Davey Dougary. Davey turned up every morning at the office as prompt as any businessman, parking his BMW 635CSi beside the battered mini-cabs. On the way from car to office, if the weather was warm he would slip his jacket off and roll up his shirt-sleeves. Yes, Trading Standards had been watching Davey for quite some time.

There would be Trading Standards officers involved in both surveillances. The police were really only there to enforce the law; it was a Trading Standards operation in name. The name they had chosen was Moneybags. Another interesting choice, thought Rebus, so original. Keeping surveillance in the pub would mean sitting around reading newspapers, circling the names of horses on the betting sheet, playing pool or the jukebox or dominoes. Oh yes, and drinking beer; after all, they didn't want to stand out in the crowd.

Keeping surveillance on the office meant sitting in the window of a disused first floor room in the tenement block across the road. The place was without charm, toilet facilities, or heating. (The bathroom fittings had been stolen during a break-in earlier in the year, down to the very toilet-pan.) A happy prospect, especially for Holmes and Clarke who would bear the burden of the surveillance, always supposing Holmes recovered in time. He thought of his two junior officers spending long days huddling for warmth in a double sleeping-bag. Hell's bells. Thank God Dougary didn't work nights. And thank God there'd be some Trading Standards bodies around too.

Still, the thought of nabbing Davey Dougary warmed Rebus's heart. Dougary was bad the way a rotten apple was. There was no repairing the damage, though the surface might seem untainted. Of course, Dougary was one of Big Ger Cafferty's 'lieutenants'. Cafferty had even turned up once at the office, captured on film. Much good would it do; he'd have a thousand good reasons for that visit. There'd be no pinning him in court. They might get Dougary, but Cafferty was a long way off, so far ahead of them they looked like they were pushing their heap of a car while he cruised in fifth gear.

'So,' Lauderdale was saying. 'We can start with this as of next Monday, yes?'

Rebus awoke from his reverie. It was clear that much had been discussed in his spiritual absence. He wondered if he'd agreed to any of it. (His silence had no doubt been received as tacit consent.)

'I've no problem with that,' said Flower.

Rebus moved again in his seat, knowing that escape was close now. 'I'll probably need someone to fill in for DS Holmes.'

'Ah yes, how is he doing?'

'I haven't heard today, sir,' Rebus admitted. 'I'll call before I clock off.'

'Well, let me know.'

'We're putting together a collection,' Flower said.

'For Christ's sake, he's no' deid yet!'

Flower took the explosion without flinching. 'Well, all the same.'

'It's a nice gesture,' Lauderdale said. Flower shrugged his shoulders modestly. Lauderdale opened his wallet and dug out a reluctant fiver, which he handed to Flower.

51

Hey, big spender, thought Rebus. Even Flower looked startled.

'Five quid,' he said, unnecessarily.

Lauderdale didn't want any thanks. He just wanted Flower to take the money. His wallet had disappeared back into its cave. Flower stuck the note in his shirt pocket and rose from his chair. Rebus stood too, not looking forward to being in the corridor alone with Flower. But Lauderdale stopped him.

'A word, John.'

Flower sniffed as he left, probably thinking Rebus was to receive a dressing down for his outburst. In fact, this wasn't what Lauderdale had in mind.

'I was passing your desk earlier. I see you've got the files on the Central Hotel fire. Old news, surely?' Rebus said nothing. 'Anything I should know about?'

'No, sir,' said Rebus, rising and making for the door. He reckoned Flower would be on his way by now. 'Nothing you should know about. Just some reading of mine. You could call it a history project.'

'Archaeology, more like.'

True enough: old bones and hieroglyphs; trying to make the dead come to life.

'The past is important, sir,' said Rebus, taking his leave.

# 4

The past was certainly important to Edinburgh. The city fed on its past like a serpent with its tail in its mouth. And Rebus's past seemed to be circling around again too. There was a message on his desk in Clarke's handwriting. Obviously she'd gone to visit Holmes, but not before taking a telephone call intended for her superior.

DI Morton called from Falkirk. He'll try again another time. He wouldn't say what it's about. Very cagey. I'll be back in two hours.

She was the sort who would make up the two hours by staying late a few nights, even though Rebus had deprived her of a reasonable lunch-break. Despite being English, there was something of the Scottish Protestant in Siobhan Clarke. It wasn't her fault she was called Siobhan either. Her parents had been English Literature lecturers at Edinburgh University back in the 1960s. They'd lumbered her with the Gaelic name, then moved south again, taking her to be schooled in Nottingham and London. But she'd come back to Edinburgh to go to college, and fallen in love (her story) with Edinburgh. Then she'd decided on the police as a career (alienating her friends and, Rebus suspected, her liberal parents). Still, the parents had bought her a New Town flat, so it couldn't be all strife.

Rebus suspected she'd do well in the police, despite

people like him. Women did have to work harder in the force to progress at the same pace as their male colleagues: everyone knew it. But Siobhan worked hard enough, and by Christ did she have a memory. A month from now, he could ask her about this note on his desk, and she'd remember the telephone conversation word for word. It was scary.

It was slightly scary too that Jack Morton's name had come up at this particular time. Another ghost from Rebus's past. When they'd worked together six years ago, Rebus wouldn't have given the younger Morton more than four or five years to live, such was his steady consumption of booze and cigarettes.

There was no contact phone number. It would have taken only a few minutes to find the number of Morton's nick, but Rebus didn't feel like it. He felt like getting back to the files on his desk. But first he phoned the Infirmary to check on Brian Holmes' progress, only to be told that there wasn't any, though there was also no decline.

'That sounds cheery.'

'It's just an expression,' the person on the phone said.

The test results wouldn't be known until next morning. He thought for a moment, then made another call, this time to Patience Aitken's group practice. But Patience was out on a call, so Rebus left a message. He got the receptionist to read it back so he could be sure it sounded right.

' "Thought I'd call to let you know how Brian's doing. Sorry you weren't in. You can call me at Arden Street if you like. John." '

Yes, that would do. She'd have to call *him* now, just to show she wasn't uncaring about Brian's condition. With a speck of hope in his heart, Rebus went back to work.

He got back to the flat at six, having done some shopping en route. Though he'd proposed taking the files home, he really couldn't be bothered. He was tired, his head ached, and his nose was stuffy from the old dust which rose from their pages. He climbed the flights of stairs wearily, opened the door, and took the grocery bags into the kitchen, where one of the students was spreading peanut butter onto a thick slice of brown bread.

'Hiya, Mr Rebus. You got a phone call.'

'Oh?'

'Some woman doctor.'

'When?'

'Ten minutes ago, something like that.'

'What did she say?'

'She said if she wanted to find out about ...'

'Brian? Brian Holmes?'

'Aye, that's it. If she wanted to find out about him, she could call the hospital, and that's exactly what she'd done twice today already.' The student beamed, pleased at having remembered the whole message. So Patience had seen through his scheme. He should have known. Her intelligence, amongst other things, had attracted him to her. Also, they were very much alike in many ways. Rebus should have learned long ago, never try to put one over on someone who knows the way your mind works. He lifted a box of eggs, tin of beans, and packet of bacon out of the bag.

'Oh my God,' said the student in disgust. 'Do you know just how intelligent pigs *are*, Mr Rebus?'

Rebus looked at the student's sandwich. 'A damned sight more intelligent than peanuts,' he said. Then: 'Where's the frying-pan?'

Later, Rebus sat watching TV. He'd nipped over to the Infirmary to visit Brian Holmes. He reckoned it was quicker to walk rather than driving around The Meadows. So he'd walked, letting his head clear. But the visit itself had been depressing. Not a bit of progress.

'How long can he stay conked out?'

'It can take a while,' a nurse had consoled.

'It's *been* a while.'

She touched his arm. 'Patience, patience.'

Patience! He almost took a taxi to her flat, but dropped the idea. Instead, he walked back to Arden Street, climbed the same old weary stairs, and flopped onto the sofa. He had spent so many evenings deep in thought in this room, but that had been back when the flat was his, only his.

Michael came into the living room, fresh from a shave and a shower. He wore a towel tight around his flat stomach. He was in good shape; Rebus hadn't noticed before. But Michael saw him noticing now, and patted his stomach.

'One thing about Peterhead, plenty of exercise.'

'I suppose you've got to get fit in there,' Rebus drawled, 'so you can fight back when someone's after your arse.'

Michael shook off the remark like it was so much water. 'Oh, there's plenty of that too. Never interested me.' Whistling, he went into the box room and started to dress.

'Going out?' Rebus called.

'Why stay in?'

'Seeing that wee girl again?'

Michael put his head around the door. 'She's a consenting adult.'

Rebus got to his feet. 'She's a wee girl.' He walked over to the box room and stared at Michael, forcing him to stop what he was doing.

'What, John? You want me to stop going out with women? If you don't like it, tough.'

Rebus thought of all the remarks he could make. This is my flat ... I'm your big brother ... you should know better ... He knew Mickey would laugh – quite rightly – at any and all of them. So he thought of something else to say.

'Fuck you, Mickey.'

Michael Rebus recommenced dressing. 'I'm sorry I'm such a disappointment, but what's the alternative? Sit here all night watching you stew or sulk or whatever it is you do inside your head? Thanks but no thanks.'

'I thought you were going to look for a job.'

Michael Rebus grabbed a book from the bed and threw it at his brother. 'I'm looking for a fucking job! What do you think I do all day? Just give it a rest, will you?' He picked up his jacket and pushed past Rebus. 'Don't wait up for me, eh?'

That was a laugh: Rebus was asleep, and alone in the flat, before the ten o'clock news. But it wasn't a sound sleep. It was a sleep filled with dreams. He was chasing Patience through some office block, always just losing her. He was eating in a restaurant with a teenage girl while the Rolling Stones entertained unnoticed on the small stage in the corner. He was watching a hotel burn to the ground, wondering if Brian Holmes, still unaccounted for, had gotten out alive . . .

And then he was awake and shivering, the room illuminated only by the street-lamp outside, burning through a chink in the curtains. He'd been reading the book Michael had thrown at him. It was about hypnotherapy and still lay in his lap, beneath the blanket someone had thrown over him. There were noises nearby, noises of pleasure. They were coming from the box room. Some therapy, no doubt. Rebus listened to them for what seemed like hours until the light outside grew pale.

# 5

Andrew McPhail sat beside his bedroom window. Across the road, the children were being lined up two by two outside the school doors. The boys had to hold hands with the girls, the whole thing supervised by two female staff members, looking hardly old enough to be parents, never mind teachers. McPhail sipped cold tea from his mug and watched. He paid very close attention to the children. Any one of the girls might have been Melanie. Except, of course, that Melanie would be older. Not much older, but older. He wasn't kidding himself. He knew the odds were Melanie wouldn't be at this school, probably wasn't even in Edinburgh any more. But he watched all the same, and imagined her down there, her hand touching the cool wet hand of one of the boys. Small delicate fingers, the beginning of fine lines on the palm. One girl was really quite similar: short straight hair curling in towards her ears and the nape of her neck. The height was familiar, too, but the face, what he could see of the face, was nothing like Melanie. Really, nothing like her. And besides, what did it matter to McPhail?

They were marching into the building now, leaving him behind with his cold tea and his memories. He could hear Mrs MacKenzie downstairs, washing dishes and probably chipping and breaking as much crockery as she got clean. Not her fault, her eyesight was failing. Everything about the old woman was failing. The house was bound to be worth £40,000, as good as money in

58

the bank. And what did he have? Only memories of the way things had been in Canada and before Canada.

A plate crashed onto the kitchen floor. It couldn't go on like this, really it couldn't. There'd be nothing left. He didn't like to think about the budgie in the living-room . . .

McPhail drained the strong tea. The caffeine made him slightly giddy, sweat breaking out on his forehead. The playground was empty, the school doors closed. He couldn't see anything through the building's few visible windows. There might be a late-arriving straggler, but he didn't have time to waste. He had work to do. It was good to keep busy. Keeping busy kept you sane.

'Big Ger,' Rebus was saying, 'real name Morris Gerald Cafferty.'

Dutifully, and despite her good memory, DC Siobhan Clarke wrote these words on her notepad. Rebus didn't mind her taking notes. It was good exercise. When she lowered her head to write, Rebus had a view of the crown of her head, light-brown hair falling forward. She was good looking in a homely sort of way. Indeed, she reminded him a bit of Nell Stapleton.

'He's the prime mover, and if we're offered him we'll take him. But Operation Moneybags will actually be focusing on David Charles Dougary, known as Davey.' Again, the words went onto the paper. 'Dougary rents office space from a dodgy mini-cab service in Gorgie Road.'

'Not far from the Heartbreak Cafe?'

The question surprised him. 'No,' he said, 'not too far.'

'And the restaurant owner hinted at a protection pay-off?'

Rebus shook his head. 'Don't get carried away, Clarke.'

'And these men are involved in protection money too, aren't they?'

'There's not much Big Ger Cafferty *isn't* involved in: money laundering, prostitution. He's a big bad bastard, but that isn't the point. The point is, this operation will concentrate on loan-sharking, period.'

'All I'm saying is maybe Sergeant Holmes was attacked by mistake instead of the Cafe's owner.'

'It's a possibility,' said Rebus. And if it's true, he thought, I'm wasting a lot of time and effort on an old case. But as Nell said, Brian was frightened of something in his black book. And all because he'd started trying to track down the mysterious R. Brothers.

'But to get back to business, we'll be setting up a surveillance across the road from the taxi firm.'

'Round the clock?'

'We'll start with working hours. Dougary has a fairly fixed routine by all accounts.'

'What's he supposed to be doing in that office?'

'The way he tells it, everything from basic entrepreneurship to arranging food parcels for the Third World. Don't get me wrong, Dougary's clever. He's lasted longer than most of Big Ger's "associates". He's also a maniac, it's worth bearing that in mind. We once arrested him after a pub brawl. He'd torn the ear off another man with his teeth. When we got there, Dougary was chomping away. The ear was never recovered.'

Rebus always expected some reaction from his favourite stories, but all Siobhan Clarke did was smile and say, 'I love this city.' Then: 'Are there files on Mr Cafferty?'

'Oh aye, there are files. By all means, plough through them. They'll give you some idea what you're up against.'

She nodded. 'I'll do that. And when do we start the surveillance, sir?'

'First thing Monday morning. Everything will be set up on Sunday. I just hope they give us a decent camera.' He noticed Clarke was looking relieved. Then the penny dropped. 'Don't worry, you won't miss the Hibs game.'

She smiled. 'They're away to Aberdeen.'

'And you're still going?'

'Absolutely.' She tried never to miss a game.

Rebus was shaking his head. He didn't know that many Hibs fans. 'I wouldn't travel that far for the Second Coming.'

'Yes you would.'

Now Rebus smiled. 'Who's been talking? Right, what's on the agenda for today?'

'I've talked to the butcher. He was no help at all. I think I'd have more chance of getting a complete sentence out of the carcases in his deep freeze. But he does drive a Merc. That's an expensive car. Butchers aren't well known for high salaries, are they?'

Rebus shrugged. 'The prices they charge, I wouldn't be so sure.'

'Anyway, I'm planning to drop in on him at home this morning, just to clear up a couple of points.'

'But he'll be at work.'

'Unfortunately yes.'

Rebus caught on. 'His wife will be home?'

'That's what I'm hoping. The offer of a cup of tea, a little chat in the living room. Wasn't it terrible about Rory? That sort of thing.'

'So you can size up his home life, and maybe get a talkative wife thrown in for good measure.' Rebus was nodding slowly. It was so devious he should have thought of it himself.

'Get tae it, lass,' he said, and she did, leaving him to reach down onto the floor and lift one of the Central Hotel files onto his desk.

He started reading, but soon froze at a certain page. It listed the Hotel's customers on the night it burnt down. One name fairly flew off the page.

'Would you credit that?' Rebus got up from the desk and put his jacket on. Another ghost. And another excuse to get out of the office.

The ghost was Matthew Vanderhyde.

61

# 6

The house next to Vanderhyde's was as mad as ever. Owned by an ancient Nationalist, it sported the saltire flag on its gate and what looked like thirty-year-old tracts taped to its windows. The owner couldn't get much light, but then the house Rebus was approaching had its curtains drawn closed.

He rang the doorbell and waited. It struck him that Vanderhyde might well be dead. He would be in his early-to mid-seventies, and though he'd seemed healthy enough the last time they'd met, well, that was over two years ago.

He had consulted Vanderhyde in an earlier case. After the case was closed, Rebus used to drop in on Vanderhyde from time to time, just casually. They only lived six streets apart, after all. But then he'd started to get serious with Dr Patience Aitken, and hadn't found time for a visit since.

The door opened, and there stood Matthew Vanderhyde, looking just the same as ever. His sightless eyes were hidden behind dark green spectacles, above which sat a high shiny forehead and long swept-back yellow hair. He was wearing a suit of beige cord with a brown waistcoat, from the pocket of which hung a watch-chain. He leaned lightly on his silver-topped cane, waiting for the caller to speak.

'Hello there, Mr Vanderhyde.'

'Ah, Inspector Rebus. I was wondering when I'd see you. Come in, come in.'

From Vanderhyde's tone, it sounded like they'd last met two weeks before. He led Rebus through the dark hallway and into the darker living room. Rebus took in the shapes of bookshelves, paintings, the large mantelpiece covered in mementoes from trips abroad.

'As you can see, Inspector, nothing has changed in your absence.'

'I'm glad to see you looking so well, sir.'

Vanderhyde shrugged aside the remark. 'Some tea?'

'No thanks.'

'I'm really quite thrilled that you've come. It must mean there's something I can do for you.'

Rebus smiled. 'I'm sorry I stopped visiting.'

'It's a free country, I didn't pine away.'

'I can see that.'

'So what sort of thing is it? Witchcraft? Devilment in the city streets?'

Rebus was still smiling. In his day, Matthew Vanderhyde had been an active white witch. At least, Rebus hoped he'd been white. It had never been discussed between them.

'I don't *think* this is anything to do with magic,' Rebus said. 'It's about the Central Hotel.'

'The Central? Ah, happy memories, Inspector. I used to go there as a young man. Tea dances, a very acceptable luncheon – they had an excellent kitchen in those days, you know – even once or twice to an evening ball.'

'I'm thinking of more recent times. You were at the hotel the night it was torched.'

'I don't recall arson was proven.'

As usual, Vanderhyde's memory was sharp enough when it suited him. 'That's true. All the same, you were there.'

'Yes, I was. But I left several hours before the fire started. Not guilty, your honour.'

'Why were you there in the first place?'

'To meet a friend for a drink.'

'A seedy place for a drink.'

'Was it? You'll have to remember, Inspector, I couldn't *see* anything. It certainly didn't *smell* or *feel* particularly disreputable.'

'Point taken.'

'I had my memories. To me, it was the same old Central Hotel I'd lunched in and danced in. I quite enjoyed the evening.'

'Was the Central your choice, then?'

'No, my friend's.'

'Your friend being ...?'

Vanderhyde considered. 'No secret, I suppose. Aengus Gibson.'

Rebus sifted through the name's connotations. 'You don't mean Black Aengus?'

Vanderhyde laughed, showing small blackened teeth. 'You'd better not let him hear you calling him that these days.'

Yes, Aengus Gibson was a reformed character, that much was public knowledge. He was also, so Rebus presumed, still one of Scotland's most eligible young men, if thirty-two could be considered young in these times. Black Aengus, after all, was sole heir to the Gibson Brewery and all that came with it.

'Aengus Gibson,' said Rebus.

'The same.'

'And this was five years ago, when he was still ...'

'High spirited?' Vanderhyde gave a low chuckle. 'Oh, he deserved the name Black Aengus then, all right. The newspapers got it just right when they came up with *that* nickname.'

Rebus was thinking. 'I didn't see his name in the records. Your name was there, but his wasn't.'

'I'm sure his family saw to it that his name never appeared in any records, Inspector. It would have given

64

the media even more fuel than they needed at the time.'

Yes, Christ, Black Aengus had been a wild one all right, so wild even the London papers took an interest. He'd looked to be spiralling out of control on ever-new excesses, but then suddenly all that stopped. He'd been rehabilitated, and was now as respectable as could be, involved in the brewing business and several prominent charities besides.

'The leopard changed its spots, Inspector. I know you policemen are dubious about such things. Every offender is a potential repeat offender. I suppose you have to be cynical in your job, but with young Aengus the leopard really *did* change.'

'Do you know why?'

Vanderhyde shrugged. 'Maybe because of our chat.'

'That night in the Central Hotel?'

'His father had asked me to talk to him.'

'You know them, then?'

'Oh, from long ago. Aengus regarded me more as an uncle than anything else. Indeed, when I heard that the Central had been razed to the ground, I saw it as symbolic. Perhaps he did too. Of course I knew the reputation it had garnered – an altogether unsavoury reputation. When it happened to burn down that night, well, I thought of the phoenix Aengus rising cleansed from its ashes. And it turned out to be true.' He paused. 'Yet now here you are, Inspector, asking questions about long forgotten events.'

'There was a body.'

'Ah yes, never identified.'

'A murdered body.'

'And somehow you've reopened that particular investigation? Interesting.'

'I wanted to ask you what you remembered from that night. Anyone you met, anything that seemed at all suspicious.'

Vanderhyde tilted his head to one side. 'There were many people in the hotel that night, Inspector. You have a list of them. Yet you choose to come to a blind man?'

'That's right,' said Rebus. 'A blind man with a photographic memory.'

Vanderhyde laughed. 'Certainly, I can give ... impressions.' He thought for a moment. 'Very well, Inspector. For you, I'll do my best. I only ask one thing.'

'What's that?'

'I've been stuck here too long. Take me out, will you?'

'Anywhere in particular?'

Vanderhyde looked surprised that he needed to ask. 'Why, Inspector, to the Central Hotel, of course!'

'Well,' said Rebus, 'this is where it used to stand. You're facing it now.' He could feel the stares of passers-by. Princes Street was lunchtime busy, office workers trying to make the most of their limited time. A few looked genuinely annoyed at having to manoeuvre past two people *daring* to stand still on the pavement! But most could see that one man was blind, the other his helper in some way, so they found charity in their souls and didn't complain.

'And what has it become, Inspector?'

'A burger joint.'

Vanderhyde nodded. 'I thought I could smell meat. Franchised, doubtless, from some American corporation. Princes Street has seen better days, Inspector. Did you know that when Scottish Sword and Shield was started up, they used to meet in the Central's ballroom? Dozens and dozens of people, all vowing to restore Dalriada to its former glory.'

Rebus remained silent.

'You don't recall Sword and Shield?'

'It must have been before my time.'

'Now that I think of it, it probably was. This was in the 1950s, an offshoot of the National Party. I attended a couple of the meetings myself. There would be some furious call to arms, followed by tea and scones. It didn't last long. Broderick Gibson was the president one year.'

'Aengus's father?'

'Yes.' Vanderhyde was remembering. 'There used to be a pub near here, famous for politics and poetry. A few of us went there after the meetings.'

'I thought you said you only went to two?'

'Perhaps a few more than two.'

Rebus grinned. If he looked into it, he knew he would probably find that a certain M. Vanderhyde had been president of Sword and Shield at some time.

'It was a fine pub,' Vanderhyde reminisced.

'In its day,' said Rebus.

Vanderhyde sighed. 'Edinburgh, Inspector. Turn your back and they change the name of a pub or the purpose of a shop.' He pointed behind him with his stick, nearly tripping someone up in the process. 'They can't change that though. *That's* Edinburgh too.' The stick was wavering in the direction of the Castle Rock. It rapped someone against their leg. Rebus tried to smile an apology, the victim being a woman.

'Maybe we should go sit across the road,' he suggested. Vanderhyde nodded, so they crossed at the traffic lights to the quieter side of the street. There were benches here, their backs to the gardens, each dedicated to someone's memory. Vanderhyde got Rebus to read the plaque on their bench.

'No,' he said, shaking his head. 'I don't recognise either of those names.'

'Mr Vanderhyde,' said Rebus, 'I'm beginning to suspect you got me to bring you here for no other reason than the outing itself.' Vanderhyde smiled but said nothing. 'What time did you go to the bar that night?'

'Seven sharp, that was the arrangement. Of course, Aengus being Aengus, he was late. I think he turned up at half past, by which time I was seated in a corner with a whisky and water. I think it was J and B whisky.' He seemed pleased by this small feat of memory.

'Anyone you knew in the bar?'

'I can hear bagpipes,' Vanderhyde said.

Rebus could too, though he couldn't see the piper. 'They play for the tourists,' he explained. 'It can be a big earner in the summer.'

'He's not very good. I should imagine he's wearing a kilt but that the tartan isn't correct.'

'Anyone in the bar you knew?' Rebus persisted.

'Oh, let me think ...'

'With respect, sir, you don't *need* to think. You either know or you don't.'

'Well, I think Tom Hendry was in that night and stopped by the table to say hello. He used to work for the newspapers.'

Yes, Rebus had seen the name on the list.

'And there was someone else ... I didn't know them, and they didn't speak. But I recall a scent of lemon. It was very vivid. I thought maybe it was a perfume, but when I mentioned it to Aengus he laughed and said it didn't belong to a woman. He wouldn't say any more, but I got the feeling it was a huge joke to him that I'd made the initial comment. I'm not sure any of this is relevant.'

'Me neither.' Rebus's stomach was growling. There was a sudden explosion behind them. Vanderhyde slipped his watch from his waistcoat pocket, opened the glass, and felt with his fingers over the dial.

'One o'clock sharp,' he said. 'As I said, Inspector, some things about our precipitous city remain immutable.'

Rebus nodded. 'Such as the precipitation, for instance?' It was beginning to drizzle, the morning sun having disappeared like a conjurer's trick. 'Anything else you can tell me?'

'Aengus and I talked. I tried to persuade him that he was on a very dangerous path. His health was failing, and so was the family's wealth. If anything, the latter argument was the more persuasive.'

'So there and then he renounced the bawdy life?'

'I wouldn't go that far. The Edinburgh establishment has never bided too far from the stews. When we parted he was setting off to meet some woman.' Vanderhyde was thoughtful. 'But if I do say so myself, my words had an effect on him.' He nodded. 'I ate alone that evening in The Eyrie.'

'I've been there myself,' said Rebus. His stomach growled again. 'Fancy a burger?'

After he'd dropped Vanderhyde home he drove back to St Leonard's – not a lot wiser for the whole exercise. Siobhan sprang from her desk when she saw him. She looked pleased with herself.

'I take it the butcher's wife was a talker,' Rebus said, dropping into his chair. There was another note on his desk telling him Jack Morton had called. But this time there was also a number where Rebus could reach him.

'A right little gossip, sir. I had trouble getting away.'

'And?'

'Something and nothing.'

'So give me the something.' Rebus rubbed his stomach. He'd enjoyed the burger, but it hadn't quite filled him up. There was always the canteen, but he was a bit worried about getting a 'dough-ring', as he termed the gut policemen specialised in.

'The something is this.' Siobhan Clarke sat down. 'Bone won the Merc in a bet.'

'A bet?'

Clarke nodded. 'He put his share of the butcher's business up against it. But he won the bet.'

'Bloody hell.'

'His wife actually sounded quite proud. Anyway, she told me he's a great one for betting. Maybe he is, but it doesn't look like he's got a winning formula.'

'How do you mean?'

She was warming to her subject. Rebus liked to see it, the gleam of successful detection. 'There were a few things not quite right in the living room. For instance, they'd videotapes but no video, though you could see where the machine used to sit. And though they had a large unit for storing the TV and video, the TV itself was one of those portable types.'

'So they've got rid of their video and their big television.'

'I'd guess to pay off a debt or debts.'

'And your money would be on gambling dues?'

'If I were the betting kind, which I'm not.'

He smiled. 'Maybe they had the stuff on tick and couldn't keep up the payments.'

Siobhan sounded doubtful. 'Maybe,' she conceded.

'Okay, well, it's interesting so far as it goes, but it doesn't go very far ... not yet. And it doesn't tell us anything about Rory Kintoul, does it?' She was frowning. 'Remember him, Clarke? He's the one who was stabbed in the street then wouldn't talk about it. *He's* the one we're interested in.'

'So what do you suggest, sir?' There was a tinge of ire to that 'sir'. She didn't like it that her good detection had not been better rewarded. 'We've already spoken to him.'

'And you're going to speak to him again.' She looked ready to protest. 'Only this time,' Rebus went on, 'you're going to be asking about his cousin, Mr Bone the butcher. I'm not sure what we're looking for exactly, so you'll have to feel your way. Just see whether anything hits the marrow.'

'Yes, sir.' She stood up. 'Oh, by the way, I got the files on Cafferty.'

'Plenty of reading in there, most of it x-rated.'

'I know, I've already started. And there's no x-rating nowadays. It's called "eighteen" instead.'

Rebus blinked. 'It's just an expression.' As she was turning away, he stopped her. 'Look, take some notes, will you? On Cafferty and his gang, I mean. Then when you're finished you can refresh my memory. I've spent a long time shutting that monster out of my thoughts; it's about time I opened the door again.'

'No problem.'

And with that she was off. Rebus wondered if he should have told her she'd done well at Bone's house. Ach, too late now. Besides, if she thought she were pleasing him, maybe she'd stop trying so hard. He picked up his phone and called Jack Morton.

'Jack? Long time no hear. It's John Rebus.'

'John, how are you?'

'No' bad, how's yourself?'

'Fine. I made Inspector.'

'Aye, me too.'

'So I heard.' Jack Morton choked off his words as he gave a huge hacking cough.

'Still on the fags, eh, Jack?'

'I've cut down.'

'Remind me to sell my tobacco shares. So listen, what's the problem?'

'It's your problem, not mine. Only I saw something from Scotland Yard about Andrew McPhail.'

Rebus tried the name out in his head. 'No,' he admitted, 'you've got me there.'

'We had him on file as a sex offender. He'd had a go at the daughter of the woman he was living with. This was about eight years back. But we never got the charge to stick.'

Rebus was remembering a little of it. 'We interviewed him when those wee girls started to disappear?' Rebus shivered at the memory: his own daughter had been one of the 'wee girls'.

'That's it, just routine. We started with convicted and suspected child offenders and went on from there.'

'Stocky guy with wiry hair?'

'You've got him.'

'So what's the point, Jack?'

'The point is, you really have got him. He's in Edinburgh.'

'So?'

'Christ, John, I thought you'd know. He buggered off to Canada after that last time we hassled him. Set himself up as a photographer, doing shots for fashion catalogues. He'd approach the parents of kids he fancied. He had business cards, camera equipment, the works, rented a studio and used to take shots of the children, promising they'd be in some catalogue or other. They'd get to dress up in fancy dresses, or sometimes maybe just in underwear ...'

'I get the picture, Jack.'

'Well, they nabbed him. He'd been touching the girls, that was all. A lot of girls, so they put him inside.'

'And?'

'And now they've let him out. But they've also deported him.'

'He's in Edinburgh?'

'I started checking. I wanted to find out where he'd ended up, because I knew if it was anywhere near my patch I'd pay him a visit some dark night. But he's on your patch instead. I've got an address.'

'Wait a second.' Rebus found a pen and copied it down.

'How did you get his address anyway? The DSS?'

'No, the files said he had a sister in Ayr. She told me he'd had her get a phone number for him, a boarding house. Know what else she said? She said we should lock him in a cellar and forget about the key.'

'Sounds like a lovely lass.'

'She's my kind of woman, all right. Of course, he's probably been rehabilitated.'

That word – rehabilitated. A word Vanderhyde had used about Aengus Gibson. 'Probably,' said Rebus, believing it about as much as Morton himself. They were professional disbelievers, after all. It was a policeman's lot.

'Still, it's good to know about. Thanks, Jack.'

'You're welcome. Any chance we'll be seeing you in Falkirk some day? It'd be good to have a drink.'

'Yes, it would. Tell you what, I might be over that way soon.'

'Oh?'

'Dropping McPhail off in the town centre.'

Morton laughed. 'Ya shite, ye.' And with that he put down the phone.

Jack Morton stared at the phone for the best part of a minute, still grinning. Then the grin melted away. He unwrapped a stick of chewing gum and started gnawing it. It's better than a cigarette, he kept telling himself. He looked at the scribbled sheet of notes in front of him on the desk. The girl McPhail had assaulted was called Melanie Maclean these days. Her mother had married, and Melanie lived with the couple in Haddington, far enough from Edinburgh so that she probably wouldn't bump into McPhail. Nor, in all probability, would McPhail be able to find her. He'd have to know the stepfather's name, and that wouldn't be easy for him. It hadn't been *that* easy for Jack Morton. But the name was here. Alex Maclean. Jack Morton had a home address, home phone number, and work number. He wondered ...

He knew too that Alex Maclean was a carpenter, and Haddington police were able to inform him that Maclean had a temper on him, and had twice (long before his marriage) been arrested after some flare-up or other. He wondered, but he knew he was going to do it. He picked up the receiver and punched in the numbers. Then waited.

'Hello, can I speak to Mr Maclean please? Mr Maclean? You don't know me, but I have some information I'd like to share with you. It concerns a man called Andrew McPhail ...'

Matthew Vanderhyde too made a telephone call that afternoon, but only after long thought in his favourite armchair. He held the cordless phone in his hand, tapping it with a long fingernail. He could hear a dog outside, the one from down the street with the nasal whine. The clock on the mantelpiece ticked, the tick seeming to slow as he concentrated on it. Time's heartbeat. At last he made the call. There was no preamble.

'I've just had a policeman here,' he said. 'He was asking about the night the Central Hotel caught fire.' He hesitated slightly. 'I told him about Aengus.' He could pause now, listening with a weary smile to the fury on the other end of the line, a fury he knew so well. 'Broderick,' he interrupted, 'if any skeletons are being uncloseted, *I* don't want to be the only one shivering.'

When the fury began afresh, Matthew Vanderhyde terminated the call.

# 7

Rebus noticed the man for the first time that evening. He thought he'd seen him outside St Leonard's in the afternoon. A young man, tall and broad-shouldered. He was standing outside the entrance to Rebus's communal stairwell in Arden Street. Rebus parked his car across the street, so that he could watch the man in his rearview mirror. The man looked agitated, pumped up about something. Maybe he was only waiting for his date. Maybe.

Rebus wasn't scared, but he started the car again and drove off anyway. He'd give it an hour and see if the man was still there. If he was, then he wasn't waiting on any date, no matter how bonny the girl. He drove along the Meadows to Tollcross, then took a right down Lothian Road. It was slow going, as per. The number of vehicles needing to get through the city of an evening seemed to grow every week. Edinburgh in the twilight looked much the same as any other place: shops and offices and crowded pavements. Nobody looked particularly happy.

He crossed Princes Street, cut into Charlotte Square, and began the crawl along Queensferry Street and Queensferry Road until he could take a merciful (if awkward) right turn into Oxford Terrace. But Patience wasn't home. He knew Patience's sister was expected this week, staying a few days then taking the girls home. Patience's cat, Lucky, sat outside, demanding entry, and Rebus for once was almost sympathetic.

'Nae luck,' he told it, before starting back up the steps.

When he got back to Arden Street, there was no sign of the skulking hulk. But Rebus would recognise him if he saw him again. Oh yes, he'd know him, all right.

Indoors, he had another argument with Michael, the two of them in the living room, everyone else in the kitchen. That was another thing: how many tenants did he have? There seemed to be a shifting population of about a dozen, where he'd rented to three with a possible fourth. He could swear he saw different faces every morning, and as a result could never remember anyone's name.

So there was another row about that, this time with the students in the kitchen while Michael sat in the box room, at the end of which Rebus said, 'Away to hell,' and proceeded to follow his own instructions by getting back in his car and making for one of the city's least respectable quarters, there to dine on pies and pints while staring at a soundless TV. He spoke with a few of his contacts, who had nothing to report regarding the assault on Brian Holmes.

So it was just another evening, really.

He got back purposely late, hoping everyone else would have gone to bed. He fumbled with the door-catch of the tenement and let the door swing shut loudly behind him, searching in his pockets for the flat key, eyes to the ground. So he didn't see the man, who must have been sitting on the bottom step of the stairs.

'Hello there.'

Rebus looked up, startled, recognised the figure, and sent small change and keys scattering as he threw a punch. He wasn't that drunk, but then his target was stone cold sober and twenty years younger. The man palmed the punch easily. He looked surprised at the attack, but also somehow excited by it. Rebus cut short the thrill of it all by sharply raising his knee into unprotected groin. The man expelled air noisily, and started to double over,

76

which gave Rebus the opportunity to punch down onto the back of his neck. He felt his knuckles crackle with the force of the blow.

'Jesus,' the man gasped. 'Stop it.'

Rebus stopped it and wagged his aching hand. But he wasn't about to offer help. He kept his distance, and asked 'Who are you?'

The man managed to stop retching for a moment. 'Andy Steele.'

'Nice to meet you, Andy. What the fuck do you want?'

The man looked up at Rebus with tears in his eyes. It took him a while to catch his breath. When he spoke, Rebus either couldn't understand the accent or else just didn't believe what he was saying. He asked Steele to repeat himself.

'Your auntie sent me,' said Steele. 'She's got a message for you.'


Rebus sat Andy Steele down on the sofa with a cup of tea, including the four sugars Steele himself had requested.

'Can't be good for your teeth.'

'They're not my own,' Steele replied, huddled over the hot mug.

'Then whose are they?' asked Rebus. Steele gave the flicker of a smile. 'You've been following me all day.'

'Not exactly. Maybe if I had a car, but I don't.'

'You don't have a car?' Steele shook his head. 'Some private detective.'

'I didn't say I was a private detective exactly. I mean, I *want* to be one.'

'A sort of trainee, then?'

'Aye, that's right. Testing the water, so to speak.'

'And how's the water, Andy?'

Another smile, a sip of tea. 'A bit hot. But I'll be more careful next time.'

'I didn't even know I had an aunt. Not up north.' Steele's accent was a giveaway.

Andy Steele nodded. 'She lives next door to my mum and dad, just across the road from Pittodrie.'

'Aberdeen?' Rebus nodded to himself. 'It's coming back to me. Yes, an uncle and aunt in Aberdeen.'

'Your dad and Jimmy – that's your uncle – fell out years ago. You're probably too young to remember.'

'Thanks for the compliment.'

'It's just what Ena told me.'

'And now Uncle Jimmy's dead?'

'Three weeks past.'

'And Aunt Ena wants to see me?' Steele nodded. 'What about?'

'I don't know. She was just talking about how she'd like to see you again.'

'Just me? No mention of my brother?'

Steele shook his head. Rebus had checked to see if Michael was in the box room. He wasn't. But the other bedrooms seemed to be occupied.

'Right enough,' said Rebus, 'if they argued when I was wee, maybe it was before Michael was born.'

'They might no' even know about him,' Steele conceded. Well, that was families for you. 'Anyway, Ena kept harping on about you, so I told her I'd come south and have a look. I got laid off from the fishing boats six months ago, and I've been going up the wall ever since. Besides, I told you I've always fancied being a private eye. I love all those films.'

'Films don't get you a knee in the balls.'

'True enough.'

'So how *did* you find me?'

Steele's face brightened. 'I went to the address Ena gave me, where you and your dad used to live. All the neighbours knew was that you were a policeman in Edinburgh. So I got the directory out and phoned every station I could find, asking for John Rebus.' He shrugged and returned to his tea.

'But how did you get my home address?'

'Someone in CID gave it to me.'

'Don't tell me, Inspector Flower?'

'A name like that, aye.'

Seated on the sofa, Andy Steele looked to be in his mid-twenties. He had the sort of large frame which could be kept in shape only through hard work, such as that found on a North Sea fishing boat. But already, deprived of work for six months, that frame was growing heavy with disuse. Rebus felt sorry for Andy Steele and his dreams of becoming a private eye. The way he stared into space as he drank the tea, he looked lost, his immediate life without form or plan.

'So are you going to go and see her?'

'Maybe at the weekend,' said Rebus.

'She'd like that.'

'I can give you a lift back.'

But the young man was shaking his head. 'No, I'd like to stay in Edinburgh for a bit.'

'Suit yourself,' said Rebus. 'Just be careful.'

'Careful? I could tell you stories about Aberdeen that would make your hair stand on end.'

'And could they thicken it a bit at the temples while they're at it?'

It took Andy Steele a minute to get the joke.


The next day, Rebus paid a visit to Andrew McPhail. But McPhail wasn't home, and his landlady hadn't seen him since the previous evening.

'Usually he comes down at seven sharp for a wee bitty breakfast. So I went upstairs and there was no sign of him. Is he in any trouble, Inspector?'

'No, nothing like that, Mrs MacKenzie. This is a lovely Madiera by the way.'

'Ach, it's a few days since I made it, it's probably a bit dry by now.'

Rebus shook his head and gulped at the tea, hoping to wash the crumbs down his throat. But they merely formed into a huge solid lump which he had to force down by degrees, and without a public show of gagging.

There was a bird-cage standing in one corner of the room, boasting mirrors and cuttle-fish and millet spray. But no sign of any bird. Maybe it had escaped.

He left his card with Mrs MacKenzie, telling her to pass it on to Mr McPhail when she saw him. He didn't doubt that she would. It had been unfair of him to introduce himself as a policeman to the landlady. She would probably become suspicious, and might even give McPhail a week's notice on the strength of those suspicions. That would be a terrible shame.

Actually, it didn't look to Rebus as though Mrs MacKenzie would twig. And McPhail would doubtless come up with some reason for Rebus's visit. Probably the City of Edinburgh Police were about to award him a commendation for saving some puppies from the raging torrents of the Water of Leith. McPhail was good at making up stories, after all. Children just loved to hear stories.

Rebus stood outside Mrs MacKenzie's house and looked across the road. It had to be coincidence that McPhail had chosen a boarding house within ogling distance of a primary school. Rebus had seen it on his arrival; it had been enough to decide him on identifying himself to the landlady. After all, he didn't believe in coincidence.

And if McPhail couldn't be persuaded to move, well, maybe the neighbours would find out the true story of Mrs MacKenzie's lodger. Rebus got into his car. He didn't always like himself or his job.

But some bits were okay.

Back at St Leonard's, Siobhan Clarke had nothing new to

report on the stabbing. Rory Kintoul was being very cagey about another interview. He'd cancelled one arranged meeting, and she'd not been able to contact him since.

'His son's seventeen and unemployed, spends most of the day at home, I could try talking to him.'

'You could.' But it was a lot of trouble. Maybe Holmes was right. 'Just do your best,' said Rebus. 'After you've talked with Kintoul, if we're no further forward we'll drop the whole thing. If Kintoul wants to get himself stabbed, that's fine with me.'

She nodded and turned away.

'Any news on Brian?'

She turned back. 'He's been talking.'

'Talking?'

'In his sleep. I thought you'd know.'

'What's he been saying?'

'Nothing they can make out, but it means he's slowly regaining consciousness.'

'Good.'

She started to turn away again, but Rebus thought of something. 'How are you getting to Aberdeen on Saturday?'

'Driving, why?'

'Any room in the car?'

'There's just me.'

'Then you won't mind giving me a lift.'

She looked startled. 'Not at all. Where to?'

'Pittodrie.'

Now she looked even more surprised. 'I wouldn't have taken you for a Hibs fan, sir.'

Rebus screwed up his face. 'No, you're all alone in that category. I just need a lift, that's all.'

'Fine.'

'And on the way, you can tell me what you've learned from the files on Big Ger.'

# 8

By Saturday, Rebus had argued three times with Michael (who was talking about moving out anyway), once with the students (also talking about moving), and once with the receptionist at Patience's surgery when she wouldn't put Rebus through. Brian Holmes had opened his eyes briefly, and it was reckoned by the doctors that he was on his way to recovery. None of them, however, hazarded the phrase 'full recovery'. Still, the news had cheered Siobhan Clarke, and she was in a good mood when she arrived at Rebus's Arden Street flat. He was waiting for her at street level. She drove a two-year-old cherry-red Renault 5. It looked young and full of life, while Rebus's car (parked next to it) looked to be in terminal condition. But Rebus's car had been looking like this for three or four years now, and just when he'd determined to get rid of it it always seemed to go into remission. Rebus had the feeling the car could read his mind.

'Morning, sir,' said Siobhan Clarke. There was pop music coming from the stereo. She saw Rebus cringe as he got into the passenger seat, and turned the volume down. 'Bad night?'

'People always seem to ask me that.'

'Now why could that be?'

They stopped at a bakery so Rebus could buy some breakfast. There had been nothing in the flat worth the description 'food', but then Rebus couldn't really complain. His contribution to the larder so far had filled a single shopping basket. And most of that had been meat, something the students didn't touch. He noticed Michael had gone vegetarian too, at least in public.

'It's healthier, John,' he'd told his brother, slapping his stomach.

'What's that supposed to mean?' Rebus had snapped.

Michael had merely shaken his head sadly. 'Too much caffeine.'

That was another thing, the kitchen cupboards were full of jars of what looked like coffee but turned out to be 'infusions' of crushed tree bark and chicory. At the bakery, Rebus bought a polystyrene beaker of coffee and two sausage rolls. The sausage rolls turned out to be a bad mistake, the flakes of pastry breaking off and covering the otherwise pristine car interior – despite Rebus's best attempts with the paper bag.

'Sorry about the mess,' he offered to Siobhan, who was driving with her window conspicuously open. 'You're not vegetarian, are you?'

She laughed. 'You mean you haven't noticed?'

'Can't say I have.'

She nodded towards a sausage roll. 'Well, have you heard of mechanically recovered meat?'

'Don't,' warned Rebus. He finished the sausage rolls quickly, and cleared his throat.

'Anything I should know about between you and Brian?'

The look on her face told him this was not the year's most successful conversational gambit. 'Not that I know of.'

'It's just that he and Nell were ... well, there's still a good chance –'

'I'm not a monster, sir. And I know the score between Brian and Nell. Brian's just a nice guy. We get along.' She glanced away from the windscreen. 'That's all there is to it.' Rebus was about to say something. 'But if there *was* more to it than that,' she went on, 'I don't see that it would be any of your business, with respect, sir. Not unless it was interfering with our work, which I wouldn't let happen. I don't suppose Brian would either.'

Rebus stayed silent.

'I'm sorry, I shouldn't have said that.'

'What you said was fair enough. The problem was the *way* you said it. A police officer's never off duty, and I'm your boss – even on a jaunt like this. Don't forget that.'

There was more silence in the car, until Siobhan broke it. 'It's a nice part of town, Marchmont.'

'Almost as nice as the New Town.'

She glared at him, her grip on the steering-wheel as determined as any strangler's.

'I thought,' she said slyly, 'you lived in Oxford Terrace these days, sir.'

'You thought wrong. Now, what about turning that bloody music off? After all, we've got a lot to talk about.'

The 'lot', of course, being Morris Gerald Cafferty.

Siobhan Clarke hadn't brought her notes with her. She didn't need them. She could recite the salient details from memory, along with a lot of detail that might not be salient but was certainly interesting. Certainly she'd done her homework. Rebus thought how frustrating the job could be. She'd swotted up on Big Ger as background to Operation Moneybags, but Operation Moneybags almost certainly wouldn't trap Cafferty. And she'd spent a lot of hours on the Kintoul stabbing, which might also turn out to be nothing.

'And another thing,' she said. 'Apparently Cafferty's got a little diary of sorts, all of it in code. We've never been able to crack his code, which means it must be highly personal.'

Yes, Rebus remembered. Whenever they brought Big Ger into custody, the diary would be collected along with his other possessions. Then they'd photocopy the pages of the diary and try to decipher them. They'd never been successful.

'Rumour has it,' Siobhan was saying, 'the diary's a record of bad debts, debts Cafferty takes care of personally.'

'A man like that garners a lot of rumours. They help make him larger than life. In life, he's just another witless gangster.'

'A code takes wits.'

'Maybe.'

'In the file, there's a recent clipping from the *Sun*. It's all about how bodies keep washing up on the coastline.'

Rebus nodded. 'On the Solway coast, not far from Stranraer.'

'You think it's Cafferty's doing?'

Rebus shrugged. 'The bodies have never been identified. Could be anything. Could be people pushed off the Larne ferry. Could be some connection with Ulster. There are some weird currents between Larne and Stranraer.' He paused. 'Could be anything.'

'Could be Cafferty, in other words.'

'Could be.'

'It's a long way to go to dispose of a body.'

'Well, he's not going to shit in his own nest, is he?'

She considered this. 'There was mention in one of the papers of a van spotted on that coastline, too early in the morning to be delivering anything.'

Rebus nodded. 'And there was nowhere along the road for it to be delivering *to*. I read the papers sometimes, Clarke. The Dumfries and Galloway Police have patrols along there now.'

Siobhan drove for a while, gathering her thoughts. 'He's just been lucky so far, hasn't he, sir? I mean, I can understand that he's a clever villain, and clever villains are harder to catch. But he has to delegate, and usually even though a villain's clever his underlings are so stupid or lazy they *would* shit in the nest.'

85

'Language, Clarke, language.' He got a smile from her. 'Point taken, though.'

'Reading all about Cafferty's "associates" I didn't get an impression of many "O" Grades. They've all got names like Slink and Codge and the Radiator.'

Rebus grinned. 'Radiator McCallum, I remember him. He was supposed to be descended from a family of Highland cannibals. He did research and everything, he was so proud of his ancestors.'

'He disappeared from the scene, though.'

'Yes, three or four years ago.'

'Four and a half, according to the records. I wonder what happened to him.'

Rebus shrugged. 'He tried to doublecross Big Ger, got scared and ran off.'

'Or didn't get the chance to run off.'

'That too, of course. Or else he just got fed up, or had another job offer. It's a very mobile profession, being a thug. Wherever the work is ...'

'Cafferty certainly gets through the personnel. McCallum's cousins disappeared from view just before McCallum himself did.'

Rebus frowned. 'I didn't know he had any cousins.'

'Known colloquially as the Bru-head Brothers. Something to do with a penchant for Irn-Bru.'

'Altogether understandable. What were their real names, though?'

She thought for a moment. 'Tam and Eck Robertson.'

Rebus nodded. 'Eck Robertson, yes. I didn't know about the other one, though. Hang on a minute ...'

Tam and Eck Robertson. The R. Brothers. Which would mean that Mork was ...

'Morris bloody Cafferty!' Rebus slapped the dashboard. Brian shortened the name and used a k for the c. Christ ... If Brian Holmes was on to something involving Cafferty and his gang, no wonder he was scared. Something to do

86

with the night the Central Hotel caught fire. Did they start the blaze because the hotel hadn't been paying its protection dues? What about the body, maybe it'd been some debtor or other. And soon afterwards, Radiator McCallum and his cousins left the scene. Bloody hell.

'If you're going to have a seizure,' said Siobhan, 'I'm trained in cardiac resuscitation.'

Rebus wasn't listening. He stared at the road ahead, one fist around the coffee cup, the other pounding his knee. He was thinking of Brian's note. He hadn't said for sure that Cafferty was there that night, only that the brothers were. And something about a poker game. He was going to try to find the Robertson brothers; that was his final comment. After which, someone came along and hit him on the head. Maybe it was beginning to come together.

'I'm not sure I can deal with catatonia though.'

'What?'

'Was it something that I said?'

'Yes, it was.'

'The Bru-Head Brothers?'

'The very same. What else can you tell me about them?'

'Born in Niddrie, petty thieves from the time they left the pram –'

'They probably stole the pram, too. Anything else?'

Siobhan knew that she'd hit some nerve. 'Plenty. Both had long records. Eck liked flashy clothes, Tam always wore jeans and a T-shirt. The funny thing is, though, Tam kept scrupulously clean. He even took his own soap everywhere with him. I thought that was strange.'

'If I were the gambling kind,' said Rebus, 'I'd bet the soap was lemon-scented.'

'How did you know that?'

'Instinct. Not mine, someone else's.' Rebus frowned. 'How come I never heard of Tam?'

'He moved to Dundee when he left school, or rather

when he was *asked* to leave school. He only came back to Edinburgh years later. The records have him down as working for the gang for about six months, maybe even less.' She waited. 'Are you going to tell me what this is all about?'

'It's all about a hotel fire.'

'You mean those files on the floor behind your desk?'

'I mean those files on the floor behind my desk.'

'I couldn't help taking a peek.'

'They might tie in with the attack on Brian.' She turned to him. 'Keep your eyes on the road. You concentrate on the driving, and I'll tell you a story. It might even keep us going till Aberdeen.'

And it did.


'In ye come, Jock. My, my, I wouldn't have recognised ye.'

'I was in shorts the last time you saw me, Auntie Ena.'

The old woman laughed. She used a zimmer frame to walk back through the narrow musty hall and into a small back room. The room was crammed with furniture. There would be a front room, too, another lounge kept for the most special occasions. But Rebus was family, and family were greeted in the back room.

She was frail-looking and hunch-backed and wore a shawl over her angular shoulders. Her silver hair had been pulled back severely and pinned tight against her head, and her eyes were sunken dots in a parchment face. Rebus couldn't remember her at all.

'You must have been three when we were last in Fife. You could talk the hind legs off a donkey, but with such a thick accent, I could hardly make out a word of it. Always wanting to tell a joke or sing a song.'

'I've changed,' Rebus said.

'Eh?' She had dumped herself into a chair beside the

fireplace, and craned her head forward. 'My hearing's not so good, Jock.'

'I said, nobody calls me Jock!' Rebus called. 'It's John.'

'Oh aye, John. Right you are.' She pulled a travel-rug over her legs. In the fireplace stood an electric fire, the kind with fake coals, fake flames, and, so far as Rebus could tell, fake heat. There was one pale orange bar on, but he couldn't feel anything.

'Danny found you, then?'

'You mean Andy?'

'He's a good laddie. Such a shame he got made redundant. Did he come back with you?'

'No, he's still in Edinburgh.' She was resting her head against the back of the chair. Rebus got the impression she was about to drift off to sleep. The walk to the front door and back had probably exhausted her.

'His parents are nice folk, always so kind to me.'

'You wanted to see me about something, Auntie Ena?'

'Eh?'

He crouched down in front of her, resting his hands on the side of the chair. 'You wanted to see me.' Well, she could see him ... and then she couldn't, as her eyes glazed over and, mouth wide open, she started to snore.

Rebus stood up and gave a loud sigh. The clock over the mantelpiece had stopped, but he knew he had at least two hours to kill. Talking over the Central Hotel case with Siobhan had made him agitated. He wanted to get back to work on it. And here he was, trapped in this miniature museum. He looked around, wrinkling his nose at a chrome commode in one dark corner. There were photos inside a glass-fronted china cabinet. He went over and examined them. He recognised a picture of his grandparents on his father's side, but there were no photos of his father. The feud, or whatever it had been, had seen to that.

The Scots never forgot. It was a burden and a gift. The

living-room led directly onto a small scullery. Rebus looked in the antique fridge and found a piece of brisket, which he sniffed. There was bread in a large tin in the pantry, and butter in a dish on the draining-board. It took him ten minutes to make the sandwiches, and five minutes to find out which of the many caddies contained the tea.

He found a radio beside the sink and tried to find commentary on a football game, but the batteries were weaker than his tea. So he tiptoed back through to where Auntie Ena was still sleeping and sat down in the chair opposite her. He hadn't come up here expecting an inheritance, exactly, but he had bargained for more than this. A particularly loud snore brought Auntie Ena wriggling towards consciousness.

'Eh? Is that you, Jimmy?'

'It's John, your nephew.'

'Gracious, John, did I nod off?'

'Just forty winks.'

'Isn't that terrible of me, with a visitor here and everything.'

'I'm not a visitor, Auntie Ena, I'm family.'

'Aye, son, so you are. Now, listen to me. There's some beef in the fridge. Shall I go and –?'

'They're already made.'

'Eh?'

'The sandwiches. I've made them up.'

'You have? You always were a bright one. Now what about some tea?'

'Sit where you are, I'll make some fresh.'

He made a pot of tea and brought the sandwiches through on a plate, setting them in front of her on a footstool. 'There we are.' He was about to hand her one, when she made a grab for his wrists, nearly toppling the plate. He saw that her eyes were shut, and though she looked frail enough her grip was strong. She'd started speaking before Rebus realised she was saying grace.

'Some hae meat and cannae eat, and some hae nane that want it. But we hae meat and we can eat, so let the Lord be thankit.'

Rebus almost burst out laughing. Almost. But inside, he was touched too. He handed her a smile along with her sandwich, then went to fetch the tea.

The meal revived her, and she seemed to remember why she'd wanted to see him.

'Your faither and my husband fell out very many years ago. Maybe forty or more years ago. They never exchanged a letter, a Christmas card, or a civil word ever again. Now, don't you think that's stupid? And do you know what it was about? It was about the fact that though we invited your faither and mither to our Ishbel's wedding, we didn't invite you. We'd decided there would be no children, you see. But then a friend of mine, Peggy Callaghan, brought her son along uninvited, and we could hardly turn him away, since there was no way for him to get back home on his own. When your faither saw this, he argued with Jimmy. A real blazing row. And then your faither stormed out, leaving your mither to follow him. A sweet woman she was. So that's that.'

She sat back in her chair, breadcrumbs prominent on her lower lip.

'That was all?'

She nodded. 'Doesn't seem like much, does it? Not from this distance. But it was enough. And the both of them were too stubborn ever to make it up.'

'And you wanted to see me so you could tell me this?'

'Partly, yes. But also, I wanted to give you something.' She rose slowly from her chair, using the zimmer-frame for support, and leaned up towards the mantelpiece. Rebus half-rose to help her, but she didn't need his help. She found the photograph and handed it down to him. He looked at it. In fading black and white, it showed two grinning schoolboys, not exactly dressed to the nines.

They had their arms casually slung around one another's necks, and their faces were close together. Best friends, but more than that: brothers.

'He kept that, you see. He told me once that he'd thrown out all the photos of your faither. But when we were going through his things, we found that in the bottom of a shoebox. I wanted you to have it, Jock.'

'It's not Jock, it's John,' said Rebus, his eyes not entirely dry.

'Of course it is,' said his Auntie Ena. 'Of course it is.'

Earlier that afternoon, Michael Rebus had lain along the couch asleep and unaware that he was missing one of his favourite films, *Double Indemnity*, on BBC2. He'd gone to the pub for a lunchtime drink: alone, as it turned out. The students weren't into it. Instead, they'd gone shopping, or to the launderette, or home for the weekend to see parents and friends. So Michael drank only two lagers topped with lemonade and returned to the flat, where he promptly fell asleep in front of the TV.

He'd been thinking about John recently. He knew he was imposing on his big brother, but didn't reckon on doing so much longer. He had spoken on the phone to Chrissie. She was still in Kirkcaldy with the kids. She'd wanted nothing to do with him after the bust, and was especially disgusted that his own brother had given evidence against him. But Michael didn't blame John for that. John had principles. And besides, some of the evidence had worked – deliberately, he was sure – in Michael's favour.

Now Chrissie was talking to him again. He'd written to her all through his incarceration, then had written from London too; not knowing whether she'd received any of his letters. But she had. She told him that when they spoke. And she didn't have a boyfriend, and the kids were fine, and did he want to see them some time?

'I want to see you,' he'd told her. It sounded right.

He was dreaming about her when the doorbell went. Well ... her and Gail the student, if truth be told. He staggered to his feet. The bell was insistent.

It took a second to turn the snib-lock, after which Michael's world imploded.


With another Hibernian defeat behind her, Siobhan Clarke was quiet on the way home, which suited Rebus. He had some thinking to do, and not about work, for a change. He thought about the job too much as it was, gave himself to it the way he had never given himself to any *person* in his life. Not his ex-wife, not his daughter, not Patience, not Michael.

He'd come into the police prematurely weary and cynical. Then he watched recruits like Holmes and Clarke and saw their best intentions thwarted by the system and the public's attitude. There were times you'd feel more welcome if you were painting plague markers on people's doors.

'A penny for them,' said Siobhan Clarke.

'Don't waste your money.'

'Why not? Look how much I've wasted already today.'

Rebus smiled at that. 'Aye,' he said, 'I keep forgetting, there's always someone in the world worse off than yourself ... Unless you're a Hibs supporter.'

'Ha bloody ha.'

Siobhan Clarke reached for the stereo and tried to find a station that didn't run the day's classified results.

# 9

Full of good intentions, Rebus opened the door of the flat, sensing immediately that nobody was home. Well, it was Saturday night, after all. But they might at least have turned the TV off.

He went into the box room and placed the old photograph on Michael's unmade bed. The room smelt faintly of perfume, reminding Rebus of Patience. He missed her more than he liked to admit. When they'd first started seeing one another, they'd agreed that they were both too old for anything that could be called 'love'. They'd also agreed that they were more than ready for lashings of sex. Then, when Rebus had moved in, they'd talked again. It didn't really mean commitment, they were agreed on that; it was just handier for the moment. Ah, but when Rebus had rented out his own flat ... *that* had meant commitment, commitment to sleeping on the sofa should Patience ever kick him out.

He lay along the sofa now, noticing that he had all but annexed what had been the flat's main communal space. The students tended to sit around in the kitchen now, talking quietly with the door closed. Rebus didn't blame them. It was all a mess in here, and all *his* mess. His suitcase lay wide open on the floor beside the window, ties and socks trickling from it. The holdall was tucked behind the sofa. His two suits hung limply from the picture-rail next to the box room, partially blocking out a psychedelic poster which had been making Rebus's eyes hurt. The place had a feral smell from lack of fresh air. The smell suited it, though. After all, wasn't this Rebus's lair?

He picked up the telephone and rang Patience. Her taped voice spoke to him; the message was new.

'I'm going with Susan and Jenny back to their mother's. Any messages, leave them after the tone.'

Rebus's first thought was how stupid Patience had been. The message let any caller – *any* caller – know she wasn't home. He knew that burglars often telephoned first. They might even go through the phone book more or less at random, finding phones that rang and rang, or answering machines. You had to make your message vague.

He guessed that if she'd gone to her sister's, she wouldn't be back until tomorrow night at the earliest, and might even stay over on the Monday.

'Hi, Patience,' he said to the machine. 'It's me. I'm ready to talk when you are. I ... miss you. Bye.'

So, the girls had gone. Maybe now things could get back to normal. No more smouldering Susan, no more gentle Jenny. They weren't the cause of the rift between Rebus and Patience, but maybe they hadn't helped. No, they definitely hadn't helped.

He made himself a cup of 'coffee substitute', all the time thinking of wandering down to the late-opening shop at the corner of Marchmont Road. But their coffee was instant and expensive, and besides, maybe this stuff would taste okay.

It tasted awful, and was absolutely caffeine-free, which was probably why he fell asleep during a dreary mid-evening movie on the television.

And awoke to a ringing telephone. Someone had switched the TV off, and perhaps that same person had thrown the blanket over him. It was getting to be a regular thing. He was stiff as he sat up and reached for the receiver. His watch told him it was one-fifteen a.m.

'Hello?'

'Is that Inspector Rebus?'

'Speaking.' Rebus rubbed at his hair.

'Inspector, this is PC Hart. I'm in South Queensferry.'

'Yes?'

'There's someone here claims he's your brother.'

'Michael?'

'That's the name he gave.'

'What's up? Is he guttered?'

'Nothing like that, sir.'

'What is it then?'

'Well, sir, we've just found him ...'

Rebus was very awake now. 'Found him where?'

'He was hanging from the Forth Rail Bridge.'

'What?' Rebus felt his hand squeezing the telephone receiver to death. *'Hanging?'*

'I don't mean like that, sir. Sorry if I ...' Rebus's grip relaxed.

'No, I mean he was hanging by his feet, sort of suspended, like. Just hanging in mid-air.'

'We thought it was some sort of joke gone wrong at first. You know, bungee jumper, that kind of thing.' PC Hart was leading Rebus to a hut on the quayside at South Queensferry. The Firth of Forth was dark and quiet in front of them, but Rebus could make out the rail bridge lowering far above them. 'But that's not the story he gave us. Besides, it was clear he hadn't taken the dive on his own.'

'How clear?'

'His hands were tied together, sir. And his mouth had been taped shut.'

'Christ.'

'Doctor says he'll be all right. If they'd tipped him over the side, his legs could've come out of the sockets, but the

96

doc reckons they must have lowered him over.'

'How did they get onto the bridge in the first place?'

'It's easy enough, if you've a head for heights.'

Rebus, who had no head for heights, had already declined the offer of a visit to the spot where Michael had been found, up on the ochre-coloured iron construction.

'Looks like they waited till they knew there'd be no trains about. But a boat was going under the bridge, and the skipper thought he saw something, so he radioed in. Otherwise, well, he could have been up there all night.' Hart shook his head. 'A cold night, I can't say I'd fancy it.'

They were at the hut now. There was only enough room inside for two men. One of these, seated with a blanket over his shoulders, was Michael. The other was a local doctor, called from his bed by the look of him. Other men stood around: police, the proprietor of a hotel on the waterfront, and the boat skipper who might just have saved Michael's life, or at the very least his sanity.

'John, thank Christ.' Michael was trembling, and seemed to have no colour in him at all. The doctor was holding a hot cup of something, from which he was coaxing Michael to drink.

'Drink up, Mickey,' said Rebus. Michael looked pathetic, like the victim of some terrible tragedy. Rebus felt a tremendous sadness overwhelm him. Michael had spent years in jail, where God knows what had happened to him. Then, released, he'd had no luck at all until he'd come to Edinburgh. The bravado, the nights out with the students – Rebus suddenly saw it for what it really was, a front, an attempt to put behind him all that Michael had feared these past few years. And now this had happened, reducing him to the crouched shivering animal in the hut.

'I'll be back in a second, Mickey.' Rebus pulled Hart

around the side of the hut. 'What has he told you?' He was trying to control the fury inside him.

'He said he was in your flat, sir, on his own.'

'When?'

'This afternoon, about four. There was a ring at the doorbell, so he answered, and three men pushed their way in. The first thing they did was put a cloth bag over his head. Then they held him down and tied him up, took the bag off and taped shut his mouth, then put the bag back.'

'He didn't see them?'

'They kept his face against the hall carpet. He just got the quick glimpse of them when he opened the door.'

'Go on.' Rebus was trying not to look up at the rail bridge. Instead, he focused on the flashing red lights on top of the more distant road bridge.

'They seem to have wrapped something like a carpet around him and taken him downstairs and into a van. It was pretty cramped in there, according to your brother. Narrow, like. He reckoned there were boxes either side of him.' Hart paused. He didn't like the look of concentration on the Inspector's face.

'Well?' Rebus snapped.

'He says they drove around for hours, not saying anything. Then he was lifted out of the van and taken into something like a cellar or a storeroom. They never took the bag off his head, so he can't be sure.' Hart paused. 'I didn't want to question him too closely, sir, in his present condition.'

Rebus nodded.

'Anyway, finally they brought him up here. Tied him to the side of the bridge, and lowered him over it. They still hadn't said anything. But when they started to lower away, they finally took the bag off his head.'

'Christ.' Rebus screwed shut his eyes. It brought back the grimmest memories of his own SAS training, the way they'd tried to get him to hand over information. Taking him up in a helicopter with a bag over his head, then threatening to drop him out, and carrying out their threat ... But only eight feet off the ground, not the hundreds of feet he'd visualised. Horrible, all of it. He pushed past Hart, pulled the doctor out of the way, and bent down to hug Michael, keeping him close against his chest as he heard Michael start to bawl. The crying lasted for many minutes, but Rebus wasn't about to let go.

And then at last, it was over. Racking dry coughs, the breathing slowing, and a sort of calm. Michael's face was a mess of tear tracks and mucus. Rebus handed him a handkerchief.

'The ambulance is waiting,' the doctor said quietly. Rebus nodded. Michael was obviously in shock; they'd keep him in the Infirmary overnight.

Two patients to visit, thought Rebus. What was more, he suspected similar motives behind the attacks. Very similar motives, if it came down to it. The rage began in him all over again, and his scalp prickled like hell. But he calmed a little as he helped Michael over to the ambulance.

'Do you want me to come with you?' he asked.

'Absolutely not,' said Michael. 'Just go home, eh?'

Part of the way to the ambulance, Michael's legs gave way, his knees refusing to lock. They carried him instead, like taking an injured player off the field, closed the door on him, and took him away. Rebus thanked the doctor, the skipper, and Hart.

'Hellish thing to happen,' Hart said. 'Any idea why it did?'

'A few,' said Rebus.

He went home to brood in his darkened living room. His whole life seemed shot to hell. Someone had been sending him a message tonight. They'd either decided to send it *via* Michael, or else they'd simply mistaken Michael for him. After all, people said they looked alike. Since the men had come to Arden Street, they were either working on very old information, or else they knew all about his separation from Patience, which meant they were very well-informed indeed. But Rebus suspected the former. The name on the doorbell still said Rebus, though it also listed on a scrap of paper four other names. That must have confused them for a minute. Yet they'd decided to attack anyway. Why? Did it mean they were desperate? Or was it just that any hostage would do to get the message across?

Message received.

And almost understood. Almost. This was serious, deadly serious. First Brian, now Michael. He had so few doubts that the two were connected. It felt like it was time to do something, not just wait for their next move. He knew what he wanted to do, too. That one phrase had brought it to mind: *shot to hell*. A part of him wanted to be holding a gun. A gun would even the odds very nicely indeed. He even knew where he could get one, didn't he? *Anything from a shag to a shooter*. He found that he'd been pacing the floor in front of the window. He felt caged, unwilling to sleep and unable to act against his invisible foe. But he had to do *some*thing ... so he went for a drive.

He drove to Perth. It didn't take long on the motorway in the middle of the night. In the city itself, he got lost once or twice (with no one about to ask directions of, not even a policeman) before finding the street he wanted. It was sited on a ridge of land, with houses on the one side only. This was where Patience's sister lived. Rebus spotted Patience's car and found a parking space two cars away from it. He turned off his lights and engine and reached into the back seat for the blanket he'd brought, pulling the blanket over as much of him as it would cover. He sat for a while, feeling more relaxed than in ages. He'd thought of bringing some whisky with him, but knew the kind of head it would give him in the morning. And tomorrow he wanted to be clear-headed if nothing else. He thought of Patience asleep in the spare room, just through the wall from Susan. She slept soundly, the moon lighting her forehead and her cheeks. It seemed a long way from Edinburgh, a long way from the shadow of the Forth Rail Bridge. John Rebus drifted into sleep, and slept well for once.

When he awoke, it was six-thirty on Sunday morning. He threw aside the blanket and started the car, turning the heating all the way up. He felt chilled but rested. The street was quiet, except for a man walking his ugly white poodle. The man seemed to find Rebus's presence there curious. Rebus smiled steadily at him as he shifted the gearstick into first and drove away.

# 10

He went straight to the Infirmary where, despite the early hour, pre-breakfast tea was being served. Michael was sitting up in bed with the cup on the tray in front of him. He seemed like a statue, staring at the surface of the dark brown liquid, his face blank. He didn't move as Rebus approached, pulled a chair noisily from a pile beside one wall, and sat down.

'Hiya, Mickey.'

'Hello, John.' Michael continued to stare. Rebus hadn't seen him blink yet.

'Going through it again and again, eh?' Michael didn't answer. 'I've been there myself, Mickey. Something terrible happens, you play it over in your mind. Eventually it fades. You might not believe that just now.'

'I'm trying to understand who did it, *why* they did it.'

'They wanted you scared, Mickey. I think it was a message for me.'

'Couldn't they have written instead? They got me scared all right. I could have shit through a Polo mint.'

Rebus laughed loudly at this. If Michael was getting back a sense of humour, the rest couldn't be far behind. 'I brought you this,' he said.

It was the photograph from Aberdeen. Rebus placed it on the tray beside the untouched tea.

'Who are they?'

'Dad and Uncle Jimmy.'

'Uncle Jimmy? I don't remember an Uncle Jimmy.'

'They fell out a long time ago, never spoke again.'

'That's a shame.'

'Uncle Jimmy died a few weeks ago. His widow – Auntie Ena – wanted us to have this photo.'

'Why?'

'Maybe because we're blood,' Rebus said.

Michael smiled. 'You wouldn't always know it.' He looked up at Rebus with wet shining eyes.

'We'll know it from now on,' said Rebus. He nodded towards the cup. 'Can I have that tea if you're not drinking it? My tongue feels like a happy hour's welcome-mat.'

'Help yourself.'

Rebus drank the tea in two swallows. 'Jesus,' he said, 'I was doing you a favour, believe me.'

'I know all about the tea they serve in institutions.'

'You're not as daft as you look then.' Rebus paused. 'You didn't see much of them, eh?'

'Who?'

'The men who grabbed you.'

'I saw bodies coming through the door. The first one was about my height, but a lot broader. The others, who knows. I never saw any faces. Sorry.'

'No problem. Can you tell me *any*thing?'

'No more than I told the constable last night. What was his name again?'

'Hart.'

'That's it. He thought I'd been bungee-jumping.' Michael gave a low laugh. 'I told him, no, I was just hanging around.'

Rebus smiled. 'But thankfully not at a loose end, eh?'

But Michael had stopped laughing. 'I had a nightmare about it. They had to give me something to make me sleep. I don't know what it was, but I still feel doped.'

'Get them to give you a prescription, you can sell tabs to the students.'

'They're good kids, John.'

'I know.'

'It'd be a shame if they moved out.'

'I know that, too.'

'You remember Gail?'

'The girl you've been seeing?'

'I've seen every inch of her. Strictly past tense now. But she has a boyfriend in Auchterarder. You don't suppose he's the jealous type?'

'I don't think he's behind last night.'

'No? Only, I've not been around Edinburgh long enough to make any enemies.'

'Don't worry,' said Rebus. 'I've got enemies enough for both of us.'

'That's very reassuring. Meanwhile ...'

'Yes?'

'What about getting a spyhole for your door? Just think if one of the lassies had answered.'

Oh, Rebus had thought about it. 'And a chain,' he said. 'I'm getting them this afternoon.' He paused. 'Hart said something about the van.'

'When they pushed me in, it was like I was fitting into a narrow space. Yet I got the feeling the van itself was a decent size.'

'So it had stuff in the back then?'

'Maybe. Bloody solid, whatever it was. I bruised both knees.' Michael shrugged. 'That's about it.' Then he thought of something. 'Oh yes, and it had a bad smell. Either that or something had died in the carpet they wrapped me in ...'

They sat talking for another quarter of an hour or so, until Michael closed his eyes and went to sleep. He wouldn't be asleep for long: they were starting to serve breakfast. Rebus got up and moved the chair back, then placed the photograph on Michael's bedside cabinet. He had another call to pay, while he was here.

But there were doctors with Brian Holmes, and the nurse didn't know how long they'd be. She only knew that Brian had woken again in the night for almost a minute. Rebus wished he'd been there: a minute would be long enough for the question he wanted to ask. Brian had also been talking in his sleep, but his words had been mumbled at best, and no one had any record of what he'd said. So Rebus gave up and went off to do some shopping. If he phoned around noon they'd let him know when Michael was likely to be getting home.

He went back to the flat by way of the corner shop, where he bought a week's worth of groceries. He was finishing breakfast when the first student wandered into the kitchen and drank three glassfuls of water.

'You're supposed to do that *before* you go to bed,' Rebus advised.

'Thank you, Sherlock.' The young man groaned. 'Got any paracetamol?' Rebus shook his head. 'Definitely a bad keg of beer last night. I thought the first pint tasted ropey.'

'Aye, but I'll bet the second tasted better and the sixth tasted great.'

The student laughed. 'What're you eating?'

'Toast and jam.'

'No bacon or sausages?'

Rebus shook his head. 'I've decided to lay off meat for a while.'

The student seemed unnaturally pleased.

'There's orange juice in the fridge,' Rebus continued. The student opened the fridge door and gave a gasp.

'There's enough stuff in here to feed a lecture hall!'

'Which is why,' said Rebus, 'I reckon it'll do us for at least a day or two.'

The student lifted a letter from the top of the fridge. 'This came for you yesterday.'

It was from the Inland Revenue. They were thinking of coming to check on the flat.

'Remember,' Rebus told the student, 'anyone asks, you're my nephews and nieces.'

'Yes, uncle.' The student recommenced rummaging in the refrigerator. 'Where did Mickey and you get to last night?' he asked. 'I crept in at two and there was no sign of life.'

'Oh, we were just ...' But Rebus couldn't find any words. So the student supplied them for him.

'Shooting the breeze?'

'Shooting the breeze,' agreed Rebus.

He drove to a DIY superstore on the edge of the city and bought a chain for the door, a spy-hole, and the tools a helpful assistant suggested would be needed for both jobs. (A lot more tools than Rebus used, as it turned out.) Since there was a supermarket nearby, Rebus did a bit more grocery shopping, by which time the pubs were open for business. He looked in a few places, but couldn't find who he was looking for. But he was able to put word out with a couple of useful barmen, who said they would pass the message along.

Back at the flat, he called the Infirmary, who told him Michael could come home this afternoon. Rebus arranged to pick him up at four. He then got to work. He drilled the necessary hole in the door, only to find he'd drilled it too high for the girl student, who had to stand on tiptoe even to get close. So he drilled another hole, filled in the first with wood putty, and then fitted the spy-hole. It was a bit askew, but it would work. Fitting the sliding chain was easier, and left him with two tools and a drill-bit unused. He wondered if the DIY store would take them back.

Next he tidied the box room and put Michael's stuff into the washing machine, after which he shared the macaroni cheese which the students had prepared for lunch. He didn't quite apologise to them for the past week, but he insisted they use the living room whenever they liked, and he told them also that he was reducing their rent – news they took unsurprisingly well. He didn't say anything about Michael; he didn't reckon Michael would want them to know. And he'd already explained away the extra security on the door by citing several recent burglaries in the locality.

He brought Michael and a large bottle of sleeping tablets back from the hospital, having first bribed the students to be out of the flat for the rest of the afternoon and evening. If Michael needed to cry again, he wouldn't want an audience.

'Look, our new peephole,' said Rebus at the door of the flat.

'That was quick.'

'Protestant work ethic. Or is it Calvinist guilt? I can never remember.' Rebus opened the door. 'Please also note the security chain on the inside.'

'You can tell it's a rush job, look where the paint's all scored.'

'Don't push your luck, brother.'

Michael sat in the living room while Rebus made two mugs of tea. The stairwell had seemed full of menace for both brothers, each sensing the other's disquiet. And even now Rebus didn't feel completely safe. This was not, however, something he wished to share with Michael.

'Just the way you like it,' he said, bringing the tea in. He could see Michael was weepy again, though trying to hide it.

'Thanks, John.'

The phone rang before Rebus could say anything. It was Siobhan Clarke, checking details of the following morning's surveillance operation.

Rebus assured her that everything was in hand; all she

had to do was turn up and freeze her bum off for a few hours.

'You're a great one for motivation, sir,' was her final comment.

'So,' Rebus asked Michael, 'what do you want to do?'

Michael was shaking a large round pill out of the brown bottle. He put it on his tongue with a wavering hand, and washed it down with tea.

'A quiet night in would suit me fine,' he said.

'A quiet night in it is,' agreed Rebus.

# 11

Operation Moneybags began quietly enough at eight-thirty on Monday morning, thirty minutes before Davey Dougary's BMW bumped its way into the pot-holed parking lot of the taxi-cab firm. Alister Flower and his team, of course, wouldn't be starting work till eleven or a little after, but it was best not to think about that, especially if, like Siobhan Clarke, you were already cold and stiff by opening time, and dreading your next visit to the chemical toilet which had been installed, for want of any other facilities, in a broom closet.

She was bored, too. DC Peter Petrie (from St Leonard's) and Elsa-Beth Jardine from Trading Standards appeared to be nursing post-weekend hangovers and resultant blues. She got the feeling that Jardine and her might actually have a lot to talk about – both were women fighting for recognition in what was perceived as a male profession – but the presence of Petrie ruled out discussion.

Peter Petrie was one of those basically intelligent but not exactly perceptive officers who climbed the ladder by passing the exams (though never with brilliant marks) and not getting in anyone's way. Petrie was quiet and methodical; she didn't doubt his competence, it was just that he lacked any spark of inspiration or instinct. And probably, she thought, he was sitting there with his thermos summing her up as an over-talkative smart-arse with a university degree. Well, whatever he was he was no John Rebus.

She had accused her superior of not exactly motivating those who worked for him, but this was a lie. He could draw you into a case, and into his way of thinking about a case, merely by being so narrow-minded about the investigation. He was secretive – and that drew you in. He was tenacious – and that drew you in. Above all, though, he had the air of knowing exactly where he was going. And he wasn't all that bad looking either. She'd learned a lot about him by sticking close to Brian Holmes, who had been only too willing to chat about past cases and what he knew of his boss's history.

Poor Brian. She hoped he was going to be all right. She had thought a lot last night about Brian, but even more about Cafferty and his gang. She hoped she could be of help to Inspector John Rebus. She already had a few ideas about the fire at the Central Hotel …

'Here comes someone,' said Petrie. He was squatting behind the tripod and busily adjusting the focus on the camera. He fired off half a dozen shots. 'Unidentified male. Denim jacket and light-coloured trousers. Approaching the office on foot.'

Siobhan took up her pad and copied down Petrie's description, noting the time alongside.

'He's entering the office … now.' Petrie turned away from the camera and grinned. 'This is what I joined the police for: a life of adventure.' Having said which, he poured more hot chocolate from his thermos into a cup.

'I can't use that loo,' said Elsa-Beth Jardine. 'I'll have to go out.'

'No can do,' said Petrie, 'it would attract too much attention, you tripping in and out every time you needed a piss.'

Jardine turned to Siobhan. 'He's got a way with words, your colleague.'

'Oh, he's a right old romantic. But it's true enough about going to the toilet.' The bathroom had flooded during the previous year's break-in, leaving the floor unsafe. Hence the broom closet.

Jardine flipped over a page of her magazine. 'Burt Reynolds has seven bathrooms in his home,' she commented.

'One for every dwarf,' muttered Petrie.

Rebus might, in Siobhan's phrase, have an air of knowing exactly where he was going, but in fact he felt like he was going round in circles. He'd visited a few early-opening pubs (near the offices of the daily newspaper; down towards the docks at Leith), social clubs and betting shops, and had asked his question and left his message in all of them. Deek Torrance was either keeping a low profile, or else he'd left the city. If still around, it was unfeasible that he wouldn't at some point stagger into a bar and loudly introduce himself and his thirst. Few people, once introduced, could forget Deek Torrance.

He'd also opened communications with hospitals in Edinburgh and Dundee, to see if either of the Robertson brothers had received surgery for a broken right arm, the old injury found on the Central Hotel corpse.

But now it was time to give up and go check out Operation Moneybags. He'd left Michael still asleep this morning, and likely to remain asleep for quite some time if those pills were anything to go by. The students had tiptoed in at a minute past midnight, 'well kettled' as one of them termed it, having spent Rebus's thirty quid on beverages at a local hostelry. They too had been asleep when Rebus had let himself out of the flat. He hardly dared admit to himself that he liked sleeping rough in his own living-room.

The whole weekend seemed like a strange bad dream now. The drive to Aberdeen, Auntie Ena, Michael ... then the drive to Perth, the lock-fitting, and too much spare time (even after all that) in which to brood. He wondered how Patience's weekend had gone. She'd be back later today for sure. He'd try phoning again.

He parked in one of the many side streets off Gorgie Road and locked his car. This was not one of the city's safest areas. He hoped Siobhan hadn't worn a green and white scarf to work this morning ... He walked down onto Gorgie Road, where buses were spraying the pavement with some of the morning's rainwater, and was careful not to pause outside the door, careful not to glance across the street at the cab offices. He just pushed the door open and climbed the stairs, then knocked at another door.

Siobhan Clarke herself opened it. 'Morning, sir.' She looked cold, though she had wrapped up well enough. 'Coffee?'

The offer was from her thermos, and Rebus shook his head. Normally during a surveillance, drinks and food could be brought in, but not to *this* surveillance. There wasn't supposed to be any activity in the building, so it would look more than a mite suspicious if someone suddenly appeared at the door with three beakers of tea and a home-delivery pizza. There wasn't even a back entrance to the building.

'How's it going?'

'Slow.' This from Elsa-Beth Jardine, who didn't look at all comfortable. There was an open magazine on her lap. 'Thank God I'm relieved at one o'clock.'

'Think yourself lucky, then,' commented DC Petrie.

Ah, how Rebus liked to see a happy crew. 'It's not supposed to be fun,' he told them. 'It's supposed to be work. If and when we nab Dougary and Co., *that's* when the party begins.' They had nothing to add to this, and neither did Rebus. He walked over to the window and peered out. The window itself was so grimy he doubted anyone could see them through it, and especially not from across the street. But a square had been cleaned off just a little, enough so that any photos would be recognisable.

'Camera working okay?'

'So far,' said Petrie. 'I don't really trust these motorised jobs. If the motor goes, you're buggered. You can't wind on by hand.'

'Got enough batteries?'

'Two back-up sets. They're not going to be a problem.'

Rebus nodded. He knew Petrie's reputation as a solid detective who might climb a little higher up the ladder yet. 'How about the phone?'

'It's connected, sir,' said Siobhan Clarke.

Usually, there would be radio contact between any stake-out and headquarters, but not for Moneybags. The problem was the cab company. The cabs and their home base were equipped with two-way radios, so it was possible that communications from Moneybags to HQ could actually be picked up across the road. There was the added complication, too, that the cab radios might interfere with Moneybags' transmissions.

To avoid these potential disasters, a telephone line had been installed early on Sunday morning. The telephone apparatus sat on the floor near the door. So far it had been used twice: once by Jardine to make a hairdresser's appointment; and once by Petrie to make a bet after he'd checked the day's horse-racing tips in his tabloid. Siobhan intended using it this afternoon to check on Brian's condition. But now Rebus was actually using it to phone St Leonard's.

'Any messages for me?' He waited. 'Oh? That's interesting. Anything else? *What?* Why the hell didn't you tell me that first?' He slammed the phone down. 'Brian's awake,' he said. 'He's sitting up in bed eating chicken soup and watching daytime TV.'

'Either of which could give him a relapse,' said Siobhan. She was wondering what the other message had been.

*

'Hello, Brian.'

'Hello, sir.' Holmes had been listening to a personal hi-fi. He switched it off and slipped the headphones down around his neck. 'Patsy Cline,' he said. 'I've been listening to a lot of her since Nell booted me out.'

'Where did the tape come from?'

'My aunt brought it in, bless her. She knows what I like. It was waiting for me when I woke up.'

Rebus had a sudden thought. They played music to coma victims, didn't they? Maybe they'd been playing Patsy Cline to Holmes. No wonder he'd been a long time waking up.

'I'm finding it hard to take in, though,' Holmes went on. 'I mean, whole days of my life, just gone like that. I wouldn't mind, I mean I like a good sleep. Only I can't remember a bloody thing I dreamt about.'

Rebus sat down by the bedside. The chair was already in place. 'Been having visitors?'

'Just the one. Nell looked in.'

'That's nice.'

'She spent the whole time crying. My face isn't horribly scarred and no one's telling me?'

'Looks as ugly as ever. What about amnesia?'

Holmes smiled. 'Oh no, I remember the whole thing, not that it'll help.'

Holmes really did look fine. It was like the doctors said, the brain shuts all systems down, thinks what damage has been done, effects repairs, and then you wake up. Policeman heal thyself.

'So?'

'So,' said Holmes, 'I'd spent the evening in the Heartbreak Cafe. I can even tell you what I ate.'

'Whatever it was, I'll bet you finished with Blue Suede Choux.'

Holmes shook his head. 'They'd none left. Like Eddie said, it's the fastest mover since the King himself.'

'So what happened after you ate?'

'The usual, I sat at the bar drinking and chatting, wondering if any gorgeous young ladies were going to slip onto the stool beside mine and ask if I came there often. I talked with Pat for a while. He was on bar duty that night.' Holmes paused. 'I should explain, Pat is –'

'Eddie's business partner, and maybe a *sleeping* partner too.'

'Now now, no homophobia.'

'Some of my best friends know gays,' Rebus said. 'You've mentioned Calder in the past. I can also tell you he doesn't drive.'

'That's right, Eddie does.'

'Even when he's shit-faced.'

Holmes shrugged. 'I've never made it my business.'

'You will when he knocks some poor old lady down.'

Holmes smiled. 'That car of his might look like a hot-rod, but it's in terrible shape. It barely does forty on the open road. Besides, Eddie's the most, if you will, *pedestrian* driver I know. He's so slow I've seen him overtaken by a skateboard – and that was being carried under somebody's arm at the time.'

'So it was just you and Calder at the bar?'

'Until Eddie joined us, after he'd finished cooking. I mean, there were other people in the place, but no obvious villains.'

'Pray continue.'

'Well, I went to go home. Someone must have been waiting behind the dustbins. Next thing I knew there was a draught up my kilt. I opened my eyes and saw these two nurses washing my tadger.'

'What?'

'That's what woke me up, I swear.'

'It's a medical miracle.'

'The magic sponge,' said Holmes.

'So who thumped you, any ideas?'

'I've been mulling it over. Maybe they were after Eddie or Pat.'

'And why would that be?'

Holmes shrugged.

'Don't keep secrets from old Uncle Rebus, Brian. You forget, I can read your mind.'

'Well, you tell *me* then.'

'Could be they've not been paying their dues.'

'You mean protection?'

'Insurance, as people like to call it.'

'Well, maybe.'

'The dynamic duo at the Heartbreak Cafe seem to think maybe it's an unholy alliance of curry house owners disgruntled at the fall-off in trade.'

'I can't see that.'

'Neither can I. Maybe it was nobody, Brian. Maybe nobody was after Eddie and Pat. Maybe they were after *you*. Now why would that be?'

The pink in Holmes' cheeks grew slightly redder. 'You've seen the Black Book?'

'Of course I have. I was looking for clues, so I had a rifle through your stuff. And there it was, all in code, too. Or at least in shorthand, so nobody but another copper would know what you were on about. But I'm another copper, Brian. Now there were a lot of cases in there, but only one that stood out.'

'The Central Hotel.'

'Give the man a cigar. Yes, the Central. A poker game took place, and in attendance were Tam and Eck Robertson, neither of whom crop up in the list of punters at the Central that night. You've been trying to find them. No luck so far?' Holmes shook his head. 'But someone told you all this, didn't they? There's no mention in the files of any poker game. Now,' Rebus leaned closer, 'would I be right in thinking that the person who told you is the

116

mysterious El?' Holmes nodded. 'Then that's all you need to tell me, Brian. Who the hell is El?'

At that moment, a nurse pushed open the door and came in bearing medicine and a lunch tray for Holmes.

'I'm starving,' he explained to Rebus. 'This is my second meal since I woke up.' He lifted the metal cover from the plate. A pale pink slice of meat, watery mashed spuds, and sliced green beans.

'Yum yum,' said Rebus. But Holmes looked keen enough. He scooped some mash and gravy into his mouth and swallowed it down.

'I'd have thought,' he said, 'that since you've figured out the hard part, you wouldn't have had any trouble with El.'

'Sorry to disappoint you. Who is he?'

'It's Elvis,' said Brian Holmes. 'Elvis himself told me.' He lifted another forkful of mush to his lips and started to slurp it down.

# 12

Rebus studied the menu, finding little to his liking beyond the often painful puns. The Heartbreak Cafe was open all day, but he'd arrived just in time for the special luncheon menu. A foot-long sausage on a roll was predictably if unappetisingly a 'Hound Dog'. Rebus could only hope that there was no literal truth to the appelation. More obscure was the drinks list, with one wine called 'Mama Liked the Rosé'. Rebus decided that he wasn't so hungry after all. Instead, he nursed his 'Teddy' beer at the bar and handed the menu back to the teenage barman.

'Pat's not in then?' he asked casually.

'Doing some shopping. He'll be back later.'

Rebus nodded. 'But Eddie's around?'

'In the kitchen, yeah.' The barman glanced towards the restaurant area. He wore three gold studs in his left ear. 'He won't be much longer, unless he's making something special for tonight.'

'Right,' said Rebus. A few minutes later, he picked up his beer glass and wandered over to a huge jukebox near the toilets. Finding it to be ornamental only, he studied some of the Presley mementoes on the walls, including a signed photograph of the Vegas Elvis and what looked like a rare Sun Records pressing. Both were protected by thick framed glass, and both were picked out by spotlights from the surrounding gloom. Finding himself, as if by chance, at the door to the kitchen, Rebus pushed it open with his shoulder and let it swing shut behind him.

Eddie Ringan was creating. Sweat glistened on his face, thin strands of hair sticking to his brow, as he shook a small frying pan over a gas flame. The set-up was impressive: cleaner than Rebus had expected, with many more cookers and pots and work surfaces. A lot of money had been spent; the Cafe wasn't just a designer façade. Amusingly, it seemed to Rebus, there was different music here from the constant diet of Presley served at the bar. Eddie Ringan was listening to Miles Davis.

The chef hadn't noticed Rebus yet, and Rebus hadn't noticed a trainee chef who'd been fetching something from one of several fridges at the back of the kitchen.

Rebus watched as Eddie, pausing from his work, grabbed a bottle of Jim Beam by its neck and upended it into his mouth, taking it away again with a satisfied exhalation.

'Hey,' said the trainee chef, 'no one's allowed in here.' Eddie looked up from the pan and gave a whoop.

'You're just the man!' he cried. 'The very man! Come over here.'

If anything, he sounded drunker than at their first meeting. But then, at their first meeting there had been the civilising (or at least restricting) presence of Pat Calder, as well as the sobering fact of Brian Holmes's attack.

Rebus walked over to the cooker. He too was starting to sweat in the heat.

'This,' said Eddie Ringan, nodding towards the pan, 'is my latest dish. Pieces of Roquefort cheese *imprisoned* in breadcrumb and spice and fried. Either pan-fried or deep-fried, that's what I'm deciding.'

'Jailhouse Roquefort,' Rebus guessed. Ringan whooped again, losing his balance slightly and sliding back with one foot.

'*Your* idea, Inspector Rabies.'

'I'm flattered, but the name's Rebus.'

'Aye, well, you should be flattered. Maybe we'll gie you a wee mention on the menu. How about that, eh?' He studied the golden nuggets, turning them expertly with a fork. 'I'm giving this lot six minutes. Willie!'

'I'm right here.'

'How long's that been?'

The protégé checked his watch. 'Three and a half. I've put the butter down there next to the eggs.'

'Willie's my assistant, Inspector.'

The exasperation in Willie's voice and expressions made Rebus doubt he would be assisting for much longer. Though younger than Ringan, Willie was about the same size. You wouldn't call him slender. Rebus reckoned chefs were partial to too much R&D. 'Can we talk for a minute?'

'Two and a half minutes if you like.'

'I'd like to know about the Central Hotel.' Ringan didn't seem to hear this, his attention on the contents of the frying-pan. 'You were there the night it burned down.'

El was short for Elvis, and Elvis was code for Eddie Ringan. Holmes hadn't wanted the wrong people getting hold of the Black Book and being able to identify the person who'd been talking. That's why he'd gone an extra step in disguising Ringan's identity.

He'd also made Rebus promise that he wouldn't tell the chef Holmes had shared their secret. It *was* to have been a secret, a little tale spilt from a bottle of bourbon. But Ringan hadn't poured out nearly enough, he'd just given Holmes a taste.

'Did you hear me, Eddie?'

'A minute left, Inspector.'

'You never cropped up on the list of staff because you were moonlighting, working there some nights without the other place you worked at knowing anything about it. So you were able to give a false name, and nobody ever found out it was you there that night, the night of the poker game.'

'Nearly done.' There was more sweat on Eddie Ringan's

face now, and his mouth seemed stiff with suppressed anger.

'I'm nearly done too, Eddie. When did you start on the booze, eh? Just after that night, wasn't it? Because something happened in that hotel. I wonder what it was. Whatever it was, you saw it, and if you don't tell me about it, I'm going to find out anyway, and then I'm going to come back here for you.' To emphasise this, Rebus pushed a finger against the chef's arm.

Ringan snatched the frying-pan and swung it at Rebus, sending bits of Jailhouse Roquefort flying in arcs across the kitchen.

'Get the fuck away from me!'

Rebus dodged the frying-pan, but Ringan was still holding it in front of him, ready to lunge.

'Just you get the fuck out of here! Who told you, anyway?'

'Nobody needed to tell me, Eddie. I worked it out for myself.'

Willie meantime was down on one knee. A hot cube of cheese had caught him smack in the eye.

'I'm dying!' he called. 'Get an ambulance, get a lawyer! This is an industrial injury.'

Eddie Ringan glanced towards the trainee chef, then back at the frying-pan in his hand, then at Rebus, and he began to laugh, the laughter becoming uproarious, hysterical. But at least he put down the pan. He even picked up one of the cheese cubes and took a bite out of it.

'Tastes like shite,' he said, still laughing and spluttering bits of breadcrumb at Rebus.

'Are you going to tell me, Eddie?' Rebus asked calmly.

'I'm going to tell you this: get the fuck out.'

Rebus stood his ground, though Eddie had already turned his back. 'Tell me where I can find the Bru-Head Brothers.'

This brought more laughter.

'Just give me a start, Eddie. Then it'll be off your conscience.'

'I lost my conscience a long time ago, Inspector. Willie, let's get a fresh batch going.'

The young man was still checking for damage. He held one hand across his good eye like a patch. 'I cannae see a thing,' he complained. 'I think the retina's cracked.'

'And the cornea's melted,' added Ringan. 'Come on, I'm hoping to have this on the menu tonight.' He turned to Rebus, making a show of astonishment. 'Still here? A definite case of too many cooks.'

Rebus looked at him with sad, steady eyes. 'Just a start, Eddie.'

'Away tae fuck.'

Slowly, Rebus turned around and pushed open the door.

'Inspector!' He turned his head towards the chef. 'There's a pub in Cowdenbeath called The Midtown. The locals call it the Midden. I wouldn't eat the food there.'

Rebus nodded slowly. 'Thanks for the tip.'

'It's *you* that's supposed to give *me* the tip!' he heard Ringan roar as he exited from the kitchen. He placed his empty glass on the bartop.

'Kitchen's off limits,' the barman informed him.

'More like the outer bloody limits.'

But no, he knew that only now would he be going to the outer limits, back to the haunts of his youth.

# 13

He had only dropped into St Leonard's to pick up a few things from his desk, but the duty sergeant stopped him short.

'Gentleman here has been waiting to see you. He seems a bit anxious.'

The 'gentleman' in question had been standing in a corner, but was now directly in front of Rebus. 'You don't recognise me?'

Rebus studied the man for a moment longer, and felt an old loathing. 'Oh yes,' he said, 'I recognise you all right.'

'Didn't you get my message?'

This had been the other message relayed to him when he'd called in from Gorgie Road. He nodded.

'Well, what are you going to do?'

'What would you like me to do, Mr McPhail?'

'You've got to stop him!'

'Stop who exactly? And from what?'

'You said you got the message.'

'All I was told was that someone called Andrew McPhail had phoned wanting to speak to me.'

'What I want is bloody protection!'

'Calm down now.' Rebus saw that the desk sergeant was getting ready for action, but he didn't think there would be any need for that.

'What have I got to do?' McPhail was saying. 'You want me to hit you? That'd get me a night in the cells, wouldn't it? I'd be safe there.'

Rebus nodded. 'You'd be safe all right, until we told your cell mates about your past escapades.'

This seemed to calm McPhail down like a bucket of ice. Maybe he was remembering particular incidents during his spell in the Canadian prison. Or maybe it was a less localised fear. Whatever it was, it worked. His tone became quietly plaintive. 'But he'll kill me.'

'Who will?'

'Stop pretending! I know you set him on to me. It had to be you.'

'Humour me,' said Rebus.

'Maclean,' said McPhail. 'Alex Maclean.'

'And who is Alex Maclean?'

McPhail looked disgusted. He spoke in an undertone. 'The wee girl's stepfather. Melanie's stepfather.'

'Ah,' said Rebus, nodding now. He knew immediately what Jack Morton had done, bugger that he was. No wonder McPhail got in touch. And as Rebus had been round to see Mrs MacKenzie, he'd thought Rebus must be behind the whole scheme.

'Has he threatened you?'

McPhail nodded.

'In what way?'

'He came to the house. I wasn't there. He told Mrs MacKenzie he'd be back to get me. Poor woman's in a terrible state.'

'You could always move, get out of Edinburgh.'

'Christ, is that what you want? That's why you've set Maclean on me. Well, I'm staying put.'

'Heroic of you, Mr McPhail.'

'Look, I know what I've done, but that's behind me.'

Rebus nodded. 'And all you've got in front of you is the view from your bedroom.'

'Jesus, I didn't know Mrs MacKenzie lived across from a primary school!'

124

'Still, you could move. A location like that, it's bound to rile Maclean further.'

McPhail stared at Rebus. 'You're repulsive,' he said. 'Whatever I've done in my life, I'm willing to bet you've done worse. Never mind about me, I'll look after myself.' McPhail made show of pushing past Rebus towards the door.

'Ca' canny, Mr McPhail,' Rebus called after him.

'Christ,' said the desk sergeant, 'who was that?'

'That,' said Rebus, 'was someone finding out how it feels to be a victim.'

All the same, he felt a bit guilty. What if McPhail *had* been rehabilitated, and Maclean *did* do him some damage? Scared as he was, McPhail might even decide a first strike was his only form of defence. Well, Rebus had slightly more pressing concerns, hadn't he?

In the CID room, he studied the only available mug-shots of Tam and Eck Robertson, taken over five years ago. He got a DC to make him some photocopies, but then had a better idea. There was no police artist around, but that didn't bother Rebus. He knew where an artist could always be found.

It was five o'clock when he got to McShane's Bar near the bottom of the Royal Mile. McShane's was a haven for bearded folk fans and their woolly sweaters. Upstairs, there was always music, be it a professional performer or some punter who'd taken the stage to belt out 'Will Ye Go Lassie Go' or 'Both Sides O' The Tweed'.

Midgie McNair did good business in McShane's sketching flattering likenesses of acquiescent customers, who paid for the privilege and often bought the drinks as well.

At this early hour, Midgie was downstairs, reading a paperback at a corner table. His sketch-pad sat on the table beside him, along with half a dozen pencils. Rebus placed two pints on the table, then sat down and produced the photos of the Bru-Head Brothers.

'Not exactly Butch and Sundance, are they?' said Midgie McNair.

'Not exactly,' said Rebus.

# 14

John Rebus had once known Cowdenbeath very well indeed, having gone to school there. It was one of those Fife mining communities which had grown from a hamlet in the late nineteenth or early twentieth centuries when coal was in great demand, such demand that the cost of digging it out of the ground hardly entered the equation. But the coalfields of Fife didn't last long. There was still plenty of coal deep underground, but the thin warped strata were difficult (and therefore costly) to mine. He supposed some opencast mining might still be going on – at one time west central Fife had boasted Europe's biggest hole in the ground – but the deep pitshafts had all been filled in. In Rebus's youth there had been three obvious career choices for a fifteen-year-old boy: the pits, Rosyth Dockyard, or the Army. Rebus had chosen the last of these. Nowadays, it was probably the only choice on offer.

Like the towns and villages around it, Cowdenbeath looked and felt depressed: closed down shops and drab chainstore clothes. But he knew that the people were stronger than their situation might suggest. Hardship bred a bitter, quickfire humour and a resilience to all but the most terminal of life's tragedies. He didn't like to think about it too deeply, but inside he felt like he really was 'coming home'. Edinburgh might have been his base for twenty years, but he was a Fifer. 'Fly Fifers', some people called them. Rebus was ready to do battle with some very fly people indeed.

Monday night was the quietest of the week for pubs across the land. The pay packets or dole money had disappeared over the course of the weekend. Monday was for staying in. Not that you would know this from the scene that greeted Rebus as he pushed open the door to the Midden. Its name belittled it; its interior was no worse than many a bar in Edinburgh and elsewhere. Basic, yes, with a red linoleum floor spotted black from hundreds of cigarette dowps. The tables and chairs were functional, and though the bar was not large enough space had been found for a pool table and dartboard. A game of darts was in progress when Rebus entered, and one young man marched around the pool table, potting shot after shot as he squinted through the smoke which rose from the cigarette in his mouth. At a corner table three old men, all wearing flat bunnets, were playing a tense game of dominoes, groups of steady drinkers filling the other tables.

So Rebus had no choice but to stand at the bar. There was just room for one more, and he nodded a greeting to the pint drinkers either side of him. A greeting no one bothered to return.

'Pint of special, please,' he said to the slick-haired barman.

'Special, son, right you are.'

Rebus got the feeling this fiftyish bartender would call even the domino players 'son'. The drink was poured with the proper amount of care, like the ritual it was in this part of the world.

'Special, son, there you are.'

Rebus paid for the beer. It was the cheapest pint he'd bought in months. He started to think about how easy it would be to commute to work from Fife . . .

'Pint of spesh, Dod.'

'Spesh, son, right you are.'

The pool player stood just behind Rebus, not quite menacingly. He placed his empty glass on the bartop and

128

waited for it to be refilled. Rebus knew the youth was interested, maybe waiting to see whether Rebus would speak. But Rebus didn't say anything. He just took photocopies of the two drawings out of his jacket pocket and unfolded them. He'd had ten copies of each made up at a newsagent's on the Royal Mile. The originals were safe in the glove compartment of his car; though how safe his car itself was, parked on the poorly lit street outside, was another matter.

He could feel the drinkers either side of him glance at the drawings, and didn't doubt that the youth was having a look too. Still nobody said anything.

'Spesh, son, there you are.' The pool player picked up the glass, spilling some beer onto the sheets of paper. Rebus turned his head towards him.

'Sorry about that.'

Rebus had seldom heard a less sincere tone of voice. 'That's all right,' he said, matching the tone. 'I've got plenty more copies.'

'Oh aye?' The youth took his change from the barman and went back to the pool table, crouching to load coins into the slot. The balls fell with a dull rumble and he started to rack them up, staring at Rebus.

'You do a bit of drawing, eh?'

Rebus, who had been wiping the drawings with his hand, turned to Dod the barman. 'Not me, no. Good though, aren't they?' He turned the drawings around slowly so Dod could get a better look.

'Oh aye, no' bad. I'm no' an expert, like. The only things anybody around here draws are the pension or the dole.' There was laughter at this.

'Or a bowl,' added one drinker. He made the word sound like 'bowel', but Rebus knew what he meant.

'Or a cigarette,' somebody else suggested, but the joke was by now history. The barman nodded towards the drawings. 'Anybody in particular, like?'

Rebus shrugged.

'Could be brothers, eh?'

Rebus turned to the drinker on his left, who had just spoken. 'What makes you say that?'

The drinker twitched and turned to stare at the row of optics behind the bar. 'They look similar.'

Rebus examined the two drawings. As requested, Midgie had aged the brothers five or six years. 'You could be right.'

'Or cousins maybe,' said the drinker on his right.

'Related, though,' Rebus mused.

'I cannae see it myself,' said Dod the barman.

'Look a bit closer,' Rebus advised. He ran his finger over the sheets of paper. 'Same chins, eyes look the same too. Maybe they *are* brothers.'

'Who are they, then?' asked the drinker on his right, a middle-aged man with square unshaven jaw and lively blue eyes.

But Rebus just shrugged again. One of the domino players came to the bar to order a round. He looked like he'd just won a rubber, and clapped his hands together.

'How's it going then, James?' he asked the drinker on Rebus's right.

'No' bad, Matt. Yourself?'

'Ach, just the same.' He smiled at Rebus. 'Havenae seen you in here afore, son.'

Rebus shook his head. 'I've been away.'

'Oh aye?' Three pints had appeared on a metal tray.

'There you go, Matt.'

'Thanks, Dod.' Matt handed over a ten-pound note. As he waited for change, he saw the drawings. 'Butch and Sundance, eh?' He laughed. Rebus smiled warmly. 'Or more like Steptoe and Son.'

'Steptoe and Brother,' Rebus suggested.

'Brothers?' Matt studied the drawings. He was still studying them when he asked, 'Are you the polis then, son?'

'Do I look like the polis?'

'No' exactly.'

'No' fat enough for a start,' said Dod. 'Eh, son?'

'You get skinny polis, though,' argued James. 'What about Stecky Jamieson?'

'Right enough,' said Dod. 'Thon bugger could hide behind a lamp post.'

Matt had picked up the tray of drinks. The other domino players at his table called out that they were 'gasping'. Matt nodded towards the drawings. 'I've seen yon buggers afore,' he said, before moving off.

Rebus drained his glass and ordered another. The drinker on his left finished and, fixing a bunnet to his head, started to make his goodbyes.

'Cheerio then, Dod.'

'Aye, cheerio.'

'Cheerio, James.'

This went on for minutes. The long cheerio. Rebus folded the drawings and put them in his pocket. He took his time over the second pint. There was some talk of football, extra-marital affairs, the nonexistent job market. Mind you, the amount of affairs that seemed to be going on, Rebus was surprised anyone found the time or energy for a job.

'You know what this part of Fife's become?' offered James. 'A giant DIY store. You either work in one, or you shop there. That's about it.'

'True enough,' said Dod, though there was little conviction in his voice.

Rebus finished the second pint and went to visit the gents'. The place stank to high heaven, and the graffiti was poor. Nobody came in for a quiet word, not that he'd been expecting it. On his way back from bathroom to bar he stopped at the dominoes game.

'Matt?' he asked. 'Sorry to interrupt. You didn't say where you thought you'd seen Butch and Sundance.'

'Maybe just the one o' them,' said Matt. The doms had been shuffled and he picked up seven, three in one hand and four in the other. 'It wasnae here, though. Maybe Lochgelly. For some reason, I think it was Lochgelly.' He put the dominoes face down on the tabletop and picked out the one he wished to play. The man next to him chapped.

'Bad sign that, Tam, this early on.'

Bad sign indeed. Rebus would have to go to Lochgelly. He returned to the bar and said his own brief cheerio.

'Or you could draw a fire,' someone at the bar was saying, poking the embers of that long-dead joke.

The drive from Cowdenbeath to Lochgelly took Rebus through Lumphinnans. His father had always made jokes about Lumphinnans; Rebus wasn't sure why, and certainly couldn't recall any of them. When he'd been young, the skies had been full of smoke, every house heated by a coal fire in the sitting room. The chimneys sent up a grey plume into the evening air, but not now. Now, central heating and gas had displaced Old King Coal.

It saddened Rebus, this silence of the lums.

It saddened him, too, that he would have to repeat his performance with the drawings. He'd hoped the Midden would be the start and finish of his quest. Of course, it was always possible Eddie had been setting a false trail in the first place. If so, Rebus would see he got his just deserts, and it wouldn't be Blue Suede Choux.

He did his act in three pubs nursing three half-pints, with no reaction save the usual bad jokes including the 'drawing the pension' line. But in the fourth bar, an understandably understated shack near the railway station, he drew the attention of a keen-eyed old man who had been cadging drinks all round the pub. At the time, Rebus was showing the drawings to a cluster of painters and decorators at the corner of the L-shaped bar.

He knew they were decorators because they'd asked him if he needed any work doing. 'On the fly, like. Cheaper that way.' Rebus shook his head and showed them the drawings.

The old man pushed his way into the group. He looked up at all the faces around him. 'All right, lads? Here, I was decorated in the war.' He cackled at his joke.

'So you keep telling us, Jock.'

'Every fuckin' night.'

'Without fuckin' fail.'

'Sorry, lads,' Jock apologised. He thrust a short thick finger at one of the drawings. 'Looks familiar.'

'Must be a bloody jockey then.' The decorator winked at Rebus. 'I'm no' joking, mister. Jock would recognise a racehorse's bahookey quicker than a human face.'

'Ach,' said Jock dismissively, 'away tae hell wi' you.' And to Rebus: 'Sure you dinnae owe me a drink fae last week ...?'

Five minutes after Rebus glumly left this last pub, a young man arrived. It had taken him some time, visiting all the bars between the Midden and here, asking whether a man had been in with some drawings. He was annoyed, too, at having to break off his pool practice so early. His screwball needed work. There was a competition on Sunday, and he had every intention of winning the £100 prize. If he didn't, there'd be trouble. But meantime, he knew he could do someone a favour by trailing this man who claimed not to be a copper. He knew it because he'd made a phone call from the Midden.

'You'd be doing me a favour,' the person on the other end of the line had said, when the pool player had finally been put through to him, having had to relate his story to two other people first.

It was useful to be owed a favour, so he'd taken off from the Midden, knowing that the man with the drawings was on his way to Lochgelly. But now here he was at the far end of the town; there were no pubs after this until Lochore. And the man had gone. So the pool player made another call and gave his report. It wasn't much, he knew, but it had been time-consuming work all the same.

'I owe you one, Sharky,' the voice said.

Sharky felt elated as he got back into his rusty Datsun. And with luck, he'd still have time for a few games of pool before closing time.

John Rebus drove back to Edinburgh with just desserts on his mind. And Andrew McPhail, and Michael with his tranquillisers, and Patience, and Operation Moneybags, and many other things besides.

Michael was sound asleep when he arrived at the flat. He checked with the students, who were worried that his brother was maybe on some sort of drugs. He assured them the drugs were prescribed rather than proscribed. Then he telephoned Siobhan Clarke at home.

'How did it go today?'

'You had to be there, sir – I could write the book on boredom. Dougary had five visitors all day. He had pizza delivered lunch. Drove home at five-thirty.'

'Any of the visitors interesting?'

'I'll let you see the photographs. Customers, maybe. But they came out with as many limbs as they went in with. Will you be joining us tomorrow?'

'Probably.'

'Only I thought maybe we could talk about the Central Hotel.'

'Speaking of which, have you seen Brian?'

'I popped in after work. He looks great.' She paused. 'You sound tired. Have you been working?'

'Yes.'

'The Central?'

'Christ knows. I suppose so.' Rebus rubbed the back of

his neck. The hangover was starting already.

'You had to buy a few drinks?' Siobhan guessed.

'Yes.'

'And drink a few?'

'Right again, Sherlock.'

She laughed, then tutted. 'And afterwards you drove home. I'd be happy to chauffeur you if it would help.' She sounded like she meant it.

'Thanks, Clarke. I'll bear it in mind.' He paused. 'Know what I'd like for Christmas?'

'It's a long way off.'

'I'd like someone to *prove* that the corpse belongs to one of the Bru-Head Brothers.'

'The body had a broken –'

'I know, I've checked. The hospitals came up with spit.' He paused again. 'Not your problem,' he said. 'I'll see you tomorrow.'

'Good night, sir.'

Rebus sat in silence for a minute or two. Something about his conversation with Siobhan Clarke made him want to talk with Patience. He picked up the receiver again and rang her.

'Hello?'

Ye Gods, not an answering machine!

'Hello, Patience.'

'John.'

'I'd like to talk. Are you ready?'

There was silence, then: 'Yes, I think so. Let's talk.'

John Rebus lay down on the sofa, one hand behind his head. Nobody else used the phone that night.

# 15

John Rebus was in a good mood that Tuesday morning, for no other reason than that he'd spent what seemed like half the previous night on the phone with Patience. They were going to meet for a drink; he just had to wait for her to get back to him with a place and a time. He was still in a good mood when he opened the ground floor door and started up the stairs towards Operation Moneybags' Gorgie centre of operations.

He could hear voices; nothing unusual about that. But the voices grew in intensity as he climbed, and he opened the door just in time to see a man lunge at DC Petrie and butt him square on the nose. Petrie fell back against the window, knocking over the camera tripod. Blood gushed from his nostrils. Rebus only half took in that two small boys were watching, along with Siobhan Clarke and Elsa-Beth Jardine. The man was pulling Petrie upright when Rebus got an arm lock around him, pinning the man's arms to his side. He pulled Rebus to right and left, trying to throw him off, all the time yelling so loudly it was a wonder nobody on the street below could hear the commotion.

Rebus heaved the man backwards and turned him, so that he lost balance and fell to the floor, where Rebus sat on top of him. Petrie started forward, but the man lashed out with his legs and sent Petrie back into the window, where his elbow smashed the glass. Rebus did what he had to do. He punched the man in the throat.

'What the hell's going on here?' he asked. The man was gasping but still struggling. 'You, stop it!' Then something hit Rebus on the back of his head. It was the clenched fist of one of the boys, and it hit him right on his burnt patch of scalp. He screwed shut his eyes, fighting the stinging pain of the blow and a nausea in his gut, right where his muesli and tea with honey were sitting.

'Leave my dad alone!'

Siobhan Clarke grabbed the boy and dragged him off.

'Arrest that little bugger,' Rebus said. Then, to the boy's father: 'I mean it, too. If you don't calm down, I'm going to have *him* charged with assault. How would you like that?'

'He's too young,' gasped the man.

'Is he?' said Rebus. 'Are you sure?'

The man thought about it and calmed down.

'That's better.' Rebus rose from the man's chest. 'Now is *someone* going to explain all this to me?'


It was quickly explained, once Petrie had been sent off to find a doctor for his nose and the boys had been sent home. The man was called Bill Chilton, and Bill Chilton didn't like squatters.

'Squatters?'

'That's what Wee Neilly told me.'

'Squatters?' Rebus turned to Siobhan Clarke. She'd been downstairs to check no passers-by had been injured by falling glass, and more importantly to explain the 'accident'.

'The two boys,' she said now, 'came barging in. They said they sometimes played here.'

Rebus stopped her and turned to Chilton. 'Why isn't Neil at school?'

'He's been suspended for fighting.'

Rebus nodded. 'He's got a fair punch on him.' The

back of his head throbbed agreement. He turned back to Siobhan.

'They asked us what we were doing, and Ms Jardine' – at this Elsa-Beth Jardine lowered her head – 'told them we were squatters.'

'Just joking,' Jardine found it necessary to add. Rebus feigned surprise, and she lowered her eyes again, blushing furiously.

'DC Petrie joined in, the boys cleared out, and we all had a laugh about it.'

'A laugh?' Rebus said. 'It wasn't a laugh, it was a breach of security.' He sounded as furious as he looked, so that even Siobhan turned her eyes away from his. He now turned his gaze on Bill Chilton.

'Well,' Chilton continued, 'Neil came home and told me there were squatters here. We've had a lot of that going on this past year or two, deserted tenement flats being broken open and used for all sorts of things . . . drug pushing and that. Some of us are doing something about it.'

'What are we talking about here, Mr Chilton? Vigilante tactics? Pickaxe handles at dawn?'

Chilton was unabashed. '*You* lot are doing bugger all!'

'So you came up here looking to scare the squatters off?'

'Before they got a toe-hold, aye.'

'And?'

Chilton said nothing.

'And,' Rebus said for him, 'you started shouting the odds at DC Petrie, who started shouting back that he was a police officer and you'd better bugger off. Only by that time you were too fired up to back off. Got a bit of a temper, Mr Chilton? Maybe it's rubbed off on Neilly, eh? Did *you* get into a lot of fights at school?'

'What the hell's that got to do with anything?' Chilton's anger was rising again. Rebus raised a pacifying hand.

'It's a serious offence, assaulting a police officer.'

'Mistaken identity,' said Chilton.

'Even after he'd identified himself?'

Chilton shrugged. 'He never showed me any ID.'

Rebus raised an eyebrow. 'You're very knowledgeable about procedure. Maybe you've been in this sort of trouble before, eh?' This shut Chilton's mouth. 'Maybe if I go down the station and look you up on the computer ... what would this be, second offence? Third? Might we be talking about a wee trip to Saughton jail?' Chilton was looking decidedly uncomfortable, which was exactly what Rebus wanted.

'Of course,' he said, 'we could always shut the book on this one.' Chilton looked interested. '*If*,' Rebus warned, 'you could keep your gob shut about it. *And* get Neil and his pal to forget they saw anything.'

Chilton nodded towards the camera. 'You're watching somebody, eh? A stake-out?'

'Best if you don't know, Mr Chilton. Do we have a deal?'

Chilton thought about it, then nodded.

'Good,' said Rebus, 'now get the fuck out of here.'

Chilton knew when he was being made an offer. He got the fuck out of there. Rebus shook his head.

'Sir –'

'Shut up and listen,' Rebus told Siobhan Clarke. 'This could've blown the whole thing. Maybe it has, we won't know for a day or two. Meanwhile, get that camera set up again and get back to work. Phone HQ and get someone in here to board up the window, leaving a big enough hole for the camera. Either that or we need a new pane of glass.

'And listen to me, the two of you.' He raised a warning finger. 'Nobody gets to know about this, *nobody*. It's forgotten as of now, understand?'

They understood. What they did not understand perhaps was exactly why Rebus wanted it kept quiet. It wasn't that he feared the early termination of Operation Moneybags – as far as he was concerned, the whole project was doomed to failure anyway. No, it was another fear altogether, the fear that Detective Inspector Alister Flower, safe and snug in the Firth Pub with his own surveillance crew, would find out. By God, that would mean trouble, more trouble than Rebus was willing to contemplate.

A pity then that he hadn't managed to say anything to DC Peter Petrie, who went back to St Leonard's for a change of shirt. The blood on his T-shirt might have been mistaken for tomato sauce or old tea, but there was no doubting the cause of the white gauze pad which had been taped across his nose and half his face. And when questioned, Peter Petrie quite gladly told his story, embellishing it only a little – as, for example, in exaggerating his assailant's size, skill, and speed of attack. There were sympathetic smiles and shakes of the head, and the same comment was uttered by more than one fellow officer.

'Wait till Flower hears about this.'

By lunchtime, Flower had heard from several sources about the giant who had wreaked such havoc to the Gorgie surveillance.

'Dearie me,' he said, sipping an orange juice laced with blue label vodka. 'That's terrible. I wonder if Chief Inspector Lauderdale knows? Ach, of course he does, Rebus wouldn't try to keep a thing like that from him, would he?' And he smiled so warmly at the DC seated beside him that the DC got quite worried, really quite worried about his boss ...


Siobhan picked up the telephone.

'Hello?' She watched John Rebus staring out of the broken window. He'd been watching the taxi offices for half an hour, so deep in thought that neither she nor Jardine had uttered a word to one another above a whisper. 'It's for you, sir.'

Rebus took the receiver from her. It was CID with a message to relay.

'Go ahead.'

'From someone called Pat Calder. He says a Mr Ringan has disappeared.'

'Disappeared?'

'Yes, and he wanted you to know. Do you want us to do anything this end?'

'No thanks, I'll go have a word myself. Thanks for letting me know.' Rebus put down the phone.

'Who's disappeared?' Siobhan asked.

'Eddie Ringan.'

'The Heartbreak Cafe?'

Rebus nodded. 'I was only speaking to him yesterday. He threatened me with a panful of hot cheese.' Siobhan was looking interested, but Rebus shook his head. 'You stay here, at least until Petrie gets back.' The Heartbreak Cafe was only five minutes away. Rebus wondered if Calder would be there. A kitchen without a chef, after all, it was hardly worth opening for the day ...

But when Rebus arrived, the Cafe was doing a brisk trade in early lunches. Calder, acting as maitre d', waved to Rebus when he entered. Passing the same young barman as yesterday, Rebus gave him a wink. Calder was looking frantic.

'What the hell did you say to Eddie yesterday?'

'What do you mean?'

'Come off it, you had a stand-up row, didn't you? I knew something was wrong. He was edgy as hell all last night, and his cooking went to pot.' Calder saw no humour in this. 'You must have said *something*.'

'Who told you?'

Calder cocked his head towards the kitchen. 'Willie.'

Rebus nodded understanding. 'And today, Willie gets his chance for fame and fortune.'

'He's doing the lunches, if that's what you mean.'

'So when did Eddie go missing?'

'After we closed last night, he went off to look for some club or other. One of those moveable feasts that takes over a warehouse for one night a week.'

'You didn't fancy it yourself?'

Calder wrinkled his nose in distaste.

'Would this be a club for gentlemen, Mr Calder?'

'A gay club, yes. No secret there, Inspector. It's all quite legit.'

'I'm sure it is. And Mr Ringan didn't come home?'

'No.'

'So maybe he found someone else to go home with ...?'

'Eddie's not that type.'

'Then what type is he?'

'The *faithful* type, believe me. He often goes out drinking, but he always comes back.'

'Until now.'

'Yes.'

Rebus considered. 'Bit early yet to start a missing person file. We usually give it at least forty-eight hours, if there's no other evidence.'

'What sort of evidence?'

'Well, a body, for example.'

Calder turned his head away. 'Christ,' he said.

'Look, I'm sure there's nothing to worry about.'

'I'm not,' said Pat Calder.

No, and neither was John Rebus.

Calder slapped a smile on his face as a couple entered the Cafe. He picked up two menus and asked them to follow him to a table. They were in their early twenties and dressed fashionably, the man looking like he'd walked out of a 1930s gangster flick, the woman like she'd put on her wee sister's skirt by mistake.

When Calder came back he spoke in an undertone. 'Someone should tell her you can't hide acne with pan-stick. You know, Eddie hasn't been the same since the night Brian was attacked.'

'Brian's okay now, by the way.'

'Yes, Eddie rang the hospital yesterday.'

'He didn't visit, though?'

'We hate hospitals, too many friends dying in them lately.'

'The news about Brian didn't cheer him up?'

Calder pursed his lips. 'I suppose it did for a little while.' He pulled a notebook and pen out of his pocket. 'Must go and see what they want to drink.'

Rebus nodded. 'I'll just have a word with Willie and your barman, see what they think.'

'Fine. Lunch is on the house.' Rebus shook his head. 'We won't poison you, Inspector.'

'It's not that,' said Rebus. 'It's all this Presley stuff on the walls. It fair takes away my appetite.'


Willie the trainee chef looked like he was enjoying his day as ruler of all he surveyed. Flustered as he was, with no one to help him, still he gave off an air of never wanting things to change.

'Remember me, Willie?'

Willie glanced up. 'Jailhouse Roquefort?' He went back to shimmying pans, then started to chop a bunch of fresh parsley. Rebus marvelled at how speedily he worked with the knife mere millimetres from his fingertips.

'You here about Eddie? He's a mad bastard that, but a brilliant chef.'

'Must be fun to be in charge though?'

'It would be if I got the credit, but those buggers out there probably think the great Eduardo's prepared each dish of the day. Like Pat says, if they knew he wisnae here, they'd go off for a tandoori businessman's lunch at half the price.'

Rebus smiled. 'Still, being in charge ...'

Willie stopped chopping. 'What? You think I've got Eddie stashed away in my coal bunker? Just so I can have a day of tearing around like a mad-arsed fly?' He waved his knife towards the kitchen door. 'Pat might lend a hand, but no, he's got to be out there buttering up the clientele. Butter Pat, that's his name. If I was going to do away with either one of them, it'd be the one right outside that door.'

'You're taking it very seriously, Willie. Eddie's only been missing overnight. Could be sleeping it off in the gutter somewhere.'

'That's not what Pat thinks.'

'And what do *you* think?'

Willie tasted from a steaming vat. 'I think I've put too much cream in the *potage*.'

'It's the way Elvis would have wanted it,' commented Rebus.

The barman, whose name was Toni ('with an i'), poured Rebus a murky half pint of Cask Conditioned.

'This looks as conditioned as my hair.'

'I know a good hairdresser if you're interested.'

Rebus ignored the remark, then decided to ignore the beer too. He waited while Toni chattily served two student types at the other end of the bar.

'How did Eddie seem after I left yesterday?'

'What's the name of that Scorsese film?'

'*Taxi Driver?*'

The barman shook his head. '*Raging Bull*. That was Eddie.'

'He was like that all evening?'

'I didn't see him much. By the time he comes out of the kitchen, I'm putting on my coat to go home.'

'Was there anyone ... *unusual* in the bar last night?'

'You get a mixed crowd in here. Any particular *type* of unusual?'

'Forget it.'

It looked like Toni-with-an-i already had.

# 16

It was beginning to look like the circle was now complete. Eddie told Holmes something about the body in the Central Hotel. Holmes tried to find out more, by going after the Bru-Head Brothers. Then Rebus came along to offer help. Now all three had been warned off in some way or other. Well, he *hoped* Eddie was just being warned off. He hoped it wasn't more drastic. Everyone knew the chef had trouble keeping his mouth shut after a drink, and 'after a drink' seemed to be his permanent state. Yes, Rebus was worried. They'd tried scaring him off and only made him more determined. So would they now pull another stunt? Or would they perhaps revert to more certain means of silence?

Rebus's face was as dark as the sky when he walked back into St Leonard's, only to be ordered immediately to Lauderdale's office. Lauderdale was pouring whisky into three glasses.

'Ah, there you are.'

Rebus could not deny it. 'Summoned by Bell's, sir.' He accepted the glass, trying not to look at Alister Flower's beaming face. The three men sat down.

'Cheers,' offered Lauderdale.

'Here's tae us,' said Flower.

Rebus just drank.

'Been having a bit of bother, John?' Lauderdale was positioning his half-empty glass on the desk. When he used Rebus's first name, Rebus knew he was in trouble.

'I don't know about that, sir. There was a minor hiccup this morning, all taken care of.'

Lauderdale nodded, still seeming affable. Flower had crossed his legs, at ease with the world. When Lauderdale next spoke, he held up a finger to accompany each point.

'Two schoolkids barge in on you. Then DC Petrie gets into a punch-up with a complete stranger. A window is smashed, and so is Petrie's nose. DC Clarke's down at street level trying to brush away broken glass and curious passers-by.' He looked up from his full hand. 'Any possibility, John, that Operation Moneybags has been placed in jeopardy?'

'No possibility, sir.' Rebus held up one finger. 'The man won't talk, because if he does we'll charge him with assault.' A second finger. 'And the boys won't talk because the father will warn them not to.' He held his two fingers in the air, then lowered his hand.

'With all due respect, sir,' the Little Weed was saying, 'we've got a fight and a broken window in what was supposed to be a deserted building. People are nosy, it's human nature. They'll be looking up at that window tomorrow, and they'll be wondering. Any movement behind the window will be noticed.'

Lauderdale turned to Rebus. 'John?'

'What Inspector Flower says is true, sir, as far as it goes. But people are quick to forget. What they'll see tomorrow is a new window, end of story. Nobody saw anything from the taxi offices, and even if they heard the glass, it's not like it doesn't happen every day along Gorgie.'

'Even so, John . . .'

'Even so, sir, it was a mistake. I've already made that clear to DC Clarke.' He could have told them that it was all the fault of the woman from Trading Standards, but making excuses made you seem weak. Rebus could take this on the chin. He'd even take it on the back of his scalp if it would get him out of the office any faster. The aromas of whisky and body odour were making him slightly queasy.

'Alister?'

'Well, sir, you know my view on the subject.'

Lauderdale nodded. 'John,' he said, 'a lot of planning has gone into Operation Moneybags, and there's a lot at stake. If you're going to let a couple of kids wander into the middle of the surveillance, maybe it's time you rethought your priorities. For example, those files beside your desk. That stuff's five years old. Get your brain back to the here and now, understand?'

'Yes, sir.'

'We know you must have been affected by the attack on DS Holmes. What I'm asking is, are you up to helping run Operation Moneybags?'

Ah, here it was. The Little Weed wanted the surveillance for himself. He wanted to be the one to bring in Dougary.

'I'm up to it, sir.'

'No more fuck-ups then, understood?'

'Understood, sir.'

Rebus would have said anything to shorten the meeting; well, just about anything. But he was damned if he was going to hand *anything* to Flower, least of all a case like this, even if he *did* think it a waste of time. Get back to the here and now, Lauderdale had said. But when Rebus left the office, he knew exactly where his brain was heading: back to the there and then.

By late afternoon, he decided that he had only two options regarding the Central Hotel, only two people left who might help. He telephoned one, and after a little persuasion was able to arrange an immediate interview.

'There may be interruptions,' the secretary warned. 'We're very busy just now.'

'I can put up with interruptions.'

Twenty minutes later, he was ushered into a small wood-panelled office in a well-maintained old stone building. The windows looked out onto uglier new constructions of corrugated metal and shining steel. Steam billowed from pipes, but indoors you miraculously lost that strong brewery smell.

The door opened and a thirtyish man ambled into the room.

'Inspector Rebus?'

They shook hands. 'Good of you to see me at such short notice, sir.'

'Your call was intriguing. I still like a bit of intrigue.'

Close up, Rebus saw that Aengus Gibson was probably still in his twenties. The sober suit, the spectacles and short sleek hair made him seem older. He went to his desk, slipped off his jacket, and placed it carefully over the back of a large padded chair. Then he sat down and began rolling up his shirtsleeves.

'Sit yourself down, Inspector, please. Now, something to do with the Central Hotel, you said?'

There were papers laid out on the desk, and Gibson appeared to be browsing through them as Rebus spoke, but Rebus knew the man was taking in every word.

'As you know, Mr Gibson, the Central burnt down five years ago. The cause of the fire was never satisfactorily explained, but more disturbing still was the finding of a body, a body with a bullet-hole through the heart. The body has never been identified.'

Rebus paused. Gibson took off his glasses and laid them on top of the papers. 'I knew the Central quite well, Inspector. I'm sure my reputation precedes you into this office.'

'Past and present reputations, sir.'

Gibson made no show of hearing this. 'I was a bit wild in my youth, and a wilder crowd you'd be hard pressed to find than that congregating in the Central Hotel in *those* days.'

'You'd be in your early twenties, sir, hardly a "youth".'

'Some of us take longer to grow up than others.'

'Why did you arrange to meet Matthew Vanderhyde there?'

Gibson sat back in his chair. 'Ah, now I see why you're here. Well, I thought Uncle Matthew might appreciate the seedy glory of the Central. He was wild himself in years past.'

'And maybe also you thought it might shock him?'

'Nobody could shock Matthew Vanderhyde, Inspector.' He smiled. 'But perhaps you're right. Yes, I'm sure there was an element of that. I knew damned fine that my father had asked him to talk to me. So I arranged to meet in the worst place I could think of.'

'I could probably have helped find a few worse places than the Central.'

'Me too, really. But the Central was ... well, *central*.'

'And the two of you talked?'

'He talked. I was supposed to listen. But when you're with a blind man, Inspector, you don't need to put up any pretence. No need for glazed eyes and all that. I think I read the paper, tried the crossword, watched the TV. It didn't seem to matter to him. He was doing my father a favour, that was all.'

'But pretty soon afterwards you put your "Black Aengus" days behind you.'

'That's true, yes. Maybe Uncle Matthew's words had an effect after all.'

'And after the meeting?'

'We thought of having dinner together – not, I might add, in the Central. Filthiest kitchens I've ever seen. But I think I had a prior appointment with a young lady. Well, not that young, actually. Married, I seem to recall. Sometimes I miss those days. The media call me a reformed character. It's an easy cliché, but damned hard to live up to.'

'Your name never appeared on the official list of the Central's customers that night.'

'An oversight.'

'One you could have corrected by coming forward.'

'Giving yet more fuel to the newspapers.'

'What if they found out now that you *were* there?'

'Well, Inspector, that wouldn't be fuel.' Aengus Gibson's eyes were warm and clear. 'That would be an incendiary.'

'Is there anything you can tell me about that night, sir?'

'You seem to know all of it. I was in the bar with Matthew Vanderhyde. We left hours before the place caught fire.'

Rebus nodded. 'Have you ever been on the hotel's first floor, sir?'

'What an extraordinary question. It was *five years ago*.'

'A long time, certainly.'

'And now the case is being reopened?'

'In a way, sir, yes. We can't give too many details.'

'That's all right, I'll get my father to ask the Chief Constable. They're good friends, you know.'

Rebus kept silent. There was no case. Nothing he could present to his superiors would cause them to reopen it. He knew he was in this all on his own, and for not very good reasons. There was a brisk tap at the door, and an older man came into the office. His face strongly resembled Aengus Gibson's, but both face and body were much leaner. Ascetic was the word that came to mind. Broderick Gibson would rarely loosen his tight-knotted tie or undo the top button of his shirt. He wore a woollen V-neck below his suit jacket. Rebus had seen church elders like him. Their faces persuaded more guilt-money into the collection.

'Sorry to butt in,' Broderick Gibson said. 'These need a

look-over before tomorrow morning.' He placed a folder on the desk.

'Father, this is Inspector Rebus. Inspector, Broderick Gibson, my father.'

And the man who had started Gibson's Brewing from his garden shed back in the 1950s. Rebus shook the firm hand.

'No trouble I hope, Inspector?'

'None at all, sir,' replied Rebus.

Broderick Gibson turned to his son. 'You haven't forgotten that do tonight for the SSPCC?'

'No, father. Eight o'clock?'

'Damned if I can remember.'

'I think it's eight o'clock.'

'You're right, sir,' said Rebus.

'Oh?' Aengus Gibson looked surprised. 'Will you be there yourself?'

But Rebus shook his head. 'I read a piece about it in the paper.' He was so far below these people on the social ladder, he wondered if they could see him at all. As they'd climbed, they'd sawn off the rungs behind them. Rebus could only peer up into the clouds, catching a glimpse every now and then. But they *all* liked to be liked by the police. Which was probably why Broderick Gibson insisted on shaking Rebus's hand again before leaving.

With his father gone, Aengus Gibson seemed to relax. 'I'm sorry, I should have asked you before – would you like tea or coffee? I know you're on duty, so I won't ask if you'd like to try a beer.'

'Actually, sir,' said Rebus, glancing at the clock on the wall, 'I finished work five minutes ago.'

Aengus Gibson laughed and went to a large cupboard which, when opened, revealed three bar-pumps and a gathering of sparkling pint and half-pint glasses. 'The Dark is very good today,' he said.

'Dark's fine, but just a half.'

'A half of Dark it is.'

In fact, Rebus managed another half, this time of the pale ale. But it was the taste of the Dark that stayed with him as he drove back out through the brewery's wrought-iron gates. Gibson's Dark. The Gibsons, father and son, were dark, all right. You had to look beneath the surface to see it, but it was there. To the outside world, Aengus Gibson might be a changed man, but Rebus could see the young man was just barely in control of himself. He even wondered if Gibson might be on mood control drugs of some kind. He had spent some time in a private 'nursing' home – euphemism for psychiatric care. At least, that was the story Rebus had heard. He thought maybe he'd do a bit of digging, just to satisfy his curiosity. He was curious about one small detail in particular, one thing Aengus Gibson had said. He not only knew the kitchens of the Central Hotel were filthy – he'd *seen* them.

John Rebus found that very interesting indeed.

He returned to St Leonard's and was relieved to find no sign of Lauderdale or Little Weed. He'd forgotten to visit Holmes, so telephoned the hospital instead. He knew how it went at the Infirmary; they could wheel a payphone to your bed.

'Brian?'

'Hello there. I've just had a visit from Nell.' He sounded bright. Rebus hoped he wasn't just getting her sympathy vote.

'How is she?'

'She's okay. Any progress?'

Rebus thought about the past twenty-four hours. A lot of work. 'No,' he said, 'no progress.' He decided not to tell Holmes that Eddie Ringan was missing: he might worry himself back into relapse.

'Are you thinking of giving up?'

'I've got a lot on my plate, Brian, but no, I'm not giving up.'

'Thanks.'

Rebus almost blurted out, It's not just for you now, it's for my brother too. Instead, he told Holmes to take care, and promised him a visit soon.

'Better make it *very* soon, they're letting me out tomorrow or the day after.'

'That's good.'

'I don't know ... there's this nurse in here ...'

'Ach, away with ye!' But Rebus remembered a nurse who had treated his scalp, a nurse he'd become too friendly with. That had been the start of the trouble with Patience. 'Be careful,' he ordered, putting down the phone.

His next call was to the local newspaper. He spoke to someone there for a few minutes, after which he tried calling Siobhan Clarke in Gorgie. But there was no answer. Obviously Dougary had clocked off for the day, and with him her surveillance. Well, it was time for Inspector Rebus to clock off too. On his way out, he heard the unmistakable brag of Alister Flower's voice heading towards him. Rebus dodged into another office and waited for Flower and his underlings to pass. They hadn't been talking about him, which was something. He felt only a little ashamed at hiding. Every good soldier knew when to hide.

# 17

Michael was up and about that evening, doing a fair imitation of a telly addict. He held the remote control like it was a pacemaker, and stared deeply at anything on the screen. Rebus began to wonder about the dosages he'd been taking. But there still seemed to be a fair number of tablets in the bottle.

He went out and bought fish suppers from the local chip shop. It wasn't the best of stuff, but Rebus didn't feel like driving the distance to anywhere better. He remembered the chip shop in their home town, where the fryer would spit into the fat to check how hot it was. Michael smiled at the story, but his eyes never left the TV. He pushed chips into his mouth, chewing slowly, picking batter off the fish and eating that before attacking the fatty white flesh.

'Not bad chips,' Rebus commented, pouring Irn-Bru for both of them. He was waiting for Patience's phone call, giving the time and place for their meet. But whenever the phone did ring, it was for the students.

It rang for a fifth or sixth time, and Rebus picked up the receiver. 'Edinburgh University answering service?'

'It's me,' said Siobhan Clarke.

'Oh, hello there.'

'Don't sound *too* excited.'

'What can I do for you, Clarke?'

'I wanted to apologise for this morning.'

'Not entirely your fault.'

'I should have told those boys who we really were. I've been going over it again and again in my head, what I should have done.'

'Well, you won't do it again.'

'No, sir.' She paused. 'I heard you were carpeted.'

'You mean by the Chief Inspector?' Rebus smiled. 'More like a fireside rug than a length of Wilton. How's the window?'

'Boarded up. The glass'll be replaced overnight.'

'Anything of interest today?'

'You were there for it, sir. Petrie came back in the afternoon.'

'Oh yes, how was he?'

'Bandaged up like the Elephant Man.'

Rebus knew that if anyone had talked about the morning's incident – and someone had – it must be Petrie. He'd little sympathy. 'I'll see you tomorrow.'

'Yes, sir. Goodnight.'

'What was all that about?' asked Michael.

'Nothing.'

'I thought that's what you'd say. Is there any more Irn-Bru?'

Rebus passed him the bottle.

When Patience hadn't phoned by ten, he gave up and started to concentrate on the TV. He had half a mind to leave the receiver off its cradle. The next call came ten minutes later. There was tremendous background noise, a party or a pub. A bad song was being badly sung nearby.

'Turn that down a bit, Mickey.' Michael hit the mute button, silencing a politician on the news. 'Hello?'

'Is that you, Mr Rebus?'

'It's me.'

'Chick Muir here.' Chick was one of Rebus's contacts.

'What is it, Chick?' The song had come to an end, and Rebus heard clapping, laughter, and whistles.

'That fellow you were wanting to see, he's about twenty feet away from me with a treble whisky up at his nose.'

'Thanks, Chick. I'll be right there.'

'Wait a second, don't you want to know where I am?'

'Don't be stupid, Chick. I *know* where you are.'

Rebus put the receiver down and looked over at Mickey, who seemed to have fallen asleep. He switched off the television, and went to get his jacket.

It was a nap Chick Muir had been calling from the Bowery, a late-opening dive near the bottom of Easter Road. The pub had been called Finnegan's until a year ago, when a new owner had come up with the 'inspired' change of name, because, as he explained, he wanted to see loads of bums on seats.

He got bums all right, some of whom wouldn't have looked amiss in the original Bowery. He also got some students and perennial hard drinkers, partly because of the pub's location but mostly because of the late licence. There had never been any trouble though, well, none to speak of. Half the drinkers in the Bowery feared the other half, who meantime were busy fearing *them*. Besides which, it was rumoured Big Ger gave round-the-clock insurance – for a price.

Chick Muir often drank there, though he managed not to participate in what was reckoned to be Edinburgh's least musical karaoke. Eddie Ringan for one would have died on the spot at the various awful deaths suffered by 'Hound Dog' and 'Wooden Heart'. Off-key and out of condition, the singers could transform a simple word like 'crying' into a multi-syllabled meaningless drawl. Huh-kuh-rye-a-yeng was an approximation of the sound that greeted Rebus as he pulled at the double doors to the pub and slitted his eyes against the cigarette fug.

As 'Crying in the Chapel' came to its tearful end, Rebus felt a hand squeeze his arm.

157

'You made it then.'

'Hullo, Chick. What are you having?'

'A double Grouse would hit the spot, not that I believe they keep real Grouse in their Grouse bottles.' Chick Muir grinned, showing two rows of dull gold teeth. He was a foot and a half shorter than Rebus, and looked in this crowd like a wee boy lost in the woods. 'Still,' he said, 'it might not be Grouse, but it's a quarter gill.'

Well, there was logic in that somewhere. So Rebus pushed his way to the bar and shouted his order. There was applause all around as a favourite son of song took the stage. Rebus glanced along the bar and saw Deek Torrance, looking no more drunk or sober than the last time they'd met. As Rebus was paying for his drinks (he'd never to wait; they knew him in here) Torrance saw him, and gave a nod and a wave. Rebus indicated that he had to take the drinks but would be back, and Torrance nodded again.

The music had started up. Oh please, no, thought Rebus. Not 'Little Red Rooster'. On the video, a cockerel seemed to be taking an interest in the blonde farm-girl who had come out to collect the morning eggs.

'Here you are, Chick. Cheers.'

'Slainte.' Chick took a sip, savoured, then shook his head. 'I'm sure this isn't Grouse. Did you see him?'

'I saw him.'

'And it's the right chap?'

Rebus handed over a folded tenner, which Chick pock-eted. 'It's him, all right.'

And indeed, Deek Torrance was squeezing his way towards them through the crush. But he stopped short and leaned over another drinker to tap Rebus's shoulder.

'John, just going –' He yanked his head towards the toilets at the side of the stage. 'Back in a min.' Rebus nodded his understanding and Torrance moved away again through the tide. Chick Muir sank his whisky. 'I'll make myself scarce,' he said.

'Aye, see you around, Chick.' Chick nodded and, placing his glass on a table, made for the exit. Rebus tried to shut out 'Little Red Rooster', and when this failed he followed Torrance to the toilets. He saw Deek having a word with the DJ on the stage, then pushing open the door of the gents'. Rebus glared at the singer as he passed, but the crowd was whipping the middle-aged man to greater and greater depths.

Deek was at the communal urinal, laughing at a cartoon on the wall. It showed two football players in Hearts strips involved in an act of buggery, and above it was the caption 'Jam Tarts – Well Stuffed!' It was the sort of thing you had to expect on Easter Road. In a pub somewhere in Gorgie there would be a similar cartoon portraying two Hibernian players. Rebus checked that no one else was in the gents'. Deek, looking over his shoulder, spotted him.

'John, I thought for a minute you were a willie-watcher.'

But Rebus was in serious mood. 'I need you to get me something, Deek.'

Torrance grunted.

'Remember when you said you could lay your hands on anything?'

'Anything from a shag to a shooter,' quoted Deek.

'The latter,' Rebus said simply. Deek Torrance looked like he might be about to comment. Instead, he grunted, zipped his fly, and went over to the washbasin.

'You could get into trouble.'

'I could.'

Torrance dried his hands on the filthy roller-towel. 'When would you need it?'

'ASAP.'

'Any particular model?' They were both serious now, talking in quiet, level tones.

'Whatever you can get will be fine. How much?'

'Anything up to a couple of hundred. You sure you want to do this?'

'I'm sure.'

'You could get a licence, make it legit.'

'I could.'

'But you probably won't.'

'You don't want to know, Deek.'

Deek grunted again. The door swung open and a young man, grinning from one side of his mouth while holding a cigarette in the other, breezed in. He ignored the two men and made for the urinal.

'Give me a phone number.' The youth half-glanced over his shoulder at them. 'Eyes front, son!' Torrance snarled at him. 'Guide dogs are gey expensive these days!'

Rebus tore a sheet from his notepad. 'Two numbers,' he said. 'Home and work.'

'I'll be in touch.'

Rebus pulled open the door. 'Buy you a drink?'

Torrance shook his head. 'I'm heading off.' He paused. 'You're sure about this?'

John Rebus nodded.

When Deek had gone, he bought himself another drink. He was shaking, his heart racing. A good-looking woman had been singing 'Band of Gold', and adequately too. She got the biggest cheer of the night. The DJ came to the microphone and repeated her name. There were more cheers as her boyfriend helped her down from the stage. His fingers were covered with gold rings. Now the DJ was introducing the next act.

'He's chosen to sing for us that great old number "King of the Road". So let's have a big hand for John Rebus!'

There was some applause, and the people who knew him lowered their drinks and looked towards where Rebus stood at the bar.

'You bastard, Deek!' he hissed. The DJ was looking out over the crowd.

'John, are you still with us?' The audience were looking around too. Someone, Rebus realised later, must have pointed him out, for suddenly the DJ was announcing that John was a shy one but he was standing at the bar with the black padded jacket on and his head buried in his glass. 'So let's coax him up here with an extra big hand.'

There was an extra big hand for John Rebus as he turned to face the crowd. It was fortunate indeed, he later decided, that Deek hadn't given him a gun then and there. Just the one bullet would have done.

Deek Torrance hated himself, but he made the phone call anyway. He made it from a public box beside a patch of waste ground. Despite the late hour, some children were riding their bikes noisily across the churned-up tarmac. They had set up a ramp from two planks and a milk crate, and launched themselves into darkness, landing heavily on their suffering tyres.

'It's Deek Torrance,' he said when the telephone was answered. He knew he would have to wait while his name was passed along. He rested his forehead against the side of the call-box. The plastic was cool. We all grow up, he said to himself. It's not much fun, but we all do it. No Peter Pans around these days.

Someone was on the line now. The telephone had been picked up at the other end.

'It's Deek Torrance,' he repeated, quite unnecessarily. 'I've got a bit of news ...'

# 18

Rebus was at work surprisingly early on Wednesday morning. He'd never been known as the earliest of arrivals, and his presence in the CID room made his more punctual colleagues look twice, just to be sure they weren't still warm and safe and dreaming in their beds.

They didn't get too close though, an early morning Rebus not being in the best of humours. But he'd wanted to get here before the day's swarm began: he didn't want too many people seeing just what information he was calling up on the computer.

Not that there was much on Aengus Grahame Fairmile Gibson. Public drunkenness mostly, usually with associated high jinks. Knocking the policeman's helmet off seemed to be a game enjoyed by youthful Gibson and his cronies. Other indiscretions included kerb-crawling in a part of town not renowned for its prostitutes, and an attempt to enter a friend's flat by the window (the key having been lost) which landed him in the wrong flat.

But it all came to a stop five years ago. From then till now, Gibson had received not so much as a parking ticket or a speeding fine. So much for his police files. Rebus punched in Broderick Gibson, too, not expecting anything. His expectations were fulfilled. The elder Gibson's 'youthful indiscretions' would be the stuff of musty old files in an annexe somewhere – always supposing there were any to begin with. Rebus had the feeling that anyone associated with Scottish Sword & Shield would probably have been arrested for disorderly conduct or breach of the peace at *some* point in their career. The possible exception, perhaps, being Matthew Vanderhyde.

He made a phone call to check that the meeting he'd arranged yesterday was still on, then switched off the computer and headed out of the building, just as a bleary Chief Superintendent Watson was coming in.

He waited in the newspaper office's public area, flipping through the past week's editions. A few early punters came in with Spot the Ball coupons or the like, and a few more hopefuls were checking copy with the people on the classified ads desk.

'Inspector Rebus.' She'd come from behind the main desk, where a stern security man had been keeping a watchful eye on Rebus. She was already wearing her raincoat, so there was to be no tour of the premises today, though she'd been promising him for weeks.

Her name was Mairie Henderson and she was in her early twenties. Rebus had come up against her when she was compiling a postmortem feature on the Gregor Jack case. Rebus had just wanted to forget about the whole ugly episode, but she'd been persistent ... and persuasive. She was just out of college, where she'd won awards for her student journalism and for pieces she'd contributed to the daily and weekly press. She hadn't yet forgotten how to be hungry; Rebus liked that.

'Come on,' she said. 'I'm starving. I'll buy you breakfast.'

So they went to a little cafe/bakery on South Bridge, where there were difficult choices to be made. Was it too early for pies and bridies? Too early for a fruit scone? Well then, they'd be like everyone else and settle for sliced sausage, black pudding and fried eggs.

'No haggis or dumpling?' Mairie was so imploring, the woman at the counter went off to ask the chef. Which made Rebus make a mental note to phone Pat Calder sometime today. But there was no haggis or dumpling, not even for ready money. So they took their trays to the cash till, where Mairie insisted on paying.

'After all, you're going to give me the story of the decade.'

'I don't know about that.'

'One of these days you will, trust me.'

They squeezed into a booth and she reached for the brown sauce, then for the ketchup. 'I can never decide between the two. Shame about the fried dumpling, that's my favourite.'

She was about five feet five inches and had about as much fat on her as a rabbit in a butcher's window. Rebus looked down at his fry-up and suddenly didn't feel very hungry. He sipped the weak coffee.

'So what's it all about?' she asked, having made a good start into the food on her plate.

'You tell me.'

She waved a no-no with her knife. 'Not till you tell me why you want to know.'

'That's not the way the game's played.'

'We'll change the rules, then.' She scooped up some egg-white with her fork. She had her coat wrapped tight around her, though it was steamy in the cafe. Good legs too; Rebus missed seeing her legs. He blew on the coffee, then sipped again. She'd be willing to wait all day for him to say something.

'Remember the fire at the Central Hotel?' he said at last.

'I was still at school.'

'A body turned up in the ruins.' She nodded encouragement. 'Well, maybe there's new evidence ... no, not new evidence. It's just that some things have been happening, and I think they've got something to do with that fire and that shooting.'

'This isn't an official investigation, then?'

'Not yet.'

'And there's no story?'

Rebus shook his head. 'Nothing that wouldn't get you pasted in a libel court.'

'I could live with that, if the story was good enough.'

'It isn't, not yet.'

She began mopping-up operations with a triangle of buttered bread. 'So let me get this straight: you're on your own looking into a fire from five years ago?'

A fire which turned one man to drink, he could have said, and led another to the path of self-righteousness. But all he did was nod.

'And what's Gibson got to do with it?'

'Strictly between us, he was there that night. Yet he was kept off the list of the hotel's customers.'

'His father pulled some strings?'

'Could be.'

'Well, that's already a story.'

'I've nothing to back it up.' This was a lie, there was always Vanderhyde; but he wasn't going to tell her that. He didn't want her getting ideas. The way she was staring, she was getting plenty of those anyway.

'Nothing?'

'Nothing,' he repeated.

'Well, I don't know that this will help.' She opened her coat and pulled out the file which she'd been hiding, tucked down the front of her fashion-cut denims. He accepted the file from her, looking around the cafe. Nobody seemed to be paying attention.

'A bit cloak and dagger,' he told her. She shrugged.

'So I've seen too many films.'

Rebus opened the file. It bore no title, but inside were cuttings and 'spiked' stories concerning Aengus Gibson.

'Those are only from five years ago to the present. There isn't much, mostly charity work, giving to good

165

causes. A little bit about the brewery's rising image and ditto profits.'

He glanced through the stuff. It was worthless. 'I was hoping to find out something about him from just after the fire.'

Mairie nodded. 'So you said on the phone. That's why I talked to a few people, including our chief sub. He says Gibson went into a psychiatric hospital. Nervous breakdown was the word.'

'Were the words,' corrected Rebus.

'Depends,' she said cryptically. Then: 'He was there the best part of three months. There was never a story, the father kept it out of the papers. When Aengus reappeared, *that's* when he started working in the business, and that's when he started all the do-gooding.'

'Shouldn't that be good-doing?'

She smiled. 'Depends,' she said. Then, of the file, 'It's not much, is it?' Rebus shook his head. 'I thought not. Still, it's all there was.'

'What about your chief sub? Would he be able to say *exactly* when Gibson went into that hospital?'

'I don't know. No harm in asking. Do you want me to?'

'Yes, I do.'

'All right then. And one more question.'

'Yes?'

'Aren't you going to eat any of that?'

Rebus pushed his plate across to her and watched her take her fill.

When he got back to St Leonard's, there was a call from the Chief Super's office. Chief Superintendent Watson wanted to see him straight away, as in ten minutes ago. Rebus checked that there were no messages for him, and called Siobhan Clarke in Gorgie to make sure the new window had been fitted.

'It's perfect,' she told him. 'It's got white gunk on it, window polish or something. We just didn't bother wiping it off. We can take shots through it, but from the outside it just looks like a new window that's waiting to be cleaned.'

'Fine,' said Rebus. He wanted to make sure he was up to date. If Watson intended to carpet him over yesterday, it would be considerably more than Lauderdale's fireside rug.

But Rebus had got it way wrong.

'What the hell are you up to?' Watson looked like he'd run a half-marathon gobbling down chilli peppers all the way. His breathing was raspy, his cheeks a dark cherry colour. If he walked into a hospital, they'd have him whisked to emergency on a two-man stretcher.

No, better make that a four-man.

'I'm not sure what you mean, sir.'

Watson fairly pounded the desk with his fist. A pencil dropped onto the floor. 'You're not sure what I mean!'

Rebus moved forward to pick up the pencil.

'Leave it! Just sit down.' Rebus went to sit. 'No, better yet, keep standing.' Rebus stood up. 'Now, just tell me why.' Rebus remembered a science teacher at his secondary school, a man with an evil temper who had spoken to the teenage Rebus just like this. 'Just tell me why.'

'Yes, sir.'

'Go on then.'

'With respect, sir, why what?'

The words came out through gritted teeth. 'Why you've seen fit to start pestering Broderick Gibson.'

'With respect, sir –'

'Stop all that "with respect" shite! Just give me an answer.'

'I'm not pestering Broderick Gibson, sir.'

'Then what *are* you doing, wooing him? The Chief

167

Constable phoned me this morning in absolute fucking apoplexy!' Watson, being a Christian of no mean persuasion, didn't swear often. It was a bad sign.

Rebus saw it all. The bash for the SSPCC. Yes, and Broderick Gibson collaring his friend the Chief Constable. One of your minions has been on to me, what's it all about? The Chief Constable not knowing anything about it, stuttering and spluttering and saying he'd get to the bottom of it. Just give me the officer's name ...

'It's his son I'm interested in, sir.'

'But you looked both of them up on the computer this morning.'

Ah, so *some*one had taken notice of his early shift. 'Yes, I did, but I was really only interested in Aengus.'

'You still haven't explained why.'

'No, sir, well, it's a bit ... nebulous.'

Watson frowned. *'Nebulous?* When's the graduation party?' Rebus didn't get it. 'Since you've obviously,' Watson was happy to explain, 'just got your astronomy degree!' He poured himself coffee from the machine on the floor, offering none to Rebus who could just use a cup.

'It was the word that came to mind, sir,' he said.

'I can think of a few words too, Rebus. Your mother wouldn't like to hear them.'

No, thought Rebus, and yours would wash your mouth out with soap.

The Chief Super slurped his coffee. They didn't call him 'Farmer' for nothing; he had many ways and predilections that could only be described as agricultural.

'But before I say any of them,' he went on, 'I'm a generous enough man to say that I'll listen to your explanation. Just make it bloody convincing.'

'Yes, sir,' said Rebus. How could he make *any* of it sound convincing? He supposed he'd have to try.

So he tried, and halfway through Watson even told

him he could sit if he liked. At the end of fifteen minutes, Rebus placed his hands out in front of him, palms up, as if to say: that's all, folks.

Watson poured another cup of coffee and placed it on the desk in front of Rebus.

'Thank you, sir.' Rebus gulped it down black.

'John, have you ever thought you might be paranoid?'

'All the time, sir. Show me two men shaking hands and I'll show you a Masonic conspiracy.'

Watson almost smiled, before recalling that this was no joking matter. 'Look, let me put it like this. What you've got so far is ... well, it's ...'

'Nebulous, sir?'

'Piss and wind,' corrected Watson. 'Somebody died five years ago. Was it anyone important? Obviously not, or we'd know who they were by now. So we assume it was somebody the world had hardly known and was happy to forget. No grieving widow or weans, no family asking questions.'

'You're saying let it die, sir? Let somebody get away with murder?'

Watson looked exasperated. 'I'm saying we're stretched as it is.'

'All Brian Holmes did was ask a few questions. Somebody brained him for it. I take over, my flat's invaded and my brother half scared to death.'

'My point exactly, it's all become *personal*. You can't allow that to happen. Look at the other stuff on your plate. Operation Moneybags for a start, and I'm sure there's more besides.'

'You're asking me to drop it, sir? Might I ask if you're under any personal pressure?'

There was personal pressure aplenty as Watson's blood rose, his face purpling. 'Now wait just one second, that's not the sort of comment I can tolerate.'

'No, sir. Sorry, sir.' But Rebus had made his point. The

clever soldier knows when to duck. Rebus had taken his shot, and now he was ducking.

'I should think so,' said Watson, wriggling in his chair as though his trousers were lined with scouring-pads. 'Now here's what I think. I think that if you can bring me something concrete, the dead man's identity perhaps, within twenty-four hours, then we'll reopen the case. Otherwise, I want the whole thing dropped until such time as new evidence *does* come forward.'

'Fair enough, sir,' said Rebus. It wasn't much good arguing the point. Maybe twenty-four hours would be enough. And maybe Charlie Chan had a clan tartan. 'Thanks for the coffee, much appreciated.'

When Watson started to make his joke about feeling 'full of beans', Rebus made his excuses and left.

# 19

He was seated at his desk, glumly examining all the dead ends in the case, when he happened to catch word of an 'altercation' at a house in Broughton. He caught the address, but it took a few seconds for it to register with him. Minutes later, he was in his car heading into the east end of town. The traffic was its usual self, with agonisingly slow pockets at the major junctions. Rebus blamed the traffic lights. Why couldn't they just do away with them and let the pedestrians take their chances? No, there'd only be more hold-ups, what with all the ambulances they'd need to ferry away the injured and the dead.

Still, why was he hurrying? He thought he knew what he was going to find. He was wrong. (It was turning out to be one of those weeks.) A police car and an ambulance sat outside Mrs MacKenzie's two-storey house, and the neighbours were out in a show of conspicuous curiosity. Even the kids across the road were interested. It must be a break-time, and some of them pushed their heads between the vertical iron bars and stared open-mouthed at the brightly marked vehicles.

Rebus thought about those railings. Their intention was to keep the kids *in*, keep them safe. But could they keep anybody *out*?

Rebus flashed his ID at the constable on door duty and entered Mrs MacKenzie's house. She was wailing loudly, so that Rebus started to think of murder. A WPC comforted her, while trying to have a conversation with her own over-amplified shoulder radio. The WPC saw Rebus.

'Make her some tea, will you?' she pleaded.

'Sorry, hen, I'm only CID. Needs someone a bit more senior to mash a pot of Brooke Bond.' Rebus had his hands in his pockets, the casually informed observer, distanced from the mayhem into which he walked. He wandered over to the bird cage and peered in. On the sand floor, amidst feathers and husks and droppings, lay a mummified budgie.

'Away the crow road,' he muttered to himself, moving out of the living room. He saw the ambulancemen in the kitchen, and folowed them. There was a body on the floor, hands and face heavily bandaged. He couldn't see any blood, though. He nearly skited on wet linoleum, and steadied himself by gripping the edge of the antiquated gas cooker. It was warm to the touch. A police constable stood by the open back door, looking out to right and left. Rebus squeezed past the carers and their patient and joined the PC.

'Nice day, eh?'

'What?'

'I see you're admiring the weather.' Rebus showed his ID again.

'No, not that. Just seeing the way he went.'

Rebus nodded. 'How do you mean?'

'The neighbours say he climbed three fences, then ran down a close and away.' The PC pointed. 'That close there, just past the line full of washing.'

'Behind the clothes-pole?'

'Aye, that must be the one. Three fences ... one, two, three. It's got to be that close over there.'

'Well done, son, that really gets us a long way.'

The constable stared at him. 'My Inspector's a stickler for notes. You're from St Leonard's? Not quite your patch is it, sir?'

'Everywhere's my patch, son, and everybody's my constable. Now what happened here?'

'The gentleman on the floor was attacked. The attacker ran off.'

Rebus nodded. 'I can tell you the how and the who already.' The PC looked dubious. 'The attacker was a man called Alex Maclean, and he almost certainly punched or headbutted Mr McPhail there.'

The constable blinked, then shook his head. '*That's* Maclean lying there.' Rebus looked down, and for the first time took in the size of the man, a good forty pounds heavier than McPhail. 'And he wasn't punched or butted. He had a pot of boiling water thrown over him.'

Just a little abashed, Rebus listened without comment to the PC's version of events. McPhail, who had been steering well clear of the house, had at last telephoned to say he'd be popping over for some clothes and things. He'd fobbed Mrs MacKenzie off with some story about working long shifts in a supermarket. He'd arrived, and was in the kitchen chatting to his landlady while she put on the water for her boiled eggs (boiled eggs every Wednesday lunchtime; poached on Thursdays – this was one part of Mrs MacKenzie's statement she wanted to get absolutely clear). But Maclean had been watching the house, and saw McPhail go in. He opened the unlocked front door and ran into the kitchen. 'A terrifying sight,' according to Mrs MacKenzie. 'I'll never forget it if I live to be a hundred.'

It was at this point that McPhail lifted the pan and swung it at Maclean, showering him with boiling water. Then he'd opened the back door and fled. Over three fences and through a close. End of melodrama.

Rebus watched them lift Maclean into the back of the ambulance. They'd be taking him to the Infirmary. Soon everyone Rebus knew in Edinburgh would be lying in the

Infirmary. McPhail had been lucky this time. If he knew what was good for him, he would now take Rebus's advice and flee the city, dodging the police who would be looking for him.

Rebus wondered if McPhail really did know what was good for him. This, after all, was a man who thought little girls were good for him. He wondered this as he sat in heavy lunchtime traffic, slowly oozing towards St Leonard's. The route he'd taken to Broughton had been so slow, he saw little to lose by sticking to the bigger roads – Leith Street, The Bridges, and Nicolson Street. Something made him stay on this road till he came to the butcher's shop where Rory Kintoul had ended up, bleeding beneath the meat counter.

He registered only slight surprise at the wooden board which had been placed across the entire front window of the shop. Pinned to the board was a large white sheet of paper with thick felt-pen writing. The sign said simply 'Business as Usual'. Interesting, thought Rebus, parking his car. He noticed that rain or general wear underfoot had done away with the splashes of blood which had once left a crimson trail along the pavement.

Mr Bone the butcher was slicing corned beef with a manual machine whose circular blade hissed through the meat. He was smaller and thinner than most butchers Rebus had come across, his face all cheekbone and worry line, hair thinning and grey. There was no one else in the front of the shop, though Rebus could hear someone whistling as they worked in the back. Bone noticed that he had a customer.

'And what'll it be today, sir?'

Rebus noticed that the display cases just inside the front window were empty, doubtless waiting to be checked for slivers of glass before restocking. He nodded towards the wooden board. 'When did that happen?'

'Ach, last night.' Bone placed the sliced corned beef in

an unsullied section of the display case, then skewered the price marker into it. He wiped his hands on his white apron. 'Kids or drunks.'

'What was it, a brick?'

'Search me.'

'Well, if there was nothing lying in the shop it must have been a sledgehammer. I can't see a kick with a steel toecap doing that sort of damage.'

Now Bone looked at him properly, and recognised him. 'You were here when Rory ...'

'That's right, Mr Bone. They didn't use a sledgehammer on him though, did they?'

'I don't know what you mean.'

'Pound of beef links, by the way.'

Bone hesitated, then took out the string of sausages and cut a length from it.

'You could be right, of course,' Rebus continued. 'Could have been kids or drunks. Did anyone see anything?'

'I don't know.'

'You didn't report it?'

'Didn't have to. Police phoned me at two this morning to tell me about it.' He sounded disgruntled.

'All part of the service, Mr Bone.'

'That's just over the pound,' Bone said, looking at the weighing scales. He wrapped the sausages in white paper, then in brown, marking the price with a pencil on this outer wrapper. Rebus handed over a five-pound note.

'Insurance will take care of it, I suppose,' he said.

'Bloody hope so, the money they charge.'

Rebus accepted his change, and made sure to catch Bone's eye. 'But I meant the *real* insurance people, Mr Bone.' An elderly couple were coming into the shop.

'What happened, Mr Bone?' the woman asked, her husband shuffling along behind her.

'Just kids, Mrs Dowie,' said Bone in the voice he used with customers, a voice he hadn't been using with Rebus.

175

He was staring at Rebus, who gave him a wink, picked up his package, and left. Outside, he looked down at the brown paper parcel. It was chill in his hand. He was supposed to be cutting down on meat, wasn't he? Not that there was much meat in sausages anyway. Another passing shopper stopped to examine the boarded-up window, then went into the shop. Jim Bone would do good business today. Everyone would want to know what had happened. Rebus was different; he *knew* what had happened, though proving it wasn't going to be easy. Siobhan Clarke hadn't managed to talk to the stabbing victim yet. Maybe Rebus should push her along, especially now that she could tell Rory Kintoul all about his cousin's broken window.

Next to his car someone had parked a Land Rover-style 4×4, inside which a huge black dog was ravening to get out. Pedestrians were giving the car a wide berth, and quite right too: the whole vehicle rocked on its axle when the dog lunged at the back window. Rebus noticed that the considerate owner had left the window open an inch. Maybe it was a trap intended for a particularly stupid car thief.

Rebus stopped in front of the open window and unrolled the package of sausages into the car. They fell onto the seat where the dog sniffed them for a nanosecond before starting to dine.

The street was blessedly quiet as Rebus unlocked his own car.

'All part of the service,' he said to himself.

At the station, he telephoned the Heartbreak Cafe, where what sounded like a hastily recorded message told him the place would be shut 'due to convalescence'. In Brian Holmes' desk drawer, he found a print-out of names and phone numbers, those most often used by Holmes himself. Some numbers had been added at the bottom in blue biro, including one for Eddie Ringan marked (h).

Rebus returned to his desk and made the call. Pat Calder answered on the third ring.

'Mr Calder, it's DI Rebus.'

'Oh.' The hope left Calder's voice.

'No sign of him then?'

'None.'

'Right, let's make it official, then. He's a missing person. I'll have someone come over and –'

'Why can't you come?'

Rebus thought about it. 'No reason at all, sir.'

'Make it anytime you like, we're shut today.'

'What happened to wonderchef Willie?'

'We had a busy night, busier than usual.'

'He cracked up?'

'Came flying out of the kitchen yelling, "I'm the chef! I'm the chef!" Lifted some poor woman's entrée and started eating it himself with his face in the bowl. I think he'd been taking drugs.'

'Sounds like he was just doing a good impersonation of late-period Elvis. I'll be there in half an hour, if that's all right.'

Stockbridge's 'Colonies' had been constructed to house the working poor, but were now much desired by young professional types. They were designed as maisonettes, with steep flights of stone stairs leading to the first floor properties. Rebus found the proportions mean in comparison with his Marchmont tenement. No high ceilings here, and no huge rooms with splendid windows and original shutters.

But he could see miners and their families being cosy here a hundred years ago. His own father had been born in a miners' row in Fife. Rebus imagined it must have been very like this ... at least on the outside.

On the inside, Pat Calder had done incredible things. (Rebus didn't doubt that his was the designing and decorating hand.) There were wooden and brass ship's trunks, black anglepoise lamps, Japanese prints in ornate frames, a dinner table whose candelabra resembled some Jewish icon, and a huge TV/hi-fi centre. But of Elvis there was nary a jot. Rebus, seated in a black leather sofa, nodded towards one of the coffin-sized loudspeakers.

'Neighbours ever complain?'

'All the time,' admitted Calder. 'Eddie's proudest moment was when the guy from four doors down phoned to tell us he couldn't hear his TV.'

'Considerate, eh?'

Calder smiled. 'Eddie's never been exactly "politic".'

'Have you known one another long?'

Calder, lying stretched on the floor with his bum on a beanbag, blew nervous smoke from a black Sobranie cigarette. 'Two years casually. We moved in together about the time we had the idea for the Heartbreak.'

'What's he like? I mean, outside the restaurant?'

'Brilliant one minute, a spoilt brat the next.'

'Do you spoil him?'

'I buffer him from the world. At least, I used to.'

'So what was he like when you met?'

'Drinking more than he does now, if you can believe that.'

'Ever tell you why he started?' Rebus had refused a cigarette, but the smoke was getting to him. Maybe he'd have to change his mind.

'He said he drank to forget. Now you're going to ask, Forget what? And I'm going to say that he never told me.'

'He never even hinted?'

'I think he told Brian Holmes more than he told me.'

Jesus, was there a hint of jealousy there? Rebus had a sudden vision of Calder bashing Holmes on the napper . . . and maybe even doing away with Fast Eddie too . . .?

Calder laughed. 'I couldn't hurt him, Inspector. I know what you're thinking.'

'It must be frustrating, though? This genius, you call him, wasting it all for booze. People like that take a lot of looking after.'

'And you're right, it *can* become frustrating.'

'Especially when they're gassed all the time.'

Calder frowned, peering through the smoke from his nostrils. 'Why do you say "gassed"?'

'It means drunk.'

'I know it does. So do a lot of other words. It's just that Eddie used to have these nightmares. About being gassed or gassing people. You know, with *real* gas, like in the concentration camps.'

'He told you about these dreams?'

'Oh no, but he used to shout out in his sleep. A lot of gays went to the gas chambers, Inspector.'

'You think that's what he meant?'

Calder stubbed out the cigarette into a porcelain bedpan beside the fireplace. He got up awkwardly from the floor. 'Come on, I want to show you something.'

Rebus had already seen the kitchen and the bathroom, and so realised that the door Calder was leading him towards must be to the only bedroom. He didn't know quite what to expect.

'I know what you've been thinking,' Calder said, swinging the door wide open. 'This is all Eddie's work.'

And what a work it was. A huge double bed covered with what looked like several zebra-skins. And on the walls, several large paintings of the rhinestone Elvis at work, the face an intentional blur of pink and sheen. Rebus looked up. There was a mirror on the ceiling. He guessed that pretty much any position you took on that bed, you'd be able to watch a white one-piece suit at work with a microphone-hand raised high.

'Whatever turns you on,' he commented.

He visited Clarke and Petrie for a couple of hours, just to

show willing. Unsurprisingly, Jardine had been replaced by a young man called Madden with a stock of puns not heard since the days of valve radio.

'Madden by name,' the Trading Standards officer said by way of introduction, 'mad 'un by nature.'

Make that *steam* radio. Rebus began to wonder if it had been such a good idea, phoning Jardine's boss and swearing exotically at him for twenty minutes.

'I make the jokes around here, son,' he warned.

Rebus had spent more exciting afternoons in his life. For example, being taken by his father to watch Cowdenbeath reserves at home to Dundee. He managed to break the monotony only by stepping out to buy buns at a nearby bakery, though this sort of activity was supposed to be *verboten*. He kept the custard slice for himself, peeling away and discarding the icing. Madden asked if he could have it, and Rebus nodded.

Siobhan Clarke looked like she'd stepped under a gardyloo bucket. She tried not to show it, and smiled whenever she saw him looking in her direction, but there was definitely something up with her. Rebus couldn't be bothered asking what. He got the idea it was to do with Brian ... maybe Brian and Nell. He told her about Bone's window.

'Make some time,' he said. 'Track down Kintoul, if not at home then at the Infirmary. He works in the labs there, right?'

'Right.' Definitely something up with her.

As was his prerogative, Rebus eventually made his excuses and left. Back at St Leonard's, there was a message for him to call Mairie Henderson at work.

'Mairie?'

'Inspector, that didn't take long.'

'You're about the only lead I've got.'

'It's nice to feel wanted.' She had one of those accents that could sound sarcastic without really flexing any muscle. 'Don't get too excited, though.'

'Your Chief Sub didn't remember?'

'Only that it was around August, making it three months after the Central burnt down.'

'Could mean something or nothing.'

'I did my best.'

'Yes, thanks, Mairie.'

'Hold on, don't hang up!' Rebus wasn't about to. 'He did tell me something. Apparently some snippet that's stuck with him.' She paused.

'In your own time, Mairie.'

'This *is* my time, Inspector.' She paused again.

'Are you drawing on a fag?'

'What if I am?'

'Since when did you start smoking?'

'It beats chewing the ends off pencils.'

'You'll stunt your growth.'

'You sound like my dad.'

Well, that brought him back to earth. Here he'd thought they were ... what? Chatting away? Chatting one another *up*? Aye, in your dreams, John Rebus. Now she'd reminded him of the not insignificant age gap between them.

'Are you still there, Inspector?'

'Sorry, my hearing aid slipped out. What did the Chief Sub say?'

'Remember that story about Aengus Gibson entering the wrong flat?'

'I remember.'

'Well, the woman whose flat he broke into was called Mo Johnson.'

Rebus smiled. But then the smile faded. 'That name almost rings a bell.'

'He's a football player.'

'I *know* he's a football player. But a female Mo Johnson, *that's* what rings bells.' But they were faint, too faint.

'Let me know if you come up with anything.'

'I will, Mairie. And Mairie?'

'What?'

'Don't stay out too late.' Rebus terminated the call.

Mo Johnson. He supposed it must be short for Maureen. Where had he come across that name? He knew how he might check. But if Watson found out, it would mean more trouble. Ach, to hell with Watson anyway. He wasn't much more than slave to a coffee bean. Rebus went to the computer console and punched in the details, bringing up Aengus Gibson's record. The anecdote was there, but no charges had ever been pressed. The woman was not mentioned by name, and there was no sign of her address. But, since Gibson was involved, CID had taken an interest. You couldn't always depend on the lower ranks to hush things up properly.

And look who the investigating officer was: DS Jack Morton. Rebus closed the file and got back on the phone. The receiver was still warm.

'You're in luck, he got back from the pub five minutes ago.'

'Away, ya gobshite,' Rebus heard Morton say as he grabbed at the receiver. 'Hello?' Two minutes later, thanks to what was left of Jack Morton's memory, Rebus had an address for Mo Johnson.

A day of contrasts. From bakery to butchery, from The Colonies to Gorgie Road. And now to the edge of Dean Village. Rebus hadn't been down this way since the Water of Leith drowning. He had forgotten how beautiful it was. Tucked down a steep hill from Dean Bridge, the Village gave a good impression of rural peace. Yet it was a five-minute walk from the West End and Princes Street.

They were spoiling it, of course. The developers had squeezed their hands around vacant lots and decaying buildings and choked them into submission. The prices asked for the resultant 'apartments', prices as steep as Bell's Brae, boggled Rebus's mind. Not that Mo Johnson lived in one of the new buildings. No, her flat was a chunk of an older property at the bottom of the brae, with a view of the Water of Leith and Dean Bridge. But she no longer lived there, and the people who did were reluctant to allow Rebus in. They didn't think they had a new address for her. There had been another owner between her moving out and their moving in. They might still have *that* owner's new address, though it would go back a couple of years.

Did they know when Ms Johnson herself moved out?

Four years ago, maybe five.

Which brought Rebus back to the fire at the Central Hotel. Everything he did in this case seemed to bounce straight back to a period five years ago, when something had happened which had changed a lot of people's lives, and taken away at least one life too. He sat in his car wondering what to do next. He knew what to do, but had been putting it off. If tangling with the Gibsons could earn him minus points, he dreaded to think what he might earn by talking with the only other person he could think of who might be able to help.

Help? That was a laugh. But Rebus wanted to meet him all the same. Christ, Flower would have a field day if he found out. He'd hire tents and food and drink and invite everyone to the biggest party in town. Right up from Lauderdale to the Chief Constable, they'd be blowing fuses that could have run hydro stations.

Yes, the more Rebus thought about it, the more he knew it was the right thing to do. The right thing? He had so few openings left, it was the *only* thing. And looking on the bright side, if he did get caught, at least the celebration would bankrupt Little Weed . . .

# 20

He telephoned first, Morris Cafferty not being a man you just dropped in on.

'Will I need my lawyer?' Cafferty growled, sounding amused. 'I'll answer that for you, Strawman, no I fucking won't. Because I've got something better than a lawyer here, better than a fucking judge in my pocket. I've got a dog that'll rip your oesophagus out if I tell it to lick your chops. Be here at six.' The phone went dead, leaving Rebus dry-mouthed and persuading himself all over again that this jumped-up bastard didn't scare him.

What scared him more was the realisation that someone somewhere in the ranks of the Lothian and Borders Police was probably listening in to Cafferty's telephone conversations. Rebus felt like he was in a corridor with doors locking behind him all the time. He saw a gas chamber in his mind and shivered, changing the picture.

Six o'clock wasn't very far away. And at least in dentists' waiting rooms they gave you magazines to pass the time.

Morris Gerald Cafferty lived in a mansion house in the expensive suburb of Duddingston. Duddingston was a 'suburb' by dint of having Arthur's Seat and Salisbury Crags between it and central Edinburgh. Cafferty liked living in Duddingston because it annoyed his neighbours, most of whom were lawyers, doctors and bankers, and also because it wasn't far from his actual and spiritual birthplace, Craigmillar. Craigmillar was one of the tougher

Edinburgh housing schemes. Cafferty grew up there, seeing his first trouble there and in neighbouring Niddrie. He'd led a gang of Craigmillar youths into Niddrie to sort out their rivals. There was a stabbing ... with an uprooted iron railing. Police discovered that the teenage Cafferty had already been in trouble at school for 'accidentally' jamming a ballpoint pen into the corner of a fellow pupil's eye.

It was the quiet start to a long career.

The wrought iron gates at the bottom of the driveway opened automatically as Rebus approached. He drove his car along a well-gritted private road with mature trees either side. You caught a glimpse of the house from the main road, nothing more. But Rebus had been here before; to ask questions, to make an arrest. He knew there was another smaller house behind the main house, linked by a covered walkway. This smaller house had been staff quarters in the days when a city merchant might have lived here. The gravel road forked to the front and back of the main house. A man directed Rebus towards the back: the servants' entrance. The man was very big with a biker helmet haircut, cut high at the fringe but falling over the ears. Where did Cafferty get them, these throw-backs?

The man followed him to the back of the house. Rebus knew where to park. There were three spaces, two vacant and one taken up by a Volvo estate. Rebus thought he recognised the Volvo, though it wasn't Cafferty's. Cafferty's collection of cars was kept in the vast garage. He had a Bentley and a cherry-red '63 T-Bird, neither of which he ever drove. For daily use, there was always the Jag, an XJS-HE. And for weekends there was a dependable Roller which Cafferty had owned for at least fifteen years.

The man opened Rebus's door for him, and pointed towards the small house. Rebus got out.

'Vidal Sassoon was booked up then,' he said.

185

'Uh?' The man turned his head right-side towards Rebus.

'Never mind.' He was about to walk away, but paused. 'Ever been in a fight with a man called Dougary?'

'Nane i' your business.'

Rebus shrugged. The big man closed the car door and stood watching Rebus walk away. So there was no chance to check the tax disc or anything else about the Volvo; nothing to do except memorise the number plate.

Rebus pulled open the door to the small house and was greeted by a wave of heat and steam. The whole structure had been gutted, so that a swimming pool and gymnasium could be installed. The pool was kidney-shaped, with a small circular pool off it – a jacuzzi, presumably. Rebus had always hated kidney pools: it was impossible to do laps in them. Not that he was much of a swimmer.

'Strawman! About bastardin' time!'

He didn't see Cafferty at first, though he had no trouble seeing who was standing over him. Cafferty lay on a massage table, head resting on a pile of towels. His back was being kneaded by none other than the Organ Grinder, who just happened to own a Volvo estate. The Organ Grinder sensibly pretended not to know Rebus; and when Cafferty wasn't looking, Rebus nodded almost imperceptibly his agreement with the pretence.

Cafferty had spun around on his backside and was now easing himself into a standing position. He tested his back and shoulders. 'That's magic,' he said. He removed the towel from around his loins and padded towards Rebus on bare feet.

'See, Strawman, no concealed weapons.' His laughter was like an apprentice with a rasp-file.

Rebus looked around. 'I don't see the –'

But suddenly there it was, pulling itself massively out of the swimming pool. Rebus hadn't even noticed it in there, retrieving a bone. Not a plastic bone either. The black beast dropped the bone at Cafferty's feet, sniffed at Rebus's legs, then shook itself dry onto him.

'Good boy, Kaiser,' said Cafferty. The parking attendant had joined them in the sticky heat. Rebus nodded nowhere in particular.

'I hope you got planning permission for this.'

'All above board, Strawman. Come on, you'd better get changed.'

'Changed for what?'

Laughter again. 'Don't worry, you're not staying to dinner. I'm going for a run, and so are you – if you want to talk to me.'

A run, Jesus! Cafferty turned and walked away towards what looked like a changing cubicle. He slapped the Organ Grinder as he passed him.

'Magic. Same time next week?'

He was hairily muscular, with a chest a borders farmer would be proud to own. There was flab, of course, but not as much as Rebus would have guessed. There was no doubt: Big Ger had got himself in shape. The backside and upper thighs were pockmarked, but the gut had been tightened. Rebus tried to remember when he'd last seen Cafferty. Probably in court ...

Rebus would have enjoyed a quiet word with the Organ Grinder, but now that the parking attendant gorilla was in spying distance, it just wasn't feasible. You couldn't be sure how much the one-eared man could hear.

'There's some stuff here, it should fit.'

The 'stuff' consisted of sweatshirt, running shorts, socks and trainers ... and a headband. There was no way Rebus was going to wear a headband. But when Cafferty emerged from his cubicle, *he* was wearing one, along with a white running vest and immaculate white shorts. He started to limber up while Rebus entered the cubicle to change.

What the hell am I doing? he asked himself. He had imagined a lot of things, but not this. Some things might be painful in life, but this, he had no doubt, was going to be torture.

'Where to?' he asked when they emerged from the overheated gym into the cool twilit evening. He wasn't wearing the headband. And he had put the sweatshirt on inside out. The legend across its front had read 'Kick me if I stop'. He supposed it represented Cafferty's idea of a joke.

'Sometimes I run to Duddingston Loch, sometimes up to the top of the Seat. You choose.' Big Ger was bouncing on the spot.

'The loch.'

'Right,' said Big Ger, and off they set.

Rebus spent the first few minutes checking that his body could take this sort of thing, which was why he was slow to spot the car following them. It was the Jag, driven by the parking attendant at a steady 0–5 mph.

'Remember the last time you gave evidence against me?' Big Ger said. As a conversational opening, it had its merits. Rebus merely nodded. They were running side by side, the pavements being all but deserted. He wondered if any undercover officers would be snapping photographs of this. 'Over in Glasgow, it was.'

'I remember.'

'Not guilty, of course.' Big Ger grinned. He looked like he'd had his teeth seen to as well. Rebus remembered them being greyish-green. Now they were a brilliantly capped white. And his hair ... was it thicker? One of those hair-weaves, maybe? 'Anyway, I heard afterwards you went back down to London and had a bit of a time.'

'You could say that.'

They ran another minute in silence. The pace wasn't exactly taxing, but then neither was Rebus in condition. His lungs were already passing him warnings of the red hot and burning varieties.

'You're getting thin at the back,' Cafferty noticed. 'A hair weave would sort that out.'

It was Rebus's turn to smile. 'You know damned fine I got burned.'

'Aye, and I know who burned you, too.'

Still, Rebus reckoned his own guess about the hair weave had been confirmed.

'Actually,' he said, 'I wanted to talk to you about another fire.'

'Oh aye?'

'At the Central.'

'The Central Hotel?' Rebus was pleased to notice that the words weren't coming so easily from Big Ger either now. 'That's prehistory.'

'Not as far as I'm concerned.'

'But what's it to do with me?'

'Two of your men were there that night, playing in a poker game.'

Cafferty shook his head. 'That can't be right. I won't have gamblers working for me. It's against the Bible.'

'Everything you do from waking till sleeping is against *somebody's* Bible, Cafferty.'

'Please, Strawman, call me *Mr* Cafferty.'

'I'll call you what I like.'

'And I'll call you the Strawman.'

The name jarred ... every time. It had been at the Glasgow trial, a sheet of notes wrongly glanced at by the prosecution, mistaking Rebus for the only other witness, a pub landlord called Stroman.

'Now then, Inspector Stroman ...' Oh, Cafferty had laughed at that, laughed from the dock so hard that he was in danger of contempt. His eyes had bored into Rebus like fat woodworm, and he'd mouthed the word one final time the way he'd heard it – Strawman.

'Like I say,' Rebus went on, 'two of your hired heid-the-ba's. Eck and Tam Robertson.'

189

They had just passed the Sheep's Heid pub, Rebus sorely tempted to veer inside, Cafferty knowing it.

'There'll be herbal tea when we get back. Watch out there!' His warning saved Rebus from stepping in a discreet dog turd.

'Thanks,' Rebus said grudgingly.

'I was thinking of the shoes,' Cafferty replied. 'Know what "flowers of Edinburgh" are?'

'A rock band?'

'Keech. They used to chuck all their keech out of the windows and onto the street. There was so much of it lying around, the locals called it the flowers of Edinburgh. I read that in a book.'

Rebus thought of Alister Flower and smiled. 'Makes you glad you're living in a decent society.'

'So it does,' said Cafferty, with no trace of irony. 'Eck and Tam Robertson, eh? The Bru-Heid Brothers. I won't lie to you, they used to work for me. Tam for just a few weeks, Eck for longer.'

'I won't ask what they did.'

Cafferty shrugged. 'They were general employees.'

'Covers a multitude of sins.'

'Look, I didn't ask you to come out here. But now that you are, I'm answering your questions, all right?'

'I appreciate it, really. You say you didn't know they were at the Central that night?'

'No.'

'Do you know what happened to them afterwards?'

'They stopped working for me. Not at the same time, Tam left first, I think. Tam then Eck. Tam was a dunderheid, Strawman, a real loser. I can't abide losers. I only hired him because Eck asked me to. Eck was a good worker.' He seemed lost in thought for a minute. 'You're looking for them?'

'That's it.'

'Sorry, I can't help.' Rebus wondered if Cafferty's cheeks

were half as red as his felt. He had a piercing stitch in his side, and didn't know how he was going to make the run back. 'You think they had something to do with the body?'

Rebus merely nodded.

'What makes you so sure?'

'I'm not sure. But if they *did* have something to do with it, I'm willing to bet you weren't a hundred miles behind.'

'Me?' Cafferty laughed again, but the laugh was strained. 'As I recall, I was on holiday in Malta with some friends.'

'You always seem to be with friends when anything happens.'

'I'm a gregarious man, I can't help it if I'm popular. Know something else I read about Scotland? The Pope called it "the arse of Europe".' Cafferty slowed to a stop. They'd come to near the top of Duddingston Loch, the city just visible down below them. 'Hard to believe, isn't it? The arse of Europe, it doesn't look like one to me.'

'Oh, I don't know,' said Rebus, bent over with hands on knees. 'If this is the arse ...' he looked up, 'I'd know where to stick the enema.'

Cafferty's laughter roared out all around. He was breathing deeply, trying to slow things down. When he spoke, it was in an undertone, though there was no one around to hear them. 'But we're a cruel people, Strawman. All of us, you and me. And we're ghouls.' His face was very close to Rebus's, both of them bent over. Rebus kept his eyes on the grass below him. 'When they killed the grave-robber Burke, they made souvenirs from his skin. I've got one in the house, I'll show it to you.' The voice might have been inside Rebus's own head. 'We *like* to watch, and that's the truth. I bet even you've got a taste for pain, Strawman. You're hurting all over, but you ran with me, you didn't give up. Why? Because you *like* the pain. It's what makes you a Calvinist.'

'It's what makes *you* a public menace.'

'Me? A simple businessman who has managed to survive this disease called recession.'

'No, you're more than that,' said Rebus, straightening up. 'You're the disease.'

Cafferty looked like he might throw a punch, but instead he pounded Rebus on the back. 'Come on, time to go.'

Rebus was about to plead another minute's rest, but saw Cafferty walking to the Jag. 'What?' Cafferty said. 'You think I'd run it *both ways*? Come on now, your herbal tea is waiting.'

And herbal tea it was, served up poolside after Rebus had showered and changed back into his clothes. He had the feeling someone had been through his wallet and diary in his absence, but knew they wouldn't have found much there. For one thing, he'd tucked his ID and credit cards into the front of his running shorts; for another, he'd about as much cash as would buy an evening paper and a packet of mints.

'Sorry I couldn't be more help,' said Cafferty after Rebus had sat himself down.

'You could if you tried,' Rebus replied. He was trying to stop his legs from shaking. They hadn't had this much exercise since the last time he'd flitted.

Cafferty just shrugged. He was now wearing baggy and wildly coloured swimming trunks, and had just had a dip. As he dried himself off, he showed enough anal cleavage to qualify as a construction worker.

The devil dog meantime sat by the pool licking its chops. Of the bone it had been chewing, there was not the slightest trace. Rebus suddenly placed the dog.

'Do you own a 4x4?' Cafferty nodded. 'I saw it parked across from Bone's the Butcher on South Clerk Street. This mutt was in the back.'

Cafferty shrugged. 'It's my wife's car.'

'And she often takes the dog into town?'

'She gets Kaiser's bones there. Besides, he's cheaper than a car alarm.' Cafferty smiled fondly at the dog. 'And I've never known anyone bypass him.'

'Maybe sausages would do it.' But this was lost on Cafferty. Rebus decided he was getting nowhere. It was time to try one final tactic. He finished the brew. It tasted like spearmint chewing gum. 'A colleague of mine was trying to track down the Robertson brothers. Someone put him in hospital.'

'Really?' Cafferty looked genuinely surprised. 'What happened?'

'He was attacked behind a restaurant called the Heart-break Cafe.'

'Dear me. Did he find them, Tam and Eck?'

'If he'd found them, I wouldn't have had to come here.'

'I thought maybe it was just an excuse for a blether about the good old days.'

'What good old days?'

'True enough, you look about as bad as ever. Not me, though. My wild days are behind me.' He sipped his tea to prove the point. 'I'm a changed man.'

Rebus nearly laughed. 'You tell that line so often in court, you're beginning to believe it.'

'No, it's true.'

'Then you wouldn't be trying to put the frighteners on me?'

Cafferty shook his head. He was crouching beside the dog, rubbing its head briskly. 'Oh no, Strawman, the day's long past when I'd take a set of six-inch carpentry nails and fix you to the floorboards in some derelict house. Or tickle your tonsils with jump-leads connected to a generator.' He was warming to his subject, looking almost as ready to pounce as his dog.

Rebus stayed nonchalant. Indeed, he had one to add to the list. 'Or hang me over the Forth Rail Bridge?' There was silence, except for the hum of the jacuzzi and the snuffling of the dog. Then the door swung open and a woman's head smiled heedlessly towards them.

'Morris, dinner in ten minutes.'

'Thanks, Mo.'

The door closed again, and Cafferty got up. So did the dog. 'Well, Strawman, it's been lovely chatting away like this, but I better take a shower before I eat. Mo's always complaining I smell like chlorine. I keep telling her, we wouldn't have to put chlorine in the pool if the visitors didn't piss in it, but she blames Kaiser!'

'She's your ... er ...?'

'My wife. As of four years and three months.'

Rebus was nodding. He knew Cafferty was married, of course. He'd just forgotten the name of the lucky bride.

'She's the one who's changed me if anyone has,' Cafferty was saying. 'She makes me read all these books.'

Rebus knew the Nazis had read books too. 'Just one thing, Cafferty.'

'*Mr* Cafferty. Go on, indulge me.'

Rebus swallowed hard. 'Mr Cafferty. What's your wife's maiden name?'

'Morag,' said Cafferty, puzzled by the question. 'Morag Johnson.' Then he padded away towards the shower, kicking off his trunks, mooning mightily at Rebus as he did so.

Morag Johnson. Yes, of course. Rebus would bet that not many people tried the 'Mo Johnson' gag in front of Big Ger. But that's where he'd heard the name before. The woman into whose flat Aengus Gibson had trespassed had soon afterwards married Big Ger Cafferty. So soon after, in fact, that they *must* have been going out together at the time the break-in had occurred.

Rebus had his link between Aengus Gibson, the Bru-Head Brothers and Big Ger.

Now all he had to do was figure out what the hell it meant.

He rose from his chair, eliciting a low growl from the devil dog. Slowly and quietly he made for the door, knowing all Big Ger had to do was call from the shower, and Kaiser would be on Rebus faster than piss on a lamp post. As he made his exit, he was remembering those scenarios for his painful execution, so lovingly described by Big Ger.

John Rebus was once again grateful he didn't yet have the gun.

But there was something else. The way Big Ger had seemed surprised when told about Holmes. As if he *really* hadn't known about it. Added to which how keen he'd been to find out if Holmes had had any success tracking down Tam and Eck Roberston.

Rebus drove away with more mysteries than answers. But one question he was sure had been answered: Cafferty had been behind Michael's abduction. He was certain of it now.

# 21

'You can't have,' said Siobhan Clarke.

'And yet I have,' said Peter Petrie. He had run out of film. Plenty of spare batteries. Of batteries there were plenty. But film was there none. It was first thing Thursday morning, and the last thing Clarke needed. 'So you'd better go and fetch some pronto.'

'Why me?'

'Because *I* am in pain.' This was true. He was on painkillers for his nose, and had complained about nothing else all day yesterday. So much so that the maddening Madden had lost all sense of good fun and bad puns and had told Petrie to 'shut the fuck up'. Now they weren't talking. Siobhan wondered if it was a good idea to leave them alone.

'It's special film,' Petrie was telling her. He rummaged in the camera case and came out with an empty film-box, the flap of which he tore off and handed to her. 'This is the stuff.'

'This,' she said to him, grabbing the scrap of card, 'is a pain in the arse.'

'Try Pyle's,' said Madden.

She turned on him. 'Are you being funny?'

'It's the name of a camera shop on Morrison Street.'

'That's miles away!'

'Take your car,' Petrie suggested.

Siobhan grabbed her bag. 'Stuff that, I'll find somewhere before Morrison Street.'

However, after ten filmless minutes she began to realise that there was no great demand for special high-speed film in Gorgie Road. It wasn't as if you needed high-speed to take a photo of Hearts in action. She consoled herself with this thought and resigned herself to the walk to Morrison Street. Maybe she could catch a bus back.

She saw that she was nearing the Heartbreak Cafe, and crossed the road to look at it. It had looked closed yesterday when she drove past, and there was a sign in the window. She read now that the place was closed 'due to con-valescence'. Strange, though, the door was open a couple of inches. And was there a funny smell, a smell like gas? She pushed the door open and peered in.

'Hello?'

Yes, definitely gas, and there was no one around. A woman on the street stopped to watch.

'Awfy smell o' gas, hen.'

Siobhan nodded and walked into the Heartbreak Cafe.

Without its lights on, and with little natural light, the place was all darkness and shadows. But the last thing she planned to do was flick an electric switch. She could see chinks of light through the kitchen door, and made towards it. Yes, there were windows in the kitchen, and the smell was much stronger here. She could hear the unmistakable hiss of escaping gas. With a hankie stuffed to her nose, she made for the emergency exit, and pushed at the bar which should release it. But the thing was sticking, or else ... She gave a mighty heave and the door grunted open an inch. Dustbins were being stored right against it on the outside. Fresh air started trickling in, the welcome smells of traffic exhaust and beer hops.

Now she had to find whichever cooker had been left on. Only as she turned did she see the legs and body which were lying on the floor, the head hidden inside a huge oven. She walked over and turned off the gas, then peered down. The body lay on its side, dressed in black and white check trousers and a white chef's jacket. She didn't recognise the man from his face, but the elaborately stitched name on his left breast made identification easy.

It was Eddie Ringan.

The place was still choking with gas, so she walked back to the emergency door and gave it another heave. This time it opened most of the way, scattering clanking dustbins onto the ground outside. It was then that a curious passer-by pushed open the door from the restaurant to the kitchen. His hand went to the light-switch.

'Don't touch tha –!'

There was a tremendous blast and fireball. The shock sent Siobhan Clarke flying backwards into the parking lot, where her landing was softened by the rubbish she'd scattered only seconds earlier. She didn't even suffer the same minor burns as the hapless passer-by, who went crashing back into the restaurant pursued by a blue ball of flame. But Eddie Ringan, well, he looked like he'd been done to a turn inside an oven which wasn't even hot.

By the time Rebus got there, aching after last night's exertions, the scene was one of immaculate chaos. Pat Calder had arrived in time to see his lover being carted away in a blue plastic bag. The bag was deemed necessary to stop bits of charred face breaking off and messing up the floor. The bagging itself had been overseen by a police doctor, but Rebus knew where Eddie would eventually end up: under the all-seeing scalpel of Dr Curt.

'All right, Clarke?'

Rebus affected the usual inspectorial nonchalance, hands in pockets and an air of having seen it all before.

'Apart from my coccyx, sir.' And she gave the bone a rub for luck.

'What happened?'

So she filled in the details, all the way from having no film (yes, why not drop Petrie in it?) to the passer-by who had nearly killed her. He had been seen to by the doctor too: frizzled eyebrows and lashes, some bruising from the fall. Rebus's scalp tingled at the thought. There was no smell of gas in the kitchen now. But there was a smell of cooked meat, almost inviting till you remembered its source.

Calder was seated at the bar, watching the world move past him in and out of the dream he had built with Eddie Ringan. Rebus sat down beside him, glad to take the weight off his legs.

'Those nightmares,' Calder said immediately, 'looks like he made them come true, eh?'

'Looks like it. Any idea why he'd kill himself?'

Calder shook his head. He was bearing up, but only just. 'I suppose it all got too much for him.'

'All what?'

Calder continued shaking his head. 'Perhaps we'll never know.'

'Don't you believe it,' Rebus said, trying not to make it sound like a threat. He must have failed, for suddenly Calder turned towards him.

'Can't you let it rest?' The pale eyes were glistening.

'No rest for the wicked, Mr Calder,' said Rebus. He slid off the barstool and went back into the kitchen. Siobhan was standing beside a shelf filled with basic cookery books.

'Most chefs,' she said, 'would rather die than keep this lot out on display.'

'He wasn't any ordinary chef.'

'Look at this one.' It was a school jotter, with ruled red lines about half an inch apart and an inch-wide margin. The margins were full of doodles and sketches, mostly of food and men with large quiffs. Neatly written in a large hand inside the margins were recipes. 'His own creations.' She flipped to the end. 'Oh look, here's Jailhouse Roquefort.' She quoted from the recipe. ' "With thanks to Inspector John Rebus for the idea." Well, well.' She was about to put the book back, but Rebus took it from her. He opened it at the inside cover, where he'd spotted a copious collection of doodles. Something had been written in the midst of the drawings (some of them gayly rude). But it had been scored out again with a darker pen.

'Can you make that out?'

They took the jotter to the back door and stood in the parking lot, where so recently someone had thumped Brian Holmes on the head. Siobhan started things off. 'Looks like the first word's "All".'

'And that's "turn",' said Rebus of a later word. 'Or maybe "tum".' But the rest remained beyond them. Rebus pocketed the recipe book.

'Thinking of a new career, sir?' Siobhan asked.

Rebus pondered a suitable comeback line. 'Shut up, Clarke,' he said.

Rebus dropped the jotter off at Fettes HQ, where they had people whose job it was to recover legibility from defaced and damaged writing. They were known as 'pen pals', the sort of boffins who liked to do really difficult crosswords.

'This won't take long,' one of them told Rebus. 'We'll just put it on the machine.'

'Great,' said Rebus. 'I'll come back in quarter of an hour.'

'Make it twenty minutes.'

Twenty minutes was fine by Rebus. While he was here and at a loose end, he might as well pay his respects to DI Gill Templer.

'Hello, Gill.' Her office smelt of expensive perfume. He'd forgotten what kind she wore. Chanel, was it? She slipped off her glasses and blinked at him.

'John, long time no see. Sit down.'

Rebus shook his head. 'I can't stay, the lab's going to have something for me in a minute. Just thought I'd see how you're doing.'

She nodded her answer. 'I'm doing fine. How about you?'

'Aw, not bad. You know how it is.'

'How's the doctor?'

'She's fine, aye.' He shuffled his feet. He hadn't expected this to be so awkward.

'It's not true she kicked you out, then?'

'How the hell do you know about that?'

Gill was smiling her lipsticked smile; a thin mouth, made for irony. 'Come on, John, this is *Edinburgh*. You want to keep secrets, move somewhere bigger than a village.'

'Who told you, though? How many people know?'

'Well, if they know here at Fettes, they're bound to know at St Leonard's.'

Christ. That meant Watson knew, Lauderdale knew, Flower knew. And none of them had said anything.

'It's only a temporary thing,' he muttered, shuffling his feet again. 'Patience has her nieces staying, so I moved back into my flat. Plus Michael's there just now.'

It was Gill Templer's turn to look surprised. 'Since when?'

'Ten days or so.'

'Is he back for good?'

Rebus shrugged. 'Depends, I suppose. Gill, I wouldn't want word getting round ...'

'Of course not! I can keep a secret.' She smiled again. 'Remember, I'm not *from* Edinburgh.'

'Me neither,' said Rebus. 'I just get screwed around here.' He checked his watch.

'Are my five minutes up?'

'Sorry.'

'Don't be, I've got plenty of work to be getting on with.' He turned to leave.

'John? Come up and see me again sometime.'

Rebus nodded. 'Mae West, right?'

'Right.'

'Bye, Gill.'

Halfway along her corridor, Rebus recalled that a Mae West was also the name for a life-jacket. He considered this, but shook his head. 'My life's complicated enough.'

He returned to the lab.

'You're a bit early,' he was told.

'Keen's the word you're looking for.'

'Well, speaking of words we're looking for, come and have a peek.' He was led to a computer console. The scribble had been OCR'd and fed into the computer, where it was now displayed on the large colour monitor. A lot of the overpenning had been 'erased', leaving the original message hopefully intact. The pen pal picked up a sheet of paper. 'Here are my ideas so far.' As he read them off, Rebus tried to see them in the message on the screen.

' "Ale I did, tum on the gum", "Ole I did man, term on the gam" ...' Rebus gazed up at him, and the pen pal grinned. 'Or maybe this,' he said. ' "All I did was turn on the gas".'

'What?'

' "All I did was turn on the gas".'

Rebus stared at the message on the screen. Yes, he could see it ... well, most of it. The pen pal was talking again.

'It helped that you told me he'd gassed himself. I still had that half in mind when I started working, and spotted "gas" straight off. A suicide note, maybe?'

Rebus looked disbelieving. 'What, scored out and surrounded by doodles on the inside cover of a jotter he tucked away on a shelf? Stick to what you know and you'll do fine.'

What Rebus knew was that Eddie Ringan had suffered nightmares during which he cried out the word 'gas'. Was this scribble the remnant from one of his bad nights? But then why score it out so heavily? Rebus picked up the jotter from the OCR machine. The inside cover looked old, the stuff there going back a year or more. Some of the doodles looked more recent than the defaced message. Whenever Eddie had written this, it wasn't last night. Which meant, presumably, that it had no direct connection to his gassing himself. Making it . . . a coincidence? Rebus didn't believe in coincidence, but he did believe in serendipity. He turned to the pen pal, who was looking not happy at Rebus's put-down.

'Thanks,' he said.

'You're welcome.'

Each was sure the other was being less than sincere.

Brian Holmes was waiting for him at St Leonard's, waiting to be welcomed back into the world.

'What the hell are you doing here?'

'Don't worry,' said Holmes, 'I'm just visiting. I've got another week on the sick.'

'How are you feeling?' Rebus was glancing nervously around, wondering if anyone had told Holmes about Eddie. He knew in his heart they hadn't, of course; if they had, Brian wouldn't be half as chipper.

'I get thumping headaches, but that apart I feel like I've had a holiday.' He patted his pocket. 'And DI Flower got up a collection. Nearly fifty quid.'

'The man's a saint,' said Rebus. 'I had a present I was going to bring you.'

'What?'

'A tape, the Stones' *Let it Bleed*.'

'Thanks a lot.'

'Something to cheer you up after Patsy De-Cline.'

'At least she can sing.'

Rebus smiled. 'You're fired. Are you at your aunt's?'

This quietened Holmes, as Rebus had hoped it would. Bring him down slowly, then drop the real news into his lap. 'For the meantime. Nell's ... well, she says she's not quite ready yet.'

Rebus knew the feeling; he wondered when Patience would be ready for that drink. 'Still,' he offered, 'things sound a bit brighter between the two of you.'

'Ach.' Holmes sat down opposite his superior. 'She wants me to leave the police.'

'That's a bit drastic.'

'So is separation.'

Rebus exhaled. 'I suppose so, but all the same ... What are you going to do?'

'Think it over, what else can I do?' He got back to his feet. 'Listen, I'd better get going. I only came in to –'

'Brian, sit down.' Holmes, recognising Rebus's tone, sat. 'I've got some bad news about Eddie.'

'Chef Eddie?' Rebus nodded. 'What about him?'

'There's been an accident. Well, sort of. Eddie was involved.'

There was no mistaking Rebus's meaning. He'd become good at this sort of speech through repetition over the years to the families of car crash victims, accidents at work, murders ...

'He's dead?' Holmes asked quietly. Rebus, lips pursed, nodded. 'Christ, I was going to drop in and see him. What happened?'

'We're not sure yet. The post-mortem will probably be this afternoon.'

Holmes was no fool; again he caught the gist. 'Accident, suicide or murder?'

'One of those last two.'

'And your money'd be on murder?'

'My money stays in my pocket till I've spoken to the tipster.'

'Meaning Dr Curt?'

Rebus nodded. 'Till then, there's not much we can do. Listen, let me get a car to take you home ...'

'No, no, I'll be all right.' He rose to his feet slowly, as though checking his bones for solidity. 'I'll be fine really. It's just ... poor Eddie. He was a friend of mine, you know?'

'I know,' said Rebus.

After Holmes had gone, Rebus was able to reflect that he'd gotten off lightly. Brian still wasn't operating at full throttle; partly the convalescence, partly the shock. So he hadn't asked Rebus any difficult questions. Questions like, does Eddie's death have anything to do with the person who nearly killed *me*? It was something Rebus had been wondering himself. Last night Eddie was missing, and Rebus had gone to see Cafferty. Today, first thing, Eddie was dead. Meaning one less person who could say anything about the night the Central burnt down; one less person who'd been there. But Rebus still had the gut feeling Cafferty had been surprised to learn of Holmes' attack. So what was the answer?

'I'm buggered if I know,' John Rebus said quietly to himself. His phone rang. He picked it up and heard pub noises, then Flower's voice.

'That's some team you've got there, Inspector. One gets his face mashed in, and now the other falls on her arse.' The connection was briskly severed.

'And bugger you, too, Flower,' Rebus said, all too aware that no one was listening.

# 22

Edinburgh's public mortuary was sited on the Cowgate, named for the route cattle would take when being brought into the city to be sold. It was a narrow canyon of a street with few businesses and only passing traffic. Way up above it were much busier streets, South Bridge for instance. They seemed so far from the Cowgate, it might as well have been underground.

Rebus wasn't sure the area had ever been anything other than a desperate meeting place for Edinburgh's poorest denizens, who often seemed like cattle themselves, dull-witted from lack of sunlight and grazing on begged handouts from passers-by. The Cowgate was ripe for redevelopment these days, but who would slaughter the cattle?

A fine setting for the understated mortuary where, when he wasn't teaching at the University, Dr Curt plied his trade.

'Look on the bright side,' he told Rebus. 'The Cowgate's got a couple of fine pubs.'

'And a few more you could shave a dead man with.'

Curt chuckled. 'Colourful, though I'm not sure the image conjured actually *means* anything.'

'I bow to your superior knowledge. Now, what have you got on Mr Ringan?'

'Ah, poor Orphan Eddie.' Curt liked to find names for all his cadavers. Rebus got the feeling the 'Orphan' prefix had been used many a time before. In Eddie Ringan's case, though, it was accurate. He had no living relations that anyone knew of, and so had been identified by Patrick Calder, and by Siobhan Clarke, since she'd been the one to find the body.

'Yes, that's the man I found,' she had said.

'Yes, that's Edward Ringan,' Pat Calder had said, before being led away by Toni the barman.

Rebus now stood with Curt beside the slab on which what was left of the corpse was being tidied up by an assistant. The assistant was whistling 'Those Were the Days' as he scraped miscellany into a bucket of offal. Rebus was reading through a list. He'd been through it three times already, trying to take his mind off the scene around him. Curt was smoking a cigarette. At the age of fifty-five, he'd decided he might as well start, since nothing else had so far managed to kill him. Rebus might have taken a cigarette from him, but they were Player's untipped, the smoking equivalent of paint stripper.

Maybe because he'd perused the list so often, something clicked at last. 'You know,' he said, 'we never found a suicide note.'

'They don't always leave them.'

'Eddie would have. *And* he'd have had Elvis singing *Heartbreak Hotel* on a tape player beside the oven.'

'Now that's style,' Curt said disingenuously.

'And now,' Rebus went on, 'from this list of the contents of his pockets, I see he didn't have any keys on him.'

'No keys, eh.' Curt was enjoying his break too much to bother trying to work it out. He knew Rebus would tell him anyway.

'So,' Rebus obliged, 'how did he get in? Or if he *did* use his keys to get in, where are they now?'

'Where indeed.' The attendant frowned as Curt stubbed his cigarette into the floor.

Rebus knew when he'd lost an audience. He put the list away. 'So what have you got for me?'

'Well, the usual tests will have to be carried out, of course.'

'Of course, but in the meantime ...?'

'In the meantime, a few points of interest.' Curt turned to the cadaver, forcing Rebus to do the same. There was a cover over the charred face, and the attendant had roughly sewn up the chest and stomach, now empty of their major organs, with thick black thread. The face had been badly burnt, but the rest of the body remained unaffected. The plump flesh was pale and shiny.

'Well,' Curt began, 'the burns were superficial merely. The internal organs were untouched by the blast. That made things easier. I would say he probably asphyxiated through inhalation of North Sea gas.' He turned to Rebus. 'That "North Sea" is pure conjecture.' Then he grinned again, a lopsided grin that meant one side of his mouth stayed closed. 'There was evidence of alcoholic intake. We'll have to wait for the test results to determine how much. A lot, I'd guess.'

'I'll bet his liver was a treat. He's been putting the stuff away for years.'

Curt seemed doubtful. He went to another table and returned with the organ itself, which had already been cross-sectioned. 'It's actually in pretty good shape. You said he was a spirits drinker?'

Rebus kept his eyes out of focus. It was something you learned. 'A bottle a day easy.'

'Well, it doesn't show from this.' Curt tossed the liver a few inches into the air. It slapped back down into his palm. He reminded Rebus of a butcher showing off to a potential buyer. 'There was also a bump to the head and bruising and minor burns to the arms.'

'Oh?'

'I'd imagine these are injuries often incurred by chefs in their daily duties. Hot fat spitting, pots and pans everywhere ...'

'Maybe,' said Rebus.

'And now we come to the section of the programme Hamish has been waiting for.' Curt nodded towards his assistant, who straightened his back in anticipation. 'I call him Hamish,' Curt confided, 'because he comes from the Hebrides. Hamish here spotted something *I* didn't. I've been putting off talking about it lest he become encephalitic.' He looked at Rebus. 'A little pathologist's joke.'

'You're not so small,' said Rebus.

'You need to know, Inspector, that Hamish has a fascination with teeth. Probably because his own as a child were terribly bad and he has memories of long days spent under the dentist's drill.'

Hamish looked as though this might actually be true.

'As a result, Hamish always looks in people's mouths, and this time he saw fit to inform me that there was some damage.'

'What sort of damage?'

'Scarring of the tissues lining the throat. Recent damage, too.'

'Like he'd been singing too loud?'

'Or screaming. But much more likely that something has been forced down his throat.'

Rebus's mind boggled. Curt always seemed able to do this to him. He swallowed, feeling how dry his own throat was. 'What sort of thing?'

Curt shrugged. 'Hamish suggested ... You understand, this is entirely conjecture – usually *your* field of expertise. Hamish suggested a pipe of some kind, something solid. I myself would add the possibility of a rubber or plastic tube.'

Rebus coughed. 'Not anything ... er, organic then?'

'You mean like a courgette? A banana?'

'You know damned well what I mean.'

Curt smiled and bowed his head. 'Of course I do, I'm sorry.' Then he shrugged. 'I wouldn't rule anything out.

But if you're suggesting a penis, it must have been sheathed in sandpaper.'

Behind them, Rebus heard Hamish stifle a laugh.

Rebus telephoned Pat Calder and asked if they might meet. Calder thought it over before agreeing.

'At the Colonies?' Rebus asked.

'Make it the Cafe, I'm heading over there anyway.'

So the Cafe it was. When Rebus arrived, the 'convalescence' sign had been replaced with one stating, 'Due to bereavement, this establishment has ceased trading.' It was signed Pat Calder.

As Rebus entered, he heard Calder roar, 'Do fuck off!' It was not, however, aimed at Rebus but at a young woman in a raincoat.

'Trouble, Mr Calder?' Rebus walked into the restaurant. Calder was busy taking the mementoes down off the walls and packing them in newspaper. Rebus noticed three tea chests on the floor between the tables.

'This bloody reporter wants some blood and grief for her newspaper.'

'Is that right, miss?' Rebus gave Mairie Henderson a disapproving but, yes, almost *fatherly* look. The kind that let her know she should be ashamed.

'Mr Ringan was a popular figure in the city,' she told Rebus. 'I'm sure he'd have wanted our readers to know –'

Calder interrupted. 'He'd have wanted them to stuff their faces here, leave a fat cheque, then get the fuck out. Print *that*!'

'Quite an epitaph,' Mairie commented.

Calder looked like he'd brain her with the Elvis clock, the one with the King's arms replacing the usual clock hands. He thought better of it, and lifted the Elvis mirror (one of several) off the wall instead. He wouldn't dare smash that: seven years' bad junk food.

210

'I think you'd better go, miss,' Rebus said calmly.

'All right, I'm going.' She slung her bag over her shoulder and stalked past Rebus. She was wearing a skirt today, a short one too. But a good soldier knew when to keep eyes front. He smiled at Pat Calder, whose anguish was all too evident.

'Bit soon for all this, isn't it?'

'You can cook, can you, Inspector? Without Eddie, this place is ... it's nothing.'

'Looks like the local restaurants can sleep easy, then.'

'How do you mean?'

'Remember, Eddie thought the attack on Brian was a warning.'

'Yes, but what's that ...' Calder froze. 'You think someone ...? It was suicide, wasn't it?'

'Looked that way, certainly.'

'You mean you're not sure?'

'Did he seem the type who would kill himself?'

Calder's reply was cold. 'He was killing himself every day with drink. Maybe it all got too much. Like I said, Inspector, the attack on Brian affected Eddie. Maybe more than we knew.' He paused, still with the mirror gripped in both hands. 'You think it was murder?'

'I didn't say that, Mr Calder.'

'Who would do it?'

'Maybe you were behind with your payments.'

'What payments?'

'Protection payments, sir. Don't tell me it doesn't go on.'

Calder stared at him unblinking. 'You forget, I was in charge of finances, and we always paid our bills on time. All of them.'

Rebus took this information in, wondering exactly what it meant. 'If you think you know who might have wanted Eddie dead, best tell me, all right? Don't go doing anything rash.'

'Like what?'

Like buying a gun, Rebus thought, but he said nothing. Calder started to wrap the mirror. 'This is about all a newspaper's worth,' he said.

'She was only doing her job. You wouldn't have turned down a good review, would you?'

Calder smiled. 'We got plenty.'

'What will you do now?'

'I haven't thought about it. I'll go away, that's all I know.'

Rebus nodded towards the tea chests. 'And you'll keep all that stuff?'

'I couldn't throw it away, Inspector. It's all there is.'

Well, thought Rebus, there's the bedroom too. But he didn't say anything. He just watched Pat Calder pack everything away.

Hamish, real name Alasdair McDougall, had more or less been chased from his native Barra by his contemporaries, one of whom tried to drown him during a midnight boat crossing from South Uist after a party. Two minutes in the freezing waters of the Sound of Barra and he'd have been fit for nothing but fish-food, but they'd hauled him back into the boat and explained the whole thing away as an accident. Which is also what it would have been had he actually drowned.

He went to Oban first, then south to Glasgow before crossing to the east coast. Glasgow suited him in some respects, but not in others. Edinburgh suited him better. His parents had always denied to themselves that their son was homosexual, even when he'd stood there in front of them and said it. His father had quoted the Bible at him, the same way he'd been quoting it for seventeen years, a believer's righteous tremble in his voice. It had once been a powerful and persuasive performance; but now it seemed laughable.

'Just because it's in the Bible,' he'd told his father, 'doesn't mean you should take it as gospel.'

But to his father it was and always would be the literal truth. The Bible had been in the old man's hand as he'd shooed his youngest son out of the door of the croft house. 'Never dare to blacken our name!' he'd called. And Alasdair reckoned he'd lived up to this through introducing himself as Dougall and almost never passing on a last name. He had been Dougall to the gay community in Glasgow, and he was Dougall here in Edinburgh. He liked the life he'd made for himself (there was never a dull night), and he'd only been kicked-in twice. He had his clubs and pubs, his bunch of friends and a wider circle of acquaintances. He was even beginning to think of writing to his parents. He would tell them, By the time my boss gets through with a body, believe me there isn't very much left for Heaven to take.

He thought again of the plump young man who'd been gassed, and he laughed. He should have said something at the time, but hadn't. Why not? Was it because he still had one foot in the closet? He'd been accused of it before, when he'd refused to wear a pink triangle on his lapel. Certainly, he wasn't sure he wanted a policeman to know he was gay. And what would Dr Curt do? There was all sorts of homophobia about, an almost medieval fear of AIDS and its transmission. It wasn't that he couldn't live without the job, but he liked it well enough. He'd seen plenty of sheep and cattle slaughtered and quartered in his time on the island. This wasn't so very different.

No, he would keep his secret to himself. He wouldn't let on that he *knew* Eddie Ringan. He remembered the evening a week or so back. They went to Dougall's place and Eddie cooked up a chilli from stuff he found in the cupboards. Hot stuff. It really made you sweat. He wouldn't stay the night, though, wasn't that type. There'd been a long kiss before parting, and half-promises of further trysts.

Yes, he knew Eddie, knew him well enough to be sure of one thing.

Whoever it was on the slab, it wasn't the guy who'd shared chilli in Dougall's bed.

Siobhan Clarke felt unnaturally calm and in control the rest of the day. She'd been given the day off from Operation Moneybags to get over the shock of her experience at the Heartbreak Cafe, but by late afternoon was itching to do *something*. So she drove out to Rory Kintoul's house on the half-chance. It was a neat and quite recent council semi in a cul-de-sac. The front garden was the size of a beer-mat but probably more hygienic; she reckoned she could eat her dinner off the trimmed weedless lawn without fear of food poisoning. She couldn't even say that of the plates in most police canteens. One gate led her down the path, and another brought her to Kintoul's front door. It was painted dark blue. Every fourth door in the street was dark blue. The others were plum-red, custard yellow, and battleship grey. Not exactly a riot of colour, but somehow in keeping with the pebbledash and tarmac. Some kids had chalked a complex hopscotch grid on the pavement and were now playing noisily. She'd smiled towards them, but they hadn't looked up from their game. A dog barked in a back garden a few doors down, but otherwise the street was quiet.

She rang the doorbell and waited. Nobody, it seemed, was home. She thought of the phrase 'gallus besom' as she took the liberty of peering in through the front window. A living room stretched to the back of the house. The dog was barking louder now, and through the far window she caught sight of a figure. She opened the garden gate and turned right, running through the close separating Kintoul's house from its neighbour. This led to the back gardens. Kintoul had left his kitchen door open so as not to make a noise. He had one leg over his neighbour's fence, and was trying to shush the leashed mongrel.

'Mr Kintoul!' Siobhan called. When he looked up, she waved her hand. 'Sitting on the fence, I see. How about the two of us going inside for a word?'

She wasn't about to spare him any blushes. As he slouched towards her across the back green, she grinned. 'Running away from the police, eh? What've you got to hide?'

'Nuthin'.'

'You should be careful,' she warned. 'A stunt like that could open those stitches in your side.'

'Do you want everyone to hear? Get inside.' He almost pushed her through the kitchen door. It was exactly the invitation Siobhan wanted.


Rebus got the call at six-fifteen and arranged the meeting for ten. At eight, Patience called him. He knew he wouldn't sound right to her, would sound like his thoughts were elsewhere (which they were), but he wanted to keep her talking. He was filling the time till ten o'clock and didn't want any of it left vacant. He might start to think about it otherwise, might change his mind.

Eventually, for want of other topics, he told Patience all about Michael (who was asleep in the box room). At last they were on the same wavelength. Patience suggested counselling, and was amazed no one at the hospital had mentioned the possibility. She would look into it and get back to Rebus. Meantime, he'd have to watch Michael didn't go into clinical depression. The problem with those drugs was that they not only killed your fears, they could kill your emotions stone dead.

'He was so lively when he moved in,' Rebus said. 'The

students are wondering what the hell's happened to him. I think they're as worried as I am.'

Michael's self-proclaimed 'girlfriend' had spent time trying to talk to him, coaxing him out to pubs and clubs. But Michael had fought against it, and she hadn't shown her face for at least a day. One of the male students had approached Rebus in the kitchen and asked, in tones of deepest sympathy, if a bit of 'blaw' might help Mickey. Rebus had shaken his head. Christ, it might not be a bad idea, though.

But Patience was against it. 'Mix the stuff he's on with cannabis and God knows what sort of reaction you'd get: paranoia or a complete downer would be my guess.'

She was anti-drugs anyway, and not just the proscribed kinds. She knew that the easy way out for doctors was to fill out a form for the pharmacy. Valium, moggies, whatever it took. People all over Scotland, and especially the people who needed most help, were eating tablets like they were nourishment. And the doctors pointed to their workloads and said, What else can we do?

'Want me to come over?' she was asking now. It was a big step. Yes, Rebus wanted her to come over, but it was nearly nine.

'No, but I appreciate the thought.'

'Well, try not to leave him too long on his own. He's sleeping to escape something he needs to confront.'

'Bye, Patience.' Rebus put down the phone and made ready to leave the flat.

Why had he chosen the waterfront at North Queensferry for the meeting? Well, wasn't it obvious? He stood near the same hut they'd taken Michael to, and he got cold. He'd arrived early, and Deek naturally was late. Rebus didn't really mind. It gave him time to stare up at the rail bridge, wondering how it would feel to be lowered over the side at the dead of night. Screaming dumbly into your gag as they took the bag from your face. Looking all the way down. That's where Rebus was now, though he was at sea level. He was looking all the way down.

'Cold though, eh?' Deek Torrance rubbed his hands together.

'Thanks for setting me up the other night.'

'Eh?'

'"Sailor for trade or rent".'

'Oh aye, that.' Torrance grinned. ' "King of the Road". That's not the way it goes, though ...'

'You've got it?'

Deek patted his coat pocket. He was jittery, with good cause. It wasn't every day you sold an illegal firearm to a policeman.

'Let's see it, then.'

'What? Out here?'

Rebus looked around. 'There's nobody here.'

Deek bit his lip, then resigned himself to lifting the handgun out of his pocket and placing it in John Rebus's palm.

The thing was a lifeless weight, but comfortable to hold. Rebus placed it in his own capacious pocket. 'Ammo?'

The bullets shook in their box like a baby's toy. Rebus pocketed them too, then reached into the back pocket of his trousers for the cash.

'Want to count it?'

Deek shook his head, then nodded across the road. 'I'll buy you a drink though, if you like.'

A drink sounded good to Rebus. 'I'll just get rid of this first.' He unlocked his car and slipped the gun and ammo underneath the driver's seat. He noticed he was trembling and a little dizzy as he stood back up. A drink would be good. He was hungry, too, but the thought of food made him want to boak. He looked again at the bridge. 'Come on, then,' he said to Deek Torrance.

Minus gun and with money in its place, Torrance was

more relaxed and loquacious. They sat in the Hawes Inn with their drinks. Torrance was explaining how the guns came into the country.

'See, it's easy to buy a gun in France. They even come around the towns in vans and flog them off the back. Stick a catalogue through your door to let you know what they'll have. I got to meet this French guy, not bad to say he's French. He's back and forth over the Channel, some sort of business he's in. He brings the guns with him, and I buy them. He brings Mace too, if you're interested.'

'Why didn't you say?' Rebus muttered into his pint. 'I wouldn't have needed the gun.'

'Eh?' Deek saw he was making a joke and laughed.

'So what have I got?' asked Rebus. 'It was a bit dark out there to see.'

'Well, they're all copies. Don't worry, I file off any identifiers myself. Yours is a Colt 45. It'll take ten rounds.'

'Eight millimetre?'

Deek nodded. 'There are twenty in the box. It's not the most lethal weapon around. I can get replica Uzis too.'

'Christ.' Rebus finished his pint. He suddenly wanted to be out of there.

'It's a living,' said Deek Torrance.

'Aye, right, a living,' said Rebus, getting up to go.

# 23

Next morning Rebus forced himself into the usual routine. He checked to see if there had been any sign of Andrew McPhail. There had not. Maclean hadn't been too badly hurt by the boiled water, most of which he'd deflected with his arms. Nobody was yet treating McPhail like a dangerous criminal. His description had been issued to bus and train stations, motorway service areas, and the like. If the manpower were available, Rebus knew *exactly* where he would start looking for him.

A shadow fell over his desk. It was the Little Weed.

'So,' Flower said, 'you lose a DS to a blow on the napper, and a DC to a gas explosion. What's for an encore?'

Rebus saw that they had an audience. Half the station had been waiting for a confrontation between the two inspectors. Now more detectives than usual seemed interested in the filing cabinets near Rebus's desk.

'It's easier if you do a handstand,' commented Rebus.

'What is?'

'Talking out of your arse.'

There were a few covering coughs from the filing cabinets. 'I've got some throat pastilles if you want them,' Rebus called. The cabinet doors slid shut. The audience moved away.

'You think you're God's gift, don't you?' Flower said. 'You think you're all it takes.'

'I'm better than some.'

'And a lot worse than others.'

Rebus picked up the previous evening's arrest sheet and started to read it. 'If you're finished . . .?'

Flower smiled. 'Rebus, I thought your kind went out with the dinosaurs.'

'Aye, but only because they turned *you* down when you asked them.'

Which made it two-nil as Alister Flower walked off the field. But Rebus knew there'd be another leg to the match, and another after that.

He looked again at the arrest sheet, checking he'd seen the name right, then sighed and went down to the cells. A cluster of young constables stood outside cell one, taking turns at the peephole.

'It's that guy with the tattoos,' one of them explained to Rebus.

'The Pincushion?'

The constable nodded. The Pincushion was tattooed from head to foot, not an inch unblemished. 'He's been brought in for questioning.'

Rebus nodded. Whenever they had reason to bring the Pincushion into a station, he always ended up naked.

'It's a good name, isn't it, sir?'

'What, Pincushion? It's better than my name for him, I suppose.'

'What's that.'

'Just another prick,' said Rebus, unlocking cell number two. He closed the door behind him. A young man was sitting on the bunk, unshaven and sorry-eyed.

'What happened to you, then?'

Andy Steele looked up at him, then away. The city of Edinburgh had not been kind to him during his visit. He ran a handful of fingers through his tousled hair.

'Did you go see your Auntie Ena?' he asked.

Rebus nodded. 'I didn't see your mum and dad, though.'

'Ach well, at least I managed that, eh? I managed to

'track you down and put you in touch with her.'

'So what have you been up to since?'

Flakes of scalp were being clawed to the surface of Andy Steele's head. They floated down onto his trousers. 'Well, I did a bit of sightseeing.'

'They don't arrest you for that these days, though.'

Steele sighed and stopped scratching. 'Depends what sights you see. I told a man in a pub I was a private detective. He said he had a case for me.'

'Oh aye?' Rebus's attention was momentarily drawn to a crude game of noughts and crosses on the cell wall.

'His wife was cheating him. He told me where he thought I could find her, and he gave me a description. I got ten quid, with more when I reported back.'

'Go on.'

Andy Steele stared up at the ceiling. He knew he wasn't making himself look good, but it was a bit late for that anyway. 'It was a ground floor flat. I watched all evening. I saw the woman, she was there, all right. But no man. So I went round the back to get a better look. Someone must have spotted me and phoned the police.'

'You told them your story?'

Steele nodded. 'They even took me back to the bar. He wasn't there, of course, and nobody knew him. I didn't even know his name.'

'But his description of the woman was accurate?'

'Oh aye.'

'Probably an ex-wife or some old flame. He wanted to give them a scare, and it was worth ten notes to do it.'

'Except now the woman's pressing charges. Not a very good start to my career, is it, Inspector?'

'Depends,' said Rebus. 'Your career as a private dick may not be much cop, but as a peeping-tom your star is definitely in the ascendant.' Seeing Steele's misery, Rebus winked. 'Cheer up, I'll see what I can do.'

In fact, before he could do anything, Siobhan Clarke

was on the telephone from Gorgie to tell him about her meeting with Rory Kintoul.

'I asked him if he knew anything about his cousin's heavy betting. He wouldn't say, but I get the feeling they're a close-knit family. There were hundreds of photos in the living room: aunties and uncles, brothers and sisters, nieces, cousins, grannies ...'

'I get the idea. Did you mention the broken window?'

'Oh yes. He was so interested, he had to clamp himself to the chair to stop from jumping out of it. Not a great talker, though. He reckoned it must have been a drunk.'

'The same drunk who took a knife to his gut?'

'I didn't put it quite like that, and neither did he. I don't know whether it's relevant or not, but he did say he'd driven the butcher's van for his cousin.'

'What, full time?'

'Yes. Up until about a year ago.'

'I didn't know Bone's had a van. That'll be the next to go.'

'Sir?'

'The van. Smash the shop window, and if that doesn't work, torch the van.'

'You're saying it's all about protection?'

'Maybe protection, more likely money owing on bad bets. What do you think?'

'Well, I did raise that possibility with Kintoul.'

'And?'

'He laughed.'

'That's strong language coming from him.'

'Agreed, he's not exactly the emotional type.'

'So it's not betting money. I'll have another think.'

'His son came in while we were talking.'

'Refresh my memory.'

'Seventeen and unemployed, name's Jason. When Kintoul told him I was CID, the son looked worried.'

'A natural reaction in a teenager on the dole. They think we're press-ganging these days.'

'There was more to it than that.'

'How much more?'

'I don't know. Could be the usual, drugs and gangs.'

'We'll see if he's got a record. How's Moneybags?'

'Frankly, I'd rather be sewing mailbags.'

Rebus smiled. 'All part of the learning curve, Clarke,' he said, putting down the phone.


Somehow yesterday he'd forgotten to ask Pat Calder about the message on the inside of the recipe book. He didn't like to think it had been jostled from his mind by Mairie's legs or the sight of all those Elvises. Rebus had checked before leaving the station. Jason Kintoul was not on the files. Somehow the gun beneath the driver's seat helped keep Rebus's mind sharp. The drive to the Colonies didn't take long.

Pat Calder seemed quite shocked to see him.

'Morning,' said Rebus. 'Thought I'd find you at home.'

'Come in, Inspector.'

Rebus went in. The living room was much less tidy than on his previous visit, and he began to wonder which of the couple had been the tidier. Certainly, Eddie Ringan looked and acted like a slob, but you couldn't always tell.

'Sorry for the mess.'

'Well, you've got a lot on your mind just now.' The place was stuffy, with that heavy male smell you got sometimes in shared flats and locker-rooms. But usually it took more than one person to create it. Rebus began to wonder about the lean young bartender who'd accompanied Calder to the mortuary ...

'I've just been arranging the funeral,' Pat Calder was saying. 'It's on Monday. They asked if it would be family and friends. I had to tell them Eddie didn't have any family.'

'He had good friends, though.'

Calder smiled. 'Thank you, Inspector. Thank you for that. Was there something in particular ...?'

'It was just something we found at the scene.'

'Oh?'

'A sort of a message. It said, "I only turned on the gas".'

Calder froze. 'Christ, it *was* suicide, then?'

Rebus shrugged. 'It wasn't that kind of note. We found it on the inside of a school jotter.'

'Eddie's recipe book?'

'Yes.'

'I wondered where that had got to.'

'The message had been heavily scored out. I took it away for analysis.'

'Maybe it's something to do with the nightmares.'

'That's just what I was thinking. Depends what he was dreaming *about*, though, doesn't it? Nightmares can be about things you fear, *or* things you've done.'

'I'm no psychologist.'

'Me neither,' Rebus admitted. 'I take it Eddie had keys to the restaurant?'

'Yes.'

'We didn't find any on his body. Did you come across them when you were packing things up?'

'I don't think so. But how did he get in without keys?'

'You should be in CID, Mr Calder. That's what I've been wondering.' Rebus got up from the sofa. 'Well, sorry I had to come by.'

'Oh, that's all right. Can you tell Brian about the funeral arrangements? Warriston Cemetery at two o'clock.'

'Monday at two, I'll tell him. Oh, one last thing. You keep a record of table bookings, don't you?'

Calder seemed puzzled. 'Of course.'

'Only, I'd like to take a look. There might be some

names there that don't mean anything to you but might mean something to a policeman.'

Calder nodded. 'I see what you're getting at. I'll drop it into the station. I'm going to the Heartbreak at lunchtime, I'll pick it up then.'

'Still clearing stuff away?'

'No, it's a potential buyer. One of the pizza restaurants is looking to expand ...'

Whatever it was Pat Calder was hiding, he was doing only a fair job. But Rebus really didn't have the heart to start digging. There was way too much for him to worry about as it was. Starting with the gun. He'd sat with it in his car last night, his finger on the trigger. Just the way his instructor had taught him back in the Army: firm, but not tense. Like it was an erection, one you wanted to sustain.

He had been thinking too of goodies and baddies. If you thought bad things – dreams of cruelty and lust – that didn't make you bad. But if your head was full of civilised thoughts and you spent all day as a torturer ... It came down to the fact that you were judged by your actions in society, not by the inside of your head. So he'd no reason to feel bad about thinking grim and bloody thoughts. Not unless he turned thoughts into deeds. Yet going beyond thought would feel so good. More than that, it would feel *right*.

He stopped his car at the first church he came to. He hadn't attended any kind of worship for several months, always managing to make excuses and promises to himself that he'd try harder. It was just that Patience had made Sunday mornings so good.

Someone had been busy with a marker-pen on the wooden signboard in the churchyard, turning 'Our Lady of Perpetual Help' into 'Our Lady of Perpetual Hell'. Not the greatest of omens, but Rebus went inside anyway. He sat in a pew for a while. There weren't many souls in there with him. He had picked up a prayer book on the way in, and stared long and hard at its unjudgmental black cover, wondering why it made him feel so guilty. Eventually, a woman left the confessional, pulling up her headscarf. Rebus stood up and made himself enter the small box. He sat there in silence for a minute, trying to think what it was you were supposed to say.

'Forgive me, father, I'm about to sin.'

'We'll see about that, son,' came a gruff Irish voice from the other side of the grille. There was such assurance in the voice, Rebus almost smiled.

Instead he said, 'I'm not even a Catholic.'

'I'm sure that's true. But you're a Christian?'

'I suppose so. I used to go to church.'

'Do you believe?'

'I can't not believe.' He didn't add how hard he'd tried.

'Then tell me your problem.'

'Someone's been threatening me, my friends and family.'

'Have you gone to the police?'

'I am the police.'

'Ah. And now you're thinking of taking the law into your own hands, as they say in the films.'

'How did you know?'

'You're not the first bobby I've had in this confessional. There are a *few* Catholics in the police force.' This time Rebus did smile. 'So what is it you're going to do?'

'I've got a gun.'

There was an intake of breath. 'Now that's serious. Oh yes, that's serious. But you must see that if you use a gun, you turn into that which you despise so much. You turn into *them*.' The priest managed to hiss this last word.

'So what?' Rebus asked.

'So, ask yourself this. Can you live the rest of your life with the memories and the guilt?' The voice paused. 'I know what you Calvinists think. You think you're doomed

226

from the start, so why not raise some hell before you get there? But I'm talking about *this* life, not the next. Do you want to live in Purgatory *before* you die?'

'No.'

'You'd be a bloody eejit to say anything else. Tie that gun to a rock and chuck it in the Forth, that's where it belongs.'

'Thank you, father.'

'You're more than welcome. And son?'

'Yes, father?'

'Come back and talk to me again. I like to know what madness you Prods are thinking. It gives me something to chew on when there's nothing good on the telly.'

Rebus didn't spend long at Gorgie Road. They weren't getting anywhere. The photos taken so far had been developed, and some of the faces identified. Those identified were all small-timers, old cons, or up-and-comers. They weren't so much small fish as spawn in a corner of the pond. It wasn't as if Flower was having better luck, which was just as well for Rebus. He couldn't wait for the Little Weed to put in his reimbursement claim. All those rounds of drinks ...

He felt revived by his talk with the priest, whose name he now realised he didn't even know. But then that was part of the deal, wasn't it? Sinners Anonymous. He might even grant the priest's wish and go back sometime. And tonight he'd drive out to the coast and get rid of the gun. It had been madness all along. In a sense, buying it had been enough. He'd never have used it, would he?

He parked at St Leonard's and went inside. There was a package for him at the front desk – the reservations book for the Heartbreak Cafe. Calder had put a note in with it.

'Well, Elvis ate pizza, didn't he?' So it looked like the Heartbreak was about to go Italian.

While he'd been reading the note, the desk officer had been phoning upstairs, keeping his voice low.

'What's all that about?' Rebus asked. He thought he'd overheard the distinct words 'He's here'.

'Nothing, sir,' said the desk officer. Rebus tried to stare an answer out of him, then turned away, just as the inner doors were pushed open in businesslike fashion by the Uglybug Sisters, Lauderdale and Flower.

'Can I have your car-keys?' Lauderdale demanded.

'What's going on?' Rebus looked to Flower, who resembled a preacher at a burning.

'The keys, please.' Lauderdale's hand was so steady, Rebus thought if he walked away and left the two men standing there, it would stay stretched out for hours. He handed over his keys.

'It's a pile of junk. If you don't kick it in the right place, you won't even get it to start.' He was following the two men through the doors and into the car park.

'I don't want to drive it,' Lauderdale said. He sounded threatening, but it was Flower's serene silence that most worried Rebus. Then it hit him: the gun! They knew about the gun. And yes, it was still under his driver's seat. Where else was he going to hide it – in the flat, where Michael might find it? In his trousers, where it would raise eyebrows? No, he'd left it in the car.

The door of which Lauderdale was now opening. Lauderdale turned towards him, his hand out again. 'The gun, Inspector Rebus.' And when Rebus didn't move: 'Give me the gun.'

# 24

He raised the gun and fired it – one, two, three shots. Then lowered it again.

They all took off their ear-protectors. The forensics man had fired the gun into what looked like a simple wooden crate. The bullets would be retrieved from its interior and could then be analysed. The scientist had been holding the gun's butt with a polythene glove over his hand. He dropped the gun into a polythene bag of its own before slipping off the glove.

'We'll let you know as soon as we can,' he told Chief Superintendent Watson, who nodded the man's dismissal. After he'd left the room, Watson turned to Lauderdale.

'Give it to me again, Frank.'

Lauderdale took a deep breath. This was the third time he'd told Watson the story, but he didn't mind. He didn't mind at all. 'Inspector Flower came to me late this morning and told me he'd received information –'

'What sort of information?'

'A phone call.'

'Anonymous, naturally.'

'Naturally.' Lauderdale took another breath. 'The caller told him the gun that had been used in the Central Hotel shooting five years ago was in Inspector Rebus's possession. Then he rang off.'

'And we're supposed to believe Rebus shot that man five years ago?'

Lauderdale didn't know. 'All I know is, there *was* a gun

in Rebus's car. And he says himself, it'll have his prints all over it. Whether it's the same gun or not, we'll know by the end of play today.'

'Don't sound so fucking cheerful! We both know this is a stitch-up.'

'What we know, sir,' said Lauderdale, ignoring Watson's outburst, 'is that Inspector Rebus has been carrying on a little private investigation of his own into the Central Hotel. The files are by the side of his desk. He wouldn't tell anyone why.'

'So he found something out and now somebody's worried. That's why they've planted the –'

'With respect, sir,' Lauderdale paused, 'nobody planted anything. Rebus has admitted he bought the gun from someone he calls "a stranger". He specifically *asked* this "stranger" to get a gun for him.'

'What for?'

'He says he was being threatened. Of course, he could be lying.'

'How do you mean?'

'Maybe the gun was the clue he found, the one that started him back into the Central files. Now he's spinning this story because at least then we can't accuse him of withholding evidence.'

Watson took this in. 'What do you think?'

'Without prejudice, sir –'

'Come on, Frank, we all know you hate Rebus's guts. When he saw you and Flower coming for him, he must have thought the lynch-mob had arrived.'

Lauderdale tried an easy laugh. 'Personalities aside, sir, even if we stick to the bare *facts*, Inspector Rebus is in serious trouble. Even supposing he did buy the gun, it's obviously a nasty piece of goods – it's had a file taken to it in the past.'

'He's worse than ever,' Watson mused, 'now that his girlfriend's kicked him out. I had high hopes there.'

'Sir?'

'She'd got him wearing decent clothes. Rebus was beginning to look ... promotable.'

Lauderdale nearly swallowed his tongue.

'Stupid bugger,' Watson went on. Lauderdale decided he was talking about Rebus. 'I suppose I'd better talk to him.'

'Do you want me to ...?'

'I want you to stay here and wait for those results. Where's Flower?'

'Back on duty, sir.'

'You mean back in the pub. I'll want to talk to him too. Funny how this anonymous Deep Throat just manages to talk to the one person in St Leonard's who loves Rebus as much as you do.'

'Loves, sir?'

'I said "loathes".'

But actually, as Rebus already knew, the call had been taken not by Flower himself but by a DC who just happened to know how Flower felt about Inspector John Rebus. He'd called Flower at the pub, and Flower had raced Jackie Stewart-style back to St Leonard's to tell Lauderdale.

Rebus knew this because he had time to kill at St Leonard's while everyone else was up at the forensic lab in Fettes. And he knew he had to be quick, because Watson would suspend him as soon as he came back. He found some carrier bags and put the Central Hotel files in them, along with the reservations book from the Heartbreak Cafe. Then he took the whole lot down to his car and threw them in the boot ... probably the first place Watson would want to look.

Christ, he'd been planning to get rid of that gun tonight.

Lauderdale had said it was 'suspected' of being the gun used in the Central Hotel murder. Well, that would be easy enough to prove or disprove. They still had the original bullet. Rebus wished he'd given the gun closer scrutiny. It had looked shiny new, but then maybe it had only ever been fired that one fatal time.

He didn't doubt that it *was* the gun. He just wondered how the hell they'd managed to set him up. The only answer was to work backwards. Deek had handed him the gun. So somehow they'd gotten to Deek. Well, Rebus himself had put word out that he was looking for Deek Torrance. And word got around. Someone had heard and been interested enough to track down Deek too. They'd asked him what his connection was with John Rebus. And when Rebus had then asked Deek for a gun, Deek had reported back to them.

Oh yes, that was it, all right. Rebus had set *himself* up by asking for the gun in the first place. Because then they'd known exactly what to do with him. Planting the gun was a bit *too* obvious, wasn't it? No one was going to be taken in. But it would have to be investigated, and investigations like that could take months, during which time he'd be suspended. They wanted him out of the way, that was all. Because he was getting close.

Rebus smiled to himself. He was no closer than Alaska ... unless he'd stumbled upon something without realising it. He needed to go over everything again, down to the last detail. But this would take time: time he was sure Watson would unwittingly be about to offer him.

So, when he walked into the Chief Superintendent's office, he surprised even Watson with his ease.

'John,' said Watson, after motioning for Rebus to sit, 'how come you always seem to have a banana skin up your sleeve?'

'Because I say the magic word, sir?' Rebus offered.

'And what is the magic word?'

Rebus looked surprised Watson didn't know. 'Abracadabra, sir.'

'John,' said Watson, 'I'm suspending you.'

'Thank you, sir,' said Rebus.

He spent that evening on the trail of Deek Torrance, even driving out to South Queensferry – the most forlorn hope of a forlorn night. Deek would have been paid plenty to get well away from the city. By now, he might not even be in the western hemisphere. Then again, maybe they'd have silenced him in some other more permanent way.

'Some pal you turned out to be,' Rebus muttered to himself more than once. And to complete the circle, he headed out to his favourite massage parlour. He always seemed to be the only customer, and had wondered how the Organ Grinder made his money. But now of course he knew: the Organ Grinder would come to your home. Always supposing you were wealthy enough ... or had reputation enough.

'How long have you been going out there?' Rebus asked. Prone on the table, he was aware that the Organ Grinder could break his neck or his back with consummate ease. But he didn't think he would. He hoped his instincts weren't wrong in this at least.

'Just a couple of months. Someone at a health club told his wife about me.'

'Know her, do you?'

'Not really. She thinks I'm too rough.'

'That's droll, coming from the wife of Big Ger Cafferty.'

'He's a villain, then?'

'Whatever gave you that idea?'

'You forget, I've not been up here that long.'

True, Rebus had forgotten the Organ Grinder's north London pedigree. When in the mood, he told wonderful stories of that city.

'Anything about him you want to tell me?' Rebus ventured, despite the thick hands on his neck.

'Nothing to tell,' said the Organ Grinder. 'Silence is a virtue, Inspector.'

'And there's too much of it around. You ever seen anyone out at his house?'

'Just his wife and the chauffeur.'

'Chauffeur? You mean the man mountain with the knob of gristle for a left ear?'

'That explains the haircut,' mused the Organ Grinder.

'Precious little else would,' said Rebus.

After the Organ Grinder had finished with him, Rebus went back to the flat. Michael was watching a late film, the glow from the TV set flicking across his rapt face. Rebus went over to the TV and switched it off. Michael still stared at the screen, not blinking. There was a cup of cold tea in his hand. Gently, Rebus took it from him.

'Mickey,' he said. 'I need someone to talk to.'

Michael blinked and looked up at him. 'You can always talk to me,' he said. 'You know that.'

'I know that,' said Rebus. 'We've got something else in common now.'

'What's that?'

Rebus sat down. 'We've both been recently suspended.'

# 25

Chief Superintendent Watson dreaded these Saturday mornings, when his wife would try to entice him to go shopping with her. Dreary hours in department stores and clothes shops, not to mention the supermarket, where he'd be guinea-pig for the latest microwavable Malaysian meal or some rude looking unpronounceable fruit. Worst of all, of course, he saw other men in exactly the same predicament. It was a wonder one of them didn't lose the rag and start screaming about how they used to be the hunters, fierce and proud.

But this morning he had the excuse of work. He always tried to have an excuse either for nipping into St Leonard's or else bringing work home with him. He sat in his study, listening to Radio Scotland and reading the newspaper, the house quiet and still around him. Then the telephone rang, annoying him until he remembered he was waiting for just this call. It was Ballistics at Fettes. After he took the call, he looked up a number in his card index and made another.

'I want you in my office Monday morning,' he told Rebus, 'for formal questioning.'

'From which I take it,' said Rebus, 'that I bought a lulu of a gun.'

'Lulu *and* her backing band.'

'They were called the Luvvers, sir. The bullets matched up?'

'Yes.'

'You knew they would,' said Rebus. 'And so did I.'

'It's awkward, John.'

'It's supposed to be.'

'For you as well as me.'

'With all respect, sir, I wasn't thinking of you ...'

When Siobhan Clarke woke up that morning, she glanced at the clock then shot out of bed. Christ, it was nearly nine! She had just run water for a bath, and was looking for clean underwear in the bathroom, when it hit her. It was the weekend! Nothing to rush for. In fact, quite the opposite. The relief team had taken over Moneybags, just for this first weekend, to see if there was any sign of life at Dougary's office. According to Trading Standards, Dougary's weekends were sacrosanct. He wouldn't go anywhere near Gorgie. But they had to be sure, so for this weekend only Operation Moneybags had a relief retinue, keeping an eye on the place. If nothing happened, next weekend they wouldn't bother. Dougary was blessedly fixed in his ways. She hadn't had to hang about too often on the surveillance past five-thirty, more often a bit earlier. Which suited Siobhan fine. It meant she'd managed a couple of useful trips to Dundee out of hours.

She'd arranged another trip for this morning, but didn't need to leave Edinburgh for an hour or so yet. And she was sure to be home before the Hibees kicked off.

Time now for some coffee. The living room was messy, but she didn't mind. She usually set aside Sunday morning for all the chores. That was the nice thing about living by yourself: your mess was your own. There was no one to comment on it or be disturbed by it. Crisp bags, pizza boxes, three-quarters-empty bottles of wine, old newspapers and magazines, CD cases, items of clothing, opened and unopened mail, plates and cutlery and every mug in the flat – these could all be found in her fourteen-by-twelve living room. Somewhere under the debris there was a futon and a cordless telephone.

The telephone was ringing. She reached under a pizza carton, picked up the receiver, and yanked up the aerial.

'Is that you, Clarke?'

'Yes, sir.' The last person she'd been expecting: John Rebus. She wandered through to the bathroom.

'Terrible interference,' said Rebus.

'I was just turning off the bath.'

'Christ, you're in the –'

'No, sir, not yet. Cordless phone.'

'I hate those things. You're talking for five minutes, then you hear the toilet flushing. Well, sorry to ... what time is it?'

'Just turned nine.'

'Really?' He sounded dead beat.

'Sir, I heard about your suspension.'

'That figures.'

'I know it's none of my business, but what were you doing with a gun in the first place?'

'Psychic protection.'

'Sorry?'

'That's what my brother calls it. He should know, he used to be a hypnotist.'

'Sir, are you all right?'

'I'm fine. Are you going to the game?'

'Not if you need me for anything else.'

'Well, I was wondering ... do you still have the Cafferty files?'

She had walked back into the living room. Oh, she still had the files, all right. Their contents were spread across her coffee table, her desk, and half the breakfast bar.

'Yes, sir.'

'Any chance you could bring them over to my flat? Only I've got the Central Hotel files here. Somewhere in them there's a clue I'm missing.'

'You want to cross-reference with the Cafferty files? That's a big job.'

'Not if two people are working on it.'

'What time do you want me there?'


Saturday at Brian Holmes' aunt's house in Barnton was a bit like Sunday, except that on Saturday he didn't have to deny her his company at the local presbyterian kirk. Was it any wonder that, having found the Heartbreak Cafe such a welcoming spot, he should have spent so long there? But those days were over. He tried to accept the fact that 'Elvis' was dead, but it was difficult. No more King Shrimp Creole or Blue Suede Choux or In the Gateau, no more Blue Hawaii cocktails. No more late nights of tequila slammers (with Jose Cuervo Gold, naturally) or Jim Beam (Eddie's preferred bourbon).

' "Keep on the Beam," he used to say.'

'There there, pet.' Oh great, now his aunt had caught him talking to himself. She'd brought him a cup of Ovaltine.

'This stuff's for bedtime,' he told her. 'It's not even noon.'

'It'll calm you down, Brian.'

He took a sip. Ach, it didn't taste bad anyway. Pat had dropped round to ask if he'd be a pall-bearer on Monday.

'It'd be an honour,' Holmes had told him, meaning it. Pat hadn't wanted to meet his eyes. Maybe he too was thinking of the nights they'd all spent slurring after-hours gossip at the bar. On one of those nights, when they'd been talking about great Scottish disasters, Eddie had suddenly announced that he'd been there when the Central Hotel caught fire.

'I was filling in for a guy, cash in the hand and no questions. Dead on my feet after the day-shift at the Eyrie.'

'I didn't know you'd worked at the Eyrie.'

'Assistant to the head man himself. If he doesn't get a

Michelin recommendation this year, he'd be as well giving up.'

'So what happened at the Central?' Holmes' head hadn't been entirely befuddled by spirits.

'Some poker game was going on, up in one of the rooms on the first floor.' He seemed to be losing it, drifting towards sleep. 'Tam and Eck were looking for players ...'

'Tam and Eck?'

'Tam and Eck Robertson ...'

'But what happened?'

'It's no good, Brian,' said Pat Calder, 'look at him.'

Though Eddie's eyes were open, head resting on his arms, arms spread across the bar, he was asleep.

'A cousin of mine was at Ibrox the day of the big crush,' Pat revealed, cleaning a pint glass.

'But do you remember where you were the night Jock Stein died?' Holmes asked. More stories had followed, Eddie sleeping through all of them.

Permanently asleep now. And Holmes was to be pall-bearer number four. He'd asked Pat a few questions.

'Funny,' Pat had said, 'your man Rebus asked me just the same.'

So Brian knew the case was in good hands.


Rebus drove around the lunchtime streets. On a Saturday, providing you steered clear of Princes Street, the city had a more relaxed feel. At least until about two-thirty, when either the east end or the west of the city (depending who was playing home) would fill with football fans. And on derby match days, best stay away from the centre alto-gether. But today wasn't a derby match, and Hibs were at home, so the town was quiet.

'You asked about him just the other week,' a barman told Rebus.

'And I'm asking again.'

He was again on the lookout for Deek Torrance; a seek

and destroy mission. He doubted Deek would be around, but sometimes money and alcohol did terrible things to a man, boosting his confidence, making him unwary of danger and vengeance. Rebus's hope was that Deek was still mingin' somewhere on the money he'd paid for the gun. As hopes went, it was more forlorn than most. But he did stumble upon Chick Muir in a Leith social club, and was able to tell him the news.

'That's just awfy,' Chick consoled. 'I'll keep my nose to the ground.'

Rebus appreciated the muddled sentiment. In Chick's case, it wouldn't be hard anyway. Informers were sometimes called snitches, and Chick's snitch was about as big as they came.

One-thirty found him leaving a dingy betting shop. He'd seen more hope and smiles in a hospice, and fewer tears too. Ten minutes later he was sitting down to microwaved haggis, neeps and tatties in the Sutherland Bar. Someone had left a newspaper on his chair, and he started to read it. By luck, it was open at a piece by Mairie Henderson.

'You're late,' he said as Mairie herself sat down. She nearly stood up again in anger.

'I was in here half an hour ago! Quarter past one, we arranged. I stayed till half past.'

'I thought half past was the agreement,' he said blithely.

'You weren't *here* at half past. You're lucky I came back.'

'Why did you?'

She tore the newspaper from him. 'I left my paper.'

'Not much in it anyway.' He scooped more haggis into his mouth.

'I thought you were buying me lunch.'

Rebus nodded towards the food counter. 'Help yourself. They'll add it to my tab.'

It took her a moment to decide that she was hungrier

than she was angry. She came back from the food counter with a plate of quiche and bean salad, and grabbed her purse. 'They don't *have* tabs here!' she informed him. Rebus winked.

'Just my little joke.' He tried to hand her some money, but she turned on her heels. Low heels, funny little shoes like children's Doc Marten's. And black tights. Rebus rolled the food around with his tongue. She sat down at last and took off her coat. It took her a moment to get comfortable.

'Anything to drink?' asked Rebus.

'I suppose it's my round?' she snapped.

He shook his head, so she asked for a gin and fresh orange. Rebus got the drinks, a half of Guinness for himself. There was probably more nutrition in the Guinness than in the meal he'd just consumed.

'So,' said Mairie, 'what's the big secret?'

Rebus used his little finger to draw his initials on the thick head of his drink, knowing they'd still be there when he reached the bottom. 'I've been shown the red card.'

That made her look up. 'What? Suspended?' She wasn't angry with him any more. She was a reporter, sniffing a story. He nodded. 'What happened?' Excitedly she forked up a mouthful of kidney bean and chickpea. Rebus had had a crash-course in pulses from his tenants. Never mind red kids and chicks, he could tell a borlotti from a pinto at fifty yards downwind.

'I came into possession of a handgun, a Colt 45. May or may not have been a copy.'

'And?' She nearly spattered him with pastry in her haste.

'And it was the gun used in the Central Hotel shooting.'

'No!' Her screech caused several drinkers to pause before their next swallow. The Sutherland was that kind of place. Riots in the streets would have merited a single measured comment. Rebus could see Mairie's head fairly filling to the brim with questions.

'Do you still write for the Sunday edition?' he asked her. She nodded, still busy trying to find an order for all the questions she had. 'What about doing me a favour, then? I've always wanted to be on the front page ...'

Not that he'd any intention of seeing his *own* name in the story. They went through it carefully together, back at the newspaper office. So Rebus got his tour of the building at last. It was a bit disappointing, all stairwell and open-plan and not much action. What action there was centred exclusively on Mairie's desk and its up-to-date word processor.

There was even a discussion with the editor of the Sunday. They needed to be sure of a few things. It was always like this with unattributed stories. In Scots law, there was no place for uncorroborated evidence. The press seemed to be following suit. But Rebus had a staunch defender in the woman whose byline would appear with the story. After a conference call with the paper's well-remunerated lawyer, the nod was given and Mairie started to hammer the keyboard into submission.

'I can't promise front page,' the editor warned. 'Beware the breaking story! As it is, you've just knocked a car crash and its three victims to the inside.'

Rebus stayed to watch the whole process. A series of commands on Mairie's computer sent the text to type-setting, which was done elsewhere in the building. Soon a laser printer was delivering a rough copy of how the front page might look tomorrow morning. And there along the bottom was the headline: GUN RECOVERED IN FIVE-YEAR-OLD MURDER MYSTERY.

'That'll change,' said Mairie. 'The sub will have a go at it once he's read the story.'

'Why?'

'Well, for one thing, it looks like the murder victim is a five-year-old.'

So it did. Rebus hadn't noticed. Mairie was staring at him.

'Isn't this going to get you in even *more* trouble?'

'Who's going to know it was me gave you the story?'

She smiled. 'Well, let's start with everyone in the City of Edinburgh Police.'

Rebus smiled too. He'd bought some caffeine pills this morning to keep him moving. They were working fine. 'If anyone asks,' he said, 'I'll just have to tell them the truth.'

'Which is what exactly?'

'That it wisnae me.'

# 26

Rebus dished out yet more money to the students that afternoon to get them out of the flat until midnight. He wondered if it were unique in Scottish social history for a landlord to be paying his own tenants. There were only two of them there, the other two (he'd now established that he had four permanent tenants, whose names he still had trouble with so never tried using) having headed home for purposes of cosseting and feeding-up.

Michael, however, stayed put. Rebus knew he wouldn't be any bother. He'd either be dozing in the box room or else watching the TV. He didn't seem to mind if the sound were turned off, just so long as there was a picture to stare at.

Rebus bought a bag of provisions: real coffee, milk, beer, soft drinks, and snacks. Back in the flat he remembered Siobhan was a vegetarian, and cursed himself for buying smoky bacon crisps. Bound to be artificial flavourings though, so maybe it didn't matter. She arrived at five-thirty.

'Come in, come in.' Rebus led her through the long dark hallway to the living room. 'This is my brother Michael.'

'Hello, Michael.'

'Mickey, this is DC Siobhan Clarke.' Michael nodded his head, blinking slowly. 'Here, let me take your jacket. How was the game, by the way?'

'Goalless.' Siobhan put down her two carrier-bags and

slipped off her black leather jacket. Rebus took the jacket into the hall and hung it up. When he came back, he noticed her studying the living room doubtfully.

'Bit of a tip,' he said, though he'd spent quarter of an hour tidying it.

'Big, though.' She didn't deny it was a tip. You could hardly see out of the huge sash window. And the carpet looked like it had moulted from a buffalo's back. As for the wallpaper ... she could well understand why the students had tried covering every inch with kd lang and Jesus & Mary Chain posters.

'Something to drink?'

She shook her head. 'Let's get on with it.' This wasn't quite what she'd imagined. The zombie brother didn't help, of course. But he wasn't much of a distraction either. They got down to work.

An hour later, they had scraped the surface of the files. Siobhan was lying on her side on the floor, legs curled up, one arm supporting her head. She was on her second can of cola. The file was on the floor in front of her. Rebus sat near her on the sofa, files on his lap and in a heap beside him. He had a pen behind his ear, just like a butcher or a turf accountant. Siobhan held her pen in her mouth, tapping it against her teeth when she was thinking. Some bad quiz show was playing to silent hysterics on the TV. For all the reaction on his face, Michael could have been watching a war trial.

He pulled himself out of the chair. 'I'm going to take forty winks,' he informed them. Siobhan tried not to look surprised when he made not for the living-room door but for the box room. He closed the door behind him.

'I'd like two things,' said Rebus. 'To identify the murder victim, once and for all.'

'And to identify the killer?' Siobhan guessed.

But Rebus shook his head. 'To place Big Ger at the scene.'

'There's no evidence he was anywhere near.'

'And maybe there never will be. But all the same ...
We still don't know who was at the poker game. It can't
just have been the Bru-Head Brothers.'

'We could talk to all the hotel's customers that night.'

'Yes, we could.' Rebus didn't sound enthusiastic.

'Or we could find the brothers – always supposing
they're still alive – and ask them.'

'Their cousin might know where they are.'

'Who? Radiator McCallum?'

Rebus nodded. 'But then we don't know where he is
either. Eddie Ringan was there, but he was never on the
official list. Black Aengus wasn't on the list, and neither
were the Bru-Head Brothers. I'm surprised we got any
names at all.'

'We *are* talking about a long time ago.' Siobhan sounded
more relaxed with Michael out of the room.

'We're also talking about long memories. Maybe I
should have another go at Black Aengus.'

'Not if you know what's good for you.' Siobhan could
have said something about Dundee, but she wanted it to
be confirmed first, and she wanted it to be a surprise.
She'd know by Monday.

The phone rang. Rebus picked it up.

'John? It's Patience.'

'Oh, hello there.'

'Hello yourself. I thought maybe we'd fix up that
date.'

'Oh, right. For a drink?'

'Don't tell me you've forgotten? No, I know what it is:
you're just playing hard to get. Don't push it *too* far,
Rebus.'

'No, it's not that, I'm just a bit busy right this minute.'
Siobhan seemed to take a hint, and got up, motioning
that she'd make some coffee in the kitchen. Rebus nodded.

'Well, I'm sorry to interrupt whatever it is you're –'

'Don't take it the wrong way, Patience. I've just got things on my mind.'

'And I'm not included?'

Rebus made an exasperated sound. From the kitchen there came the louder sound of a sneeze. Aye, those Easter Road terraces could be snell.

'John,' said Patience, 'is there a woman in the flat?'

'Yes,' he said.

'One of the students?'

He seldom lied to her. 'No, a colleague. We're working through some case-notes.'

'I see.'

Christ, he should have tried lying. His head was too full of the Central Hotel to be able to cope with Patience's jousting. 'Look,' he said, 'have you got a time and place in mind for that drink?'

But Patience had rung off. Rebus stared at the receiver, shrugged, and placed it on the carpet. He didn't want any more interruptions.

'Coffee's on,' said Siobhan.

'Great.'

'Was it something I said?'

'What? No, no, just ... nothing.'

But Siobhan was canny. 'She heard me sneeze and thought you had another woman here.'

'I *do* have another woman here. It's just the way her mind works ... She doesn't exactly trust me.'

'And she should trust you?'

Rebus sighed. 'Tell me about the Robertson brothers again.'

Siobhan sat down on the floor and started to read from the file. From the sofa, Rebus looked down on her. The top of her head, the nape of her neck with its fine pale hairs disappearing into her collar. Small pierced ears ...

'We know they get on well. It was a close family, six kids in a one-bedroom cottage.'

247

'What happened to the other brothers and sisters?'

'Four sisters,' Siobhan read. 'Law-abiding wives and mothers these days. The boys were the only wild ones. Both like gambling, especially cards and the horses. Tam is the better card player of the two, but Eck has more luck on the horses ... Remember this stuff is six years old, and all hearsay in the first place.'

Rebus nodded. He was remembering the old man in that last pub in Lochgelly, the one who'd come cadging drinks from the painters and decorators. He'd said one of the drawings looked familiar. Then one of the painters had cut him short with a story about how he'd recognise a horse easier than a man. So the old guy was keen on the gee-gees, and so were Eck and Tam.

'Maybe he saw him in a bookie's,' Rebus wondered aloud.

'Sorry?'

So Rebus told her.

'It's worth a try,' she conceded. 'What else do we have to go on?'

Rebus had one good contact at Dunfermline CID, Detective Sergeant Hendry. It was rumoured that Hendry was too good at his job ever to merit promotion. Only the incompetent were promoted. It shuffled them out of the way. As a DI, Rebus didn't necessarily agree. But he knew Hendry should have been an Inspector long ago, and wondered what or who was blocking him. It couldn't be that Hendry was too abrasive: he was one of the calmest people Rebus had ever met. His hobby, bird-watching, reflected his nature. They'd exchanged home phone numbers once on a case. Yes, it was worth a try.

'Hello there, Hendry,' he said. 'It's Rebus here.'

'Rebus, trust you to disturb a working man's rest.'

'Been bird-watching?'

'I saw a spotted woodpecker this morning.'

'I saw a spotted dick once.'

'Ah, but I'm not a man of the world like you. So what do you want?'

'I want you to look in your local phone directory. I'm after bookie's shops.'

'Any one in particular?'

'No, I'm not picky. I need the names and addresses of all of them.'

'Which towns?'

Rebus thought. 'Dunfermline, Cowdenbeath, Lochgelly, Cardenden, Kelty, Ballingry. That'll do for starters.'

'This could take a bit of time. Can I phone you back?'

'Aye, sure. And ponder on two names for me. Tom and Eck Robertson. They're brothers.'

'Okay. You're at Arden Street, I hear.'

'What?'

'You got the heave from the doctor. What was it, your bedside manner?'

'Who told you?'

'Word gets around. Isn't it true then?'

'No, it's not. It's just that my brother's here for a ... ach, forget it.'

'Talk to you later.'

Rebus put down the phone. 'Would you credit that? Every bugger seems to know about Patience and me. Was there a notice in the papers, or something?'

Siobhan smiled. 'What now?'

'Hendry's going to get back with the details. Meantime, we could nip out and get a curry or something.'

'What if he phones while we're out?'

'He'll try again.'

'Haven't you got an answering machine?'

'I could never get it to work, so I chucked it out. Besides, there are that many bookie's shops in Fife, Hendry'd be on it for hours.'

They walked to Tollcross, Siobhan insistent that she could do with some fresh air.

'I thought you'd have had enough of that at the game.'

'Are you joking? *Fresh air?* Between the smoking and the smells of dead beer and pie-grease ...'

'You're putting me off my curry.'

'I bet you're the vindaloo type too.'

'Strictly Madras,' said Rebus.

During the meal, he reasoned that Siobhan might as well toddle off home afterwards. It wasn't as if they could do anything tonight with the list of betting shops. And tomorrow the shops would be closed. But Siobhan wanted to stick around at least until Hendry phoned.

'We haven't covered all the files yet,' she argued.

'True enough,' said Rebus. After the meal, while Siobhan drank a cup of coffee Rebus ordered some take-away for Michael.

'Is he all right?' Siobhan asked.

'He's getting better,' Rebus insisted. 'Those pills are nearly finished. He'll be fine once he's shot of them.'

As if to prove the point, when they got back to the flat Michael was in the kitchen, dunking a teabag in a mug of hot milky water. He looked like he'd just had a shower. He'd also shaved.

'I fetched you a curry,' Rebus said.

'You must be a mind reader.' Michael sniffed into the brown paper bag. 'Rogan Josh?' Rebus nodded and turned to Siobhan. 'Michael is the city's Rogan Josh expert.'

'There was a call while you were out.' Michael lifted the cardboard containers out of the bag.

'Hendry?'

'That was the name.'

'Did he leave a message?'

Michael unpeeled both cartons, meat and rice. 'He said you should get a pen and a lot of paper ready.'

Rebus smiled at Siobhan. 'Come on,' he said, 'let's save Hendry's phone bill.'

'I'm glad you phoned back,' were Hendry's first words. 'For one thing, I'm due at an indoor bowls tourney in half an hour. For another, this is a big list.'

'So let's have it,' said Rebus.

'I could fax it to you at the station?'

'No you couldn't, I'm out of the game.'

'I hadn't heard.'

'Funny, that; you hear about my love life fast enough. Ready when you are.'

As Hendry reeled off the names, addresses and phone numbers, Rebus relayed them to Siobhan. She claimed to be a fast writer, so was given the job of transcribing. But after ten minutes they switched over, her hand being sore. The final list covered three sides of A4. As well as the basic information, Hendry dropped in snippets of his own, such as licensing wrangles, suspected handling of stolen goods, hangouts for ne'er-do-wells and the like. Rebus was grateful for all of it.

'A fine institution, the bookie's,' he commented, when Siobhan handed him the receiver.

'You bet,' said Hendry. 'Can I go now?'

'Sure, and thanks for everything.'

'So long as it helps you get back in the game. We need all the fly-halfs we can get. Those two names didn't click with me, by the way. And Rebus?'

'What?'

'She sounds a right wee smasher.'

Hendry severed the connection before Rebus could explain. When it came to gossip, Hendry was a regular sweetie-wife. Rebus dreaded to think what stories he'd be hearing about himself in the next week or two.

'What was he saying?' Siobhan asked.

'Nothing.'

She'd been running through the list for herself. 'Well,' she said, 'no names there that mean anything to me.' Rebus took the list from her.

'Me neither.'

'Next stop Fife?'

'For me, yes. On Monday, I suppose.' Except that on Monday he'd to report to Chief Superintendent Watson *and* attend Eddie Ringan's funeral. 'You,' he said, 'are going to be busy shoring up our side of Operation Money-bags.'

'Oh, I thought I might go to the funeral. That'd give us the excuse for a couple of hours' work in Fife.'

Rebus shook his head. 'I appreciate the thought, but *you're* still on the force. I'm the one with time for this sort of legwork.' She looked bitterly disappointed. 'And that's an order,' Rebus told her.

'Yes, sir,' said Siobhan.

# 27

The thought of another interminable Sunday bothered Rebus so much that, after attending Mass, he drove across the Forth Road Bridge back into Fife.

He'd been to Our Lady of Perpetual Hell, sitting at the back, watching and wondering if the priest who led the worship was *his* priest. The accent was Scots-Irish; hard to tell. His priest had spoken quietly, while this one belted everything out at the top of his voice. Maybe some of the congregation were deaf. But at least there were a fair number of young folk in attendance. He was almost alone in not accepting communion.

West-central Fife could use a spot of communion itself. It would drink the wine and pawn the chalice. He decided to leave Dunfermline till last; it was the biggest town with the most locations. He'd start small. He couldn't recall whether it was quicker to get to Ballingry by coming off the motorway at Kinross, but certainly it was a much bonnier drive. He was tempted to stop at Loch Leven, site of many a childhood picnic and game of football. He still had a lump below his knee where Michael had kicked him once. The narrow, meandering roads were busy with Sunday drivers, their cars polished like medals. There was half a chance Hendry would be at the Loch Leven bird sanctuary, but Rebus didn't stop. Soon enough he was in the glummer confines of Ballingry. He didn't loiter longer than he needed to.

He wasn't sure what this trip was supposed to

accomplish. All the betting shops would be tight shut. Maybe he'd find someone he could gossip with about this or that bookie's, but he doubted it. He knew what he was doing. He was killing time, and this was a good place for it. At least here there was the illusion that he was doing something constructive about the case. So he parked outside the closed shop and constructively marked a tick against the address on his three-page list.

Of course, there *was* one more reason for his early rise this morning and his early exit from the house. In the car with him he had the Sunday paper. The Central Hotel story had stuck tenaciously to the front page, now with the headline CENTRAL MURDER BLAZE: GUN FOUND. Once Watson and co. saw it, they'd be on the phone to each other and, naturally, to John Rebus. But for once the students would have to field *his* calls. He'd read the story through twice to himself, knowing every word by heart. He was hoping that somewhere *some*body was reading it and starting to panic ...

Next stops: Lochore, Lochgelly, Cardenden. Rebus had been born and raised in Cardenden. Well, Bowhill actually, back when there had been four parishes: Auchterderran, Bowhill, Cardenden, and Dundonald. The ABCD, people called it. Then the post office had termed it all the one town, Cardenden. It wasn't so very much changed from the place Rebus had known. He stopped the car at the cemetery and spent a few minutes by the grave of his father and mother. A woman in her forties placed some flowers against a headstone nearby and smiled at Rebus as she passed him. When Rebus got back to the cemetery gates, she was waiting there.

'Johnny Rebus?'

It was so unexpected he grinned, the grin dissolving years from his face.

'I went to school with you,' the woman stated. 'Heather Cranston.'

'Heather . . .?' He stared at her face. *'Cranny?'*

She put a hand to her mouth, blocking laughter. 'Nobody's called me that in twenty-odd years.'

He remembered her now. The way she always stifled laughs with her hand, embarrassed because her laugh sounded so funny to her. Now she nodded into the cemetery.

'I walk past your mum and dad most weeks.'

'It's more than I do.'

'Aye, but you're in Edinburgh or someplace now, aren't you?'

'That's right.'

'Just visiting?'

'Passing through.' They had come out of the cemetery now, and were walking downhill into Bowhill. They passed by Rebus's car, but he'd no wish to break off the conversation. So they walked.

'Aye,' she said, 'plenty of folk pass through. Never many stay put. I used to ken everybody in the place, but not now . . .'

*A yistiken awb-di.* Listening to her, Rebus realised how much of the accent and the dialect he'd lost over the years.

'Come round for a cup of tea,' she was saying now. He'd looked in vain for an engagement or wedding ring on her hand. She was by no means an unlovely woman. Big, whereas at school she'd been tiny and shy. Or maybe Rebus wasn't remembering right. Her cheeks were shining and there was mascara round her eyes. She was wearing black shoes with inch and a half heels, and tea-coloured tights on muscular legs. Rebus, who hadn't had breakfast or lunch, would bet that she had a pantry full of cakes and biscuits.

'Aye, why not?' he said.

She lived in a house along Craigside Road. They'd passed one betting shop on the way from the cemetery. It was as dead as the rest of the street.

'Are you going to take a look at the old house?' She meant the house he'd grown up in. He shrugged and watched her unlock her door. In the lobby, she listened for a second then yelled, 'Shug! Are you up there?' But there was no sound from upstairs. 'It's a miracle,' she said. 'Out of his bed before four o'clock. He must've gone out somewhere.' She saw the look on Rebus's face, and her hand went to her mouth. 'Don't worry, it's not a husband or boyfriend or anything. Hugh's my son.'

'Oh?'

She took off her coat. 'Away through you go.' She opened the living room door for him. It was a small room, choked with a huge three-piece suite, dining-table and chairs, wall-unit and TV. She'd had the chimney blocked off and central heating installed.

Rebus sank into one of the fireside chairs. 'But you're not married?'

She had slung her coat over the banister. 'Never really saw the point,' she said, entering the room. She devoured space as she moved, first to the radiator to check it was warm, then to the mantelpiece for cigarettes and her lighter. She offered one to Rebus.

'I've stopped,' he said. 'Doctor's orders.' Which was, in a sense, the truth.

'I tried stopping once or twice, but the weight I put on, you wouldn't credit it.' She inhaled deeply.

'So, Hugh's father ...?'

She blew the smoke out of her nostrils. 'Never knew him, really.' She saw the look on Rebus's face. 'Have I shocked you, Johnny?'

'Just a bit, Cranny. You used to be ... well ...'

'Quiet? That was a lifetime ago. What do you fancy, coffee, tea or me?' And she laughed behind her cigarette hand.

'Coffee's fine,' said John Rebus, shifting in his chair.

She brought in two mugs of bitter instant. 'No biscuits, sorry, I'm all out.' She handed him his mug. 'I've already sugared it, hope that's all right.'

'Fine,' said Rebus, who did not take sugar. The mug was a souvenir of Blackpool. They talked about people they'd known at school. Sitting opposite him, she decided at one point to cross one leg over the other. But her skirt was too tight, so she gave up and tugged at the hem of the garment.

'So what brings you here? Passing through, you said?'

'Well, sort of. I'm actually looking for a bookie's shop.'

'We passed one on the –'

'This is a particular business. It's probably either new in the past five or so years, or else has been taken over by a new operator during that time.'

'Then you're after Hutchy's.' She said this nonchalantly, sucking on her cigarette afterwards.

'Hutchy's? But that place was around when *we* were growing up.'

She nodded. 'Named after Joe Hutchinson, he started it. Then he died and his son Howie took over. Tried changing the name of the place, but everybody kept calling it Hutchy's, so he gave up. About, oh, five years ago, maybe a bit less, he sold up and buggered off to Spain. Imagine, same age as us and he's made his pile. Retired to the sun. Nearest we get to the sun here is when the toaster's on.'

'So who did he sell the business to?'

She had to think about this. 'Greenwood, I think his name is. But the place is still called Hutchy's. That's what the sign says above the door. Aye, Tommy Greenwood.'

'Tommy? You're sure of that. Not Tom or Tam?'

She shook her permed head. She'd had a salt-and-pepper dye done quite recently. Rebus supposed it was to hide some authentic grey. The style itself could only be termed Bouffant Junior. It took Rebus back in time ...

'Tommy Greenwood,' she said. 'Friend of mine used to go out with him.'

'Had he been around Cardenden for long before he bought Hutchy's?'

'No time at all. We didn't know him from Adam. Then in short order he'd bought Hutchy's *and* the old doctor's house down near the river. The story goes, he paid Howie from a suitcase stacked with cash. The story goes, he *still* doesn't have a bank account.'

'So where did the money come from?'

'Aye, now you're asking a good question.' She nodded her head slowly. 'A few folk would like to know the answer to *that* one.'

He asked a few more questions about Greenwood, but there wasn't more she could tell. He kept himself to himself, walked between his house and the bookie's every day. Didn't own a flash car. No wife, no kids. Didn't do much in the way of socialising or drinking.

'He'd be quite a catch for some woman,' she said, in tones that let Rebus know she'd tried with the rod and line. 'Oh aye, quite a catch.'

Rebus escaped twenty minutes later, but not without an exchange of addresses and phone numbers and promises to keep in touch. He walked back slowly past Hutchy's – an uninspiring little double-front with peeling paint and smoky windows – and then briskly up the brae to the cemetery. At the cemetery, he saw that another car had been parked tight in behind his. A cherry-red Renault 5. He passed his own car and tapped on the window of the Renault. Siobhan Clarke put down her newspaper and wound open the window.

'What the hell are you doing here?' Rebus demanded.

'Following a hunch.'

'I don't have a hunch.'

'Took me a while. Did you start with Ballingry?' He nodded. 'That's what threw me. I came off the motorway at Kelty.'

'Listen,' Rebus said, 'I've found a contender.'

She didn't seem interested. 'Have you seen this morning's paper?'

'Oh that, I meant to tell you about it.'

'No, not the front page, the inside.'

'Inside?'

She tapped a headline and handed the paper through the window to him. THREE INJURED IN M8 SMASH. The story told how on Saturday morning a BMW left the motorway heading towards Glasgow and ended up in a field. The family in the car had all been hospitalised – wife, teenage son, and 'Edinburgh businessman David Dougary, 41'.

'Christ,' gasped Rebus, 'I knocked that off the front page.'

'Pity you didn't read it at the time. What'll happen now?'

Rebus read the story through again. 'I don't know. It'll depend. If they shut down or transfer the Gorgie operation, either we shut down or we follow it.'

'"We"? You're suspended, remember.'

'Or else Cafferty brings someone else in to take over while Dougary's on the mend.'

'It would be short notice.'

'Which means he'll hand pick someone.'

'Or fill in for Dougary himself?'

'I doubt it,' said Rebus, 'but wouldn't it be just magic if he did? The only way of knowing is to keep the surveillance going till *something* happens one way or the other.'

'And meantime?'

'Meantime, we've got a ton more bookie's shops to check.' Rebus turned and gave Bowhill a smiling glance.

'But something tells me we've already had a yankee come up.'

'What's a yankee?' Siobhan asked, as Rebus unlocked and got into his car.

When they stopped for a bite to eat and some tea in Dunfermline, Rebus told her the story of Hutchy's and the man with the case full of cash. Her face twitched a little, as though her tea were too hot or the egg mayonnaise sandwich too strong.

'What was that name again?' she asked.

'Tommy Greenwood.'

'But he's in the Cafferty file.'

'What?' It was Rebus's turn to twitch.

'Tommy Greenwood, I'm sure it is. He's ... he *was* one of Cafferty's associates years ago. Then he disappeared from the scene, like so many others. They'd quarrelled about equal shares, or something.'

'Sounds like a boulder round the balls and the old heave-ho off a bridge.'

'As you say, it's a mobile profession.'

'Glub, glub, glub, all the way to the bottom.'

Siobhan smiled. 'So is it the real Tommy Greenwood or not?'

Rebus shrugged. 'If the bugger's had plastic surgery, it could be hard to tell. All the same, there are ways.' He was nodding to himself. 'Oh yes, there are ways.'

Ways which started with a friendly taxman ...


More than one person that Sunday read the story on the front page of their morning paper with a mixture of anguish, fear, guilt, and fury. Telephone calls were made. Words were exchanged like bullets. But being Sunday, there wasn't much anyone could do about the situation except, if they were of a mind, pray. If the off-licences had been open, or the supermarkets and grocer's shops allowed to sell alcohol, they might have drowned their sorrows or assuaged their anger. As it was, the anger just built, and so did the anguish. Block by block, the structure neared completion. A roof, that was all it lacked. Something to keep the pressure in, or nature's forces out.

And it was all because of John Rebus. This was more or less agreed. John Rebus was out there with a battering ram, and more than one person was of a mind to unlock the door and let him in – let him into *their* lair. And then lock the door after him.

# 28

The meeting in Farmer Watson's office had been arranged
for nine in the morning. Presumably, they wanted Rebus
at his groggiest and most supine. He might growl loudly
in the morning, but he didn't normally start biting till
afternoon. That everyone from Watson to the canteen
staff knew he was being fitted up didn't make things any
less awkward. For a start, the investigation into the
Central Hotel murder wasn't official, and Watson still
wasn't keen to sanction it. So Rebus had been working
rogue anyway. Give the Farmer his due, he looked after
his team. They managed between them to concoct a story
whereby Rebus had been given permission to do some
digging into the files on his own time.

'With a view towards the case perhaps being reopened
at a later date as fresh evidence allowed,' said the Farmer.
His secretary, a smart woman with a scary taste in hair
colourants, copied down these closing words. 'And date it
a couple of weeks ago.'

'Yes, sir,' she said.

When she'd left the room, Rebus said, 'Thank you, sir.'
He'd been standing throughout the proceedings, there
being space for just the one chair, the one the secretary
had been seated on. He now stepped gingerly over piles
of files and placed his bum where hers had latterly
been.

'I'm covering *my* hide as well as yours, John. And not
a word to anyone, understand?'

'Yes, sir. What about Inspector Flower, won't he suspect? He's bound to complain to Chief Inspector Lauderdale at least.'

'Good. Him and Lauderdale can have a chinwag. There's something you've got to understand, John.' Watson clasped his hands together on the desk, his head sinking into huge rounded shoulders. He spoke softly. 'I *know* Lauderdale's after my job. I know I can trust him as far as I'd trust an Irish scoor-oot.' He paused. 'Do *you* want my job, Inspector?'

'No fear.'

Watson nodded. 'That's what I mean. Now, I know you're not going to be sitting on your hands for the next week or two, so take some advice. The law can't be tinkered with the way you tinker with an old car. *Think* before you do anything. And remember, stunts like buying a gun can get you thrown off the force.'

'But I didn't buy it, sir,' said Rebus, reciting the story they'd thought up, 'it came into my possession as a potential piece of evidence.'

Watson nodded. 'Quite a mouthful, eh? But it might just save your bacon.'

'I'm vegetarian, sir,' Rebus said. A statement which caused Watson to laugh very loudly indeed.

They were both more than a little interested in what was happening in Gorgie. The initial news had not seemed promising. Nobody had turned up at the office, nobody at all. An extra detail was now keeping a watch on the hospital where Dougary lay in traction. If nothing happened at the Gorgie end, they'd switch to the hospital until Dougary was up and about. Maybe he'd keep working from his bedside. Stranger things had happened.

But at eleven-thirty, a brightly polished Jag pulled into the taxi lot. The chauffeur, a huge man with long straight hair, got out, and when he opened the back door, out stepped Morris Gerald Cafferty.

'Got you, you bastard,' hissed DS Petrie, firing off a whole roll of film in the excitement. Siobhan was already telephoning St Leonard's. And after talking with CI Lauderdale, as instructed (though *not* by Lauderdale) she phoned Arden Street. Rebus picked up the phone on its second ring.

'Bingo,' she said. 'Cafferty's come calling.'

'Make sure the photographs are dated and timed.'

'Yes, sir. How did the meeting go?'

'I think the Farmer's in love with me.'

'They're both going in,' said Petrie, at last lifting his finger from the shutter release. The camera motor stopped. Madden, who had come over to the window to watch, asked who they were.

At the same time, Rebus was asking a similar question. 'Who's with Big Ger?'

'His driver.'

'Man mountain with long hair?'

'That's him.'

'That's also the guy who got his ear eaten by Davey Dougary.'

'No love lost there, then?'

'Except now the man mountain's working for Big Ger.' He thought for a moment. 'Knowing Big Ger, I'd say he put him on the payroll just to piss off Dougary.'

'Why would he do that?'

'His idea of a joke. Let me know when they come out again.'

'Will do.'

She phoned him back half an hour later. 'Cafferty's taken off again.'

'He didn't stay long.'

'But listen, the chauffeur stayed put.'

'What?'

'Cafferty drove off alone.'

'Well, I'll be buggered. He's putting the man mountain in charge of Dougary's accounts!'

'He must trust him.'

'I suppose he must. But I can't see the big chap having much experience running a book. He's strictly a guard dog.'

'Meaning?'

'Meaning Big Ger will have to nurse him along. Meaning Big Ger will be down at that office practically every day. It couldn't be better!'

'We'd better get in some more film, then.'

'Aye, don't let that stupid bugger Petrie run out again. How's his face by the way?'

'Itchy, but it hurts when he scratches.' Petrie glanced over, so she told him, 'Inspector Rebus was just asking after you.'

'Was I buggery,' said Rebus. 'I hope his nose drops off and falls in his thermos.'

'I'll pass your good wishes on, sir,' said Siobhan.

'Do that,' replied Rebus. 'And don't be shy about it either. Right, I'm off to a funeral.'

'I was talking to Brian, he said he's a pall-bearer.'

'Good,' said Rebus. 'That means I'll have a shoulder to cry on.'

Warriston Cemetery is a sprawling mix of graves, from the ancient (and sometimes desecrated) to the brand new. There are stones there whose messages have been eroded away to faint indents only. On a sunny day, it can be an educational walk, but at nights the local Hell's Angels chapter have been known to party hard, recreating scenes more like New Orleans voodoo than Scottish country dancing.

Rebus felt Eddie would have approved. The ceremony itself was simple and dignified, if you ignored the wreath in the shape of an electric guitar and the fact that he was to be buried with an Elvis LP cover inside the casket.

Rebus stood at a distance from proceedings, and had turned down an invitation by Pat Calder to attend the reception afterwards, which was to be held not in the hollow Heartbreak Cafe but in the upstairs room of a nearby hostelry. Rebus was tempted for a moment – the chosen pub served Gibson's – but shook his head the way he'd shaken Calder's hand: with regrets.

Poor Eddie. For all that Rebus hadn't really known him, for all that the chef had tried scalping him with a panful of appetisers, Rebus had liked the man. He saw them all the time, people who could have made so much of their lives, yet hadn't. He knew he belonged with them. The losers.

But at least I'm still alive, he thought. And God willing nobody will dispatch me by funneling alcohol down my throat before turning on the gas. It struck him again: why the need for the funnel? All you had to do was take Eddie to any bar and he'd willingly render himself unconscious on tequila and bourbon. You didn't *need* to force him. Yet Dr Curt had tossed his liver in the air and proclaimed it a fair specimen. That was difficult to accept, except that he'd seen it with his own eyes.

Or had he?

He peered across the distance to where Pat Calder was taking hold of rope number one, testing it for tensile strength. Brian was number four, which meant he stood across the casket from Calder and sandwiched between two men Rebus didn't know. The barman Toni was number six. But Rebus's eyes were on Calder. Oh Jesus, you bastard, he thought. You didn't, did you? Then again, maybe you did.

He turned and ran, back to where his car was parked out on the road outside the cemetery. His destination was Arden Street.

Arden Street and the reservations book for the Heart-break Cafe.

As he saw it, Rebus had two choices. He could kick the door down, or he could try to open it quietly. It was a snib lock, the kind a stiff piece of plastic could sometimes open. Of course, there was a mortice deadlock too, but probably not engaged. When he pushed and pulled the door, there was enough give in it to suggest this was probably true. Only the snib then. But the gap where door met jamb was covered by a long strip of ornamental wood. This normally wouldn't deter a burglar, who would take a crowbar to it until he had access to the gap.

But Rebus had forgotten to pack his crowbar.

A rap with the door-knocker wouldn't elicit a response, would it? But he didn't fancy his chances of shouldering or kicking the door down, snib-lock or not. So he crouched down, opened the letterbox with one hand, put his eyes level with it, and reached up his other hand to the black iron ring, giving it five loud raps: shave-and-a-haircut, some people called it. It signalled a friend; at least, that's what Rebus hoped. There was neither sound nor move-ment from the inside of the maisonette. The Colonies was daytime quiet. He could probably crowbar the door open without anyone noticing. Instead, he tried the knocker again. The door had a spy-hole, and he was hoping someone might be intrigued enough to want to creep to the spy-hole and take a look.

Movement now, a shadow moving slowly from the living area towards the hall. Moving stealthily. And then a head sticking out of the doorway. It was all Rebus needed.

'Hello, Eddie,' he called. 'I've got your wreath here.'

Eddie Ringan let him in.

He was dressed in a red silk kimono-style gown with a fierce dragon crawling all down its back. On the arms

267

were symbols Rebus didn't understand. They didn't worry him. Eddie flopped onto the sofa, usually Rebus's perch, so Rebus made do with standing.

'I was lying about the wreath,' he said.

'It's the thought that counts. Nice suit, too.'

'I had to borrow the tie,' said Rebus.

'Black ties are cool.' Eddie looked like death warmed up. His eyes were dark-ringed and bloodshot, and his face resembled a prisoner's: sunless grey, lacking hope. He scratched himself under the armpit. 'So how did it go?'

'I left just as they were lowering you away.'

'They'll be at the reception now. Wish I could have done the catering myself, but you know how it is.'

Rebus nodded. 'It's not easy being a corpse. You'd have found that out.'

'Some people have managed quite nicely in the past.'

'Like Radiator McCallum and the Robertson brothers?'

Eddie produced a grim smile. 'One of those, yes.'

'You must be pretty desperate to stage your own death.'

'I'm not saying anything.'

'That's fine.' There was silence for a minute until Eddie broke it.

'How did you find out?'

Rebus absent-mindedly took a cigarette from the pack on the mantelpiece. 'It was Pat. He made up this unnecessarily exaggerated story.'

'That's Pat for you. Amateur fucking dramatics all the way.'

'He said Willie stormed out of the restaurant after sticking his face in some poor punter's plate. I checked with a couple of the people who ate there that night. A quick phone call was all it took. Nobody saw anything of the sort. Then there was the dead man's liver. It was in good nick, so it couldn't possibly have been yours.'

'You can say that again.'

Rebus was about to light up. He caught himself, lifted

the cigarette from his mouth, and placed it beside the packet.

'Then I checked missing persons. Seems Willie hasn't been back to his digs in a few days. The whole thing was amateurish, Eddie. If the poor bugger hadn't got his face blown away in the explosion, we'd've known straight away it wasn't you.'

'Would you? We wondered about that, we reckoned with Brian off the scene and Haymarket not your territory, it might just work.'

Rebus shook his head. 'For a start, we take photographs, and I'd have seen them sooner or later. I always do.' He paused. 'So why did you kill him?'

'It was an accident.'

'Let me guess, you came back late to the restaurant after a pretty good bender. You were angry as hell to see Willie had coped. You had a fight, he smashed his head. Then you had an idea.'

'Maybe.'

'There's only one rotten thing about the whole story,' said Rebus. Eddie shifted on the sofa. He looked ridiculous in the kimono, and had folded his arms protectively. He was staring at the fireplace, avoiding Rebus altogether.

'What?' he said finally.

'Pat said Willie ran out of the Cafe on *Tuesday* night. His body wasn't found until Thursday morning. If he'd died in a fight on Tuesday, lividity and rigor mortis would have told the pathologist the body was old. But it wasn't, it was fresh. Which means you didn't booze him up and gas him until early Thursday morning. You must've kept him alive all day Wednesday, knowing pretty well what you were going to do with him.'

'I'm not saying anything.'

'No, *I'm* saying it. Like I say, a desperate remedy, Eddie. About as desperate as they come. Now come on.'

'What?'

'We're taking a drive.'

'Where to?'

'Down to the station, of course. Get some clothes on.' Rebus watched him try to stand up. His legs took a while to lock upright. Yes, murder could do that to you. It was the opposite of rigor mortis. It was liquefaction, the jelly effect. It took him a long time to dress, Rebus watching throughout. There were tears in Eddie's eyes when he finished, and his lips were wet with saliva.

Rebus nodded. 'You'll do,' he said. He fully intended taking Eddie to St Leonard's.

But they'd be taking the scenic route.

'Where are we going?'

'A little drive. Nice day for it.'

Eddie looked out of the windscreen. It was a uniform grey outside, buildings and sky, with rain threatening and the breeze gaining force. He started to get the idea when they turned up Holyrood Park Road, heading straight for Arthur's Seat. And when Rebus took a right, away from Holyrood and in the direction of Duddingston, Eddie started to look very worried indeed.

'You know where we're going?' Rebus suggested.

'No.'

'Oh well.'

He kept driving, drove all the way up to the gates of the house and signalled with his indicator that he was turning into the drive.

'Christ, no!' yelped Eddie Ringan. He tucked his knees in front of him, wedging them against the dashboard like he thought they were about to crash. Instead of turning in at the gates, Rebus cruised past them and stopped kerbside. You caught a glimpse of Cafferty's mansion from here. Presumably, if someone up at the house were looking out of the right window, they could see the car.

'No, no.' Eddie was weeping.

'You *do* know where we are,' Rebus said, voicing surprise. 'You know Big Ger, then?' He waited till Eddie nodded. The chef had assumed a foetal position, feet on the seat beneath him, head tucked into his knees. 'Are you scared of him?' Eddie nodded again. 'Why?' Slowly, Eddie shook his head. 'Is it because of the Central Hotel?'

'Why did I have to tell Brian?' It was a loud yell, all the louder for being confined by the car. 'Why the fuck am I so stupid?'

'They've found the gun, you know.'

'I don't know anything about that.'

'You never saw the gun?'

Eddie shook his head. Damn, Rebus had been expecting more. 'So what did you see?'

'I was in the kitchens.'

'Yes?'

'This guy came running in, screaming at me to turn on the gas. He looked crazy, spots of blood on his face ... in his eyelashes.' Eddie was calming as the exorcism took effect. 'He started to turn on all the gas rings. Not lighting them. He looked so crazy, I helped him. I turned on the gas, just like he told me to.'

'And then?'

'I got out of there. I wasn't sticking around. I thought the same as everybody else: it was for the insurance money. Till they found the body. A week later, I got a visit from Big Ger. A *painful* visit. The message was: never say a word, not a word about what happened.'

'Was Big Ger there that night?'

Eddie shrugged. Damn him again! 'I was in the kitchens. I only saw the crazy guy.'

Well, Rebus knew who *that* was – someone who'd seen the state of the Central kitchens. 'Black Aengus?' he asked.

Eddie didn't say anything for a few minutes, just stared blearily out of the windscreen. Then: 'Big Ger's bound to find out I said something. Every now and then he sends another warning. Nothing physical ... not to me, at least. Just to let me know he remembers. He'll kill me.' He turned his head to Rebus. 'He'll kill me, and all I did was turn on the gas.'

'The man with the blood, it was Aengus Gibson, wasn't it?'

Eddie nodded slowly, screwing shut his eyes and wringing out tears. Rebus started the car. As he was driving off, he saw the 4x4 coming towards him from the opposite direction. It was signalling to pull into the gates, and the gates themselves were opening compliantly. The car was driven by a thug whose face was new to Rebus. In the back seat sat Mo Cafferty.

It bothered him, during the short drive back to St Leonard's, with Eddie bawling and huddled in the passenger seat. It bothered him. Could Mo Cafferty drive at all? That would be easy enough to check: a quick chat with DVLC. If she couldn't, if she needed a chauffeur, then who was driving the 4x4 that day Rebus had seen it parked outside Bone's? And wasn't *that* quite a coincidence anyway? John Rebus didn't believe in coincidences.

'The Heartbreak Cafe didn't get its meat from Bone's, did it?' he asked Eddie, who misinterpreted the question. 'I mean Bone's the butcher's shop,' Rebus explained. But Eddie shook his head. 'Never mind,' said Rebus.

Back at St Leonard's, the very person he wanted to see was waiting for him.

'Why aren't you out at Gorgie?' he asked.

'Why aren't you on suspension?' Siobhan Clarke asked back.

'That's below the belt. Besides, I asked first.'

'I had to come and pick up these.' She waved a huge brown envelope at him.

'Well, listen, I've got a little job for you. Several, in fact.

First, we need to have Eddie Ringan's casket back up out of the ground.'

'What?'

'It's not Eddie inside, I've just put him in the cells. You'll need to interview and book him. I'll tell you all about it.'

'I'm going to need to write all this down.'

'No you won't, your memory's good enough.'

'Not when my brain's in shock. You mean that wasn't Eddie in the oven?'

'That's what I mean. Next, check and see if Mo Cafferty has a driving licence.'

'What for?'

'Just do it. And do you remember telling me that when Bone won his Merc, he put up *his share* of the business to cover the bet? Your words: his share.'

'I remember. His wife told me.'

Rebus nodded. 'I want to know who owns the other half.'

'Is that all, sir?'

Rebus thought. 'No, not quite. Check Bone's Merc. See if anyone owned it before him. That way, we'll know who he won it from.' He looked at her unblinking. 'Quick as you can, eh?'

'Quick as I can, sir. Now, do you want to know what's in the envelope? It's for the man who has everything.'

'Go on then, surprise me.'

So she did.

Rebus was so surprised, he bought her coffee and a dough-ring in the canteen. The X-rays lay on the table between them.

'I don't believe this,' he kept saying. 'I really don't believe this. I put out a search for these *ages* ago.'

'They were in the records office at Ninewells.'

'But I *asked* them!'

'But did you ask nicely?'

Siobhan had explained that she'd been able to take a few trips to Dundee, chatting up anyone who might be useful, and especially in the chaotic records department, which had been moved and reorganised a few years before, leaving older records an ignored shambles. It had taken time. More than that, she'd had to promise a date to the young man who'd finally come up with the goods.

Rebus held up one of the X-rays again.

'Broken right arm,' Siobhan confirmed. 'Twelve years ago. While he was living and working in Dundee.'

'Tam Roberston,' Rebus said simply. That was that then: the dead man, the man with the bullet wound through his heart, the bullet from Rebus's Colt 45, was Tam Robertson.

'Difficult to prove in a court of law,' Siobhan suggested. True enough, you'd need more than hearsay and an X-ray to prove identity to a jury.

'There are ways,' said Rebus. 'We can try dental records again, now we've got an idea who the corpse is. Then there's superimposition. For the moment, it's enough for me that *I'm* satisfied.' He nodded. 'Well done, Clarke.' He started to get up.

'Sir?'

'Yes?'

She was smiling. 'Merry Christmas, sir.'

# 29

He phoned Gibson's Brewery, only to be told that 'Mr Aengus' was attending an ale competition in Newcastle, due back later tonight. So he called the Inland Revenue and spoke for a while to the inspector in charge of his case. If he was going to confront Tommy Greenwood, he'd need all the ammo he could gather ... bad metaphor considering, but true all the same. He left his car at St Leonard's while he went for a walk, trying to clear his head. Everything was coming together now. Aengus Gibson had been playing cards with Tam Robertson, and had shot him. Then set fire to the hotel to cover up the murder. It should all be tied up, but Rebus's brain was posing more questions than answers. Was it likely Aengus carried a gun around with him, even in his wild days? Why didn't Eck, also present, seek revenge for his brother? Wouldn't Aengus have had to shut him up somehow? Was it likely that only three of them were involved in the poker game? And who had delivered the gun to Deek Torrance? So many questions.

As he came down onto South Clerk Street, he saw that a van was parked outside Bone's. A new plate-glass window was being installed in the shop itself, and the van door was open at the back. Rebus walked over to the van and looked in the back. It had been a proper butcher's van at one time, and nobody had bothered changing it. You climbed a step into the back, where there were counters and cupboards and a small fridge-freezer. The van would have had its usual rounds of the housing schemes in the city, housewives and retired folk queuing for meat rather than travelling to a shop. A man in a white apron came out of Bone's with an ex-pig hoisted on his shoulder.

'Excuse me,' he said, carrying the carcass into the van.

'You use this for deliveries?' Rebus asked.

The man nodded. 'Just to restaurants.'

'I remember when a butcher's van used to come by our way,' Rebus reminisced.

'Aye, it's not economic these days, though.'

'Everything changes,' said Rebus. The man nodded agreement. Rebus was examining the interior again. To get behind the counter, you climbed into the van, pulled a hinged section of the counter up, and pushed open a narrow little door. Narrow: that's what the back of the van was. He remembered Michael's description of the van he'd been shunted about in. A narrow van with a smell. As the man came out of the van, he disturbed something with his foot. It was a piece of straw. Straw in a butcher's van? None of the animals carried in here had seen straw for a while.

Rebus looked into the shop. A young assistant was watching the glass being installed.

'Open for business, sir,' he informed Rebus cheerily.

'I was looking for Mr Bone.'

'He's not in this afternoon.'

Rebus nodded towards the van. 'Do you still do runs?'

'What, house-to-house?' The young man shook his head. 'Just general deliveries, bulk stuff.'

Yes, Rebus would agree with that.

He walked back up to St Leonard's, and caught Siobhan again. 'I forgot to say ...'

'More work?'

'Not much more. Pat Calder, you'll need to bring him in for questioning too. He'll be back home by now and getting frantic wondering where Eddie's sloped off to. I'm just sorry I won't be around for the reunion. I suppose I can always catch it in court ...'

It had been quite a day already, and it wasn't yet six o'clock. Back in the flat, the students were cooking a lentil curry while Michael sat in the living room reading another book on hypnotherapy. It had all become very settled in the flat, very ... well, the word that came to mind was *homely*. It was a strange word to use about a bunch of teenage students, a copper and an ex-con, yet it seemed just about right.

Michael had finished the tablets, and looked the better for it. He was supposed to arrange a check-up, but Rebus was dubious: they'd probably only stick him on more tablets. The scars would heal over naturally. All it took was time. He'd certainly regained his appetite: two helpings of curry.

After the meal they all sat around in the living room, the students drinking wine, Michael refusing it, Rebus supping beer from a can. There was music, the kind that never went away: the Stones and the Doors, Janis Joplin, very early Pink Floyd. It was one of those evenings. Rebus felt absolutely shattered, and blamed it on the caffeine tablets he'd been taking. Here he'd been worrying about Michael, and all the time he'd been swallowing down his own bad medicine. They'd seen him through the weekend, sleeping little and thinking lots. But you couldn't go on like that forever. And what with the music and the beer and the relaxed conversation, he'd almost certainly fall asleep here on the sofa ...

'What was that?'

'Sounds like somebody smashed a bottle or something.'

The students got up to look out of the window. 'Can't see anything.'

'No, look, there's glass on the road.' They turned to

Rebus. 'Someone's broken your windshield.'

Someone had indeed broken his windshield, as he found when he wandered downstairs and into the street. Other neighbours had gathered at doors and windows to check the scene. But most of them were retreating now. There was a chunk of rock on the passenger seat, surrounded by jewels of shattered glass. Nearby a car was reversing lazily out of its parking spot. It stopped in the road beside him. The passenger side window went down.

'What happened?'

'Nothing. Just a rock through the windscreen.'

'What?' The passenger turned to his driver. 'Wait here a second.' He got out to examine the damage. 'Who the hell would want to do that?'

'How many names do you want?' Rebus reached into the car to pull out the rock, and felt something collide with the back of his head. It didn't make sense for a moment, but by then he was being dragged away from the car into the road. He heard a car reverse and stop. He tried to resist, clawing at the unyielding tarmac with his fingernails. Jesus, he was going to pass out. His head was trying to close all channels. Each thud of his heart brought intense new pain to his skull. Someone had opened a window and was shouting something, some warning or complaint. He was alone in the middle of the road now. The passenger had run back to the car and slammed the door shut. Rebus pushed himself onto all fours, a baby resisting gravity for the first time. He blinked, trying to see out of cloudy eyes. He saw headlights, and knew what they were going to do.

They were going to drive straight over him.

Sucker punch, and he'd fallen for it. The offer of help from your attacker routine. Older than Arthur's Seat itself. The car's engine roared, and the tyres squealed towards him, dragging the body of the car with them. Rebus wondered if he'd get the licence number before he died.

A hand grabbed the neck of his shirt and hauled, pulling him backwards out of the road. The car caught his legs, tossing one shoe up off his foot and into the air. The car didn't stop, or even slow down, just kept on up the slope to the top of the road, where it took a right and disappeared.

'Are you okay, John?'

It was Michael. 'You saved my life there, Mickey.' Adrenalin was mixing with pain in Rebus's body, making him feel sick. He threw up undigested lentil curry onto the pavement.

'Try to stand up,' said Michael. Rebus tried and failed.

'My legs hurt,' he said. 'Christ, do my legs hurt!'


The X-rays showed no breaks or fractures, not even a bone chipped. 'Just bad bruising, Inspector,' said the woman doctor at the Infirmary. 'You were lucky. A hit like that could have done a lot of damage.'

Rebus nodded. 'I suppose I should have known,' he said. 'I've been due a visit here as a patient. Christ knows I've been here enough recently as a visitor.'

'I'll just fetch you something,' said the doctor.

'Wait a second, doctor. Are your labs open in the evening?'

She shook her head. 'Why do you ask?'

'Nothing.'

She left the room. Michael came closer. 'How do you feel?'

'I don't know which hurts worse, my head or my left leg.'

'No great loss to association football.'

Rebus almost smiled, but grimaced instead. Any movement of his face muscles sent electric spurts through his brain. The doctor came back into the room. 'Here you are,' she said. This should help.'

Rebus had been expecting painkillers. But she was holding a walking stick.

It was an aluminium walking stick, hollow and therefore lightweight, with a large rubberised grip and adjustable height courtesy of a series of holes in its shaft, into which a locking-pin could be placed. It looked like some strange wind instrument, but Rebus was glad of it as he walked out of the hospital.

Back at the flat, however, one of the solicitous students said he had something better, and came back from his bedroom with a black wooden cane with a silver and bone handle. Rebus tried it. It was a good height for him.

'I bought it in a junk shop,' the student said, 'don't ask me why.'

'Looks like it should have a concealed sword,' said Rebus. He tried twisting and pulling at the handle, but nothing happened. 'So much for that.'

The police, who had talked to Rebus at the Infirmary, had also spoken to the students.

'This constable,' related the walking-stick owner, whose name Rebus was sure was Ed, 'I mean, he was looking at us like we were squatters, and he was asking, was Inspector Rebus in here with you? And we were nodding, yes he was. And the constable couldn't figure it out at all.' He started laughing. Even Michael smiled. Someone else made a pot of herbal tea.

Great, thought Rebus. Another story that would be doing the rounds: Rebus fills his flat with students, then sits around with them of an evening with wine and beer. At the Infirmary, they'd asked if he'd recognised either of the men. The answer was no. It was a mobile profession, after all ... One of the neighbours had caught the car's number plate. It was a Ford Escort, stolen only an hour or so before from a car park near the Sheraton on Lothian Road. They would find it abandoned quite soon, probably not far from Marchmont. There wouldn't be any fingerprints.

'They must've been crazy,' Michael said on the way home, Rebus having got them a lift in the back of a patrol car. 'Thinking they could pull a stunt like that.'

'It wasn't a stunt, Michael. Somebody's desperate. That story in yesterday's paper has really shaken them up.' After all, wasn't that exactly what he'd wanted? He'd sought a reaction, and here it was.

From the flat he telephoned an emergency windscreen replacement firm. It would cost the earth, but he needed the car first thing in the morning. He just prayed his leg wouldn't seize up in the night.

# 30

Which of course it did. He was up at five, practising walking across the living room, trying to unstiffen the joints and tendons. He looked at his left leg. A spectacular blood-filled bruise stretched across his calf, wrapping itself around most of the front of the leg too. If the bony front of his leg had taken the impact rather than the fleshy back, there would have been at the very least a clean break. He swallowed two paracetamol – recommended for the pain by the Infirmary doctor – and waited for morning proper to arrive. He'd needed sleep last night, but hadn't got much. Today he'd be living on his wits. He just hoped those wits would be sharp enough.

At six-thirty he managed the tenement stairs and hobbled to his car, now boasting a windscreen worth more than the rest of it put together. Traffic wasn't quite heavy yet coming into town, and non-existent heading out, so the drive itself was mercifully shortened. Pressing down on the clutch hurt all the way up into his groin. He took the coast road out to North Berwick, letting the engine labour rather than changing gears too often. Just the other side of the town, he found the house he was looking for. Well, an estate, actually, and not a housing estate. It must have been about thirty or forty acres, with an uninterrupted view across the mouth of the Forth to the dark lump of Bass Rock. Rebus wasn't much good at architecture; Georgian, he'd guess. It looked like a lot of the houses in Edinburgh's New Town, with fluted stone columns either side of the doorway and large sash windows, nine panes of glass to each half.

Broderick Gibson had come a long way since those days in his garden shed, pottering with homebrew recipes. Rebus parked outside the front door and rang the bell. The door was opened by Mrs Gibson. Rebus introduced himself.

'It's a bit early, Inspector. Is anything wrong?'

'If I could just speak to your son, please.'

'He's eating breakfast. Why don't you wait in the sitting-room and I'll bring you –'

'It's all right, mother.' Aengus Gibson was still chewing and wiping his chin with a cloth napkin. He stood in the dining-room doorway. 'Come in here, Inspector.'

Rebus smiled at the defeated Mrs Gibson as he passed her.

'What's happened to your leg?' Gibson asked.

'I thought you might know, sir.'

'Oh? Why?' Aengus had seated himself at the table. Rebus had been entertaining an image of silver service – tureens and hot-plates, kedgeree or kippers, Wedgewood plates, and tea poured by a manservant. But all he saw was a plain white plate with greasy sausage and eggs on it. Buttered toast on the side and a mug of coffee. There were two newspapers folded beside Aengus – Mairie's paper and the *Financial Times* – and enough crumbs around the table to suggest that mother and father had eaten already.

Mrs Gibson put her head round the door. 'A cup of coffee, Inspector?'

'No, thank you, Mrs Gibson.' She smiled and retreated.

'I just thought,' Rebus said to Aengus, 'you might have arranged it.'

'I don't understand.'

'Trying to shut me up before I can ask a few questions about the Central Hotel.'

'That again!' Aengus bit into a piece of toast.

'Yes, that again.' Rebus sat down at the table, stretching his left leg out in front of him. 'You see, I *know* you were there that night, long after Mr Vanderhyde left. I know you were at a poker game set up by two villains called Tam and Eck Robertson. I know someone shot and killed Tam, and I know you ran into the kitchens covered in blood and screaming for all the gas rings to be turned on. That, Mr Gibson, is what I know.'

Gibson seemed to have trouble swallowing the chewed toast. He gulped coffee, and wiped his mouth again.

'Well, Inspector,' he said, 'if that's what you know, I suggest you don't know very much.'

'Maybe you'd like to tell me the rest, sir?'

They sat in silence. Aengus toyed with the empty mug, Rebus waiting for him to speak. The door burst open.

'Get out of here!' roared Broderick Gibson. He was wearing trousers and an open-necked shirt, whose cuffs flapped for want of their links. Obviously, his wife had disturbed him halfway through dressing. 'I could have you arrested right this minute!' he said. 'The Chief Constable tells me you've been suspended.'

Rebus stood up slowly, making much of his injured leg. But there was no charity in Broderick Gibson.

'And stay away from us, unless you have the authority! I'll be talking to my solicitor this morning.'

Rebus was at the door now. He stopped and looked into Broderick Gibson's eyes. 'I suggest you do that, sir. And you might care to tell him where *you* were the night the Central Hotel burnt down. Your son's in serious trouble, Mr Gibson. You can't hide him from the fact forever.'

'Just get out,' Gibson hissed.

'You haven't asked about my leg.'

'What?'

'Nothing, sir, just wondering aloud ...'

As Rebus walked back across the large hallway, with

its paintings and candelabra and fine curving stairwell, he felt how cold the house was. It wasn't just its age or the tiled floor either; the place was cold at its heart.

He arrived in Gorgie just as Siobhan was pouring her first cup of decaf of the day.

'What happened to your leg?' she asked.

Rebus pointed with his stick to the man stationed behind the camera.

'What the hell are you doing here?'

'I'm relieving Petrie,' said Brian Holmes.

'I wonder what any of us is doing here,' said Siobhan. Rebus ignored her.

'You're off sick.'

'I was bored, I came back early. I spoke to the Chief Super yesterday and he okayed it. So here I am.' Holmes looked fine but sounded dour. 'There was an ulterior motive, though,' he said. 'I wanted to hear from Siobhan herself the story of Eddie and Pat. It all sounds so ... incredible. I mean, I *cried* at that cemetery yesterday, and the bastard I was crying for was sitting at home playing with himself.'

'He'll be playing with himself in jail soon,' said Rebus. Then, to Siobhan: 'Give me some of that coffee.' He drank two scalding swallows before passing the plastic cup back. 'Thanks. Any progress?'

'No one's arrived yet. Not even our Trading Standards companion.'

'I meant those other things.'

'What *did* happen to your leg?' Holmes asked. So Rebus told them all about it.

'It's my fault,' Holmes said, 'for getting you into this in the first place.'

'That's right, it is,' said Rebus, 'and as penance you can keep your eyes glued to that window.' He turned to Siobhan. 'So?'

She took a deep breath. 'So I interviewed Ringan and Calder yesterday afternoon. They've both been charged. I also checked and Mrs Cafferty doesn't have a driving licence, not under her married or her maiden name. Bone's Mercedes belonged to —'

'Big Ger Cafferty.'

'You already knew?'

'I guessed,' said Rebus. 'What about the other half of Bone's business?'

'Owned by a company called Geronimo Holdings.'

'Which in turn is owned by Big Ger?'

'And sweetly, the word Geronimo includes both his and his wife's names. So what do you make of it?'

'Looks to me like Ger probably won his half of the business in a bet with Bone.'

'Either that,' added Holmes, 'or he got it in lieu of protection money Bone couldn't afford.'

'Maybe,' said Rebus. 'But the bet's more likely.'

'After all,' said Siobhan, 'Bone won the car in a bet with Cafferty. They've gambled together in the past.'

Rebus nodded. 'Well, it all adds up to a tight connection between the two of them. And there's a tighter connection too, though I can't prove it just yet.'

'Hang on,' said Siobhan, 'if the stabbing and the smashed window are to do with protection or gambling, then they're to do with Cafferty. Which means, since Cafferty owns half the business, that Cafferty smashed his *own* window.'

Rebus was shaking his head. 'I didn't say they were to do with protection or gambling.'

'And where does the cousin fit in?' Holmes interrupted.

'My my,' commented Rebus, 'you *are* keen to be back, aren't you? I'm not sure exactly where Kintoul fits in, but I'm getting a fair idea.'

'Hold on,' said Holmes, 'here we are.'

They all watched as a battered purple mini drove up to

the taxi offices. When the driver's door opened, the man mountain squeezed himself out.

'Like toothpaste from the tube,' said Rebus.

'Christ,' added Holmes, 'he must've taken out the front seats.'

'All alone today,' Siobhan noted.

'I'll bet Cafferty drops in sometime, though,' said Rebus, 'just to check. He's been ripped off badly in the past, he won't want it happening again.'

'Ripped off badly?' Siobhan echoed. 'How do you know that?'

Rebus winked at her. 'It's an odds-on bet,' he said.

He had to wait till after lunch for the information he needed. He had it faxed to him at a local newsagent's. During the long wait in Gorgie, he'd discussed the case with Holmes and Siobhan. They both were of the same mind in one particular: nobody would testify against Cafferty. And of like minds in another: they couldn't even be sure Cafferty had anything to do with it.

'I'll find out this afternoon,' Rebus told them, heading out to pick up the fax.

He was getting used to walking with the cane, and as long as he kept moving, the leg itself didn't stiffen up. But he knew the drive to Cardenden wouldn't do him much good. He considered the train, but ruled it out in short order. He might want to escape from Fife in a hurry; and Scotrail's timetables just didn't fit the bill.

It was just after two-thirty when he pushed open the door of Hutchy's betting shop. The place was airless, smelling old and undusted. The cigarette butts on the floor were probably last week's. There was a two-thirty-five race, and a few punters lined the walls waiting for the commentary. Rebus didn't let the look of the place put him off. Nobody wanted to bet in a plush establishment: it meant the bookie was making too much money. These tawdry surroundings were all psychology. You might not be winning, the bookmaker was saying, but look at me, I'm not doing any better.

Except that he was.

Rebus noticed a half-familiar face studying the form on one of the newspapers pinned to the wall. But then this town was full of half-familiar faces. He approached the glass-partitioned desk. 'I'd like a word with Mr Greenwood, please.'

'Do you have an appointment?'

But Rebus was no longer talking to the woman. His attention was on the man who'd looked up from a desk behind her. 'Mr Greenwood, I'm a police officer. Can we have a word?'

Greenwood thought about it, then got up, unlocked the door of the booth, and came out. 'Round here,' he said, leading Rebus to the rear of the shop. He unlocked another door, letting them into a much cosier and more private office.

'Any trouble?' he asked immediately, sitting down and reaching into his desk drawer for a bottle of whisky.

'Not for me, sir,' Rebus said. He sat down opposite Greenwood and stared at him. Christ, it was difficult after all these years. But Midge's portrait wasn't so far off the mark. A chess player would be making ready to play a pawn; Rebus decided to sacrifice his queen. 'So, Eck,' he said, getting comfortable, 'how've things been?'

Greenwood looked around. 'Are you talking to me?'

'I suppose I must be. My name's not Eck. Do you want to keep playing games? Fine then, let's play games.' Greenwood was pouring himself a large whisky. 'Your name is Eck Robertson. You fled from the Cafferty gang taking with you quite a lot of Big Ger's money. You also took another man's identity – Thomas Greenwood. You knew Tommy wouldn't complain because he was dead.

Another one of Big Ger's incredible disappearing acts. You took his name and his identity, and you set up for yourself in the arse-end of Fife, living out of a suitcase full of money till you got this place in profit.' Rebus paused. 'How am I doing?'

Greenwood, *aka* Eck Robertson, swallowed loudly and refilled his glass.

'You took too much of Greenwood's identity, though. When you set up here, Inland Revenue got onto you for an unpaid income tax bill. You wrote to them, and eventually you paid up.' Rebus brought the faxed sheets from his pocket. 'I've got a copy of your letter here, along with some earlier stuff from the *real* Thomas Greenwood. Wait till a handwriting expert gets hold of them in court. Have you ever seen those guys work on a jury? It's like Perry Mason. Even I can see the signatures aren't the same.'

'I changed my writing style.'

Rebus smiled. 'Changed your face too. Dyed hair, shaved off your moustache, contact lenses ... tinted. Your eyes used to be hazel, didn't they, Eck?'

'I keep telling you, my name's –'

Rebus got up. 'Whatever you say. I'm sure Big Ger will recognise you quick enough.'

'Wait a minute, sit down.' Rebus sat and waited. Eck Robertson tried to smile. He flicked on his radio for a moment and listened to the race, then flicked it off again. A six-to-one shot had romped home.

'Another win for the bookies,' Rebus said. 'Always liked the horses, didn't you? Not as much as Tam, though, Tam just loved betting. He bet you he could screw money out of Big Ger without Ger noticing. Creaming it off just a little at a time, but it all mounted up. Here.' Rebus tossed the drawing of Tam Robertson onto the desk. 'Here's what he might look like these days if Big Ger hadn't found out.'

Eck Robertson stared at the drawing, tracing a finger over it.

'You had to do a runner before Big Ger caught you, so you took the money. Then Radiator ran too. After all, he'd introduced the two of you into the gang. He'd be in for punishment too.' Rebus paused again. 'Or did Big Ger catch up with him?'

Robertson, eyes still on the drawing, shrugged.

'Well, whatever,' said Rebus. 'I think I'll have that whisky now.' His leg was hurting like blazes, his knuckles white on the handle of the cane. It took Robertson a while to pour the drink. 'So,' Rebus asked him, 'anything you want to add?'

'How did you find me?'

'Somebody spotted you.'

Robertson nodded. 'The chef, what's his name? Ringan? I saw him in some pub in Cowdenbeath. He looked like he was on a bender, so I got out fast. I didn't think he'd seen me, and if he had I didn't think he'd recognise me. I was wrong, eh?'

'You were wrong.' Rebus sipped the whisky like it was medicine on a spoon.

'It was Aengus Gibson,' Robertson said suddenly. 'Aengus Gibson had the gun.'

And then he told the rest of the story. Tam had been cheating at poker, as usual. But Aengus was on to him, and drew the gun. Shot Tam dead.

'We scarpered.'

'What?' Rebus was disbelieving. 'No thoughts of revenge? That young drunk had just killed your brother!'

'Nobody touched Black Aengus. He was Big Ger's pal. They got friendly after some misunderstanding, a break-in at Mo's flat. Big Ger had plans for him.'

'What sort of plans?'

Robertson shrugged. 'Just plans. You're right about the money. I knew I had to run while I could.'

'Why here, though?'

Robertson blinked. 'It was the last station on the line. Big Ger's never had much interest in Fife. It would mean tackling the Italians and the Orangemen.'

Rebus was doing some quick thinking. 'So what did Ger do when Aengus shot Tam?'

'How do you mean?'

'Eck, I *know* Big Ger was at the poker game. So what did he do?'

'He scarpered the same as the rest of us.'

So Big Ger *had* been there! Robertson's eyes were on his brother's portrait again. Rebus had a very good idea, too, what Cafferty's 'plans' for Aengus must have been. Imagine, having such a hold over someone who'd one day control the Gibson Brewing business. Such a hold all these years ...

'Who took away the gun, Eck?'

Eck shrugged again. Rebus got the idea he'd stopped listening. He rapped the edge of the desk with his cane. 'You went to a lot of trouble, Eck. Eddie Ringan appreciated that. He learned from you that it's possible to disappear. A handy lesson when Big Ger's after you. He *really* makes people disappear, doesn't he? Dumping them at sea like that. That's what he does, isn't it?'

'After a while, aye.'

Rebus frowned at this. But then Eck Robertson's next words hit him.

'Nobody notices a butcher's van.'

Rebus nodded, smiling. 'You're right about that.' He wet his lips. 'Eck, would you testify against him? In closed court, keep your new identity secret? Would you?'

But Eck Robertson was shaking his head. He was still shaking it when the door burst open. Ah, the half-remembered face from the form sheets. It was the pool player from the Midden.

'All right, Tommy?'

'Fine, Sharky, fine.' But 'Tommy Greenwood' didn't look it.

'Out you go, son,' said Rebus, 'Mr Greenwood and me have got business.'

Sharky ignored him. 'Want me to chuck him out, Tommy?'

Tommy Greenwood never got a chance to answer. Rebus pushed the handle of his cane hard up under Sharky's nose and then whipped it harder still against his knees. The young man crumpled. Rebus stood up. 'Handy thing, this,' he said. He pointed it at Eck Robertson. 'You can keep the picture as a reminder, Eck. Meantime, I'll be back. I want you to testify against Cafferty. Not now, not yet. Sometime after I've got him firm on a charge. And if you won't testify, I can always resurrect Eck Robertson. Think about it. One way or the other, Big Ger'll know.'

He was crossing the Forth Road Bridge when he heard the news on the radio.

'Aw Christ,' he said, stepping on the accelerator.

# 31

Rebus showed his ID as he drove through the brewery gates. There was only the one police car left at the scene, and no sign of an ambulance. Workers stood around in huddled, low-talking groups, passing round cigarettes and stories.

Rebus knew the detective sergeant. He worked out of Edinburgh West, and his unfortunate name was Robert Burns. This Burns was tall and bulky and red-haired, with freckles on his face. On Sunday afternoons, he could sometimes be found at the foot of the Mound, where he would lambast the strolling heathens. Rebus was glad to see Burns. You might get fire and brimstone with him, but you'd never get waffle.

Burns pointed to the huge aluminium tank. 'He climbed to the top.' Yes, Rebus could see all too clearly the metal stairwell which reached to the top of the tank, with walkways circling the tank every thirty feet or so. 'And when he got to the top, he jumped. A lot of the workers saw him, and they all said the same thing. He just climbed steadily till there were no more stairs, and then he threw himself off, arms stretched out. One of them said the dive was better than anything he'd seen in the Olympics.'

'That good, eh?' They weren't the only ones staring at the tank. Some of the workforce glanced up from time to time, then traced Aengus Gibson's descent. He'd hit the tarmac and crumpled like a concertina. There was a dent in the ground as though a boulder had been lifted from the spot.

'His father tried chasing after him,' Burns was saying. 'Didn't get very far. Old boy like that, it's a wonder his heart didn't give out. They had to help him down from the third circle.'

Rebus counted up three walkways. 'A bit of Dante, eh?' he said, winking at Burns.

'The old boy's saying it was an accident.'

'Of course he is.'

'It wasn't, though.'

'Of course it wasn't.'

'I've got a dozen witnesses who say he jumped.'

'A dozen witnesses,' Rebus corrected, 'who'll change their minds if their jobs are on the line.'

'Aye, right enough.'

Rebus breathed in. He'd always liked that smell of hops, but from now on he knew it would smell differently to him. It would smell like this moment, played over time and time again.

'The Lord giveth and the Lord taketh away,' said Burns. 'What happened to your leg, by the way?'

'Ingrown toenails,' said Rebus. 'The Lord gave them, the Infirmary took them away.'

Burns was shaking his head at this easy blasphemy when a window in the building behind them opened.

'You!' shouted Broderick Gibson. 'You killed him! You did it!' His crooked finger, a finger he seemed unable to straighten, was mostly pointed at Rebus. His eyes were like wet glass, his breathing strained. Someone was trying to coax him gently back into the office, hands on his shoulders. 'There'll be a reckoning!' he called to Rebus. 'Mark my words. There'll come a reckoning!'

The old man was finally pulled inside, the window falling shut after him. The workers were looking over towards the two policemen.

'He must be one of yours,' said Rebus, making for his car.

That was that then. Aengus Gibson had shot and killed Tam Robertson, and now Aengus was dead. End of story. Rebus could think of one person not in Aengus's family who was going to be very upset: Big Ger Cafferty. Cafferty had protected Black Aengus, maybe even blackmailed him, all the time waiting for the day when the young man would take over the brewery. With Aengus dead, the whole edifice fell, and good riddance to it.

Still, there was no comeback for Cafferty, no punishment.

Back at the flat, Michael had some news.

'The doc's been trying to get you.'

'Which one? I've seen so many recently.'

'Dr Patience Aitken. She seems to think you're avoiding her. Sounds like the ploy's working, too.'

'It's not a ploy. I've just had a lot on my plate.'

'And if you don't finish it, you won't get afters.' Michael smiled. 'She sounds nice, by the way.'

'She *is* nice. I'm the arsehole.'

'So go see her.'

Rebus flopped onto the sofa. 'Maybe I will. What are you reading?' Michael showed him the cover. 'Another book on hypnotherapy. You must have exhausted the field.'

'I've just been scratching the surface.' Michael paused. 'I'm going to take a course.'

'Oh?'

'I'm going to become a hypnotherapist. I mean, I know I can hypnotise people.'

'You can certainly get them to take their trousers off and bark like dogs.'

'Exactly, it's about time I put it to better use.'

'They say laughter is the best medicine.'

'Shut up, John, I'm trying to be serious. And I'm moving back in with Chrissie and the kids.'

'Oh?'

'I've talked with her. We've decided to try again.'

'Sounds romantic.'

'Well, one of us has got to have some romance in his soul.' Michael picked up the telephone and handed it to Rebus. 'Now phone the doctor.'

'Yes, sir,' said Rebus.


Broderick Gibson had clout, there was no denying it. On Wednesday morning the newspapers reported the 'tragic accident' at the Gibson Brewery near Fountainbridge, Edinburgh. There were photos of Aengus, some in his Black Aengus days, others showing the later model at charity events. There wasn't a whisper of suicide. It was another cover-up by Aengus's father, another distortion of the truth. It had become just something Broderick Gibson did, a part of the routine.

At ten-fifteen, Rebus received a phone call. It was Chief Superintendent Watson.

'There's someone here to see you,' he said. 'I told him you're under suspension, but he's bloody insistent.'

'Who is it?' asked Rebus.

'Some blind old duffer called Vanderhyde.'

Vanderhyde was still waiting when Rebus arrived. He looked quite at ease, concentrating on the sounds around him. Chatter and phone calls and the clacking of key-boards. He was seated on a chair facing Rebus's desk. Rebus tiptoed painfully around him and sat down. He watched Matthew Vanderhyde for a couple of minutes. He was dressed in a dark suit, white shirt and black tie: mourning clothes. He carried a blue cardboard folder, which he rested on his thighs. His walking-stick rested against the side of his chair.

'Well, Inspector,' said Vanderhyde suddenly, 'seen enough?'

Rebus gave a wry smile. 'Good morning, Mr Vanderhyde. What gave me away?'

'You're carrying a cane of some kind. It hit the corner of your desk.'

Rebus nodded. 'I was sorry to hear –'

'No sorrier than his parents. They've worked hard over the years with Aengus. He has *been* hard work. Devilish hard at times. Now it's all gone to waste.' Vanderhyde leaned forward in his chair. Had he been sighted, his eyes would have been boring into Rebus's. As it was, Rebus could see his own face reflected in the double mirror of Vanderhyde's glasses. 'Did he deserve to die, Inspector?'

'He had a choice.'

'Did he?'

Rebus was remembering the priest's words. *Can you live the rest of your life with the memories and the guilt?* Vanderhyde knew Rebus wasn't about to answer. He nodded slowly, and sat back a little in his chair.

'You were there that night, weren't you?' Rebus asked.

'Where?'

'At the card game.'

'Blind men make poor card-players, Inspector.'

'A sighted person could help them.' Rebus waited. Vanderhyde sat stiff and straight like the wax figure of a Victorian. 'Maybe someone like Broderick Gibson.'

Vanderhyde's fingers played over the blue folder, gripped it, and passed it over the desk.

'Broderick wanted you to have this.'

'What is it?'

'He wouldn't say. All he did say was, he hoped you'll think it was worth it, though he himself doubts it.' Vanderhyde paused. 'Of course, I was curious enough to study it in my own particular way. It's a book of some kind.' Rebus accepted the heavy folder, and Vanderhyde took his own hand away, finding his walking-stick and resting the hand there. 'Some keys were found on Aengus.

They didn't seem to match any known lock. Last night, Broderick found some bank statements detailing monthly payments to an estate office. He knows the head of the office, so he phoned him. Aengus, it seems, had been leasing a flat in Blair Street.'

Rebus knew it, a narrow passage between the High Street and the Cowgate, balanced precariously between respectability and low living. 'Nobody knew about it?'

Vanderhyde shook his head. 'It was his little den, Inspector. A real rat's nest, according to Broderick. Mouldering food and empty bottles, pornographic videos ...'

'A regular bachelor pad.'

Vanderhyde ignored his levity. 'This book was found there.'

Rebus had already opened the folder. Inside was a large ring-bound notebook. It bore no title, but its narrow lines were filled with writing. A few sentences told Rebus what it was: Aengus Gibson's journal.

# 32

Rebus sat at his desk reading. Nobody bothered him, despite the fact that he was supposed to be suspended. The day grew sunless, and the office emptied slowly. He might as well have been in solitary confinement for all the notice he took. His phone was off its hook and his head, bowed over the journal, was hidden by his hands; a clear sign that he did not want to be disturbed.

He read the journal quickly first time through. After all, only some of the pages were germane. The early entries were full of wild parties, illicit coitus in country mansions with married women who were still 'names' even today, and more often with the daughters of those women. Arguments with father and mother, usually over money. Money. There was a lot of money in these early entries, money spent on travel, cars, champagne, clothes. However, the journal itself opened quite strangely:

Sometimes, mostly when I'm alone, but occasionally in company, I catch a glimpse of someone from the corner of my eye. Or think I do. When I look properly, there's nobody there. There may be some shape there, some interesting, unconscious arrangement of the edge of an open door and the window frame beyond it, or whatever, which gives the hint of a human shape. I mention the door and the window frame because it is the most recent example.

I am becoming convinced, however, that I really am

seeing things. And what I am seeing – being shown, to be more accurate – is myself. That other part of me. I went to church when I was a child, and believed in ghosts. I still believe in ghosts ...

Rebus skipped to the start of the next entry:

I can write this journal safe in the knowledge that whoever is reading it – yes you, dear reader – does so after my death. Nobody knows it is here, and since I have no friends, no confidants or confidantes, it is unlikely that anyone will sneak a look at it. A burglar may carry it off, of course. If so, shame on you: it is the least valuable thing in this flat, though it may become more valuable the longer I write ...

There were huge gaps in the chronology. A single year might garner half a dozen dated entries. Black Aengus, it seemed, was no more regular in keeping a diary than he was in anything else. Five years ago, though, there had been a spate of entries. The accidental break-in at Mo Johnson's flat; Aengus becoming friendly with Mo and being introduced by her to a certain Morris Cafferty. After a while, Cafferty became simply 'Big Ger' as Aengus and he met at parties and in pubs and clubs.

By far the longest entry, however, belonged to the one day Rebus was really interested in:

This isn't a bad place really. The nursing staff are understanding and ready with jokes and stories. They carry me with all gentleness back to my room when I find I've wandered from it. The corridors are long and mazey. I thought I saw a tree once in one corridor, but it was a painting on the window. A nurse placed my hand on the cold glass so I could be sure in my mind.

Like the rest of them, she refused to smuggle in any vodka.

From my window I can see a squirrel – a red squirrel, I think – leaping between trees, and beyond that hills covered with stunted foliage, like a bad school haircut.

But I'm not really seeing this pastoral scene. I'm looking into a room, a room where I think I'll be spending a great deal of my time, even after I've left this hospital.

Why did I ever try to talk my father into going to the poker game? I know the answer now. Because Cafferty wanted him there. And father was keen enough – there's still a spark in him, a spark of the wildness that has been his legacy to me. But he couldn't come. Had he been there, I wonder if things would have turned out differently.

I met Uncle Matthew in the bar. God, what a bore. He thinks that because he has dabbled with demons and the hobgoblins of nationalism he has some import in the world. I could have told him, men like Cafferty have import. They are the hidden movers and shakers, the deal–makers. Simply, they get things done. And God, what things!

Tam Robertson suggested that I join the poker game which was happening upstairs. The stake money required was not high, and I knew I could always nip over to Blair Street for more cash if needed. Of course, I knew Tam Robertson's reputation. He dealt cards in a strange manner, elbow jutting out and up. Though I couldn't fathom how, some people reckoned he was able to see the underside of the cards as he dealt. His brother, Eck, explained it away by saying Tam had broken his arm as a young man. Well, I'm no card sharp, and I expected to lose a few quid, but I was sure I'd know if anyone tried to cheat me.

But then the other two players arrived, and I knew I would not be cheated. One was Cafferty. He was with a man called Jimmy Bone, a butcher by trade. He looked like a butcher, too – puffy-faced, red-cheeked, with fingers as fat as link sausages. He had a just-scrubbed look too. You often get that with butchers, surgeons, workers in the slaughterhouse. They like to look cleaner than clean.

Now that I think of it, Cafferty looked like that too. And Eck. And Tam. Tam was always rubbing his hands, giving off an aroma of lemon soap. Or he would examine his fingernails and pick beneath them. To look at his clothes, you would never guess, but he was pathologically hygienic. I realise now – blessed hindsight! – that the Robertson brothers were not pleased to see Cafferty. Nor did the butcher look happy at having been cajoled into playing. He kept complaining that he owed too much as it was, but Cafferty wouldn't hear of it.

The butcher was a dreadful poker player. He mimed dejection whenever he had a bad hand, and fidgeted, shuffling his feet, when he had a good one. As the game wore on, it was obvious there was an undercurrent between Cafferty and the Robertsons. Cafferty kept complaining about business. It was slow, money wasn't what it was. Then he turned to me abruptly and slapped his palm against the back of my hand.

'How many dead men have you seen?'

In Cafferty's company, I affected more bravado even than usual, an effect achieved in most part by seeming preternaturally relaxed.

'Not many,' I said (or something offhand like that).

'Any at all?' he persisted. He didn't wait for an answer. 'I've seen dozens. Yes, dozens. What's more, Black Aengus, I've killed my fair share of them.'

He lifted his hand away, sat back and said nothing. The next hand was dealt in silence. I wished Mo were around. She had a way of calming him down. He was drinking whisky from the bottle, sloshing it around in his mouth before swallowing noisily. Sober, he is unpredictable; drunk, he is dangerous. That's why I like him. I even admire him, in a strange sort of way. He gets what he wants by any means necessary. There is something magnetic about that singularity of mind. And of course, in his company I am someone to be respected, respected by people who would normally call me a stuck-up snob and, as one person did, 'a pissed-up piece of shite'. Cafferty took exception when I told him I'd been called this. He paid the man responsible a visit.

What makes him want to spend time with me? Before that night, I'd thought maybe we saw fire in one another's eyes. But now I know differently. He spent time with me because I was going to be another means to an end. A final, bitter end.

I was drinking vodka, at first with orange, later neat – but always from a glass and always with ice. The Robertsons drank beer. They had a crate of bottles on the floor between them. The butcher drank whisky, whenever Cafferty deigned to pour him some, which wasn't often enough for the poor butcher. I was twenty quid down within a matter of minutes, and sixty quid down after a quarter of an hour. Cafferty placed his hand on mine again.

'If I'd not strayed along,' he said, 'they'd have had the shirt off your back and the breeks off your arse.'

'I never cheat,' said Tam Robertson. I got the feeling Cafferty had been wanting him to say something all along. Robertson acknowledged this by biting his lip.

Cafferty asked him if he was sure he didn't cheat. Robertson said nothing. His brother tried to calm things down, putting our minds back onto the game. But Cafferty grinned at Tam Robertson as he picked up his cards. Later, he started again.

'I've killed a lot of men,' he said, directing his eyes at me but his voice at the Robertsons. 'But not one of those killings wasn't justified. People who owed me, people who'd done me wrong, people who'd cheated. The way I look at it, everybody knows what he's getting into. Doesn't he?'

For want of any other answer, I agreed.

'And once you're into something, there are consequences to be faced, aren't there?' I nodded again. 'Black Aengus,' he said, 'have you ever *thought* about killing someone?'

'Many a time.'

This was true, though I wish now I'd held my tongue. I'd wanted to kill men wealthier than me, more handsome than me, men possessing beautiful women, and women who rejected my advances. I'd wanted to kill people who refused me service when drunk, people who didn't smile back when I smiled at them, people who were paged in hotels and made movies in Hollywood and owned ranches and castles and their own private armies. So my answer was accurate.

'Many a time.'

Cafferty was nodding. He'd almost finished the whisky. I thought something must be about to happen, some act of violence, and I was prepared for it – or thought I was. The Robertsons looked ready either to explode or implode. Tam had his hands on the edge of the table, ready to jump to his feet. And then the door opened. It was someone from the kitchens, bringing us up the sandwiches we'd ordered earlier. Smoked salmon and roast beef. The man waited to be paid.

'Go on, Tam,' said Cafferty quietly, 'you're the one with the luck tonight. Pay the man.'

Grudgingly, Tam counted out some notes and handed them over.

'And a tip,' said Cafferty. Another note was handed over. The waiter left the room. 'A very nice gesture,' said Cafferty. It was his turn to deal. 'How much are you down now, Black Aengus?'

'I'm not bad,' I said.

'I asked how much.'

'About forty.' I'd been a hundred down at one stage, but two decent hands had repaired some of the damage. Plus – there could be no doubt about it – the best card players around the table, by which I mean the Robertson brothers, were finding it hard to concentrate. The room was not warm, but there was sweat trickling down from Eck's sideburns. He kept rubbing the sweat away.

'You're letting them cheat you out of forty?' Cafferty said conversationally.

Tam Robertson leapt to his feet, his chair tipping over behind him.

'I've heard just about enough!'

But Eck righted the chair and pulled him down into it. Cafferty had finished dealing and was studying his cards, as though oblivious to the whole scene. The butcher got up suddenly, anouncing that he was going to be sick. He walked quickly out of the room.

'He won't be back,' Cafferty announced.

I said something lame to the effect that I was thinking of an early night myself. When Cafferty turned to me, he looked and sounded unlike any of his many personalities, the many I'd encountered so far.

'You wouldn't know an early night if it kicked you in the cunt.' He had started to gather up the cards for a redeal. I could feel blood tingling in my cheeks. He'd spoken with something close to revulsion. I told myself that he'd just drunk too much. People often said things . . . etc. Look at me, I was one to be upset about the nasty things drunks could say!

He dealt the hand again. When it came time for him to make his initial bet, he threw a note into the pot, then laid his cards face down on the table. He reached into the waistband of his trousers. He'd worn a suit throughout; he always looks smart. He says the police are warier of picking up people wearing good clothes, and certainly more wary about punching or kicking them.

'They don't like to see good material ruined,' he told me. 'Canny Scots, you see.'

Now, when he withdrew his hand from the waistband, it was holding a pistol of some kind. The Robertsons started to object, while I just stared at the gun. I'd seen guns before, but never this close and in this kind of situation. Suddenly, the vodka, which had been having little or no effect all night, swam through me like waste through a sewer-pipe. I thought I was going to be sick, but swallowed it down. I even thought I might pass out. And all the time Cafferty was talking calm as you like about how Tam had been cheating him and where was the money.

'And you've been cheating Black Aengus too,' he said. I wanted to protest that this wasn't true, but still thought I might be sick if I opened my mouth, so I just shook my head, after which I felt even dizzier. You can't know the pain and frustration I'm feeling as I try to write this down candidly and exactly. Fourteen weeks have passed since that night, but every night it comes back to me, waking and sleeping. They're giving me drugs here, and strictly no alcohol. During the day I can walk in the grounds. There are 'encounter groups' where I'm supposed to talk my way out of my problem. Christ, if it were only that easy! The first thing my father did was get me out of the way. I am tempted to say *his* way. His answer was to send me on holiday. Mother chaperoned me around New England, where an aunt has a house in Bar Harbor. I tried talking to mother, but didn't seem to make much sense. She had that stupid sympathetic smile pasted onto her face.

I digress, not that it matters. Back to the poker game. You've perhaps guessed what happened next. I felt Cafferty's hand on mine, only this time he lifted my hand up in his. Then he placed the gun in my hand. I can feel it now, cold and hard. Half of me thought the gun was fake and he was just going to scare the Robertsons. The other half knew the gun was real, but didn't think he would use it.

Then I felt his fingers pushing mine until my index finger was around the trigger. His hand now fully enclosed mine, and aimed the gun. He squeezed his finger against mine, and there was an explosion in the room, and wisps of acrid powder. Blood freckled us all. It was warm for a

306

moment, then cold against my skin. Eck was leaning over his brother, speaking to him. The gun clattered onto the table. Though I didn't take it in at the time, Cafferty proceeded to wrap the gun in a polythene bag. I know that any prints on it must be mine.

I flew up from the table, panicking, hysterical. Cafferty was seated still, and looking pacified. His calm had the opposite effect on me. I threw the vodka bottle against the wall, where it smashed, dousing wallpaper and curtains in alcohol. Seeing an idea, I grabbed a lighter from the table and ignited the vodka. Only now did Cafferty get up. He was swearing at me, and tried to douse the flames, but they were licking up the curtains out of our reach, scudding across the fabric wallcovering on the ceiling. He saw the fire was moving quicker than we could. I think Eck had already forsaken his brother and fled before I ran out of the room. I took the stairs three at a time and burst into the kitchens, demanding that all the gas be turned on. If the Central was going to burn, let it take the evidence with it.

I must have looked crazy enough, for the chef followed my instructions. I think he was the same person who served us the sandwiches, only he'd changed jackets. It was late, and he was alone in the kitchen, writing something down in a book. I told him to get out. He left by the back way, and I followed, keeping my head low as I jogged back to Blair Street.

I think that's everything. It doesn't feel any better for the writing down. There's no exorcism or catharsis. Maybe there never will be. You see, they've found the body. More than that, they know the man was shot. I don't see how the devil they can know, but they do. Maybe someone told them. Eck Robertson would have reason to. He's the only one who could tell. It's all my fault. I know that Cafferty started swearing at me because I'd mucked things up by setting fire to the room. If I hadn't, he would have seen to it that Tam Robertson's body disappeared in the usual way. No one would have known. We would have gotten away with murder.

But 'getting away with it' isn't always getting away with it. The corpse haunts me. Last night I dreamt it came back to me, charred, smouldering. Pointing a finger towards me and squeezing the trigger. Oh Christ, this is agony. And they think I'm here for alcoholism. I still haven't told father all of it, not yet. He knows, though. He knows I was there. But he's not saying anything. Sometimes I wish he'd hit me more as a child and not let me misbehave. He *liked* me to misbehave! 'We'll make a man of you,' he used to say. Father, I am made.

That was that. Rebus sat back in his chair and stared at the ceiling. Eddie Ringan knew a little more than he'd been telling. He'd been a witness at the card game and could place Cafferty there. No wonder he'd been running scared. Cafferty probably hadn't known him back then, hadn't paid attention to a waiter who was moonlighting anyway and not one of the regular staff.

Rebus rubbed his eyes and returned to the journal. There was a bit about a holiday, then about the hospital again. And then a few months later:

I saw Cafferty today (Sunday). Not my idea. He must have been following me. He caught up on Blackford Hill. I'd come through the Hermitage, climbing the steep face of the hill. He must have thought I was trying to get away from him. He pulled on my arm, swinging me around. I think I nearly jumped out of my skin.

He told me I had to keep my nose clean from now on. He said it was a good idea, going into that hospital. I think he was trying to let me know that he knew everything I'd been up to. I think I know what he's doing. He's biding his time. Watching me as I take instructions in the business.

Waiting for the day when I take over from my father. I think he wants it all, body and soul.

Yes, body and soul.

There was a lot more, the style and substance of the entries changing as Aengus too tried to change. He'd found it hard work. The public face, the charity face, masked a yearning for some of that wild past. Rebus flipped to the final entry, undated:

You know, dear friend or foe, I liked the feel of that gun in my hand. And when Cafferty put my finger on the trigger ... he *did* squeeze it. I'm certain of that. But supposing he hadn't? Would I still have fired, with his strong unfailing hand on mine? After all these years, all the bad dreams, the cold sweats and sudden surges, something has happened. The case is being reopened. I've spoken with Cafferty who tells me not to worry. He says I should concentrate my energies on the brewery. He seems to know more about our finances than I do. Father is talking of retiring next year. The business will be all mine, and all Cafferty's. I've seen him at charity functions, accompanied by Mo, and at various public occasions. We've talked, but never since that night have we enjoyed one another's company. I lost my usefulness that night. Perhaps I just showed my weakness by smashing the bottle. Or perhaps that had been the plan all along. He always gives me a wink when he sees me. But then he winks at just about everyone. But when he winks at me, when he closes his eye for that second, it's as if he's taking aim, setting me in his sights. Christ, is there no end in sight? If I weren't so scared, I'd be praying the police would find me. But Cafferty won't let them. He never will let them, never.

Rebus closed the journal. His heart was beating fast, hands trembling. You poor bugger, Aengus. When you read we'd got the gun, you thought we'd fingerprint it and then we'd come looking for you.

But instead, Cafferty had blown his trump trying to incriminate Rebus, just to keep him out of the picture for a while. And the irony of it all was, with the prints messed up, Black Aengus was in the clear – in the clear for a murder he didn't really commit.

Again, though, it was all uncorroborated. Rebus imagined the field day the defence would have if he walked into the Royal Mile courts with nothing more than the journal of a recovering dipsomaniac. The Edinburgh law courts were notoriously tough at the best of times. With the sort of advocate Cafferty could afford, it was a definite loser from the word go.

Yet Rebus *knew* he had to do something about Cafferty. The man deserved punishment, a million punishments. Let the punishment fit the crime, he thought. But he shook the notion away. No more guns.

He didn't go home, not right away. He walked out of the now-empty office and got into his car. And sat there, in the car park. The key was in the ignition, but he let it sit there. His hands rested lightly on the steering-wheel. After almost an hour, he started the engine, mostly because he was getting cold. He didn't go anywhere, except inside his head, and slowly but surely, with back-tracking and rerouting along the way, the idea came to him. Let the punishment fit the crime. Yes, but not Cafferty's punishment. No, not Cafferty's.

Andrew McPhail's.

# 33

Rebus didn't go near St Leonard's for a couple of days, though he did get a message from Farmer Watson that Broderick Gibson was considering bringing an action against him, for harrying his son.

'He's been harrying himself for years,' was Rebus's only comment.

But he was waiting in his car when they released Andy Steele. The fisherman cum private eye blinked into the sun. Rebus sounded his horn, and Steele approached warily. Rebus wound down his window.

'Oh, it's you,' said Steele. There was disappointment in his voice. Rebus had said he'd see what he could do for the young man, then had left him to languish, never coming near.

'They let you out, then,' said Rebus.

'Aye, on bail.'

'That's because someone put up the money for you.'

Steele nodded, then started. 'You?'

'Me,' said Rebus. 'Now get in, I've got a job for you.'

'What sort of job?'

'Get in and I'll tell you.'

There was a bit more life in Steele as he walked round to the passenger side and opened the door.

'You want to be a private eye,' stated Rebus. 'Fair enough. I've got a job for you.'

Steele seemed unable to take it in for a moment, then

cleared his head by shaking it briskly, rubbing his hands through his hair.

'Great,' he said. 'So long as it's not against the law.'

'Oh, it's nothing illicit. All I want you to do is talk to a few folk. They're good listeners too, shouldn't be any problem.'

'What am I going to tell them?'

Rebus started the car. 'That there's a contract out on a certain individual.'

'A contract?'

'Come on, Andy, you've seen the films. A contract.'

'A contract,' Andy Steele mouthed, as Rebus pulled into the traffic.

There was still no sign of Andrew McPhail. Alex Maclean, Rebus discovered, was back in circulation though not yet back at work. When Rebus visited Mrs Mackenzie, she said she hadn't seen a man with bandaged hands and face hanging around. But one of the neighbours had. Well, it didn't matter, McPhail wouldn't be coming back here again. He would probably write or telephone with a forwarding address, asking his landlady to send on his stuff. Rebus looked towards the school as he got back into his car. The children were in their own little world ... and safe.

He did a lot of driving, visiting schools and playparks. He knew McPhail must be sleeping rough. Maybe he was well away from Edinburgh by now. Rebus had a vision of him climbing up onto a coal train headed slowly south. A hand reached out and helped McPhail into the wagon. It was Deek Torrance. The opening credits began to roll ...

It didn't matter if he couldn't find McPhail; it would just be a nice touch. A nicely cruel touch.

Wester Hailes was a good place to get lost, meaning it was an easy place to get lost. Sited to the far west of the

312

city, visible from the bypass which gave Edinburgh such a wide berth, Wester Hailes was somewhere the city put people so it could forget about them. The architecture was unenthusiastic, the walls of the flat-blocks finished off with damp and cracks.

People might leave Wester Hailes, or stay there all their lives, surrounded by roads and industrial estates and empty green spaces. It had never before struck Rebus that it would make a good hiding place. You could walk the streets, or the Kingsknowe golf course, or the roads around Sighthill, and as long as you didn't look out of place you would be safe. There were places you could sleep without being discovered. And if you were of a mind, there was a school. A school and quite a few play-parks.

This was where, on the second day, he found Andrew McPhail. Never mind watching the bus and railway stations, Rebus had known where to look. He followed McPhail for three-quarters of an hour, at first in the car and then, when McPhail took a pedestrian shortcut, awkwardly on foot. McPhail kept moving, his gait brisk. A man out for a walk, that was all. A bit shabby maybe, but these days with unemployment what it was, you lost the will to shave every morning, didn't you?

McPhail was careful not to draw attention to himself. He didn't pause to stare at any children he saw. He just smiled towards them and went on his way. When Rebus had seen enough, he gained quickly and tapped him on the shoulder. He might as well have used a cattle-prod.

'Jesus, it's you!' McPhail's hand went to his chest. 'You nearly gave me a heart attack.'

'That would have saved Alex Maclean a job.'

'How is he?'

'Minor burns. He's up and about and on the warpath.'

'Christ's sake! We're talking about something that happened *years* ago!'

'And it's not going to happen again?'

'No!'

'And it was an accident you ended up living across from a primary school?'

'Yes.'

'And I was wrong to think I'd find you somewhere near a school or a playground . . .?'

McPhail opened his mouth, then closed it again. He shook his head. 'No, you weren't wrong. I still like kids. But I never . . . I'd never do anything to them. I won't even speak to them these days.' He looked up at Rebus. 'I'm *trying*, Inspector.'

Everyone wanted a second chance: Michael, McPhail, even Black Aengus. Sometimes, Rebus could help. 'Tell you what,' he said. 'There are programmes for past offenders. You could go into one of them, not in Edinburgh, somewhere else. You could sign on for social security and look for a job.' McPhail looked ready to say something. 'I know it takes money, a wee bit of cash to get you on your feet. But I can help with that too.'

McPhail blinked, one eye staying half closed. 'Why?'

'Because I want to. And afterwards, you'll be left alone, I promise. I won't tell anyone where you are or what's happened to you. Is it a deal?'

McPhail thought about it – for two seconds. 'A deal,' he said.

'Fine then.' Rebus put his hand on McPhail's shoulder again, drawing him a little closer. 'There's just one small thing I'd like you to do for me first . . .'

It had been quiet in the social club, and Chick Muir was thinking of heading home when the young chap at the bar asked if he could buy him a drink. Chick readily agreed.

'I don't like drinking on my own,' the young man explained.

'Who can blame you?' said Chick agreeably, handing

his empty glass to the barman. 'Not from round here?'

'Aberdeen,' said the young man.

'A long way from home. Is it still like Dallas up there?'

Chick meant the oil-boom, which had actually disappeared almost as quickly as it had begun, except in the mythology of those people not living in Aberdeen.

'Maybe it is,' said the young man, 'but that didn't stop them sacking me.'

'Sorry to hear it.' Chick really was too. He'd been hoping the young man was off the oil rigs with cash to burn. He was planning to tap him for a tenner, but now shrugged away the idea.

'I'm Andy Steele, by the way.'

'Chick Muir.' Chick placed his cigarette in his mouth so he could shake Andy Steele's hand. The grip was like a rubbish-crusher.

'The money didn't bring much luck to Aberdeen, you know,' Steele was reminiscing. 'Just a load of sharks and gangsters.'

'I'll believe it.' Muir was already halfway through his drink. He wished he'd been drinking a whisky instead of the half-pint when he'd been asked about another. It didn't look good exchanging a half-pint for a nip, so he was stuck with a half.

'That's mostly why I'm here,' said Steele.

'What? Gangsters?' Muir sounded amused.

'In a way. I'm visiting a friend, too, but I thought while I was here I might pick up a few bob.'

'How's that?' Chick was beginning to feel uncomfortable, but also distinctly curious.

Steele dropped his voice, though they were alone at the bar. 'There's word going around Aberdeen that someone's out to get a certain individual in Edinburgh.'

The barman had turned on the tape machine behind the bar. The low-ceilinged room was promptly filled with a folk duet. They'd played the club last week, and the barman had made a tape of them. It sounded worse now than it had then.

'In the name of Auld Nick, turn that down!' Chick didn't have a loud voice, but no one could say it lacked authority. The barman turned the sound down a bit, and when Chick still glared at him turned it even lower. 'What was that?' he asked Andy Steele. Andy Steele, who had been enjoying his drink, put down the glass and told Chick Muir again. And a little while later, mission accomplished, he bought Chick a final drink and then left.

Chick Muir didn't touch this fresh half pint. He stared past it at his own reflection in the mirror behind the row of optics. Then he made a few phone calls, again roaring at the barman to 'turn that shite off!' The third call he made was to St Leonard's, where he was informed, a bit too light-heartedly, he thought, that Inspector Rebus had been suspended from duty pending enquiries. He tried Rebus at his flat, but no joy there either. Ach well, it wasn't so important. What mattered was that he'd talked to the big man. Now the big man owed him, and that was quite enough for the penniless Chick Muir to be going on with.

Andy Steele gave the same performance in a meanly lit pub and a betting shop, and that evening was at Powderhall for the greyhound racing. He recited to himself the description Rebus had given him, and eventually spotted the man tucking into a meal of potato crisps at a window-seat in the bar.

'Are you Shuggie Oliphant?' he asked.

'That's me,' said the huge thirtyish man. He was poking a finger into the farthest corner of the crisp-bag in search of salt.

'Somebody told me you might be interested in a bit of information I've got.'

Oliphant still hadn't looked at him. The bag emptied,

he folded it into a thin strip, then tied it in a knot and placed it on the table. There were four other granny knots just like it in a row. 'You don't get paid till I do,' Oliphant informed him, sucking on a greasy finger and smacking his lips.

Andy Steele sat down across from him. 'That's okay by me,' he said.


On Sunday morning Rebus waited at the top of a blustery Calton Hill. He walked around the observatory, as the other Sunday strollers were doing. His leg was definitely improving. People were pointing out distant landmarks. Broken clouds were moving rapidly over a pale blue sky. Nowhere else in the world, he reckoned, had this geography of bumps and valleys and outcrops. The volcanic plug beneath Edinburgh Castle had been the start of it. Too good a place *not* to build a fortress. And the town had grown around it, grown out as far as Wester Hailes and beyond.

The observatory was an odd building, if functional. The folly, on the other hand, was just that, and served no function at all save as a thing to clamber over and a place to spraypaint your name. It was one side of a projected Greek temple (Edinburgh, after all, being 'the Athens of the north'). The all-too-eccentric brain behind the scheme had run out of money after completion of this first side. And there it stood, a series of pillars on a plinth so tall kids had to stand on each other's shoulders to climb aboard.

When Rebus looked towards it, he saw a woman there swinging her legs from the plinth and waving towards him. It was Siobhan Clarke. He walked over to her.

'How long have you been here?' he called up.

'Not long. Where's your stick?'

'I can manage fine without it.' This was true, though by 'fine' he meant that he could hobble along at a reasonable pace. 'I see Hibs got a result yesterday.'

'About time.'

'No sign of himself?'

But Siobhan pointed to the car park. 'Here he comes now.'

A Mini Metro had climbed the road to the top of the hill and was squeezing into a space between two shinier larger cars. 'Give me a hand down,' said Siobhan.

'Watch for my leg,' Rebus complained. But she felt almost weightless as he lifted her down.

'Thanks,' she said. Brian Holmes had watched the performance before locking his car and coming towards them.

'A regular Baryshnikov,' he commented.

'Bless you,' said Rebus.

'So what's this all about, sir?' Siobhan asked. 'Why the secrecy?'

'There's nothing secret,' Rebus said, starting to walk, 'about an Inspector wanting to talk with two of his junior colleagues. *Trusted* junior colleagues.'

Siobhan caught Holmes's eye. Holmes shook his head: he wants something from us. As if she didn't know.

They leaned against a railing, enjoying the view, Rebus doing most of the talking. Siobhan and Holmes added occasional questions, mostly rhetorical.

'So this would be off our own bats?'

'Of course,' Rebus answered. 'Just two keen coppers with a little bit of initiative.' He had a question of his own. 'Will the lighting be difficult?'

Holmes shrugged. 'I'll ask Jimmy Hutton about that. He's a professional photographer. Does calendars and that sort of thing.'

'It's not going to be wee kittens or a Highland glen,' replied Rebus.

'No, sir,' said Holmes.

'And you think this'll work?' asked Siobhan.

Rebus shrugged. 'Let's wait and see.'

'We haven't said we'll do it, sir.'

'No,' said Rebus, turning away, 'but you will.'

# 34

Off their own initiative then, Holmes and Siobhan decided to spend Monday evening doing a surveillance shift on Operation Moneybags. Without heating, the room they crouched in was cold and damp, and dark enough to attract the odd mouse. Holmes had set the camera up, after taking advice from the calendar man. He'd even borrowed a special lens for the occasion, telephoto and night-sighted. He hadn't bothered with his Walkman and his Patsy Cline tapes: in the past, there'd always been more than enough to talk about with Siobhan. But tonight she didn't seem in the mood. She kept gnawing on her top and bottom lips, and got up every now and then to do stretching exercises.

'Don't you get stiff?' she asked him.

'Not me,' said Holmes quietly. 'I've been in training for this – years of being a couch potato.'

'I thought you kept pretty fit.'

He watched her bend forward and lay her arms down the length of one leg. 'And you must be double-jointed.'

'Not quite. You should've seen me in my teens.' Holmes' grin was illuminated by the street light's diffuse orange glow. 'Down, Rover,' said Siobhan. There was a scuttling overhead.

'A rat,' said Holmes. 'Ever cornered one?' She shook her head. 'They can jump like a Tummel salmon.'

'My parents took me to the hydro dam when I was a kid.'

'At Pitlochry?' She nodded. 'So you've seen the salmon leaping?' She nodded again. 'Well,' said Holmes, 'imagine one of those with hair and fangs and a long thick tail.'

'I'd rather not.' She watched from the window. 'Do you think he'll come.'

'I don't know. John Rebus isn't often wrong.'

'Is that why everyone hates him?'

Holmes seemed a little surprised. 'Who hates him?'

She shrugged. 'People I've talked to at St Leonard's ... and other places. They don't trust him.'

'He wouldn't have it any other way.'

'Why not?'

'Because he's thrawn.' He was remembering the first time Rebus had used him in a case. He'd spent a cold frustrating evening watching for a dog-fight that never took place. He was hoping tonight would be better.

The rat was moving again, to the back of the room now, over by the door.

'*Do* you think he'll come?' Siobhan asked again.

'He'll come, lass.' They both turned towards the shape in the doorway. It was Rebus. 'You two,' he said, 'blething like sweetiewives. I could have climbed those stairs in pit boots and you'd not have heard me.' He came over to the window. 'Anything?'

'Nothing, sir.'

Rebus angled his watch towards the light. 'I make it five to.'

The display on Siobhan's digital watch was backlit. 'Ten to, sir.'

'Bloody watch,' muttered Rebus. 'Not long now. There'll be some action by the top of the hour. Unless that daft Aberdonian's put the kibosh on it.'

But the 'daft Aberdonian' wasn't so daft. Big Ger Cafferty paid for information. Even if it was information he already knew, he tended to pay: it was a cheap way of making sure *everything* got back to him. For example, even though he'd already heard from two sources that the teuchters were planning to muscle in on him, he still paid Shug Oliphant a few notes for his effort. And Oliphant, who liked to keep his own sources sweet, handed over ten quid to Andy Steele, this representing two-fifths of Oliphant's reward.

'There you go,' he said.

'Cheers,' said Andy Steele, genuinely pleased.

'Found anything you like?'

Oliphant was referring to the videotapes which surrounded them in the small rental shop which he operated. The area behind the narrow counter was so small, Oliphant only just squeezed in there. Every time he moved he seemed to knock something off a shelf onto the floor, where it remained, since there was also no room for him to bend over.

'I've got some bits and pieces under the counter,' he went on, 'if you're interested.'

'No, I don't want a video.'

Oliphant grinned unpleasantly. 'I'm not sure the gentleman really believed your story,' Oliphant told Andy. 'But I've heard the rumour a few times since, so maybe there's something in it.'

'There is,' said Andy Steele. Rebus was right, if you told a deaf man something on Monday, by Tuesday it was in the evening paper. 'They've got a watch on his hangouts, including the operation in Gorgie.'

Oliphant looked mightily suspicious. 'How do you know?'

'Luck, really. I bumped into one of them. I knew him in Aberdeen. He told me to get out if I didn't want to get mixed up in it.'

'But you're still here.'

'I'm on the mail train tomorrow morning.'

'So something's happening tonight?' Oliphant still

322

sounded highly sceptical, but then that was his way.

Steele shrugged. 'All I know is, they're keeping watch. I think maybe they just want to talk.'

Oliphant considered, running his fingers over a video-box. 'There were two pubs last night got their windows smashed.' Steele didn't blink. 'Pubs where the gentleman drank. Could be a connection?'

Steele shrugged. 'Could be.' If he were being honest, he'd have told how he acted as getaway driver while Rebus himself tossed the large rocks through the glass. One of the pubs had been the Firth at Tollcross, the other the Bowery at the bottom of Easter Road.

But instead he said, 'Loon called McPhail, he's the one watching Gorgie. He's in charge.'

Oliphant nodded. 'You know the way it works, come back in a day or two. There'll be money if the gen's on the nail.'

But Steele shook his head. 'I'm off up to Aberdeen.'

'So you are,' said Oliphant. 'Tell you what,' he tore a sheet from a pad, 'give me your address and I'll send on the cash.'

Andy Steele had fun inventing the address.

Cafferty was playing snooker when he got the message. He had a quarter share in an upmarket snooker hall and leisure complex in Leith. The intended market had been yuppies, working class lads scraping their way up the greasy pole. But the yuppies had vanished in a puff of smoke. So now the complex was shifting cannily down-market with video bingo, happy hour, an arcade full of electronic machines, and plans for a bowling alley. Teenagers always seemed to have money in their pockets. They would carve the bowling alley out of the little-used gymnasium, the restaurant next to it, and the aerobics room beyond that.

Staying in business, Cafferty had found, was all about

remaining flexible. If the wind changed, you didn't try to steer in the opposite direction. Mooted future plans included a soul club and a 1940s ballroom, the latter complete with tea dances and 'blackout nights'. Groping nights, Cafferty called them.

He knew he was crap at snooker, but he liked the game. His theory was fine; it was the practice that was lacking. Vanity prevented him taking lessons, and his renowned lack of patience would have dissuaded all but the most foolhardy from giving them. On Mo's advice, he'd tried a few other sports – tennis, squash, even skiing one time. The only one he'd enjoyed was golf. He loved thwacking that ball all over the place. Problem was, he didn't know when to hold back, he was always overshooting. If he hadn't split at least a couple of balls after nine holes, he wasn't happy.

Snooker suited him. It had everything. Tactics, ciggies, booze, and a few sidebets. So here he was again in the hall, overhead lights flooding the green tables, dusk everywhere else. Quiet, too, therapeutic; just the clack of the balls, the occasional comment or joke, a floor-stomp with the cue to signal a worthy shot. Then Jimmy the Ear was coming towards him.

'Phone call from the house,' he told Cafferty. Then he gave him Oliphant's message.

Andrew McPhail trusted Rebus about as far as he could toss a caber into a gale. He knew he should be running for cover right now, let the caber land where it might. There were several ways it could go. Rebus might be setting up a meeting between McPhail and Maclean. Well, McPhail could prepare himself against this. Or it might be some other kind of ruse, probably ending up with a beating and the clear message to get the fuck out of Edinburgh.

Or it could be straight. Aye, if the spirit-level was bent.

Rebus had asked McPhail to deliver a message, a letter. He'd even handed over the envelope. The message was for a man called Cafferty, who would be leaving the taxi office on Gorgie Road around ten.

'So what's the message?'

'Never you mind,' Rebus had said.

'Why me?'

'It can't come from me, that's all you need to know. Just make sure it's him, and give him the envelope.'

'This stinks.'

'I can't make it any simpler. We'll meet afterwards and fix up your new future. The ball's already rolling.'

'Aye,' said McPhail, 'but where the fuck's the net?'

Yet here he was, walking up Gorgie Road. A bit cold, threatening rain. Rebus had taken him to St Leonard's this afternoon, let him shower and shave, even provided some clean clothes which he'd picked up from Mrs Mackenzie's.

'I don't want a tramp delivering my post,' he'd explained. Ah, the letter. McPhail wasn't donnert; he'd torn the envelope open earlier this evening. Inside was a smaller brown envelope with some writing on the front: NO PEEKING NOW, McPHAIL!

He'd thought about opening it anyway. It didn't feel like there was much inside, a single sheet of paper. But something stopped him, a pale spark of hope, the hope that everything was going to be all right.

He didn't have a watch, but was a good judge of time. It felt like ten o'clock. And here he was in front of the taxi office. There were lights on inside, and cabs ready and waiting outside. Their busiest shift would be starting soon, the rides home after closing time. The night air smelt like ten o'clock. Diesel from the railway lines, rain close by. Andrew McPhail waited.

He saw the headlights, and when the car – a Jag – swerved and mounted the pavement his first thought was:

drunk driver. But the car braked smoothly, stopping beside him, almost pinning him to the wire fence. The driver got out. He was big. A gust of wind flapped his long hair, and McPhail saw that one ear was missing.

'You McPhail?' he demanded. The back door of the Jag was opening slowly, another man getting out. He wasn't as big as the driver, but he somehow *seemed* larger. He was smiling unkindly.

The letter was in McPhail's pocket. 'Cafferty?' he asked, forcing the word from his lungs.

The smiling man blinked lazily in acknowledgement. In McPhail's other pocket was the broken neck of a whisky bottle he'd found beside an overflowing bottle bank. It wasn't much of a weapon, but it was all he could afford. Even so, he didn't rate his chances. His bladder felt painfully full. He reached for the letter.

The driver pinned his arms to his side and swung him around, so he was face to face with Cafferty, who swung a kick into his groin. The butt of a three-section snooker cue slipped expertly from Cafferty's coat sleeve into his hand. As McPhail doubled over, the cue caught him on the side of the jaw, fracturing it, dislodging teeth. He fell further forwards and was rewarded with the cue on the back of his neck. His whole body went numb. Now the driver was pulling his head up by the hair and Cafferty was forcing his mouth open with the cue, working it past his tongue and into his throat.

'Hold it there!' Two of them, a man and a woman, running from across the street and holding open their IDs. 'Police officers.'

Cafferty lifted both hands away, raising them head high. He had left the cue in McPhail's mouth. The driver released the battered man, who remained upright on his knees. Shakily, Andrew McPhail started to pull the snooker cue out of his throat. There were sirens close by as a police car approached.

'It's nothing, officer,' Cafferty was saying, 'a mis-understanding.'

'Some misunderstanding,' said the male police officer. His sidekick slipped her hand into McPhail's pocket. She felt a broken bottle. Wrong pocket. From the other pocket she produced the letter, crumpled now. She handed it to Cafferty.

'Open this, please, sir,' she said.

Cafferty stared at it. 'Is this a set-up?' But he opened it anyway. Inside was a scrap of paper, which he unfolded. The note was unsigned. He knew who it was from anyway. 'Rebus!' he spat. 'That bastard Rebus!'

A few minutes later, as Cafferty and his driver were being taken away, and the ambulance was arriving for Andrew McPhail, Siobhan picked up the note which Cafferty had dropped. It said simply, 'I hope they sell your skin for souvenirs.' She frowned and looked up at the surveillance window, but couldn't see anyone there.

Had she seen anything, it would have been the outline of a man making the shape of a gun from his fist, lining up the thumb so Cafferty was in its sights, and pulling the imaginary trigger.

Bang!

# 35

Nobody at St Leonard's believed Holmes and Siobhan were there that night simply out of an exaggerated sense of duty. The more credible version had them meeting for a clandestine shag and just happening upon the beating. Lucky there was film in the surveillance camera. And didn't the photos come out well?

With Cafferty in custody, they got the chance to take away his things and have yet another look at them ... including the infamous coded diary. Watson and Lauderdale were poring over xeroxed sheets from it when there was a knock at the Chief Super's door.

'Come!' called Watson.

John Rebus walked in and looked around admiringly at the sudden floorspace. 'I see you got your cabinets, sir.'

Lauderdale pulled himself up straight. 'What the hell are you doing here? You're suspended from duty.'

'It's all right, Frank,' said Watson, 'I asked Inspector Rebus to come in.' He turned the xeroxed pages towards Rebus. 'Take a look.'

It didn't take long. The problem with the code in the past was that they hadn't known *what* to look for. But now Rebus had a more than fair idea. He stabbed one entry. 'There,' he said. '3TUB SCS.'

'Yes?'

'It means the butcher on South Clerk Street owes three thousand. He's abbreviated 'butcher' and written it backwards.'

Lauderdale looked disbelieving. 'Are you sure?'

Rebus shrugged. 'Put the experts at Fettes onto it. They should be able to find at least a few more late-payers.'

'Thank you, John,' said Watson. Rebus turned smartly and left the room. Lauderdale stared at his superior.

'I get the feeling,' he said, 'something's going on here I don't know about.'

'Well, Frank,' said Watson, 'why should today be different from any other?'

Which, as the saying went, put CI Lauderdale's gas at a very low peep.

It was Siobhan Clarke who came up with the most important piece of information in the whole case.

It *was* a case now. Rebus didn't mind that the machine was in operation without him. Holmes and Clarke reported back to him at the end of each day. The code-breakers had been hard at work, as a result of which detectives were talking to Cafferty's black book victims. It would only take one or two of them in court, and Cafferty would be going down. So far, though, no one was talking. Rebus had an idea of one person who, given enough persuasion, might.

Then Siobhan mentioned that Cafferty's company Geronimo Holdings held a seventy-nine per cent share in a large farm in the south-west Borders, not so very far from the coastline where the bodies had been washing up until recently. A party was sent to the farm. They found plenty for the forensic scientists to start working on ... especially the pigsties. The sties themselves were clean enough, but there was an enclosed area of storage space above each ramshackle sty. Most of the farm had turned itself over to the latest in high-tech agriculture, but not the sties. It was this which initially alerted the police. Above the pigsties, in the dark enclosures strewn with rank straw, there was a tangible reek of something unwholesome, something putrid. Strips of cloth were found; in one corner there lay a man's trouser-belt. The area was photographed and picked over for its least congruous particles. Upstairs in the farmhouse, meanwhile, a man who claimed initially to be an agricultural labourer eventually admitted to being Derek Torrance, better known as Deek.

At the same time, Rebus was driving out to Dalkeith, to Duncton Terrace, to be precise. It was early evening, and the Kintoul family was at home. Mother, father and son took up three sides of a fold-down table in the kitchen. The chip-pan was still smouldering and spitting on the greasy gas cooker. The vinyl wallpaper was slick with condensation. Most of the food on the plates was disguised by brown sauce. Rebus could smell vinegar and washing-up liquid. Rory Kintoul excused himself and went with Rebus into the living room. Kitchen and living room were connected by a serving hatch. Rebus wondered if wife and son would be listening at the hatch.

Rebus sat in one fireside chair, Kintoul opposite him.

'Sorry if it's a bad time,' Rebus began. There was a ritual to be followed, after all.

'What is it, Inspector?'

'You'll have heard, Mr Kintoul, we've arrested Morris Cafferty. He'll be going away for quite a while.' Rebus looked at the photos on the mantelpiece, snapshots of gap-toothed kids, nephews and nieces. He smiled at them. 'I just thought maybe it was time you got it off your chest.'

He kept silent for a moment, still examining the framed photos. Kintoul said nothing.

'Only,' said Rebus, 'I know you're a good man. I mean, a *good* man. You put family first, am I right?' Kintoul nodded uncertainly. 'Your wife and son, you'd do anything for them. Same goes for your other family, parents, sisters, brothers, cousins . . .' Rebus trailed off.

'I know Cafferty's going away,' said Kintoul.

'And?'

Kintoul shrugged.

'It's like this,' said Rebus. 'We know just about all there is to know. We just need a little corroboration.'

'That means testifying?'

Rebus nodded. Eddie Ringan would be testifying too, telling all he knew about the Central Hotel, in return for a good word from the police come his own trial. 'Mr Kintoul, you've got to accept something. You've got to accept that you've changed, you're not the same man you were a year or two ago. Why did you do it?' Rebus asked the way a friend would, just curious.

Kintoul wiped a smear of sauce from his chin. 'It was a favour. Jim always needed favours.'

'So you drove the van?'

'Yes, I did his rounds.'

'But you were a lab technician!'

Kintoul smiled. 'And I could earn more on the butcher's round.' He shrugged again. 'Like you say, Inspector, I put family first, especially where money's concerned.'

'Go on.'

'How much do you know?'

'We know the van was used to dump the bodies.'

'Nobody ever notices a butcher's van.'

'Except a poor constable in north-east Fife. He ended up with concussion.'

'That was after my time. I was shot of it by then.' He waited till Rebus nodded agreement, then went on. 'Only, when I wanted out Cafferty didn't want me out. He was putting pressure on.'

'That's how you got stabbed?'

'It was that bodyguard of his, Jimmy the Ear. He lost the head. Knifed me as I was getting out of the car. Crazy bastard.' Kintoul glanced towards the serving-hatch. 'You know what Cafferty did when I said I wanted to stop driving the van? He offered Jason a job "driving" for him. Jason's my son.'

Rebus nodded. 'But why all this fuss? Cafferty could get a hundred guys to drive a van for him.'

'I thought you knew him, Inspector. Cafferty's like that. He's ... particular about his flesh.'

'He's off his head,' commented Rebus. 'How did you get sucked in in the first place?'

'I was still driving full-time when Cafferty won half the business from Jimmy. One evening, one of Cafferty's men turned up all smarmy, told me we'd be taking a run to the coast early next morning. Via some farm in the Borders.'

'You went to the farm?' So that's why there was straw in the van.

The colour was seeping from Kintoul's face like blood from a cut of meat.

'Oh aye. There was something in the pigsties, tied up in fertiliser bags. Stank to high heaven. I'd been working in a butcher's long enough to know it had been rotting in that sty for a good few weeks, months, even.'

'A corpse?'

'Easy to tell, isn't it? I threw my guts up. Cafferty's man said what a waste, I should've done it into the trough.' Kintoul paused. He was still wiping at his chin, though the sauce mark had long ago been erased. 'Cafferty liked the bodies to be rotten, less chance of them washing ashore in any recognisable state.'

'Christ.'

'I haven't come to the worst part yet.' In the next room, Kintoul's wife and son were speaking in undertones. Rebus was in no hurry, and merely watched as Kintoul got up to stare from his back window. There was a patch of garden out there he could call his own. It was small, but it was his. He came back and stood in front of the gas fire, not looking at Rebus.

'I was there one day when he killed someone,' he said

baldly. Then he screwed shut his eyes. Rebus was trying to control his own breathing. This guy would make a gem of a witness.

'Killed them how?' Still not pressing; still the friend.

Kintoul tipped his head back, feeding tears back where they had come from. 'How? With his bare hands. We'd arrived late. The van had broken down in the middle of nowhere. It was about ten in the morning. Mist all around the farm, like driving into Brigadoon. They were both wearing business suits, that's what got me. And they were up to their ankles in glaur.'

Rebus frowned, not quite comprehending. 'They were *in* the pigsty?'

Kintoul nodded. 'There's a fenced run. Cafferty was in there with this man. There were other people watching through the fence.' He swallowed. 'I swear Cafferty looked like he was enjoying it. There with the mud lapping at him, and the pigs squealing in their boxes wondering what the hell was happening, and all the silent onlookers.' Kintoul tried to shake the memory away, probably a daily event.

'They were fighting?'

'The other man looked like he'd been roughed up beforehand. Nobody'd call it a fair fight. And eventually, after Cafferty'd beaten the living shite out of him, he grabbed him by the neck and forced him down into the muck. He stood on the man's back, balancing there, and holding the face down with his hands. He looked like it was nothing new. Then the man stopped struggling ...'

Rebus and Kintoul were silent, blood pounding through them, both trying to cope with the vision of an early morning pigsty ... 'Afterwards,' said Kintoul, his voice lower than ever, 'he beamed at us like it was his coronation.'

Then, in complete grimacing silence, he started to weep.

Rebus was visiting the Infirmary so often he was considering taking out a season ticket. But he hadn't expected to see Flower there.

'Checking in? The psychiatric section's down the hall.'

'Ha ha,' said Flower.

'What are you doing here anyway?'

'I could ask you the same question.'

'I live here, what about you?'

'I came to ask some questions.'

'Of Andrew McPhail?' Flower nodded. 'Did nobody tell you his jaw's wired shut?' Flower twitched, producing a good wide grin from Rebus. 'How come it's your business anyway?'

'It involves Cafferty,' Flower said.

'Oh aye, so it does, I'd forgotten.'

'Looks like we've got him this time.'

'Looks like it. But you never know with Cafferty.' Rebus stared unblinking at Flower as he spoke. 'The reason he's lasted so long is he's clever. He's clever, and he's got the best lawyers. Plus he's got people scared of him, and he's got people in his pocket ... maybe even a copper or three.'

Flower had stared out the gaze; now he blinked. 'You think I was in Cafferty's pocket?'

Rebus had been pondering this. He had Cafferty marked down for the attack on Michael and the scam with the gun. As for the clumsy hit-and-run attempt, that was so amateurish, he guessed at Broderick Gibson for its architect. Quite simply, Cafferty would have used better men.

He'd been silent long enough, so he shook his head. 'I don't think you're that smart. Cafferty likes smart people. But I *do* think you had a word with the Inland Revenue about me.'

'I don't know what you're talking about.'

Rebus grinned. 'I do like a cliché.' Then he walked on down the hall.

Andrew McPhail was easy to find. You just looked for the broken face. He was wired up like somebody's first attempt at a junction box. Rebus thought he could see where they'd used two wires where one would have sufficed. But then he was no doctor. McPhail had his eyes closed.

'Hello there,' said Rebus. The eyes opened. There was anger there, but Rebus could cope with it. He held up a hand. 'No,' he said, 'don't bother to thank me.' Then he smiled. 'It's all set up for when they let you out. Up north for rehabilitation, maybe a job, and bracing coastal walks. Man, I envy you.' He looked around the ward. Every bed had a body in it. The nurses looked like they could use a holiday or at the very least a gin and lime with some dry-roast peanuts.

'I said I'd leave you alone,' Rebus went on, 'and I keep my word. But a piece of advice.' He rested his hands on the edge of the bed and leaned towards McPhail. 'Cafferty's the biggest villain in town. You're probably the only bugger in Edinburgh who didn't know that. Now his men know a guy called McPhail set their boss up. So don't ever think of coming back, will you?' McPhail still glared at him. 'Good,' said Rebus. He straightened up, turned, and walked away, then paused and turned. 'Oh,' he said, 'and I meant to say something.' He returned to the bed and stood at its foot, where charts showed McPhail's temperature and medicaments. Rebus waited till McPhail's wet eyes were on his, then he smiled sympathetically again.

'Sorry,' he said. This time, when he turned he kept on walking.

Andy Steele had been the necessary go-between. It was too dangerous for Rebus to put the story out first-hand. The source of the tale might have got back to Cafferty, and that would have ruined everything. McPhail hadn't been necessary, but he'd been useful. Rebus explained the ruse twice to Andy Steele, and even then the young fisherman didn't seem to take it all in. He had the look of a man with a dozen unaskable questions.

'So what are you going to do now?' Rebus asked. He'd been hoping in fact that Steele might already have left for home.

'Oh, I'm applying for a grant,' said Steele.

'You mean like university?'

But Steele hooted. 'Not likely! It's one of those schemes to get the unemployed into business.'

'Oh aye?'

Steele nodded. 'I'm eligible.'

'So what's the business?'

'A detective agency, of course!'

'Where exactly?'

'Edinburgh. I've made more money since I came here than I made in six months in Aberdeen.'

'You cannot be serious,' said Rebus. But Andy Steele was.

# 36

He had one last meeting planned, and wasn't looking forward to it. He walked from St Leonard's to the University library at George Square. The indifferent security man on the door glanced at his ID and nodded him towards the front desk, where Nell Stapleton, tall and broad-shouldered, was taking returned books from a duffel-coated student. She caught his eye and looked surprised. Pleased at first; but as she went through the books, Rebus saw her mind wasn't wholly on the job. At last, she came over to him.

'Hello, John.'

'Nell.'

'What brings you here?'

'Can we have a word?'

She checked with the other assistant that it was okay to take a five-minute break. They walked as far as a book-lined corridor.

'Brian tells me you've closed the case, the one he was so worried about.'

Rebus nodded.

'That's great news. Thanks for your help.'

Rebus shrugged.

She tilted her head slightly. 'Is something the matter?'

'I'm not sure,' said Rebus. 'Do you want to tell me?'

'*Me?*'

Rebus nodded again.

'I don't understand.'

'You've lived with a policeman, Nell. You know we deal in motives. Sometimes there isn't much else to go on. I've been thinking about motives recently.' He shut up as a female student pulled open a door, came out into the corridor, smiled briefly at Nell, and went on her way. Nell watched her go. Rebus thought she would like to swop bodies for a few minutes.

'Motives?' she said. She was leaning against the wall, but Rebus got no notion of calmness from her stance.

'Remember,' he said, 'that night in the hospital, the night Brian was attacked. You said something about an argument, and him going off to the Heartbreak Cafe?'

She nodded. 'That's right. We met that night to talk over a drink. But we argued. I don't see –'

'Only, I've been thinking about the motive behind the attack. There were too many at first, but I've narrowed them down. They're all motives *you'd* have, Nell.'

'What?'

'You told me you were scared for him, scared because *he* was scared. And he was scared because he was poking into something that could nail Big Ger Cafferty. Wouldn't it be better if there was *another* body on the case, someone else to attract the fire? Me, in other words. So you got me involved.'

'Now wait a minute –'

But Rebus held his hand up and closed his eyes, begging silence. 'Then,' he said, 'there was DC Clarke. They were getting along so famously together. Jealousy maybe? Always a good motive.'

'I don't believe this.'

Rebus ignored her. 'And of course the simplest motive. The two of you had been rowing about whether or not to have kids. That and the fact that he was overworking, not paying you enough attention.'

'Did he tell you that?'

Rebus did not sound unkind. 'You told me yourself

338

you'd had a row that evening. You knew where he was headed – same place as always. So why not wait near his car and brain him when he came out? A nice simple revenge.' Rebus paused. 'How many motives does that make? I've lost count. Enough to be going on with, eh?'

'I don't believe this.' Tears were rising into her eyes. Every time she blinked, more appeared. She ran a thumb and forefinger down her nose, clearing it, breathing in noisily. 'What are you going to do?' she asked at last.

'I'm going to lend you a hankie,' said Rebus.

'I don't want your fucking hankie!'

Rebus put a finger to his lips. 'This is a library, remember?'

She sniffed and wiped away tears.

'Nell,' he said quietly, 'I don't want you to say anything. I don't want to know. I just want *you* to know. All right?'

'You think you're so fucking smart.'

He shrugged. 'The offer of a hankie still stands.'

'Get stuffed.'

'Do you really want Brian to leave the force?'

But she was walking away from him, head held high, shoulders swinging just a little exaggeratedly. He watched her go behind the desk, where her co-worker saw something was wrong and put a comforting arm around her. Rebus examined the shelves of books in front of him in the corridor, but saw nothing to delay his leavetaking.

He sat on a bench in the Meadows, the back of the library rising up behind him. He had his hands in his pockets as he watched a hastily arranged game of football. Eight men against seven. They'd come over to him and asked if he fancied making up the numbers.

'You must be desperate,' he'd said, shaking his head. The goalposts comprised one orange and white traffic cone, one pile of coats, one pile of folders and books, and a branch stuck in the ground. Rebus glanced at his watch more often than necessary. No one on the field was worrying too much about the time taken to play the first half. Two of the players looked like brothers though they played on opposing sides. Mickey had left the flat that morning, taking the photo of their dad and Uncle Jimmy with him.

'To remind me,' he'd said.

A woman in a Burberry trenchcoat sat down on the bench beside him.

'Are they any good?' she asked.

'They'd give Hibs a run for their money.'

'How good does that make them?' she asked.

Rebus turned towards Dr Patience Aitken and smiled, reaching out to take her hand in his. 'What kept you so long?' he asked.

'Just the usual,' she said. 'Work.'

'I tried phoning you so often.'

'Put my mind at rest then,' she said.

'How?'

She moved closer. 'Tell me I'm not just a number in your little black book ...'

340

# Mortal Causes

# Acknowledgements

A lot of people helped me with this book. I'd like to thank the people of Northern Ireland for their generosity and their 'crack'. Particular thanks need to go to a few people who can't be named or wouldn't thank me for naming them. You know who you are.

Thanks also to: Colin and Liz Stevenson, for trying; Gerald Hammond, for his gun expertise; the officers of the City of Edinburgh Police and Lothian and Borders Police, who never seem to mind me telling stories about them; David and Pauline, for help at the Festival.

The best book on the subject of Protestant para-militaries is Professor Steve Bruce's *The Red Hand* (OUP, 1992). One quote from the book: 'There is no "Northern Ireland problem" for which there is a solution. There is only a conflict in which there must be winners and losers.'

The action of *Mortal Causes* takes place in a fictionalised summer, 1993, before the Shankill Road bombing and its bloody aftermath.

Perhaps Edinburgh's terrible inability to speak out,
Edinburgh's silence with regard to all it should be saying,
Is but the hush that precedes the thunder,
The liberating detonation so oppressively imminent now?

Hugh MacDiarmid

We're all gonna be just dirt in the ground.

Tom Waits

He could scream all he liked.

They were underground, a place he didn't know, a cool ancient place but lit by electricity. And he was being punished. The blood dripped off him onto the earth floor. He could hear sounds like distant voices, something beyond the breathing of the men who stood around him. Ghosts, he thought. Shrieks and laughter, the sounds of a good night out. He must be mistaken: he was having a very bad night in.

His bare toes just touched the ground. His shoes had come off as they'd scraped him down the flights of steps. His socks had followed sometime after. He was in agony, but agony could be cured. Agony wasn't eternal. He wondered if he would walk again. He remembered the barrel of the gun touching the back of his knee, sending waves of energy up and down his leg.

His eyes were closed. If he opened them he knew he would see flecks of his own blood against the whitewashed wall, the wall which seemed to arch towards him. His toes were still moving against the ground, dabbling in warm blood. Whenever he tried to speak, he could feel his face cracking: dried salt tears and sweat.

It was strange, the shape your life could take. You might be loved as a child but still go bad. You might have monsters for parents but grow up pure. His life had been neither one nor the other. Or rather, it had been both, for he'd been cherished and abandoned in equal measure. He was six,

1

and shaking hands with a large man. There should have been more affection between them, but somehow there wasn't. He was ten, and his mother was looking tired, bowed down, as she leaned over the sink washing dishes. Not knowing he was in the doorway, she paused to rest her hands on the rim of the sink. He was thirteen, and being initiated into his first gang. They took a pack of cards and skinned his knuckles with the edge of the pack. They took it in turns, all eleven of them. It hurt until he belonged.

Now there was a shuffling sound. And the gun barrel was touching the back of his neck, sending out more waves. How could something be so cold? He took a deep breath, feeling the effort in his shoulder-blades. There couldn't be more pain than he already felt. Heavy breathing close to his ear, and then the words again.

'*Nemo me impune lacessit.*'

He opened his eyes to the ghosts. They were in a smoke-filled tavern, seated around a long rectangular table, their goblets of wine and ale held high. A young woman was slouching from the lap of a one-legged man. The goblets had stems but no bases: you couldn't put them back on the table until they'd been emptied. A toast was being raised. Those in fine dress rubbed shoulders with beggars. There were no divisions, not in the tavern's gloom. Then they looked towards him, and he tried to smile.

He felt but did not hear the final explosion.

# 1

Probably the worst Saturday night of the year, which was why Inspector John Rebus had landed the shift. God was in his heaven, just making sure. There had been a derby match in the afternoon, Hibs versus Hearts at Easter Road. Fans making their way back to the west end and beyond had stopped in the city centre to drink to excess and take in some of the sights and sounds of the Festival.

The Edinburgh Festival was the bane of Rebus's life. He'd spent years confronting it, trying to avoid it, cursing it, being caught up in it. There were those who said that it was somehow atypical of Edinburgh, a city which for most of the year seemed sleepy, moderate, bridled. But that was nonsense; Edinburgh's history was full of licence and riotous behaviour. But the Festival, especially the Festival Fringe, was different. Tourism was its lifeblood, and where there were tourists there was trouble. Pickpockets and house-breakers came to town as to a convention, while those football supporters who normally steered clear of the city centre suddenly became its passionate defenders, challenging the foreign invaders who could be found at tables outside short-lease cafes up and down the High Street.

Tonight the two might clash in a big way.

'It's hell out there,' one constable had already commented as he paused for rest in the canteen. Rebus believed him all too readily. The cells were filling nicely along with the CID in-trays. A woman had pushed her drunken husband's fingers into the kitchen mincer. Someone was applying superglue to cashpoint machines then chiselling the flap open later to get at the money. Several bags had been snatched around Princes Street. And the Can Gang were on the go again.

The Can Gang had a simple recipe. They stood at bus stops and offered a drink from their can. They were imposing figures, and the victim would take the proffered drink, not knowing that the beer or cola contained crushed up Mogadon tablets, or similar fast-acting tranquillisers. When the victim passed out, the gang would strip them of cash and valuables. You woke up with a gummy head, or in one severe case with your stomach pumped dry. And you woke up poor.

Meantime, there had been another bomb threat, this time phoned to the newspaper rather than Lowland Radio. Rebus had gone to the newspaper offices to take a statement from the journalist who'd taken the call. The place was a madhouse of Festival and Fringe critics filing their reviews. The journalist read from his notes.

'He just said, if we didn't shut the Festival down, we'd be sorry.'

'Did he sound serious?'

'Oh, yes, definitely.'

'And he had an Irish accent?'

'Sounded like it.'

'Not just a fake?'

The reporter shrugged. He was keen to file his story, so Rebus let him go. That made three calls in the past week, each one threatening to bomb or otherwise disrupt the Festival. The police were taking the threat seriously. How could they afford not to? So far, the tourists hadn't been scared off, but venues were being urged to make security checks before and after each performance.

Back at St Leonard's, Rebus reported to his Chief Superintendent, then tried to finish another piece of paperwork. Masochist that he was, he quite liked the Saturday back-

shift. You saw the city in its many guises. It allowed a
salutory peek into Edinburgh's grey soul. Sin and evil
weren't black – he'd argued the point with a priest – but
were greyly anonymous. You saw them all night long, the
grey peering faces of the wrongdoers and malcontents, the
wife beaters and the knife boys. Unfocused eyes, drained of
all concern save for themselves. And you prayed, if you
were John Rebus, prayed that as few people as possible ever
had to get as close as this to the massive grey nonentity.

Then you went to the canteen and had a joke with the
lads, fixing a smile to your face whether you were listening
or not.

'Here, Inspector, have you heard the one about the squid
with the moustache? He goes into a restaurant and –'

Rebus turned away from the DC's story towards his
ringing phone.

'DI Rebus.'

He listened for a moment, the smile melting from his
face. Then he put down the receiver and lifted his jacket
from the back of his chair.

'Bad news?' asked the DC.

'You're not joking, son.'


The High Street was packed with people, most of them just
browsing. Young people bobbed up and down trying to
instil enthusiasm in the Fringe productions they were
supporting. Supporting them? They were probably the *leads*
in them. They busily thrust flyers into hands already full
of similar sheets.

'Only two quid, best value on the Fringe!'

'You won't see another show like it!'

There were jugglers and people with painted faces, and
a cacophony of musical disharmonies. Where else in the
world would bagpipes, banjos and kazoos meet to join in a
busking battle from hell?

Locals said this Festival was quieter than the last. They'd

been saying it for years. Rebus wondered if the thing had ever had a heyday. It was plenty busy enough for him.

Though it was a warm night, he kept his car windows shut. Even so, as he crawled along the setts flyers would be pushed beneath his windscreen wipers, all but blocking his vision. His scowl met impregnable drama student smiles. It was ten o'clock, not long dark; that was the beauty of a Scottish summer. He tried to imagine himself on a deserted beach, or crouched atop a mountain, alone with his thoughts. Who was he trying to kid? John Rebus was *always* alone with his thoughts. And just now he was thinking of drink. Another hour or two and the bars would sluice themselves out, unless they'd applied for (and been granted) the very late licences available at Festival time.

He was heading for the City Chambers, across the street from St Giles' Cathedral. You turned off the High Street and through one of two stone arches into a small parking area in front of the Chambers themselves. A uniformed constable was standing guard beneath one of the arches. He recognised Rebus and nodded, stepping out of the way. Rebus parked his own car beside a marked patrol car, stopped the engine and got out.

'Evening, sir.'

'Where is it?'

The constable nodded towards a door near one of the arches, attached to the side wall of the Chambers. They walked towards it. A young woman was standing next to the door.

'Inspector,' she said.

'Hello, Mairie.'

'I've told her to move on, sir,' the constable apologised.

Mairie Henderson ignored him. Her eyes were on Rebus's. 'What's going on?'

Rebus winked at her. 'The Lodge, Mairie. We always meet in secret, like.' She scowled. 'Well then, give me a chance. Off to a show, are you?'

6

'I was till I saw the commotion.'

'Saturday's your day off, isn't it?'

'Journalists don't get days off, Inspector. What's behind the door?'

'It's got glass panels, Mairie. Take a keek for yourself.'

But all you could see through the panels was a narrow landing with doors off. One door was open, allowing a glimpse of stairs leading down. Rebus turned to the constable.

'Let's get a proper cordon set up, son. Something across the arches to fend off the tourists before the show starts. Radio in for assistance if you need it. Excuse me, Mairie.'

'Then there *is* going to be a show?'

Rebus stepped past her and opened the door, closing it again behind him. He made for the stairs down, which were lit by a naked lightbulb. Ahead of him he could hear voices. At the bottom of this first flight he turned a corner and came upon the group. There were two teenage girls and a boy, all of them seated or crouching, the girls shaking and crying. Over them stood a uniformed constable and a man Rebus recognised as a local doctor. They all looked up at his approach.

'This is the Inspector,' the constable told the teenagers. 'Right, we're going back down there. You three stay here.'

Rebus, squeezing past the teenagers, saw the doctor give them a worried glance. He gave the doctor a wink, telling him they'd get over it. The doctor didn't seem so sure.

Together the three men set off down the next flight of stairs. The constable was carrying a torch.

'There's electricity,' he said. 'But a couple of the bulbs have gone.' They walked along a narrow passage, its low ceiling further reduced by air- and heating-ducts and other pipes. Tubes of scaffolding lay on the floor ready for assembly. There were more steps down.

'You know where we are?' the constable asked.

'Mary King's Close,' said Rebus.

Not that he'd ever been down here, not exactly. But he'd been in similar old buried streets beneath the High Street. He knew of Mary King's Close.

'Story goes,' said the constable, 'there was a plague in the 1600s, people died or moved out, never really moved back. Then there was a fire. They blocked off the ends of the street. When they rebuilt, they built over the top of the close.' He shone his torch towards the ceiling, which was now three or four storeys above them. 'See that marble slab? That's the floor of the City Chambers.' He smiled. 'I came on the tour last year.'

'Incredible,' the doctor said. Then to Rebus: 'I'm Dr Galloway.'

'Inspector Rebus. Thanks for getting here so quickly.'

The doctor ignored this. 'You're a friend of Dr Aitken's, aren't you?'

Ah, Patience Aitken. She'd be at home just now, feet tucked under her, a cat and an improving book on her lap, boring classical music in the background. Rebus nodded.

'I used to share a surgery with her,' Dr Galloway explained.

They were in the close proper now, a narrow and fairly steep roadway between stone buildings. A rough drainage channel ran down one side of the road. Passages led off to dark alcoves, one of which, according to the constable, housed a bakery, its ovens intact. The constable was beginning to get on Rebus's nerves.

There were more ducts and pipes, runs of electric cable. The far end of the close had been blocked off by an elevator shaft. Signs of renovation were all around: bags of cement, scaffolding, pails and shovels. Rebus pointed to an arc lamp.

'Can we plug that in?'

The constable thought they could. Rebus looked around. The place wasn't damp or chilled or cobwebbed. The air seemed fresh. Yet they were three or four storeys beneath road level. Rebus took the torch and shone it through a doorway. At the end of the hallway he could see a wooden toilet, its seat raised. The next door along led into a long vaulted room, its walls whitewashed, the floor earthen.

'That's the wine shop,' the constable said. 'The butcher's is next door.'

So it was. It too consisted of a vaulted room, again whitewashed and with a floor of packed earth. But in its ceiling were a great many iron hooks, short and blackened but obviously used at one time for hanging up meat.

Meat still hung from one of them.

It was the lifeless body of a young man. His hair was dark and slick, stuck to his forehead and neck. His hands had been tied and the rope slipped over a hook, so that he hung stretched with his knuckles near the ceiling and his toes barely touching the ground. His ankles had been tied together too. There was blood everywhere, a fact made all too plain as the arc lamp suddenly came on, sweeping light and shadows across the walls and roof. There was the faint smell of decay, but no flies, thank God. Dr Galloway swallowed hard, his Adam's apple seeming to duck for cover, then retreated into the close tō be sick. Rebus tried to steady his own heart. He walked around the carcass, keeping his distance initially.

'Tell me,' he said.

'Well, sir,' the constable began, 'the three young people upstairs, they decided to come down here. The place had been closed to tours while the building work goes on, but they wanted to come down at night. There are a lot of ghost stories told about this place, headless dogs and –'

'How did they get a key?'

'The boy's great-uncle, he's one of the tour guides, a retired planner or something.'

'So they came looking for ghosts and they found this.'

'That's right, sir. They ran back up to the High Street and bumped into PC Andrews and me. We thought they were having us on at first, like.'

But Rebus was no longer listening, and when he spoke it wasn't to the constable.

'You poor little bastard, look what they did to you.'

Though it was against regulations, he leaned forward and touched the young man's hair. It was still slightly damp. He'd probably died on Friday night, and was meant to hang here over the weekend, enough time for any trail, any clues, to grow as cold as his bones.

'What do you reckon, sir?'

'Gunshots.' Rebus looked to where blood had sprayed the wall. 'Something high-velocity. Head, elbows, knees, and ankles.' He sucked in breath. 'He's been six-packed.'

There were shuffling noises in the close, and the wavering beam of another torch. Two figures stood in the doorway, their bodies silhouetted by the arc lamp.

'Cheer up, Dr Galloway,' a male voice boomed to the hapless figure still crouched in the close. Recognising the voice, Rebus smiled.

'Ready when you are, Dr Curt,' he said.

The pathologist stepped into the chamber and shook Rebus's hand. 'The hidden city, quite a revelation.' His companion, a woman, stepped forward to join them. 'Have the two of you met?' Dr Curt sounded like the host at a luncheon party. 'Inspector Rebus, this is Ms Rattray from the Procurator Fiscal's office.'

'Caroline Rattray.' She shook Rebus's hand. She was tall, as tall as either man, with long dark hair tied at the back.

'Caroline and I,' Curt was saying, 'were enjoying supper after the ballet when the call came. So I thought I'd drag her along, kill two birds with one stone . . . so to speak.'

Curt exhaled fumes of good food and good wine. Both he and the lawyer were dressed for an evening out, and already some white plaster-dust had smudged Caroline Rattray's black jacket. As Rebus moved to brush off the dust, she caught her first sight of the body, and looked away quickly. Rebus didn't blame her, but Curt was advancing on the

10

figure as though towards another guest at the party. He paused to put on polythene overshoes.

'I always carry some in my car,' he explained. 'You never know when they'll be needed.'

He got close to the body and examined the head first, before looking back towards Rebus.

'Dr Galloway had a look, has he?'

Rebus shook his head slowly. He knew what was coming. He'd seen Curt examine headless bodies and mangled bodies and bodies that were little more than torsos or melted to the consistency of lard, and the pathologist always said the same thing.

'Poor chap's dead.'

'Thank you.'

'I take it the crew are on their way?'

Rebus nodded. The crew were on their way. A van to start with, loaded with everything they'd need for the initial scene of crime investigation. SOC officers, lights and cameras, strips of tape, evidence bags, and of course a bodybag. Sometimes a forensic team came too, if cause of death looked particularly murky or the scene was a mess.

'I think,' said Curt, 'the Procurator Fiscal's office will agree that foul play is suspected?'

Rattray nodded, still not looking.

'Well, it wasn't suicide,' commented Rebus. Caroline Rattray turned towards the wall, only to find herself facing the sprays of blood. She turned instead to the doorway, where Dr Galloway was dabbing his mouth with a handkerchief.

'We'd better get someone to fetch me my tools.' Curt was studying the ceiling. 'Any idea what this place was?'

'A butcher's shop, sir,' said the constable, only too happy to help. 'There's a wine shop too, and some houses. You can still go into them.' He turned to Rebus. 'Sir, what's a six-pack?'

'A six-pack?' echoed Curt.

11

Rebus stared at the hanging body. 'It's a punishment,' he said quietly. 'Only you're not supposed to die. What's that on the floor?' He was pointing to the dead man's feet, to the spot where they grazed the dark-stained ground.

'Looks like rats have been nibbling his toes,' said Curt.

'No, not that.' There were shallow grooves in the earth, so wide they must have been made with a big toe. Four crude capital letters were discernible.

'Is that Neno or Nemo?'

'Could even be Memo,' offered Dr Curt.

'Captain Nemo,' said the constable. 'He's the guy in *2,000 Leagues Beneath the Sea.*'

'Jules Verne,' said Curt, nodding.

The constable shook his head. 'No, sir, Walt Disney,' he said.

# 2

On Sunday morning Rebus and Dr Patience Aitken decided to get away from it all by staying in bed. He nipped out early for croissants and papers from the local corner shop, and they ate breakfast from a tray on top of the bedcovers, sharing sections of the newspapers, discarding more than they read.

There was no mention of the previous night's grisly find in Mary King's Close. The news had seeped out too late for publication. But Rebus knew there would be something about it on the local radio news, so he was quite content for once when Patience tuned the bedside radio to a classical station.

He should have come off his shift at midnight, but murder tended to disrupt the system of shifts. On a murder inquiry, you stopped working when you reasonably could. Rebus had hung around till two in the morning, consulting with the night shift about the corpse in Mary King's Close. He'd contacted his Chief Inspector and Chief Super, and kept in touch with Fettes HQ, where the forensic stuff had gone. DI Flower kept telling him to go home. Finally he'd taken the advice.

The real problem with back shifts was that Rebus couldn't sleep well after them anyway. He'd managed four hours since arriving home, and four hours would suffice. But there was a warm pleasure in slipping into bed as dawn neared, curling against the body already asleep there. And even more pleasure in pushing the cat off the bed as you did so.

Before retiring, he'd swallowed four measures of whisky. He told himself it was purely medicinal, but rinsed the glass and put it away, hoping Patience wouldn't notice. She complained often of his drinking, among other things.

'We're eating out,' she said now.

'When?'

'Lunch today.'

'Where?'

'That place out at Carlops.'

Rebus nodded. 'Witch's Leap,' he said.

'What?'

'That's what Carlops means. There's a big rock there. They used to throw suspected witches from it. If you didn't fly, you were innocent.'

'But also dead?'

'Their judicial system wasn't perfect, witness the ducking-stool. Same principle.'

'How do you know all this?'

'It's amazing what these young constables know nowadays.' He paused. 'About lunch ... I should go into work.'

'Oh no, you don't.'

'Patience, there's been a —'

'John, there'll be a murder *here* if we don't start spending some time together. Phone in sick.'

'I can't do that.'

'Then *I'll* do it. I'm a doctor, they'll believe me.'

They believed her.


They walked off lunch by taking a look at Carlops Rock, and then braving a climb onto the Pentlands, despite the fierce horizontal winds. Back in Oxford Terrace, Patience eventually said she had some 'office things' to do, which meant filing or tax or flicking through the latest medical journals. So Rebus drove out along Queensferry Road and parked outside the Church of Our Lady of Perpetual Hell, noting with guilty pleasure that no one had yet corrected the mischievous graffiti on the noticeboard which turned 'Help' into 'Hell'.

Inside, the church was empty, cool and quiet and flooded with coloured light from the stained glass. Hoping his timing was good, he slipped into the confessional. There was someone on the other side of the grille.

'Forgive me, father,' said Rebus, 'I'm not even a Catholic.'

'Ah good, it's you, you heathen. I was hoping you'd come. I want your help.'

'Shouldn't that be my line?'

'Don't be bloody cheeky. Come on, let's have a drink.'


Father Conor Leary was between fifty-five and seventy and had told Rebus that he couldn't remember which he was nearer. He was a bulky barrelling figure with thick silver hair which sprouted not only from his head but also from ears, nose and the back of his neck. In civvies, Rebus guessed he would pass for a retired dockworker or skilled labourer of some kind who had also been handy as a boxer, and Father Leary had photos and trophies to prove that this last was incontrovertible truth. He often jabbed the air to make a point, finishing with an upper-cut to show that there could be no comeback. In conversation between the two men, Rebus had often wished for a referee.

But today Father Leary sat comfortably and sedately enough in the deckchair in his garden. It was a beautiful early evening, warm and clear with the trace of a cool sea-borne breeze.

'A great day to go hot-air ballooning,' said Father Leary, taking a swig from his glass of Guinness. 'Or bungee jumping. I believe they've set up something of the sort on The Meadows, just for the duration of the Festival. Man, I'd like to try that.'

Rebus blinked but said nothing. His Guinness was cold

enough to double as dental anaesthetic. He shifted in his own deckchair, which was by far the older of the two. Before sitting, he'd noticed how threadbare the canvas was, how it had been rubbed away where it met the horizontal wooden spars. He hoped it would hold.

'Do you like my garden?'

Rebus looked at the bright blooms, the trim grass. 'I don't know much about gardens,' he admitted.

'Me neither. It's not a sin. But there's an old chap I know who does know about them, and he looks after this one for a few bob.' He raised his glass towards his lips. 'So how are you keeping?'

'I'm fine.'

'And Dr Aitken?'

'She's fine.'

'And the two of you are still...?'

'Just about.'

Father Leary nodded. Rebus's tone was warning him off. 'Another bomb threat, eh? I heard on the radio.'

'It could be a crank.'

'But you're not sure?'

'The IRA usually use codewords, just so we know they're serious.'

Father Leary nodded to himself. 'And a murder too?'

Rebus gulped his drink. 'I was there.'

'They don't even stop for the Festival, do they? Whatever must the tourists think?' Father Leary's eyes were sparkling.

'It's about time the tourists learned the truth,' Rebus said, a bit too quickly. He sighed. 'It was pretty gruesome.'

'I'm sorry to hear that. I shouldn't have been so flippant.'

'That's all right. It's a defence.'

'You're right, it is.'

Rebus knew this. It was the reason behind his many little jokes with Dr Curt. It was their way of avoiding the obvious, the undeniable. Even so, since last night Rebus had held in his mind the picture of that sad strung-up

16

figure, a young man they hadn't even identified yet. The picture would stay there forever. Everybody had a photographic memory for horror. He'd climbed back out of Mary King's Close to find the High Street aglow with a firework display, the streets thronged with people staring up open-mouthed at the blues and greens in the night sky. The fireworks were coming from the Castle; the night's Tattoo display was ending. He hadn't felt much like talking to Mairie Henderson. In fact, he had snubbed her.

'This isn't very nice,' she'd said, standing her ground.

'This is very nice,' Father Leary said now, relaxing back further into his seat.

The whisky Rebus had drunk hadn't rubbed out the picture. If anything, it had smeared the corners and edges, which only served to highlight the central fact. More whisky would have made this image sharper still.

'We're not here for very long, are we?' he said now.

Father Leary frowned. 'You mean here on earth?'

'That's what I mean. We're not around long enough to make any difference.'

'Tell that to the man with a bomb in his pocket. Every one of us makes a difference just by being here.'

'I'm not talking about the man with the bomb, I'm talking about stopping him.'

'You're talking about being a policeman.'

'Ach, maybe I'm not talking about anything.'

Father Leary allowed a short-lived smile, his eyes never leaving Rebus's. 'A bit morbid for a Sunday, John?'

'Isn't that what Sundays are for?'

'Maybe for you sons of Calvin. You tell yourselves you're doomed, then spend all week trying to make a joke of it. Others of us give thanks for *this* day and its meaning.'

Rebus shifted in his chair. Lately, he didn't enjoy Father Leary's conversations so much. There was something proselytising about them. 'So when do we get down to business?' he said.

Father Leary smiled. 'The Protestant work ethic.'

'You haven't brought me here to convert me.'

'We wouldn't want a dour bugger like you. Besides, I'd more easily convert a fifty-yard penalty in a Murrayfield cross-wind.' He took a swipe at the air. 'Ach, it's not really your problem. Maybe it isn't a problem at all.' He ran a finger down the crease in his trouser-leg.

'You can still tell me about it.'

'A reversal of roles, eh? Well, I suppose that's what I had in mind all along.' He sat further forward in the deckchair, the material stretching and sounding a sharp note of complaint. 'Here it is then. You know Pilmuir?'

'Don't be daft.'

'Yes, stupid question. And Pilmuir's Garibaldi Estate?'

'The Gar-B, it's the roughest scheme in the city, maybe in the country.'

'There are good people there, but you're right. That's why the Church sent an outreach worker.'

'And now he's in trouble?'

'Maybe.' Father Leary finished his drink. 'It was my idea. There's a community hall on the estate, only it had been locked up for months. I thought we could reopen it as a youth club.'

'For Catholics?'

'For both faiths.' He sat back in his chair. 'Even for the faithless. The Garibaldi is predominantly Protestant, but there are Catholics there too. We got agreement, and set up some funds. I knew we needed someone special, someone really dynamic in charge.' He punched the air. 'Someone who might just draw the two sides together.'

Mission impossible, thought Rebus. This scheme will self-destruct in ten seconds.

Not least of the Gar-B's problems was the sectarian divide, or the lack of one, depending on how you looked at it. Protestants and Catholics lived in the same streets, the same tower blocks. Mostly, they lived in relative harmony and shared poverty. But, there being little to do on the estate, the youth of the place tended to organise into opposing gangs and wage warfare. Every year there was at least one pitched battle for police to contend with, usually in July, usually around the Protestant holy day of the 12th.

'So you brought in the SAS?' Rebus suggested. Father Leary was slow to get the joke.

'Not at all,' he said, 'just a young man, a very ordinary young man but with inner strength.' His fist cut the air. 'Spiritual strength. And for a while it looked like a disaster. Nobody came to the club, the windows were smashed as soon as we'd replaced them, the graffiti got worse and more personal. But then he started to break through. *That* seemed the miracle. Attendance at the club increased, and both sides were joining.'

'So what's gone wrong?'

Father Leary loosened his shoulders. 'It just wasn't quite right. I thought there'd be sports, maybe a football team or something. We bought the strips and applied to join a local league. But the lads weren't interested. All they wanted to do was hang around the hall itself. And the balance isn't there either, the Catholics have stopped joining. Most of them have even stopped attending.' He looked at Rebus. 'That's not just sour grapes, you understand.'

Rebus nodded. 'The Prod gangs have annnexed it?'

'I'm not saying that exactly.'

'Sounds like it to me. And your ... outreach worker?'

'His name's Peter Cave. Oh, he's still there. Too often for my liking.'

'I still don't see the problem.' Actually he could, but he wanted it spelling out.

'John, I've talked to people on the estate, and all over Pilmuir. The gangs are as bad as ever, only now they seem to be working together, divvying the place up between them. All that's happened is that they've become more

19

organised. They have meetings in the club and carve up the surrounding territory.'

'It keeps them off the street.' Father Leary didn't smile. 'So close the youth club.'

'That's not so easy. It would look bad for a start. And would it solve anything?'

'Have you talked with Mr Cave?'

'He doesn't listen. He's changed. That's what troubles me most of all.'

'You could kick him out.'

Father Leary shook his head. 'He's lay, John. I can't *order* him to do anything. We've cut the club's funding, but the money to keep it going comes from somewhere nevertheless.'

'Where from?'

'I don't know.'

'How much?'

'It doesn't take much.'

'So what do you want me to do?' The question Rebus had been trying not to ask.

Father Leary gave his weary smile again. 'To be honest, I don't know. Perhaps I just needed to tell someone.'

'Don't give me that. You want me to go out there.'

'Not if you don't want to.'

It was Rebus's turn to smile. 'I've been in safer places.'

'And a few worse ones, too.'

'I haven't told you about half of them, Father.' Rebus finished his drink.

'Another?'

He shook his head. 'It's nice and quiet here, isn't it?'

Father Leary nodded. 'That's the beauty of Edinburgh, you're never far from a peaceful spot.'

'And never far from a hellish one either. Thanks for the drink, Father.' Rebus got up.

'I see your team won yesterday.'

'What makes you think I support Hearts?'

'They're Prods, aren't they? And you're a Protestant yourself.'

'Away to hell, Father,' said John Rebus, laughing.

Father Leary pulled himself to his feet. He straightened his back with a grimace. He was acting purposely aged. Just an old man. 'About the Gar-B, John,' he said, opening his arms wide, 'I'm in your hands.'

Like nails, thought Rebus, like carpentry nails.

# 3

Monday morning saw Rebus back at work and in the Chief Super's office. 'Farmer' Watson was pouring coffee for himself and Chief Inspector Frank Lauderdale, Rebus having refused. He was strictly decaf these days, and the Farmer didn't know the meaning of the word.

'A busy Saturday night,' said the Farmer, handing Lauderdale a grubby mug. As inconspicuously as he could, Lauderdale started rubbing marks off the rim with the ball of his thumb. 'Feeling better, by the way, John?'

'Scads better, sir, thank you,' said Rebus, not even close to blushing.

'A grim business under the City Chambers.'

'Yes, sir.'

'So what do we have?'

It was Lauderdale's turn to speak. 'Victim was shot seven times with what looks like a nine-millimetre revolver. Ballistics will have a full report for us by day's end. Dr Curt tells us that the head wound actually killed the victim, and it was the last bullet delivered. They wanted him to suffer.'

Lauderdale sipped from the cleaned rim of his mug. A Murder Room had been set up along the hall, and he was in charge. Consequently, he was wearing his best suit. There would be press briefings, maybe a TV appearance or two. Lauderdale looked ready. Rebus would gladly have tipped the mug of coffee down the mauve shirt and paisley-pattern tie.

'Your thoughts, John,' said Farmer Watson. 'Someone mentioned the words "six-pack".'

'Yes, sir. It's a punishment routine in Northern Ireland, usually carried out by the IRA.'

'I've heard of kneecappings.'

Rebus nodded. 'For minor offences, there's a bullet in each elbow or ankle. For more serious crimes, there's a kneecapping on top. And finally there's the six-pack: both elbows, both knees, both ankles.'

'You know a lot about it.'

'I was in the army, sir. I still take an interest.'

'You were in Ulster?'

Rebus nodded slowly. 'In the early days.'

Chief Inspector Lauderdale placed his mug carefully on the desktop. 'But they normally wouldn't then kill the person?'

'Not normally.'

The three men sat in silence for a moment. The Farmer broke the spell. 'An IRA punishment gang? *Here?*'

Rebus shrugged. 'A copycat maybe. Gangs aping what they've seen in the papers or on TV.'

'But using serious guns.'

'Very serious,' said Lauderdale. 'Could be a tie-in with these bomb threats.'

The Farmer nodded. 'That's the line the media are taking. Maybe our would-be bomber had gone rogue, and they caught up with him.'

'There's something else, sir,' said Rebus. He'd phoned Dr Curt first thing, just to check. 'They did the knees from behind. Maximum damage. You sever the arteries before smashing kneecaps.'

'What's your point?'

'Two points, sir. One, they knew exactly what they were doing. Two, why bother when you're going to kill him anyway? Maybe whoever did it changed his mind at the last minute. Maybe the victim was meant to live. The probable handgun was a revolver. Six shots. Whoever did it must have stopped to reload before putting that final bullet in the head.'

Eyes were avoided as the three men considered this, putting themselves in the victim's place. You've been six-packed. You think it's over. Then you hear the gun being reloaded . . .

'Sweet Jesus,' said the Farmer.

'There are too many guns around,' Lauderdale said matter-of-factly. It was true: over the past few years there had been a steady increase in the number of firearms on the street.

'Why Mary King's Close?' asked the Farmer.

'You're not likely to be disturbed there,' Rebus guessed. 'Plus it's virtually soundproof.'

'You could say the same about a lot of places, most of them a long way from the High Street in the middle of the Festival. They were taking a big risk. Why bother?'

Rebus had wondered the same thing. He had no answer to offer.

'And Nemo or Memo?'

It was Lauderdale's turn, another respite from the coffee. 'I've got men on it, sir, checking libraries and phone directories, digging up meanings.'

'You've talked to the teenagers?'

'Yes, sir. They seem genuine enough.'

'And the person who gave them the key?'

'He didn't give it to them, sir, they took it without his knowledge. He's in his seventies and straighter than a plumb-line.'

'Some builders I know,' said the Farmer, 'could bend even a plumb-line.'

Rebus smiled. He knew those builders too.

'We're talking to everyone,' Lauderdale went on, 'who's been working in Mary King's Close.' It seemed he hadn't got the Farmer's joke.

'All right, John,' said the Farmer. 'You were in the army, what about the tattoo?'

Yes, the tattoo. Rebus had known the conclusion everyone would jump to. From the case notes, they'd spent most of Sunday jumping to it. The Farmer was examining a photograph. It had been taken during Sunday's post-mortem examination. The SOCOs on Saturday night had taken photos too, but those hadn't come out nearly as clearly.

The photo showed a tattoo on the victim's right forearm. It was a rough, self-inflicted affair, the kind you sometimes saw on teenagers, usually on the backs of hands. A needle and some blue ink, that's all you needed; that and a measure of luck that the thing wouldn't become infected. Those were all the victim had needed to prick the letters SaS into his skin.

'It's not the Special Air Service,' said Rebus.

'No?'

Rebus shook his head. 'For all sorts of reasons. You'd use a capital A for a start. More likely, if you wanted an SAS tattoo you'd go for the crest, the knife and wings and "Who dares wins", something like that.'

'Unless you didn't know anything about the regiment,' offered Lauderdale.

'Then why sport a tattoo?'

'Do we have any ideas?' asked the Farmer.

'We're checking,' said Lauderdale.

'And we still don't know who he is?'

'No, sir, we still don't know who he is.'

Farmer Watson sighed. 'Then that'll have to do for now. I know we're stretched just at the minute, with the Festival threat and everything else, but it goes without saying this takes priority. Use all the men you have to. We need to clean this up quickly. Special Branch and the Crime Squad are already taking an interest.'

Ah, thought Rebus, so that was why the Farmer was

25

being a bit more thorough than usual. Normally, he'd just let Lauderdale get on with it. Lauderdale was good at running an office. You just didn't want him out there on the street with you. Watson was shuffling the papers on his desk.

'I see the Can Gang have been at it again.'

It was time to move on.

Rebus had had dealings in Pilmuir before. He'd seen a good policeman go wrong there. He'd tasted darkness there. The sour feeling returned as he drove past stunted grass verges and broken saplings. Though no tourists ever came here, there was a welcome sign. It comprised somebody's gable-end, with white painted letters four feet high: ENJOY YOUR VISIT TO THE GAR-B.

Gar-B was what the kids (for want of a better term) called the Garibaldi estate. It was a mish-mash of early-'60s terraced housing and late-'60s tower blocks, every-thing faced with grey harling, with boring swathes of grass separating the estate from the main road. There were a lot of orange plastic traffic cones lying around. They would make goalposts for a quick game of football, or chicanes for the bikers. Last year, some enterprising souls had put them to better use, using them to divert traffic off the main road and into the Gar-B, where youths lined the slip-road and pelted the cars with rocks and bottles. If the drivers ran from their vehicles, they were allowed to go, while the cars were stripped of anything of value, right down to tyres, seat-covers and engine parts.

Later in the year, when the road needed digging up, a lot of drivers ignored the genuine traffic cones and as a result drove into newly dug ditches. By next morning, their abandoned vehicles had been stripped to the bone. The Gar-B would have stripped the paint if they could.

You had to admire their ingenuity. Give these kids money and opportunity and they'd be the saviours of the capitalist state. Instead, the state gave them dole and daytime TV. Rebus was watched by a gang of pre-teens as he parked. One of them called out.

'Where's yir swanky car?'

'It's no' him,' said another, kicking the first lazily in the ankle. The two of them were on bicycles and looked like the leaders, being a good year or two older than their cohorts. Rebus waved them over.

'What is it?' But they came anyway.

'Keep an eye on my car,' he told them. 'Anyone touches it, you touch them, okay? There's a couple of quid for you when I get back.'

'Half now,' the first said quickly. The second nodded. Rebus handed over half the money, which they pocketed.

'Naebody'd touch *that* car anyway, mister,' said the second, producing a chorus of laughter from behind him.

Rebus shook his head slowly: the patter here was probably sharper than most of the stand-ups on the Fringe. The two boys could have been brothers. More than that, they could have been brothers in the 1930s. They were dressed in cheap modern style, but had shorn heads and wide ears and sallow faces with dark-ringed eyes. You saw them staring out from old photographs wearing boots too big for them and scowls too old. They didn't just seem older than the other kids; they seemed older than Rebus himself.

When he turned his back, he imagined them in sepia.

He wandered towards the community centre. He'd to pass some lock-up garages and one of the three twelve-storey blocks of flats. The community centre itself was no more than a hall, small and tired looking with boarded windows and the usual indecipherable graffiti. Surrounded by concrete, it had a low flat roof, asphalt black, on which lay four teenagers smoking cigarettes. Their chests were naked, their t-shirts tied around their waists. There was so much broken glass up there, they could have doubled as fakirs in a magic show. One of them had a pile of sheets of paper, and was folding them into paper planes which he released from the roof. Judging by the number of planes littering the grass, it had been a busy morning at the control tower.

Paint had peeled in long strips from the centre's doors, and one layer of the plywood beneath had been punctured by a foot or a fist. But the doors were locked fast by means of not one but two padlocks. Two more youths sat on the ground, backs against the doors, legs stretched in front of them and crossed at the ankles, for all the world like security guards on a break. Their trainers were in bad repair, their denims patched and torn and patched again. Maybe it was just the fashion. One wore a black t-shirt, the other an unbuttoned denim jacket with no shirt beneath.

'It's shut,' the denim jacket said.

'When does it open?'

'The night. No polis allowed though.'

Rebus smiled. 'I don't think I know you. What's your name?'

The smile back at him was a parody. Black t-shirt grunted an undeveloped laugh. Rebus noticed flecks of white scale in the youth's hair. Neither youth was about to say anything. The teenagers on the roof were standing now, ready to leap in should anything develop.

'Hard men,' said Rebus. He turned and started to walk away. Denim jacket got to his feet and came after him.

'What's up, Mr Polisman?'

Rebus didn't bother looking at the youth, but he stopped walking. 'Why should anything be up?' One of the paper planes, aimed or not, hit him on the leg. He picked it up. On the roof, they were laughing quietly. 'Why should anything be up?' he repeated.

'Behave. You're not our usual plod.'

'A change is as good as a rest.'

'Arrest? What for?'

Rebus smiled again. He turned to the youth. The face

was just leaving acne behind it, and would be good looking for a few more years before it started to decline. Poor diet and alcohol would be its undoing if drugs or fights weren't. The hair was fair and curly, like a child's hair, but not thick. There was a quick intelligence to the eyes, but the eyes themselves were narrow. The intelligence would be narrow too, focusing only on the main chance, the next deal. There was quick anger in those eyes too, and something further back that Rebus didn't like to think about.

'With an act like yours,' he said, 'you should be on the Fringe.'

'I fuckn *hate* the Festival.'

'Join the club. What's your name, son?'

'You like names, don't you?'

'I can find out.'

The youth slipped his hands into his tight jeans pockets. 'You don't want to.'

'No?'

A slow shake of the head. 'Believe me, you really don't want to.' The youth turned, heading back to his friends. 'Or next time,' he said, 'your car might not be there at all.'

Sure enough, as Rebus approached he saw that his car was sinking into the ground. It looked like maybe it was taking cover. But it was only the tyres. They'd been generous; they'd only slashed two of them. He looked around him. There was no sign of the pre-teen gang, though they might be watching from the safe distance of a tower-block window.

He leaned against the car and unfolded the paper plane. It was the flyer for a Fringe show, and a blurb on the back explained that the theatre group in question were uprooting from the city centre in order to play the Garibaldi Community Centre for one night.

'You know not what you do,' Rebus said to himself.

Some young mothers were crossing the football pitch. A crying baby was being shaken on its buggy springs. A toddler was being dragged screaming by the arm, his legs frozen in protest so that they scraped the ground. Both baby and toddler were being brought back into the Gar-B. But not without a fight.

Rebus didn't blame them for resisting.

# 4

Detective Sergeant Brian Holmes was in the Murder Room, handing a polystyrene cup of tea to Detective Constable Siobhan Clarke, and laughing about something.

'What's the joke?' asked Rebus.

'The one about the hard-up squid,' Holmes answered.

'The one with the moustache?'

Holmes nodded, wiping an imaginary tear from his eye. 'And Gervase the waiter. Brilliant, eh, sir?'

'Brilliant.' Rebus looked around. The Murder Room was all purposeful activity. Photos of the victim and the locus had been pinned up on one wall, a staff rota not far from it. The staff rota was on a plastic wipe-board, and a WPC was checking names from a list against a series of duties and putting them on the board in thick blue marker-pen. Rebus went over to her. 'Keep DI Flower and me away from one another, eh? Even if it means a slip of the pen.'

'I could get into trouble for that, Inspector.' She was smiling, so Rebus winked at her. Everyone knew that having Rebus and Flower in close proximity, two detectives who hated one another, would be counter productive. But of course Lauderdale was in charge. It was Lauderdale's list, and Lauderdale liked to see sparks fly, so much so that he might have been happier in a foundry.

Holmes and Clarke knew what Rebus had been talking about with the WPC, but said nothing.

'I'm going back down Mary King's Close,' Rebus said quietly. 'Anyone want to tag along?'

He had two takers.

Rebus was keeping an eye on Brian Holmes. Holmes hadn't tendered his resignation yet, but you never knew when it might come. When you joined the police, of course, you signed on for the long haul, but Holmes's significant other was pulling on the other end of the rope, and it was hard to tell who'd win the tug o' war.

On the other hand, Rebus had stopped keeping an eye on Siobhan Clarke. She was past her probation, and was going to be a good detective. She was quick, clever and keen. Police officers were seldom all three. Rebus himself might pitch for thirty per cent on a good day.

The day was overcast and sticky, with lots of bugs in the air and no sign of a dispersing breeze.

'What are they, greenfly?'

'Maybe midges.'

'I'll tell you what they are, they're disgusting.'

The windscreen was smeared by the time they reached the City Chambers, and there being no fluid in the wiper bottle, the windscreen stayed that way. It struck Rebus that the Festival really was a High Street thing. Most of the city centre streets were as quiet or as busy as usual. The High Street was the hub. The Chambers' small car park being full, he parked on the High Street. When he got out, he brought a sheet of kitchen-towel with him, spat on it, and cleaned the windscreen.

'What we need is some rain.'

'Don't say that.'

A transit van and a flat-back trailer were parked outside the entrance to Mary King's Close, evidence that the builders were back at work. The butcher's shop would still be taped off, but that didn't stop the renovations.

'Inspector Rebus?'

An old man had been waiting for them. He was tall and fit looking and wore an open cream-coloured raincoat despite the day's heat. His hair had turned not grey or silver but a kind of custard yellow, and he wore half-moon glasses most of the way down his nose, as though he needed them only to check the cracks in the pavement.

'Mr Blair-Fish?' Rebus shook the brittle hand.

'I'd like to apologise again. My great-nephew can be such a –'

'No need to apologise, sir. Your great-nephew did us a favour. If he hadn't gone down there with those two lassies, we wouldn't have found the body so fast as we did. The quicker the better in a murder investigation.'

Blair-Fish inspected his oft-repaired shoes, then accepted this with a slow nod. 'Still, it's an embarrassment.'

'Not to us, sir.'

'No, I suppose not.'

'Now, if you'll lead the way . . . ?'

Mr Blair-Fish led the way.

He took them in through the door and down the flights of stairs, out of daylight and into a world of low-wattage bulbs beyond which lay the halogen glare of the builders. It was like looking at a stage-set. The workers moved with the studied precision of actors. You could charge a couple of quid a time and get an audience, if not a Fringe First Award. The gaffer knew police when he saw them, and nodded a greeting. Otherwise, nobody paid much attention, except for the occasional sideways and appraising glance towards Siobhan Clarke. Builders were builders, below ground as above.

Blair-Fish was providing a running commentary. Rebus reckoned he'd been the guide when the constable had come on the tour. Rebus heard about how the close had been a thriving thoroughfare prior to the plague, only one of many such plagues to hit Edinburgh. When the denizens moved back, they swore the close was haunted by the spirits of those who had perished there. They all moved out again and the street fell into disuse. Then came a fire, leaving only the first few storeys untouched. (Edinburgh tenements back then could rise to a precarious twelve storeys or more.) After which, the city merely laid slabs across what remained and built again, burying Mary King's Close.

'The old town was a narrow place, you must remember, built along a ridge or, if you enjoy legend, on the back of a buried serpent. Long and narrow. Everyone was squeezed together, rich and poor living cheek by jowl. In a tenement like this you'd have your paupers at the top, your gentry in the middle floors, and your artisans and commercial people at street level.'

'So what happened?' asked Holmes, genuinely interested.

'The gentry got fed up,' said Blair-Fish. 'When the New Town was built on the other side of Nor' Loch, they were quick to move. With the gentry gone, the old town became dilapidated, and stayed that way for a long time.' He pointed down some steps into an alcove. 'That was the baker's. See those flat stones? That's where the oven was. If you touch them, they're still warmer than the stones around them.'

Siobhan Clarke had to test this. She came back shrugging. Rebus was glad he'd brought Holmes and Clarke with him. They kept Blair-Fish busy while he could keep a surreptitious eye on the builders. This had been his plan all along: to appear to be inspecting Mary King's Close, while really inspecting the builders. They didn't look nervous; well, no more nervous than you would expect. They kept their eyes away from the butcher's shop, and whistled quietly as they worked. They did not seem inclined to discuss the murder. Someone was up a ladder dismantling a run of pipes. Someone else was mending brickwork at the top of a scaffold.

Further into the tour, away from the builders, Blair-Fish took Siobhan Clarke aside to show her where a child had been bricked up in a chimney, a common complaint among eighteenth-century chimney sweeps.

'The Farmer asked a good question,' Rebus confided to Holmes. 'He said, why would you bring anyone down here?

Think about it. It shows you must be local. Only locals know about Mary King's Close, and even then only a select few.' It was true, the public tour of the close was not common knowledge, and tours themselves were by no means frequent. 'They'd have to have been down here themselves, or know someone who had. If not, they'd more likely get lost than find the butcher's.'

Holmes nodded. 'A shame there's no record of the tour parties.' This had been checked, the tours were informal, parties of a dozen or more at a time. There was no written record. 'Could be they knew about the building work and reckoned the body would be down here for weeks.'

'Or maybe,' said Rebus, 'the building work is the reason they were down here in the first place. Someone might have tipped them off. We're checking everyone.'

'Is that why we're here just now? Giving the crew a once-over?' Rebus nodded, and Holmes nodded back. Then he had an idea. 'Maybe it was a way of sending a message.'

'That's what I've been wondering. But what kind of message, and who to?'

'You don't go for the IRA idea?'

'It's plausible and implausible at the same time,' Rebus said. 'We've got nothing here to interest the paramilitaries.'

'We've got Edinburgh Castle, Holyrood Palace, the Festival...'

'He has a point.'

They turned towards the voice. Two men were standing in torchlight. Rebus recognised neither of them. As the men came forwards, Rebus studied both. The man who had spoken, the slightly younger of the two, had an English accent and the look of a London copper. It was the hands in the trouser pockets that did it. That and the air of easy superiority that went with the gesture. Plus of course he was wearing old denims and a black leather bomber-jacket. He had close cropped brown hair spiked with gel, and a heavy pockmarked face. He was probably in his late-thirties but looked like a fortysomething with coronary problems. His eyes were a piercing blue. It was difficult to meet them. He didn't blink often, like he didn't want to miss any of the show.

The other man was well-built and fit, in his late-forties, with ruddy cheeks and a good head of black hair just turning silver at the edges. He looked as if he needed to shave two or even three times a day. His suit was dark blue and looked straight off the tailor's dummy. He was smiling.

'Inspector Rebus?'

'The same.'

'I'm DCI Kilpatrick.'

Rebus knew the name of course. It was interesting at last to have a face to put to it. If he remembered right, Kilpatrick was still in the SCS, the Scottish Crime Squad.

'I thought you worked out of Stuart Street, sir,' Rebus said, shaking hands.

'I moved back from Glasgow a few months ago. I don't suppose it made the front page of the *Scotsman*, but I'm heading the squad here now.'

Rebus nodded. The SCS took on serious crimes, where cross-force investigations were necessary. Drugs were their main concern, or had been. Rebus knew men who'd been seconded to the SCS. You stayed three or four years and came out two things: unwillingly, and tough as second-day bacon. Kilpatrick was introducing his companion.

'This is DI Abernethy from Special Branch. He's come all the way from London to see us.'

'That takes the biscuit,' said Rebus.

'My grandad was a Jock,' Abernethy answered, gripping Rebus's hand and not getting the joke. Rebus introduced Holmes and, when she returned, Siobhan Clarke. From the colouring in Clarke's cheeks, Rebus reckoned someone along the way had made a pass at her. He decided to rule out Mr Blair-Fish, which still left plenty of suspects.

36

'So,' said Abernethy at last, rubbing his hands, 'where's this slaughterhouse?'

'A butcher's actually,' Mr Blair-Fish explained.

'I know what I mean,' said Abernethy.

Mr Blair-Fish led the way. But Kilpatrick held Rebus back.

'Look,' he whispered, 'I don't like this bastard being here any more than you do, but if we're tolerant we'll get rid of him all the quicker, agreed?'

'Yes, sir.' Kilpatrick's was a Glaswegian accent, managing to be deeply nasal even when reduced to a whisper, and managing, too, to be full of irony and a belief that Glasgow was the centre of the universe. Usually, Glaswegians somehow added to all this a ubiquitous chip on their shoulder, but Kilpatrick didn't seem the type.

'So no more bloody cracks about biscuits.'

'Understood, sir.'

Kilpatrick waited a moment. 'It was you who noticed the paramilitary element, wasn't it?' Rebus nodded. 'Good work.'

'Thank you, sir.' Yes, and Glaswegians could be patronising bastards, too.

When they rejoined the group, Holmes gave Rebus a questioning look, to which Rebus replied with a shrug. At least the shrug was honest.

'So they strung him up here,' Abernethy was saying. He looked around at the setting. 'Bit melodramatic, eh? Not the IRA's style at all. Give them a lock-up or a warehouse, something like that. But someone who likes a bit of drama set this up.'

Rebus was impressed. It was another possible reason for the choice of venue.

'Bang-bang,' Abernethy continued, 'then back upstairs to melt into the crowd, maybe take in a late-night revue before toddling home.'

Clarke interrupted. 'You think there's some connection with the Festival?'

Abernethy studied her openly, causing Brian Holmes to straighten up. Not for the first time, Rebus wondered about Clarke and Holmes.

'Why not?' Abernethy said. 'It's every bit as feasible as anything else I've heard.'

'But it was a six-pack.' Rebus felt obliged to defend his corner.

'No,' Abernethy corrected, 'a *seven*-pack. And that's not paramilitary style at all. A waste of bullets for a start.' He looked to Kilpatrick. 'Could be a drug thing. Gangs like a bit of melodrama, it makes them look like they're in a film. Plus they do like to send messages to each other. Loud messages.'

Kilpatrick nodded. 'We're considering it.'

'My money'd still be on terrorists,' Rebus added. 'A gun like that –'

'Dealers use guns, too, Inspector. They *like* guns. Big ones to make a big loud noise. I'll tell you something, I'd hate to have been down here. The report from a nine-millimetre in an enclosed space like this. It could blow out your eardrums.'

'A silencer,' Siobhan Clarke offered. It wasn't her day. Abernethy just gave her a look, so Rebus provided the explanation.

'Revolvers don't take silencers.'

Abernethy pointed to Rebus, but his eyes were on Clarke's. 'Listen to your Inspector, darling, you might learn something.'

Rebus looked around the room. There were six people there, four of whom would gladly punch another's lights out.

He didn't think Mr Blair-Fish would enter the fray.

Abernethy meantime had sunk to his knees, rubbing his fingers over the floor, over ancient dirt and husks.

'The SOCOs took off the top inch of earth,' Rebus said, but Abernethy wasn't listening. Bags and bags of the stuff had been taken to the sixth floor of Fettes HQ to be sieved and analysed and God knew what else by the forensics lab.

It occurred to Rebus that all the group could now see of Abernethy was a fat arse and brilliant white Reeboks. Abernethy turned his face towards them and smiled. Then he got up, brushing his palms together.

'Was the deceased a drug user?'

'No signs.'

'Only I was thinking, SaS, could be Smack and Speed.'

Again, Rebus was impressed, thoroughly despite himself. Dust had settled in the gel of Abernethy's hair, small enough motes of comfort.

'Could be Scott and Sheena,' offered Rebus. In other words: could be anything. Abernethy just shrugged. He'd been giving them a display, and now the show was over.

'I think I've seen enough,' he said. Kilpatrick nodded with relief. It must be hard, Rebus reflected, being a top cop in your field, a man with a rep, sent to act as tour guide for a junior officer ... and a Sassenach at that.

Galling, that was the word.

Abernethy was speaking again. 'Might as well drop in on the Murder Room while I'm here.'

'Why not?' said Rebus coldly.

'No reason I can think of,' replied Abernethy, all sweetness and bite.

# 5

St Leonard's police station, headquarters of the city's B Division, boasted a semi-permanent Murder Room. The present inquiry looked like it had been going on forever. Abernethy seemed to favour the scene. He browsed among the computer screens, telephones, wall charts and photographs. Kilpatrick touched Rebus's arm.

'Keep an eye on him, will you? I'll just go say hello to your Chief Super while I'm here.'

'Right, sir.'

Chief Inspector Lauderdale watched him leave. 'So that's Kilpatrick of the Crime Squad, eh? Funny, he looks almost mortal.'

It was true that Kilpatrick's reputation – a hard one to live up to – preceded him. He'd had spectacular successes in Glasgow, and some decidedly public failures too. Huge quantities of drugs had been seized, but a few terrorist suspects had managed to slip away.

'At least he looks human,' Lauderdale went on, 'which is more than can be said for our cockney friend.'

Abernethy couldn't have heard this – he was out of earshot – but he looked up suddenly towards them and grinned. Lauderdale went to take a phone call, and the Special Branch man sauntered back towards Rebus, hands stuffed into his jacket pockets.

'It's a good operation this, but there's not much to go on, is there?'

'Not much.'

'And what you've got doesn't make much sense.'

'Not yet.'

'You worked with Scotland Yard on a case, didn't you?'

'That's right.'

'With George Flight?'

'Right again.'

'He's gone for retraining, you know. I mean, at *his* age. Got interested in computers, I don't know, maybe he's got a point. They're the future of crime, aren't they? Day's coming, the big villains won't have to move from their living rooms.'

'The big villains never have.'

This earned a smile from Abernethy, or at least a lopsided sneer. 'Has my minder gone for a jimmy?'

'He's gone to say hello to someone.'

'Well tell him ta-ta from me.' Abernethy looked around, then lowered his voice. 'I don't think DCI Kilpatrick will be sorry to see the back of me.'

'What makes you say that?'

Abernethy chuckled. 'Listen to you. If your voice was any colder you could store cadavers in it. Still think you've got terrorists in Edinburgh?' Rebus said nothing. 'Well, it's *your* problem. I'm well shot of it. Tell Kilpatrick I'll talk to him before I head south.'

'You're supposed to stay here.'

'Just tell him I'll be in touch.'

There was no painless way of stopping Abernethy from leaving, so Rebus didn't even try. But he didn't think Kilpatrick would be happy. He picked up one of the phones. What did Abernethy mean about it being Rebus's problem? If there *was* a terrorist connection, it'd be out of CID's hands. It would become Special Branch's domain, M15's domain. So what did he mean?

He gave Kilpatrick the message, but Kilpatrick didn't seem bothered after all. There was relaxation in his voice, the sort that came with a large whisky. The Farmer had stopped drinking for a while, but was back off the wagon again. Rebus wouldn't mind a drop himself...

Lauderdale, who had also just put down a telephone, was staring at a pad on which he'd been writing as he took the call.

'Something?' Rebus asked.

'We may have a positive ID on the victim. Do you want to check it out?' Lauderdale tore the sheet from the pad.

'Do Hibs fans weep?' Rebus answered, accepting it.


Actually, not all Hibs fans were prone to tears. Siobhan Clarke supported Hibernian, which put her in a minority at St Leonard's. Being English-educated (another minority, much smaller) she didn't understand the finer points of Scottish bigotry, though one or two of her fellow officers had attempted to educate her. She wasn't Catholic, they explained patiently, so she should support Heart of Midlothian. Hibernian were the Catholic team. Look at their name, look at their green strip. They were Edinburgh's version of Glasgow Celtic, just as Hearts were like Glasgow Rangers.

'It's the same in England,' they'd tell her. 'Wherever you've got Catholics and Protestants in the same place.' Manchester had United (Catholic) and City (Protestant), Liverpool had Liverpool (Catholic) and Everton (Protestant). It only got complicated in London. London even had Jewish teams.

Siobhan Clarke just smiled, shaking her head. It was no use arguing, which didn't stop her trying. They just kept joking with her, teasing her, trying to convert her. It was light-hearted, but she couldn't always tell how light-hearted. The Scots tended to crack jokes with a straight face and be deadly serious when they smiled. When some officers at St Leonard's found out her birthday was coming, she found herself unwrapping half a dozen Hearts scarves. They all went to a charity shop.

She'd seen the darker side of football loyalty, too. The

collection tins at certain games. Depending on where you were standing, you'd be asked to donate to either one cause or the other. Usually it was for 'families' or 'victims' or 'prisoners' aid', but everyone who gave knew they might be perpetuating the violence in Northern Ireland. Fearfully, most gave. One pound sterling towards the price of a gun.

She'd come across the same thing on Saturday when, with a couple of friends, she'd found herself standing at the Hearts end of the ground. The tin had come round, and she'd ignored it. Her friends were quiet after that.

'We should be doing something about it,' she complained to Rebus in his car.

'Such as?'

'Get an undercover team in there, arrest whoever's behind it.'

'Behave.'

'Well why not?'

'Because it wouldn't solve anything and there'd be no charge we could make stick other than something paltry like not having a licence. Besides, if you ask me most of that cash goes straight into the collector's pocket. It never reaches Northern Ireland.'

'But it's the *principle* of the thing.'

'Christ, listen to you.' Principles: they were slow to go, and some coppers never lost them entirely. 'Here we are.'

He reversed into a space in front of a tenement block on Mayfield Gardens. The address was a top floor flat.

'Why is it always the top floor?' Siobhan complained.

'Because that's where the poor people live.'

There were two doors on the top landing. The name on one doorbell read MURDOCK. There was a brown bristle welcome-mat just outside the door. The message on it was GET LOST!

'Charming.' Rebus pressed the bell. The door was opened by a bearded man wearing thick wire-framed glasses. The beard didn't help, but Rebus would guess the man's age at mid-twenties. He had thick shoulder-length black hair, through which he ran a hand.

'I'm Detective Inspector Rebus. This is –'

'Come in, come in. Mind out for the motorbike.'

'Yours, Mr Murdock?'

'No, it's Billy's. It hasn't worked since he moved in.'

The bike's frame was intact, but the engine lay disassembled along the hall carpet, lying on old newspapers turned black from oil. Smaller pieces were in polythene bags, each bag tied at the neck and marked with an identifying number.

'That's clever,' said Rebus.

'Oh aye,' said Murdock, 'he's organised is Billy. In here.' He led them into a cluttered living area. 'This is Millie, she lives here.'

'Hiya.'

Millie was sitting on the sofa swathed in a sleeping bag, despite the heat outside. She was watching the television and smoking a cigarette.

'You phoned us, Mr Murdock.'

'Aye, well, it's about Billy.' Murdock began to pad around the room. 'See, the description in the paper and on the telly, well ... I didn't think about it at the time, but as Millie says, it's not like Billy to stay away so long. Like I say, he's organised. Usually he'd phone or something, just to let us know.'

'When did you last see him?'

Murdock looked to Millie. 'When was it, Thursday night?'

'I saw him Friday morning.'

'So you did.'

Rebus turned to Millie. She had short fair hair, dark at the roots, and dark eyebrows. Her face was long and plain, her chin highlighted by a protruding mole. Rebus reckoned she was a few years older than Murdock. 'Did he say where he was going?'

'He didn't say anything. There's not a lot of conversation in this flat at that hour.'

'What hour?'

She flicked ash into the ashtray which was balanced on her sleeping bag. It was a nervous habit, the cigarette being tapped even when there was no ash for it to surrender. 'Seven thirty, quarter to eight,' she said.

'Where does he work?'

'He doesn't,' said Murdock, resting his hand on the mantelpiece. 'He used to work in the Post Office, but they laid him off a few months back. He's on the dole now, along with half of Scotland.'

'And what do you do, Mr Murdock?'

'I'm a computer consultant.'

Sure enough, some of the living room's clutter was made up of keyboards and disk drives, some of them dismantled, piled on top of each other. There were piles of fat magazines too, and books, hefty operating manuals.

'Did either of you know Billy before he moved in?'

'I did,' said Millie. 'A friend of a friend, casual acquaintance sort of thing. I knew he was looking for a room, and there was a room going spare here, so I suggested him to Murdock.' She changed channels on the TV. She was watching with the sound turned off, watching through a squint of cigarette smoke.

'Can we see Billy's room?'

'Why not?' said Murdock. He'd been glancing nervously towards Millie all the time she'd been talking. He seemed relieved to be in movement. He took them back into where the narrow entrance hall became a wider rectangle, off which were three doors. One was a cupboard, one the kitchen. Back along the narrow hall they'd passed the bathroom on one side and Murdock's bedroom on the other. Which left just this last door.

It led them into a very small, very tidy bedroom. The room itself would be no more than ten feet by eight, yet it managed to contain single bed, wardrobe, a chest of drawers and a writing desk and chair. A hi-fi unit, including speakers, sat atop the chest of drawers. The bed had been made, and there was nothing left lying around.

'You haven't tidied up, have you?'

Murdock shook his head. 'Billy was always tidying. You should see the kitchen.'

'Do you have a photograph of Billy?' Rebus asked.

'I might have some from one of our parties. You want to look at them?'

'Just the best one will do.'

'I'll fetch it then.'

'Thank you.' When Murdock had gone, Siobhan squeezed into the room beside Rebus. Until then, she'd been forced to stay just outside the door.

'Initial thoughts?' Rebus asked.

'Neurotically tidy,' she said, the comment of one whose own flat looked like a cross between a pizza franchise and a bottle bank.

But Rebus was studying the walls. There was a Hearts pennant above the bed, and a Union Jack flag on which the Red Hand of Ulster was centrally prominent, with above it the words 'No Surrender' and below it the letters FTP. Even Siobhan Clarke knew what those stood for.

'Fuck the Pope,' she murmured.

Murdock was back. He didn't attempt to squeeze into the narrow aisle between bed and wardrobe, but stood in the doorway and handed the photo to Siobhan Clarke, who handed it to Rebus. It showed a young man smiling manically for the camera. Behind him you could see a can of beer held high, as though someone were about to pour it over his head.

'It's as good a photo as we've got,' Murdock said by way of apology.

'Thank you, Mr Murdock.' Rebus was almost sure. Almost. 'Billy had a tattoo?'

46

'On his arm, aye. It looked like one of those things you do yourself when you're a daft laddie.'

Rebus nodded. They'd released details of the tattoo, looking for a quick result.

'I never really looked at it close up,' Murdock went on, 'and Billy never talked about it.'

Millie had joined him in the doorway. She had discarded the sleeping bag and was wearing a modestly long t-shirt over bare legs. She put an arm around Murdock's waist. 'I remember it,' she said. 'SaS. Big S, small a.'

'Did he ever tell you what it stood for?'

She shook her head. Tears were welling in her eyes. 'It's him, isn't it? He's the one you found dead?'

Rebus tried to be non-committal, but his face gave him away. Millie started to bawl, and Murdock hugged her to him. Siobhan Clarke had lifted some cassette tapes from the chest of drawers and was studying them. She handed them silently to Rebus. They were collections of Orange songs, songs about the struggle in Ulster. Their titles said it all: *The Sash and other Glories*, *King Billy's Marching Tunes*, *No Surrender*. He stuck one of the tapes in his pocket.

They did some more searching of Billy Cunningham's room, but came up with little excepting a recent letter from his mother. There was no address on the letter, but it bore a Glasgow postmark, and Millie recalled Billy saying something about coming from Hillhead. Well, they'd let Glasgow deal with it. Let Glasgow break the news to some unsuspecting family.

In one of the drawers, Siobhan Clarke came up with a Fringe programme. It contained the usual meltdown of *Abigail's Party*s and *Krapp's Last Tapes*, revues called things like *Teenage Alsatian Orgy*, and comic turns on the run from London fatigue.

'He's ringed a show,' said Clarke.

So he had, a country and western act at the Crazy Hose

Saloon. The act had appeared for three nights back at the start of the Festival.

'There's no country music in his collection,' Clarke commented.

'At least he showed taste,' said Rebus.

On the way back to the station, he pushed the Orange tape into his car's antiquated machine.

The tape played slow, which added to the grimness. Rebus had heard stuff like it before, but not for a wee while. Songs about King Billy and the Apprentice Boys, the Battle of the Boyne and the glory of 1690, songs about routing the Catholics and why the men of Ulster would struggle to the end. The singer had a pub vibrato and little else, and was backed by accordion, snare and the occasional flute. Only an Orange marching band could make the flute sound martial to the ears. Well, an Orange marching band or Iain Anderson from Jethro Tull. Rebus was reminded that he hadn't listened to Tull in an age. Anything would be better than these songs of . . . the word 'hate' sprang to mind, but he dismissed it. There was no vitriol in the lyrics, just a stern refusal to compromise in any way, to give ground, to accept that things could change now that the 1690s had become the 1990s. It was all blinkered and backward-looking. How narrow a view could you get?

'The sod is,' said Siobhan Clarke, 'you find yourself humming the tunes after.'

'Aye,' said Rebus, 'bigotry's catchy enough all right.'

And he whistled Jethro Tull all the way back to St Leonard's.

Lauderdale had arranged a press conference and wanted to know what Rebus knew.

'I'm not positive,' was the answer. 'Not a hundred per cent.'

'How close?'

'Ninety, ninety-five.'

Lauderdale considered this. 'So should I say anything?'

'That's up to you, sir. A fingerprint team's on its way to the flat. We'll know soon enough one way or the other.'

One of the problems with the victim was that the last killing shot had blown away half his face, the bullet entering through the back of the neck and tearing up through the jaw. As Dr Curt had explained, they could do an ID covering up the bottom half of the face, allowing a friend or relative to see just the top half. But would that be enough? Before today's potential break, they'd been forced to consider dental work. The victim's teeth were the usual result of a Scottish childhood, eroded by sweets and shored up by dentistry. But as the forensic pathologist had said, the mouth was badly damaged, and what dental work remained was fairly routine. There was nothing unusual there for any dentist to spot definitively as his or her work.

Rebus arranged for the party photograph to be reprinted and sent to Glasgow with the relevant details. Then he went to Lauderdale's press conference.

Chief Inspector Lauderdale loved his duels with the media. But today he was more nervous than usual. Perhaps it was that he had a larger audience than he was used to, Chief Superintendent Watson and DCI Kilpatrick having emerged from somewhere to listen. Both sported faces too ruddy to be natural, whisky certainly the cause. While the journalists sat towards the front of the room, the police officers stood to the back. Kilpatrick saw Rebus and sidled over to him.

'You may have a positive ID?' he whispered.

'Maybe.'

'So is it drugs or the IRA?' There was a wry smile on his face. He didn't really expect an answer, it was the whisky asking, that was all. But Rebus had an answer for him anyway.

'If it's anybody,' he said, 'it's not the IRA but the other lot.' There were so many names for them he didn't even begin to list them: UDA, UVF, UFF, UR ... The U stood for Ulster in each case. They were proscribed organisations, and they were all Protestant. Kilpatrick rocked back a little on his heels. His face was full of questions, fighting their way to the surface past the burst blood vessels which cherried nose and cheeks. A drinker's face. Rebus had seen too many of them, including his own some nights in the bathroom mirror.

But Kilpatrick wasn't so far gone. He knew he was in no condition to ask questions, so he made his way back to the Farmer instead, where he spoke a few words. Farmer Watson glanced across to Rebus, then nodded to Kilpatrick. Then they turned their attention back to the press briefing.

Rebus knew the reporters. They were old hands mostly, and knew what to expect from Chief Inspector Lauderdale. You might walk into a Lauderdale session sniffing and baying like a bloodhound, but you shuffled out like a sleepy-faced pup. So they stayed quiet mostly, and let him have his insubstantial say.

Except for Mairie Henderson. She was down at the front, asking questions the others weren't bothering to ask; weren't bothering for the simple reason that they knew the answer the Chief Inspector would give.

'No comment,' he told Mairie for about the twentieth time. She gave up and slumped in her chair. Someone else asked a question, so she looked around, surveying the room. Rebus jerked his chin in greeting. Mairie glared and stuck her tongue out at him. A few of the other journalists looked around in his direction. Rebus smiled out their inquisitive stares.

The briefing over, Mairie caught up with him in the corridor. She was carrying a legal notepad, her usual blue fineliner pen, and a recording walkman.

'Thanks for your help the other night,' she said.

'No comment.'

She knew it was a waste of time getting angry at John

Rebus, so exhaled noisily instead. 'I was first on the scene, I could have had a scoop.'

'Come to the pub with me and you can have as many scoops as you like.'

'That one's so weak it's got holes in its knees.' She turned and walked off, Rebus watching her. He never liked to pass up the opportunity of looking at her legs.

# 6

Edinburgh City Mortuary was sited on the Cowgate, at the
bottom of High School Wynd and facing St Ann's Community Centre and Blackfriars Street. The building was
low-built red brick and pebbledash, purposely anonymous
and tucked in an out of the way place. Steep sloping roads
led up towards the High Street. For a long time now, the
Cowgate had been a thoroughfare for traffic, not pedestrians. It was narrow and deep like a canyon, its pavements offering scant shelter from the taxis and cars
rumbling past. The place was not for the faint-hearted.
Society's underclass could be found there, when it wasn't
yet time to shuffle back to the hostel.

But the street was undergoing redevelopment, including
a court annexe. First they'd cleaned up the Grassmarket,
and now the city fathers had the Cowgate in their sights.

Rebus waited outside the mortuary for a couple of
minutes, until a woman poked her head out of the door.

'Inspector Rebus?'

'That's right.'

'He told me to tell you he's already gone to Bannerman's.'

'Thanks.' Rebus headed off towards the pub.

Bannerman's had been just cellarage at one time, and
hadn't been altered much since. Its vaulted rooms were
unnervingly like those of the shops in Mary King's Close.
Cellars like these formed connecting burrows beneath the
Old Town, worming from the Lawnmarket down to the
Canongate and beyond. The bar wasn't busy yet, and Dr

Curt was sitting by the window, his beer glass resting on a barrel which served as table. Somehow, he'd found one of the few comfortable chairs in the place. It looked like a minor nobleman's perch, with armrests and high back. Rebus bought a double whisky for himself, dragged over a stool, and sat down.

'Your health, John.'

'And yours.'

'So what can I do for you?'

Even in a pub, Rebus would swear he could smell soap and surgical alcohol wafting up from Curt's hands. He took a swallow of whisky. Curt frowned.

'Looks like I might be examining your liver sooner than I'd hoped.'

Rebus nodded towards the pack of cigarettes on the table. They were Curt's and they were untipped. 'Not if you keep smoking those.'

Dr Curt smiled. He hadn't long taken up smoking, having decided to see just how indestructible he was. He wouldn't call it a death wish exactly; it was merely an exercise in mortality.

'How long have you and Ms Rattray been an item then?'

Curt laughed. 'Dear God, is that why I'm here? You want to ask me about Caroline?'

'Just making conversation. She's not bad though.'

'Oh, she's quite something.' Curt lit a cigarette and inhaled, nodding to himself. 'Quite something,' he repeated through a cloud of smoke.

'We may have a name for the victim in Mary King's Close. It's up to fingerprints now.'

'Is that why you wanted to see me? Not just to discuss Caro?'

'I want to talk about guns.'

'I'm no expert on guns.'

'Good. I'm not after an expert, I'm after someone I can talk to. Have you seen the ballistics report?' Curt shook his

53

head. 'We're looking at something like a Smith and Wesson model 547, going by the rifling marks – five grooves, right-hand twist. It's a revolver, takes six rounds of nine millimetre parabellum.'

'You've lost me already.'

'Probably the version with the three-inch rather than four-inch barrel, which means a weight of thirty-two ounces.' Rebus sipped his drink. There were whisky fumes in his nostrils now, blocking any other smells. 'Revolvers don't accept silencers.'

'Ah.' Curt nodded. 'I begin to see some light.'

'A confined space like that, shaped the way it was ...' Rebus nodded past the bar to the room beyond. 'Much the same size and shape as this.'

'It would have been loud.'

'Bloody loud. Deafening, you might say.'

'Meaning what exactly?'

Rebus shrugged. 'I'm just wondering how professional all of this really was. I mean, on the surface, if you look at the *style* of execution, then yes, it was a pro job, no question. But then things start to niggle.'

Curt considered. 'So what now? Do we scour the city for recent purchasers of hearing-aids?'

Rebus smiled. 'It's a thought.'

'All I can tell you, John, is that those bullets did damage. Whether meant to or not, they were messy. Now, we've both come up against messy killers before. Usually the facts of the mess make it easier to find them. But this time there doesn't seem to be much evidence left lying around, apart from the bullets.'

'I know.'

Curt slapped his hand on the barrel. 'Tell you what, I've got a suggestion.'

'What is it?'

He leaned forward, as if to impart a secret. 'Let me give you Caroline Rattray's phone number.'

'Bugger off,' said Rebus.

That evening, a marked patrol car picked him up from Patience's Oxford Terrace flat. The driver was a Detective Constable called Robert Burns, and Burns was doing Rebus a favour.

'I appreciate it,' said Rebus.

Though Burns was attached to C Division in the west end, he'd been born and raised in Pilmuir, and still had friends and enemies there. He was a known quantity in the Gar-B, which was what mattered to Rebus.

'I was born in one of the pre-fabs,' Burns explained. 'Before they levelled them to make way for the high-rises. The high-rises were supposed to more "civilised", if you can believe that. Bloody architects and town planners. You never find one admitting he made a mistake, do you?' He smiled. 'They're a bit like us that way.'

'By "us" do you mean the police or the Wee Frees?' Burns was more than just a member of the Free Church of Scotland. On Sunday afternoons he took his religion to the foot of The Mound, where he spouted hellfire and brimstone to anyone who'd listen. Rebus had listened a few times. But Burns took a break during the Festival. As he'd pointed out, even his voice would be fighting a losing battle against steel bands and untuned guitars.

They were turning into the Gar-B, passing the gable end again with its sinister greeting.

'Drop me as close as you can, eh?'

'Sure,' said Burns. And when they came to the dead end near the garages, he slowed only fractionally as he bumped the car up first onto the pavement and then onto the grass. 'It's not my car,' he explained.

They drove beside the path past the garages and a high-rise, until there was nowhere else to go. When Burns stopped, the car was resting about twelve feet from the community centre.

'I can walk from here,' said Rebus.

Kids who'd been lying on the centre's roof were standing now, watching them, cigarettes hanging from open mouths. People watched from the path and from open windows, too. Burns turned to Rebus.

'Don't tell me you wanted to sneak up on them?'

'This is just fine.' He opened his door. 'Stay with the car. I don't want us losing any tyres.'

Rebus walked towards the community centre's wide open doors. The teenagers on the roof watched him with practised hostility. There were paper planes lying all around, some of them made airborne again temporarily by a gust of wind. As Rebus walked into the building, he heard grunting noises above him. His rooftop audience were pretending to be pigs.

There was no preliminary chamber, just the hall itself. At one end stood a high basketball hoop. Some teenagers were in a ruck around the grounded ball, feet scraping at ankles, hands pulling at arms and hair. So much for non-contact sports. On a makeshift stage sat a ghetto blaster, blaring out the fashion in heavy metal. Rebus didn't reckon he'd score many points by announcing that he'd been in at the birth. Most of these kids had been born after *Anarchy in the UK*, never mind *Communication Breakdown*.

There was a mix of ages, and it was impossible to pick out Peter Cave. He could be nodding his head to the distorted electric guitar. He could be smoking by the wall. Or in with the basketball brigade. But no, he was coming towards Rebus from the other direction, from a tight group which included black t-shirt from Rebus's first visit.

'Can I help?'

Father Leary had said he was in his mid-twenties, but he could pass for late-teens. The clothes helped, and he wore them well. Rebus had seen church people before when they wore denim. They usually looked as if they'd be more comfortable in something less comfortable. But Cave, in

56

faded denim jeans and denim shirt, with half a dozen thin leather and metal bracelets around his wrists, he looked all right.

'Not many girls,' Rebus stated, playing for a little more time.

Peter Cave looked around. 'Not just now. Usually there are more than this, but on a nice night...'

It was a nice night. He'd left Patience drinking cold rose wine in the garden. He had left her reluctantly. He got no initial bad feelings from Cave. The young man was fresh-faced and clear-eyed and looked level headed too. His hair was long but by no means untidy, and his face was square and honest with a deep cleft in the chin.

'I'm sorry,' Cave said, 'I'm Peter Cave. I run the youth club.' His hand shot out, bracelets sliding down his wrist. Rebus took the hand and smiled. Cave wanted to know who he was, a not unreasonable request.

'Detective Inspector Rebus.'

Cave nodded. 'Davey said a policeman had been round earlier. I thought probably he meant uniformed. What's the trouble, Inspector?'

'No trouble, Mr Cave.'

A circle of frowning onlookers had formed itself around the two of them. Rebus wasn't worried, not yet.

'Call me Peter.'

'Mr Cave,' Rebus licked his lips, 'how are things going here?'

'What do you mean?'

'A simple question, sir. Only, crime in Pilmuir hasn't exactly dropped since you started this place up.'

Cave bristled at that. 'There haven't been any gang fights.'

Rebus accepted this. 'But housebreaking, assaults ... there are still syringes in the playpark and aerosols lying –'

'Aerosols to you too.'

57

Rebus turned to see who had entered. It was the boy with the naked chest and denim jacket.

'Hello, Davey,' said Rebus. The ring had broken long enough to let denim jacket through.

The youth pointed a finger. 'I thought I said you didn't want to know my name?'

'I can't help it if people tell me things, Davey.'

'Davey Soutar,' Burns added. He was standing in the doorway, arms folded, looking like he was enjoying himself. He wasn't of course, it was just a necessary pose.

'Davey Soutar,' Rebus echoed.

Soutar had clenched his fists. Peter Cave attempted to intercede. 'Now, please. Is there a problem here, Inspector?'

'You tell me, Mr Cave.' He looked around him. 'Frankly, we're a little bit concerned about this gang hut.'

Colour flooded Cave's cheeks. 'It's a youth centre.'

Rebus was now studying the ceiling. Nobody was playing basketball any more. The music had been turned right down. 'If you say so, sir.'

'Look, you come barging in here –'

'I don't recall barging, Mr Cave. More of a saunter. I didn't ask for trouble. If Davey here can be persuaded to unclench his fists, maybe you and me can have a quiet chat outside.' He looked at the circle around them. 'I'm not one for playing to the cheap seats.'

Cave stared at Rebus, then at Soutar. He nodded slowly, his face drained of anger, and eventually Soutar let his hands relax. You could tell it was an effort. Burns hadn't put in an appearance for nothing.

'There now,' said Rebus. 'Come on, Mr Cave, let's you and me go for a walk.'

They walked across the playing fields. Burns had returned to the patrol car and moved it to a spot where he could watch them. Some teenagers watched from the back of the community centre and from its roof, but they didn't venture any closer than that.

'I really don't see, Inspector –'

'You think you're doing a good job here, sir?'

Cave thought about it before answering. 'Yes, I do.'

'You think the experiment is a success?'

'A limited success so far, but yes, once again.' He had his hands behind his back, head bowed a little. He looked like he didn't have a care in the world.

'No regrets?'

'None.'

'Funny then...'

'What?'

'Your church doesn't seem so sure.'

Cave stopped in his tracks. 'Is that what this is about? You're in Conor's congregation, is that it? He's sent you here to ... what's the phrase? Come down heavy on me?'

'Nothing like that.'

'He's paranoid. *He* was the one who wanted me here. Now suddenly he's decided I should leave, *ipso facto* I *must* leave. He's used to getting his way after all. Well, I don't choose to leave. I like it fine here. Is that what he's afraid of? Well there's not much he can do about it, is there? And as far as I can see, Inspector, there's nothing you can do about it either, unless someone from the club is found breaking the law.' Cave's face had reddened, his hands coming from behind his back so he could gesture with them.

'That lot break the law every day.'

'Now just a –'

'No, listen for a minute. Okay, you got the Jaffas and the Tims together, but ask yourself why they were amenable. If they're not divided, they're united, and they're united for a *reason*. They're the same as before, only stronger. You must see that.'

'I see nothing of the sort. People can change, Inspector.'

Rebus had been hearing the line all his professional life. He sighed and toed the ground.

'You don't believe that?'

'Frankly, sir, not in this particular case, and the crime stats back me up. What you've got just now is a truce of sorts, and it suits them because while there's a truce they can get busy carving up territory between them. Anyone threatens them, they can retaliate in spades ... or even *with* spades. But it won't last, and when they split back into their separate gangs, there's going to be blood spilled, no way round it. Because now there'll be more at stake. Tell me, in your club tonight, how many Catholics were there?'

Cave didn't answer, he was too busy shaking his head. 'I feel sorry for you, really I do. I can smell cynicism off you like sulphur. I don't happen to believe anything you've just said.'

'Then you're every bit as naive as I am cynical, and that means they're just using you. Which is good, because the only way of looking at this is that you've been sucked into it and you accept it, knowing the truth.'

Cave's cheeks were red again. 'How dare you say that!' And he punched Rebus in the stomach, hard. Rebus had been punched by professionals, but he was unprepared and felt himself double over for a moment, getting his wind back. There was a burning feeling in his gut, and it wasn't whisky. He could hear cheering in the distance. Tiny figures were dancing up and down on the community centre roof. Rebus hoped they'd fall through it. He straightened up again.

'Is that what you call setting a good example, Mr Cave?'

Then he punched Cave solidly on the jaw. The young man stumbled backwards and almost fell.

He heard a double roar from the community centre. The youth of the Gar-B were clambering down from the roof, starting to run in his direction. Burns had started the car and was bumping it across the football pitch towards him. The car was outpacing the crowd, but only just. An empty can bounced off its rear windscreen. Burns barely braked as he caught up with Rebus. Rebus yanked the door open and got in, grazing a knee and an elbow. Then they were off again, making for the roadway.

'Well,' Burns commented, checking the rearview, 'that seemed to go off okay.' Rebus was catching his breath and examining his elbow.

'How did you know Davey Soutar's name?'

'He's a maniac,' Burns said simply. 'I try to keep abreast of these things.'

Rebus exhaled loudly, rolling his sleeve back down. 'Never do a favour for a priest,' he said to himself.

'I'll bear that in mind, sir,' said Burns.

# 7

Rebus walked into the Murder Room next morning with a cup of delicatessen decaf and a tuna sandwich on whole-meal. He sat at his desk and peeled off the top from the styrofoam cup. From the corner of his eye he could see the fresh mound of paperwork which had appeared on his desk since yesterday. But he could ignore it for another five minutes.

The victim's fingerprints had been matched with those taken from items in Billy Cunningham's room. So now they had a name for the body, but precious little else. Murdock and Millie had been interviewed, and the Post Office were looking up their personnel files. Today, Billy's room would be searched again. They still didn't know who he was really. They still didn't know anything about where he came from or who his parents were. There was so much they didn't know.

In a murder investigation, Rebus had found, you didn't always need to know everything.

Chief Inspector Lauderdale was standing behind him. Rebus knew this because Lauderdale brought a smell with him. Not everyone could distinguish it, but Rebus could. It was as if talcum powder had been used in a bathroom to cover some less acceptable aroma. Then there was a click and the buzz of Lauderdale's battery-shaver. Rebus straightened at the sound.

'Chief wants to see you,' Lauderdale said. 'Breakfast can wait.'

Rebus stared at his sandwich.

'I said it can wait.'

Rebus nodded. 'I'll bring you back a mug of coffee, shall I, sir?'

He took his own coffee with him, sipping it as he listened for a moment at Farmer Watson's door. There were voices inside, one of them more nasal than the other. Rebus knocked and entered. DCI Kilpatrick was sitting across the desk from the Farmer.

'Morning, John,' said the Chief Super. 'Coffee?'

Rebus raised his cup. 'Got some, sir.'

'Well, sit down.'

He sat next to Kilpatrick. 'Morning, sir.'

'Good morning, John.' Kilpatrick was nursing a mug, but he wasn't drinking. The Farmer meantime was pouring himself a refill from his personal machine.

'Right, John,' he said at last, sitting down. 'Bottom line, you're being seconded to DCI Kilpatrick's section.' Watson took a gulp of coffee, swilling it around his mouth. Rebus looked to Kilpatrick, who obliged with a confirmation.

'You'll be based with us at Fettes, but you're going to be our eyes and ears on this murder inquiry, liaison if you like, so you'll still spend most of your time here at St Leonard's.'

'But why?'

'Well, Inspector, this case might concern the Crime Squad.'

'Yes, sir, but why me in particular?'

'You've been in the Army. I notice you served in Ulster in the late '60s.'

'That was quarter of a century ago,' Rebus protested. An age spent forgetting all about it.

'Nevertheless, you'll agree there seem to be paramilitary aspects to this case. As you commented, the gun is not your everyday hold-up weapon. It's a type of revolver used by terrorists. A lot of guns have been coming into the UK recently. Maybe this murder will connect us to them.'

'Wait a second, you're saying you're not interested in the shooting, you're interested in the *gun?*'

'I think it will become clearer when I show you our operation at Fettes. I'll be through here in –' he looked at his watch '– say twenty minutes. That should give you time to say goodbye to your loved ones.' He smiled.

Rebus nodded. He hadn't touched his coffee. A cooling scum had formed on its surface. 'All right, sir,' he said, getting to his feet.

He was still a little dazed when he got back to the Murder Room. Two detectives were being told a joke by a third. The joke was about a squid with no money, a restaurant bill, and the guy from the kitchen who washed up. The guy from the kitchen was called Hans.

Rebus was joining the SCS, the Bastard Brigade as some called it. He sat at his desk. It took him a minute to work out that something was missing.

'Which bollocks of you's eaten my sandwich?'

As he looked around the room, he saw that the joke had come to an untimely end. But no one was paying attention to him. A message was being passed through the place, changing the mood. Lauderdale came over to Rebus's desk. He was holding a sheet of fax paper.

'What is it?' Rebus asked.

'Glasgow have tracked down Billy Cunningham's mother.'

'Good. Is she coming here?'

Lauderdale nodded distractedly. 'She'll be here for the formal ID.'

'No father?'

'The father and mother split up a long time ago. Billy was still an infant. She told us his name though.' He handed over the fax sheet. 'It's Morris Cafferty.'

'What?' Rebus's hunger left him.

'Morris Gerald Cafferty.'

64

Rebus read the fax sheet. 'Say it ain't so. It's just Glasgow having a joke.' But Lauderdale was shaking his head.

'No joke,' he said.

Big Ger Cafferty was in prison, had been for several months, would be for many years to come. He was a dangerous man, runner of protection rackets, extortioner, murderer. They'd pinned only two counts of murder on him, but there had been others, Rebus knew there had been others.

'You think someone was sending him a message?' he asked.

Lauderdale shrugged. 'This changes the case slightly, certainly. According to Mrs Cunningham, Cafferty kept tabs on Billy all the time he was growing up, made sure he didn't want for anything. She still gets money from time to time.'

'But did Billy know who his father was?'

'Not according to Mrs Cunningham.'

'Then would anyone else have known?'

Lauderdale shrugged again. 'I wonder who'll tell Cafferty.'

'They better do it by phone. I wouldn't want to be in the same room with him.'

'Lucky my good suit's in my locker,' said Lauderdale. 'There'll have to be another press conference.'

'Best tell the Chief Super first though, eh?'

Lauderdale's eyes cleared. 'Of course.' He lifted Rebus's receiver to make the call. 'What did he want with you, by the way?'

'Nothing much,' said Rebus. He meant it too, now.

'But maybe this changes things,' he persisted to Kilpatrick in the car. They were seated in the back, a driver taking them the slow route to Fettes. He was sticking to the main roads, instead of the alleys and shortcuts and fast stretches unpoliced by traffic lights that Rebus would have used.

'Maybe,' said Kilpatrick. 'We'll see.'

Rebus had been telling Kilpatrick all about Big Ger Cafferty. 'I mean,' he went on, 'if it's a gang thing, then it's nothing to do with paramilitaries, is it? So I can't help you.'

Kilpatrick smiled at him. 'What is it, John? Most coppers I know would give their drinking arm for an assignment with SCS.'

'Yes, sir.'

'But you're not one of them?'

'I'm quite attached to my drinking arm. It comes in handy for other things.' Rebus looked out of the window. 'The thing is, I've been on secondment before, and I didn't like it much.'

'You mean London? The Chief Superintendent told me all about it.'

'I doubt that, sir,' Rebus said quietly. They turned off Queensferry Road, not a minute's walk from Patience's flat.

'Humour me,' said Kilpatrick stiffly. 'After all, it sounds like you're an expert on this man Cafferty too. I'd be daft not to use a man like you.'

'Yes, sir.'

And they left it at that, saying nothing as they turned into Fettes, Edinburgh's police HQ. At the end of the long road you got a good view of the Gothic spires of Fettes School, one of the city's most exclusive. Rebus didn't know which was uglier, the ornate school or the low anonymous building which housed police HQ. It could have been a comprehensive school, not so much a piece of design as a lack of it. It was one of the most unimaginative buildings Rebus had ever come across. Maybe it was making a statement about its purpose.

The Scottish Crime Squad's Edinburgh operation was run from a cramped office on the fifth floor, a floor shared with the city's Scene of Crime unit. One floor above worked the forensic scientists and the police photographers. There was a lot of interaction between the two floors.

The Crime Squad's real HQ was Stuart Street in Glasgow, with other branches in Stonehaven and Dunfermline, the latter being a technical support unit. Eighty-two officers in total, plus a dozen or so civilian staff.

'We've got our own surveillance and drugs teams,' Kilpatrick added. 'We recruit from all eight Scottish forces.' He kept his spiel going as he led Rebus through the SCS office. A few people looked up from their work, but by no means all of them. Two who did were a bald man and his freckle-faced neighbour. Their look wasn't welcoming, just interested.

Rebus and Kilpatrick were approaching a very large man who was standing in front of a wall-map. The map showed the British Isles and the north European mainland, stretching east as far as Russia. Some sea routes had been marked with long narrow strips of red material, like something you'd use in dressmaking. Only the big man didn't look the type for crimping-shears and tissue-paper cut-outs. On the map, the ports had been circled in black pen. One of the routes ended on the Scottish east coast. The man hadn't turned round at their approach.

'Inspector John Rebus,' said Kilpatrick, 'this is Inspector Ken Smylie. He never smiles, so don't bother joking with him about his name. He doesn't say much, but he's always thinking. And he's from Fife, so watch out. You know what they say about Fifers.'

'I'm from Fife myself,' said Rebus. Smylie had turned round to grip Rebus's hand. He was probably six feet three or four, and had the bulk to make the height work. The bulk was a mixture of muscle and fat, but mostly muscle. Rebus would bet the guy worked out every day. He was a few years younger than Rebus, with short thick fair hair and a small dark moustache. You'd take him for a farm labourer, maybe even a farmer. In the Borders, he'd definitely have played rugby.

'Ken,' Kilpatrick said to Smylie, 'I'd like you to show

John around. He's going to be joining us temporarily. He's ex-Army, served in Ulster.' Kilpatrick winked. 'A good man.' Ken Smylie looked appraisingly at Rebus, who tried to stand up straight, inflating his chest. He didn't know why he wanted to impress Smylie, except that he didn't want him as an enemy. Smylie nodded slowly, sharing a look with Kilpatrick, a look Rebus didn't understand.

Kilpatrick touched Smylie's arm. 'I'll leave you to it.' He turned and called to another officer. 'Jim, any calls?' Then he walked away from them.

Rebus turned to the map. 'Ferry crossings?'

'There isn't a ferry sails from the east coast.'

'They go to Scandinavia.'

'This one doesn't.' He had a point. Rebus decided to try again.

'Boats then?'

'Boats, yes. We think boats.' Rebus had expected the voice to be *basso profondo*, but it was curiously high, as though it hadn't broken properly in Smylie's teens. Maybe it was the reason he didn't say much.

'You're interested in boats then?'

'Only if they're bringing in contraband.'

Rebus nodded. 'Guns.'

'Maybe guns.' He pointed to some of the east European ports. 'See, these days things being what they are, there are a lot of weapons in and around Russia. If you cut back your military, you get excess. And the economic situation there being what it is, you get people who need money.'

'So they steal guns and sell them?'

'If they need to steal them. A lot of the soldiers kept their guns. Plus they picked up souvenirs along the way, stuff from Afghanistan and wherever. Here, sit down.'

They sat at Smylie's desk, Smylie himself spilling from a moulded plastic chair. He brought some photographs out of a drawer. They showed machine guns, rocket launchers, grenades and missiles, armour-piercing shells, a whole dusty armoury.

'This is just some of the stuff that's been tracked down. Most of it in mainland Europe: Holland, Germany, France. But some of it in Northern Ireland of course, and some in England and Scotland.' He tapped a photo of an assault rifle. 'This AK 47 was used in a bank hold-up in Hillhead. You know Professor Kalashnikov is a travelling salesman these days? Times are hard, so he goes to arms fairs around the world flogging his creations. Like this.' Smylie picked out another photograph. 'Later model, the AK 74. The magazine's made of plastic. This is actually the 74S, still quite rare on the market. A lot of the stuff travels across Europe courtesy of motorcycle gangs.'

'Hell's Angels?'

Smylie nodded. 'Some of them are in this up to their tattooed necks, and making a fortune. But there are other problems. A lot of stuff comes into the UK direct. The armed forces, they bring back souvenirs too, from the Falklands or Kuwait. Kalashnikovs, you name it. Not everyone gets searched, a lot of stuff gets in. Later, it's either sold or stolen, and the owners aren't about to report the theft, are they?'

Smylie paused and swallowed, maybe realising how much he'd been talking.

'I thought you were the strong silent type,' Rebus said.

'I get carried away sometimes.'

Rebus wouldn't fancy being on stretcher detail. Smylie began to tidy up the photographs.

'That's basically it,' he said. 'The material that's already here we can't do much about, but with the help of Interpol we're trying to stop the trafficking.'

'You're not saying Scotland is a target for this stuff?'

'A conduit, that's all. It comes through here on its way to Northern Ireland.'

'The IRA?'

69

'To whoever has the money to pay for it. Right now, we think it's more a Protestant thing. We just don't know why.'

'How much evidence do you have?'

'Not enough.'

Rebus was thinking. Kilpatrick had kept very quiet, but all along he'd thought there was a paramilitary angle to the murder, because it tied in with all of this.

'You're the one who spotted the six-pack?' Smylie asked. Rebus nodded. 'You might well be right about it. If so, the victim must've been involved.'

'Or just someone who got caught up in it.'

'That tends not to happen.'

'But there's another thing. The victim's father is a local gangster, Big Ger Cafferty.'

'You put him away a while back.'

'You're well informed.'

'Well,' said Smylie, 'Cafferty adds a certain symmetry, doesn't he?' He rose briskly from his chair. 'Come on, I'll give you the rest of the tour.'

Not that there was much to see. But Rebus was introduced to his colleagues. They didn't look like supermen, but you wouldn't want to fight them on their terms. They all looked like they'd gone the distance and beyond.

One man, a DS Claverhouse, was the exception. He was lanky and slow-moving and had dark cusps beneath his eyes.

'Don't let him fool you,' Smylie said. 'We don't call him Bloody Claverhouse for nothing.'

Claverhouse's smile took time forming. It wasn't that he was slow so much as that he had to calculate things before he carried them out. He was seated at his desk, Rebus and Smylie standing in front of him. He was tapping his fingers on a red cardboard file. The file was closed, but on its cover was printed the single word SHIELD. Rebus had just seen the word on another file lying on Smylie's desk.

'Shield?' he asked.

'The Shield,' Claverhouse corrected. 'It's something we keep hearing about. Maybe a gang, maybe with Irish connections.'

'But just now,' interrupted Smylie, 'all it is is a name.'

Shield, the word meant something to Rebus. Or rather, he knew it should mean something to him. As he turned from Claverhouse's desk, he caught something Claverhouse was saying to Smylie, saying in an undertone.

'We don't need him.'

Rebus didn't let on he'd heard. He knew nobody liked it when an outsider was brought in. Nor did he feel any happier when introduced to the bald man, a DS Blackwood, and the freckled one, DC Ormiston. They were as enthusiastic about him as dogs welcoming a new flea to the area. Rebus didn't linger; there was a small empty desk waiting from him in another part of the room, and a chair which had been found in some cupboard. The chair didn't quite have three legs, but Rebus got the idea: they hadn't exactly stretched themselves to provide him with a wholesome working environment. He took one look at desk and chair, made his excuses and left. He took a few deep breaths in the corridor, then descended a few floors. He had one friend at Fettes, and saw no reason why he shouldn't visit her.

But there was someone else in DI Gill Templer's office. The nameplate on the door told him so. Her name was DI Murchie and she too was a Liaison Officer. Rebus knocked on the door.

'Enter!'

It was like entering a headmistress's office. DI Murchie was young; at least, her face was. But she had made determined efforts to negate this fact.

'Yes?' she said.

'I was looking for DI Templer.'

Murchie put down her pen and slipped off her half-moon glasses. They hung by a string around her neck. 'She's moved on,' she said. 'Dunfermline, I think.'

'Dunfermline? What's she doing there?'

'Dealing with rapes and sexual assaults, so far as I know. Do you have some business with Inspector Templer?'

'No, I just ... I was passing and ... Never mind.' He backed out of the room.

DI Murchie twitched her mouth and put her glasses back on. Rebus went back upstairs feeling worse than ever.

He spent the rest of the morning waiting for something to happen. Nothing did. Everyone kept their distance, even Smylie. And then the phone rang on Smylie's desk, and it was a call for him.

'Chief Inspector Lauderdale,' Smylie said, handing over the receiver.

'Hello?'

'I hear you've been poached from us.'

'Sort of, sir.'

'Well, tell them I want to poach you back.'

I'm not a fucking salmon, thought Rebus. 'I'm still on the investigation, sir,' he said.

'Yes, I know that. The Chief Super told me all about it.' He paused. 'We want you to talk to Cafferty.'

'He won't talk to me.'

'We think he might.'

'Does he know about Billy?'

'Yes, he knows.'

'And now he wants someone he can use as a punch-bag?' Lauderdale didn't say anything to this. 'What good will it do talking to him?'

'I'm not sure.'

'Then why bother?'

'Because he's insisting. He wants to talk to CID, and not just any officer will do. He's asked to speak to *you*.' There was silence between them. 'John? Anything to say?'

'Yes, sir. This has been a very strange day.' He checked his watch. 'And it's not even one o'clock yet.'

# 8

Big Ger Cafferty was looking good.

He was fit and lean and had purpose to his gait. A white t-shirt was tight across his chest, flat over the stomach, and he wore faded work denims and new-looking tennis shoes. He walked into the Visiting Room like he was the visitor, Rebus the inmate. The warder beside him was no more than a hired flunkey, to be dismissed at any moment. Cafferty gripped Rebus's hand just a bit too hard, but he wasn't going to try tearing it off, not yet.

'Strawman.'

'Hello, Cafferty.' They sat down at opposite sides of the plastic table, the legs of which had been bolted to the floor. Otherwise, there was little to show that they were in Barlinnie Jail, a prison with a tough reputation from way back, but one which had striven to remake itself. The Visiting Room was clean and white, a few public safety posters decorating its walls. There was a flimsy aluminium ashtray, but also a No Smoking sign. The tabletop bore a few burn marks around its rim from cigarettes resting there too long.

'They made you come then, Strawman?' Cafferty seemed amused by Rebus's appearance. He knew, too, that as long as he kept using his nickname for Rebus, Rebus would be needled.

'I'm sorry about your son.'

Cafferty was no longer amused. 'Is it true they tortured him?'

'Sort of.'

'Sort of?' Cafferty's voice rose. 'There's no halfway house with torture!'

'You'd know all about that.'

Cafferty's eyes blazed. His breathing was shallow and noisy. He got to his feet.

'I can't complain about this place. You get a lot of freedom these days. I've found you can *buy* freedom, same as you can buy anything else.' He stopped beside the warder. 'Isn't that right, Mr Petrie?'

Wisely, Petrie said nothing.

'Wait for me outside,' Cafferty ordered. Rebus watched Petrie leave. Cafferty looked at him and grinned a humourless grin.

'Cosy,' he said, 'just the two of us.' He started to rub his stomach.

'What do you want, Cafferty?'

'Stomach's started giving me gyp. What's my point, Strawman? My point's this.' He was standing over Rebus, and now leant down, his hands pressing Rebus's shoulders. 'I want the bastard found.' Rebus found himself staring at Cafferty's bared teeth. 'See, I can't have people fucking with my family, it's bad for *my* reputation. Nobody gets away with something like that ... it'd be bad for business.'

'Nice to see the paternal instinct's so strong.'

Cafferty ignored this. 'My men are out there hunting, understood? And they'll be keeping an eye on *you*. I want a result, Strawman.'

Rebus shrugged off Cafferty's pressure and got to his feet. 'You think we're going to sit on our hands because the victim was your son?'

'You better not ... *that's* what I'm saying. Revenge, Strawman, I'll have it one way or the other. I'll have it on *some*body.'

'Not on me,' Rebus said quietly. He held Cafferty's stare, till Cafferty opened his arms wide and shrugged, then went

74

to his chair and sat down. Rebus stayed standing.

'I need to ask you a few questions,' he said.

'Fire away.'

'Did you keep in touch with your son?'

Cafferty shook his head. 'I kept in touch with his mum. She's a good woman, too good for me, always was. I send her money for Billy, at least I did while he was growing up. I still send something from time to time.'

'By what means?'

'Someone I can trust.'

'Did Billy know who his father was?'

'Absolutely not. His mum wasn't exactly proud of me.' He started rubbing his stomach again.

'You should take something for that,' Rebus said. 'So, could anyone have got to him as a way of getting at you?'

Cafferty nodded. 'I've thought about it, Strawman. I've thought a lot about it.' Now he shook his head. 'I can't see it. I mean, it was my first thought, but nobody knew, nobody except his mum and me.'

'And the intermediary.'

'He didn't have anything to do with it. I've had people ask him.'

The way Cafferty said this sent a shiver through Rebus.

'Two more things,' he said. 'The word Nemo, mean anything?'

Cafferty shook his head. But Rebus knew that by tonight villains across the east of Scotland would be on the watch for the name. Maybe Cafferty's men *would* get to the killer first. Rebus had seen the body. He didn't much care who got the killer, so long as someone did. He guessed this was Cafferty's thinking too.

'Second thing,' he said, 'the letters SaS on a tattoo.'

Cafferty shook his head again, but more slowly this time. There was something there, some recognition.

'What is it, Cafferty?'

But Cafferty wasn't saying.

'What about gangs, was he in any gangs?'

'He wasn't the type.'

'He had the Red Hand of Ulster on his bedroom wall.'

'I've got a Pirelli calendar on mine, doesn't mean I use their tyres.'

Rebus walked towards the door. 'Not much fun being a victim, is it?'

Cafferty jumped to his feet. 'Remember,' he said, 'I'll be watching.'

'Cafferty, if one of your goons so much as asks me the time of day, I'll throw him in a cell.'

'You threw me in a cell, Strawman. Where did it get you?'

Unable to bear Cafferty's smile, the smile of a man who had drowned people in pigshit and shot them in cold blood, a cold devious manipulator, a man without morals or remorse, unable finally to bear any of this, Rebus left the room.

The prison officer, Petrie, was standing outside, shuffling his feet. His eyes couldn't meet Rebus's.

'You're an absolute disgrace,' Rebus told him, walking away.

While he was in Glasgow, Rebus could have talked to the boy's mother, only the boy's mother was in Edinburgh giving an official ID to the top half of her dead son's face. Dr Curt would be sure she never saw the bottom half. As he'd said to Rebus, if Billy had been a ventriloquist's dummy, he'd never have worked again.

'You're a sick man, doctor,' John Rebus had said.

He drove back to Edinburgh weary and trembling. Cafferty had that effect on him. He'd never thought he'd have to see the man again, at least not until both of them were of pensionable age. Cafferty had sent him a postcard the day he'd arrived in Barlinnie. But Siobhan Clarke had intercepted it and asked if he wanted to see it.

'Tear it up,' Rebus had told her. He still didn't know what the message had been.

Siobhan Clarke was still in the Murder Room when he got back.

'You're working hard,' he told her.

'It's a wonderful thing, overtime. Besides, we're a bit short of hands.'

'You've heard then?'

'Yes, congratulations.'

'What?'

'SCS, it's like a lateral promotion, isn't it?'

'It's only temporary, like a run of good games to Hibs. Where's Brian?'

'Out at Cunningham's digs, talking to Murdock and Millie again.'

'Was Mrs Cunningham up to questioning?'

'Just barely.'

'Who talked to her?'

'I did, the Chief Inspector's idea.'

'Then for once Lauderdale's had a good idea. Did you ask her about religion?'

'You mean all that Orange stuff in Billy's room? Yes, I asked. She just shrugged like it was nothing special.'

'It *is* nothing special. There are hundreds of people with the same flag, the same music-tapes. Christ, I've seen them.'

And this was the truth. He'd seen them at close quarters, not just as a kid, hearing the Sash sung by drunks on their way home, but more recently. He'd been visiting his brother in Fife, just over a month ago, the weekend before July 12th. There'd been an Orange march in Cowdenbeath. The pub they were in seemed to be hosting a crowd of the marchers in the dance hall upstairs. Sounds of drums, especially the huge drum they called the *lambeg*, and flutes and penny whistles, bad choruses repeated time and again. They'd gone upstairs to investigate, just as the thing was winding down. *God Save the Queen* was being destroyed on a dozen cheap flutes.

And some of the kids singing along, sweaty brows and shirts open, some of them had their arms raised, hands straight out in front of them. A Nazi-style salute.

'Nothing else?' he asked. Clarke shook her head. 'She didn't know about the tattoo?'

'She thinks he must have done it in the last year or so.'

'Well, that's interesting in itself. It means we're not dealing with some ancient gang or old flame. SaS was something recent in his life. What about Nemo?'

'It didn't mean anything to her.'

'I've just been talking to Cafferty, SaS meant something to him. Let's pull his records, see if they tell us anything.'

'*Now?*'

'We can make a start. By the way, remember that card he sent me?' Clarke nodded. 'What was on it?'

'It was a picture of a pig in its sty.'

'And the message?'

'There wasn't any message,' she said.


On the way back to Patience's he dropped into the video store and rented a couple of movies. It was the only video store nearby that he hadn't turned over at one time or another with vice or Trading Standards, looking for porn and splatter and various bootleg tapes. The owner was a middle-aged fatherly type, happy to tell you that some comedy was particularly good or some adventure film might prove a bit strong for 'the ladies'. He hadn't commented on Rebus's selections: *Terminator 2* and *All About Eve*. But Patience had a comment.

'Great,' she said, meaning the opposite.

'What's wrong?'

'You hate old movies and I hate violence.'

Rebus looked at the Schwarzenegger. 'It's not even an 18. And who says I don't like old films?'

'What's your favourite black and white movie?'

'There are hundreds of them.'

'Name me five. No, three, and don't say I'm not fair.'

He stared at her. They were standing a few feet apart in the living room, Rebus with the videos still in his hands, Patience with her arms folded, her back erect. He knew she could probably smell the whisky on his breath, even keeping his mouth shut and breathing through his nose. It was so quiet, he could hear the cat washing itself somewhere behind the sofa.

'What are we fighting about?' he asked.

She was ready for this. 'We're fighting about consideration, as usual. To wit, your lack of any.'

'*Ben Hur*.'

'Colour.'

'Well, that courtroom one then, with James Stewart.' She nodded. 'And that other one, with Orson Welles and the mandolin.'

'It was a zither.'

'Shite,' said John Rebus, throwing down the videos and making for the front door.

Millie Docherty waited until Murdock had been asleep for a good hour. She spent the hour thinking about the questions the police had asked both of them, and thinking further back to good days and bad days in her life. She spoke Murdock's name. His breathing remained regular. Only then did she slip out of bed and walk barefoot to Billy's bedroom door, touching the door with her fingertips. Christ, to think he wasn't there, would never be there again. She tried to control her breathing, fast in, slow out. Otherwise she might hyperventilate. Panic attacks, they called them. For years she'd suffered them not knowing she was not alone. There were lots of people out there like her. Billy had been one of them.

She turned the doorknob and slipped into his room. His

79

mother had been round earlier on, hardly in a state to cope with any of it. There had been a policewoman with her, the same one who'd come to the flat that first time. Billy's mum had looked at his room, but then shook her head.

'I can't do this. Another time.'

'If you like,' Millie had offered, 'I can bag everything up for you. All you'd have to do is have his things collected.' The policewoman had nodded her gratitude at that. Well, it was the least ... She felt the tears coming and sat down on his narrow bed. Funny how a bed so narrow could be made wide enough for two, if the two were close. She did the breathing exercises again. Fast in, slow out, but those words, her instructions to herself, reminded her of other things, other times. Fast in, slow out.

'I've got this self-help book,' Billy had said. 'It's in my room.' He'd gone to find it for her, and she'd followed him into his room. Such a tidy room. 'Here it is,' he'd said, turning towards her quickly, not realising how close behind him she was.

'What's all this Red Hand stuff?' she'd asked, looking past him at his walls. He'd waited till her eyes returned to his, then he'd kissed her, tongue rubbing at her teeth till she opened her mouth to him.

'Billy,' she said now, her hands filling themselves with his bedcover. She stayed that way for a few minutes, part of her mind staying alert, listening for sounds from the room she shared with Murdock. Then she moved across the bed to where the Hearts pennant was pinned to the wall. She pushed it aside with a finger.

Underneath, taped flat against the wall, was a computer disk. She'd left it here, half hoping the police would find it when they searched the room. But they'd been hopeless. And watching them search, she'd become suddenly afraid for herself, and had started to hope they wouldn't find it. Now, she got her fingernails under it and unpeeled it, looking at the disk. Well, it was hers now, wasn't it? They might kill her for it, but she could never let it go. It was part of her memory of him. She rubbed her thumb across the label. The streetlight coming through the unwashed window wasn't quite enough for her to read by, but she knew what the label said anyway.

It was just those three letters, SaS.

Dark, dark, dark.

Rebus recalled that line at least. If Patience had asked him to quote from a poem instead of giving her movie titles, he'd have been all right. He was standing at a window of St Leonard's, taking a break from his deskful of work, all the paperwork on Morris Gerald Cafferty.

Dark, dark, dark.

She was trying to civilise him. Not that she'd admit it. What she said instead was that it would be nice if they liked the same things. It would give them things to talk about. So she gave him books of poetry, and played classical music at him, bought them tickets for ballet and modern dance. Rebus had been there before, other times, other women. Asking for something more, for commitment beyond the commitment.

He didn't like it. He enjoyed the basic, the feral. Cafferty had once accused him of liking cruelty, of being attracted to it; his natural right as a Celt. And hadn't Rebus accused Peter Cave of the same thing? It was coming back to him, pain on pain, crawling back along his tubes from some place deep within him.

His time in Northern Ireland.

He'd been there early in the history of 'the Troubles', 1969, just as it was all boiling over; so early that he hadn't really known what was going on, what the score was; none of them had, not on any side. The people were pleased to see them at first, Catholic and Protestant, offering food and drink and a genuine welcome. Then later the drinks were laced with weedkiller, and the welcome might be

81

leading you into a 'honey trap'. The crunching in the sponge cake might only be hard seeds from the raspberry jam. Then again, it might be powdered glass.

Bottles flying through the dark, lit by an arc of flame. Petrol spinning and dripping from the rag wick. And when it fell on a littered road, it spread in an instant pool of hate. Nothing personal about it, it was just for a cause, a troubled cause, that was all.

And later still it was to defend the rackets which had grown up around that aged cause. The protection schemes, black taxis, gun-running, all the businesses which had spread so very far away from the ideal, creating their own pool.

He'd seen bullet wounds and shrapnel blasts and gashes left by hurled bricks, he'd tasted mortality and the flaws in both his character and his body. When not on duty, they used to hang around the barracks, knocking back whisky and playing cards. Maybe that was why whisky reminded him he was still alive, where other drinks couldn't.

There was shame too: a retaliatory strike against a drinking club which had gotten out of hand. He'd done nothing to stop it. He'd swung his baton and even his SLR with the rest of them. Yet in the middle of the commotion, the sound of a rifle being cocked was enough to bring silence and stillness . . .

He still kept an interest in events across the water. Part of his life had been left behind there. Something about his tour of duty there had made him apply to join the Special Air Service. He went back to his desk and lifted the glass of whisky.

Dark, dark, dark. The sky quiet save for the occasional drunken yell.

No one would ever know who called the police.

No one except the man himself and the police themselves.

He'd given his name and address, and had made his complaint about the noise.

'And do you want us to come and see you afterwards, sir, after we've investigated?'

'That won't be necessary.' The phone went dead on the desk officer, who smiled. It was very seldom necessary. A visit from the police meant you were involved. He wrote on a pad then passed the note along to the Communications Room. The call went out at ten to one.

When the Rover patrol car got to the community centre, it was clear that things were winding down. The officers debated heading off again, but since they were here ... Certainly there had been a party, a function of some kind. But as the two uniformed officers walked in through the open doors, only a dozen or so stragglers were left. The floor was a mess of bottles and cigarette butts, probably a few roaches in there too if they cared to look.

'Who's in charge?'

'Nobody,' came the sharp response.

There were flushing sounds from the toilets. Evidence being destroyed, perhaps.

'We've received complaints about the noise.'

'No noise here.'

The patrolman nodded. On a makeshift stage a ghetto-blaster had been hooked up to a guitar amplifier, a large Marshall job with separate amp and speaker-bin. Probably a hundred watts, none of it built for subtlety. The amplifier was still on, emitting an audible buzz. 'This thing belongs out at the Exhibition Centre.'

'Simple Minds let us borrow it.'

'Whose is it really though?'

'Where's your search warrant?'

The officer smiled again. He could see that his partner was itching for trouble, but though neither of them had a welter of experience, they weren't stupid either. They knew where they were, they knew the odds. So he stood there smiling, legs apart, arms by his side, not looking for aggro.

He seemed to be having a dialogue with one of the group, a guy with a denim jacket and no shirt underneath. He was wearing black square-toed biker boots with straps and a round silver buckle. The officer had always liked that style, had even considered buying himself a pair, just for the weekends.

Then maybe he'd start saving for the bike to go with them.

'Do we need a search warrant?' he said. 'We're called to a disturbance, doors wide open, no one barring our entry. Besides, this is a community centre. There are rules and regulations. Licences need to be applied for and granted. Do you have a licence for this ... soirée?'

'Swaah-ray?' the youth said to his pals. 'Fuckin' listen to that! Swaaah-rrray!' And he came sashaying over towards the two uniforms, like he was doing some old-fashioned dance step. He turned behind and between them. 'Is that a dirty word? Something I'm not supposed to understand? This isn't your territory, you know. This is the Gar-B, and we're having our own wee festival, since nobody bothered inviting us to the other one. You're not in the real world now. You better be careful.'

The first officer could smell alcohol, like something from a chemistry lab or a surgery: gin, vodka, white rum.

'Look,' he said, 'there has to be someone running the show, and it isn't you.'

'Why not?'

'Because you're a short-arsed wee prick.'

There was stillness in the hall. The other officer had spoken, and now his partner swallowed, trying not to look at him, keeping all his concentration on the denim jacket. Denim jacket was considering, a finger to his lips, tapping them.

'Mmm,' he said at last, nodding. 'Interesting.' He started moving back towards the group. He seemed to be wiggling his bum as he moved. Then he stooped forward, pretending to tie a shoe-lace, and let rip with a loud fart. He straightened up as his gang enjoyed the joke, their laughter subsiding only when denim jacket spoke again.

'Well, sirs,' he said, 'we're just packing everything away.' He faked a yawn. 'It's well past our bedtimes and we'd like to go home. If you don't mind.' He opened his arms wide to them, even bowed a little.

'I'd like to –'

'That'll be fine.' The first officer touched his partner's arm and turned away towards the doors. They were going to get out. And when they got out, he was going to have words with his partner, no doubt about that.

'Right then, lads,' said denim jacket, 'let's get this place tidy. We'll need to put this somewhere for a start.'

The constables were near the door when, without warning, the ghetto-blaster caught both of them a glancing blow to the back of their skulls.

# 9

Rebus heard about it on the morning news. The radio came on at six twenty-five and there it was. It brought him out of bed and into his clothes. Patience was still trying to rouse herself as he placed a mug of tea on the bedside table and a kiss on her hot cheek.

'*Ace in the Hole* and *Casablanca*,' he said. Then he was out of the door and into his car.

At Drylaw police station, the day shift hadn't come on yet, which meant that he heard it from the horses' mouths, so to speak. Not a big station, Drylaw had requested reinforcements from all around, as what had started as an assault on two officers had turned into a miniature riot. Cars had been attacked, house windows smashed. One local shop had been ram-raided, with consequent looting (if the owner was to be believed). Five officers were injured, including the two men who had been coshed with a hi-fi machine. Those two constables had escaped the Gar-B by the skin of their arses.

'It was like Northern bloody Ireland,' one veteran said. Or Brixton, thought Rebus, or Newcastle, or Toxteth...

The TV news had it on now, and police heavy-handedness was being discussed. Peter Cave was being interviewed outside the youth club, saying that his had been the party's organising hand.

'But I had to leave early. I thought I had flu coming on or something.' To prove it, he blew his nose.

'At breakfast-time, too,' complained someone beside Rebus.

'I know,' Cave went on, 'that I bear a certain amount of responsibility for what happened.'

'That's big of him.'

Rebus smiled, thinking: we police invented irony, we live by its rules.

'But,' said Cave, 'there are still questions which need answering. The police seem to think they can rule by threat rather than law. I've talked to a dozen people who were in the club last night, and they've told me the same thing.'

'Surprise, surprise.'

'Namely, that the two police officers involved made threats and menacing actions.'

The interviewer waited for Cave to finish. Then: 'And what do you say, Mr Cave, to local people who claim the youth club is merely a sort of hang-out, a gang headquarters for juveniles on the estate?'

Juveniles: Rebus liked that.

Cave was shaking his head. They'd brought the camera in on him for the shot. 'I say rubbish.' And he blew his nose again. Wisely, the producer switched back to the studio.

Eventually, the police had managed to make five arrests. The youths had been brought to Drylaw. Less than an hour later, a mob from the Gar-B had gathered outside, demanding their release. More thrown bricks, more broken glass, until a massed charge by the police ranks dispersed the crowd. Cars and foot patrols had cruised Drylaw and the Gar-B for the rest of the night. There were still bricks and strewn glass on the road outside. Inside, a few of the officers involved looked shaken.

Rebus looked in on the five youths. They sported bruised faces, bandaged hands. The blood had dried to a crust on them, and they'd left it there, like war paint, like medals.

'Look,' one of them said to the others, 'it's the bastard who took a poke at Pete.'

'Keep talking,' retorted Rebus, 'and you'll be next.'

'I'm quaking.'

The police had stuck a video camera onto the rioters outside the station. The picture quality was poor, but after a few viewings Rebus made out that one of the stone throwers, face hidden by a football scarf, was wearing an open denim jacket and no shirt.

He stuck around the station a bit longer, then got back in his car and headed for the Gar-B. It didn't look so different. There was glass in the road, sounds of brittle crunching under his tyres. But the local shops were like fortresses: wire mesh, metal screens, padlocks, alarms. The would-be looters had run up and down the main road for a while in a hot-wired Ford Cortina, then had launched it at the least protected shop, a place specialising in shoe repairs and key-cutting. Inside, the owner's own brand of security, a sleepy-eyed Alsatian, had thrown itself into the fray before being beaten off and chased away. As far as anyone knew, it was still roaming the wide green spaces.

A few of the ground floor flats were having boards hammered into place across their broken windows. Maybe one of them had made the initial call. Rebus didn't blame the caller; he blamed the two officers. No, that wasn't fair. What would he have done if he'd been there? Yes, exactly. And there'd have been more trouble than this if he had...

He didn't bother stopping the car. He'd only be in the way of the other sight-seers and the media. With not much happening on the IRA story, reporters were here in numbers. Plus he knew he wasn't the Gar-B's most popular tourist. Though the constables couldn't swear who'd thrown the ghetto-blaster, they knew the most likely suspect. Rebus had seen the description back at Drylaw. It was Davey Soutar of course, the boy who couldn't afford a shirt. One of the CID men had asked Rebus what his interest was.

'Personal,' he'd said. A few years back, a riot like this would have prompted the permanent closure of the community hall. But these days it was more likely the Council would bung some more cash at the estate, guilt money. Shutting the hall down wouldn't do much good anyway. There were plenty of empty flats on the estate – flats termed 'unlettable'. They were kept boarded up and padlocked, but could soon be opened. Squatters and junkies used them; gangs could use them too. A couple of miles away in different directions, middle class Barnton and Inverleith were getting ready for work. A world away. They only ever took notice of Pilmuir when it exploded.

It wasn't much of a drive to Fettes either, even with the morning bottlenecks starting their day's business. He wondered if he'd be first in the office; that might show *too* willing. Well, he could check, then nip out to the canteen until everyone started arriving. But when he pushed open the office door, he saw that there was someone in before him. It was Smylie.

'Morning,' Rebus said. Smylie nodded back. He looked tired to Rebus, which was saying something, the amount of sleep Rebus himself had had. He rested against one of the desks and folded his arms. 'Do you know an Inspector called Abernethy?'

'Special Branch,' said Smylie.

'That's him. Is he still around?'

Smylie looked up. 'He went back yesterday, caught an evening plane. Did you want to see him?'

'Not really.'

'There was nothing here for him.'

'No?'

Smylie shook his head. 'We'd know about it if there was. We're the best, we'd've spotted it before him. QED.'

'*Quod erat demonstrandum.*'

89

Smylie looked at him. 'You're thinking of Nemo, aren't you? Latin for nobody.'

'I suppose I am.' Rebus shrugged. 'Nobody seems to think Billy Cunningham knew any Latin.' Smylie didn't say anything. 'I'm not wanted here, am I?'

'How do you mean?'

'I mean, you don't need me. So why did Kilpatrick bring me in? He must've known it'd cause nothing but aggro.'

'Best ask him yourself.'

'Maybe I will. Meantime, I'll be at St Leonard's.'

'We'll be pining away in your absence.'

'I don't doubt it, Smylie.'


'What does the woman do?'

'Her name's Millie Docherty,' said Siobhan Clarke. 'She works in a computer retailer's.'

'And her boyfriend's a computer consultant. And they shared their flat with an unemployed postie. An odd mix?'

'Not really, sir.'

'No? Well, maybe not.' They were in the canteen, facing one another across the small table. Rebus took occasional bites from a damp piece of toast. Siobhan had finished hers.

'What's it like over at Fettes?' she asked.

'Oh, you know: glamour, danger, intrigue.'

'Much the same as here then?'

'Much the same. I read some of Cafferty's notes last night. I've marked the place, so you can take over.'

'Three's more fun,' said Brian Holmes, dragging over a chair. He'd placed his tray on the table, taking up all the available room. Rebus gave Holmes's fry-up a longing look, knowing it wouldn't square with his diet. All the same ... Sausage, bacon, eggs, tomato and fried bread.

'Ought to carry a government health warning,' said the vegetarian Clarke.

'Hear about the riot?' Holmes asked.

'I went out there this morning,' Rebus admitted. 'The place looked much the same.'

'I heard they threw an amplifier at a couple of our lads.' The process of exaggeration had begun.

'So, about Billy Cunningham,' Rebus nudged, none too subtly.

Holmes forked up some tomato. 'What about him?'

'What have you found out?'

'Not a lot,' Holmes conceded. 'Unemployed deliverer of the royal mail, the only regular job he's ever had. Mum was overfond of him and kept gifting him money to get by on. Bit of a loyalist extremist, but no record of him belonging to the Orange Lodge. Son of a notorious gangster, but didn't know it.' Holmes thought for a second, decided this was all he had to say, and cut into his sliced sausage.

'Plus,' said Clarke, 'the anarchist stuff we found.'

'Ach, that's nothing,' Holmes said dismissively.

'What anarchist stuff?' asked Rebus.

'There were some magazines in his wardrobe,' Clarke explained. 'Soft porn, football programmes, a couple of those survivalist mags teenagers like to read to go with their diet of *Terminator* films.' Rebus almost said something, but stopped himself. 'And a flimsy little pamphlet called ...' She sought the title. '*The Floating Anarchy Factfile*.'

'It was years old, sir,' said Holmes. 'Not relevant.'

'Do we have it here?'

'Yes, sir,' said Siobhan Clarke.

'It's from the Orkneys,' said Holmes. 'I think it's priced in old money. It belongs in a museum, not a police station.'

'Brian,' said Rebus, 'all that fat you're eating is going to your head. Since when do we dismiss *anything* in a murder inquiry?' He picked a thin rasher of streaky from the plate and dropped it into his mouth. It tasted wonderful.

*The Floating Anarchy Factfile* consisted of six sheets of A4 paper, folded over with a single staple through the middle

91

to keep it from falling apart. It was typed on an old and irregular typewriter, with hand printed titles to its meagre articles and no photographs or drawings. It was priced not in old money but in new pence: five new pence to be exact, from which Rebus guessed it to be fifteen to twenty years old. There was no date, but it proclaimed itself 'issue number three'. To a large extent Brian Holmes was right: it belonged in a museum. The pieces were written in a style that could be termed 'Celtic hippy', and this style was so uniform (as were the spelling mistakes) that the whole thing looked to be the work of a single individual with access to a copying machine, something like an old Roneo.

As for the content, there were cries of nationalism and individualism in one paragraph, philosophical and moral lethargy the next. Anarcho-syndicalism was mentioned, but so were Bakunin, Rimbaud and Tolstoy. It wasn't, to Rebus's eye, the sort of stuff to boost advertising revenue. For example:

'What Dalriada needs is a new commitment, a new set of mores which look to the existent and emerging youth culture. What we need is action by the individual without recourse or prior thought to the rusted machinery of law, church, state.

'We need to be free to make our own decisions about our nation and then act self-consciously to make those decisions a reality. The sons and daughters of Alba are the future, but we are living in the mistakes of the past and must change those mistakes in the present. If you do not act then remember: Now is the first day of the rest of your strife. And remember too: inertia corrodes.'

Except that 'mores' was spelt 'moeres' and 'existent' as 'existant'. Rebus put the pamphlet down.

'A psychiatrist could have a field day,' he muttered. Holmes and Clarke were seated on the other side of his desk. He noticed that while he'd been at Fettes, people had been using his desktop as a dumping ground for sandwich wrappers and polystyrene cups. He ignored these and turned the pamphlet over. There was an address at the bottom of the back page: Zabriskie House, Brinyan, Rousay, Orkney Isles.

'Now that's what I call dropping out,' said Rebus. 'And look, the house is named after *Zabriskie Point*.'

'Is that in the Orkneys too?' asked Holmes.

'It's a film,' said Rebus. He'd gone to see it a long long time ago, just for the '60s soundtrack. He couldn't remember much about it, except for an explosion near the end. He tapped his finger against the pamphlet. 'I want to know more about this.'

'You're kidding, sir,' said Holmes.

'That's me,' said Rebus sourly, 'always a smile and a joke.'

Clarke turned to Holmes. 'I think that means he's serious.'

'In the land of the blind,' said Rebus, 'the one-eyed man is king. And even *I* can see there's more to this than meets your eyes, Brian.'

Holmes frowned. 'Such as, sir?'

'Such as its provenance, its advanced years. What would you say, 1973? '74? Billy Cunningham wasn't even born in 1974. So what's this doing in his wardrobe beside up-to-date scud mags and football programmes?' He waited. 'Answer came there none.'

Holmes looked sullen; an annoying trait whenever Rebus showed him up. But Clarke was ready. 'We'll get Orkney police to check, sir, always supposing the Orkneys possess any police.'

'Do that,' said Rebus.

# 10

Like a rubber ball, he thought as he drove, I'll come bouncing back to you. He'd been summoned back to Fettes by DCI Kilpatrick. In his pocket there was a message from Caroline Rattray, asking him to meet her in Parliament House. He was curious about the message, which had been taken over the phone by a Detective Constable in the Murder Room. He saw Caroline Rattray as she'd been that night, all dressed up and then dragged down into Mary King's Close by Dr Curt. He saw her strong masculine face with its slanting nose and high prominent cheekbones. He wondered if Curt had said anything to her about him ... He would definitely make time to see her.

Kilpatrick had an office of his own in a corner of the otherwise open-plan room used by the SCS. Just outside it sat the secretary and the clerical assistant, though Rebus couldn't work out which was which. Both were civilians, and both operated computer consoles. They made a kind of shield between Kilpatrick and everyone else, a barrier you passed as you moved from your world into his. As Rebus passed them, they were discussing the problems facing South Africa.

'It'll be like on Uist,' one of them said, causing Rebus to pause and listen. 'North Uist is Protestant and South Uist is Catholic, and they can't abide one another.'

Kilpatrick's office itself was flimsy enough, just plastic partitions, see-through above waist height. The whole thing could be dismantled in minutes, or wrecked by a few judicious kicks and shoulder-charges. But it was definably an office. It had a door which Kilpatrick told Rebus to close. There was a certain amount of sound insulation. There were two filing-cabinets, maps and print-outs stuck to the walls with Blu-Tak, a couple of calendars still showing July. And on the desk a framed photograph of three grinning gap-toothed children.

'Yours, sir?'

'My brother's. I'm not married.' Kilpatrick turned the photo around, the better to study it. 'I try to be a good uncle.'

'Yes, sir.' Rebus sat down. Beside him sat Ken Smylie, hands crossed in his lap. The skin on his wrists had wrinkled up like a bloodhound's face.

'I'll get straight to the point, John,' said Kilpatrick. 'We've got a man undercover. He's posing as a long-distance lorry driver. We're trying to pick up information on arms shipments: who's selling, who's buying.'

'Something to do with The Shield, sir?'

Kilpatrick nodded. 'He's the one who's heard the name mentioned.'

'So who is he?'

'My brother,' Smylie said. 'His name's Calumn.'

Rebus took this in. 'Does he look like you, Ken?'

'A bit.'

'Then I dare say he'd pass as a lorry driver.'

There was almost a smile at one corner of Smylie's mouth.

'Sir,' Rebus said to Kilpatrick, 'does this mean you think the Mary King's Close killing had something to do with the paramilitaries?'

Kilpatrick smiled. 'Why do you think you're here, John? *You* spotted it straight off. We've got three men working on Billy Cunningham, trying to track down friends of his. For some reason they had to kill him, I'd like to know why.'

'Me too, sir. If you want to find out about Cunningham, try his flatmate first.'

'Murdock? Yes, we're talking to him.'

'No, not Murdock, Murdock's girlfriend. I went round there when they reported him missing. There was something about her, something not quite right. Like she was holding back, putting on an act.'

Smylie said, 'I'll take a look.'

'Her and her boyfriend both work with computers. Think that might mean something?'

'I'll take a look,' Smylie repeated. Rebus didn't doubt that he would.

'Ken thinks you should meet Calumn,' Kilpatrick said.

Rebus shrugged. 'Fine by me.'

'Good,' said Kilpatrick. 'Then we'll take a little drive.'

Out in the main office they all looked at him strangely, like they knew precisely what had been said to him in Kilpatrick's den. Well, of course they knew. Their looks told Rebus he was resented more than ever. Even Claverhouse, usually so laid back, was managing a snide little grin.

DI Blackwood rubbed a smooth hand over the hairless crown of his head, then tucked a stray hair back behind his ear. His tonsure was positively monasterial, and it bothered him. In his other hand he held his telephone receiver, listening to someone on the line. He ignored Rebus as Rebus walked past.

At the next desk along, DS Ormiston was squeezing spots on his forehead.

'You two make a picture,' Rebus said. Ormiston didn't appear to get it, but that wasn't Rebus's problem. His problem was that Kilpatrick was taking him into his confidence, and Rebus still didn't know why.

There are lots of warehouses in Sighthill, most of them anonymous. They weren't exactly advertising that one of them had been leased by the Scottish Crime Squad. It was a big old prefabricated building surrounded by a high wire fence and protected by a high barred gate. There was barbed wire strung out across the top of the fence and the gate, and the gatehouse was manned. The guard unlocked the gate and swung it open so they could drive in.

'We got this place for a song,' Kilpatrick explained. 'The market's not exactly thriving just now.' He smiled. 'They even offered to throw in the security, but we didn't think we'd need any help with that.'

Kilpatrick was sitting in the back with Rebus, Smylie acting as chauffeur. The steering wheel was like a frisbee in his paws. But he was a canny driver, slow and considerate. He even signalled as he turned into a parking bay, though there was only one other car in the whole forecourt, parked five bays away. When they got out, the Sierra's suspension groaned upwards. They were standing in front of a normal sized door whose nameplate had been removed. To its right were the much bigger doors of the loading bay. From the rubbish lying around, the impression was of a disused site. Kilpatrick took two keys from his pocket and unlocked the side door.

The warehouse was just that, no offices or partitions off, just one large space with an oily concrete floor and some empty packing cases. A pigeon, disturbed by their entrance, fluttered near the ceiling for a moment before settling again on one of the iron spars supporting the corrugated roof. It had left its mark more than once on the HGV's windshield.

'That's supposed to be lucky,' said Rebus. Not that the articulated lorry looked clean anyway. It was splashed with pale caked-on mud and dust. It was a Ford with a UK licence plate, K registration. The cab door opened and a large man heaved himself out.

He didn't have his brother's moustache and was probably a year or two younger. But he wasn't smiling, and when he spoke his voice was high-pitched, almost cracking from effort.

97

'You must be Rebus.'

They shook hands. Kilpatrick was doing the talking.

'We impounded this lorry two months back, or rather Scotland Yard did. They've kindly loaned it to us.'

Rebus hoisted himself onto the running-plate and peered in the driver's window. Behind the driving seat had been fixed a nude calendar and a dog-eared centrefold. There was space for a bunk, on which a sleeping bag was rolled up ready for use. The cab was bigger than some of the caravans Rebus had stayed in for holidays. He climbed back down.

'Why?'

There was a noise from the back of the lorry. Calumn Smylie was opening its container doors. By the time Rebus and Kilpatrick got there, the two Smylies had swung both doors wide and were standing inside the back, just in front of a series of wooden crates.

'We've taken a few liberties,' said Kilpatrick, hoisting himself into the back beside them, Rebus following. 'The stuff was originally hidden beneath the floor.'

'False fuel tanks,' explained Ken Smylie. 'Good ones too, welded and bolted shut.'

'The Yard cut into them from up here.' Kilpatrick stamped his foot. 'And inside they found what the tip-off had told them they'd find.'

Calumn Smylie lifted the lid off a crate so Rebus could look in. Inside, wrapped in oiled cloths, were eighteen or so AK 47 assault rifles. Rebus lifted one of them out by its folded metal butt. He knew how to handle a gun like this, even if he didn't like doing it. Rifles had gotten lighter since his Army days, but they hadn't gotten any more comfortable. They'd also gotten a deal more lethal. The wooden hand-grip was as cold as a coffin handle.

'We don't know exactly where they came from,' Kilpatrick explained. 'And we don't even know where they were headed. The driver wouldn't say anything, no matter how scary the Anti-Terrorist Branch got with him. He denied all knowledge of the load, and wasn't about to point a finger anywhere else.'

Rebus put the gun back in its crate. Calumn Smylie leaned past him to wipe off any fingerprints with a piece of rag.

'So what's the deal?' Rebus asked. Calumn Smylie gave the answer.

'When the driver was pulled in, there were some phone numbers in his pocket, two in Glasgow, one in Edinburgh. All three of them were bars.'

'Could mean nothing,' Rebus said.

'Or everything,' commented Ken Smylie.

'See,' Calumn added, 'could be those bars are his contacts, maybe his employers, or the people his employers are selling to.'

'So,' said Kilpatrick, leaning against one of the crates, 'we've got men watching all three pubs.'

'In the hope of what?'

It was Calumn's turn again. 'When Special Branch stopped the lorry, they managed to keep it quiet. It's never been reported, and the driver's tucked away somewhere under the Prevention of Terrorism Act and a few minor offences.'

Rebus nodded. 'So his employers or whoever won't know what's happened?' Calumn was nodding too. 'And they might get antsy?' Now Rebus shook his head. 'You should be a sniper.'

Calumn frowned. 'Why?'

'Because that's the longest shot I've ever heard.'

Neither Smylie seemed thrilled to hear this. 'I've already overheard a conversation mentioning The Shield,' Calumn said.

'But you've no idea what The Shield *is*,' Rebus countered. 'Which pub are we talking about anyway?'

'The Dell.'

It was Rebus's turn to frown. 'Just off the Garibaldi Estate?'

'That's the one.'

'We've had some aggro there.'

'Yes, so I hear.'

Rebus turned to Kilpatrick. 'Why do you need the lorry?'

'In case we can operate a sting.'

'How long are you going to give it?'

Calumn shrugged. His eyes were dark and heavy from tension and a lack of sleep. He rubbed a hand through his uncombed hair, then over his unshaven face.

'I can see it's been like a holiday for you,' Rebus said. He knew the plan must have been cooked up by the Smylie brothers. They seemed its real defenders. Kilpatrick's part in it was more uncertain.

'Better than that,' Calumn was saying.

'How so?'

'The holiday I'm having, you don't need to send post-cards.'

Not many people know of Parliament House, home of the High Court of Justiciary, Scotland's highest court for criminal cases. There are few signposts or identifying markers outside, and the building itself is hidden behind St Giles, separated from it by a small anonymous car park containing a smattering of Jaguars and BMWs. Of the many doors facing the prospective visitor, only one normally stands open. This is the public entrance, and leads into Parliament Hall, from off which stretch the Signet Library and Advocates Library.

There were fourteen courts in all, and Rebus guessed he'd been in all of them over the years. He sat on one of the long wooden benches. The lawyers around him were wearing dark pinstripe suits, white shirts with raised collars and white bow ties, grey wigs, and long black cloaks like those his teachers had worn. Mostly the lawyers were talking, either with clients or with each other. If with each other, they might raise their voices, maybe even share a joke. But with clients they were more circumspect. One well-dressed woman was nodding as her advocate talked in an undertone, all the while trying to stop the many files under his arm from wriggling free.

Rebus knew that beneath the large stained glass window there were two corridors lined with old wooden boxes. Indeed, the first corridor was known as the Box Corridor. Each box was marked with a lawyer's name, and each had a slat in the top, though the vast majority of boxes were kept open more or less permanently. Here documents awaited collection and perusal. Rebus had wondered at the openness of the system, the opportunities for theft and espionage. But there had never been any reports of theft, and security men were in any case never far away. He got up now and walked over to the stained glass. He knew the King portrayed was supposed to be James V, but wasn't sure about the rest of it, all the figures or the coats of arms. To his right, through a wooden swing door with glass windows, he could see lawyers poring over books. Etched in gold on the glass were the words PRIVATE ROOM.

He knew another private room close to here. Indeed, just on the other side of St Giles and down some flights of stairs. Billy Cunningham had been murdered not fifty yards from the High Court.

He turned at the sound of heels clicking towards him. Caroline Rattray was dressed for work, from black shoes and stockings to powder-grey wig.

'I wouldn't have recognised you,' he said.

'Should I take that as a compliment?' She gave him a big smile, and held it as she held his gaze. Then she touched his arm. 'I see you've noticed.' She looked up at the stained glass. 'The royal arms of Scotland.' Rebus looked up too. Beneath the large picture there were five smaller square windows, each showing a coat of arms. Caroline Rattray's eyes were on the central panel. Two unicorns held the shield of the red Lion Rampant. Above on a scroll were the words IN DEFENCE, and at the bottom a Latin inscription. Rebus read it.

'*Nemo me impune lacessit.*' He turned to her. 'Never my best subject.'

'You might know it better as "Wha daur meddle wi' me?". It's the motto of Scotland, or rather, the motto of Scotland's kings.'

'A while since we've had any of them.'

'*And* of the Order of the Thistle. Sort of makes you the monarch's private soldier, except they only give it to crusty old sods. Sit down.' She led them back to the bench Rebus had been sitting on. She had files with her, which she placed on the floor rather than the bench, though there was space. Then she gave him her full attention. Rebus didn't say anything, so she smiled again, tipping her head slightly to one side. 'Don't you see?'

'Nemo,' he guessed.

'Yes! Latin for nobody.'

'We already know that, Miss Rattray. Also a character in Jules Verne and in Dickens, plus the letters make the word "omen" backwards.' He paused. 'We've been working, you see. But does it get us any further forward? I mean, was the victim trying to tell us that no one killed him?'

She seemed to puncture, her shoulders sagging. It was like watching an old balloon die after Christmas.

'It could be something,' he offered. 'But it's hard to know what.'

'I see.'

'You could have told me about it on the phone.'

'Yes, I could.' She straightened her back. 'But I wanted you to see for yourself.'

'You think the Order of the Thistle ganged up and murdered Billy Cunningham?' Her eyes were holding his again, no smile on her lips. He broke free, staring past her

102

at the stained glass. 'How's the prosecution game?'

'It's a slow day,' she said. 'I hear the victim's father is a convicted murderer. Is there a connection?'

'Maybe.'

'No concrete motive yet?'

'No motive.' The longer Rebus looked at the royal arms, the more his focus was drawn to its central figure. It was definitely a shield. 'The Shield,' he said to himself.

'Sorry?'

'Nothing, it's just ...' He turned back to her. She was looking eager about something, and hopeful too. 'Miss Rattray,' he said, 'did you bring me here to chat me up?'

She looked horrified, her face reddening; not just her cheeks, but forehead and chin too, even her neck coloured. 'Inspector Rebus,' she said at last.

'Sorry, sorry.' He bowed his head and raised his hands. 'Sorry I said that.'

'Well, I don't know ...' She looked around. 'It's not every day I'm accused of being ... well, whatever. I think I need a drink.' Then, reverting to her normal voice: 'I think you'd better buy me one, don't you?'

They crossed the High Street, dodging the leafleters and mime artists and clowns on stilts, and threaded their way through a dark close and down some worn stone steps into Caro Rattray's preferred bar.

'I hate this time of year,' she said. 'It's such a hassle getting to and from work. And as for parking in town ...'

'It's a hard life, all right.'

She went to a table while Rebus stood at the bar. She had taken a couple of minutes to change out of her gown and wig, had brushed her hair out, though the sombre clothes that remained – the accent on black with touches of white – still marked her out as a lawyer in this lawyer's howff.

The place had one of the lowest ceilings of any pub Rebus had ever been in. When he considered, he thought they must be almost directly above some of the shops which led off Mary King's Close. The thought made him change his order.

'Make that whisky a double.' But he added plenty of water.

Caroline Rattray had ordered lemonade with lots of ice and lemon. As Rebus placed her drink on the table, he laughed.

'What's so funny?'

He shook his head. 'Advocate and lemonade, that makes a snowball.' He didn't have to explain to her. She managed a weary smile. 'Heard it before, eh?' he said, sitting beside her.

'And every person who says it thinks they've just invented it. Cheers.'

'Aye, *slainte*.'

'*Slainte*. Do you speak Gaelic?'

'Just a couple of words.'

'I learnt it a few years ago, I've already forgotten most of it.'

'Ach, it's not much use anyway, is it?'

'You wouldn't mind if it died out?'

'I didn't say that.'

'I thought you just did.'

Rebus gulped at his drink. 'Never argue with a lawyer.'

Another smile. She lit a cigarette, Rebus declining.

'Don't tell me,' he said, 'you still see Mary King's Close in your head at night?'

She nodded slowly. 'And during the day. I can't seem to erase it.'

'So don't try. Just file it away, that's all you can do. Admit it to yourself, it happened, you were there, then file it away. You won't forget, but you won't harp on it either.'

'Police psychology?'

'Common sense, hard learnt. That's why you were so excited about the Latin inscription?'

'Yes, I thought I was ... *involved*.'

'You'll be involved if we ever catch the buggers. It'll be your job to put them away.'

'I suppose so.'

'Until then, leave it to us.'

'Yes, I will.'

'I'm sorry though, sorry you had to see it. Typical of Curt, dragging you down there. There was no need to. Are you and him ... ?'

Her whoop filled the bar. 'You don't think ... ? We're just acquaintances. He had a spare ticket, I was on hand. Christ almighty, you think I could ... with a *pathologist?*'

'They're human, despite rumours to the contrary.'

'Yes, but he's twenty years older than me.'

'That's not always a consideration.'

'The thought of those hands on me ...' She shivered, sipped her drink. 'What did you say back there about a shield?'

He shook his head. He saw a shield in his mind, and you never got a shield without a sword. *With sword and shield*, that was a line from an Orange song. He slapped the table with his fist, so hard that Caroline Rattray looked frightened.

'Was it something I said?'

'Caroline, you're brilliant. I've got to go.' He got up and walked past the bar, then stopped and came back, taking her hand in his, holding it. 'I'll phone you,' he promised. Then: 'If you like.'

He waited till she'd nodded, then turned again and left. She finished her lemonade, smoked another cigarette, and stubbed it into the ashtray. His hand had been hot, not like a pathologist's at all. The barman came to empty her ashtray into a pail and wipe the table.

'Out hunting again I see,' he said quietly.

'You know too much about me, Dougie.'

'I know too much about everyone, hen,' said Dougie, picking up both glasses and taking them to the bar.

*

105

Several months back, Rebus had been talking to an acquaintance of his called Matthew Vanderhyde. Their conversation had concerned another case, one involving, as it turned out, Big Ger Cafferty, and apropos of very little Vanderhyde, blind for many years and with a reputation as a white witch, had mentioned a splinter group of the Scottish National Party. The splinter group had been called Sword and Shield, and they'd existed in the late 1950s and early 1960s.

But as a phone call to Vanderhyde revealed, Sword and Shield had ceased to exist around the same time the Rolling Stones were putting out their first album. And at no time, anyway, had they been known as SaS.

'I do believe,' Vanderhyde said, and Rebus could see him in his darkened living room, its curtains shut, slumped in an armchair with his portable phone, 'there exists in the United States an organisation called Sword and Shield, or even Scottish Sword and Shield, but I don't know anything about them. I don't think they're connected to the Scottish Rites Temple, which is a sort of North American Free-masons, but I'm a bit vague.'

Rebus was busy writing it all down. 'No you're not,' he said, 'you're a bloody encyclopaedia.' That was the problem with Vanderhyde: he seldom gave you just the one answer, leaving you more confused than before you'd asked your question.

'Is there anything I can read about Sword and Shield?' Rebus asked.

'You mean histories? I wouldn't know, I shouldn't think they'd bother to issue any as braille editions or talking books.'

'I suppose not, but there must have been something left when the organisation was wound up, papers, docu-ments...?'

'Perhaps a local historian might know. Would you like me to do some sleuthing, Inspector?'

'I'd appreciate it,' said Rebus. 'Would Big Ger Cafferty have had anything to do with the group?'

'I shouldn't think so. Why do you ask?'

'Nothing, forget I said it.' He terminated the call with promises of a visit, then scratched his nose, wondering who to take all this to: Kilpatrick or Lauderdale? He'd been seconded to SCS, but Lauderdale was in charge of the murder inquiry. He asked himself a question: would Lauderdale protect me from Kilpatrick? The answer was no. Then he changed the names around. The answer this time was yes. So he took what he had to Kilpatrick.

And then had to admit that it wasn't much.

Kilpatrick had brought Smylie into the office to join them. Sometimes Rebus wasn't sure who was in charge. Calumn Smylie would be back undercover, maybe drinking in The Dell.

'So,' said Kilpatrick, 'summing up, John, we've got the word Nemo, we've got a Latin phrase –'

'Much quoted by nationalists,' Smylie added, 'at least in its Scots form.'

'And we've got a shield on this coat of arms, all of which reminds you of a group called Sword and Shield who were wound up in the early '60s. You think they've sprung up again?'

Rebus visualised a spring suddenly appearing through the worn covering of an old mattress. He shrugged. 'I don't know, sir.'

'And then this source of yours mentions an organisation in the USA called Sword and Shield.'

'Sir, all I know is, SaS must stand for something. Calumn Smylie's been hearing about an outfit called The Shield who might be in the market for arms. There's also a shield on the Scottish royal arms, as well as a phrase with the word Nemo. I know these are all pretty weak links, but all the same...'

Kilpatrick looked to Smylie, who gave a look indicating he was on Rebus's side.

'Maybe,' Smylie said in proof, 'we could ask our friends in the States to check for us. They'd be doing the work, there's nothing to lose, and with the back-up they've got they could probably give us an answer in a few days. As I say, we haven't lost anything.'

'I suppose not. All right then.' Kilpatrick's hands were ready for prayer. 'John, we'll give it a go.'

'Also, sir,' Rebus added, just pushing his luck a bit, 'we might do some digging into the original Sword and Shield. If the name's been revived, it wasn't just plucked out of the air.'

'Fair point, John. I'll put Blackwood and Ormiston onto it.'

Blackwood and Ormiston: they'd thank him for this, they'd bring him flowers and chocolates.

'Thank you, sir,' said Rebus.

# 11

Ever since the riot, Father Leary had been trying to contact Rebus, leaving message after message at St Leonard's. So when he got to St Leonard's, Rebus relented and called the priest.

'It hasn't gone too well, father,' he said gamely.

'Then it's God's will.'

For a second, Rebus heard it as God swill. He stuck in his own apostrophe and said, 'I knew you'd say that.' He was watching Siobhan Clarke striding towards him. She had her thumbs up and a big grin spread across her face.

'Got to go, father. Say one for me.'

'Don't I always?'

Rebus put down the receiver. 'What've you got?'

'Cafferty,' she said, throwing the file onto his desk. 'Buried way back.' She produced a sheet of paper and handed it to him. Rebus read through it quickly.

Yes, buried, because it was only a suspicion, one of hundreds that the police had been unable to prove over the course of Cafferty's career.

'Handling dirty money,' he said.

'For the Ulster Volunteer Force.'

Cafferty had formed an unholy alliance with a Glasgow villain called Jinky Johnson, and between them they'd offered a service, turning dirty money into clean at the behest of the UVF. Then Johnson disappeared. Rumour had it he'd either fled with the UVF's cash, or else he'd been skimming a bit and they'd found out and done away with him. Whatever, Cafferty broke his connection.

'What do you think?' Clarke asked.

'It ties Cafferty to the Protestant paramilitaries.'

'And if they thought he knew about Johnson, it'd mean there was no love lost.'

But Rebus had doubts about the time scale. 'They wouldn't wait ten years for revenge. Then again, Cafferty *did* know what SaS stood for. He's heard of it.'

'A new terrorist group?'

'I think so, definitely. And they're here in Edinburgh.' He looked up at Clarke. 'And if we're not careful, Cafferty's men are going to get to them first.' Then he smiled.

'You don't sound overly concerned.'

'I'm so bothered by it all, I think I'll buy you a drink.'

'Deal,' said Siobhan Clarke.


As he drove home, he could smell the cigarettes and booze on his clothes. More ammo for Patience. Christ, there were those videos to take back too. She wouldn't do it, it was up to him. There'd be extra to pay, and he hadn't even watched the bloody things yet.

To defer the inevitable, he stopped at a pub. They didn't come much smaller than the Oxford Bar, but the Ox managed to be cosy too. Most nights there was a party atmosphere, or at the very least some entertaining patter. And there were quarter gills too, of course. He drank just the one, drove the rest of the way to Patience's, and parked in his usual spot near the sports Merc. Someone on Queensferry Road was trying to sing *Tie a Yellow Ribbon*. Overhead, the streetlighting's orange glow picked out the top of the tenements, their chimney pots bristling. The warm air smelt faintly of breweries.

'Rebus?'

It wasn't dark yet, not quite. Rebus had seen the man

waiting across the road. Now the man was approaching, hands deep in jacket pockets. Rebus tensed. The man saw the change and brought his hands out to show he was unarmed.

'Just a word,' the man said.

'What about?'

'Mr Cafferty's wondering how things are going.'

Rebus studied the man more closely. He looked like a weasel with misshapen teeth, his mouth constantly open in something that was either a sneer or a medical problem. He breathed in and out through his mouth in a series of small gasps. There was a smell from him that Rebus didn't want to place.

'You want a trip down the station, pal?'

The man grinned, showing his teeth again. Close up, Rebus saw that they were stained so brown from nicotine they might have been made of wood.

'What are the charges?' the weasel said.

Rebus looked him up and down. 'Offence against public decency for a start. They should have kept you in your cage, right at the back of the pet shop.'

'He said you had a way with words.'

'Not just with words.' Rebus started to cross the road to Patience's flat. The man followed, so close he might have been on a leash.

'I'm trying to be pleasant,' the weasel said.

'Tell the charm school to give you a refund.'

'He said you'd be difficult.'

Rebus turned on the man. 'Difficult? You don't know just how difficult I can get if I really try. If I see you here again, you'd better be ready to square off.'

The man narrowed his eyes. 'That'd suit me fine. I'll be sure to mention your co-operation to Mr Cafferty.'

'Do that.' Rebus started down the steps to the garden flat. The weasel leaned down over the rails.

'Nice flat.' Rebus stopped with his key in the lock. He

looked up at the man. 'Shame if anything happened to it.'

By the time Rebus ran back up the steps, the weasel had disappeared.

# 12

'Have you heard from your brother?'

It was next morning, and Rebus was at Fettes, talking with Ken Smylie.

'He doesn't phone in that often.'

Rebus was trying to turn Smylie into someone he could trust. Looking around him, he didn't see too many potential allies. Blackwood and Ormiston were giving him their double-act filthy look, from which he deduced two things. One, they'd been assigned to look into what, if anything, remained of the original Sword and Shield.

Two, they knew whose idea the job had been.

Rebus, pleased at their glower, decided he wouldn't bother mentioning that Matthew Vanderhyde was looking into Sword and Shield too. Why give them shortcuts when they'd have had him run the marathon?

Smylie didn't seem in the mood for conversation, but Rebus persisted. 'Have you talked to Billy Cunningham's flatmate?'

'She kept going on about his motorbike and what was she supposed to do with it?'

'Is that all?'

Smylie shrugged. 'Unless I want to buy a stripped down Honda.'

'Careful, Smylie, I think maybe you've caught something.'

'What?'

'A sense of humour.'

As Rebus drove to St Leonard's, he rubbed at his jaw

and chin, enjoying the feel of the bristles under his fingertips. He was remembering the very different feel of the AK 47, and thinking of sectarianism. Scotland had enough problems without getting involved in Ireland's. They were like Siamese twins who'd refused the operation to separate them. Only one twin had been forced into a marriage with England, and the other was hooked on self-mutilation. They didn't need politicians to sort things out; they needed a psychiatrist.

The marching season, the season of the Protestant, was over for another year, give or take the occasional small fringe procession. Now it was the season of the International Festival, a festive time, a time to forget the small and insecure country you lived in. He thought again of the poor sods who'd decided to put on a show in the Gar-B.

St Leonard's looked to be joining in the fun. They'd even arranged for a pantomime. Someone had owned up to the Billy Cunningham murder. His name was Unstable from Dunstable.

The police called him that for two reasons. One, he was mentally unstable. Two, he claimed he came from Dunstable. He was a local tramp, but not without resources. With needle and thread he had fashioned for himself a coat constructed from bar towels, and so was a walking sandwich-board for the products which kept him alive and kept him dying.

There were a lot of people out there like him, shiftless until someone (usually the police) shifted them. They'd been 'returned to the community' – a euphemism for dumped – thanks to a tightening of the government's heart and purse-strings. Some of them couldn't tighten their shoe laces without bursting into tears. It was a crying shame.

Unstable was in an interview room now with DS Holmes, being fed hot sweet tea and cigarettes. Eventually they'd turf him out, maybe with a couple of quid in his hand, his technicolor beercoat having no pockets.

Siobhan Clarke was at her desk in the Murder Room. She was being talked at by DI Alister Flower.

So someone had forgotten Rebus's advice regarding the duty roster.

'Well,' Flower said loudly, spotting Rebus, 'if it isn't our man from the SCS. Have you brought the milk?'

Rebus was too slow getting the reference, so Flower obliged.

'The Scottish Co-Operative Society. SCS, same letters as the Scottish Crime Squad.'

'Wasn't Sean Connery a milkman with the Co-Op,' said Siobhan Clarke, 'before he got into acting?' Rebus smiled towards her, appreciating her effort to shift the gist of the conversation.

Flower looked like a man who had comebacks ready, so Rebus decided against a jibe. Instead he said, 'They think very highly of you.'

Flower blinked. 'Who?'

Rebus twitched his head. 'Over at SCS.'

Flower stared at him, then narrowed his eyes. 'Do tell.'

Rebus shrugged. 'What's to tell? I'm serious. The high hiedyins know your record, they've been keeping an eye on you ... that's what I hear.'

Flower shuffled his feet, relaxing his posture. He almost became shy, colour showing in his cheeks.

'They told me to tell you ...' Rebus leaned close, Flower doing likewise, '... that as soon as there's a milk round to spare, they'll give you a call.'

Flower showed two rows of narrow teeth as he growled. Then he stalked off in search of easier prey.

'He's easy to wind up, isn't he?' said Siobhan Clarke.

'That's why I call him the Clockwork Orangeman.'

'Is he an Orangeman?'

'He's been known to march on the 12th.' He considered. 'Maybe Orange Peeler would be a better name for him, eh?'

Clarke groaned. 'What have you got for me from our teuchter friends?'

'You mean the Orkneys. I don't think they'd appreciate being called teuchters.' She tried hard to pronounce the word, but being mostly English, she just failed.

'Remember,' said Rebus, 'teuch is Scots for tough. I don't think they'd mind me calling them tough.' He dragged a chair over to her desk. 'So what did you get?'

She flicked open a paper pad, finding the relevant page. 'Zabriskie House is actually a croft. There's a small cottage, one bedroom and one other room doubling as –'

'I'm not thinking of buying the place.'

'No, sir. The current owners didn't know anything about its past history, but neighbours remembered a chap renting the place for a year or two back in the '70s. He called himself Cuchullain.'

'What?'

'A mythical warrior, Celtic I think.'

'And that was all he called himself?'

'That was all.'

It fitted with the tone of the *Floating Anarchy Factfile*: Celtic hippy. Rebus knew that in the early '70s a lot of young Scots had emulated their American and European cousins by 'dropping out'. But then years later they tended to drop back in again, and did well for themselves in business. He knew because he'd almost dropped out himself. But instead he'd gone to Northern Ireland.

'Anything else?' he asked.

'Bits and pieces. A description that's twenty-odd years old now from a woman who's been blind in one eye since birth.'

'This is your source, is it?'

'Mostly, yes. A police constable went sniffing. He also talked to the man who used to run the sub-post office, and a couple of boatmen. You need a boat to get provisions across to Rousay, and the postman comes by his own boat.

He kept himself to himself, grew his own food. There was talk at the time, because people used to come and go at Zabriskie House, young women with no bras on, men with beards and long hair.'

'The locals must've been mortified.'

Clarke smiled. 'The lack of bras was mentioned more than once.'

'Well, a place like that, you have to make your own entertainment.'

'There's one lead the constable is still following up. He'll get back to me today.'

'I won't hold my breath. Have you ever been to the Orkneys?'

'You're not thinking of –' She was interrupted by her telephone. 'DC Clarke speaking. Yes.' She looked up at Rebus and pulled her notepad to her, starting to write. Presumably it was the Old Policeman of Hoy, so Rebus took a stroll around the room. He was reminded again just why he didn't fit, why he was so unsuited to the career life had chosen for him. The Murder Room was like a production line. You had your own little task, and you did it. Maybe someone else would follow up any lead you found, and then someone else after that might do the questioning of a suspect or potential witness. You were a small part of a very large team. It wasn't Rebus's way. He wanted to follow up every lead personally, cross referencing them all, taking them through from first principle to final reckoning. He'd been described, not unkindly, as a terrier, locking on with his jaws and not letting go.

Some dogs, you had to break the jaw to get them off.

Siobhan Clarke came up to him. 'Something?' he asked.

'My constable friend found out Cuchullain used to keep a cow and a pig, plus some chickens. Part of the self-sufficiency thing. He wondered what might have happened to them when Cuchullain moved away.'

'He sounds bright.'

'Turns out Cuchullain sold them on to another crofter, and this crofter keeps records. We got lucky, Cuchullain had to wait for his money, and he gave the crofter a forwarding address in the Borders.' She waved a piece of paper at him.

'Don't get too excited,' warned Rebus. 'We're still talking a twenty year old address for a man whose name we don't know.'

'But we do know. The crofter had a note of that too. It's Francis Lee.'

'Francis Lee?' Rebus sounded sceptical. 'Wasn't he playing for Manchester City in the '70s? Francis Lee ... as in Frank Lee? As in Frank Lee, my dear, I don't give a damn?'

'You think it's another alias?'

'I don't know. Let's get the Borders police to take a look.' He studied the Murder Room. 'Ach, no, on second thoughts, let's go take a look ourselves.'

118

# 13

Whenever John Rebus had cause or inclination to drive through any town in the Scottish Borders, one word came to his mind.

Neat.

The towns were simply laid out and almost pathologically tidy. The buildings were constructed from unadorned stone and had a square-built no-nonsense quality to them. The people walking briskly from bank to grocer's shop to chemist's were rosy cheeked and bursting with health, as though they scrubbed their faces with pumice every morning before sitting down to farmhouse fare. The men's limbs moved with the grace of farm machinery. You could present any of the women to your own mother. She'd tell them you weren't good enough for them.

Truth be told, the Borderers scared Rebus. He couldn't understand them. He understood though, that placed many more miles from any large Scottish conurbation than from the English border, there was bound to be some schizophrenia to the towns and their inhabitants.

Selkirk however was definably Scots in character, architecture, and language. Its annual Lammas Fair was not yet just a memory to see the townfolk through the winter. There were still rows of pennants waiting to be taken down, flapping in the slightest breeze. There were some outside the house which abutted the kirkyard wall. Siobhan Clarke checked the address and shrugged.

'It's the manse, isn't it?' Rebus repeated, sure that they had something wrong.

'It's the address I've got here.'

The house was large with several prominent gables. It was fashioned from dull grey stone, but boasted a lush and sweet-smelling garden. Siobhan Clarke pushed open the gate. She searched the front door for a bell but found none, so resorted to the iron knocker which was shaped like an open hand. No one answered. From nearby came the sound of a manual lawnmower, its pull and push as regular as a pendulum. Rebus looked in through the front window of the house, and saw no sign of movement.

'We're wasting our time,' he said. A waste of a long car journey too. 'Let's leave a note and get out of here.'

Clarke peered through the letterbox, then stood up again. 'Maybe we could ask around, now we're here.'

'Fine,' said Rebus, 'let's go talk to the lawnmower man.'

They walked round to the kirkyard gate and took the red gravel path around the perimeter of the church itself. At the back of the soot-blackened building they saw an old man pushing a mower which in Edinburgh might have graced a New Town antique shop.

The gentleman stopped his work when he saw them crossing the trimmed grass towards him. It was like walking on a carpet. The grass could not have been shorter if he'd been using nail scissors. He produced a voluminous handkerchief from his pocket and mopped his suntanned brow. His face and arms were as brown as oak, the face polished with sweat. The elderly skin was still tight across the skull, shiny like a beetle's back. He introduced himself as Willie McStay.

'Is it about the vandalism?' he asked.

'Vandalism? *Here?*'

'They've been desecrating the graves, daubing paint on the headstones. It's the skinheads.'

120

'Skinheads in Selkirk?' Rebus was not convinced. 'How many skinheads are there, Mr McStay?'

McStay thought about it, grinding his teeth together as though he were chewing tobacco or a particularly tough piece of phlegm. 'Well,' he said, 'there's Alec Tunnock's son for a start. His hair's cropped awful short and he wears those boots wi' the laces.'

'Boots with laces, eh?'

'He hasna had a job since he left school.'

Rebus was shaking his head. 'We're not here about the headstones, Mr McStay. We were wondering about that house.' He pointed towards it.

'The manse?'

'Who lives there, Mr McStay?'

'The minister, Reverend McKay.'

'How long has he lived there?'

'Gracious, I don't know. Fifteen years maybe. Before him it was Reverend Bothwell, and the Bothwells were here for a quarter century or more.'

Rebus looked to Siobhan Clarke. A waste of time.

'We're looking for a man called Francis Lee,' she said.

McStay chomped on the name, jaw chewing from side to side, cheekbones working. He reminded Rebus of a sheep. The old man shook his head. 'Nobody I know of,' he said.

'Well, thanks anyway,' said Rebus.

'A minute,' McStay ordered. Meaning that he wanted to think about it for a minute more. Finally he nodded. 'You've got it the wrong way round.' He leant a hand against the mower's black rubber grip. 'The Bothwells were a lovely couple, Douglas and Ina. Couldn't do enough for this town. When they died, their son sold the house straight off. He wasn't supposed to, Reverend Bothwell told me that often enough. He was supposed to keep it in the family.'

'But it's a manse,' Clarke said. 'Church of Scotland property. How could he sell it?'

'The Bothwells loved the house so much, they bought it

off the Church. They were going to live there when Reverend Bothwell retired. The thing is, the son sold it back to the Church. He was a wastrel, that one, took the money and ran. Nobody'd look after their grave if it wasn't for me and a few other old folk here who remember them fondly.' He shook his head. 'Young people, they've no sense of history or commitment.'

'What's this got to do with Francis Lee?' Siobhan Clarke asked. McStay looked at her like she was a child who'd spoken out of turn, and addressed his answer to Rebus.

'Their son was called Lee. I think his middle name was Francis.'

Lee Francis Bothwell: Francis Lee. It was too close to be mere coincidence. Rebus nodded slowly.

'I don't suppose you've any idea,' he said, 'where we might find –' He broke off. 'Frankie Bothwell? Thanks, Mr McStay, thanks for your help.' And he walked towards the gate. It took Siobhan Clarke a moment to catch up with him.

'So are you going to tell me?'

'You don't know Frankie Bothwell?' He watched her try out the name in her mind. She shook her head furiously. 'He owns the Crazy Hose Saloon.'

Now she nodded. 'That Fringe programme in Billy Cunningham's room.'

'Yes, with a show at the Crazy Hose circled. Nice coincidence, eh?' They were at the car now. Rebus opened the passenger door but didn't get in. Instead he rested his elbow on the roof and looked across at her. 'If you believe in coincidence.'

She'd driven them twenty or thirty yards when Rebus ordered her to stop. He'd been looking in his wing mirror, and now got out of the car and started back towards the gates. Siobhan cursed under her breath, drew the car in to the kerb, and followed him. Idling by the gates was a red estate car she'd seen parked further away when they were leaving. Rebus had stopped two men who'd been walking towards Willie McStay.

Neither of the two would have looked out of place in the back of a scrum. Siobhan was in time to catch the end of her superior's argument.

'– and if you don't lay off, so help me, I'll drop you so far in it you'll wish you'd brought a diving bell.' To reinforce this point, Rebus jabbed his finger into the larger man's gut, all the way up to the second joint. The man didn't look like he was enjoying it. His face was a huge ripe plum. But he kept his hands clasped behind his back throughout. He was showing such self control, Siobhan might have taken him for a Buddhist.

Only she'd yet to come across a Buddhist with razor scars carved down both cheeks.

'And what's more,' Rebus was saying, 'you can tell Cafferty we know all about him and the UVF, so he needn't go on acting the innocent about terrorism.'

The bigger of the two men spoke. 'Mr Cafferty's getting very impatient. He wants a result.'

'I don't care if he wants world peace. Now get out of here, and if I hear you've been back asking questions, I'll see you both put away, and I don't care what I've got to do, understood?'

They didn't look overly impressed, but the two men walked away anyway, back to the gates and through them.

'Your fan club?' Siobhan Clarke guessed.

'Ach, they only want me for my body.'

Which, in a sense, was true.

It was late afternoon, and the Crazy Hose was doing no trade at all.

Those in the know just called it the Hose; those not in the know would say, 'Shouldn't it be Horse?' But it was the Hose because its premises were an old decommissioned fire station, left vacant when they built a new edifice just up the street. And it was the Crazy Hose Saloon because it had a wild west theme and country and western music. The main doors were painted gloss black and boasted small square barred windows. Rebus knew the place was doing no trade, because Lee Francis Bothwell was sitting on the steps outside smoking a cigarette.

Although Rebus had never met Frankie Bothwell, he knew the reputation, and there was no mistaking the mess on the steps for anything else. He was dressed like a Las Vegas act, with the face and hair of McGarrett in *Hawaii 5–0*. The hair had to be fake, and Rebus would lay odds some of the face was fake too.

'Mr Bothwell?'

The head nodded without the hair moving one millimetre out of coiffeured place. He was wearing a tan-coloured leather safari jacket, tight white trousers, and an open-necked shirt. The shirt would offend all but the colour blind and the truly blind. It had so many rhinestones on it, Rebus was in no doubt the rhine mines were now exhausted as a result. Around Bothwell's neck hung a simple gold chain, but he would have been better off with a neck-cast. A neck-cast would have disguised the lines, the wrinkles and sags which gave away Bothwell's not insubstantial age.

'I'm Inspector Rebus, this is Detective Constable Clarke.' Rebus had briefed Clarke on the way here, and she didn't look too stunned by the figure in front of her.

'You want a bottle of rye for the police raffle?'

'No, sir. We're trying to complete a collection of magazines.'

'Huh?' Bothwell had been studying the empty street. Just along the road was Tollcross junction, but you couldn't see it from the front steps of the Crazy Hose. Now he looked up at Rebus.

'I'm serious,' Rebus said. 'We're missing a few back issues, maybe you can help.'

'I don't get it.'

'*The Floating Anarchy Factfile.*'

Frankie Bothwell took off his sunglasses and squinted at Rebus. Then he ground his cigarette-end under the heel of a cowboy boot. 'That was a lifetime ago. How do you know about it?' Rebus shrugged. Frankie Bothwell grinned. He was perking up again. 'Christ, that *was* a long time ago. Up in the Orkneys, peace and love, I had some fun back then. But what's it got to do with anything?'

'Do you know this man?' Rebus handed over a copy of the photo Murdock had given him, the one from the party. It had been cropped to show Billy Cunningham's face only. 'His name's Billy Cunningham.'

Bothwell took a while studying the photo, then shook his head.

'He came here to see a country and western show a couple of weeks back.'

'We're packed most nights, Inspector, especially this time of year. I can ask the bar staff, the bouncers, see if they know him. Is he a regular?'

'We don't know, sir.'

'See, if he's a regular, he'll carry the Cowpoke Card. You get one after three visits in any one month, entitles you to thirty per cent off the admission.' Rebus was shaking his head. 'What's he done anyway?'

'He's been murdered, Mr Bothwell.'

Bothwell screwed up his face. 'Bad one.' Then he looked at Rebus again. 'Not the kid in that underground street?'

Rebus nodded.

Bothwell stood up, brushing dirt from his backside. '*Floating Anarchy* hasn't been in circulation for twenty years. You say this kid had a copy?'

'Issue number three,' Siobhan Clarke confirmed.

Bothwell thought about it. 'Number three, that was a big printing, a thousand or so. There was momentum behind number three. After that ... not so much momentum.' He smiled ruefully. 'Can I keep the photo? Like I say, I'll ask around.'

'Fine, Mr Bothwell. We've got copies.'

'Secondhand shops maybe.'

'Pardon?'

'The magazine, maybe he got it secondhand.'

'That's a thought.'

'A kid that age, Christ.' He shook his head. 'I love kids, Inspector, that's what this place is all about. Giving kids a good time. There's nothing like it.'

'Really, sir?'

Bothwell spread his hands. 'I don't mean anything ... you know ... nothing like that. I've always liked kids. I used to run a football team, local youth club thing. Anything for kids.' He smiled again. 'That's because I'm still a kid myself, Inspector. Me, I'm Peter bloody Pan.'

Still holding the photo, he invited them in for a drink. Rebus was tempted, but declined. The bar would be an empty barn; no place for a drink. He handed Bothwell a card with his office number.

'I'll do my best,' Bothwell said.

Rebus nodded and turned away. He didn't say anything to Siobhan Clarke till they were back in her car.

'Well, what do you think?'

'Creepy,' she said. 'How can he dress like that?'

'Years of practice, I suppose.'

'So what do you reckon to him?'

Rebus thought about this. 'I'm not sure. Let me think about it over a drink.'

'That's very kind, sir, but I'm going out.' She made a show of checking her watch.

'A Fringe show?' She nodded.

'Early Tom Stoppard,' she said.

'Well,' Rebus sniffed, 'I didn't say you were invited anyway.' He paused. 'Who are you going with?'

126

She looked at him. 'I'm going on my own, not that it's any of your business ... sir.'

Rebus shifted a little. 'You can drop me off at the Ox.'

As they drove past, there was no sign of Frankie Bothwell on the steps of the Crazy Hose Saloon.

The Ox gave Rebus a taste. He phoned Patience, but got the answer-phone. He seemed to remember she was going out tonight, but couldn't recall where. He took the slow route home. In Daintry's Lounge, he stood at the bar listening in on its tough wit. The Festival only touched places like Daintry's insofar as providing posters to advertise the shows. These were as much decoration as the place ever had. He stared at a sign above the row of optics. It said, 'If arseholes could fly, this place would be an airport'.

'Ready for take-off,' he said to the barmaid, proffering his empty glass.

A little later, he found himself approaching Oxford Terrace from Lennox Street, so turned into Lennox Street Lane. What had once been stables in the Lane had now become first floor homes with ground floor garages. The place was always dead. Some of the tenements on Oxford Terrace backed onto the lane. Rebus had a key to Patience's garden gate. He'd let himself in the back door to the flat. As shortcuts went, it wasn't much of one, but he liked the lane.

He was about a dozen paces from the gate when somebody grabbed him. They got him from behind, pulling him by the coat, keeping the grip tight so that he might as well have been wearing a straitjacket. The coat came up over Rebus's head, trapping him, binding his arms. A knee came up into his groin. He lashed out with a foot, which only made it all the easier to unbalance him. He was shouting and swearing as he fell. The attacker had released his grip on the coat. While Rebus struggled to get out of it, a foot caught him on the side of the head. The foot was wearing a plimsoll, which explained why Rebus hadn't heard his attacker following him. It also explained why he was still conscious after the kick.

Another kick dug into his side. And then, just as his head was emerging from his coat, the foot caught him on the chin, and all he could see were the setts beneath him, slick and shining from what light there was. The attacker's hands were on him, rifling pockets. The man was breathing hard.

'Take the money,' Rebus said, trying to focus his eyes. He knew there wasn't much money to take, less than a fiver, all of it in small change. The man didn't seem happy with his haul. It wasn't much for a night's work.

'A'm gonny put you in the hospital.' The accent was Glaswegian. Rebus could make out the man's build – squat – but not yet his face. There was too much shadow. He was rearing up again, coins spilling from his hands to rain down on Rebus.

He'd given Rebus just enough time to shake off the alcohol. Rebus sprang from his crouch and hit the man square in the stomach with his head, propelling his assailant backwards. The man kept his balance, but Rebus was standing too now, and he was bigger than the Glaswegian. There was a glint in the man's hand. A cutthroat razor. Rebus hadn't seen one in years. It flashed in an arc towards him, but he dodged it, then saw that there were two other figures in the lane. They were watching, hands in pockets. He thought he recognised them as Cafferty's men, the ones from the churchyard.

The razor was swinging again, the Glaswegian almost smiling as he went about his business. Rebus slipped his coat all the way off and wrapped it around his left arm. He met the blade with his arm, feeling it cut into the cloth, and lashed out with the sole of his right foot, connecting with the man's knee. The man took a step back, and Rebus struck out again, connecting with a thigh this time. When the man attempted to come back at him, he was limping and easy to sidestep. But instead of aiming with the razor he barrelled into Rebus, pushing him hard against some garage doors. Then he turned and ran.

There was only one exit from the alley, and he took it, running past Cafferty's men. Rebus took a deep breath, then sank to his knees and threw up onto the ground. His coat was ruined, but that was the least of his problems. Cafferty's men were strolling towards him. They lifted him to his feet like he was a bag of shopping.

'You all right?' one asked.

'Winded,' Rebus said. His chin hurt too, but there was no blood. He puked up more alcohol, feeling better for it. The other man had stooped to pick up the money. Rebus didn't get it.

'Your man?' he said. They were shaking their heads. Then the bigger one spoke.

'He just saved us the bother.'

'He was trying to hospitalise me.'

'I think I'd have done the same,' said the big man, holding out Rebus's coins. 'If this is all I'd found.'

Rebus took the money and pocketed it. Then he took a swing at the man. It was slow and tired and didn't connect. But the big man connected all right. His punch took all the remaining fight out of Rebus. He fell to his knees again, palms on the cold ground.

'That's by way of an incentive,' the man said. 'Just in case you were needing one. Mr Cafferty'll be talking to you soon.'

'Not if I can help it,' spat Rebus, sitting with his back to the garage. They were walking away from him, back towards the mouth of the lane.

'He'll be talking to you.'

Then they were gone.

A Glaswegian with a razor, Rebus thought to himself,

happy to sit here till the pain went away. If not Cafferty's
man, then whose?

And why?

# 14

Rebus struggled towards consciousness, even as he picked up the telephone.

'Heathen!' he gasped into it.

'Pardon?'

'To call at this ungodly hour.' He'd recognised DCI Kilpatrick's voice. He ran the palm of his hand down his face, pulling open his eyelids. When he could focus, he tried finding the time on the clock, but in his struggle for the receiver he'd knocked it to the floor. 'What do you want ... sir?'

'I was hoping you could come in a bit early.'

'What? Cleaners on strike and you're looking for a relief?'

'He sounds like the dead, but he's still cracking jokes.'

'When do you want me?'

'Say, half an hour?'

'You say it, I'll do what I can.' He put down the receiver and found his watch. It was on his wrist. The time was five past six. He hadn't so much slept as drifted into coma. Maybe it was the drink or the vomiting or the beating. Maybe it was just too many late nights catching up with him. Whatever, he didn't feel the worse for it. He checked his side: it was bruised, but not badly. His chin and face didn't feel too bad either, just grazed.

'Who the hell was that?' Patience growled sleepily from beneath her pillow.

'Duty calls,' said Rebus, swinging his unwilling legs out of bed.

131

They were seated in Kilpatrick's office, Rebus and Ken Smylie. Rebus held his coffee cup the way a disaster victim would, cradling this smallest of comforts. He couldn't have looked worse if there'd been a blanket around his shoulders and a reporter in front of him asking how he felt about the plane crash. His early morning buzz had lasted all the way from the bed to the bathroom. It had been an effort to look in the mirror. Unshaven, you hardly noticed the bruises, but he could feel them on the inside.

Smylie seemed alert enough, not needing the caffeine. And Rebus shouldn't have been drinking it either; it would play merry hell with him later.

It was a minute short of seven o'clock, and they were watching Kilpatrick pretend to reread some fax sheets. At last he was ready. He put down the sheets and interlocked the fingers of both hands. Rebus and Smylie were trying to get a look at what the fax said.

'I've heard from the United States. You were right, Ken, they're quick workers. The gist is, there are two fairly widespread but above board organisations in the US, one's called the Scottish Rites Temple.'

'That's a kind of masonic lodge for Scots,' Rebus said, remembering Vanderhyde's words.

Kilpatrick nodded. 'The other is called Scottish Sword and Shield.' He watched Rebus and Smylie exchange a look. 'Don't get excited. It's much more low-key than Scottish Rites, but it's not into the financing of gun-running. However,' he picked up the fax again, 'there's one final group. It has its main headquarters in Toronto, Canada, but also has branches in the States, particularly in the south and the north-west. It's called The Shield, and you won't find it in any phone book. The FBI have been investigating the US operation for just over a year, as have the American tax people. I had a chat with an FBI agent at their headquarters in Washington.'

'And?'

'And, the Shield is a fund-raiser, only nobody's quite sure what for. Whatever it is, it isn't Catholic. The FBI agent said he'd already passed a lot of this information on to the Royal Ulster Constabulary, in the event of their becoming cognisant of the organisation.'

Ten minutes on the phone to Washington, and already Kilpatrick was aping American speech.

'So,' Rebus said, 'now we talk to the RUC.'

'I already have. That's why I called this meeting.'

'What did they say?'

'They were pretty damned cagey.'

'No surprises there, sir,' said Smylie.

'They did admit to having some information on what they called Sword and Shield.'

'Great.'

'But they won't release it. Usual RUC runaround. They don't like sharing things. Their line is, if we want to see it, we have to go there. Those bastards really are a law unto themselves.'

'No point going higher up with this, sir? *Some*one could order the information out of them.'

'Yes, and it could get lost, or they could lift out anything they didn't feel like letting us see. No, I think we show willing on this.'

'Belfast?'

Kilpatrick nodded. 'I'd like you both to go, it'll only be a day trip.' Kilpatrick checked his watch. 'There's a Loganair flight at seven-forty, so you'd best get going.'

'No time to pack my tour guides,' said Rebus. Inside, two old dreads were warming his gut.

They banked steeply coming down over Belfast harbour, like one of those fairground rides teenagers take to prove themselves. Rebus still had a hum of caffeine in his ears.

'Pretty good, eh?' said Smylie.

'Aye, pretty good.' Rebus hadn't flown in a few years. He'd had a fear of flying ever since his SAS training. Already he was dreading the return trip. It wasn't when he was high up, he didn't mind that. But the take-off and landing, that view of the ground, so near and yet far enough to kill you stone dead if you hit it. Here it came again, the plane dropping fast now, too fast. His fingers were sore against the armrests. There was every chance of them locking there. He could see a surgeon amputating at the wrists . . .

And then they were down. Smylie was quick to stand up. The seat had been too narrow for him, with not enough legroom. He worked his neck and shoulders, then rubbed his knees.

'Welcome to Belfast,' he said.


'We like to give visitors the tour,' Yates said.

He was Inspector Yates of the Royal Ulster Constabulary, and both he and his car were in mufti. He had a face formed of fist-fights or bad childhood infections, scar tissue and things not quite in their right place. His nose veered leftwards, one earlobe hung lower than the other, and his chin had been stitched together not altogether successfully. You'd look at him in a bar and then look away again quickly, not risking the stare he deserved. He had no neck, that was another thing. His head sat on his shoulders like a boulder on the top of a hill.

'That's very kind,' said Smylie, as they sped into town, 'but we'd –'

'Lets you see what we're dealing with.' Yates kept looking in his rearview, conducting a conversation with the mirror. 'The two cities. It's the same in any war zone. I knew this guy, height of the trouble in Beirut, he was recruited as a croupier there. Bombs falling, gunmen on the rampage, and the casinos were still open. Now these,' he nodded out of the windscreen, 'are the recruiting stations.'

They had left the City Airport behind, shaved the city's

commercial centre, and were passing through a wasteland. Until now, you couldn't have said which British city you were in. A new road was being built down by the docks. Old flats, no worse than those in the Gar-B, were being demolished. As Yates had commented, sometimes the divide was hidden.

Not far away, a helicopter hovered high in the sky, watching someone or something. Around them, whole streets had been bulldozed. The kerbstones were painted green and white.

'You'll see red, white and blue ones in other areas.'

On the gable-end of a row of houses was an elaborate painting. Rebus could make out three masked figures, their automatic weapons raised high. There was a tricolour above them, and a phoenix rising from flames above this.

'A nice piece of propaganda,' said Rebus.

Yates turned to Smylie. 'Your man knows what he's talking about. It's a work of art. These are some of the poorest streets in Europe, by the way.'

They didn't look so bad to Rebus. The gable-end had reminded him again of the Gar-B. Only there was more rebuilding going on here. New housing developments were rising from the old.

'See that wall?' said Yates. 'That's called an environmental wall built and maintained by the Housing Executive.' It was a red brick wall, functional, with a pattern in the bricks. 'There used to be houses there. The other side of the wall is Protestant, once you get past the wasteland. They knock down the houses and extend the wall. There's the Peace Line too, that's an ugly old thing, made from iron rather than bricks. Streets like these, they're meat and drink to the paramilitaries. The loyalist areas are the same.'

Eyes were following their slow progress, the eyes of teenagers and children grouped at street corners. The eyes held neither fear nor hate, only mistrust. On a wall, someone had daubed painted messages, old references to the H Block and Bobby Sands, newer additions in praise of the IRA, and promising revenge against the loyalist paramilitaries, the UVF and UFF predominantly. Rebus saw himself patrolling these streets, or streets like them, back when there had been more houses, more people on the move. He'd often been the 'back walker', which meant he stayed at the back of the patrol and faced the rear, his gun pointing towards the people they'd just passed, men staring at the ground, kids making rude gestures, shows of bravado, and mothers pushing prams. The patrol moved as cautiously as in any jungle.

'See, here we are,' Yates was saying, 'we're coming into Protestant territory now.' More gable-ends, now painted with ten-foot-high Williams of Orange riding twenty-foot-high white horses. And then the cheaper displays, the graffiti, exhorting the locals to 'Fuck the Pope and the IRA'. The letters FTP were everywhere. Five minutes before, they had been FKB: Fuck King Billy. They were just routine, a reflex. But of course they were more. You couldn't laugh them off as name-calling, because the people who'd written them wouldn't let you. They kept shooting each other, and blowing each other up.

Smylie read one of the slogans aloud. ' "Irish Out".' He turned to Yates. 'What? All of them?'

Yates smiled. 'The Catholics write "Troops Out", so the loyalists write "Irish Out". They don't see themselves as Irish, they're British.' He looked in the mirror again. 'And they're getting more vicious, loyalist paramilitaries killed more civvies last year than the IRA did. That's a first, so far as I know. The loyalists hate us now, too.'

'Who's us?'

'The RUC. They weren't happy when the UDA was outlawed. Your man, Sir Patrick Mayhew, he lit the fuse.'

'I read about some riots.'

'Only last month, here in the Shankill and elsewhere. They say we're harassing them. We can't really win, can we?'

'I think we get the picture,' said Smylie, anxious to get to work. But Rebus knew the point the RUC man was making: this *was* their work.

'If you think you get the picture,' Yates said, 'then you're not getting the picture. You're to blame, you know.'

'Eh?'

'The Scots. You settled here in the seventeenth century, started pushing around the Catholics.'

'I don't think we need a history lesson,' Rebus said quietly. Smylie was looking like he might explode.

'But it's all about history,' Yates said levelly. 'On the surface at least.'

'And underneath?'

'Paramilitaries are in the business of making money. They can't exist without money. So now they've become gangsters, pure and simple, because that's the easy way to make the money they need. And then it becomes self-perpetuating. The IRA and UDA get together now and then and discuss things. They sit around a table together, just like the politicians want them to, but instead of talking about peace, they talk about carving up the country. You can extort from these taxi firms if we can extort from the building sites. You even get cases where the stuff the one side has stolen is passed on to the other for them to sell in their areas. You get times when the tension's high, then it's back to business as usual. It's like one of those mafia films, the money these bastards are making . . .' Yates shook his head. 'They can't *afford* peace. It'd be bad for business.'

'And bad for your business too.'

Yates laughed. 'Aye, right enough, overtime wouldn't be easy to come by. But then we might live to retirement age, too. That doesn't always happen just now.' Yates had lifted his radio transmitter. 'Two-Six-Zero, I'm about five minutes from base. Two passengers.' The radio spat static.

'Received and understood.'

He put down the receiver. 'Now this,' he said, 'this is

137

Belfast too. South Belfast, you don't hear much about it because hardly anything ever happens here. See what I mean about two cities?'

Rebus had been noticing the change in their surroundings. Suddenly it looked prosperous, safe. There were wide tree-lined avenues, detached houses, some of them very new-looking. They'd passed the university, a red-brick replica of some older college. Yet they were still only ten minutes from 'the Troubles'. Rebus knew this face of the city, too. He'd only spent the one tour of duty here, but he remembered the big houses, the busy city centre, the Victorian pubs whose interiors were regarded as national treasures. He knew the city was surrounded by lush green countryside, winding lanes and farm tracks, at the end of which might sit silent milk-churns packed with explosives.

The RUC station on the Malone Road was a well-disguised affair, tucked away behind a wooden fence, with a discreet lookout tower.

'We have to keep up appearances for the locals,' Yates explained. 'This is a nice part of town, no mesh fences and machine guns.'

The gates had been opened for them, and closed quickly again.

'Thanks for the tour,' Rebus said as they parked. He meant it, something Yates acknowledged with a nod. Smylie opened his door and prised himself out. Yates glanced at the upholstery, then opened the glove compartment and lifted out his holstered pistol, bringing it with him.

'Is your accent Irish?' Rebus asked.

'Mostly. There's a bit of Liverpool in there too. I was born in Bootle, we moved here when I was six.'

'What made you join the RUC?' Smylie asked.

'I've always been a stupid bastard, I suppose.'

He had to sign both visitors into the building, and their identities were checked. Later, Rebus knew, some clerical assistant would add them to a computer file.

Inside, the station looked much like any police station, except that the windows were heavily protected and the beat patrols carried padded vests with them and wore holsters. They'd seen policemen during their drive, but had acknowledged none of them. And they'd passed a single Army patrol, young squaddies sitting at the open rear door of their personnel carrier (known as a 'pig' in Rebus's day, and probably still), automatic rifles held lightly, faces trained not to show emotion. In the station, the windows might be well protected but there seemed little sign of a siege mentality. The jokes were just as blue, just as black, as the ones told in Edinburgh. People discussed TV and football and the weather. Smylie wasn't watching any of it. He wanted the job done and out again as quick as could be.

Rebus wasn't sure about Smylie. The man might be a wonder in the office, as efficient as the day was long, but here he seemed less sure of himself. He was nervous, and showed it. When he took his jacket off, complaining of the heat, there were large sweat marks spreading from beneath his arms. Rebus had thought *he'd* be the nervous one, yet he felt detached, his memories bringing back no new fears. He was all right.

Yates had a small office to himself. They'd bought beakers of tea at a machine, and now sat these on the desk. Yates put his gun into a desk drawer, draped his jacket over his chair, and sat down. Pinned above him on the wall behind the desk was a sheet of computer print-out bearing the oversized words *Nil Illegitimum Non Carborundum*. Smylie decided to take a poke.

'I thought Latin was for the Catholics?'

Yates stared at him. 'There *are* Catholics in the RUC. Don't get us confused with the UDR.' Then he unlocked another drawer and pulled out a file, pushing it across the desk towards Rebus. 'This doesn't leave the room.' Smylie drew his chair towards Rebus's, and they read the contents together, Smylie, the faster reader, fidgeting as he waited for Rebus to catch up.

'This is incredible,' Smylie said at one point. He was right. The RUC had evidence of a loyalist paramilitary force called Sword and Shield (usually just referred to as The Shield), and of a support group working out of the mainland, acting as a conduit through which money and arms could pass, and also raising funds independently.

'By mainland do you mean Scotland?' Rebus asked.

Yates shrugged. 'We're not really taking them seriously, it's just a cover name for the UVF or UFF, got to be. That's the way it works. There are so many of these wee groups, Ulster Resistance, the Red Hands Commando, Knights of the Red Hand, we can hardly keep up with them.'

'But this group is on the mainland,' Rebus said.

'Yes.'

'And we've maybe come up against them.' He tapped the folder. 'Yet nobody thought to tell us any of this.'

Yates shrugged again, his head falling further into his body. 'We leave that to Special Branch.'

'You mean Special Branch were told about this?'

'Special Branch here would inform Special Branch in London.'

'Any idea who the contact would be in London?'

'That's classified information, Inspector, sorry.'

'A man called Abernethy?'

Yates pushed his chair back so he could rock on it, the front two legs coming off the floor. He studied Rebus.

'That's answer enough,' Rebus said. He looked to Smylie, who nodded. They were being screwed around by Special Branch. But why?

'I see something's on your mind,' said Yates. 'Want to tell me about it? I'd like to hear what you know.'

Rebus placed the folder on the desk. 'Then come to Edinburgh some time, maybe we'll tell you.'

Yates placed all four legs of his chair on the floor. When

140

he looked at Rebus, his face was stone, his eyes fire. 'No need to be like that,' he said quietly.

'Why not? We've wasted a whole day for four sheets of filing paper, all because you wouldn't send it to us!'

'It's nothing personal, Inspector, it's security. Wouldn't matter if you were the Chief fucking Constable. Perspectives tend to change when your arse is in the line of fire.'

If Yates was looking for the sympathy vote, Rebus wasn't about to place a cross in his box. 'The Prods haven't always been as keen as the Provos, have they? What's going on?'

'First off, they're loyalists, not Prods. Prods means Protestants, and we're dealing only with a select few, not with all of them. Second, they're Provies, not Provos. Third ... we're not sure. There's a younger leadership, a keener leadership. Plus like I say, they're not happy just to let the security forces get on with it. See, the loyalist paramilitaries have always had a problem. They're supposed to be on the same side as the security forces, they're supposed to be law-abiding. That's changed. They feel threatened. Just now they're the majority, but it won't always be that way. Plus the British government's more concerned with its international image than with a few hard-line loyalists, so it's paying more attention to the Republic. Put all that together and you get disillusioned loyalists, and plenty of them. The loyalist paramilitaries used to have a bad image. A lot of their operations went wrong, they didn't have the manpower or the connections or the international support of the IRA.

'These days they seem to be better organised though, not so much blatant racketeering. A lot of the thugs have been put off the Road ... that is, put off the Shankill Road, as in banished.'

'But at the same time they're arming themselves,' Rebus said.

'It's true,' added Smylie. 'In the past, whenever we caught them red-handed on the mainland, we used to find gelignite or sodium chlorate, now we're finding rocket launchers and armour-piercing shells.'

'Red-handed.' Yates smiled at that. 'Oh, it's getting heavy duty,' he agreed.

'But you don't know why?'

'I've given you all the reasons I can.'

Rebus wondered about that, but didn't say anything.

'Look, this is a new thing for us,' Yates said. 'We're used to facing off the Provies, not the loyalists. But now they've got Kalashnikovs, RPG-7s, frag grenades, Brownings.'

'And you're taking them seriously?'

'Oh yes, Inspector, we're taking them seriously. That's why I want to know what *you* know.'

'Maybe we'll tell you over a beer,' Rebus said.


Yates took them to the Crown Bar. Across the street, most of the windows in the Europa Hotel were boarded up, the result of another bomb. The bomb had damaged the Crown, too, but the damage hadn't been allowed to linger. It was a Victorian pub, well preserved, with gas lighting and a wall lined with snugs, each with its own table and its own door for privacy. The interior reminded Rebus of several Edinburgh bars, but here he drank stout rather than heavy, and whiskey rather than whisky.

'I know this place,' he said.

'Been here before, eh?'

'Inspector Rebus,' Smylie explained, 'was in the Army in Belfast.'

So then Rebus had to tell Yates all about it, all about 1969. He wasn't getting it out of his system; he could still feel the pressure inside him. He remembered the republican drinking club again, and the way they'd gone in there swinging wildly, some of the toms more enthusiastic than others. What would he say if he met any of the men they'd beaten? Sorry didn't seem enough. He wouldn't talk about it, but he told Yates a few other stories. Talking was okay, and drinking was okay too. The thought of the return flight didn't bother him so much after two pints and a nip. By the time they were in the Indian restaurant eating an early lunch in a private booth a long way from any other diners, Smylie had grown loquacious, but it was all mental arm-wrestling, comparing and contrasting the two police forces, discussing manpower, back-up, arrest sheets, drug problems.

As Yates pointed out, leaving aside terrorism, Northern Ireland had one of the lowest crime rates going, certainly for serious crimes. There were the usual housebreakings and car-jackings, but few rapes and murders. Even the rougher housing schemes were kept in check by the para-militaries, whose punishments went beyond incarceration.

Which brought them back to Mary King's Close. Were they any nearer, Rebus wondered, to finding out why Billy Cunningham had been tortured and killed and who had killed him? The letters SaS on an arm, the word Nemo on the floor, the style of the assassination and Cunningham's own sympathies. What did it all add up to?

Yates meantime talked a little more freely, while helping Smylie polish off the remaining dishes. He admitted they weren't all angels in the RUC, which did not exactly surprise Rebus and Smylie, but Yates said they should see some of the men in the Ulster Defence Regiment, who were so fair-minded that their patrols had to be accompanied by RUC men keeping an eye on them.

'You were here in '69, Inspector, you'll remember the B Specials? The UDR was formed to replace the B Spesh. The same madmen joined. See, if a loyalist wants to do something for his cause, all he has to do is join the UDR or the RUC Reserve. That fact has kept the UDA and UVF small.'

'Is there still collusion between the security forces and the loyalists?'

Yates pondered that one over a belch. 'Probably,' he said, reaching for his lager. 'The UDR used to be terrible, so did the Royal Irish Rangers. Now, it's not so widespread.'

'Either that or better hidden,' said Rebus.

'With cynicism like that, you should join the RUC.'

'I don't like guns.'

Yates wiped at his plate with a final sliver of nan bread. 'Ah yes,' he said, 'the essential difference between us. I get to shoot people.'

'It's a big difference,' Rebus suggested.

'All the difference in the world,' Yates agreed.

Smylie had gone quiet. He was wiping his own plate with bread.

'Do the loyalists get aid from overseas?' Rebus asked.

Yates sat back contentedly. 'Not as much as the republicans. The loyalists probably rake in £150,000 a year from the mainland, mostly to help families and convicted members. Two-thirds of that comes from Scotland. There are pockets of sympathisers abroad – Australia, South Africa, the US and Canada. Canada's the big one. The UVF have some Ingrams submachine guns just now that were shipped from Toronto. Why do you want to know?'

Rebus and Smylie shared a look, then Smylie started to talk. Rebus was happy to let him: this way, Yates only got to know what Smylie knew, rather than what Rebus suspected. Toronto: headquarters of The Shield. When Smylie had finished, Rebus asked Yates a question.

'This group, Sword and Shield, I didn't see any names on the file.'

'You mean individuals?' Rebus nodded. 'Well, it's all pretty low-key. We've got suspicions, but the names wouldn't mean anything to you.'

'Try me.'

Yates considered, then nodded slowly. 'Okay.'

'For instance, who's the leader?'

'We haven't breached their command structure ... not yet.'

'But you have your suspicions?'

Yates smiled. 'Oh yes. There's one bastard in particular.' His voice, already low, dropped lower still. 'Alan Fowler. He was UVF, but left after a disagreement. A right bad bastard, I think the UVF were glad to be shot of him.'

'Can I have a photo? A description?'

Yates shrugged. 'Why not? He's not my problem just now anyway.'

Rebus put down his glass. 'Why's that?'

'Because he took the ferry to Stranraer last week. A car picked him up and drove him to Glasgow.' Yates paused. 'And that's where we lost him.'

# 15

Ormiston was waiting at the airport with a car.

Rebus didn't like Ormiston. He had a huge round face marked with freckles, and a semi-permanent grin too close to a sneer for comfort. His hair was thickly brown, always in need of a comb or a cut. He reminded Rebus of an overgrown schoolboy. Seeing him at his desk next to the bald and schoolmasterly Blackwood was like seeing the classroom dunce placed next to the teacher so an eye could be kept on his work.

But there was something particularly wrong with Ormiston this afternoon. Not that Rebus really cared. All he cared about was the headache which had woken him on the approach to Edinburgh. A midday drinking headache, a glare behind the eyes and a stupor further back in the brain. He'd noticed at the airport, the way Ormiston was looking at Smylie, Smylie not realising it.

'Got any paracetamol on you?' Rebus asked.

'Sorry.' And he caught Rebus's eye again, as if trying to communicate something. Normally he was a nosy bugger, yet he hadn't asked about their trip. Even Smylie noticed this.

'What is it, Ormiston? A vow of *omerta* or something?'

Ormiston still wasn't talking. He concentrated on his driving, giving Rebus plenty of time for thought. He had things to tell Kilpatrick ... and things he wanted to keep to himself for the time being.

When Ormiston stopped the car at Fettes, he turned to Rebus.

'Not you. We've got to meet the Chief somewhere.'

'What?'

Smylie, half out of his door, stopped. 'What's up?'

Ormiston just shook his head. Rebus looked to Smylie. 'See you later then.'

'Aye, sure.' And Smylie got out, relieving the car's suspension. As soon as he'd closed the door, Ormiston moved off.

'What is it, Ormiston?'

'Best if the Chief tells you himself.'

'Give me a clue then.'

'A murder,' Ormiston said, changing up a gear. 'There's been a murder.'


The scene had been cordoned off.

It was a narrow street of tall tenements. St Stephen Street had always enjoyed a rakish reputation, something to do with its mix of student flats, cafes and junk shops. There were several bars, one of them catering mainly to bikers. Rebus had heard a story that Nico, ex-Velvet Underground, had lived here for a time. It could be true. St Stephen Street, connecting the New Town to Raeburn Place, was a quiet thoroughfare which still managed to exude charm and seediness in equal measures.

The tenements either side of the street boasted basements, and a lot of these were flats with their own separate stairwells and entrances. Patience lived in just such a flat not seven minutes' walk away. Rebus walked carefully down the stone steps. They were often worn and slippy. At the bottom, in a sort of damp courtyard, the owner or tenant of the flat had attempted to create a garden of terracotta pots and hanging baskets. But most of the plants had died, probably from lack of light, or perhaps from rough treatment at the hands of the builders. Scaffolding stretched up the front of the tenement, much of it covered with thick polythene, crackling in the breeze.

'Cleaning the façade,' someone said. Rebus nodded. The front door of the flat faced a whitewashed wall, and in the wall were set two doors. Rebus knew what these were, they were storage areas, burrowed out beneath the surface of the pavement. Patience had almost identical doors, but never used the space for anything; the cellars were too damp. One of the doors stood open. The floor was mostly moss, some of which was being scraped into an evidence-bag by a SOCO.

Kilpatrick, watching this, was listening to Blackwood, who ran his left hand across his pate, tucking an imaginary hair behind his ear. Kilpatrick saw Rebus.

'Hello, John.'

'Sir.'

'Where's Smylie?'

Ormiston was coming down the steps. Rebus nodded towards him. 'The Quiet Man there dropped him at HQ. So what's the big mystery?'

Blackwood answered. 'Flat's been on the market a few months, but not selling. Owner decided to tart it up a bit, see if that would do the trick. Builders turned up yesterday. Today one of them decided to take a look at the cellars. He found a body.'

'Been there long?'

Blackwood shook his head. 'They're doing the post-mortem this evening.'

'Any tattoos?'

'No tattoos,' said Kilpatrick. 'Thing is, John, it was Calumn.' The Chief Inspector looked genuinely troubled, almost ready for tears. His face had lost its colour, and had lengthened as though the muscles had lost all motivation. He massaged his forehead with a hand.

'Calumn?' Rebus shook away his hangover. 'Calumn Smylie?' He remembered the big man, in the back of the

HGV with his brother. Tried to imagine him dead, but couldn't. Especially not here, in a cellar...

Kilpatrick blew his nose loudly, then wiped it. 'I suppose I'd better get back and tell Ken.'

'No need, sir.'

Ken Smylie was standing at street level, gripping the gloss-black railings. He looked like he might uproot the lot. Instead he arched back his head and gave a high-pitched howl, the sound swirling up into the sky as a smattering of rain began to fall.

Smylie had to be ordered to go home, they couldn't shift him otherwise. Everyone else in the office moved like automatons. DCI Kilpatrick had some decisions to make, chief among them whether or not to tie together the two murder inquiries.

'He was stabbed,' he told Rebus. 'No signs of a struggle, certainly no torture, nothing like that.' There was relief in his voice, a relief Rebus could understand. 'Stabbed and dumped. Whoever did it probably saw the For Sale sign outside the flat, didn't reckon on the body being found for a while.' He had produced a bottle of Laphroaig from the bottom drawer of his desk, and poured himself a glass.

'Medicinal,' he explained. But Rebus declined the offer of a glass. He'd taken three paracetamol washed down with Irn-Bru. He noticed that the level in the Laphroaig bottle was low. Kilpatrick must have a prescription.

'You think he was rumbled?'

'What else?' said Kilpatrick, dribbling more malt into his glass.

'I'd have expected another punishment killing, something with a bit of ritual about it.'

'Ritual?' Kilpatrick considered this. 'He wasn't killed there, you know. The pathologist said there wasn't enough blood. Maybe they held their "ritual" wherever they killed him. Christ, and I let him go out on a limb.' He took out a handkerchief and blew his nose, then took a deep breath. 'Well, I've got a murder inquiry to start up, the high hiedyins are going to be asking questions.'

'Yes, sir.' Rebus stood up, but stopped at the door. 'Two murders, two cellars, two lots of builders.'

Kilpatrick nodded, but said nothing. Rebus opened the door.

'Sir, who knew about Calumn?'

'How do you mean?'

'Who knew he was undercover? Just this office, or anyone else?'

Kilpatrick furrowed his brow. 'Such as?'

'Special Branch, say.'

'Just this office,' Kilpatrick said quietly. Rebus turned to leave. 'John, what did you find out in Belfast?'

'That Sword and Shield exists. That the RUC know it's operating here on the mainland. That they told Special Branch in London.' He paused. 'That DI Abernethy probably knows all about it.'

Having said which, Rebus left the room. Kilpatrick stared at the door for a full minute.

'Christ almighty,' he said. His telephone was ringing. He was slow to answer it.


'Is it true?' Brian Holmes asked. Siobhan Clarke was waiting for an answer too.

'It's true,' said Rebus. They were in the Murder Room at St Leonard's. 'He was working on something that might well be connected to Billy Cunningham.'

'So what now, sir?'

'We need to talk to Millie and Murdock again.'

'We've talked to them.'

'That's why I said "again". Don't you listen? And after that, let's fix up a little chat with some of the Jaffas.'

'Jaffas?'

150

Rebus tutted at Siobhan Clarke. 'How long have you lived here? Jaffas are Orangemen.'

'The Orange Lodge?' said Holmes. 'What can they tell us?'

'The date of the Battle of the Boyne for a start.'

'1690, Inspector.'

'Yes, sir.'

'The date, of course, means more than a mere *annus mirabilis*. One-six-nine-o. One and six make seven, nine plus nought equals nine, seven and nine being crucial numbers.' He paused. 'Do you know anything of numerology, Inspector?'

'No, sir.'

'What about the lassie?'

Siobhan Clarke bristled visibly. 'It's sort of a crank science, isn't it?' she offered. Rebus gave her a cooling look. Humour him, the look ordered.

'Not crank, no. It's ancient, with the ring of truth. Can I get you something to drink?'

'No, thanks, Mr Gowrie.'

They were seated in Arch Gowrie's 'front room', a parlour kept for visitors and special occasions. The real living room, with comfortable sofa, TV and video, drinks cabinet, was elsewhere on this sprawling ground floor. The house was at least three storeys high, and probably boasted an attic conversion too. It was sited in The Grange, a leafy backwater of the city's southern side. The Grange got few visitors, few strangers, and never much traffic, since it was not a well-known route between any two other areas of the city. A lot of the huge detached houses, one-time merchants' houses with walled grounds and high wooden or metal gates, had been bought by the Church of Scotland or other religious denominations. There was a retirement home to one side of Gowrie's own residence, and what Rebus thought was a convent on the other side.

Archibald Gowrie liked to be called 'Arch'. Everyone knew him as Arch. He was the public face of the Orange Lodge, an eloquent enough apologist (not that he thought there was anything to apologise for), but by no means that organisation's most senior figure. However, he was high enough, and he was easy to find – unlike Millie and Murdock, who weren't home.

Gowrie had agreed readily to a meeting, saying he'd be free between seven and quarter to eight.

'Plenty of time, sir,' Rebus had said.

He studied Arch Gowrie now. The man was big and fiftyish and probably attractive to women in that way older men could be. (Though Rebus noticed Siobhan Clarke didn't seem too enthralled.) Though his hair – thinning nicely – was silver, his thick moustache was black. He wore his shirt with the sleeves rolled up, showing darkly haired arms. He was always ready for business. In fact, 'open for business' had been his public motto, and he worked tirelessly whenever he got his teeth into a new development.

From what Rebus knew, Gowrie had made his money initially as director of a company which had nippily shifted its expertise from ships and pipelines to building exploration platforms and oil rigs for the North Sea. That was back in the early '70s. The company had been sold at vast profit, and Gowrie had disappeared for several years before reappearing in the guise of property developer and invest-ment guru. He was still a property developer, his name on several projects around the city as well as further afield. But he had diversified into wildly different areas: film production, hi-fi design, edible algae, forestry, two country house hotels, a woollen mill, and the Eyrie restaurant in the New Town. Probably Arch was best known for his part-ownership of the Eyrie, the city's best restaurant, certainly its most exclusive, by far its most expensive. You wouldn't find nutritious Hebridean Blue Algae on its menu, not even written in French.

Rebus knew of only one large loss Gowrie had taken, as money man behind a film set predominantly in Scotland. Even boasting Rab Kinnoul as its star, the film had been an Easter turkey. Still, Gowrie wasn't shy: there was a framed poster for the film hanging in the entrance hall.

'*Annus mirabilis*,' Rebus mused. 'That's Latin, isn't it?'

Gowrie was horrified. 'Of course it's Latin! Don't tell me you never studied Latin at school? I though we Scots were an educated bunch. Miraculous year, that's what it means. Sure about that drink?'

'Maybe a small whisky, sir.' Kill or cure.

'Nothing for me, sir,' said Siobhan Clarke, her voice coming from the high moral ground.

'I won't be a minute,' said Gowrie. When he'd left the room, Rebus turned to her.

'Don't piss him off!' he hissed. 'Just keep your gob shut and your ears open.'

'Sorry, sir. Have you noticed?'

'What?'

'There's nothing green in this room, nothing at all.'

He nodded again. 'The inventor of red, white and blue grass will make a fortune.'

Gowrie came back into the room. He took a look at the two of them on the sofa, then smiled to himself and handed Rebus a crystal tumbler.

'I won't offend you by offering water or lemonade with that.'

Rebus sniffed the amber liquid. It was a West Highland malt, darker, more aromatic than the Speysides. Gowrie held his own glass up.

'*Slainte.*' He took a sip, then sat in a dark blue armchair. 'Well now,' he said, 'how exactly can I help you?'

'Well, sir –'

'It's nothing to do with us, you know. We've told the Chief Constable that. They're an offshoot of the Grand Lodge, less than that even, now that we've disbarred them.'

Rebus suddenly knew what Gowrie was talking about. There was to be a march along Princes Street on Saturday, organised by the Orange Loyal Brigade. He'd heard about it weeks ago, when the very idea had provoked attacks from republican sympathisers and anti-right wing associations. There were expected to be confrontations during the march.

'When did you disbar the group exactly, sir?'

'April 14th. That was the day we had the disciplinary hearing. They belonged to one of our district lodges, and at a dinner-dance they'd sent collecting tins round for the LPWA.' He turned to Siobhan Clarke. 'That's the Loyalist Prisoners' Welfare Association.' Then back to Rebus. 'We can't have that sort of thing, Inspector. We've denounced it in the past. We'll have no truck with the paramilitaries.'

'And the disbarred members set up the Orange Loyal Brigade?'

'Correct.'

Rebus was feeling his way. 'How many do you think will be on the march?'

'Ach, a couple of hundred at most, and that's including the bands. I think they've got bands coming from Glasgow and Liverpool.'

'You think there'll be trouble?'

'Don't you? Isn't that why you're here?'

'Who's the Brigade's leader?'

'Gavin MacMurray. But don't you know all this already? Your Chief Constable asked if I could intervene. But I told him, they're nothing to do with the Orange Lodge, nothing at all.'

'Do they have connections with the other right-wing groups?'

'You mean with fascists?' Gowrie shrugged. 'They deny it, of course, but I wouldn't be surprised to see a few skinheads on the march, even ones with Sassenach accents.'

Rebus left a pause before asking, 'Do you know if there's any link-up between the Orange Brigade and The Shield?'

Gowrie frowned. 'What shield?'

'Sword and Shield. It's another splinter group, isn't it?'

Gowrie shook his head. 'I've never heard of it.'

'No?'

'Never.'

Rebus placed his whisky glass on a table next to the sofa. 'I just assumed you'd know something about it.' He got to his feet, followed by Clarke. 'Sorry to have bothered you, sir.' Rebus held out his hand.

'Is that it?'

'That's all, sir, thanks for your help.'

'Well ...' Gowrie was clearly troubled. 'Shield ... no, means nothing to me.'

'Then don't worry about it, sir. Have a good evening now.'

At the front door, Clarke turned and smiled at Gowrie. 'We'll let you get back to your wee numbers. Goodbye, sir.'

They heard the door close behind them with a solid click as they walked back down the short gravel path to the driveway.

'I've only got one question, sir: what was all that about?'

'We're dealing with lunatics, Clarke, and Gowrie isn't a lunatic. A zealot maybe, but not a madman. Tell me, what do you call a haircut in an asylum?'

By now Clarke knew the way her boss's mind worked. 'A lunatic fringe?' she guessed.

'*That's* who I want to talk to.'

'You mean the Orange Loyal Brigade?'

Rebus nodded. 'And every one of them will be taking a stroll along Princes Street on Saturday.' He smiled without humour. 'I've always enjoyed a parade.'

# 16

Saturday was hot and clear, with a slight cooling breeze, just enough to make the day bearable. Shoppers were out on Princes Street in numbers, and the lawns of Princes Street Gardens were as packed as a seaside beach, every bench in full use, a carousel attracting the children. The atmosphere was festive if frayed, with the kids squealing and tiring as their ice-cream cones melted and dropped to the ground, turning instantly into food for the squirrels, pigeons, and panting dogs.

The parade was due to set off from Regent Road at three o'clock, and by two-fifteen the pubs behind Princes Street were emptying their cargo of brolly-toting white-gloved elders, bowler hats fixed onto their sweating heads, faces splotched from alcohol. There was a show of regalia, and a few large banners were being unfurled. Rebus couldn't remember what you called the guy at the front of the march, the one who threw up and caught the heavy ornamental staff. He'd probably known in his youth. The flute players were practising, and the snare drummers adjusted their straps and drank from cans of beer.

People outside the Post Office on Waterloo Place could hear the flutes and drums, and peered along towards Regent Road. That the march was to set off from outside the old Royal High School, mothballed site for a devolved Scottish parliament, added a certain something to the affair.

Rebus had been in a couple of the bars, taking a look at the Brigade members and supporters. They were a varied crew, taking in a few Doc Marten-wearing skinheads (just as Gowrie had predicted) as well as the bowler hats. There were also the dark suit/white shirt/dark tie types, their shoes as polished as their faces. Most of them were drinking like fury, though they didn't seem completely mortal yet. Empty cans were being kicked along Regent Road, or trodden on and left by the edges of the pavement. Rebus wasn't sure why these occasions always carried with them the air of threat, of barely suppressed violence, even before they started. Extra police had been drafted in, and were readying to stop traffic from coming down onto Princes Street. Metal-grilled barriers waited by the side of the road, as did the small groups of protesters, and the smaller group of protesters who were protesting against the protesters. Rebus wondered, not for the first time, which maniac on the Council had pushed through the okay for the parade.

The marching season of course had finished, the main parades being on and around the 12th of July, date of the Battle of the Boyne. Even then the biggest marches were in Glasgow. What was the point of this present parade? To stir things up, of course, to make a noise. To be noticed. The big drum, the *lambeg*, was being hammered now. There was competition from a few bagpipe buskers near Waverley Station, but they'd be silenced by the time the parade reached them.

Rebus wandered freely among the marchers as they drank and joked with each other and adjusted their uniforms. A Union Jack was unfurled, then ordered to be rolled up again, bearing as it did the initials of the British National Party. There didn't seem to be any collecting tins or buckets, the police having pressed for a quick march with as little interaction with the public as possible. Rebus knew this because he'd asked Farmer Watson, and the Farmer had confirmed that it would be so.

'Here's tae King Billy!' A can was raised. 'God bless the Queen and King William of Orange!'

'Well said, son.'

The bowler hats said little, standing with the tips of their umbrellas touching the ground, hands resting lightly on the curved wooden handles. It was easy to dismiss these unsmiling men too lightly. But God help you if you started an argument with one of them.

'Why dae yis hate Catholics?' a pedestrian yelled.

'We don't!' somebody yelled back, but she was already bustling away with her shopping bags. There were smiles, but she'd made her point. Rebus watched her go.

'Hey, Gavin, how long now?'

'Five minutes, just relax.'

Rebus looked towards the man who had just spoken, the man who was probably called Gavin MacMurray and therefore in charge. He seemed to have appeared from nowhere. Rebus had read the file on Gavin MacMurray: two arrests for breach of the peace and actual bodily harm, but a lot more information to his name than that. Rebus knew his age (38), that he was married and lived in Currie, and that he ran his own garage. He knew Inland Revenue had no complaints against him, that he drove a red Mercedes Benz (though he made his money from more prosaic Fords, Renaults and the like), and that his teenage son had been in trouble for fighting, with two arrests after pitched battles outside Rangers matches and one arrest after an incident on the train home from Glasgow.

So Rebus assumed the teenager standing close beside Gavin MacMurray must be the son, Jamesie. Jamesie had pretensions of all obvious kinds. He wore sunglasses and a tough look, seeing himself as his father's lieutenant. His legs were apart, shoulders back. Rebus had never seen anyone itching so badly for action of some kind. He had his father's low square jaw, the same black hair cut short at the front. But while Gavin MacMurray was dressed in chainstore anonymity, Jamesie wanted people to look at him. Biker boots, tight black jeans, white t-shirt and black leather jacket. He wore a red bandana around his right wrist, a studded leather strap around the left. His hair, long and curling at the back, had been shaved above both ears.

Turning from son to father was like turning from overt to covert strength. Rebus knew which he'd rather tackle. Gavin MacMurray was chewing gum with his front teeth, his head and eyes constantly in movement, checking things, keeping things in check. He kept his hands in ·his wind-cheater pockets, and wore silver-framed spectacles which magnified his eyes. There seemed little charisma about him, little of the rouser or orator. He looked chillingly ordinary.

Because he *was* ordinary, they all were, all these semi-inebriated working men and retired men, quiet family types who might belong to the British Legion or their local Ex-Servicemen's Club, who might inhabit the bowling green on summer evenings and go with their families on holiday to Spain or Florida or Largs. It was only when you saw them in groups like this that you caught a whiff of something else. Alone, they had nothing but a nagging complaint; together, they had a voice: the sound of the *lambeg*, dense as a heartbeat; the insistent flutes; the march. They always fascinated Rebus. He couldn't help it. It was in his blood. He'd marched in his youth. He'd done a lot of things back then.

There was a final gathering of lines, MacMurray readying his troops. A word with the policeman in charge, a con-versation by two-way radio, then a nod from MacMurray. The opening fat-fry of snare drums, the *lambeg* pumping away, and then the flutes. They marched on the spot for a few moments, then moved off towards Princes Street, where traffic had been stopped for them, where the Castle glared down on them, where a lot of people but by no means everyone paused to watch.

A few months back, a pro-republican march had been banned from this route. That was why the protesters were particularly loud in their jeers, thumbs held down. Some of them were chanting Na-Zis, Na-Zis, and then being told to shut up by uniformed police. There would be a few arrests, there always were. You hadn't had a good day out at a march unless there'd been at least the threat of arrest.

Rebus followed the march from the pavement, sticking to the Gardens side, which was quieter. A few more marchers had joined in, but it was still small beer, hardly worth the bother. He was beginning to wonder what he'd thought would happen. His eyes moved back through the procession from the tosser at the front, busy with his muckle stick, through the flutes and drums, past bowler hats and suits, to the younger marchers and stragglers. A few pre-teenage kids had joined in on the edges, loving every minute. Jamesie, right near the back, told them in no uncertain terms that they should leave, but they didn't listen to him.

'Tough' always was a relative term.

But now one of the stragglers clutched Jamesie's arm and they shared a few words, both of them grinning. The straggler was wearing sunglasses with mirrored lenses, and a denim jacket with no shirt beneath.

'Hello,' said Rebus quietly. He watched Jamesie and Davey Soutar have their conversation, saw Jamesie pat Davey on the shoulder before Davey moved away again, falling back until he left the procession altogether, squeezing between two of the temporary barriers and vanishing into the crowd.

Jamesie seemed to relax a bit after this. His walk became looser, less of an act, and he swung his arms in time to the music. He seemed to be realising that it was a bright summer's day, and at last peeled off his leather jacket, slinging it over one shoulder, showing off his arm muscles and several tattoos. Rebus walked a bit faster, keeping close to the edge of the pavement. One of the tattoos was professional, and showed the ornately overlaid letters RFC: Rangers Football Club. But there was also the maroon emblem of Heart of Midlothian FC, so obviously Jamesie liked to play safe. Then there was a kilted, busby-wearing piper, and further down his arm towards the leather wristband a much more amateur job, the usual shaky greenyblue ink.

The letters SaS.

Rebus blinked. It was almost too far away for him to be sure. Almost. But he *was* sure. And suddenly he didn't want to talk to Gavin MacMurray any more. He wanted a word with his son.

He stopped on the pavement, letting the march pull away from him. He knew where they were heading. A left turn into Lothian Road, passing the windows of the Caledonian Hotel. Something for the rich tourists to get a picture of. Then another left into King's Stables Road, stopping short of the Grassmarket. Afterwards, they'd probably head down into the Grassmarket itself for the post-march analysis and a few more beers. The Grassmarket being trendy these days, there'd be a lot of Fringe drinkers there too. A fine cocktail of cultures for a Saturday afternoon.

He followed the trail to one of the rougher pubs on the Cowgate, just the other side of Candlemaker Row from the Grassmarket. At one time, they'd hung miscreants from the gallows in the Grassmarket. It was a cheerier prospect these days, though you wouldn't necessarily know it from a visit to the Merchant's Bar where, at ten p.m. each night, the pint glasses were switched for flimsy plastic imposters, relieving the bar of ready weapons. It was that kind of place.

Inside, the bar was airless, a drinkers' fug of smoke and television heat. You didn't come here for a good time, you came out of necessity. The regulars were like dragons, each mouthful cooling the fire inside them. As he entered the bar, he saw no one he recognised, not even the barman. The barman was a new face, just out of his teens. He poured pints with an affected disdain, and took the money like it was a bribe. From the sounds of atonal song, Rebus knew the marchers were upstairs, probably emptying the place.

Rebus took his pint – still in a glass glass – and headed up to the dance hall. Sure enough, the marchers were about all there was. They'd shed jackets, ties, and inhibitions, and were milling around, singing to off-key flutes and downing pints and shorts. Getting the drink in had become a logistical nightmare, and more marchers were coming in all the time.

Rebus took a deep breath, carved a smile into his face, and waded in.

'Magic, lads.'

'Aye, ta, pal.'

'Nae bother, eh?'

'Aye, nae bother right enough.'

'All right there, lads?'

'Fine, aye. Magic.'

Gavin MacMurray hadn't arrived yet. Maybe he was off elsewhere with his generals. But his son was on the stage pretending he held a microphone stand and a crowd's attention. Another lad clambered onto the stage and played an invisible guitar, still managing to hold his pint glass. Lager splashed over his jeans, but he didn't notice. That was professionalism for you.

Rebus watched with the smile still on his face. Eventually they gave up, as he'd known they would, there being no audience, and leapt down from the stage. Jamesie landed just in front of Rebus. Rebus held his arms wide.

'Whoah there! That was brilliant.'

Jamesie grinned. 'Aye, ta.' Rebus slapped him on the shoulder.

'Get you another?'

'I think I'm all right, ta.'

'Fair enough.' Rebus looked around, then leant close to Jamesie's ear. 'I see you're one of us.' He winked.

'Eh?'

The tattoo had been covered by the leather jacket, but Rebus nodded towards it. 'The Shield,' he said slyly. Then he nodded again, catching Jamesie's eye, and moved away. He went back downstairs and ordered two pints. The bar was busy and noisy, both TV and jukebox blaring, a couple of arguments rising above even these. Half a minute later, Jamesie was standing beside him. The boy wasn't very bright, and Rebus weighed up how much he could get away with.

'How do you know?' Jamesie asked.

'There's not much I don't know, son.'

'But I don't know you.'

Rebus smiled into his drink. 'Best keep it that way.'

'Then how come you know me?'

Rebus turned towards him. 'I just do.' Jamesie looked around him, licking his lips. Rebus handed him one of the pints. 'Here, get this down you.'

'Ta.' He lowered his voice. 'You're in The Shield?'

'What makes you think that?' Now Jamesie smiled. 'How's Davey, by the way?'

'Davey?'

'Davey Soutar,' said Rebus. 'You two know each other, don't you?'

'I know Davey.' He blinked. 'Christ, you *are* in The Shield. Hang on, did I see you at the parade?'

'I bloody hope so.'

Now Jamesie nodded slowly. 'I thought I saw you.'

'You're a sharp lad, Jamesie. There's a bit of your dad in you.'

Jamesie started at this. 'He'll be here in five minutes. You don't want him to see us . . .'

'You're right. He doesn't know about The Shield then?'

'Of course not.' Jamesie looked slighted.

'Only sometimes the lads tell their dads.'

'Not me.'

163

Rebus nodded. 'You're a good one, Jamesie. We've got our eyes on you.'

'Really?'

'Absolutely.' Rebus supped from his pint. 'Shame about Billy.'

Jamesie became a statue, the glass inches from his lips. He recovered with effort. 'Pardon?'

'Good lad, say nothing.' Rebus took another sup. 'Good parade, wasn't it?'

'Oh aye, the best.'

'Ever been to Belfast?'

Jamesie looked like he was having trouble keeping up with the conversation. Rebus hoped he was. 'Naw,' he said at last.

'I was there a few days ago, Jamesie. It's a proud city, a lot of good people there, *our* people.' Rebus was wondering, how long can I keep this up? A couple of teenagers, probably a year or two beneath the legal drinking age, had already come to the stairs looking for Jamesie to join them.

'True,' Jamesie said.

'We can't let them down.'

'Absolutely not.'

'Remember Billy Cunningham.'

Jamesie put down his glass. 'Is this ...' his voice had become a little less confident, 'is this a ... some sort of warning?'

Rebus patted the young man's arm. 'No, no, you're all right, Jamesie. It's just that the polis are sniffing around.' It was amazing where a bit of confident bull's keech could get you.

'I'm no squealer,' said Jamesie.

The way he said it, Rebus knew. 'Not like Billy?'

'Definitely not.'

Rebus was nodding to himself when the doors burst open and Gavin MacMurray swaggered in, a couple of his generals squeezing through the doorway in his wake. Rebus became just another punter at the bar, as MacMurray slung a heavy arm around his son's neck.

'Awright, Jamesie boy?'

'Fine, Dad. My shout.'

'Three export then. Bring them up back, aye?'

'No bother, Dad.'

Jamesie watched the three men walk to the stairs. He turned towards his confidant, but John Rebus had already left the bar.

# 17

Every chain, no matter how strong, has one link weaker than the rest. Rebus had hopes of Jamesie MacMurray, as he walked out of the Merchant's. He was halfway to his car when he saw Caro Rattray walking towards him.

'You were going to call me,' she said.

'Work's been a bit hectic.'

She looked back at the pub. 'Call that work, do you?'

He smiled. 'Do you live here?'

'On the Canongate. I've just been walking my dog.'

'Your dog?' There was no sign of a leash, never mind the animal. She shrugged.

'I don't actually like dogs, I just like the idea of walking them. So I have an imaginary dog.'

'What's he called?'

'Sandy.'

Rebus looked down at her feet. 'Good boy, Sandy.'

'Actually, Sandy's a girl.'

'Hard to tell at this distance.'

'And I don't talk to her.' She smiled. 'I'm not mad, you know.'

'Right, you just go walking with a pretend dog. So what are you and Sandy doing now?'

'Going home and having a drink. Fancy joining us?'

Rebus thought about it. 'Sure,' he said. 'Drive or walk?'

'Let's walk,' said Caroline Rattray. 'I don't want Sandy shedding on your seats.'

\*

166

She lived in a nicely furnished flat, tidy but not obsessive. There was a grandfather clock in the hall, a family heirloom. Her surname was engraved on the brass face.

A dividing wall had been taken away so that the living room had windows to front and back. A book lay open on the sofa, next to a half-finished box of shortbread. Solitary pleasures, thought Rebus.

'You're not married?' he said.

'God, no.'

'Boyfriend?'

She smiled again. 'Funny word that, isn't it? Especially when you get to my age. I mean, a boyfriend should be in his teens or twenties.'

'Gentleman friend then,' he persisted.

'Doesn't have the same connotations though, does it?' Rebus sighed. 'I know, I know,' she said, 'never argue with an advocate.'

Rebus looked out of the back window onto a drying-green. Overhead, the few clouds were basking in the space they had. 'Sandy's digging up your flower bed.'

'What do you want to drink?'

'Tea, please.'

'Sure? I've only got decaf.'

'That's perfect.' He meant it. While she made noises in the kitchen, he walked through the living room. Dining-table and chairs and wall units at the back, sofa, chairs, bookcases towards the front. It was a nice room. From the small front window, he looked down onto slow-walking tourists and a shop selling tartan teddy-bears.

'This is a nice part of town,' he said, not really meaning it.

'Are you kidding? Ever tried parking round here in the summer?'

'I never try parking anywhere in the summer.'

He moved away from the window. A flute and some sheet music sat on a spindly music-stand in one corner. On a unit were small framed photos of the usual gap-toothed kids and kind-looking old people.

'Family,' she said, coming back into the room. She lit a cigarette, took two deep puffs on it, then stubbed it into an ashtray, exhaling and wafting the smoke away with her hand. 'I hate smoking indoors,' she explained.

'Then why do it?'

'I smoke when I'm nervous.' She smiled slyly and returned to the kitchen, Rebus following. The aroma of the cigarette mingled with the richer aroma of the perfume she wore. Had she just applied some? It hadn't been this strong before.

The kitchen was small, functional. The whole flat had the look of recent but not radical redecoration.

'Milk?'

'Please. No sugar.' Their conversation, he realised, was assuming a studied banality.

The kettle clicked off. 'Can you take the mugs?'

She had already poured a splash of milk into either plain yellow mug. There wasn't much room at all in the kitchen, something Rebus realised as he went to pick up the mugs. He was right beside her as she stirred the teabags in the pot. Her head was bent down, affording a view of the long black hairs curling from her nape, and the nape of her neck itself. She half turned her face towards him, smiling, her eyes finally finding his. Then she moved her body around too. Rebus kissed her forehead first, then her cheek. She had closed her eyes. He burrowed his face in her neck, inhaling deeply: shampoo and perfume and skin. He kissed her again, then came up for air. Caroline opened her eyes slowly.

'Well now,' she said.

He felt suddenly as though he'd been flung down a tunnel, watching the circle of light at the entrance shrink to a full stop. He tried desperately to think of something to say. There was perfume in his lungs.

'Well now,' she repeated. What did that mean? Was she pleased, shocked, bemused? She turned back to the teapot and put its lid on.

'I better go,' Rebus said. She became very still. He couldn't see her face, not enough of it. 'Hadn't I?'

'I've no commitments, John.' Her hands were resting lightly on the work surface, either side of the pot. 'What about you?'

He knew what she meant; she meant Patience. 'There's someone,' he said.

'I know, Dr Curt told me.'

'I'm sorry, Caroline, I shouldn't have done that.'

'What?' She turned to him.

'Kissed you.'

'I didn't mind.' She gave him her smile again. 'I'll never drink a whole pot of tea on my own.'

He nodded, realising he was still holding the mugs. 'I'll take them through.'

He walked out of the kitchen on unsteady legs, his heart shimmying. He'd kissed her. Why had he kissed her? He hadn't meant to. But it had happened. It was real now. The photographs smiled at him as he put the mugs down on a small table which already had coffee-rings on it. What was she doing in the kitchen? He stared at the doorway, willing her to come, willing her not to come.

She came. The teapot was on a tray now, a tea-cosy in the shape of a King Charles spaniel keeping in the heat.

'Is Sandy a King Charles?'

'Some days. How strong do you like it?'

'As it comes.'

She smiled again and poured, handed him a mug, then took one herself and sat in her chair. She didn't look very comfortable. Rebus sat opposite her on the sofa, not resting against the back of it but leaning forward.

'There's some shortbread,' she said.

'No, thanks.'

'So,' she said, 'any progress on Nemo?'

'I think so.' This was good; they were talking. 'SaS is a loyalist support group. They're buying and shipping arms.'

'And the victim in Mary King's Close, he was killed by paramilitaries, nothing to do with his father?'

Rebus shrugged again. 'There's been another murder. It could be linked.'

'That man they found in the cellar?' Rebus nodded. 'Nobody told me they were connected.'

'It's being kept a bit quiet. He was working undercover.'

'How was he found?'

'The flat was having some building work done. One of the labourers opened the cellar door.'

'That's a coincidence.'

'What?'

'There was building work going on in Mary King's Close too.'

'Not the same firm.'

'You've checked?'

Rebus frowned. 'Not me personally, but yes, we've checked.'

'Oh well.' She took another cigarette from her packet and made to light it, but stopped herself. She took the cigarette from her mouth and examined it. 'John,' she said, 'if you'd like to, we can make love any time you want.'

There were none of Cafferty's men waiting for him outside Patience's flat, nothing to delay him. He'd been hoping for the Weasel. Right now, he felt ready for some hands-on with the Weasel.

But it wasn't Cafferty's man he was angry with.

Inside, the long hallway was cool and dark, the only light coming from three small panes of glass above the front door. 'Patience?' he called, hoping she'd be out. Her car was outside, but that didn't mean anything. He wanted to run a bath, steep in it. He turned on both taps, then

went to the bedroom, picked up the phone, and rang Brian
Holmes at home. Holmes's partner Nell picked up the call.

'It's John Rebus,' he told her. She said nothing, just put
the receiver to one side and went off to fetch Brian.
There was no love lost these days between Rebus and Nell
Stapleton, something Holmes himself realised but couldn't
bring himself to query...

'Yes, sir?'

'Brian, those two building companies.'

'Mary King's Close and St Stephen Street?'

'How thoroughly have we checked them?'

'Pretty well.'

'And we've cross-referenced? There's no connection
between them.'

'No, why?'

'Can you check them again yourself?'

'I can.'

'Humour me then. Do it Monday.'

'Anything in particular I should be looking for?'

'No.' He paused. 'Yes, start with casual labour.'

''I thought you wanted Siobhan and me to go see
Murdock?'

'I did. I'll take your place. Have a nice evening.' Rebus
put down the phone and went back to the bathroom. There
was good pressure in the pipes, and the bath was practically
full already. He turned off the cold and reduced the hot to
a trickle. The kitchen was through the living room, and he
fancied some milk from the fridge.

Patience was in the kitchen, chopping vegetables.

'I didn't know you were here,' Rebus said.

'I live here, remember? This is my flat.'

'Yes, I know.' She was angry with him. He opened the
fridge door, took out the milk, and managed to pass her
without touching her. He put the milk on the breakfast
table and got a glass from the draining board. 'What are
you cooking?'

'Why the interest? You never eat here.'

'Patience...'

She came to the sink, scraping peelings into a plastic container. It would all go onto her compost heap. She turned to him. 'Running a bath?'

'Yes.'

'It's Giorgio, isn't it?'

'Sorry?'

'That perfume.' She leaned close, sniffed his shirt. 'Giorgio of Beverly Hills.'

'Patience...'

'You'll have to tell me about her one of these days.'

'You think I'm seeing someone?'

She threw the small sharp kitchen knife at the sink and ran from the room. Rebus stood there, listening until he heard the front door slam. He poured the milk down the sink.

He took back the videos – still unwatched – then went for a drive. The Dell Bar sat on an unlovely stretch of main road outside the Gar-B. It didn't get much passing trade, but there was a line of cars parked outside. Rebus slowed as he drove past. He could go in, but what good would it do? Then he saw something, and pulled his car up kerbside. Next to him a van was parked, with fly-posters pasted on its sides. The posters advertised the play which was soon to go on in the Gar-B gang hut. The theatre group was called Active Resistance. Some of them must be drinking inside. A few vehicles further on was the car he wanted. He bent down at the driver's side window. Ken Smylie tried to ignore him, then wound the window down angrily.

'What are you doing here?' he asked.

'I was about to ask the same,' said Rebus.

Smylie nodded towards the Dell. He had his hands on the steering-wheel. They weren't just resting on it, they were squeezing it. 'Maybe there's someone drinking in there killed Calumn.'

172

'Maybe there is,' Rebus said quietly: he didn't fancy being Smylie's punchbag. 'What are you going to do about it?'

Smylie stared at him. 'I'm going to sit here.'

'And then what? Break the neck of every man who comes out? You know the score, Ken.'

'Leave me alone.'

'Look, Ken –' Rebus broke off as the Dell's door swung open and two punters sauntered out, cigarettes in mouths, sharing some joke between them. 'Look,' he said, 'I know how you feel. I've got a brother too. But this isn't doing any good.'

'Just go away.'

Rebus sighed, straightened up. 'Fair enough then. But if there's any hassle, radio for assistance. Just do that for me, okay?'

Smylie almost smiled. 'There won't be any trouble, believe me.'

Rebus did, the way he believed TV advertising and weather reports. He walked back towards his car. The two drinkers were getting into their Vauxhall. As the passenger yanked open his door, it nearly caught Rebus.

The man didn't bother to apologise. He gave Rebus a look like it was Rebus's fault, then got into his seat.

Rebus had seen the man before. He was about five-ten, broad in the chest, wearing jeans and black t-shirt and a denim jacket. He had a face shiny with drink, sweat on his forehead and in his wavy brown hair. But it wasn't until Rebus was back in his own car and halfway home that he put a name to the face.

The man Yates had told him about, shown him a photo of, the ex-UVF man they'd lost in Glasgow. Alan Fowler. Drinking in the Gar-B like he owned the place.

Maybe he did at that.

Rebus retraced his route, cruising some of the narrow streets, checking parked cars. But he'd lost the Vauxhall. And Ken Smylie's car was no longer outside the Dell.

# 18

Monday morning at St Leonard's, Chief Inspector Lauderdale was having to explain a joke he'd just made.

'See, the squid's so meek, Hans can't bring himself to thump it either.' He caught sight of Rebus walking into the Murder Room. 'The prodigal returns! Tell us, what's it like working with the glamour boys?'

'It's all right,' said Rebus. 'I've already had one return flight out of them.'

Lauderdale clearly had not been expecting this...

'So it's true then,' he said, recovering well, 'they're all high flyers over at SCS.' He captured a few laughs for his trouble. Rebus didn't mind being the butt. He knew the way it was. In a murder inquiry, you worked as a team. Lauderdale, as team manager, had the job of boosting morale, keeping things lively. Rebus wasn't part of the team, not exactly, so he was open to the occasional low tackle with studs showing.

He went to his desk, which more than ever resembled a rubbish tip, and tried to see if any messages had been left for him. He had spent the rest of his weekend, when not avoiding Patience, trying to track down Abernethy or anyone else in Special Branch who'd talk to him. Rebus had left message after message, so far without success.

DI Flower, teeth showing, advanced on Rebus's desk.

'We've got a confession,' he said, 'to the stabbing in St Stephen Street. Want to talk to the man?'

Rebus was wary. 'Who is it?'

'Unstable from Dunstable. He's off his trolley this time, keeps asking for a curry and talking about cars. I told him he'd have to settle for a bridie and his bus fare.'

'You're all heart, Flower.' Rebus saw that Siobhan Clarke had finished getting ready. 'Excuse me.'

'Ready, sir?' Clarke asked.

'Plenty ready. Let's go before Lauderdale or Flower can think of another gag at my expense. Not that *their* jokes ever cost me more than small change.'

They took Clarke's cherry-red Renault 5, following bus after bus west through the slow streets until they could take a faster route by way of The Grange, passing the turn-off to Arch Gowrie's residence.

'And you said The Grange didn't lead anywhere,' Clarke said, powering through the gears. True enough, it was the quickest route between St Leonard's and Morningside. It was just that as a policeman, Rebus had never had much cause to heed Morningside, that genteel backwater where old ladies in white face powder, like something out of a Restoration play, sat in tea shops and pondered aloud their next choice from the cake-stand.

Morningside wasn't exclusive the way Grange was. There were students in Morningside, living at the top of roadside tenements, and people on the dole, in rented flats housing too many bodies, keeping the rent down. But when you thought of Morningside you thought of old ladies and that peculiar pronunciation they had, like they'd all under-studied Maggie Smith in *The Prime of Miss Jean Brodie*. The Glaswegians joked about it. They said Morningside people thought sex was what the coal came in. Rebus doubted there were coal fires in Morningside any longer, though there would certainly be some wood-burning stoves, brought in by the young professionals who probably out-numbered the old ladies these days, though they weren't nearly so conspicuous.

It was to serve these young professionals, as well as to

cater for local businesses, that a thriving little computer shop had opened near the corner of Comiston Road and Morningside Drive.

'Can I help you?' the male assistant asked, not looking up from his keyboard.

'Is Millie around?' Rebus asked.

'Through the arch.'

'Thanks.'

There was a single step up to the arch, through which was another part of the shop, specialising in contract work and business packages. Rebus almost didn't recognise Millie, though there was no one else there. She was seated at a terminal, thinking about something, tapping her finger against her lips. It took her a second to place Rebus. She hit a key, the screen went blank, and she rose from her seat.

She was dressed in an immaculate combination of brilliant white skirt and bright yellow blouse, with a single string of crystals around her neck.

'I just can't shake you lot off, can I?'

She did not sound unhappy. Indeed, she seemed almost *too* pleased to see them, her smile immense. 'Can I fix you some coffee?'

'Not for me, thanks.'

Millie looked to Siobhan Clarke, who shook her head. 'Mind if I make some for myself?' She went to the arch. 'Steve? Cuppa?'

'Wouldn't say no.'

She came back. 'No, but he might say please, just once.' There was a cubby-hole at the back of the shop, leading to a toilet cubicle. In the cubbyhole sat a percolator, a packet of ground coffee, and several grim-looking mugs. Millie got to work. While she was occupied, Rebus asked his first question.

'Billy's mum tells us you were good enough to pack up all his stuff.'

176

'It's still sitting in his room, three bin liners. Not a lot to show for a life, is it?'

'What about his motorbike?'

She smiled. 'That thing. You could hardly call it a bike. A friend of his asked if he could have it. Billy's mum said she didn't mind.'

'You liked Billy?'

'I liked him a lot. He was genuine. You never got bullshit with Billy. If he didn't like you, he'd tell you to your face. I hear his dad's some kind of villain.'

'They didn't know one another.'

She slapped the coffee-maker. 'This thing takes ages. Is that what you want to ask me about, Billy's dad?'

'Just a few general questions. Before he died, did Billy seem worried about anything?'

'I've been asked already, more than once.' She looked at Clarke. 'You first, and then that big bastard with the voice like something caught in a mousetrap.' Rebus smiled: it was a fair description of Ken Smylie. 'Billy was just the same as ever, that's all I can say.'

'Did he get along okay with Mr Murdock?'

'What sort of question is that? Christ, you're scraping the barrel if you think Murdock would've done anything to Billy.'

'You know what it's like in mixed flats though, where there's a couple plus one, jealousy can be a problem.'

An electric buzzer announced the arrival of a customer. They could hear Steve talking to someone.

'We've got to ask, Millie,' Clarke said soothingly.

'No you don't. It's just that you *like* asking!'

So much for the good mood. Even Steve and the customer seemed to be listening. The coffee machine started dolloping boiled water into the filter.

'Look,' said Rebus, 'let's calm down, eh? If you like, we can come back. We could come to the flat –'

'It never ends, does it? What is this? Trying to get a

confession out of me?' She clasped her hands together. 'Yes, I killed him. It was me.'

She held her hands out, wrists prominent.

'I've forgotten my cuffs,' Rebus said, smiling. Millie looked to Siobhan Clarke, who shrugged.

'Great, I can't even get myself arrested.' She sloshed coffee into a mug. 'And I thought it was the easiest thing in the world.'

'Are we really so bad, Millie?'

She smiled, looked down at her mug. 'I suppose not, sorry about that.'

'You're under a lot of strain,' said Siobhan Clarke, 'we appreciate that. Maybe if we sit down, eh?'

So they sat at Millie's desk, like customers and assistant. Clarke, who liked computers, had actually picked up a couple of brochures.

'That's got a twenty-five megahertz microprocessor,' Millie said, pointing to one of the brochures.

'What size memory?'

'Four meg RAM, I think, but you can select a hard disk up to one-sixty.'

'Does this one have a 486 chip?'

Good girl, thought Rebus. Clarke was calming Millie down, taking her mind off both Billy Cunningham and her recent outburst. Steve brought the customer through to show him a certain screen. He gave the three of them a look full of curiosity.

'Sorry, Steve,' said Millie, 'forgot your coffee.' Her smile would not have passed a polygraph.

Rebus waited till Steve and the customer had retreated. 'Did Billy ever bring friends back to the flat?'

'I've given you a list.'

Rebus nodded. 'Nobody else you've thought of since?'

'No.'

'Can I try you with a couple of names? Davey Soutar and Jamesie MacMurray.'

178

'Last names don't mean much in our flat. Davey and Jamesie ... I don't think so.'

Rebus willed her to look at him. She did so, then looked away again quickly. You're lying, he thought.

They left the shop ten minutes later. Clarke looked up and down the pavement. 'Want to go see Murdock now?'

'I don't think so. What do you suppose it was she didn't want us to see?'

'Sorry?'

'You look up, see the police coming towards you, why do you blank your computer screen pronto and then come flying off your seat all bounce and flounce?'

'You think there was something on the computer she didn't want us to see?'

'I thought I just said that,' said Rebus. He got into the Renault's passenger seat and waited for Clarke. 'Jamesie MacMurray knows about The Shield. They killed Billy.'

'So why aren't we pulling him in?'

'We've nothing on him, nothing that would stick. That's not the way to work it.'

She looked at him. 'Too mundane?'

He shook his head. 'Like a golf course, too full of holes. We need to get him scared.'

She thought about this. 'Why did they kill Billy?'

'I think he was about to talk, maybe he'd threatened to come to us.'

'Could he be that stupid?'

'Maybe he had insurance, something he thought would save his skin.'

Siobhan Clarke looked at him. 'It didn't work,' she said.

Back at St Leonard's, there was a message for him to call Kilpatrick.

'Some magazine,' Kilpatrick said, 'is about to run with a story about Calumn Smylie's murder, specifically that he was working undercover at the time.'

'How did they get hold of that?'

'Maybe someone talked, maybe they just burrowed deep enough. Whatever, a certain local reporter has made no friends for herself.'

'Not Mairie Henderson?'

'That's the name. You know her, don't you?'

'Not particularly,' Rebus lied. He knew Kilpatrick was fishing. If someone in the notoriously tight-lipped SCS was blabbing, who better to point the finger at than the new boy?

He phoned the news desk while Siobhan fetched them coffee. 'Mairie Henderson, please. What? Since when? Right, thanks.' He put the phone down. 'She's resigned,' he said, not quite believing it. 'Since last week. She's gone freelance apparently.'

'Good for her,' said Siobhan, handing over a cup. But Rebus wasn't so sure. He called Mairie's home number, but got her answering machine. Its message was succinct:

'I'm busy with an assignment, so I can't promise a quick reply unless you're offering work. If you *are* offering work, leave your number. You can see how dedicated I am. Here comes the beep.'

Rebus waited for it. 'Mairie, it's John Rebus. Here are three numbers you can get me on.' He gave her St Leonard's, Fettes, and Patience's flat, not feeling entirely confident about this last, wondering if any message from a woman would reach him with Patience on the intercept.

Then he made an internal call to the station's liaison officer.

'Have you seen Mairie Henderson around?'

'Not for a wee while. The paper seems to have switched her for someone else, a right dozy wee nyaff.'

'Thanks.'

Rebus thought about the last time he'd seen her, in the corridor after Lauderdale's conference. She hadn't mentioned any story, or any plan of going freelance. He made one more call, external this time. It was to DCI Kilpatrick.

'What is it, John?'

'That magazine, sir, the one doing the story about Calumn Smylie, what's it called?'

'It's some London rag ...' There were sounds of papers being shuffled. 'Yes, here it is. *Snoop.*'

'*Snoop?*' Rebus looked to Siobhan Clarke, who nodded, signalling she'd heard of it. 'Right, thank you, sir.' He put the receiver down before Kilpatrick could ask any questions.

'Want me to phone them and ask?'

Rebus nodded. He saw Brian Holmes come into the room. 'Just the man,' he said. Holmes saw them and wiped imaginary sweat from his brow.

'So,' said Rebus, 'what did you get from the builders?'

'Everything but an estimate for repointing my house.' He took out his notebook. 'Where do you want me to start?'

# 19

Davey Soutar had agreed to meet Rebus in the community hall.

On his way to the Gar-B, Rebus tried not to think about Soutar. He thought instead about building firms. All Brian Holmes had been able to tell him was that the two firms were no cowboys, and weren't admitting to use of casual, untaxed labour. Siobhan Clarke's call to the office of *Snoop* magazine had been more productive. Mairie Henderson's piece, which they intended publishing in their next issue, had not been commissioned specially. It was part of a larger story she was working on for an American magazine. Why, Rebus wondered, would an American magazine be interested in the death of an Edinburgh copper? He thought he had a pretty good idea.

He drove into the Gar-B car park, bumped his car up onto the grass, and headed slowly past the garages towards the community hall. The theatre group hadn't bothered with the car park either. Maybe someone had had a go at their van. It was now parked close by the hall's front doors. Rebus parked next to it.

'It's the filth,' someone said. There were half a dozen teenagers on the roof of the building, staring down at him. And more of them sitting and standing around the doors. Davey Soutar had not come alone.

They let Rebus past. It was like walking through hate. Inside the hall, there was an argument going on.

'I never touched it!'

'It was there a minute ago.'

'You calling me a liar, pal?'

Three men, who'd been constructing a set on the stage, had stopped to watch. Davey Soutar was talking with another man. They were standing close, faces inches apart. Clenched fists and puffed-out chests.

'Is there a problem?' Rebus said.

Peter Cave, who'd been sitting with head in hands, now stood up.

'No problem,' he said lightly.

The third man thought there was. 'The wee bastard,' he said, meaning Davey Soutar, 'just lifted a packet of fags.'

Soutar looked ready to hit something. It was interesting that he didn't hit his accuser. Rebus didn't know what he'd been expecting from the theatre company. He certainly hadn't been expecting this. The accuser was tall and wiry with long greasy hair and several days' growth of beard. He didn't look in the least scared of Soutar, whose reputation must surely have preceded him. Nor did the workers on the stage look unwilling to enter any fray. He reached into his pocket and brought out a fresh pack of twenty, which he handed to Davey Soutar.

'Here,' he said, 'take these, and give the gentleman back his ciggies.'

Soutar turned on him like a zoo leopard, not happy with its cage. 'I don't need your . . .' The roar faded. He looked at the faces around him. Then he laughed, a hysterical giggling laugh. He slapped his bare chest and shook his head, then took the cigarettes from Rebus and tossed another pack onto the stage.

Rebus turned to the accuser. 'What's your name?'

'Jim Hay.' The accent was west coast.

'Well, Jim, why don't you take those cigarettes outside, have a ten-minute break?'

Jim Hay looked ready to protest, but then thought better of it. He gestured to his crew and they followed him outside.

Rebus could hear them getting into the van. He turned his attention to Davey Soutar and Peter Cave.

'I'm surprised you came,' said Soutar, lighting up.

'I'm full of surprises, me.'

'Only, last time I saw you here, you were heading for the hills. You owe Peter an apology, by the way.' Soutar had changed completely. He looked like he was enjoying himself, like he hadn't lost his temper in weeks.

'I don't think that's strictly necessary,' Peter Cave said into the silence.

'Apology accepted,' said Rebus. He dragged over a chair and sat down. Soutar decided this was a good idea. He found a chair for himself and sat with a hard man's slump, legs wide apart, hands stuffed into the tight pockets of his denims, cigarette hanging from his lips. Rebus wanted a cigarette, but he wasn't going to ask for one.

'So what's the problem, Inspector?'

Soutar had agreed to a meeting here, but hadn't mentioned Peter Cave would be present. Maybe it was coincidence. Whatever, Rebus didn't mind an audience. Cave looked tired, pale. There was no question who was in charge, who had power over whom.

'I just have a few things to ask, there's no question of charges or anything criminal, all right?' Soutar obliged with a grunt, examining the laces of his basketball boots. He was shirtless again, still wearing the worn denim jacket. It was filthy, and had been decorated with pen drawings and dark-inked words, names mostly. Grease and dirt were erasing most of the messages and symbols, a few of which had already been covered with fresh hieroglyphs in thicker, darker ink. Soutar slid a hand from his pocket and ran it down his chest, rubbing the few fair curling hairs over his breast bone. He was giving Rebus a friendly look, his lips slightly parted. Rebus wanted to smash him in the face.

'I can walk any time I want?' he said to Rebus.

'Any time.'

The chair grated against the floor as Soutar pushed it back and stood up. Then he laughed and sat down again, wriggling to get comfortable, making sure his crotch was visible. 'Ask me a question then,' he said.

'You know the Orange Loyal Brigade?'

'Sure. That was easy, try another.'

But Rebus had turned to Cave. 'Have you heard of it, too?'

'I can't say I –'

'Hey! It's me the questions are for!'

'In a second, Mr Soutar.' Davey Soutar liked that: *Mr* Soutar. Only the dole office and the census taker had ever called him Mr. 'The Orange Loyal Brigade, Mr Cave, is an extreme hardline Protestant group, a small force but an organised one, based in east central Scotland.'

Soutar confirmed this with a nod.

'The Brigade were kicked out of the Orange Lodge for being too extreme. This may give you some measure of them. Do you know what they're committed to, Mr Cave? Maybe Mr Soutar can answer.'

*Mr* again! Soutar chuckled. 'Hating the Papes,' he said.

'Mr Soutar's right.' Rebus's eyes hadn't moved from Cave's since he'd first turned to him. 'They hate Catholics.'

'Papes,' said Soutar. 'Left-footers, Tigs, bogmen, Paddies.'

'And a few more names beside,' added Rebus. He left a measured pause. 'You're a Roman Catholic, aren't you?' As if he'd forgotten. Cave merely nodded, while Soutar slid his eyes sideways to look at him. Suddenly Rebus turned to Soutar. 'Who's head of the Brigade, Davey?'

'Er ... Ian Paisley!' He laughed, and got a smile from Rebus.

'No, but really.'

'I haven't a clue.'

'No? You don't know Gavin MacMurray?'

'MacMurray? Is he the one with the garage in Currie?'

'That's him. He's the Supreme Commander of the Orange Loyal Brigade.'

'I'll take your word for it.'

'And his son's the Provost-Marshall. Lad called Jamesie, be a year or two younger than you.'

'Oh aye?'

Rebus shook his head. 'Short term memory loss, that's what a bad diet does.'

'Eh?'

'All the chips and crisps, the booze you put away, not exactly brain food, is it? I know what it's like on estates like the Gar-B, you eat rubbish and you inject yourselves with anything you can get your paws on. Your body'll wither and die, probably before your brain does.'

The conversation had clearly taken an unexpected turn. 'What are you talking about?' Soutar yelled. 'I don't do drugs! I'm as fit as fuck, pal!'

Rebus looked at Soutar's exposed chest. 'Whatever you say, Davey.'

Soutar sprang to his feet, the chair tumbling behind him. He threw off his jacket and stood there, chest inflated, pulling both arms up and in to show the swell of muscle.

'You could punch me in the guts and I wouldn't flinch.'

Rebus could believe it, too. The stomach was flat except for ripples of musculature, looking so solid they might have been sculpted from marble. Soutar relaxed his arms, held them in front of him.

'Look, no tracks. Drugs are for mugs.'

Rebus held up a pacifying hand. 'You've proved your point, Davey.'

Soutar stared at him for a moment longer, then laughed and picked his jacket up off the floor.

'Interesting tattoos, by the way.'

They were the usual homemade jobs in blue ink, with one larger professional one on the right upper arm. It showed the Red Hand of Ulster, with the words No Surrender beneath. Below it the self-inflicted tattoos were just letters and messages: UVF, UDA, FTP, and SaS.

Rebus waited till Soutar had put on his jacket. 'You know Jamesie MacMurray,' he stated.

'Do I?'

'You bumped into him last Saturday when the Brigade was marching on Princes Street. You were there for the march, but you had to leave. However, you said hello to your old friend first. You knew Mr Cave was a Catholic right from the start, didn't you? I mean, he didn't hide the fact?'

Soutar was looking confused. The questions were all over the place, it was hard to keep up.

'Pete was straight with us,' he admitted. He was staying on his feet.

'And that didn't bother you? I mean, you came to his club, bringing your gang with you. And the Catholic gang came along too. What did Jamesie say about that?'

'It's nothing to do with him.'

'You could see it was a good thing though, eh? Meeting the Catholic gang, divvying up the ground between you. It's the way it works in Ulster, that's what you've heard. Who told you? Jamesie? His dad?'

'His *dad*?'

'Or was it The Shield?'

'I never even –' Davey Soutar stopped. He was breathing hard as he pointed at Rebus. 'You're in shite up past the point of breathing.'

'Then I must be standing on your shoulders. Come on, Davey.'

'It's *Mr* Soutar.'

'Mr Soutar then.' Rebus had his hands open, palms up. He was sitting back in his chair, rocking it on its back legs. 'Come on, sit down. It's no big deal. Everybody knows about The Shield, knows you're part of it. Everybody except Mr Cave here.' He turned to Peter Cave. 'Let's just say that

The Shield is even more extreme than the Orange Loyal Brigade. The Shield collects money, mostly by violence and extortion, and it sends arms to Northern Ireland.' Soutar was shaking his head.

'You're nothing, you've *got* nothing.'

'But you've got something, Davey. You've got your hate and your anger.' He turned to Cave again. 'See, Mr Cave? You've got to be asking, how come Davey puts up with a committed worker for the Church of Rome, or the Whore of Rome as Davey himself might put it? A question that has to be answered.'

When he looked round, Soutar was on the stage. He pushed over the sets, kicking them, stomping them, then jumped down again and made for the doors. His face was orange with anger.

'Was Billy a friend too, Davey?' That stopped him dead. 'Billy Cunningham, I mean.'

Soutar was on the move.

'Davey! You've forgotten your fags!' But Davey Soutar was out the door and screaming things which were unintelligible. Rebus lit a cigarette for himself.

'That laddie's got too much testosterone for his own good,' he said to Cave.

'Look who's talking.'

Rebus shrugged. 'Just an act, Mr Cave. Method acting, you might say.' He blew out a plume of smoke. Cave was staring at his hands, which were clasped in his lap. 'You need to know what you've gotten into.'

Cave looked up. 'You think I condone sectarian hate?'

'No, my theory's much simpler. I think you get off on violence and young men.'

'You're sick.'

'Then maybe all you are, Mr Cave, is misguided. Get out while you can. A policeman's largesse never lasts.' He walked over to Cave and bent down, speaking quietly. 'They've swallowed you, you're in the pit of the Gar-B's stomach. You can still crawl out, but maybe there's not as much time as you think.' Rebus patted Cave's cheek. It was cold and soft, like chicken from the fridge.

'Look at yourself some time, Rebus. You might find you'd make a bloody good terrorist yourself.'

'Thing is, I'd never be tempted. What about you?'

Cave stood up and walked past him towards the doors. Then he walked through them and kept going. Rebus blew smoke from his nose, then sat on the edge of the stage, finishing the cigarette. Maybe he'd tripped Soutar's fuse too early. If it had come out right, he'd have learned something more about The Shield. At the moment, it was all cables and coiled springs, junctions from which spread different coloured wires. Hard to defuse when you didn't know which wire to attack first.

The doors were opening again, and he looked up. Davey Soutar was standing there. Behind him there were others, more than a dozen of them. Soutar was breathing hard. Rebus glanced at his watch and hoped it was right. There was an Emergency Exit at the other end of the hall, but where did Rebus go from there? Instead, he climbed onto the stage and watched them advance. Soutar wasn't saying anything. The whole procession took place in silence, except for breathing and the shuffle of feet on the floor. They were at the front of the stage now. Rebus picked up a length of wood, part of the broken set. Soutar, his eyes on the wood, began to climb onto the stage.

He stopped when he heard the sirens. He froze for a moment, staring up at Rebus. The policeman was smiling.

'Think I'd come here without my cavalry, Davey?' The sirens were drawing closer. 'Your call, Davey,' Rebus said, managing to sound relaxed. 'If you want another riot, here's your chance.'

But all Davey Soutar did was ease himself back off the stage. He stood there, eyes wide and unblinking, as if sheer will of thought might cause Rebus to implode. A final snarl, and he turned and walked away. They followed him, all of them. Some looked back at Rebus. He tried not to look too relieved, lit another cigarette instead. Soutar was crazy, a force gone mad, but he was strong too. Rebus was just beginning to realise how very strong he was.

He went home exhausted that evening, 'home' by now being a very loose term for Patience's flat.

He was still shaking a bit. When Soutar had left the hall that first time, he'd taken it all out on Rebus's car. There were fresh dents, a smashed headlamp, a chipped windscreen. The actors in the van looked like they'd witnessed a frenzy. Then Rebus had told them about their sets.

He'd thought about the theatre group on his way, under police escort, out of the Gar-B. They'd been parked outside the Dell the night he'd seen the Ulsterman there. He still had their flyer, the one that had doubled as a paper plane.

At St Leonard's, he found them in the Fringe programme, Active Resistance Theatre; active as opposed to passive, Rebus supposed. He placed a couple of calls to Glasgow. Someone would get back to him. The rest of the day was a blur.

As he was locking what was left of his car, he sensed a shape behind him.

'Damn you, weasel-face!'

But he turned to see Caroline Rattray.

'Weasel-face?'

'I thought you were someone else.'

She put her arms round him. 'Well I'm not, I'm me. Remember me? I'm the one who's being trying to phone you for God knows how long. I know you got my messages, because someone in your office told me.'

That would be Ormiston. Or Flower. Or anyone else with a grudge.

'Christ, Caro.' He pulled away from her. 'You must be crazy.'

'For coming here?' She looked around. 'This is where she lives?'

She sounded completely unconcerned. Rebus didn't need this. His head felt like it was splitting open above the eyes. He needed to bathe and to stop thinking, and it would take a great effort to stop him thinking about this case.

'You're tired,' she said. Rebus wasn't listening. He was too busy looking at Patience's parked car, at her gateway, then along the street, willing her not to appear. 'Well, I'm tired too, John.' Her voice was rising. 'But there's always room in the day for a little consideration!'

'Keep your voice down,' he hissed.

'Don't you dare tell me what to do!'

'Christ, Caro ...' He squeezed shut his eyes and she relented for a moment. It was long enough to appraise his physical and psychic state.

'You're exhausted,' she concluded. She smiled and touched his face. 'I'm sorry, John. I just thought you'd been avoiding me.'

'Who'd want to do that, Caro?' Though he was starting to wonder.

'What about a drink?' she said.

'Not tonight.'

'All right,' she said, pouting. A moment ago, she had been all tempest and cannon fire, and now she was a surface as calm as any doldrums could produce. 'Tomorrow?'

'Fine.'

'Eight o'clock then, in the Caly bar.' The Caly being the Caledonian Hotel. Rebus nodded assent.

'Great,' he said.

'See you then.' She leaned into him again, kissing his lips. He drew away as quickly as he could, remembering her perfume. One more waft of that, and Patience would go nuclear.

'See you, Caro.' He watched her get into her car, then walked quickly down the steps to the flat.

The first thing he did was run a bath. He looked at himself in the mirror and got a shock. He was looking at his father. In later years, his father had grown a short grey beard. There was grey in Rebus's stubble too.

'I look like an old man.'

There was a knock at the bathroom door. 'Have you eaten?' Patience called.

'Not yet. Have you?'

'No, shall I stick something in the microwave?'

'Sure, great.' He added foam-bath to the water.

'Pizza?'

'Whatever.' She didn't sound too bad. That was the thing about being a doctor, you saw so much pain every day, it was easy to shrug off the more minor ailments like arguments at home and suspected infidelities. Rebus stripped off his clothes and dumped them in the laundry basket. Patience knocked again.

'By the way, what are you doing tomorrow?'

'You mean tomorrow night?' he called back.

'Yes.'

'Nothing I know of. I might be working...'

'You better not be. I've invited the Bremners to dinner.'

'Oh, good,' said Rebus, putting his foot in the water without checking the temperature. The water was scalding. He lifted the foot out again and screamed silently at the mirror.

# 20

They had breakfast together, talking around things, their conversation that of acquaintances rather then lovers. Neither spoke his or her thoughts. We Scots, Rebus thought, we're not very good at going public. We store up our true feelings like fuel for long winter nights of whisky and recrimination. So little of us ever reaches the surface, it's a wonder we exist at all.

'Another cup?'

'Please, Patience.'

'You'll be here tonight,' she said. 'You won't be working.' It was neither question nor order, not explicitly.

So he tried phoning Caro from Fettes, but now she was the one having messages left for her: one on her answering machine at home, one with a colleague at her office. He couldn't just say, 'I'm not coming', not even to a piece of recording tape. So he'd just asked her to get in touch. Caro Rattray, elegant, apparently available, and mad about him. There *was* something of the mad in her, something vertiginous. You spent time with her and you were standing on a cliff edge. And where was Caro? She was standing right behind you.

When his phone rang, he leapt for it.

'Inspector Rebus?' The voice was male, familiar.

'Speaking.'

'It's Lachlan Murdock.' Lachlan: no wonder he used his last name.

'What can I do for you, Mr Murdock?'

'You saw Millie recently, didn't you?'

'Yes, why?'

'She's gone.'

'Gone where?'

'I don't know. What the hell did you say to her?'

'Are you at your flat?'

'Yes.'

'I'm coming over.'

He went alone, knowing he should take some back-up, but loath to approach anyone. Out of the four – Ormiston, Blackwood, 'Bloody' Claverhouse, Smylie – Smylie would still be his choice, but Smylie was as predictable as the Edinburgh weather, even now turning overcast. The pavements were still Festival busy, but not for much longer, and as recompense September would be quiet. It was the city's secret month, a retreat from public into private.

As if to reassure him, the cloud swept away again and the sun appeared. He wound down his window, until the bus fumes made him roll it back up again. The back of the bus advertised the local newspaper, which led him to thoughts of Mairie Henderson. He needed to find her, and it wasn't often a policeman thought that about a reporter.

He parked the car as close to Murdock's tenement as he could find a space, pressed the intercom button beside the main door, and got the answering buzz which unlocked the door.

Your feet made the same sound on every tenement stairwell, like sandpaper on a church floor. Murdock had opened the door to his flat. Rebus walked in.

Lachlan Murdock did not look in good fettle. His hair was sprouting in clumps from his head, and he pulled on his beard like it was a fake he'd glued on too well. They were in the living room. Rebus sat down in front of the TV. It was where Millie had been sitting the first time he'd visited. The ashtray was still there, but the sleeping bag had gone. And so had Millie.

'I haven't seen her since yesterday.' Murdock was standing, and showed no sign of sitting down. He walked to the window, looked out, came back to the fireplace. His eyes were everywhere that wasn't Rebus.

'Morning or evening?'

'Morning. I got back last night and she'd packed and left.'

'Packed?'

'Not everything, just a holdall. I thought maybe she'd gone to see a pal, she does that sometimes.'

'Not this time?'

Murdock shook his head. 'I phoned Steve at her work this morning, and he said the police had been to see her yesterday, a young woman and an older man. I thought of you. Steve said she was in a terrible state afterwards, she'd to come home early. What did you say to her?'

'Just a few questions about Billy.'

'Billy.' The dismissive shake of the head told Rebus something.

'She got on better with Billy than you did, Mr Murdock?'

'I didn't dislike the guy.'

'Was there anything between the two of them?'

But Murdock wasn't about to answer that. He paced the room again, flapping his arms as though attempting flight. 'She hasn't been the same since he died.'

'It was upsetting for her.'

'Yes, it was. But to run off ...'

'Can I see her room?'

'What?'

Rebus smiled. 'It's what we usually do when someone goes missing.'

Murdock shook his head again. 'She wouldn't want that. What if she comes back, and sees someone's been through her stuff? No, I can't let you do that.' Murdock looked ready for physical resistance if necessary.

'I can't force you,' Rebus said calmly. 'Tell me a bit more about Billy.'

This quietened Murdock. 'Like what?'

'Did he like computers?'

'Billy? He liked video games, so long as they were violent. I don't know, I suppose he was interested in computers.'

'He could work one?'

'Just about. What are you getting at?'

'Just interested. Three people sharing a flat, two of them work with computers, the third doesn't.'

Murdock nodded. 'You're wondering what we had in common. Look around the city, Inspector, you'll see flats full of people who're only there because they need a room or the rent money. In an ideal world, I wouldn't have needed someone in the spare room at all.'

Rebus nodded. 'So what should we do about Miss Docherty?'

'What?'

'You called me, I came, where do we go from here?' Murdock shrugged. 'Normally we'd wait another day or so before listing her missing.' He paused. 'Unless there's reason to suspect foul play.'

Murdock seemed lost in thought, then recovered. 'Let's wait another day then.' He started nodding. 'Maybe I'm overreacting. I just ... when Steve told me...'

'I'm sure it wasn't anything I said to her,' Rebus lied, getting to his feet. 'Can I have another look at Billy's room while I'm here?'

'It's been gutted.'

'Just to refresh my memory.' Murdock said nothing. 'Thanks,' said Rebus.

The small room had indeed been gutted, the bed stripped of duvet and sheet and pillowcase, though the pillow still lay there. It was stained brown, leaking feathers. The bare mattress was pale blue with similar brown patches. There seemed a little more space in the room, but not much. Still,

Rebus doubted Murdock would have any trouble finding a new tenant, not with the student season approaching.

He opened the wardrobe to a clanging of empty wire hangers. There was a fresh sheet of newspaper on the floor. He closed the wardrobe door. Between the corner of the bed and the wardrobe there was a clear patch of carpet. It lay hard up against the skirting-board beneath the still unwashed window. Rebus crouched down and tugged at the carpet's edge. It wasn't tacked, and lifted an inch or so. He ran his fingers underneath it, finding nothing. Still crouched, he lifted the mattress, but saw only bedsprings and the carpet beneath, thick balls of dust and hair marking the furthest reach of the hoover.

He stood up, glancing at the bare walls. There were small rips in the wallpaper where Blu-Tak had been removed. He looked more closely at one small pattern of these. The wallpaper had come away in two longer strips. Wasn't this where the pennant had hung? Yes, you could see the hole made by the drawing-pin. The pennant had hung from a maroon cord which had been pinned to the wall. Meaning the pennant had been hiding these marks. They didn't look so old. The lining paper beneath was clean and fresh, as though the Sellotape had been peeled off recently.

Rebus put his fingers to the two stripes. They were about three inches apart and three inches long. Whatever had been taped there, it had been square and thin. Rebus knew exactly what would fit that description.

Out in the hall, Murdock was waiting to leave.

'Sorry to keep you waiting, sir,' Rebus said.

The Carlton sounded like another old ladies' tea-room, but in fact was a transport cafe with famed large helpings. When Mairie Henderson finally got back to Rebus, he suggested taking her to lunch there. It was on the shore at Newhaven, facing the Firth of Forth just about where that broad inlet became inseparable from the North Sea.

Lorries bypassing Edinburgh or heading to Leith from the north would usually pause for a break outside the Carlton. You saw them in a line by the sea wall, between Starbank Road and Pier Place. The drivers thought the Carlton well worth a detour, even if other road users and the police didn't always appreciate their sentiments.

Inside, the Carlton was a clean well-lit place and as hot as a truck engine. For air conditioning, they kept the front door wedged open. You never ate alone, which was why Rebus phoned in advance and booked a table for two.

'The one between the counter and the toilets,' he specified.

'Did I hear you right? *Book* a table?'

'You heard me.'

'Nobody's *booked* a table all the years we've been open.' The chef held the phone away from his face. 'Hiy, Maggie, there's somebody here wants tae *book* a table.'

'Cut the shite, Sammy, it's John Rebus speaking.'

'Special occasion is it, Mr Rebus? Anniversary? I'll bake yis a cake.'

'Twelve o'clock,' said Rebus, 'and make sure it's the table I asked for, okay?'

'Yes, sir.'

So when Rebus walked into the Carlton, and Sammy saw him, Sammy whipped a dishtowel off the stove and came sauntering between the tables, the towel over his arm.

'Your table is ready, sir, if you'll follow me.'

The drivers were grinning, a few of them offering encouragement. Maggie stood there holding a pillar of empty white plates, and attempted a curtsy as Rebus went past. The small Formica-topped table was laid for two, with a bit of card folded in half and the word RESERVED written in blue biro. There was a clean sauce bottle, into the neck of which someone had pushed a plastic carnation.

He saw Mairie look through the cafe window, then come in through the door. The drivers looked up.

'Room here, sweetheart.'

'Hiy, hen, sit on my lap, no' his.'

They grinned through the smoke, cigarettes never leaving their mouths. One of them ate camel-style, lower jaw moving in sideways rotation while his upper jaw chewed down. He reminded Rebus so strongly of Ormiston, he had to look away. Instead he looked at Mairie. Why not, everyone else was. They were staring without shame at her bum as she moved between the tables. True to form, Mairie had worn her shortest skirt. At least, Rebus hoped it was her shortest. And it was tight, one of those black Lycra numbers. She wore it with a baggy white t-shirt and thick black tights whose vertical seams showed pinpricks of white leg flesh. She'd pushed her sunglasses onto the top of her head, and swung her shoulder-bag onto the floor as she took her seat.

'I see we're in the members' enclosure.'

'It took money but I thought it was worth it.'

Rebus studied her while she studied the wall-board which constituted the Carlton's menu.

'You look good,' he lied. Actually, she looked exhausted.

'Thanks. I wish I could say the same.'

Rebus winced. 'I looked as good as you at your age.'

'Even in a mini-skirt?' She leaned down to lift a pack of cigarettes from her bag, giving Rebus a view of her lace-edged bra down the front of her t-shirt. When she came up again he was frowning.

'Okay, I won't smoke.'

'It stunts your growth. And speaking of health warnings, what about that story of yours?'

But Maggie came over, so they went through the intricacies of ordering. 'We're out of Moët Shandy,' Maggie said.

'What was that about?' Mairie asked after Maggie had gone.

'Nothing,' he said. 'You were about to tell me...?'

'Was I?' She smiled. 'How much do you know?'

199

'I know you've been working on a story, a chunk of which you've sold to *Snoop* but the bulk of which is destined for some US magazine.'

'Well, you know quite a lot then.'

'You took the story to your own paper first?'

She sighed. 'Of course I did, but they wouldn't print it. The company lawyers thought it was close to libel.'

'Who were you libelling?'

'Organisations rather than individuals. I had a blow-up with my editor about it, and handed in my resignation. His line was that the lawyers were paid to be over-cautious.'

'I bet their fees aren't over-cautious.' Which reminded him: Caro Rattray. He still had to contact her.

'I was planning on going freelance anyway, just not quite so soon. But at least I'm starting with a strong story. A few months back I got a letter from a New York journalist. His name's Jump Cantona.'

'Sounds like a car.'

'Yes, a four-by-four, that's just what I thought. Anyway, Jump's a well known writer over there, investigations with a capital I. But then of course it's easier in the US.'

'How's that?'

'You can go further before someone starts issuing writs. Plus you've got more freedom of information. Jump needed someone this end, following up a few leads. His name comes first in the main article, but any spin-offs I write, I get sole billing.'

'So what have you found?'

'A can of worms.' Maggie was coming with their food. She heard Mairie's closing words and gave her a cold look as she placed the fry-up in front of her. For Rebus, there was a half-portion of lasagne and a green salad.

'How did Cantona find you?' Rebus asked.

'Someone I met when I was on a journalism course in New York. This guy knew Cantona was looking for someone who could do some digging in Scotland. I was the obvious

200

choice.' She attacked four chips with her fork. Chewing, she reached for the salt, vinegar, and tomato sauce. After momentary consideration, she poured some brown sauce on as well.

'I knew you'd do that,' Rebus said. 'And it still disgusts me.'

'You should see me with mustard and mayonnaise. I hear you got moved to SCS.'

'It's true.'

'Why?'

'If I didn't know better, I'd say they were keeping an eye on me.'

'Only, they were there at Mary King's Close, a murder that looks like an execution. Then next thing you're off to SCS, and I know SCS are investigating gun-running with an Irish slant.' Maggie arrived with two cans of Irn-Bru. Mairie checked hers was cold enough before opening it. 'Are we working on the same story?'

'The police don't have stories, Mairie, we have cases. And it's hard to answer your question without seeing your story.'

She slipped a hand into her shoulder-bag and pulled out several sheets of neatly typed paper. The document had been stapled and folded in half. Rebus could see it was a photocopy.

'Not very long,' he said.

'You can read it while I eat.'

He did. But all it did was put a lot of speculative meat on the bones he already had. Mostly it concentrated on the North American angle, mentioning the IRA fundraising in passing, though the Orange Loyal Brigade was mentioned, as was Sword and Shield.

'No names,' Rebus commented.

'I can give you a few, off the record.'

'Gavin and Jamesie MacMurray?'

'You're stealing my best lines. Do you have anything on them?'

'What do you think we'll find, a garden shed full of grenade launchers?'

'That could be pretty close.'

'Tell me.'

She took a deep breath. 'We can't put anything in print yet, but we think there's an Army connection.'

'You mean stuff from the Falklands and the Gulf? Souvenirs?'

'There's too much of it for it to be souvenirs.'

'What then? The stuff from Russia?'

'Much closer to home. You know stuff walks out of Army bases in Northern Ireland?'

'I've heard of it happening.'

'Same thing happened in the '70s in Scotland, the Tartan Army got stuff from Army bases. We think it's happening again. At least, Jump thinks it is. He's spoken to someone who used to be in American Shield, sending money over here. It's easier to send money here than arms shipments. This guy told Jump the money was buying *British* armaments. See, the IRA has good links with the East and Libya, but the loyalist paramilitaries don't.'

'You're telling me they're buying guns from the Army?' Rebus laughed and shook his head. Mairie managed a small smile.

'There's another thing. I know there's nothing to back this up. Jump knows it too. It's just one man's word, and that man isn't even willing to go public. He's afraid American Shield would get to him. Anyway, who'd believe him: he's being paid to tell Jump this stuff. He could be making it all up. Journalists like a juicy conspiracy, we lap them up like cream.'

'What are you talking about, Mairie?'

'A policeman, a detective, someone high up in The Shield.'

'In America?'

She shook her head. 'At the UK end, no name or anything. Like I say, just a story.'

'Aye, just a story. How did you find out we had a man undercover?'

'That was strange. It was a phone call.'

'Anonymous of course?'

'Of course. But who could have known?'

'Another policeman, obviously.'

Mairie pushed her plate away. 'I can't eat all these chips.'

'They should put up a plaque above the table.'

Rebus needed a drink, and there was a good pub only a short walk away. Mairie went with him, though she complained she didn't have room for a drink. Still, when they got there she found space for a white wine and soda. Rebus had a half-pint and a nip. They sat by the window, with a view out over the Forth. The water was battleship grey, reflecting the sky overhead. Rebus had never seen the Forth look other than forbidding.

'What did you say?' He'd missed it completely.

'I said, I forgot to say.'

'Yes, but the bit after that?'

'A man called Moncur, Clyde Moncur.'

'What about him?'

'Jump has him pegged as one of The Shield's hierarchy in the US. He's also a big-time villain, only it's never been proven in a court of law.'

'And?'

'And he flies into Heathrow tomorrow.'

'To do what?'

'We don't know.'

'So why aren't you down in London waiting for him?'

'Because he's booked on a connecting flight to Edinburgh.'

Rebus narrowed his eyes. 'You weren't going to tell me.'

'No, I wasn't.'

'What changed your mind?'

She gnawed her bottom lip. 'It may be I'll need a friend sometime soon.'

'You're going to confront him?'

'Yes ... I suppose so.'

'Jesus, Mairie.'

'It's what journalists do.'

'Do you know anything about him? I mean *anything*?'

'I know he's supposed to run drugs into Canada, brings illegal immigrants in from the Far East, a real Renaissance man. But on the surface, all he does is own a fish-processing plant in Seattle.' Rebus was shaking his head. 'What's wrong?'

'I don't know,' he said. 'I suppose I just feel ... gutted.'

It took her a moment to get the joke.

# 21

'Caro, thank God.'

Rebus was back in Fettes, at his desk, on the phone, having finally tracked Caroline Rattray to ground.

'You're calling off our drink,' she said coldly.

'I'm sorry, something's cropped up. Work, you know how it is. The hours aren't always social.' The phone went dead in his hand. He replaced the receiver like it was spun sugar. Then, having requested five minutes of his boss's time, he went to Kilpatrick's office. As ever there was no need to knock; Kilpatrick waved him in through the glass door.

'Take a seat, John.'

'I'll stand, sir, thanks all the same.'

'What's on your mind?'

'When you spoke to the FBI, did they mention a man called Clyde Moncur?'

'I don't think any names were mentioned.' Kilpatrick wrote the name on his pad. 'Who is he?'

'He's a Seattle businessman, runs his own fish-processing plant. Possibly also a gangster. He's coming to Edinburgh on holiday.'

'Well, we need the tourist dollars.'

'And he may be high up in The Shield.'

'Oh?' Kilpatrick casually underlined the name. 'What's your source?'

'I'd rather not say.'

'I see.' Kilpatrick underlined the name one last time. 'I don't like secrets, John.'

'Yes, sir.'

'Well, what do you want to do?'

'Put a tail on him.'

'Ormiston and Blackwood are good.'

'I'd prefer someone else.'

Kilpatrick threw down his pen. 'Why?'

'I just would.'

'You can trust me, John.'

'I know that, sir.'

'Then tell me why you don't want Ormiston and Blackwood on the tail.'

'We don't get on. I get the feeling they might muck things up just to make me look bad.' Lying was easy with practice, and Rebus had years of practice at lying to superiors.

'That sounds like paranoia to me.'

'Maybe it is.'

'I've got a *team* here, John. I need to know that they can work as a team.'

'You brought me in, sir. I didn't ask for secondment. Teams always resent the new man, it just hasn't worn off yet.' Then Rebus played his ace. 'You could always move me back to St Leonard's.' Not that he wanted this. He liked the freedom he had, flitting between the two stations, neither Chief Inspector knowing where he was.

'Is that what you want?' Kilpatrick asked.

'It's not down to me, it's what *you* want that matters.'

'Quite right, and I want you in SCS, at least for the time being.'

'So you'll put someone else on the tail?'

'I take it you've got people in mind?'

'Two more from St Leonard's. DS Holmes and DC Clarke. They work well together, they've done this sort of thing before.'

'No, John, let's keep this to SCS.' Which was Kilpatrick's way of reasserting his authority. 'I know two good men over in Glasgow, no possible grudge against you. I'll get them over here.'

'Right, sir.'

'Sound all right to you, Inspector?'

'Whatever you think, sir.'

When Rebus left the office, the two typists were discussing famine and Third World debt.

'Ever thought of going into politics, ladies?'

'Myra's a local councillor,' one of them said, nodding to her partner.

'Any chance of getting my drains cleared?' Rebus asked Myra.

'Join the queue,' Myra said with a laugh.

Back at his desk Rebus phoned Brian Holmes to ask him a favour, then he went to the toilets down the hall. The toilet was one of those design miracles, like Dr Who's time machine. Somehow two urinals, a toilet cubicle, and washhand basin had been squeezed into a space smaller than their total cubic volume.

So Rebus wasn't thrilled when Ken Smylie joined him. Smylie was supposed to be taking time off work, only he insisted on coming in.

'How are you doing, Ken?'

'I'm all right.'

'Good.' Rebus turned from his urinal and headed for the sink.

'You seem to be working hard,' Smylie said.

'Do I?'

'You're never here, I assume you're working.'

'Oh, I'm working.' Rebus shook water from his hands.

'Only I never see any notes.'

'Notes?'

'You never write down your case notes.'

'Is that right?' Rebus dried his hands on the cotton roller-towel. This was his lucky day: a fresh roll had just been fitted. He still had his back to Smylie. 'Well, I like to keep my notes in my head.'

'That's not procedure.'

'Tough.'

He'd just got the word out, and was preparing for another intake of breath, when Smylie's arms gripped him with the force of a construction crane around his chest. He couldn't breathe, and felt himself being lifted off the ground. Smylie pushed his face against the wall next to the roller-towel. His whole weight was sandwiching Rebus against the wall.

'You're on to something, aren't you?' Smylie said in his high whistling voice. 'Tell me who it is.' He released his bear hug just enough so Rebus could speak.

'Get the fuck off me!'

The grip tightened again, Rebus's face pressing harder into the wall. I'll go through it in a minute, he thought. My head'll be sticking out into the corridor like a hunting trophy.

'He was my brother,' Smylie was saying. '*My* brother.'

Rebus's face was full of blood which wanted to be somewhere else. He could feel his eyes bulging out of their sockets, his eardrums straining. My last view, he thought, will be of this damned roller-towel. Then the door swung inwards, and Ormiston was standing there, cigarette gawping. The cigarette dropped to the floor as Ormiston flung his own arms around Smylie's. He couldn't reach all the way round, but enough to dig his thumbs into the soft flesh of the inner elbows.

'Let go, Smylie!'

'Get off me!'

Rebus felt the pressure on him ease, and used his own shoulders to throw Smylie off. There was barely room for all three men, and they danced awkwardly, Ormiston still holding Smylie's arms. Smylie threw him off with ease. He was on Rebus again, but now Rebus was ready. He kneed the big man in the groin. Smylie groaned and slumped to his knees. Ormiston was picking himself up.

'What the hell sparked this?'

Smylie pulled himself to his feet. He looked angry, frustrated. He nearly took the handle off the door as he pulled it open.

Rebus looked in the mirror. His face was that sunburnt cherry colour some fair-skinned people go, but at least his eyes had retreated back into their sockets.

'Wonder what my blood pressure got up to,' he said to himself. Then he thanked Ormiston.

'I was thinking of me, not you,' Ormiston retorted. 'With you two wrestling,' he stooped to pick up his cigarette, 'there wasn't room for me to have a quiet puff.'

The cigarette itself survived the mêlée, but after inspecting it Ormiston decided to flush it anyway and light up a fresh one.

Rebus joined him. 'That may be the first time smoking's saved someone's life.'

'My grandad smoked for sixty years, died in his sleep at eighty. Mind you, he was bedridden for thirty of them. So what was all that about?'

'Filing. Smylie doesn't like my system.'

'Smylie likes to know everything that's going on.'

'He shouldn't even be here. He should be at home, bereaving.'

'But that's what he *is* doing,' argued Ormiston. 'Just because he looks like a big cuddly bear, a gentle giant, don't be fooled.' He took a drag on his cigarette. 'Let me tell you about Smylie.'

And he did.

Rebus was home at six o'clock, much to Patience Aitken's surprise. He had a shower rather than a bath and came into the living room dressed in his best suit and wearing a shirt Patience had given him for Christmas. It wasn't till

209

he'd tried it on that they both discovered it required cuff links, so then he'd had to buy some.

'I can never do these up by myself,' he said now, flapping his cuffs and brandishing the links. Patience smiled and came to help him. Close up, she smelt of perfume.

'Smells wonderful,' he said.

'Do you mean me or the kitchen?'

'Both,' said Rebus. 'Equally.'

'Something to drink?'

'What are you having?'

'Fizzy water till the cooking's done.'

'Same for me.' Though really he was dying for a whisky. He'd lost the shakes, but his ribs still hurt when he inflated his lungs. Ormiston said he'd once seen Smylie bear-hug a recalcitrant prisoner into unconsciousness. He also told Rebus that before Kilpatrick had come on the scene, the Smylie brothers had more or less run the Edinburgh Crime Squad.

He drank the water with ice and lime and it tasted fine. When the preparations were complete and the table laid and the dishwasher set to work on only the first of the evening's loads, they sat down together on the sofa and drank gin with tonic.

'Cheers.'

'Cheers.'

And then Patience led him by the hand out into the small back garden. The sun was low over the tops of the tenements, the birds easing off into evensong. She examined every plant as she passed it, like a general assessing her troops. She'd trained Lucky the cat well; it now went over the wall into the neighbouring garden when it needed the toilet. She named some of the flowers for him, like she always did. He could never remember them from one day to the next.

The ice clinked in Patience's glass as she moved. She had changed into a long patterned dress, all flowing folds and

210

squares of colour. With her hair up at the back, the dress worked well, showing off her neck and shoulders and the contours of her body. It had short sleeves to show arms tanned from gardening.

Though the bell was a long way off, he heard it. 'Front door,' he said.

'They're early.' She looked at her watch. 'Well, not much actually. I'd better get the potatoes on.'

'I'll let them in.'

She squeezed his arm as they separated, and Rebus made his way down the hallway towards the front door. He straightened himself, readying the smile he'd be wearing all evening. Then he opened the door.

'Bastard!'

Something hissed, a spray-can, and his eyes stung. He'd closed them a moment too late, but could still feel the spray dotting his face. He thought it must be Mace or something similar, and swiped blindly, trying to knock the can out of his assailant's hand. But the feet were already on the stone steps, shuffling upwards and away. He didn't want to open his eyes, so staggered blindly towards the bathroom, his hands feeling the hallway walls, past the bedroom door then hitting the lightswitch. He slammed the door and locked it as Patience was coming into the hall.

'John? John, what is it?'

'Nothing,' he said through his teeth. 'It's all right.'

'Are you sure? Who was at the door?'

'They were looking for the upstairs neighbours.' He was running water into the sink. He got his jacket off and plunged his head into the warm water, letting the sink fill, wiping at his face with his hands.

Patience was still waiting on the other side of the bathroom door. 'Something's wrong, John, what is it?'

He didn't say anything. After a few moments, he pried open one eye, then shut it again. Shit, that stung! He swabbed again with the water, opening his eyes underwater

211

this time. The water seemed murky to him. And when he looked at his hands, they were red and sticky.

Oh Christ, he thought. He forced himself to look in the mirror above the sink. He was bright red. It wasn't like earlier in the day when Smylie had attacked him. It was ... paint. That's what it was, red paint. From an aerosol can. Jesus Christ. He staggered out of his clothes and got into the shower, turning his face up to the spray, shampooing his hair as hard as he could, then doing it again. He scrubbed at his face and neck. Patience was at the door again, asking him what the hell he was up to. And then he heard her voice change, rising on the final syllable of a name.

The Bremners had arrived.

He got out of the shower and rubbed himself down with a towel. When he looked at himself again, he'd managed to get a lot of the colour off, but by no means all of it. Then he looked at his clothes. His jacket was dark, and didn't show the paint too conspicuously; conspicuously enough though. As for his good shirt, it was ruined, no question about that. He unlocked the bathroom door and listened. Patience had taken the Bremners into the living room. He padded down the hall into the bedroom, noticing on the way that his hands had left red smears on the wallpaper. In the bedroom he changed quickly into chinos, yellow t-shirt and a linen jacket Patience had bought him for summer walks by the river which they never took.

He looked like a has-been trying to look trendy. It would do. The palms of his hands were still red, but he could say he'd been painting. He popped his head round the living room door.

'Chris, Jenny,' he said. The couple were seated on the sofa. Patience must be in the kitchen. 'Sorry, I'm running a bit late. I'll just dry my hair and I'll be with you.'

'No rush,' said Jenny as he retreated into the hall. He took the telephone into the bedroom and called Dr Curt at home.

'Hello?'

'It's John Rebus here, tell me about Caroline Rattray.'

'Pardon?'

'Tell me what you know about her.'

'You sound smitten,' Curt said, amusement in his voice.

'I'm smitten all right. She's just sprayed me with a can of paint.'

'I'm not sure I caught that.'

'Never mind, just tell me about her. Like for instance, is she the jealous type?'

'John, you've met her. Would you say she's attractive?'

'Yes.'

'And she has a very good career, plenty of money, a lifestyle many would envy?'

'Yes.'

'But does she have any beaux?'

'You mean boyfriends, and the answer is I don't know.'

'Then take it from me, she does not. That's why she can be at a loose end when I have ballet tickets to spare. Ask yourself, why should this be? Answer, because she scares men off. I don't know *what's* wrong with her, but I know that she's not very good at relationships with the opposite sex. I mean, she *has* relationships, but they never last very long.'

'You might have told me.'

'I didn't realise you two were an item.'

'We're not.'

'Oh?'

'Only she thinks we are.'

'Then you're in trouble.'

'It looks like it.'

'Sorry I can't be more help. She's always been all right with me, perhaps I could have a word with her ... ?'

'No thanks, that's my department.'

'Goodbye then, and good luck.'

Rebus waited till Curt had put his receiver down. He

listened to the line, then heard another click. Patience had been listening on the kitchen extension. He sat on the bed, staring at his feet, till the door opened.

'I heard,' she said. She had an oven glove in one hand. She knelt down in front of him, her hands on his knees. 'You should have told me.'

He smiled. 'I just did.'

'Yes, but to my face.' She paused. 'There was nothing between the two of you, nothing happened?'

'Nothing happened,' he said without blinking. There was another moment's silence.

'What are we going to do?'

He took her hands. 'We,' he said, 'are going to join our guests.' Then he kissed her on the forehead and pulled her with him to her feet.

# 22

At nine-thirty next morning, Rebus was sitting in his car outside Lachlan Murdock's flat.

When he'd washed his eyes last night, it had been like washing behind them as well. Always it came to this, he tried to do things by the books and ended up cooking them instead. It was easier, that was all. Where would the crime detection rates be without a few shortcuts?

He had tried Murdock's number from a callbox at the end of the road. There was no one there, just an answering machine. Murdock was at work. Rebus got out of the car and tried Murdock's intercom. Again, no answer. So he picked the lock, the way he'd been taught by an old lag when he'd gone to the man for lessons. Once inside, he climbed the stairwell briskly, a regular visitor rather than an intruder. But no one was about.

Murdock's flat was on the Yale rather than a deadlock, so it was easy to open too. Rebus slipped inside and closed the door after him. He went straight to Murdock's bedroom. He didn't suppose Millie would have left the computer disk behind, but you never knew. People with no access to safe deposit boxes sometimes mistook their homes for one.

The postman had been, and Murdock had left the mail strewn on the unmade bed. Rebus glanced at it. There was a letter from Millie. The envelope was postmarked the previous day, the letter itself written on a single sheet of lined writing paper.

'Sorry I didn't say anything. Don't know how long I'll

215

be away. If the police ask, say nothing. Can't say more just now. Love you. Millie.'

Rebus left the letter lying where it was and pulled on a pair of surgical gloves stolen from Patience. He walked over to Murdock's workdesk and switched on the computer, then started going through the computer disks. There were dozens of them, kept in plastic boxes, most of them neatly labelled. The majority had labels with spidery black handwriting, which Rebus guessed was Murdock's. The few that remained he took to be Millie's.

He went through these first, but found nothing to interest him. The unlabelled disks proved to be either blank or corrupted. He started searching through drawers for other disks. Parked on the floor one side of the bed were the plastic binliners containing Billy's things. He looked through these, too. Murdock's side of the bed was a chaos of books, ashtray, empty cigarette packets, but Millie's side was a lot neater. She had a bedside cupboard on which sat a lamp, alarm clock, and a packet of throat lozenges. Rebus crouched down and opened the cupboard door. Now he knew why Millie's side of the bed was so neat: the cupboard was like a wastepaper bin. He sifted through the rubbish. There were some crumpled yellow Post-It notes in amongst it. He picked them out and unpeeled them. They were messages from Murdock. The first one contained a seven-digit phone number and beneath it the words 'Why don't you call this bitch?' As Rebus unpeeled the others, he began to understand. There were half a dozen telephone messages, all from the same person. Rebus had thought he recognised the phone number, but on the rest of the messages the caller's name was printed alongside.

Mairie Henderson.

Back at St Leonard's he was pleased to find that both Holmes and Clarke were elsewhere. He went to the toilets and splashed water on his face. His eyes were still irritated, red at their rims and bloodshot. Patience had taken a close look at them last night and pronounced he'd live. After the Bremners had gone home happy, she'd also helped him scrub the rest of the red out of his hair and off his hands. Actually, there was still some on his right palm.

'Cuchullain of the Red Hand,' Patience had said. She'd been great really, considering. Trust a doctor to be calm in a crisis. She'd even managed to calm him down when, late in the evening, he'd considered going round to Caroline Rattray's flat and torching it.

'Here,' she'd said, handing him a whisky, 'set fire to yourself instead.'

He smiled at himself in the toilet mirror. There was no Smylie here, about to grope him to death, no jeering Ormiston or preening Blackwood. This was where he belonged. He wondered again just what he was doing at Fettes. Why had Kilpatrick scooped him up?

He thought now that he had a bloody good idea.

Edinburgh's Central Lending Library is situated on George IV Bridge, across the street from the National Library of Scotland. This was student territory, and just off the Royal Mile, and hence at the moment also Festival Fringe territory. Pamphleteers were out in force, still enthusing, sensing audiences to be had now that the least successful shows had packed up and headed home. For the sake of politeness, Rebus took a lurid green flyer from a teenage girl with long blonde hair, and read it as far as the first litter bin, where it joined many more identical flyers.

The Edinburgh Room was not so much a room as a gallery surrounding an open space. Far below, readers in another section of the library were at their desks or browsing among the bookshelves. Not that Mairie Henderson was reading books. She was poring over local newspapers, seated at one of the few readers' tables. Rebus stood beside Mairie, reading over her shoulder. She had a neat portable computer with her, flipped open and plugged into a socket in the library floor. Its screen was milky grey and filled with notes. It took her a minute to sense that there was someone standing over her. She looked round slowly, expecting a librarian.

'Let's talk,' said Rebus.

She saved what she'd been writing and followed him out onto the library's large main staircase. A sign told them not to sit on the window ledges, which were in a dangerous condition. Mairie sat on the top step, and Rebus sat a couple of steps down from her, leaving plenty of room for people to get past.

'I'm in a dangerous condition, too,' he said angrily.

'Why? What's happened?' She looked as innocent as stained glass.

'Millie Docherty.'

'Yes?'

'You didn't tell me about her.'

'What exactly should I have told you?'

'That you'd been trying to talk to her. Did you succeed?'

'No, why?'

'She's run off.'

'Really?' She considered this. 'Interesting.'

'What did you want to talk to her about?'

'The murder of one of her flatmates.'

'That's all?'

'Shouldn't it be?' She was looking interested.

'Funny she does a runner when you're after her. How's the research?' She'd told him over their drink in Newhaven that she was looking into what she called 'past loyalist activity' in Scotland.

'Slow,' she admitted. 'How's yours?'

'Dead stop,' he lied.

'Apart from Ms Docherty's disappearance. How did you know I wanted to talk to her?'

'None of your business.'

She raised her eyebrows. 'Her flatmate didn't tell you?'

'No comment at this time.'

She smiled.

'Come on,' said Rebus, 'maybe you'll talk over a coffee.'

'Interrogation by scone,' Mairie offered.

They walked the short walk to the High Street and took a right towards St Giles Cathedral. There was a coffee shop in the crypt of St Giles, reached by way of an entrance which faced Parliament House. Rebus glanced across the car park, but there was no sign of Caroline Rattray. The coffee shop though was packed, having not many tables to start with and this still being the height of the tourist season.

'Try somewhere else?' Mairie suggested.

'Actually,' said Rebus, 'I've gone off the idea. I've got a bit of business across the road.' Mairie tried not to look relieved. 'I'd caution you,' he warned her, 'not to piss me about.'

'Caution received and understood.'

She waved as she walked off back towards the library. Rebus watched her good legs recede from view. They stayed good-looking all the way out of his vision. Then he threaded his way between the lawyers' cars and entered the court building. He had an idea he was going to leave a note for Caroline Rattray in her box, always supposing she had one. But as he walked into Parliament Hall he saw her talking with another lawyer. There was no chance to retreat; she spotted him immediately. She kept up the conversation for a few more moments, then put her hand on her colleague's shoulder, said a brief farewell, and headed towards Rebus.

It was hard to reconcile her, in her professional garb, with the woman who had spray-painted him the previous night. She left her colleague with a faint smile on her lips, and met Rebus with that same smile. Under her arm were the regulation files and documents.

'Inspector, what brings you here?'

'Can't you guess?'

'Ah yes, of course, I'll send a cheque.'

He had kept telling himself all the way across the car park that he wasn't going to let her get under his skin. Now he found she was already there, like a half inch of syringe.

'Cheque?'

'For the dry cleaning or whatever.' A passing lawyer nodded to her. 'Hullo, Mansie. Oh, Mansie?' She spoke with the lawyer for a few moments, her hand on his elbow.

She was offering a cheque for the dry cleaning. Rebus was glad of a few moments in which to cool off. But now someone was tapping his shoulder. He turned to find Mairie Henderson standing there.

'I forgot,' she said, 'the American's in town.'

'Yes, I know. Have you done anything about him?'

She shook her head. 'Biding my time.'

'Good, no use scaring him off.' Caroline Rattray was looking interested in this new arrival, so much so that she was losing the thread of her own conversation. She dismissed Mansie halfway through a sentence and turned to Rebus and Mairie. Mairie smiled at her, the two women waiting for an introduction.

'See you then,' Rebus said to Mairie.

'Oh, right.' Mairie walked backwards a step or two, just in case he'd change his mind, then turned. As she turned, Caroline Rattray took a step forward, her hand out as though she were about to make her own introduction, but Rebus really didn't want her to, so he grabbed the hand and held her back. She shrugged his grip off and glared at him, then looked back through the doorway. Mairie had already left the building.

'You seem to have quite a little stable, Inspector.' She tried rubbing at her wrist. It wasn't easy with the files still precariously pressed between her elbow and stomach

'Better stable than unstable,' he said, regretting the dig

immediately. He should just have denied the charge.

'Unstable?' she echoed. 'I don't know what you mean.'

'Look, let's forget it, eh? I mean, forget *everything*. I've told Patience all about it.'

'I find that difficult to believe.'

'That's your problem, not mine.'

'You think so?' She sounded amused.

'Yes.'

'Remember something, Inspector.' Her voice was level and quiet. '*You* started it. And then *you* told the lie. My conscience is clear, what about yours?'

She gave him a little smile before walking away. Rebus turned and found himself confronting a statue of Sir Walter Scott, seated with his feet crossed and a walking-cane held between his open knees. Scott looked as though he'd heard every word but wasn't about to pass judgment.

'Keep it that way,' Rebus warned, not caring who might hear.


He phoned Patience and invited her to an early evening drink at the Playfair Hotel on George Street.

'What's the occasion?' she asked.

'No occasion,' he said.

He was restless the rest of the day. Glasgow came back to him, but only to say that they'd nothing on either Jim Hay or Active Resistance Theatre. He turned up early at the Playfair, making across its entrance hall (all faded glory, but *studied* faded glory, almost too perfect) to the bar beyond. It called itself a 'wet bar', which was okay with Rebus. He ordered a Talisker, hoisted himself onto a well-padded barstool and dipped a hand into the bowl of peanuts which had appeared at his approach.

The bar was empty, but would be filled soon enough with prosperous businessmen on their way home, other businessmen who wanted to look prosperous and didn't mind spending money on it, and the hotel clientele, enjoying a snifter before a pre-dinner stroll. A waitress stood idly against the end of the bar, not far from the baby grand. The piano was kept covered with a dustsheet until evening, so for now there was wallpaper music, except that whoever was playing trumpet wasn't half bad. He wondered if it was Chet Baker.

Rebus paid for his drink and tried not to think about the amount of money he'd just been asked for. After a bit, he changed his mind and asked if he could have some ice. He wanted the drink to last. Eventually a middle-aged couple came into the bar and sat a couple of seats away from him. The woman put on elaborate glasses to study the cocktail list, while her husband ordered Drambuie, pronouncing it Dramboo-i. The husband was short but bulky, given to scowling. He was wearing a white golfing cap, and kept glancing at his watch. Rebus managed to catch his eye, and toasted him.

'*Slainte.*'

The man nodded, saying nothing, but the wife smiled. 'Tell me,' she said, 'are there many Gaelic speakers left in Scotland?'

Her husband hissed at her, but Rebus was happy to answer. 'Not many,' he conceded.

'Are you from Edinburgh?' Head-in-burrow, it sounded like.

'Pretty much.'

She noticed that Rebus's glass was now all melting ice. 'Will you join us?' The husband hissed again, something about her not bothering people who only wanted a quiet drink.

Rebus looked at his watch. He was calculating whether he could afford to buy a round back. 'Thank you, yes, I'll have a Talisker.'

'And what is that?'

'Malt whisky, it comes from Skye. There are some Gaelic speakers over there.'

The wife started humming the first few notes of the *Skye Boat Song*, all about a French Prince who dressed in drag. Her husband smiled to cover his embarrassment. It couldn't be easy, travelling with a madwoman.

'Maybe you can tell me something,' said Rebus. 'Why is a wet bar called a wet bar?'

'Could be because the beer's draught,' the husband offered grudgingly, 'not just bottled.'

The wife had perched her shiny handbag on the bar and now opened it, taking out a compact so she could check her face. 'You're not the mystery man, are you?' she asked.

Rebus put down his glass. 'Sorry?'

'Ellie!' her husband warned.

'Only,' she said, putting away her compact, 'Clyde had a message to meet someone in the bar, and you're the only person here. They didn't leave a name or anything.'

'A misunderstanding, that's all,' said Clyde. 'They got the wrong room.' But he looked at Rebus anyway. Rebus obliged with a nod.

'Mysterious, certainly.'

The fresh glass was put before Rebus, and the barman decided he merited another bowl of nuts too.

'*Slainte*,' said Rebus.

'*Slainte*,' said husband and wife.

'Am I late?' said Patience Aitken, running her hands up Rebus's spine. She slipped onto the stool which separated Rebus from the tourists. For some reason, the man now removed his cap, showing a good amount of hair slicked back from the forehead.

'Patience,' Rebus said, 'I'd like to introduce you to . . .'

'Clyde Moncur,' said the man, visibly relaxing. Rebus obviously posed no threat. 'This is my wife Eleanor.'

Rebus smiled. 'Dr Patience Aitken, and I'm John.'

Patience looked at him. He seldom used 'Dr' when introducing her, and why had he left out his own surname?

'Listen,' Rebus was saying, staring right past her,

223

'wouldn't we be more comfortable at a table?'

They took a table for four, the waitress appearing with a little tray of nibbles, not just nuts but green and black olives and chipsticks too. Rebus tucked in. The drinks might be expensive, but you had to say the food was cheap.

'You're on holiday?' Rebus said, opening the conversation.

'That's right,' said Eleanor Moncur. 'We just love Scotland.' She then went on to list everything they loved about it, from the skirl of the bagpipes to the windswept west coast. Clyde let her run on, taking sips from his drink, occasionally swirling the ice around. He sometimes looked up from the drink to John Rebus.

'Have you ever been to the United States?' Eleanor asked.

'No, never,' said Rebus.

'I've been a couple of times,' Patience said, surprising him. 'Once to California, and once to New England.'

'In the fall?' Patience nodded. 'Isn't that just heaven?'

'Do you live in New England?' Rebus asked.

Eleanor smiled. 'Oh no, we're way over the other side. Washington.'

'Washington?'

'She means the state,' her husband explained, 'not Washington DC.'

'Seattle,' said Eleanor. 'You'd like Washington, it's wild.'

'As in wilderness,' Clyde Moncur added. 'I'll put that on our room, miss.'

Patience had ordered lager and lime, which the waitress had just brought. Rebus watched as Moncur took a room key from his pocket. The waitress checked the room number.

'Clyde's ancestors came from Scotland,' Eleanor was saying. 'Somewhere near Glasgow.'

'Kilmarnock.'

'That's right, Kilmarnock. There were four brothers, one went to Australia, two went to Northern Ireland, and Clyde's great-grandfather sailed from Glasgow to Canada with his wife and children. He worked his way across Canada and settled in Vancouver. It was Clyde's grandfather who came down into the United States. There are still offshoots of the family in Australia and Northern Ireland.'

'Where in Northern Ireland?' Rebus asked casually.

'Portadown, Londonderry,' she went on, though Rebus had directed the question at her husband.

'Ever visit them?'

'No,' said Clyde Moncur. He was interested in Rebus again. Rebus met the stare squarely.

'The north west's full of Scots,' Mrs Moncur rattled on. 'We have ceilidhs and clan gatherings and Highland Games in the summer.'

Rebus lifted his glass to his lips and seemed to notice it was empty. 'I think we need another round,' he said. The drinks arrived with their own scalloped paper coasters, and the waitress took away with her nearly all the money John Rebus had on him. He'd used the anonymous message to get Moncur down here, and Patience to put him off his guard. In the event, Moncur was sharper than Rebus had given him credit for. The man didn't need to say a word, his wife spoke enough for two, and nothing she said could prove remotely useful.

'So you're a doctor?' she asked Patience now.

'General practice, yes.'

'I admire doctors,' said Eleanor. 'They keep Clyde and me alive and ticking.' And she gave a big grin. Her husband had been watching Patience while she'd been speaking, but as soon as she finished he turned his gaze back to Rebus. Rebus lifted his glass to his lips.

'For some time,' Eleanor Moncur was saying now, 'Clyde's grandaddy was captain of a clipper. His wife gave birth on board while the boat was headed to pick up ... what was it, Clyde?'

'Timber,' Clyde said. 'From the Philippines. She was eighteen and he was in his forties. The baby died.'

'And know what?' said Eleanor. 'They preserved the body in brandy.'

'Embalmed it?' Patience offered.

Eleanor Moncur nodded. 'And if that boat had been a temperance vessel, they'd've used tar instead of brandy.'

Clyde Moncur spoke to Rebus. 'Now *that* was hard living. Those are the people who built America. You had to be tough. You might be conscientious, but there wasn't always room for a conscience.'

'A bit like in Ulster,' Rebus offered. 'They transplanted some pretty hard Scots there.'

'Really?' Moncur finished his drink in silence.

They decided against a third round, Clyde reminding his wife that they had yet to take their pre-prandial walk down to Princes Street Gardens and back. They exchanged handshakes outside, Rebus taking Patience's arm and leading her downhill, as though they were heading into the New Town.

'Where's your car?' he asked.

'Back on George Street. Where's yours?'

'Same place.'

'Then where are we going?'

He checked over his shoulder, but the Moncurs were out of sight. 'Nowhere,' he said, stopping.

'John,' said Patience, 'next time you need me as a cover, have the courtesy to ask first.'

'Can you lend me a few quid, save me finding a cash-point?'

She sighed and dug into her bag. 'Twenty enough?'

'Hope so.'

'Unless you're thinking of returning to the Playfair bar.'

'I've been up braes that weren't as steep as that place.'

He told her he'd be back late, perhaps very late, and pecked her on the cheek. But she pulled him to her and took her fair share of mouth to mouth.

'By the way,' she said, 'did you talk to the action painter?'

'I told her to get lost. That doesn't mean she will.'

'She better,' said Patience, pecking him a last time on the cheek before walking away.

He was unlocking his car when a heavy hand landed on his own. Clyde Moncur was standing next to him.

'Who the fuck are you?' the American spat, looking around him.

'Nobody,' Rebus said, shaking off the hand.

'I don't know what all that shit was about at the hotel, but you better stay far away from me, friend.'

'That might not be easy,' said Rebus. 'This is a small place. *My* town, not yours.'

Moncur took a step back. He'd be in his late-60s, but the hand he'd placed on Rebus's had stung. There was strength there, and determination. He was the sort of man who normally got his own way, whatever the cost.

'Who *are* you?'

Rebus pulled open the car door. He drove away without saying anything at all. Moncur watched him go. The American stood legs apart, and raised a hand to pat his jacket at chest height, nodding slowly.

A gun, Rebus thought. He's telling me he's got a gun.

And he's telling me he'd use it, too.

# 23

Mairie Henderson had a flat in Portobello, on the coast east of the city. In Victorian times a genteel bathing resort, 'Porty' was still used by day trippers in summer. Mairie's tenement was on one of the streets between High Street and the Promenade. With his window rolled down, Rebus caught occasional wafts of salt air.

When his daughter Sammy was a kid they'd come to Porty beach for walks. The beach had been cleaned up by then, or at least covered with tons of sand from elsewhere. Rebus used to enjoy those walks, trouser legs rolled up past the ankles, feet treading the numbing water at the edge of the louring North Sea.

'If we kept walking, Daddy,' Sammy would say, pointing to the skyline, 'where would we go?'

'We'd go to the bottom of the sea.'

He could still see the dreadful look on her face. She'd be twenty this year. Twenty. He reached under his seat and let his hand wander till it touched his emergency pack of cigarettes. One wouldn't do any harm. Inside the pack, nestling amongst the cigarettes, was a slim disposable lighter.

The light was still on in Mairie's first-floor window. Her car was parked right outside the tenement's front door. He knew the back door led to a small enclosed drying-green. She'd have to come out the front. He hoped she'd bring Millie Docherty with her.

He didn't quite know why he thought Mairie was hiding

Millie; it was enough that he thought it. He'd had wrong hunches before, enough for a convention of the Quasimodo fan club, but you always had to follow them up. If you stopped being true to instinct, you were lost. His stomach rumbled, reminding him that olives and chipsticks did not a meal make. He thought of the Portobello chip shops, but sucked on his cigarette instead. He was across the road from the tenement and about six cars down. It was eleven o'clock and dark; no chance of Mairie spotting him.

He thought he knew why Clyde Moncur was in town. Same reason the ex-UVF man was here. He just didn't want to go public with his thoughts, not when he didn't know who his friends were.

At quarter past eleven, the tenement door opened and Mairie came out. She was alone, wearing a Burberry-style raincoat and carrying a bulging shopping bag. She looked up and down the street before unlocking her car and getting in.

'What are you nervous about, kid?' Rebus asked, watching her headlights come on. He lit another cigarette, just to wash down the first, and started his engine.

She took the Portobello Road back into the city. He hoped she wasn't going far. Tailing a car, even in the dark, wasn't as easy as the movies made it look, especially when the person you were tailing knew your car. The roads were quiet, making things trickier still, but at least she stuck to the main routes. If she'd used side streets and rat runs, she'd have spotted him for sure.

On Princes Street, the bikers were out in summer-night force, hitting the late-opening burger bars and revving up and down the straight. He wondered if Clyde Moncur was out for a post-prandial stroll. With the burgers and bikes, he'd probably feel right at home. Moncur was tough the way old people could get; seeming to shrink as they got older but that was only because they were losing juice, becoming rock-hard as a result. There was nothing soft left of Clyde Moncur. He had a handshake like a saloon-bar challenge. Even Patience had complained of it.

The night was delicious, perfect for a walk, and that's what most people were enjoying. Too bad for the Fringe shows: who wanted to sit in an airless, dark theatre for two hours while the real show was outside, continuous and absolutely free?

Mairie turned left at the west end, heading up Lothian Road. The street was already reeling with drunks. They'd probably be heading for a curry house or pizza emporium. Later, they'd regret this move. You saw the evidence each morning on the pavements. Just past the Tollcross lights, Mairie signalled to cross the oncoming traffic. Rebus wondered where the hell she was headed. His question was soon answered. She parked by the side of the road and turned off her lights. Rebus hurried past while she was locking her door, then stopped at the junction ahead. There was no traffic coming, but he sat there anyway, watching in his rearview.

'Well, well,' he said as Mairie crossed the road and went into the Crazy Hose Saloon. He put the car into reverse, brought it back, and squeezed in a few cars ahead of Mairie. He looked across at the Crazy Hose. The sign above was yellow and red flashing neon, which must be fun for the people in the tenement outside which Rebus was parked. A short flight of steps led to the main doors, and on these steps stood two bouncers. The Hose's wild west theme had passed the bouncers by, and they were dressed in regulation black evening suits, white shirts and black bow ties. Both had cropped hair to match their IQs, and held their hands behind their backs, swelling already prodigious chests. Rebus watched them open the doors for a couple of stetson-tipping cowpokes and their mini-dressed partners.

'In for a dime, I suppose.' He locked his car and walked purposefully across the road, trying to look like a man looking for a good time. The bouncers eyed him suspiciously, and did not open the door. Rebus decided he'd played enough games today, so he opened his ID and stuck it in the tallest bouncer's face. He wondered if the man could read.

'Police,' he said helpfully. 'Don't I get the door opened for me?'

'Only on your way out,' the smaller bouncer said. So Rebus pulled open the door and went in. The admission desk had been done up like an old bank, with vertical wooden bars in front of the smiling female face.

'Platinum Cowpoke Card,' Rebus said, again showing his ID. Past the desk was a fair-sized hallway where people were playing one-armed bandits. There was a large crowd around an interactive video game, where some bearded actor on film invited you to shoot him dead if you were quick enough on the draw. Most of the kids in front of the machine were dressed in civvies, though a few sported cowboy boots and bootlace ties. Big belt-buckles seemed mandatory, and both males and females wore Levi and Wrangler denims with good-sized turn-ups. The toilets were out here too, always supposing you could work out which you were, a Honcho or Honchette.

A second set of doors led to the dance hall and four bars, one in each corner of the vast arena. Plenty of money had been spent on the decor, with the choicest pieces being spotlit behind Perspex high up out of reach on the walls. There was a life-size cigar-store Indian, a lot of native head-dresses and jackets and the like, and what Rebus hoped was a replica of a Gatling-gun. Old western films played silently on a bank of TV screens set into one wall, and there was a bucking bronco machine against another wall. This was disused now, ever since a teenager had fallen from it and been put in a coma. They'd nearly shut the place down for that. Rebus didn't like to think about why they hadn't. He kept coming up with friends in the right places and money changing hands. There was something that looked like a font near one of the bars, but Rebus knew it was a spittoon. He noticed that the bar closest to it wasn't doing great business.

Rebus wasn't hard to pick out in a crowd. Although there were people there his own age, they were all wearing western dress to some degree, and they were nearly all dancing. There was a stage which was spotlit and full of instruments but empty of bodies. Instead the music came through the PA. A DJ in an enclosed box next to the stage babbled between songs; you could have heard him halfway to Texas.

'Can I help you?'

Not hard to pick out in the crowd, and of course the bouncers had sent word to the floor manager. He was in his late-twenties with slick black hair and a rhinestone waistcoat. The accent was strictly Lothian.

'Is Frankie in tonight?' If Bothwell were in the dancehall, he'd have spotted him. Bothwell's clothes would have drowned out the PA.

'I'm in charge.' The smile told Rebus he was as welcome as haemorrhoids at a rodeo.

'Well, there's no trouble, son, so I can put your mind at rest straight off. I'm just looking for a friend, only I didn't fancy paying the admission.'

The manager looked relieved. You could see he hadn't been in the job long. He'd probably been promoted from behind the bar. 'My name's Lorne Strang,' he said.

'And mine's Lorne Sausage.'

Strang smiled. 'My real name's Kevin.'

'Don't apologise.'

'Drink on the house?'

'I'd rather drink on a bar-stool, if that's all right with you.'

Rebus had given the dance floor a good look, and Mairie wasn't there, which meant she was either trapped in the Honchettes' or was somewhere behind the scenes. He wondered what she could be doing behind the scenes at Frankie Bothwell's club.

'So,' said Kevin Strang, 'who are you looking for?'

'Like I say, a friend. She said she'd be here. Maybe I'm a bit late.'

'The place is only just picking up now. We're open another two hours. What'll you have?' They were at the bar. The bar staff wore white aprons covering chest and legs and gold-coloured bands around their sleeves to keep their cuffs out of the way.

'Is that so they can't palm any notes?' asked Rebus.

'Nobody cheats the bar here.' One of the staff broke off serving someone to attend to Kevin Strang.

'Just a beer, please,' Rebus said.

'Draught? We only serve half pints.'

'Why's that?'

'There's more profit in it.'

'An honest answer. I'll have a bottle of Beck's.' He looked back to the dance floor. 'The last time I saw this many cowboys was at a builders' convention.'

The record was fading out. Strang patted Rebus's back. 'That's my cue,' he said. 'Enjoy yourself.'

Rebus watched him move through the dancers. He climbed onto the stage and tapped the microphone, sending a whump through the on-stage PA. Rebus didn't know what he was expecting. Maybe Strang would call out the steps of the next barn dance. But instead all he did was speak in a quiet voice, so people had to be quiet to hear him. Rebus didn't think Kevin Strang had much future as floor manager at the Crazy Hose.

'Dudes and womenfolk, it's a pleasure to see you all here at the Crazy Hose Saloon. And now, please welcome onto the Deadwood Stage our band for this evening's hoedown ... Chaparral!'

There was generous applause as the band emerged through a door at the back of the stage. A few of the arcade junkies had come in from the foyer. The band was a six-piece, barely squeezing onto the stage. Guitar/vocals, bass, drums, another guitar and two backing singers. They started into their first number a little shakily, but had warmed up by the end, by which time Rebus was finishing his drink and thinking about heading back to the car.

Then he saw Mairie.

No wonder she'd had a raincoat around her. Underneath she must have been wearing a tasselled black skirt, brown leather waistcoat, white blouse cut just above the chest and up around the shoulders, leaving a lot of bare flesh. She wasn't wearing a stetson, but there was a red kerchief around her throat and she was singing her heart out.

She was one of the backing singers.

Rebus ordered another drink and gawped at the stage. After a few songs, he could differentiate between Mairie's voice and that of the other backing singer. He noticed that most of the men were watching this singer. She was much taller than Mairie and had long straight black hair, plus she was wearing a much shorter skirt. But Mairie was the better singer. She sang with her eyes closed, swaying from the hips, knees slightly bent. Her partner used her hands a lot, but didn't gain much from it.

At the end of their fourth song, the male singer/guitarist gave a short spiel while the others in the band caught their breath, retuned, swigged drinks or wiped their faces. Rebus didn't know about C&W, but Chaparral seemed pretty good. They didn't just play mush about pet dogs, dying spouses or standing by your lover. Their songs had a harder, much urban feel, with lyrics to match.

'And if you don't know Hal Ketchum,' the singer was saying, 'you better get to know him. This is one of his, it's called Small Town Saturday Night.'

Mairie took lead vocal, her partner patting a tambourine and looking on. At the end of the song, the cheers were loud. The singer came back to his mike and raised his arm towards Mairie.

'Katy Hendricks, ladies and gentlemen.' The cheers resumed while Mairie took her bow.

After this they started into their own material, two songs whose intention was always ahead of ability. The singer mentioned that both were available on the band's first cassette, available to buy in the foyer.

'We're going to take a break now. So you can all go away for the next fifteen minutes, but be sure to come back.'

Rebus went into the foyer and dug six pounds out of his pocket. When he came back in, the band were at one of the bars, hoping to be bought drinks if half-time refreshments weren't on the house. Rebus shook the cassette in Mairie's ear.

'Miss Hendricks, would you autograph this, please?'

The band looked at him and so did Mairie. She took him by the lapels and propelled him away from the bar.

'What are you doing here?'

'Didn't you know? I'm a big country and western fan.'

'You don't like anything but sixties rock, you told me so yourself. Are you following me?'

'You sang pretty well.'

'*Pretty* well? I was great.'

'That's my Mairie, never one to hide her light under a tumbleweed. Why the false name?'

'You think I wanted those arseholes at the paper to find out?' Rebus tried to imagine the Hose full of drunken journos cheering their singer-scribe.

'No, I don't suppose so.'

'Anyway, everyone in the band uses an alias, it makes it harder for the DSS to find out they've been working.' She pointed at the tape. 'You bought that?'

'Well, they didn't hand it over as material evidence.'

She grinned. 'You liked us then?'

'I really did. I know I shouldn't be, but I'm amazed.'

She was almost persuaded onto this tack, but not quite. 'You still haven't said why you're following me.'

He put the tape in his pocket. 'Millie Docherty.'

'What about her?'

'I think you know where she is.'

'What?'

'She's scared, she needs help. She might just run to the reporter who's being wanting to see her. Reporters have been known to hide their sources away, protect them.'

'You think I'm hiding her?'

He paused. 'Has she told you about the pennant?'

'What pennant?'

Mairie had lost her cowgirl singer look. She was back in business.

'The one on Billy Cunningham's wall. Has she told you what he had hidden behind it?'

'What?'

Rebus shook his head. 'I'll make a deal,' he said. 'We'll talk to her together, that way neither of us is hiding anything. What do you say?'

The bassist handed Mairie an orange juice.

'Thanks, Duane.' She gulped it down until only ice was left. 'Are you staying for the second set?'

'Will it be worth my while?'

'Oh yes, we do a cracking version of "Country Honk".'

'That'll be the acid test.'

She smiled. 'I'll see you after the set.'

'Mairie, do you know who owns this place?'

'A guy called Boswell.'

'It's Bothwell. You don't know him?'

'Never met him. Why?'

The second set was paced like a foxtrot: two slow dances, two fast, then a slow, sad rendering of 'Country Honk' to end with. The floor was packed for the last dance, and

Rebus was flattered when a woman a good few years younger than him asked him up. But then her man came back from the Honchos', so that was the end of that.

As the band played a short upbeat encore, one fan climbed onstage and presented the backing singers with sheriff's badges, producing the loudest cheer of the night as both women pinned them on their chests. It was a good natured crowd, and Rebus had spent worse evenings. He couldn't see Patience enjoying it though.

When the band finished, they went back through the door they'd first appeared through. A few minutes later, Mairie reappeared, still dressed in all her gear and with the raincoat folded up in her shopping bag along with her flat-soled driving shoes.

'So?' Rebus said.

'So let's go.'

He started for the exit, but she was making towards the stage, gesturing for him to follow.

'I don't really want her to see me like this,' she said. 'I'm not sure the outfit conveys journalistic clout and professionalism. But I can't be bothered changing.'

They climbed onto the stage, then through the door. It led into a low-ceilinged passage of broom closets, crates of empty bottles, and a small room where in the evening the band got ready and during the day the cleaner could stop for a cup of tea. Beyond this was a dark stairwell. Mairie found the light switch and started to climb.

'Where exactly are we going?'

'The Sheraton.'

Rebus didn't ask again. The stairs were steep and twisting. They reached a landing where a padlocked door faced them, but Mairie kept climbing. At the second landing she stopped. There was another door, this time with no lock. Inside was a vast dark space, which Rebus judged to be the building's attic. Light infiltrated from the street through a skylight and some gaps in the roof, showing the solid forms of rafters.

'Watch you don't bump your head.'

The roofspace, though huge, was stifling. It seemed to be filled with tea chests, ladders, stacks of cloth which might have been old firemen's uniforms.

'She's probably asleep,' Mairie whispered. 'I found this place the first night we played here. Kevin said she could stay here.'

'You mean Lorne? He knows?'

'He's an old pal, he got us this residency. I told him she was a friend who'd come up for the Fringe but had nowhere to stay. I said I had eight people in my flat as it was. That's a lie by the way, I like my privacy. Where else was she going to stay? The city's bursting at the seams.'

'But what does she do all day?'

'She can go downstairs and boil a kettle, there's a loo there too. The club itself's off limits, but she's so scared I don't think she'd risk it anyway.'

She had led them past enough obstacles for a game of crazy golf, and now they were close to the front of the building. There were some small window panes here, forming a long thin arch. They were filthy, but provided a little more light.

'Millie? It's only me.' Mairie peered into the gloom. Rebus's eyes had become accustomed to the dark, but even so there were places enough she could be hiding. 'She's not here,' Mairie said. There was a sleeping bag on the floor: Rebus recognised it from the first time he'd met Millie. Beside it lay a torch. Rebus picked it up and switched it on. A paperback book lay face down on the floor.

'Where's her bag?'

'Her bag?'

'Didn't she have a bag of stuff?'

'Yes.' Mairie looked around. 'I don't see it.'

'She's gone,' said Rebus. But why would she leave the

sleeping-bag, book and torch? He moved the beam around the walls. 'This place is a junk shop.' An old red rubberised fire-hose snaked cross the floor. Rebus followed it with the beam all the way to a pair of feet.

He moved the beam up past splayed legs to the rest of the body. She was propped against the corner in a sitting position. 'Stay here,' he ordered, approaching the body, trying to keep the torch steady. The fire-hose was coiled around Millie Docherty's neck. Someone had tried strangling her with it, but they hadn't succeeded. The perished rubber had snapped. So instead they'd taken the brass nozzle and stuffed it down her throat. It was still there, looking like the mouth of a funnel. And that's what they'd used it as. Rebus put his nose close to the funnel and sniffed.

He couldn't be sure, but he thought they'd used acid. They'd tipped it down into her while she'd been choking on the nozzle. If he looked closer, he'd see her throat burnt away. He didn't look. He shone the torch on the floor instead. Her bag was lying there, its contents emptied onto the floorboards. There was something small and crumpled beside a wooden chest. He picked it up and flattened it out. It was the sleeve for a computer disk. Written on it were the letters SaS.

'Looks like they got what they wanted,' he said.


Nobody was dancing in the Crazy Hose Saloon.

Everyone had been sent home. Because the Hose was in Tollcross, it was C Division's business. They'd sent officers out from Torphichen Place.

'John Rebus,' one of the CID men said. 'You get around more than a Jehovah's Witness.'

'But I never try to sell you religion, Shug.'

Rebus watched DI Shug Davidson climb onto the stage and disappear through the door. They were all upstairs; the action was upstairs. They were setting up halogen lamps on tripods to assist the photographers. No key could be found for the first floor padlock, so they'd taken a sledgehammer to it. Rebus didn't like to ask who or what they thought they'd find hidden behind a door padlocked from the outside. He doubted it would be germane to the case. Only one thing was germane, and it was standing at the bar near the spittoon, drinking a long cold drink. Rebus walked over.

'Have you talked to your boss yet, Kevin?'

'I keep getting his answering machine.'

'Bad one.'

Kevin Strang nearly bit through the glass. 'How do you mean?'

'Bad for business.'

'Aye, right enough.'

'Mairie tells me you and her are friends?'

'Went to school together. She was a couple of years above me, but we were both in the school orchestra.'

'That's good, you'll have something to fall back on.'

'Eh?'

'If Bothwell sacks you, you can always busk for a living. Did you ever see her? Talk to her?'

Kevin knew who he meant. He was shaking his head before Rebus had finished asking.

'No?' Rebus persisted. 'You weren't even a wee bit curious? Didn't want to see what she looked like?'

'Never thought about it.'

Rebus looked across to the distant table where Mairie was being questioned by one of the Torphichen squad, with a WPC in close attendance. 'Bad one,' he said again. He leaned closer to Kevin Strang. 'Just between us, Kevin, who did you tell?'

'I didn't tell anyone.'

'Then you're going down, son.'

'How do you mean?'

'They didn't find her by accident, Kevin. They *knew* she

was there. Only two people could have provided that information: Mairie or you. C Division are hard bastards. They'll want to know all about you, Kevin. You're about the only suspect they've got.'

'I'm not a suspect.'

'She died about six hours ago, Kevin. Where were you six hours ago?' Rebus was making this up: they wouldn't know for sure until the pathologist took body temperature readings. But he reckoned it was a fair guess all the same.

'I'm telling you nothing.'

Rebus smiled. 'You're just snot, Kevin. Worse, you're hired snot.' He made to pat Kevin Strang's face, but Strang flinched, staggered back, and hit the spittoon. They watched it tip with a crash to the floor, rock to and fro, and then lie there. Nothing happened for a second, then with a wet sucking sound a thick roll of something barely liquid oozed out. Everyone looked away. The only thing Strang found to look at was Rebus. He swallowed.

'Look, I had to tell Mr Bothwell, just to cover myself. If I hadn't told him, and he'd found out...'

'What did he say?'

'He just shrugged, said she was *my* responsibility.' He shuddered at the memory.

'Where were you when you told him?'

'In the office, off the foyer.'

'This morning?' Strang nodded. 'Tell me, Kevin, did Mr Bothwell go check out the lodger?'

Strang looked down at his empty glass. It was answer enough for Rebus.

There were strict rules covering the investigation of a serious crime such as murder. For one, Rebus should talk to the officer in charge and tell him everything he knew about Millie Docherty. For two, he should also mention his conversation with Kevin Strang. For three, he should then leave well alone and let C Division get on with it.

But at two in the morning, he was parked outside Frankie Bothwell's house in Ravelston Dykes, giving serious thought to going and ringing the doorbell. If nothing else, he might learn whether Bothwell's night attire was as gaudy as his daywear. But he dismissed the idea. For one thing, C Division would be speaking with Bothwell before the night was out, always supposing they managed to get hold of him. They would not want to be told by Bothwell that Rebus had beaten them to it.

For another, he was too late. He heard the garage doors lift automatically, and saw the dipped headlights as Bothwell's car, a gloss-black Merc with custom bodywork, bounced down off the kerb onto the road and sped away. So he'd finally got the message, and was on his way to the Hose. Either that or he was fleeing.

Rebus made a mental note to do yet more digging on Lee Francis Bothwell.

But for now, he was relieved the situation had been taken out of his hands. He drove back to Oxford Terrace at a sedate pace, trying hard not to fall asleep at the wheel. No one was waiting in ambush outside, so he let himself in quietly and went to the living room, his body too tired to stay awake but his mind too busy for sleep. Well, he had a cure for that: a mug of milky tea with a dollop of whisky in it. But there was a note on the sofa in Patience's handwriting. Her writing was better than most doctors', but not by much. Eventually Rebus deciphered it, picked up the phone, and called Brian Holmes.

'Sorry, Brian, but the note said to call whatever the time.'

'Hold on a sec.' He could hear Holmes getting out of bed, taking the cordless phone with him. Rebus imagined Nell Stapleton awake in the bed, rolling back over to sleep and cursing his name. The bedroom door closed. 'Okay,' said Holmes, 'I can talk now.'

'What's so urgent? Is it about our friend?'

'No, all's quiet on that front. I'll tell you about it in the morning. But I was wondering if you'd heard the news?'

'I was the one who found her.'

Rebus heard a fridge opening, a bottle being taken out, something poured into a glass.

'Found who?' Brian asked.

'Millie Docherty. Isn't that what we're talking about?' But of course it wasn't; Brian couldn't possibly know so soon. 'She's dead, murdered.'

'They're piling up, aren't they? What happened to her?'

'It's not a bedtime story. So what's your news?'

'A breakout from Barlinnie. Well, from a van actually, stopped between Barlinnie and a hospital. The whole thing was planned.'

Rebus sat down on the sofa. 'Cafferty?'

'He does a good impersonation of a perforated ulcer. It happened this evening. The prison van was sandwiched between two lorries. Masks, sawn-offs and a miracle recovery.'

'Oh Christ.'

'Don't worry, there are patrols all up and down the M8.'

'If he's coming back to Edinburgh, that's the last road he'll use.'

'You think he'll come back?'

'Get a grip, Brian, of course he's coming back. He's going to have to kill whoever butchered his son.'

# 24

He didn't get much sleep that night, in spite of the tea and whisky. He sat by the recessed bedroom window wondering when Cafferty would come. He kept his eyes on the stairwell outside until dawn came. His mind made up, he started packing. Patience sat up in bed.

'I hope you've left a note,' she said.

'We're both leaving, only not together. What's the score in an emergency?'

'My dream was making more sense than this.'

'Say you had to go away at very short notice?'

She was rubbing her hair, yawning. 'Someone would cover for me. What did you have in mind, elopement?'

'I'll put the kettle on.'

When he came back from the kitchen carrying two mugs of coffee, she was in the shower.

'What's happening?' she asked afterwards, rubbing herself dry.

'You're going to your sister's,' he told her. 'So drink your coffee, phone her, get dressed, and start packing.'

She took the mug from him. 'In that order?'

'Any order you like.'

'And where are you going?'

'Somewhere else.'

'Who'll feed the pets?'

'I'll get someone to do it, don't worry.'

'I'm not worried.' She took a sip of coffee. 'Yes I am. What *is* going on?'

'A bad man's coming to town.' Something struck him. 'There you are, that's another old film I like: *High Noon*.'

Rebus booked into a small hotel in Bruntsfield. He knew the night manager and phoned first, checking they had a room.

'You're lucky, we've one single.'

'How come you're not full?'

'The old gent who was in it, he's been coming here for years, he died of a stroke yesterday afternoon.'

'Oh.'

'You're not superstitious or anything?'

'Not if it's your only room.'

He climbed the steps to street level and looked around. When he was happy, he gestured for Patience to join him. She carried a couple of bags. Rebus was already holding her small suitcase. They put the stuff in the back of her car and embraced hurriedly.

'I'll call you,' he said. 'Don't try phoning me.'

'John . . .'

'Trust me on this if on nothing else, Patience, please.'

He watched her drive off, then hung around to make sure no one was following her. Not that he could be absolutely sure. They could pick her up on Queensferry Road. Cafferty wouldn't hesitate to use her, or anyone, to get to him. Rebus got his own bag from the flat, locked the flat tight, and headed for his car. On the way he stopped at the next door neighbour's door, dropping an envelope through the letterbox. Inside were keys to the flat and feeding instructions for Lucky the cat, the budgie with no name, and Patience's goldfish.

It was still early morning, the quiet streets unsuitable for a tail. Even so, he took every back route he could think of. The hotel was just a big family house really, converted into a small family hotel. Out front, where a garden once separated it from the pavement, tarmac had been laid, making a car park for half a dozen cars. But Rebus drove round the back and parked where the staff parked. Monty, the night manager, brought him in the back way, then led him straight up to his room. It was at the top of the house, all the way up one of the creakiest staircases Rebus had ever climbed. No one would be able to tiptoe up there without him and the woodworm knowing about it.

He lay on the solid bed wondering if lying on a dead man's bed was like stepping into his shoes. Then he started to think about Cafferty. He knew he was taking half-measures only. How hard would it be for Cafferty to track him down? A few men staked outside Fettes and St Leonard's and in a few well-chosen pubs, and Rebus would be in the gangster's hands by the end of the day. Fine, he just didn't want Patience involved, or Patience's home, or those of his friends.

Didn't most suicides do the same thing, come to hotels so as not to involve family and friends?

He could have gone home of course, back to his flat in Marchmont, but it was still full of students working in Edinburgh over the summer. He liked his tenants, and didn't want them meeting Cafferty. Come to that, he didn't want Monty the night manager meeting Cafferty either.

'He's not after *me*,' he kept reminding himself, hands behind his head as he stared at the ceiling. There was a clock radio by the bed, and he switched it on, catching the news. Police were still searching for Morris Gerald Cafferty. 'He's not after me,' he repeated. But in a sense, Cafferty *was*. He'd know Rebus was his best bet to finding the killers. There was a short item about the body at the Crazy Hose, though no gruesome details. Not yet, anyway.

When the news finished, he washed and went downstairs. He got a black cab to take him to St Leonard's. Once told the destination, the driver switched off his meter.

'On the house,' he said.

Rebus nodded and sat back. He'd commandeer someone's

car during the course of the day, either that or find a spare car from the pool. No one would complain. They all knew who'd put Cafferty in Barlinnie. At St Leonard's, he walked smartly into the station and went straight to the computer, tapping into Brains. Brains had a direct link to PNC2, the UK mainland police database at Hendon. As he'd expected, there wasn't much on Lee Francis Bothwell, but there was a note referring him to files kept by Strathclyde Police in Partick.

The officer he talked to in Partick was not thrilled.

'All that old stuff's in the attic,' he told Rebus. 'I'll tell you, one of these days the ceiling'll come down.'

'Just go take a look, eh? Fax it to me, save yourself a phone call.'

An hour later, Rebus was handed several fax sheets relating to activities of the Tartan Army and the Workers' Party in the early 1970s. Both groups had enjoyed short anarchic lives, robbing banks to finance their arms purchases. The Tartan Army had wanted independence for Scotland, at any price. What the Workers' Party had wanted Rebus couldn't recall, and there was no mention of their objectives in the fax. The Tartan Army had been the bigger terror of the two, breaking into explosives stores and Army bases, building up an arms cache for an insurrection which never came.

Frankie Bothwell was mentioned as a Tartan Army supporter, but with no evidence against him of illegal acts. Rebus reckoned this would be just before his move to the Orkneys and rebirth as Cuchullain. Cuchullain of the Red Hand.

Arch Gowrie was probably at breakfast when Rebus caught him. He could hear the clink of cutlery on plate.

'Sorry to disturb you so early, sir.'

'More questions, Inspector? Maybe I should start charging a consultancy fee.'

'I was hoping you could help me with a name.' Gowrie

made a noncommittal noise, or maybe he was just chewing.

'Lee Francis Bothwell.'

'Frankie Bothwell?'

'You know him?'

'I used to.'

'He was a member of the Orange Lodge?'

'Yes, he was.'

'But he got kicked out?'

'Not quite. He left voluntarily.'

'Might I ask why, sir?'

'You might.' There was a pause. 'He was ... unpredictable, had a temper on him. Most of the time he was fine. He coached the youth football teams for a couple of district lodges, he seemed to enjoy that.'

'Was he interested in history?'

'Yes, Scottish and Irish history.'

'Cuchullain?'

'Amongst other things. I think he wrote a couple of articles for *Ulster*, that's the magazine of the UDA. He did them under a pseudonym, so we couldn't discipline him, but the style was his. Loyalists, Inspector, are very interested in Irish pre-history. Bothwell was writing about the Cruithin. He was very bright like that, but he –'

'Did he have any links with the Orange Loyal Brigade?'

'Not that I know of, but it wouldn't surprise me. Gavin MacMurray's interested in pre-history too.' Gowrie sighed. 'Frankie left the Orange Lodge because he didn't feel we went far enough. That's as much as I'll say, but maybe it tells you something about him.'

'It does, Mr Gowrie, yes. Thanks for your help.'

Rebus put the phone down and thought it over. Then he shook his head sadly.

'You picked some place to hide her, Mairie. Some fucking place.'

His desk now looked like a skip, and he decided to do something about it. He filled his waste bin with empty cups, plates, crumpled papers and packets. Until, only slightly buried, he came to an A4-size manila envelope. His name was written on it in black marker pen. The envelope was fat. It hadn't been opened.

'Who left this here?'

But nobody seemed to know. They were too busy discussing another call made to the newspaper by the lunatic with the Irish accent. Nobody knew about The Shield, of course, not the way Rebus knew. The media had stuck to the theory that the body in Mary King's Close was that of the caller, a rogue from an IRA unit who'd been disciplined by his masters. It didn't make any sense now, but that didn't matter. There'd been another call now, another morning headline. ' "Shut the Whole Thing Down," says Threat Man.' Rebus had considered what benefit SaS could derive from disrupting the Festival. Answer: none.

He looked at the envelope a final time, then ran his finger under the flap and eased out a dozen sheets of paper, photocopies of reports, news stories. American, the lot of them, though whoever had done the copying had been careful, leaving off letter headings, addresses, phone numbers. As Rebus read, he couldn't be sure where half the stories originated. But one thing *was* clear, they were all about one man.

Clyde Moncur.

There were no messages, nothing handwritten, nothing to identify the sender. Rebus checked the envelope. It hadn't been posted. It had been delivered by hand. He asked around again, but nobody owned up to having ever seen the thing before. Mairie was the only source he could think of, but she wouldn't have sent the stuff like this.

He read through the file anyway. It reinforced his impression of Clyde Moncur. The man was a snake. He ran drugs up into Vancouver and across to Ontario. His boats brought in immigrants from the Far East, or often didn't, though they were known to have picked up travellers along the way. What happened to them, these people who paid to be transported to a better life? The bottom of the deep blue sea, seemed to be the inference.

There were other murky areas to Moncur's life, like his undeclared interest in a fish processing plant outside Toronto ... Toronto, home of The Shield. The US Internal Revenue had been trying for years to get to the bottom of it all, and failing.

Buried in all the clippings was the briefest mention of a Scottish salmon farm.

Moncur had imported Scottish smoked salmon into the USA, though the Canadian stuff was just a mite closer to hand. The salmon farm he used was just north of Kyle of Lochalsh. Its name struck home. Rebus had come across the name very recently. He went back to the files on Cafferty, and there it was. Cafferty had been legitimate part-owner of the farm in the 1970s and early 80s ... around the time him and Jinky Johnson were washing and drying dirty money for the UVF.

'This is beautiful,' Rebus said to himself. He hadn't just squared the circle, he'd created an unholy triangle out of it.

He got a patrol car to take him to the Gar-B.

From the back seat, he had a more relaxed view of the whole of Pilmuir. Clyde Moncur had talked about the early Scottish settlers. The new settlers, of course, took on just as tough a life, moving into the private estates which were being built around and even *in* Pilmuir. This was a frontier life, complete with marauding natives who wanted the intruders gone, border skirmishes, and wilderness experiences aplenty. These estates provided starter homes for those making the move from the rented sector. They also provided starter courses in basic survival.

Rebus wished the settlers well.

When they got to the Gar-B, Rebus gave the uniforms their instructions and sat in the back seat enjoying the stares of passers-by. They were away a while, but when they came back one of them was pulling a boy by his forearm and pushing the boy's bike. The other one had two kids, no bikes. Rebus looked at them. He recognised the one with the bike.

'You can let the others go,' he said. 'But him, I want in here with me.'

The boy got into the car reluctantly. His pals ran as soon as the officers released them. When they were far enough away, they turned to watch. They wanted to know what would happen.

'What's your name, son?' Rebus asked.

'Jock.'

Maybe it was true and maybe it wasn't. Rebus wasn't bothered. 'Shouldn't you be at school, Jock?'

'We've no' started back yet.'

This too could be true; Rebus didn't know. 'Do you remember me, son?'

'It wasnae me did your tyres.'

Rebus shook his head. 'That's all right. I'm not here about that. But you remember when I came here?' The boy nodded. 'Remember you were with a pal, and he thought I was someone else. Remember? He asked me where my flash car was.' The boy shook his head. 'And you told him that I wasn't who he thought I was. Who did he think I was, son?'

'I don't know.'

'Yes you do.'

'I don't.'

'But someone a bit like me, eh? Similar build, age, height? Fancier clothes though, I'll bet.'

'Maybe.'

'What about his car, the swanky car?'

'A custom Merc.'

Rebus smiled. There were some things boys just had eyes and a memory for. 'What colour Merc?'

'Black, all of it. The windows too.'

'Seen him here a lot?'

'Don't know.'

'Nice car though, eh?'

The boy shrugged.

'Right, son, on you go.'

The boy knew from the pleased look on the policeman's face that he'd made a mistake, that he'd somehow helped. His cheeks burned with shame. He snatched his bike from the constable and ran with it, looking back from time to time. His pals were waiting to question him.

'Get what you were looking for, sir?' asked one of the uniforms, getting back into the car.

'Exactly what I was looking for,' said Rebus.

# 25

He went to see Mairie, but a friend was looking after her and Mairie herself was sleeping. The doctor had given her a few sleeping pills. Left alone in the flat with an unconscious Mairie, he could have gone through her notes and computer files, but the friend didn't even let him over the threshold. She had a pinched face with prominent cheeks and a few too many teeth in her quiet but determined mouth.

'Tell her I called,' Rebus said, giving up. He had retrieved his car from the back of the hotel. Cafferty would find him, with or without the rust-bucket to point the way. He drove to Fettes where DCI Kilpatrick had an update on the Clyde Moncur surveillance.

'He's acting the tourist, John, no more or less. He and his wife are admiring the sights, taking bus tours, buying souvenirs.' Kilpatrick sat back in his chair. 'The men I put on it are restless. Like they say, it's hardly likely he's here on business when his wife's with him.'

'Or else it's the perfect cover.'

'A couple more days, John, that's all we can give it.'

'I appreciate it, sir.'

'What about this body at the Crazy Hose?'

'Millie Docherty, sir.'

'Yes, any ideas?'

Rebus just shrugged. Kilpatrick didn't seem to expect an answer. Part of his mind was still on Calumn Smylie. They were about to open an internal inquiry. There would be questions to answer about the whole investigation.

'I hear you had a run in with Smylie,' Kilpatrick said.

So Ormiston had been talking. 'Just one of those things, sir.'

'Watch out for Smylie, John.'

'That's all I seem to do these days, sir, watch out for people.' But he knew now that Smylie was the least of his problems.

At St Leonard's, DCI Lauderdale was fighting his corner, arguing that his team should take on the Millie Docherty investigation from C Division. So he was too busy to come bothering Rebus, and that was fine by Rebus.

Officers were out at Lachlan Murdock's flat, talking to him. He was being treated as a serious suspect now; you didn't lose two flatmates to hideous deaths and not come under the microscope. Murdock would be on the petri dish from now till the case reached some kind of conclusion. Rebus returned to his desk. Since he'd last been there, earlier in the day, people had started using it as a rubbish bin again.

He phoned London, and waited to be passed along the line. It was not a call he could have made from Fettes.

'Abernethy speaking.'

'About bloody time. It's DI Rebus here.'

'Well well. I wondered if I'd hear from you.'

Rebus could imagine Abernethy leaning back in his chair. Maybe his feet were up on the desk in front of him. 'I must have left a dozen messages, Abernethy.'

'I've been busy, what about you?' Rebus stayed silent. 'So, Inspector Rebus, how can I help?'

'I've got a few questions. How much stuff is the Army losing?'

'You've lost me.'

'I don't think so.' Someone walking past offered Rebus a cigarette. Without thinking he accepted it. But then the donor walked away, leaving Rebus without a light. He sucked on the filter anyway. 'I think you know what I'm talking about.' He opened the desk drawers, looking for matches or a lighter.

'Well, I don't.'

'I think material has been going missing.'

'Really?'

'Yes, really.' Rebus waited. He didn't want to speculate too wildly, and he certainly didn't want Abernethy to know any more than was necessary. But there was silence on the other end of the line. 'Or you suspect it's going missing.'

'That would be a matter for Army Intelligence or the security service.'

'Yes, but you're Special Branch, aren't you? You're the public arm of the security service. I think you came up here in a hurry because you damned well know what's going on. The question is, why did you disappear again in such a hurry too?'

'You've lost me again. Maybe I'd better pack my bag for a trip, what do you say?'

Rebus didn't say anything, he just put down the phone. 'Anyone got a light?' Someone tossed a box of matches onto the desk. 'Cheers.' He lit the cigarette and inhaled, the smoke rattling his nerves like they were dice in a cup.

He knew Abernethy would come.

He kept moving, the most difficult kind of target. He was trusting to his instincts; after all, he had to trust something. Dr Curt was in his office at the university. To get to the office you had to walk past a row of wooden boxes marked with the words 'Place Frozen Sections Here'. Rebus had never looked in the boxes. In the Pathology building, you kept your eyes front and your nostrils tight. They were doing some work in the quadrangle. Scaffolding had been erected, and a couple of workmen were belying their name by sitting on it smoking cigarettes and sharing a newspaper.

'Busy, busy, busy,' Curt said, when Rebus reached his office. 'You know, most of the university staff are on holiday.

I've had postcards from the Gambia, Queensland, Florida.' He sighed. 'I am cursed with a vocation while others get a vacation.'

'I bet you were awake all night thinking up that one.'

'I was awake half the night thanks to your discovery at the Crazy Hose Saloon.'

'Post-mortem?'

'Not yet complete. It was a corrosive of some kind, the lab will tell us exactly which. I am constantly surprised by the methods murderers will resort to. The fire hose was new to me.'

'Well, it stops the job becoming routine, I suppose.'

'How's Caroline?'

'I'd forgotten all about her.'

'You must pray that she'll let you.'

'I stopped praying a long time ago.'

He walked back down the stairs and out into the quadrangle, wondering if it was too soon in the day for a drink at Sandy Bell's. The pub was just round the corner, and he hadn't been there in months. He noticed someone standing in front of the Frozen Sections boxes. They had the flap open, like they'd just made a deposit. Then they turned around towards Rebus and smiled.

It was Cafferty.

'Dear God.'

Cafferty closed the flap. He was dressed in a baggy black suit and open-necked white shirt, like an undertaker on his break. 'Hello, Strawman.' The old nickname. It was like an ice-pack on Rebus's spine. 'Let's talk.' There were two men behind Rebus, the two from the churchyard, the two who'd watched him taking a beating. They escorted him back to a newish Rover parked in the quadrangle. He caught the licence number, but felt Cafferty's hand land on his shoulder.

'We'll change plates this afternoon, Strawman.' Someone was getting out of the car. It was weasel-face. Rebus and Cafferty got into the back of the car, weasel-face and one of the heavies into the front. The other heavy stood outside, blocking Rebus's door. He looked towards where the scaffolding stood. The workmen had vanished. There was a sign on the scaffolding, just the name of a firm and their telephone number. A light came on in practically the last dark room in Rebus's head.

Big Ger Cafferty had made no effort at disguise. His clothes didn't look quite right – a bit large and not his style – but his face and hair were unchanged. A couple of students, one Asian and one Oriental, walked across the quadrangle towards the Pathology building. They didn't so much as glance at the car.

'I see your stomach cleared up.'

Cafferty smiled. 'Fresh air and exercise, Strawman. You look like you could do with both.'

'You're crazy coming back here.'

'We both know I had to.'

'We'll have you inside again in a matter of days.'

'Maybe I only need a few days. How close are you?'

Rebus stared through the windscreen. He felt Cafferty's hand cover his knee.

'Speaking as one father to another . . .'

'You leave my daughter out of this!'

'She's in London, isn't she? I've a lot of friends in London.'

'And I'll tear them to shreds if she so much as stubs a toe.'

Cafferty smiled. 'See? See how easy it is to get worked up when it's family?'

'It's not family with you, Cafferty, you said so yourself. It's business.'

'We could do a trade.' Cafferty looked out of his window, as though thinking. 'Say someone's been bothering you, could be an old flame. Let's say she's been disrupting your life, making things awkward.' He paused. 'Making you see red.'

Rebus nodded to himself. So weasel-face had witnessed the little scene with the spray-can.

'My problem, not yours.'

Cafferty sighed. 'Sometimes I wonder how hard you really are.' He looked at Rebus. 'I'd like to find out.'

'Try me.'

'I will, Strawman, one day. Trust me on that.'

'Why not now? Just you and me?'

Cafferty laughed. 'A square go? I haven't the time.'

'You used to shuffle cash around for the UVF, didn't you?'

The question caught Cafferty unaware. 'Did I?'

'Till Jinky Johnson disappeared. You were in pretty tight with the terrorists. Maybe that's where you heard of the SaS. Billy was a member.'

Cafferty's eyes were glassy. 'I don't know what you're saying.'

'No, but you know what I'm talking about. Ever heard the name Clyde Moncur?'

'No.'

'That sounds like another lie to me. What about Alan Fowler?'

Now Cafferty nodded. 'He was UVF.'

'Not now he isn't. Now he's SaS, and he's here. They're *both* here.'

'Why are you telling me?' Rebus didn't answer. Cafferty moved his face closer. 'It's not because you're scared. There's something else ... What's on your mind, Rebus?' Rebus stayed silent. He saw Dr Curt coming out of the Pathology building. Curt's car, a blue Saab, was parked three cars away from the Rover.

'You've been busy,' Cafferty said.

Now Curt was looking over towards the Rover, at the big man standing there and the men seated inside.

'Any more names?' Cafferty was beginning to sound impatient, losing all his cool veneer. 'I want *all of them*!' His right hand lashed around Rebus's throat, his left hand pushing him deep into the corner of the seat. 'Tell me all of it, all of it!'

Curt had turned as though forgetting something, and was walking back towards the building. Rebus blinked away the water in his eyes. The stooge outside thumped on the bodywork. Cafferty released his grip and watched Curt going back into Pathology. He used both hands to grasp Rebus's face, turning it towards his, holding Rebus with the pressure of his palms on Rebus's cheekbones.

'We'll meet again, Rebus, only it won't be like in the song.' Rebus felt like his head was going to crack, but then the pressure stopped.

The heavy outside opened the door and he got out fast. As the heavy got in, the driver gunned the engine. The back window went down, Cafferty looking at him, saying nothing.

The car sped off, tyres screeching as it turned into the one-way traffic on Teviot Place. Dr Curt appeared in the Pathology doorway, then came briskly across the quadrangle.

'Are you all right? I've just phoned the police.'

'Do me a favour, when they get here tell them you were mistaken.'

'What?'

'Tell them anything, but don't tell them it was me.'

Rebus started to move off. Maybe he'd have that drink at Sandy Bell's. Maybe he'd have three.

'I'm not a very good liar,' Dr Curt called after him.

'Then the practice will be good for you,' Rebus called back.


Frankie Bothwell shook his head again.

'I've already spoken with the gentlemen from Torphichen Place. You want to ask anyone, ask them.'

He was being difficult. He'd had a difficult night, what with being dragged from his bed and then staying up till all hours dealing with the police, answering their questions, explaining the stash of cased spirits they'd found on the first floor. He didn't need this.

259

'But you knew Miss Murdoch was upstairs,' Rebus persisted.

'Is that right?' Bothwell wriggled on his barstool and tipped ash onto the floor.

'You were told she was upstairs.'

'Was I?'

'Your manager told you.'

'You've only got his word for that.'

'You deny he said it? Maybe if we could get the two of you together?'

'You can do what you like, he's out on his ear anyway. I sacked him first thing. Can't have people dossing upstairs like that, bad for the club's image. Let them sleep on the streets like everyone else.'

Rebus tried to imagine what resemblance the kid at the Gar-B had seen between himself and Frankie Bothwell. He was here because he was feeling reckless. Plus he'd put a few whiskies away in Sandy Bell's. He was here because he quite fancied beating Lee Francis Bothwell to a bloody mush on the dance floor.

Stripped of music and flashing lights and drink and dancers, the Crazy Hose had as much life as a warehouse full of last year's fashions. Bothwell, appearing to dismiss Rebus from his mind, lifted one foot and began to rub some dust from a cowboy boot. Rebus feared the white trousers would either split or else eviscerate their wearer. The boot was black and soft with small puckers covering it like miniature moon craters. Bothwell caught Rebus looking at it.

'Ostrich skin,' he explained.

Meaning the craters were where each feather had been plucked. 'Look like a lot of little arseholes,' Rebus said admiringly. Bothwell straightened up. 'Look, Mr Bothwell, all I want are a couple of answers. Is that so much to ask?'

'And then you'll leave?'

'Straight out the door.'

Bothwell sighed and flicked more ash onto the floor. 'Okay then.'

Rebus smiled his appreciation. He rested his hand on the bar and leaned towards Bothwell.

'Two questions,' he said. 'Why did you kill her and who's got the disk?'

Bothwell stared at him, then laughed. 'Get out of here.'

Rebus lifted his hand from the bar. 'I'm going,' he said. But he stopped at the doors to the foyer, holding them open. 'You know Cafferty's in town?'

'Never heard of him.'

'That's not the point. The point is, has *he* heard of *you*? Your father was a minister. Did you ever learn Latin?'

'What?'

'*Nemo me impune lacessit.*' Bothwell didn't even blink. 'Never mind, it won't worry Cafferty one way or the other. See, you didn't just meddle with him, you meddled with his family.'

He let the doors swing shut behind him. This was the way he should have worked it throughout, using Cafferty – the mere threat of Cafferty – to do his work for him. But would Cafferty be enough to scare the American and the Ulsterman?

Somehow, John Rebus doubted it.

Back at St Leonard's, Rebus first phoned the scaffolding company, then placed a call to Peter Cave.

'Something I've been meaning to ask you, sir,' he said.

'Yes?' Cave sounded tired, deep down inside.

'Since the Church stopped supporting the youth club, how do you survive?'

'We manage. Everyone who comes along has to pay.'

'Is it enough?'

'No.'

'You're not subsidising the place out of your own pocket?' Cave laughed at this. 'What then? Sponsorship?'

'In a way, yes.'

'What sort of way?'

'Just someone who saw the good the club was doing.'

'Someone you know?'

'Never met him, as a matter of fact.'

Rebus took a stab. 'Francis Bothwell?'

'How did you know that?'

'Someone told me,' Rebus lied.

'Davey?'

So Davey Soutar *did* know Bothwell. Yes, it figured. Maybe from a district lodge football team, maybe some other way. Time to change track.

'What does Davey do by the way?'

'Works in an abattoir.'

'He's not a builder then?'

'No.'

'One last thing, Mr Cave. I got a name from a scaffolding company: Malky Haston. He's eighteen, lives in the Gar-B.'

'I know Malky, Inspector. And he knows you.'

'How's that?'

'Heavy metal fan, always wears a band t-shirt. You've spoken with him.'

Black t-shirt, thought Rebus, Davey Soutar's pal. With white flecks in his hair that Rebus had mistaken for dandruff.

'Thank you, Mr Cave,' Rebus said, 'I think that's everything.'

Everything he needed.

A uniform approached as he put down the phone, and handed Rebus the information he'd requested on recent and not-so-recent break-ins. Rebus knew what he was looking for, and it didn't take long. Acid wasn't that easy to come by, not unless you had a plausible reason for wanting it. Easier to steal the stuff if you could. And where could you find acid?

Break-ins at Craigie Comprehensive School were fairly

262

standard. It was like pre-employment training for the unrulier pupils. They learned to slip a window-catch and jemmy open a door, some graduated to lock-picking, and others became fences for the stolen goods. It was always a buyers' market, but then economics was not a strong point with these junior careerists. Three months back, Craigie had been entered at the dead of night and the tuck shop emptied.

They'd also broken into the science rooms, physics and chemistry. The chemistry stock room had a different lock, but they took that out too, and made off with a large jar of methylated spirits, a few other choice cocktail ingredients, and three thick glass jars of various acids.

The caretaker, who lived in a small pre-fabricated house on the school grounds, saw and heard nothing. He'd been watching a special comedy night on the television. Probably he wouldn't have ventured out of doors anyway. Craigie Comprehensive wasn't exactly full of pupils with a sense of humour or love for their elders.

What could you expect from a school whose catchment area included the infamous Garibaldi Estate?

He was putting the pieces together when Chief Inspector Lauderdale came over.

'As if we're not stretched thin enough,' Lauderdale complained.

'What's that?'

'Another anonymous threat, that's twice today. He says our time's up.'

'Shame, I was just beginning to enjoy myself. Any specifics?'

Lauderdale nodded distractedly. 'A bomb. He didn't say where. He says it's so big there'll be no hiding place.'

'Festival's nearly over,' Rebus said.

'I know, that's what worries me.' Yes, it worried Rebus too.

Lauderdale turned to walk away, just as Rebus's phone rang.

'Inspector, my name's Blair-Fish, you won't remember me...'

'Of course I remember you, Mr Blair-Fish. Have you called to apologise about your grand-nephew again?'

'Oh no, nothing like that. But I'm a bit of a local historian, you see.'

'Yes.'

'And I was contacted by Matthew Vanderhyde. He said you wanted some information about Sword and Shield.'

Good old Vanderhyde: Rebus had given up on him. 'Go on, please.'

'It's taken me a while. There was thirty years of detritus to wade through...'

'What have you got, Mr Blair-Fish?'

'Well, I've got notes of some meetings, a treasurer's report, minutes and things like that. Plus the membership lists. I'm afraid they're not complete.'

Rebus sat forward in his chair. 'Mr Blair-Fish, I'd like to send someone over to collect everything from you. Would that be all right?' Rebus was reaching for pen and paper.

'Well, I suppose ... I don't see why not.'

'Let's look on it as final atonement for your grand-nephew. Now if you'll just give me your address...'

Locals called it the Meat Market, because it was sited close to the slaughterhouse. Workers from the slaughterhouses wandered in at lunchtime for pints, pies and cigarettes. Sometimes they wore flecks of blood; the owner didn't mind. He'd been one of them once, working the jet-air gun at a chicken factory. The pistol, hooked up to a compressor, had taken the heads off several hundred stunned chickens per hour. He ran the Meat Market with the same unruffled facility.

It wasn't lunchtime, so the Market was quiet – two old

men drinking slow half pints at opposite ends of the bar, ignoring one another so studiously that there had to be a grudge between them, and two unemployed youths shooting pool and trying to make each game last, their pauses between shots the stuff of chess games. Finally, there was a man with sparks in his eyes. The proprietor was keeping a watch on him. He knew trouble when he saw it. The man was drinking whisky and water. He looked the sort of drinker, when he was mortal you wouldn't want to get in his way. He wasn't getting mortal just now; he was making the one drink last. But he didn't look like he was enjoying anything about it. Finally he finished the quarter gill.

'Take care,' the proprietor said.

'Thanks,' said John Rebus, heading for the door.

Slaughterhouse workers are a different breed.

They worked amid brain and offal, thick blood and shit, in a sanitised environment of whitewash and piped radio music. A huge electrical unit reached down from the ceiling to suck the smell away and pump in fresh air. The young man hosing blood into a drain did so expertly, spraying none of the liquid anywhere other than where he wanted it. And afterwards he turned down the pressure at the nozzle and hosed off his black rubber boots. He wore a white rubberised apron round his neck and stretching down to his knees, as did most of those around him. Aprons to Rebus meant barmen, masons and butchers. He was reminded only of this last as he walked across the floor.

They were working with cattle. The cows looked young and fearful, eyes bulging. They'd probably already been injected with muscle relaxants, so moved drunkenly along the line. A jolt of electricity behind either ear numbed them, and quickly the wielder of the bolt-gun took aim with the cold muzzle hard against each skull. Their back legs seemed to crumple first. Already the light was vanishing from behind their eyes.

He'd been told Davey Soutar was working near the back of the operation, so he had to pick his way around the routine. Men and women speckled with blood smiled and nodded as he passed. They all wore hats to keep their hair off the meat.

Or perhaps to keep the meat off their hair.

Soutar was by the back wall, resting easily against it, hands tucked into the front of his apron. He was talking to a girl, chatting her up perhaps.

So romance isn't dead, thought Rebus.

Then Soutar saw him, just as Rebus slipped on a wet patch of floor. Soutar placed him immediately, and seemed to raise his head and roll his eyes in defeat. Then he ran forward and picked something up from a shiny metal table. He was fumbling with it as Rebus advanced. It was only when Soutar took aim and the girl screamed that Rebus realised it was a bolt-gun. There was the sound of a two-pound hammer hitting a girder. The bolt flew, but Rebus dodged it. Soutar threw the gun at him and dived for the rear wall, hitting the bar of the emergency exit. The door swung open then closed again behind him. The girl was still screaming as Rebus ran towards her, pushed the horizontal bar to unlock the door, and stumbled into the abattoir's back yard.

There were a couple of large transporters in the middle of disgorging their doomed cargo. The animals were sending out distress calls as they were fed into holding pens. The entire rear area was walled in, so nobody from the outside world could glimpse the spectacle. But if you went around the transporters, a lane led back to the front of the building. Rebus was about to head that way when the blow felled him. It had come from behind. On his hands and knees, he half-turned his head to see his attacker. Soutar had been hiding behind the door. He was holding a long metal stick, a cattle prod. It was this which he had swung at Rebus's head, catching him on the left ear. Blood dropped onto the ground. Soutar lunged with the pole, but Rebus caught it and managed to pull himself up. Soutar kept moving forwards, but though wiry and young he did not possess the older man's bulk and strength. Rebus twisted the pole from his hands, then dodged the kick which Soutar aimed at him. Kick-fighting wasn't so easy with rubber boots on.

Rebus wanted to get close enough to land a good punch or kick of his own, or even to wrestle Soutar to the ground. But Soutar reached into his apron and came out with a gold-coloured butterfly knife, flicking its two moulded wings to make a handle for the vicious looking blade.

'There's more than one way to skin a pig,' he said, grinning, breathing hard.

'I like it when there's an audience,' Rebus said. Soutar turned for a second to take in the sight of the cattle herders, all of whom had stopped work to watch the fight. By the time he looked back, Rebus had caught the knife hand with the toe of his shoe, sending the knife clattering to the ground. Soutar came straight for him then, butting him on the bridge of the nose. It was a good hit. Rebus's eyes filled with tears, he felt energy earth out of him into the ground, and blood ran down his lips and chin.

'You're dead!' Soutar screamed. 'You just don't know it yet!' He picked up his knife, but Rebus had the metal pole, and swung it in a wide arc. Soutar hesitated, then ran for it. He took a short cut, climbing the rail which funnelled the cattle into the pens, then leaping one of the cows and clearing the rail at the other side.

'Stop him!' Rebus called, spraying blood. 'I'm a police officer!' But by then Davey Soutar was out of sight. All you could hear were his rubber boots flapping as he ran.

The doctor at the Infirmary had seen Rebus several times before, and tutted as usual before getting to work. She confirmed what he knew: the nose was not broken. He'd been lucky. The cut to his ear required two stitches, which she did there and then. The thread she used was thick and black and ugly.

'Whatever happened to invisible mending?'

'It wasn't a deterrent.'

'Fair point.'

'If it stings, you can always get your girlfriend to lick your wounds.'

Rebus smiled. Was that a chat-up line? Well, he had enough problems without adding another to the inventory. So he didn't say anything. He acted the good patient, then went to Fettes and filed the assault.

'You look like Ken Buchanan on a good night,' said Ormiston. 'Here's the stuff you wanted. Claverhouse has gone off in a huff; he didn't like being turned into a messenger boy.'

Ormiston patted the heavy package on Rebus's desk. It was a large brown cardboard box, smelling of dust and old paper. Rebus opened it and took out the ledger book which served as a membership record for the original Sword and Shield. The blue fountain-ink had faded, but each surname was in capitals so it didn't take him long. He sat staring at the two names, managing a short-lived smile. Not that he'd anything to smile about, not really. There was nothing to be proud of. His desk drawer didn't lock, but Ormiston's did. He took the ledger with him.

'Has the Chief seen this?' Ormiston shook his head.

'He's been out of the office since before it arrived.'

'I want it kept safe. Can you lock it in your drawer?' He watched Ormiston open the deep drawer, drop the package in, then shut it again and lock it.

'Tighter than a virgin's,' Ormiston confirmed.

'Thanks. Listen, I'm going out hunting.'

Ormiston drew the key out of the lock and pocketed it. 'Count me in,' he said.

# 26

Not that Rebus expected to find Davey Soutar at home; he doubted Soutar was quite that daft. But he did want to take a look, and now he had the excuse. He also had Ormiston, who looked threatening enough to dissuade anyone who might look like complaining. Ormiston, cheered by the story of how Rebus came by his cuts and bruises (his eyes were purpling and swelling nicely, a consequence of the head butt), was further cheered by the news that they were headed for the Gar-B.

'They should open the place as a safari park,' he opined. 'Remember those places? They used to tell you to keep your car doors locked and your windows rolled up. Same advice I'd give to anyone driving through the Gar-B. You never know when the baboons will stick their arses in your face.'

'Did you ever find anything about Sword and Shield?'

'You never expected us to,' Ormiston said. When Rebus looked at him, he laughed coldly. 'I might look daft, but I'm not. You're not daft either, are you? Way you're acting, I'd say you think you've cracked it.'

'Paramilitaries in the Gar-B,' Rebus said quietly, keeping his eyes on the road. 'And Soutar's in it up to his neck and beyond.'

'He killed Calumn?'

'Could be. A knife's his style.'

'Not Billy Cunningham though?'

'No, he didn't kill Billy.'

'Why are you telling me all this?'

Rebus turned to him for a moment. 'Maybe I just want someone else to know.'

Ormiston weighed this remark. 'You think you're in trouble?'

'I can think of half a dozen people who'd throw confetti at my funeral.'

'You should take this to the Chief.'

'Maybe. Would you?'

Ormiston thought about this. 'I haven't known him long, but I heard good things from Glasgow, and he seems pretty straight. He expects us to show initiative, work off our own backs. That's what I like about SCS, the leeway. I hear you like a bit of leeway yourself.'

'That reminds me, Lee Francis Bothwell: know him?'

'He owns that club, the one with the body in it?'

'That's him.'

'I know he should change the music.'

'What to?'

'Acid house.'

It was worth a laugh, but Rebus didn't oblige. 'He's an acquaintance of my assailant.'

'What is he, slumming it?'

'I'd like to ask him, but I can't see him answering. He's been putting money into the youth club.' Rebus was measuring each utterance, wondering how much to feed Ormiston.

'Very civic minded of him.'

'Especially for someone who got kicked out of the Orange Lodge on grounds of zeal.'

Ormiston frowned. 'How are you doing for evidence?'

'The youth club leader's admitted the connection. Some kids I spoke to a while back thought I was Bothwell, only my car wasn't flash enough. He drives a customised Merc.'

'How do you read it?'

'I think Peter Cave blundered with good intention into

something that was already happening. I think something very bad is happening in the Gar-B.'

They had to take a chance on parking the car and leaving it. If Rebus had thought about it, he'd have brought one other man, someone to guard the wheels. There were kids loitering by the parking bays, but not the same kids who'd done his tyres before, so he handed over a couple of quid and promised a couple more when he came back.

'It's dearer than the parking in town,' Ormiston complained as they headed for the high-rises. The Soutars' high-rise had been renovated, with a sturdy main door added to stop undesirables congregating in the entrance hall or on the stairwells. The entrance hall had been decorated with a green and red mural. Not that you would know any of this to look at the place. The lock had been smashed, and the door hung loosely on its hinges. The mural had been all but blocked out by penned graffiti and thick black coils of spray paint.

'Which floor are they on?' Ormiston asked.

'The third.'

'Then we'll take the stairs. I don't trust the lifts in these places.'

The stairs were at the end of the hall. Their walls had become a winding scribble-pad, but they didn't smell too bad. At each turn in the stairs lay empty cider cans and cigarette stubs. 'What do they need a youth club for when they've got the stairwell?' Ormiston asked.

'What've you got against the lift?'

'Sometimes the kids'll wait till you're between floors then shut off the power.' He looked at Rebus. 'My sister lives in one of those H-blocks in Oxgangs.'

They entered the third floor at the end of a long hallway which seemed to be doubling as a wind tunnel. There were fewer scribbles on the walls, but there were also smeared patches, evidence that the inhabitants had been cleaning the stuff off. Some of the doors offered polished brass name plaques and bristle doormats. But most were also protected by a barred iron gate, kept locked shut when the flats were empty. Each flat had a mortice deadlock as well as a Yale, and a spyhole.

'I've been in jails with laxer security.'

But conspicuously, the door with the name Soutar on it had no extra security, no gate or spyhole. This fact alone told Rebus a lot about Davey Soutar, or at least about his reputation amongst his peers. Nobody was going to break into Davey's flat.

There was neither bell nor knocker, so Rebus banged his fist against the meat of the door. After a wait, a woman answered. She peered out through a chink, then opened the door wide.

'Fuckin' polis,' she said. It was a statement of fact rather than a judgment. 'Davey, I suppose?'

'It's Davey,' said Rebus.

'He did that to you?' She meant Rebus's face, so he nodded. 'And what were you doing to him?'

'Just the usual, Mrs Soutar,' Ormiston interrupted. 'A length of lead pipe on the soles of the feet, a wet towel over the face, you know how it is.'

Rebus nearly said something, but Ormiston had judged her right. Mrs Soutar smiled tiredly and stepped back into her hall. 'You'd better come in. A bit of steak would stop those eyes swelling, but all I've got is half a pound of mince, and it's the economy stuff. You'd get more meat from a butcher's pencil. This is my man, Dod.'

She had led them along the short narrow hall and into a small living room where a venerable three-piece suite took up too much space. Along the sofa, his shoeless feet resting on one arm of it, lay an unshaven man in his forties, or perhaps even badly nurtured thirties. He was reading a war comic, his lips moving with the words on the page.

'Hiy, Dod,' Mrs Soutar said loudly, 'these are the polis. Davey's just put the heid on one of them.'

'Good for him,' Dod said without looking up. 'No offence, like.'

'None taken.' Rebus had wandered over to the window, wondering what the view was like. The window, however, was a botched piece of double glazing. Condensation had crept between the panes, frosting the glass.

'It wasn't much of a view to start with,' Mrs Soutar said. He turned and smiled at her. He didn't doubt she would see through any scheme, any lie. She was a short, strong-looking woman, big boned with a chiselled jaw but a pleasant face. If she didn't smile often, it was because she had to protect herself. She couldn't afford to look weak. In the Gar-B, the weak didn't last long. Rebus wondered how much influence she'd had over her son while he was growing up here. A lot, he'd say. But then the father would be an influence too.

She kept her arms folded while she talked, unfolding them only long enough to slap Dod's feet off the end of the sofa so she could sit herself down on the arm.

'So what's he done this time?'

Dod put down his comic and reached into his packet of cigarettes, lighting one for himself and handing the pack to Mrs Soutar.

'He's assaulted a police officer for a start,' Rebus said. 'That's a pretty serious offence, Mrs Soutar. It could land him a spell in the carpentry shop.'

'You mean the jail?' Dod pronounced it, 'jyle'.

'That's what I mean.'

Dod stood up, then half doubled over, seized by a cough which crackled with phlegm. He went into the kitchenette, separated from the living room by a breakfast bar, and spat into the sink.

'Run the tap!' Mrs Soutar ordered. Rebus was looking at her. She was looking sad but resilient. It took her only a moment to shrug off the idea of the prison sentence. 'He'd be better off in jail.'

'How's that?'

'This is the Gar-B, or hadn't you noticed? It does things to you, to the young ones especially. Davey'd be better off out of the place.'

'What has it done to him, Mrs Soutar?'

She stared at him, considering how long an answer to give. 'Nothing,' she said finally. Ormiston was standing by the wall unit, studying a pile of cassettes next to the cheap hi-fi system. 'Put some music on if you like,' she told him. 'Might cheer us up.'

'Okay,' said Ormiston, opening a cassette case.

'I was joking.'

But Ormiston just smiled, slammed the tape home, and pressed play. Rebus wondered what he was up to. Then the music started, an accordion at first, joined by flutes and drums, and then a quavering voice, using vibrato in place of skill.

The song was 'The Sash'. Ormiston handed the cassette case to Rebus. The cover was a cheap Xeroxed drawing of the Red Hand of Ulster, the band's name scratched on it in black ink. They were called the Proud Red Hand Marching Band, though it was hard to conceive of anyone marching to an accordion.

Dod, who had returned from the sink, started whistling along and clapping his hands. 'It's a grand old tune, eh?'

'What do you want to put that on for?' Mrs Soutar asked Ormiston. He shrugged, saying nothing.

'Aye, a grand old tune.' Dod collapsed onto the sofa. The woman glared at him.

'It's bigotry's what it is. I've nothing against the Catholics.'

'Well neither have I,' Dod countered. He winked at Ormiston. 'But there's no shame in being proud of your roots.'

274

'What about Davey, Mr Soutar? Does he have anything against Catholics?'

'No.'

'No? He seems to run around with Protestant gangs.'

'It's the Gar-B,' Mr Soutar said. 'You have to belong.'

Rebus knew what he was saying. Dod Soutar sat forward on the sofa.

'Ye see, it's history, isn't it? The Protestants have run Ulster for hundreds of years. Nobody's going to give that up, are they? Not if the other lot are sniping away and planting bombs and that.' He realised that Ormiston had turned off the tape. 'Well, isn't that right? It's a religious war, you can't deny it.'

'Ever been there?' Ormiston asked. Dod shook his head. 'Then what the fuck do you know about it?'

Dod gave a challenging look, and stood up. 'I know, pal, don't think I don't.'

'Aye, right,' Ormiston said.

'I thought you were here to talk about my Davey?'

'We are talking about Davey, Mrs Soutar,' Rebus said quietly. 'In a roundabout way.' He turned to Dod Soutar. 'There's a lot of you in your son, Mr Soutar.'

Dod Soutar turned his combative gaze from Ormiston. 'Oh aye?'

Rebus nodded. 'I'm sorry, but there it is.'

Dod Soutar's face creased into an angry scowl. 'Wait a fuckn minute, pal. Think you can walk in here and fuckn –'

'People like you terrify me,' Rebus said coolly. He meant it, too. Dod Soutar, hacking cough and all, was a more horrifying prospect than a dozen Caffertys. You couldn't change him, couldn't argue with him, couldn't touch his mind in any way. He was a closed shop, and the management had all gone home.

'My son's a good boy, brought up the right way,' Soutar was saying. 'Gave him everything I could.'

'Some folk are just born lucky,' said Ormiston.

That did it. Soutar launched himself across the narrow width of the room. He went for Ormiston with his head low and both fists out in front of him, but collided with the shelf unit when Ormiston stepped smartly aside. He turned back towards the two policemen, swinging wildly, swearing barely coherent phrases. When he went for Rebus, and Rebus arched back so that the swipe missed, Rebus decided he'd had enough. He kneed Soutar in the crotch.

'Queensferry Rules,' he said, as the man went down.

'Dod!' Mrs Soutar ran to her husband. Rebus gestured to Ormiston.

'Get out of my house!' Mrs Soutar screamed after them. She came to the front door and kept on yelling and crying. Then she went indoors and slammed her door.

'The cassette was a nice touch,' Rebus said on his way downstairs.

'Thought you'd appreciate it. Where to now?'

'While we're here,' said Rebus, 'maybe the youth club.'

They walked outside and didn't hear anything until the vase hit the ground beside them, smashing into a thousand pieces of shrapnel. Mrs Soutar was at her window.

'Missed!' Rebus yelled at her.

'Jesus Christ,' Ormiston said, as they walked away.

The usual lacklustre teenagers sat around outside the community hall, propping their backs against its door and walls. Rebus didn't bother to ask about Davey Soutar. He knew what the response would be; it had been drilled into them like catechism. His ear was tingling, not hurting exactly, but there was a dull throbbing pain in his nose. When they recognised Rebus, the gang got to their feet.

'Afternoon,' Ormiston said. 'You're right to stand up, by the way. Sitting on concrete gives you piles.'

In the hall, Jim Hay and his theatre group were sitting on the stage. Hay too recognised Rebus.

'Guess what?' he said. 'We have to mount a guard, otherwise they rip the stuff off.'

Rebus didn't know whether to believe him or not. He was more interested in the youth sitting next to Hay.

'Remember me, Malky?'

Malky Haston shook his head.

'I've got a few questions for you, Malky. Want to do it here or down the station?'

Haston laughed. 'You couldn't take me out of here, not if I didn't want to go.'

He had a point. 'We'll do it here then,' said Rebus. He turned to Hay, who raised his hands.

'I know, you want us to take a fag break.' He got up and led his troupe away. Ormiston went to the door to stop anyone else coming in.

Rebus sat on the stage next to Haston, getting close, making the teenager uncomfortable.

'I've done nothing, and I'm saying nothing.'

'Have you known Davey a while?'

Haston said nothing.

'I'd imagine since you were kids,' Rebus answered. 'Remember the first time we met? You had bits in your hair. I thought it was dandruff, but it was plaster. I spoke to ScotScaf. They hire out scaffolding to building contractors, and when it comes back it's your job to clean it. Isn't that right?'

Haston just looked at him.

'You're under orders not to talk, eh? Well, I don't mind.' Rebus stood up, facing Haston. 'There was ScotScaf scaffolding at the two murder sites, Billy's and Calumn Smylie's. You told Davey, didn't you? You knew where building work was going on, empty sites, all that.' He leaned close to Haston's face. 'You *knew*. That makes you an accessory at the very least. And that means we're going to throw you in jail. We'll pick out a nice Catholic wing for you, Malky, don't worry. Plenty of the green and white.'

277

Rebus turned his back and lit a cigarette. When he turned back to Haston, he offered him one. Ormiston was having a bit of bother at the door. The gang wanted in. Haston took a cigarette. Rebus lit it for him.

'Doesn't matter what you do, Malky. You can run, you can lie, you can say nothing at all. You're going away, and we're the only friends you'll ever have.'

He turned away and walked towards Ormiston. 'Let them in,' he ordered. The gang came crashing through the doors, fanning out across the hall. They could see Malky Haston was all right, though he was sitting very still on the edge of the stage. Rebus called to him.

'Thanks for the chat, Malky. We'll talk again, any time you want.' Then he turned to the gang. 'Malky's got his head screwed on,' he told them. '*He* knows when to talk.'

'Lying bastard!' Haston roared, as Rebus and Ormiston walked into the daylight.


Rebus met Lachlan Murdock at the Crazy Hose, despite Bothwell's protests.

Murdock's uncombed hair was wilder than ever, his clothes sloppy. He was waiting in the foyer when Rebus arrived.

'They all think I had something to do with it,' Murdock protested as Rebus led him into the dancehall.

'Well, you did, in a way,' Rebus said.

'What?'

'Come on, I want to show you something.'

He led Murdock up to the attic. In the daytime, the attic was a lot lighter. Even so, Rebus had brought a torch. He didn't want Murdock to miss anything.

'This,' he said, 'is where I found her. She'd suffered, believe me.' Already, Murdock was close to fresh tears, but sympathy could wait, the truth couldn't. 'I found this on the floor.' He handed over the disk cover. 'This is what they killed her for. A computer disk, same size as would fit your machine at home.' He walked up close to Murdock's slouched figure. 'They killed her for *this*!' he hissed. He waited a moment, then moved away towards the windows.

'I thought maybe she'd have made a copy. She wasn't daft, was she? But I went to the shop, and there's nothing there. Maybe in your flat?' Murdock just sniffed. 'I can't believe she –'

'There was a copy,' Murdock groaned. 'I wiped it.'

Rebus walked back towards him. 'Why?'

Murdock shook his head. 'I didn't think it . . .' He took a deep breath. 'It reminded me . . .'

Rebus nodded. 'Ah yes, Billy Cunningham. It reminded you of the pair of them. When did you begin to suspect?'

Murdock shook his head again.

'See,' said Rebus, 'I know most of it. I know enough. But I don't know it all. Did you look at the files on the disk?'

'I looked.' He wiped his red-rimmed eyes. 'It was Billy's disk, not hers. But a lot of the stuff on it was hers.'

'I don't understand.'

Murdock managed a weak smile. 'You're right, I did know about the two of them. I didn't want to know, but I knew all the same. When I wiped the disk, I was angry, I was *so* angry.' He turned to look at Rebus. 'I don't think he could have done it without Millie. You need quite a set-up to hack into the kinds of systems they were dealing with.'

'Hacking?'

'They probably used the stuff in her shop. They hacked into Army and police computers, bypassed security, invaded datafiles, then marched out again without leaving any trace.'

'So what did they do?'

Murdock was talking now, enjoying the release. He wiped tears from below his glasses. 'They monitored a couple of police investigations and altered a few inventories. Believe me, once they were in, they could have done a lot more.'

The way Murdock went on to explain it, it was almost ludicrously simple. You could steal from the Army (with inside assistance, there had to be inside assistance), and then erase the theft by altering the computer records to show stocks as they stood, not as they had been. Then, if SCS or Scotland Yard or anyone else took an interest, you could monitor their progress or lack of it. Millie: Millie had been the key throughout. Whether or not she knew what she was doing, she got Billy Cunningham in. He placed her in the lock and turned. The disk had contained instructions on their hacking procedures, tips for bypassing security checks, the works.

Rebus didn't doubt that the further Billy Cunningham got in, the more he wanted out. He'd been killed because he wanted out. He'd probably mentioned his little insurance policy in the hope they would let him leave quietly. Instead, they'd tried to torture its whereabouts out of him, before delivering the final silencing bullet. Of course, The Shield knew Billy wasn't hacking alone. It wouldn't have taken them long to get to Millie Docherty. Billy had stayed silent to protect her. She must have known. That's why she'd run.

'There was stuff about this group, too, The Shield,' Murdock was saying. 'I thought they were just a bunch of hackers.'

Rebus tried him with a few names. Davey Soutar and Jamesie MacMurray hit home. Rebus reckoned that in an interview room he could crack Jamesie like a walnut under a hammer. But Davey Soutar ... well, he might need a real hammer for that. The final file on the computer was all about Davey Soutar and the Gar-B.

'This Soutar,' Murdock said, 'Billy seemed to think he'd been skimming. That was the word he used. There's some stuff stashed in a lock-up out at Currie.'

Currie: the lock-up would belong to the MacMurrays.

Murdock looked at Rebus. 'He didn't say what was being skimmed. Is it money?'

'I underestimated you, Davey,' Rebus said aloud. 'All down the line. It might be too late now, but I swear I won't underestimate you again.' He thought of how Davey and his kind hated the Festival. Hated it with a vengeance. He thought of the anonymous threats.

'Not money, Mr Murdock. Weapons and explosives. Come on, let's get out of here.'

Jamesie talked like a man coming out of silent retreat, especially when his father, hearing the story from Rebus, ordered him to. Gavin MacMurray was incensed, not that his son should be in trouble, but that the Orange Loyal Brigade hadn't been enough for him. It was a betrayal.

Jamesie led Rebus and the other officers to a row of wooden garages on a piece of land behind MacMurray's Garage. Two Army men were on hand. They checked for booby traps and trip wires and it took them nearly half an hour to get round to going in. Even then, they did not enter by the door. Instead, they climbed a ladder to the roof and cut through the asphalt covering, then dropped through and into the lock-up. A minute later, they gave the all clear, and a police constable broke open the door with a crowbar. Gavin MacMurray was with them.

'I haven't been in here for years,' he said. He'd said it before, as if they didn't believe him. 'I never use these garages.'

They had a good look round. Jamesie didn't know the precise location of the cache, only that Davey had said he needed a place to keep it. The garage had operated as a motorcycle workshop – that was how Billy Cunningham had got to know Jamesie, and through him Davey Soutar, in the first place. There were long rickety wooden shelves groaning with obscure metal parts, a lot of them rusted brown with age, tools covered with dust and cobwebs, and tins of paint and solvent. Each tin had to be opened, each tool examined. If you could hide Semtex in a transistor radio, you could certainly hide it in a tool shed. The Army had offered a specialised sniffer dog, but it would have to come from Aldershot. So instead they used their own eyes and noses and instinct.

Hanging from nails on the walls were old tyres and wheels and chains. Forks and handlebars lay on the floor along with engine parts and mouldy boxes of nuts, bolts and screws. They scraped at the floor, but found no buried boxes. There was a lot of oil on the ground.

'This place is clean,' said a smudged Army man. Rebus nodded agreement.

'He's been and cleared the place out. How much was there, Jamesie?'

But Jamesie MacMurray had been asked this before, and he didn't know. 'I swear I don't. I just said he could use the space. He got his own padlock fitted and everything.'

Rebus stared at him. These young hard men, Rebus had been dealing with them all his life and they were pathetic, like husks in suits of armour. Jamesie was about as hard as the *Sun* crossword. 'And he never showed you?'

Jamesie shook his head. 'Never.'

His father was staring at him furiously. 'You stupid wee bastard,' Gavin MacMurray said. 'You stupid, stupid wee fool.'

'We'll have to take Jamesie down the station, Mr Mac-Murray.'

'I know that.' Then Gavin MacMurray slapped his son's face. With a hand callused by years of mechanical work, he loosened teeth and sent blood curdling from Jamesie's mouth. Jamesie spat on the dirt floor but said nothing. Rebus knew Jamesie was going to tell them everything he knew.

Outside, one of the Army men smiled in relief. 'I'm glad we didn't find anything.'

'Why?'

'Keeping the stuff in an environment like that, it's bound to be unstable.'

'Just like the guy who's got it.' Unstable . . . Rebus thought of Unstable from Dunstable, confessing to the St Stephen Street killing, raving to DI Flower about curry and cars . . . He walked back into the garage and pointed to the stain on the floor.

'That's not oil,' he said, 'not all of it.'

'What?'

'Everybody out, I want this place secured.'

They all got out. Flower should have listened to Unstable from Dunstable. The tramp had been talking about Currie, not curry. And he'd said cars because of the garages. He must have been sleeping rough nearby and seen or heard something that night.

'What is it, sir?' one of the officers asked Rebus.

'If I'm right, this is where they killed Calumn Smylie.'


That evening, Rebus moved out of the hotel and back into Patience's flat. He felt exhausted, like a tool that had lost its edge. The stain on the garage floor had been a mixture of oil and blood. They were trying to separate the two so they could DNA-test the blood against Calumn Smylie's. Rebus knew already what they'd find. It all made sense when you thought about it.

He poured a drink, then thought better of it. Instead he phoned Patience and told her she could come home in the next day or two. But she was determined to return in the morning, so he told her why she shouldn't. She was very quiet for a moment.

'Be careful, John.'

'I'm still here, aren't I?'

'Let's keep it that way.'

He rang off when he heard the doorbell. The manhunt for Davey Soutar was in full swing, under the control of CI

Lauderdale at St Leonard's. Arms would be issued as and when necessary. Though they didn't know the extent of Soutar's cache, no chances would be taken. Rebus had been asked if he'd like a bodyguard.

'I'll trust to my guardian angel,' he'd said.

The doorbell rang again. He felt naked as he walked down the long straight hall towards the door. The door itself was inch-and-a-half thick wood, but most guns could cope with that and still leave enough velocity in the bullet to puncture human flesh. He listened for a second, then put his eye to the spy-hole. He let his breath out and unlocked the door.

'You've got things to tell me,' he said, opening the door wide.

Abernethy produced a bottle of whisky from behind his back. 'And I've brought some antiseptic for those cuts.'

'Internal use only,' Rebus suggested.

'The money it cost me, you better believe it. Still, a nice drop of Scotch is worth all the tea in China.'

'We call it whisky up here.' Rebus closed the door and led Abernethy back down the hall into the living room. Abernethy was impressed.

'Been taking a few back-handers?'

'I live with a doctor. It's her flat.'

'My mum always wanted me to be a doctor. A respectable job, she called it. Got some glasses?'

Rebus fetched two large glasses from the kitchen.

# 27

Frankie Bothwell couldn't afford to close the Crazy Hose.

The Festival and Fringe had only a couple more days to go. All too soon the tourists would be leaving. But over the past fortnight he'd really been packing them in. Advertising and word of mouth helped, as had a three-night residency by an American country singer. The club was making more money than ever before, but it wouldn't last. The Crazy Hose was unique, every bit as unique as Frankie himself. It deserved to do well. It *had* to do well. Frankie Bothwell had commitments, financial commitments. They couldn't be broken or excused because of low takings. Every week needed to be a good week.

So he was not best pleased to see Rebus and another cop walk into the bar. You could see it in his eyes and the smile as frozen as a Crazy Hose daiquiri.

'Inspector, how can I help you?'

'Mr Bothwell, this is DI Abernethy. We'd like a word.'

'It's a bit hectic just now. I haven't had a chance to replace Kevin Strang.'

'We insist,' said Abernethy.

With two conspicuous police officers on the premises, trade at the bars wasn't exactly brisk, and nobody was dancing. They were all waiting for something to happen. Bothwell took this in.

'Let's go to my office.'

Abernethy waved bye-bye to the crowd as he followed Rebus and Bothwell into the foyer. They went behind the admission desk and Bothwell unlocked a door. He sat behind his desk and watched them squeeze their way into the space that was left.

'A big office is a waste of space,' he said by way of apology. The place was like a cleaning cupboard. There were spare till rolls and boxes of glasses on a shelf above Bothwell's head, framed cowboy posters stacked against a wall, bric-a-brac and debris like everything had just spilled out of a collision at a car boot sale.

'We might be more comfortable talking in the toilets,' Rebus said.

'Or down the station,' offered Abernethy.

'I don't think we've met,' Bothwell said to him, affably enough.

'I usually only meet shit when I wipe my arse.'

That took the smile off Bothwell's face.

'Inspector Abernethy,' Rebus said, 'is Special Branch. He's here investigating The Shield.'

'The Shield?'

'No need to be coy, Mr Bothwell. You're not being charged, not yet. We just want you to know we're on to you in a big way.'

'And we're not about to let go,' Abernethy said on cue.

'Though it might help your case if you told us about Davey Soutar.' Rebus placed his hands in his lap and waited. Abernethy lit a cigarette and blew the smoke across the strewn desk. Frankie Bothwell looked from one man to the other and back again.

'Is this a joke? I mean, it's a bit early for Halloween, that's when you're supposed to scare people without any reason.'

Rebus shook his head. 'Wrong answer. What you should have said was, "Who's Davey Soutar?"'

Bothwell sat back in his chair. 'All right then, who's Davey Soutar?'

'I'm glad you asked me that,' said Rebus. 'He's your

286

lieutenant. Maybe he's also your recruiting officer. And now he's on the run. Did you know he's been keeping back some of the explosives and guns for himself? We've got a confession.' It was a blatant lie, and caused Bothwell to smile. That smile sealed Bothwell's guilt in Rebus's mind.

'Why have you been funding the Gar-B youth centre?' he asked. 'Is it a useful recruiting station? You took the name Cuchullain when you were an anarchist. He's the great Ulster hero, the original Red Hand. That was no accident. You were dismissed from the Orange Lodge for being a bit over-zealous. In the early '70s your name was linked to the Tartan Army. They used to break into Army bases and steal weapons. Maybe that's what gave you the idea.'

Bothwell was still smiling as he asked, 'What idea?'

'You know.'

'Inspector, I haven't understood a word you've said.'

'No? Then understand this, we're a bollock-hair's breadth away from you. But more importantly, we want to find Davey Soutar, because if he's gone rogue with rifles and plastic explosives...'

'I still don't know what you're –'

Rebus jumped from his seat and grabbed Bothwell's lapels, pulling him tight against the desk. Bothwell's smile evaporated.

'I've been to Belfast, Bothwell, I've spent time in the North. The last thing that place needs is cowboys like you. So put away your forked tongue and tell us where he is!'

Bothwell wrenched himself out of Rebus's grip, his lapel tearing down the middle in the process. His face was purple, eyes blazing. He stood with his knuckles on the edge of the desk, leaning over it, his face close to Rebus's.

'Nobody meddles wi' me!' he spat. 'That's my motto.'

'Aye,' said Rebus, 'and you know the Latin for it too. Did you get a kick that night in Mary King's Close?'

'You're crazy.'

'We're the police,' Abernethy said lazily. 'We're paid to be crazy, what's your excuse?'

Bothwell considered the two of them and sat down slowly. 'I don't know anyone called Davey Soutar. I don't know anything about bombs or Sword and Shield or Mary King's Close.'

'I didn't say Sword and Shield,' said Rebus. 'I just said The Shield.'

Bothwell sat in silence.

'But now you mention it, I see your father the minister was in the original Sword and Shield. His name's on file. It was an offshoot of the Scottish National Party; I don't suppose you know anything about it?'

'Nothing.'

'No? Funny, you were in the youth league.'

'Was I?'

'Did your dad get you interested in Ulster?'

Bothwell shook his head slowly. 'You never stop, do you?'

'Never,' said Rebus.

The door opened. The two bouncers from the main door stood there, hands clasped in front of them, legs apart. They'd obviously been to the bouncers' school of etiquette. And, just as obviously, Bothwell had summoned them with some button beneath the lip of his desk.

'Escort these bastards off the premises,' he ordered.

'Nobody escorts me anywhere,' said Abernethy, 'not unless she's wearing a tight skirt and I've paid for her.' He got up and faced the bouncers. One of them made to take his arm. Abernethy grabbed the bouncer at the wrist and twisted hard. The man fell to his knees. There wasn't much room for the other bouncer, and he looked undecided. He was still looking blank as Rebus pulled him into the room and threw him over the desk. Bothwell was smothered beneath him. Abernethy let the other bouncer go and followed Rebus outside with a real spring in his step, breathing deeply of Edinburgh's warm summer air. 'I enjoyed that.'

'Aye, me too, but do you think it worked?'

'Let's hope so. We're making liabilities of them. I get the feeling they're going to implode.'

Well, that was the plan. Every good plan, however, had a fall-back. Theirs was Big Ger Cafferty.

'Is it too late to grab a curry?' Abernethy added.

'You're not in the sticks now. The night's young.'

But as Rebus led Abernethy towards a good curry house, he was thinking about liabilities and risks ... and dreading tomorrow's showdown.

# 28

The day dawned bright, with blue skies and a breeze which would soon warm. It was expected to stay good all day, with a clear night for the fireworks. Princes Street would be bursting at the seams, but it was quiet as DCI Kilpatrick drove along it. He was an early riser, but even he had been caught by Rebus's wake-up call.

The industrial estate was quiet too. After being cleared by the guard on the gate, he drove up to the warehouse and parked next to Rebus's car. The car was empty, but the warehouse door stood open. Kilpatrick went inside.

'Morning, sir.' Rebus was standing in front of the HGV.

'Morning, John. What's with all the cloak and dagger?'

'Sorry about that, sir. I hope I can explain.'

'I hope so too, going without breakfast never puts me in the best of moods.'

'It's just that there's something I had to tell you, and this seems as quiet a place as any.'

'Well, what is it?'

Rebus had started walking around the lorry, Kilpatrick following him. When they were at the back of the vehicle, Rebus pulled on the lever and swung the door wide open. On top of the boxes inside sat Abernethy.

'You didn't warn me it was a party,' Kilpatrick said.

'Here, let me help you up.'

Kilpatrick looked at Rebus. 'I'm not a pensioner.' And he pulled himself into the back, Rebus clambering after him.

'Hello again, sir,' Abernethy said, putting his hand out

for Kilpatrick to shake. Kilpatrick folded his arms instead.

'What's this all about, Abernethy?'

But Abernethy shrugged and nodded towards Rebus.

'Notice anything, sir?' said Rebus. 'I mean, about the load.'

Kilpatrick put on a thoughtful face and looked around. 'No,' he said finally, adding: 'I never was one for party games.'

'No games, sir. Tell me, what happens to all this stuff if we're not going to use it in a sting operation?'

'It goes to be destroyed.'

'That's what I thought. And the papers go with it, don't they?'

'Of course.'

'But since the stuff has been under our stewardship, those papers will be from the City of Edinburgh Police?'

'I suppose so. I can't see —'

'You will, sir. When the stuff came here, there was a record with it, detailing what it was and how much of it there was. But we replace that record with one of our own, don't we? And if the first record goes astray, well, there's always *our* record.' Rebus tapped one of the boxes. 'There's less here than there was.'

'What?'

Rebus lifted the lid from a crate. 'When you showed me around before with Smylie, there were more AK 47s than this.'

Kilpatrick looked horrified. 'Are you sure?' He looked inside the crate.

'Yet the current inventory shows twelve AK 47s, and that's how many are here.'

'Twelve,' Abernethy confirmed, as Rebus got out the sheet of paper and handed it to Kilpatrick.

'Then you must have made a mistake,' said Kilpatrick.

'No, sir,' said Rebus, 'with all due respect. I've checked with Special Branch. They hold a record of the original delivery. Two dozen AK 47s. The other dozen are missing. There's other stuff too: a rocket launcher, some of the ammo...'

'You see, sir,' said Abernethy, 'normally nobody would bother to backtrack, would they? The stuff is going for disposal, and there's a chitty says everything checks. No one ever looks back down the line.'

'But it's impossible.' Kilpatrick still held the sheet of paper, but he wasn't looking at it.

'No, sir,' said Rebus, 'it's dead easy. *If* you can alter the record. You're in charge of this load, it's your name on the sheet.'

'What are you saying?'

Rebus shrugged and slipped his hands into his pockets. 'The surveillance on the American, that was your operation too, sir.'

'As requested by you, Inspector.'

Rebus nodded. 'And I appreciated it. It's just, I can't understand a few things. Such as how your trusted team from Glasgow didn't spot me and a friend of mine having a drink with Clyde Moncur and his wife.'

'What?'

'The details you gave me, sir, there was nothing about that. I didn't think there would be. That's partly why I did it. Nor was there any mention of a meeting between Clyde Moncur and Frankie Bothwell. All your men say is that Moncur and his wife go for walks, see the sights, act the perfect tourists. But there *is* no surveillance, is there? I know because I put a couple of colleagues onto Moncur myself. You see, I knew something was up the minute I met Inspector Abernethy here.'

'You put an unofficial surveillance on Moncur?'

'And I've the pictures to prove it.' On cue, Abernethy rustled a white paper bag, one side of which was clear cellophane. The black and white photos could be seen inside.

'There's even one here,' Abernethy said, 'of you meeting Moncur in Gullane. Maybe you were talking about golf?'

'You must have promised The Shield some of these arms before I came along,' Rebus went on. 'You brought me into the investigation to keep an eye on me.'

'But why would I bring you here in the first place?'

'Because Ken Smylie asked you to. And you didn't want to raise *his* suspicions. There's not much gets past Ken.'

Rebus had expected Kilpatrick to deflate, but he didn't, if anything he grew bigger. He plunged his hands into his jacket pockets and slid his shoulders back. His face showed no emotion, and he wasn't about to talk.

'We've been looking at you for a while,' Abernethy continued. 'Those Prod terrorists you let slip through your fingers in Glasgow ...' He shook his head slowly. 'That's one reason we moved you from Glasgow, to see if you could still operate. When news of the six-pack reached me, I knew you were still lending a hand to your friends in The Shield. They've always relied on inside help, and by Christ they've been getting it.'

'You thought it was a drugs hit,' Kilpatrick argued.

Abernethy shrugged. 'I'm a good actor. When you seconded Inspector Rebus, I knew it was because you saw him as a threat. You needed to keep an eye on him. Luckily he came to the same conclusion.' Abernethy peered into the bag of photographs. 'And here's the result.'

'Funny, sir,' said Rebus, 'when we were talking about Sword and Shield, the old Sword and Shield I mean, you never mentioned that you were a member.'

'What?'

'You didn't think there were any records, but I managed to track some down. Back in the early '60s you were in their youth league. Same time Frankie Bothwell was. Like I say, funny you never mentioned it.'

'I didn't think it was relevant.'

'Then I was attacked by someone trying to put me out

293

of the game. The man was a pro, I'd swear to that, a street-slugger with a cutthroat razor. He had a Glasgow accent. You must have met a few hard men during your stint over there.'

'You think I hired him?'

'With all respect,' Rebus locked eyes with Kilpatrick, 'you must be off your rocker.'

'Madness comes from the head, not the blood, not the heart.' Kilpatrick rested against a box. 'You think you can trust Abernethy, John? Well, good luck to you. I'm waiting.'

'For what?'

'Your next gimmick.' He smiled. 'If you wanted to make a case against me, we wouldn't be meeting like this. You know as well as I do that a filing mistake and an innocent photograph don't make a case. They don't make anything.'

'You could be kicked off the force.'

'With my record? No, I might retire early, say on health grounds, but no one's going to sack me. It doesn't happen that way, I thought two experienced officers would know that. Now answer me this, Inspector Rebus, you set up an illicit surveillance: how much trouble can that get *you* in? With your record of insubordination and bucking the rules, we could kick you off the force for not wiping your arse properly.' He rose from the box and walked to the edge of the lorry, then dropped to the ground and turned towards them. 'You haven't proved anything to me. If you want to try your act with someone else, be my guests.'

'You cold bastard,' Abernethy said. He made it sound like a compliment. He walked to the edge of the lorry and faced Kilpatrick, then slowly began to pull his shirt out from his trousers. He lifted it up, showing bare flesh and sticking plasters and wires. He was miked up. Kilpatrick stared back at him.

'Anything to add, sir?' Abernethy said. Kilpatrick turned and walked away. Abernethy turned to Rebus. 'Quiet all of a sudden, isn't it?'

Rebus leapt from the lorry and walked briskly to the door. Kilpatrick was getting into his car, but stopped when he saw him.

'Three murders so far,' Rebus said. 'Including a police officer, one of your own. That's a madness of the blood.'

'That wasn't me,' Kilpatrick said quietly.

'Yes, it was,' Rebus said. 'There'd be none of it without you.'

'I don't know how they got to Calumn Smylie.'

'They hack into computers. Your secretary uses one.'

Kilpatrick nodded. 'And there's a file on the operation in the computer.' He shook his head slowly. 'Look, Rebus...' But Kilpatrick stopped himself. He shook his head again and got into the car, shutting the door.

Rebus bent down to the driver's-side window, and waited for Kilpatrick to wind it down.

'Abernethy's told me what it's about, why the loyalists are suddenly arming themselves. It's Harland and Wolff.' This being a shipyard, one of the biggest employers in the province, its workforce predominantly Protestant. 'They think it's going to be wound up, don't they? The loyalists are taking it as a symbol. If the British government lets Harland and Wolff go to the wall, then it's washing its hands of the Ulster Protestants. Basically, it's pulling out.' Hard to know whether Kilpatrick was listening. He was staring through the windscreen, hands on the steering wheel. 'At which point,' Rebus went on anyway, 'the loyalists are set to explode. You're arming them for civil war. But worse than that, you've armed Davey Soutar. He's a walking anti-personnel mine.'

Kilpatrick's voice was hard, unfeeling. 'Soutar's not my problem.'

'Frankie Bothwell can't help. Maybe he could control Soutar once upon a time, but not now.'

'There's only one person Soutar respects,' Kilpatrick said quietly, 'Alan Fowler.'

'The UVF man?'

Kilpatrick had started the engine.

'Wait a minute,' said Rebus. As Kilpatrick moved off, Rebus kept a grip of the window-frame. Kilpatrick turned to him.

'Nine tonight,' he said. 'At the Gar-B.'

Then he sped out of the compound.

Abernethy was just behind Rebus.

'What was he telling you?' he asked.

'Nine o'clock at the Gar-B.'

'Sounds like a nice little trap to me.'

'Not if we take the cavalry.'

'John,' Abernethy said with a grin, 'I've got all the cavalry we'll need.'

Rebus turned to face him. 'You've been playing me like a pinball machine, haven't you? That first time we met, all that stuff you told me about computers being the future of crime. You knew back then.'

Abernethy shrugged. He pulled up his shirt again and started to pull off the wires. 'All I did was point you in the general direction. Look at the way I got on your tits that first time. *That's* how I knew I could trust you. I nettled you and you let it show. You'd nothing to hide.' He nodded to himself. 'Yes, I knew, I've known for a long time. Proving it was the bugger.' Abernethy looked at the compound gates. 'But Kilpatrick's got enemies, remember that, not just you and me any more.'

'What do you mean?'

But Abernethy just winked and tapped his nose. 'Enemies,' he said.


Rebus had pulled Siobhan Clarke off the Moncur surveillance and put her on to Frankie Bothwell. But Frankie Bothwell had disappeared. She apologised, but Rebus only shrugged. Holmes had kept with Clyde Moncur, but Moncur and his wife were off on some bus tour, a two-day trip to the Highlands. Moncur could always get off the bus and double back, but Rebus discontinued the tail anyway.

'You seem a bit glum, sir,' Siobhan Clarke told him. Maybe she was right. The world seemed upside down. He'd seen bad cops before, of course he had. But he had never before seen anything like Kilpatrick's lack of an explanation or a decent defence. It was as if he didn't feel he needed one, as if he'd just been doing the right thing; in the wrong way perhaps, but the right thing all the same.

Abernethy had told him how deep the suspicions went, how long they'd been accumulating. But it was hard to investigate a policeman who, on the surface, seemed to be doing nearly everything right. Investigation required co-operation, and the co-operation wasn't there. Until Rebus had come along.

At the Gar-B lock-ups, outside the blocks of flats, police and Army experts were opening doors, just in case the stolen cache was inside one of the garages. Door to door inquiries were going on, trying to pin down Davey's friends, trying to get someone to talk or to admit they were hiding him. Meantime, Jamesie MacMurray was already being charged. But they were minnows, their flesh not enough to merit the hook. Kilpatrick, too, had disappeared. Rebus had phoned Ormiston and found that the CI hadn't returned to his office, and no one answered at his home.

Holmes and Clarke returned from the warrant search of Soutar's home, Holmes toting a plain cardboard box, obviously not empty. Holmes put the box on Rebus's desk.

'Let's start,' Holmes said, 'with a jar of acid, carefully concealed under Soutar's bed.'

'His mother says he never lets her in to clean his room,' Clarke explained. 'He's got a padlock on the door to prove it. We had to break the lock. His mum wasn't best pleased.'

'She's a lovely woman, isn't she?' said Rebus. 'Did you meet the dad?'

'He was at the bookie's.'

'Lucky for you. What else have you got?'

'Typhoid probably,' Holmes complained. 'The place was like a Calcutta rubbish tip.'

Clarke dipped in and pulled out a few small polythene bags; everything in the box had been wrapped first and labelled. 'We've got knives, most of them illegal, one still with what looks like dried blood on it.' Some of it Calumn Smylie's blood, Rebus didn't doubt. She dipped in again. 'Mogadon tablets, about a hundred of them, and some unopened cans of cola and beer.'

'The Can Gang?'

Clarke nodded. 'Looks like it. There are wallets, credit cards ... it'll take us two minutes to check. Oh, and we found this little booklet.' She held it up for him. It was poorly Xeroxed, with its A4-sized sheets folded in half and stapled. Rebus read the title.

'*The Total Anarchy Primer.* Wonder who gave him this?'

'Looks like it's been translated from another language, maybe German. Some of the words they couldn't find the English for, so they've left them in the original.'

'Some primer.'

'It tells you how to make bombs,' said Clarke, 'in case you were wondering. Mostly fertiliser bombs, but there's a section on timers and detonators, just in case you found yourself with any plastique.'

'The perfect Christmas gift. Are they checking the bedroom for traces?'

Holmes nodded. 'They were at it when we left.'

Rebus nodded. A special forensic unit had been sent in to test for traces of explosive materials. The same unit had been working at the MacMurray lock-up. They knew now that the garage had held a quantity of plastic explosive, probably Semtex. But they couldn't say how much. Usually, as one of the team had explained, Semtex was quite difficult to prove, being colourless and fairly scentless. But it looked like Soutar had been playing with his toys, unwrapping at least one of the packages the better to have a look at it. Traces had been left on the surface of the workbench.

'Were there detonators in the cache?' Rebus asked. 'That's the question.'

Holmes and Clarke looked at one another.

'A rhetorical one,' Rebus added.

# 29

The city was definitely coming out to play.

It was the start of September, and therefore the beginning of that slow slide into chill autumn and long dark winter. The Festival was winding down for another year, and everyone was celebrating. It was on days like this that the city, so often submerged like Atlantis or some subaqua Brigadoon, bubbled to the surface. The buildings seemed less dour and the people smiled, as though cloud and rain were unknowns.

Rebus might have been driving through a thunderstorm for all the notice he took. He was a hunter, and hunters didn't smile. Abernethy had just admitted being Marie's anonymous caller, the one who'd put her on to Calumn Smylie.

'You knew you were putting his life in danger?' Rebus asked.

'Maybe I thought I was saving it.'

'How did you know about Mairie anyway? I mean, how did you know to contact *her*?'

Abernethy just smiled.

'You sent me that stuff about Clyde Moncur, didn't you?'

'Yes.'

'You could have warned me what I was getting into.'

'You were more effective the way you were.'

'I've been a walking punch-bag.'

'But you're still here.'

'I bet you'd lose a lot of sleep if I wasn't.'

The sun had finally given up. The street lights were on. There were a lot of people on the streets tonight. Hogmanay apart, it was the city's biggest night of the year. The traffic was all headed into town, where most of the parking spaces had been grabbed hours ago.

'Families,' Rebus explained, 'on their way to the fireworks.'

'I thought *we* were on our way to the fireworks,' Abernethy said, smiling again.

'We are,' said Rebus quietly.

There were never signposts to places like the Gar-B, the inference being that if you wanted to go there, you must already know the place. People didn't just visit on a whim. Rebus took the slip-road past the gable end – ENJOY YOUR VISIT TO THE GAR-B – and turned into the access road.

'Nine o'clock, he said.'

Abernethy checked his watch. 'Nine it is.'

But Rebus wasn't listening. He was watching a van roaring towards them. The road was barely wide enough for two vehicles, and the van driver didn't seem to be paying much attention. He was crouched down, eyes on his wing mirror. Rebus slammed on the brakes and the horn and whipped the steering wheel around. The rust bucket slew sideways like it was on ice. That was the problem with bald tyres.

'Out!' Rebus called. Abernethy didn't need telling twice. The driver had finally seen them. The van was skidding to an uncertain stop. It hit the driver's side door, shuddered, and was still. Rebus pulled open the van door and hauled out Jim Hay. He'd heard of people looking white as a sheet, white as a ghost, but Jim Hay looked whiter than that. Rebus held him upright.

'He's gone off his fucking head!' Hay yelled.

'Who has?'

'Soutar.' Hay was looking behind him, back down the

road which curled snake-like into the Gar-B. 'I'm only the delivery man, not this ... not this.'

Dusting himself off, Abernethy joined them. He'd lost the knees out of his denims.

'You deliver the stuff,' Rebus was saying to Hay, 'the explosives, the arms?'

Hay nodded.

Yes, the perfect delivery man, in his little theatre van, all boxes and props, costumes and sets, guns and grenades. Delivered east coast to west, where another connection would be made, another switch.

'Hold him,' Rebus ordered. Abernethy looked like he didn't understand. 'Hold him!'

Then Rebus let Jim Hay go, got into the van, and reversed it out of his car's bodywork and back into the Gar-B. When he reached the car park, he turned the van and bumped it at speed onto the grass, heading for the youth centre.

There was nobody about, not a soul. The door-to-door had been wound up for the day, having yielded nothing. The Gar-B simply didn't speak to the 'polis'. It was a rule of life, like remembering to breathe. Rebus was breathing hard. The garages he passed had been searched and declared safe, though one of them had contained a suspicious number of TV sets, videos, and camcorders, and another showed evidence of sniffed glue and smoked crack.

No neighbours were out discussing the day's events. There was even silence at the community centre. He doubted the Gar-B tribe were the kind to be attracted to a firework display ... not normally.

The doors were open, so Rebus walked in. A bright trail of blood led in an arc across the floor from the stage to the far wall. Kilpatrick was slumped against the wall, almost but not quite sitting up. He'd removed his necktie halfway across the room, maybe to help him breathe. He was still alive, but he'd lost maybe a pint of blood already. When Rebus crouched down beside him, Kilpatrick clutched at him with wet red fingers, leaving a bloody handprint on Rebus's shirt. His other hand was protecting his own stomach, source of the wound.

'I tried to stop him,' he whispered.

Rebus looked around him. 'Was the stuff hidden here?'

'Under the stage.'

Rebus looked at the small stage, a stage he'd sat on and stood on.

'Hay's gone to fetch an ambulance,' Kilpatrick said.

'He was running like a rabbit,' Rebus said.

Kilpatrick forced a smile. 'I thought he might.' He licked his lips. They were cracked, edged with white like missed toothpaste. 'They've gone with him.'

'Who? His gang?'

'They'll follow Davey Soutar to hell. He made those phone calls. He told me so. Just before he did this.' Kilpatrick tried to look down at his stomach. The effort was almost too much for him.

Rebus stood up. Blood flushed around his system, making him dizzy. 'The Fireworks? He's going to blow up the Fireworks?' He ran out of the hall and into the nearest tower block. The first front door he came to, he kicked it in. It took him three good hits. Then he marched into the living room, where two terrified pensioners were watching TV.

'Where's your phone?'

'We dinnae have one,' the man eventually said.

Rebus walked back out and kicked in the next door. Same procedure. This time the single mother with the two shrieking kids did have a phone. She hurled abuse at Rebus as he pressed the buttons.

'I'm the police,' he told her. It made her angrier still. She quietened, though, when she heard Rebus order an ambulance. She was shushing the kids as he made his second call.

'It's DI Rebus here,' he said. 'Davey Soutar and his gang

are on their way to Princes Street with a load of high explosives. We need that area *sealed*.'

He half-smiled an apology as he left the flat and half-ran back to the van. Still nobody had come to investigate, to see what all the noise and the fuss were. Like Edinburghers of old, they could become invisible to trouble. In olden times, they'd hidden in the catacombs below the Castle and the High Street. Now they just shut their windows and turned up the TV. They were Rebus's employers, whose taxes paid his salary. They were the people he was paid to protect. He felt like telling them all to go to hell.

When he got back to his car, Abernethy was standing there with Jim Hay, not a clue what to do with him. Rebus yanked the steering wheel and pulled the van onto the grass.

'An ambulance is on its way,' he said, trying to pull open his car door. It groaned like something in a scrapyard crusher, but eventually gave, and he squeezed through the gap into his seat, brushing aside the glass chippings.

'Where are you going?' Abernethy asked.

'Stay here with him,' Rebus said, starting the car and reversing back up the access road.

The Glenlivet Fireworks: every year there was a firework display from the Castle ramparts, accompanied by a chamber orchestra in Princes Street Gardens' bandstand and watched by crowds in the Gardens and packed into Princes Street itself. The concert usually started around ten-fifteen, ten-thirty. It was now ten o'clock on a balmy dry evening. The area would be full to bursting.

Wild Davey Soutar. He and his kind detested the Festival. It took away from them *their* Edinburgh and propped something else in its place, a façade of culture which they didn't need and couldn't understand. There was no underclass in Edinburgh, they'd all been pushed out into schemes on the city boundaries. Isolated, exiled, they had every right to resent the city centre with its tourist traps and temporary playtime.

Not that that's why Soutar was doing it. Rebus thought Soutar had some simpler reasons. He was showing off, he was showing even his elders in The Shield that they couldn't control him, that *he* was the boss. He was, in fact, quite mad.

'Make a run for it, Davey,' Rebus said to himself. 'Get a grip. Use your sense. Just ...' But he couldn't think of the words.

He didn't often drive fast; dangerously ... almost never. It was car smashes that did it, being on the scene at car smashes. You saw heads so messed up you didn't know which side was the face until it opened its mouth to scream.

Nevertheless, Rebus drove back into town like he was attempting the land-speed record.

His car seemed to sense the absolute urgency, the necessity, and for once didn't black out or choke up. It whined its own argument, but kept moving.

Princes Street and the three main streets leading down to it from George Street had been cordoned off as a matter of course, stopping traffic from coming anywhere near the thousands of spectators. On a night like this, there'd be quarter of a million souls watching the display, the majority of them in and around Princes Street. Rebus took his car as far as he could, then simply stopped in the middle of the road, got out, and ran. Police were setting up new barriers. Lauderdale and Flower were there. He made straight for them.

'Any news?' he spat.

Lauderdale nodded. 'There was a convoy of cars on West Coates, running red lights, travelling at speed.'

'That's them.'

'We've put up a diversion to bring them here.'

Rebus looked around, wiping sweat from his eyes. The

street was lined with shops at street level, offices above. Uniformed officers were moving civilians out of the area. An Army vehicle sat roadside.

'Bomb disposal,' Lauderdale explained. 'Remember, we've been ready for this.'

More barriers were being erected, and Rebus saw van doors open and half a dozen police marksmen appear, their chests covered by black body armour.

'Is Kilpatrick okay?' Lauderdale asked.

'Should be, depends on the ambulance.'

'How much stuff does Soutar have?'

Rebus tried to remember. 'It's not just explosives, he's probably toting AK 47s, pistols and ammo, maybe grenades . . .'

'Christ almighty.' Lauderdale spoke into his radio. 'Where are they?'

The radio crackled to life. 'Can't you see them yet?'

'No.'

'They're right in front of you.'

Rebus looked up. Yes, here they came. Maybe they were expecting a trap, maybe not. Whichever, it was still a suicide mission. They might get in, but they weren't going to get out.

'Ready!' Lauderdale called. The marksmen checked their guns and pointed them ahead. There were police cars behind the barriers. The uniforms had stopped moving people away. They wanted to watch. More onlookers were arriving all the time, keen for this preliminary event.

In the lead car, Davey Soutar was alone. He seemed to think about ramming the barricade, then braked hard instead, bringing his car to a stop. Behind him, four other cars slowed and halted. Davey sat frozen in his seat. Lauderdale lifted a megaphone.

'Bring your hands where we can see them.'

The car doors behind Davey were opening. Metal clattered to the ground as guns were thrown down. Some of the

Gar-B started to run for it, others, seeing the armed police, got out slowly with hands held high. Others were awaiting instructions. One of them, a young kid, no older than fourteen, lost his nerve and ran straight for the police lines.

Overhead, the first fireworks burst into brief life with a noise like old-fashioned gunfire and mortar. The sky sizzled, the glow lighting the scene.

At the first noise, most people flinched instinctively. The armed police dropped to a crouch, others spread themselves on the ground. The kid who'd been running towards the barriers started screaming in fright, then fell to his hands and knees.

Behind him, Davey Soutar's car was empty.

He'd shuffled into the passenger seat, opened the door, and made a dash to the pavement. Running low, it took him only seconds to disappear into the mass of pedestrians.

'Did anyone see? Did he have a gun?'

The Army personnel moved in warily on the lead car, while police started rounding up the Gar-B. More weapons were jettisoned. Lauderdale moved in to supervise his men.

And John Rebus was after Soutar.

The one place there wasn't much of a crowd was George Street: you couldn't see the fireworks from there. So Rebus had little trouble following Soutar. The sky turned from red to green to blue, with small pops and the occasional huge explosion. Each explosion had Rebus squirming, thinking of the bomb disposal unit busy back at Soutar's car. When the wind changed, it carried with it wafts of musical accompaniment from the orchestra in the Gardens. Chase music it wasn't.

Soutar ran with loose energy, almost bouncing. He covered a lot of ground, but it wasn't a straight line. He did a lot of weaving from side to side, covering most of the width of the pavement. Rebus concentrated on closing the gap, moving forwards like he was on rails. His eyes were on Soutar's hands. As long as he could see those hands, see they weren't carrying anything, he was content.

For all Soutar's crazy progress, Rebus was losing ground on the younger man, except when Soutar turned to look back at his pursuer. That's what he was doing when he ran out into the road and bounced off a taxi cab. The cab was on St Andrew's Square. The driver stuck his head out the window, then pulled it in again fast when Soutar drew his gun.

It looked like a service revolver to Rebus. Soutar fired a shot through the cab window, then started running again. He was slower now, with a slouch announcing a damaged right leg.

Rebus glanced in at the cab driver. He'd thrown up all over his knees, but was unhurt.

Give it up, Rebus thought, his lungs on fire. Give it up.

But Soutar kept moving. He ran through the bus station, dodging the single-deckers as they moved in and out of their ranks. The few waiting passengers could see he was armed, and stared in horror as he flew past them, jacket flapping, for all the world like a scarecrow come to life.

Rebus followed him up James Craig Walk, across the top of Leith Street, and into Waterloo Place. Soutar stopped for a moment, as though trying to come to a decision. His right hand still gripped the revolver. He saw Rebus moving steadily in his direction, and dropped to one knee, taking two-handed aim with the revolver. Rebus stepped into a doorway and waited for a shot that didn't come. When he peered out again, Soutar had vanished.

Rebus walked slowly towards where Soutar had been. He was nowhere on the street, but a couple of yards further on was a gateway, and beyond it some steps. The steps led to the top of Calton Hill. Rebus took a final deep breath and accepted the challenge.

The rough steps up to the summit were busy with people climbing and descending. Most of them were young and had been drinking. Rebus couldn't even summon the breath to yell something, 'Stop him' or 'Get out of his way'. He knew if he tried to spit, the stuff would be like paste. All he could do was follow.

At the top, Calton Hill was crowded with people sitting on the grass, all eyes turned towards the Castle. The view would have been breathtaking, had Rebus had any breath to spare. The music was being piped up here too. Smoke drifted south across the city, followed by more tinsel colour and rockets. It was like being the onlooker at a medieval siege. A lot of people were drunk. Some were stoned. It wasn't gunpowder you could smell up here.

Rebus had a good look around. He'd lost Davey Soutar.

There was no street lighting here, and crowds of people, mostly young and dressed in denim. Easy to lose someone.

Too damned easy.

Soutar could be heading down the other side of the hill, or snaking back down the roadway to Waterloo Place. Or he could be hiding amongst people who looked just like him. Except that the night air was chill. Rebus could feel it turning his sweat cold. And Soutar was only wearing a denim jacket.

As a huge firework burst over the Castle, and everyone stared up at the sky and gasped and cheered, Rebus looked for the one person who wasn't watching. The one person with his head down. The one person shivering like he'd never get warm again. He was sitting on the grass verge, next to a couple of girls who were drinking from cans and waving what looked like luminous rubber tubes. The girls had moved away from him a little, so that he looked the way he was: all alone in the world. Behind him on the grass was a gang of bikers, all muscle and gut. They were shouting and swearing, proclaiming hate of the English and all things foreign.

Rebus walked up to Davey Soutar, and Davey Soutar looked up.

And it wasn't him.

This kid was a couple of years younger, strung out on something, his eyes unable to focus.

'Hey,' one of the bikers yelled, 'you trying to pick up my pal?'

Rebus held up his hands. 'My mistake,' he said.

He turned around fast. Davey Soutar was behind him. He'd slipped off his jacket and had wound it around his right arm, all the way down to the wrist and the hand. Rebus knew what was in the hand, disguised now by the grubby denim.

'Okay, pigmeat, let's walk.'

Rebus knew he had to get Soutar away from the crowd. There were probably five bullets still in the revolver. Rebus didn't want any more bodies, not if he could help it.

They walked to the car park. There was a hot-food van doing good business, and a few cars, their drivers and passengers biting into burgers. It was darker here, and quieter. There wasn't much action here.

'Davey,' Rebus said, coming to a stop.

'This as far as you want to go?' Soutar said. He'd turned to face Rebus.

'No point me answering that, Davey, you're in charge now.'

'I've been in charge all along!'

Rebus nodded. 'That's right, skimming without your bosses knowing about it. Planning all this.' He nodded towards the fireworks. 'Could have been quite something.'

Soutar soured his face. 'You couldn't let it go, could you? Kilpatrick knew you were trouble.'

'You didn't have to stab him.' A car was making its way slowly up to the car park from Regent Road. Soutar had his back to it, but Rebus could see it. It was a marked police car, its headlights off.

'He tried to stop me,' Soutar sneered. 'No guts.'

If the music was anything to go by, the fireworks were coming to their climax. Rebus fixed his eyes on Soutar,

310

watching the face turn from gold to green to blue.

'Put the gun away, Davey. It's finished.'

'Not till I say so.'

'Look, enough! Just put it down.'

The police car was at the top of the rise now. Davey Soutar unwound the jacket from his arm and threw it to the ground. A girl at the hot-food van started to scream. Behind Soutar, the police driver switched his headlamps on full-beam, lighting Soutar and Rebus like they were on stage. The passenger door was open, someone leaning out of it. Rebus recognised Abernethy. Soutar pivoted, aiming the gun. It was all the incentive Abernethy needed. The report from his gun was as loud as anything from the Castle. Meantime, the crowd was applauding again, unaware of the drama behind them.

Soutar was knocked backwards, taking Rebus with him. They fell in a heap, Rebus feeling the young man's damp hair brushing his face, his lips. He swore impressively as he pulled himself out from under the suddenly prone, suddenly still figure. Abernethy was pulling the revolver from Soutar's hand, his foot heavy on the youth's wrist.

'No need for that,' Rebus hissed. 'He's dead.'

'Looks like,' said Abernethy, putting away his own gun. 'So here's my story: I saw a flash, heard a bang, and assumed he'd fired. Sound reasonable?'

'Are you authorised to carry that cannon?'

'What do you think?'

'I think you're...'

'As bad as him?' Abernethy raised an eyebrow. 'I don't think so. And hey, don't mention it.'

'What?'

'Saving your fucking life! After that stunt you pulled, leaving me in the Gar-B.' He paused. 'You've got blood on you.'

Rebus looked. There was plenty of blood. 'There goes another shirt.'

'Trust a Jock to make a comment like that.'

The police driver had got out of the car to look, and a useful crowd was growing, now that the fireworks had finished. Abernethy began to check Soutar's pockets. Best get it over with while the body was warm. It was more pleasant that way. When he got to his feet again, Rebus was gone, and so was the car. He looked in disbelief at his driver.

'Not again.'

Yes, again.

# 30

Rebus had the police radio on as he drove. The bomb disposal team were halfway through lifting five small packages from the boot of Soutar's car. The packages had been fitted with detonators, and the Semtex was of advanced age, possibly unstable. There were pistols, automatic and bolt-action rifles too. God knew what he'd been planning to use them for.

The fireworks over, the buildings no longer glowed. They'd returned to their normal sooty hue. Crowds were moving through the streets, making their way home or towards last drinks, late suppers. People were smiling, wrapping arms around themselves to keep warm. They'd all enjoyed a good night out. Rebus didn't like to think about how close the whole night had come to disaster.

He switched on his siren and emergency lights to clear people from the roadway, then pulled past the line of cars in front of him. It was a few minutes before he realised he was shivering. He pulled the damp shirt away from his back and turned up the heating in the car. Not that heat would stop him shivering. He wasn't shivering from cold. He was headed for Tollcross, the Crazy Hose. He was headed for final business.

But when he arrived, siren and lights off, he saw smoke seeping out through the front doors. He pulled his car hard onto the pavement and ran to the doors, kicking them open. It wasn't rule one in the firefighter's manual, but he didn't have much choice. The fire was in the dancehall.

Only the smoke had so far reached the foyer and beyond. There was no one about. A sign on the front door gave abrupt notice that the club was closed 'due to unforeseen circumstances'.

That's me, thought Rebus, I'm unforeseen circumstances.

He headed for Frankie Bothwell's office. Where else was he going to go?

Bothwell was sitting in his chair, prevented from movement by a sudden case of death. His neck flopped over to one side in a way necks shouldn't. Rebus had seen broken necks before. There was bruising on the throat. Strangulation. He hadn't been dead long, his forehead was still warm. But then it was getting warm in the office. It was getting warm everywhere.

The new fire station was at the top of the road. Rebus wondered where the fire crew was.

As he came back into the foyer, he saw that more smoke was belching from the dance hall. The door had been opened. Clyde Moncur was dragging himself into the foyer. He was still alive and wanted to stay that way. Rebus checked Moncur wasn't carrying a gun, then got hold of him by the neck of his jacket and hauled him across the floor. Moncur was trying hard to breathe. He was having a little trouble. He felt light as Rebus dragged him. He kicked open the doors and deposited Moncur at the top of the steps.

Then he went in again.

Yes, the blaze had started here, here in the dance hall. Flames had taken control of the walls and ceiling. All Bothwell's gewgaws and furnishings were melting or turning to ash. The carpet in the seating area had caught. The bottles of alcohol hadn't exploded yet, but they would. Rebus looked around, but couldn't see much. The smoke was too thick, there was too much of it. He wrapped his handkerchief around his face, but even so he couldn't stop coughing. He could hear a rhythmic thumping sound coming from somewhere. Somewhere up ahead.

It was the little self-contained box where the DJ sat, over beyond the stage. There was someone in there now. He tried the door. It was locked, so sign of a key. He took a few steps back so he could run at it.

Then the door flew open. Rebus recognised the Ulsterman, Alan Fowler. He's used his head to butt the door open, his arms being tied firmly to the back of a chair. They were still tied to the chair as, head low, he came barrelling from the box. He caught Rebus a blow to the stomach and Rebus went down. Rebus rolled and came to his knees, but Fowler was up too, and he was blind mad. For all he knew, it was Rebus who was trying to roast him. He butted Rebus again, this time in the face. It was a sore one, but Rebus had ridden a Glasgow Kiss before. The blow caught him on his cheek.

The power of it snapped Rebus's head back, sending him staggering. Fowler was like a bull, the chair legs sticking up like swords from his back. Now that he was more or less upright, he went for Rebus with his feet. One caught Rebus on his damaged ear, tearing it, sending a white jab of pain bouncing through his brain. That gave Fowler time for another kick, and this one was going to shatter Rebus's knee ... Until a blow in the face with an empty bottle knocked him sideways. Rebus looked up to see his saviour, his knight in shining armour. Big Ger Cafferty was still wearing his funeral suit and open shirt. He was busy making sure Fowler was down and out. Then he took one look at Rebus, and produced the hint of a smile, looking every bit as amused as a butcher who finds the carcass he's working on is still alive.

He spent a precious few seconds, life and death seconds, weighing up his options. Then he slung Rebus's arm over his shoulder and walked with him out of the dance hall, through the foyer, and into the night air, the clean, breathable air. Rebus took in huge gulps of it, falling onto the pavement, sitting there, head bowed, his feet on the road. Cafferty sat down beside him. He seemed to be studying his own hands. Rebus knew why, too.

And now the fire engines were arriving, men leaping out of cabs, doing things with hoses. One of them complained about the police car. The keys were in the ignition, so the fireman backed it up.

At last Rebus could speak. 'You did that?' he asked. It was a stupid question. Hadn't he given Cafferty nearly all the information he'd needed?

'I saw you going in,' Cafferty said, his voice raw. 'You were gone a long time.'

'You could have let me die.'

Cafferty looked at him. 'I didn't come in for *you*. I came in to stop you bringing out that bastard Fowler. As it is, Moncur's done a runner.'

'He can't run far.'

'He better try. He knows I won't give up.'

'You knew him, didn't you? Moncur, I mean. He's an old pal of Alan Fowler's. When Fowler was UVF, the UVF laundered money using your salmon farm. Moncur bought the salmon with his good US dollars.'

'You never stop.'

'It's my business.'

'Well,' said Cafferty, glancing back at the club, 'this was business, too. Only, sometimes you have to cut a few corners. I know *you* have.'

Rebus was wiping his face. 'Problem is, Cafferty, when you cut a corner, it bleeds.'

Cafferty studied him. There was blood on Rebus's ear, sweat cloying his hair. Davey Soutar's blood still spattered his shirt, mixed now with smoke. And Kilpatrick's handprint was still there. Cafferty stood up.

'Not thinking of going anywhere?' Rebus said.

'You going to stop me?'

'You know I'll try.'

A car drew up. In it were Cafferty's men, the two from the kirkyard plus weasel-face. Cafferty walked to the car. Rebus was still sitting on the pavement. He got up slowly now, and walked towards the police car. He heard Cafferty's car door shutting, and looked at it, noting the licence plate. As the car passed him, Cafferty was looking at the road ahead. Rebus opened his own car and got on the radio, giving out the licence number. He thought about starting his engine and giving chase, but just sat there instead, watching the firemen go about their business.

I played it by the rules, he thought. I cautioned him and then I called in. It didn't say in the rules that you had to have a go when there were four of them and only one of you.

Yes, he'd played it by the rules. The good feeling started to wear off after only minutes, and damned few minutes at that.


They finally picked Clyde Moncur up at a ferry port. Special Branch in London were dealing with him. Abernethy was dealing with him. Before he'd left, Rebus had asked a simple question.

'Will it happen?'

'Will what happen?'

'Civil war.'

'What do you think?'

So much for that. The story was simple. Moncur was visiting town to see how the money from US Shield was being spent. Fowler was around to make sure Moncur was happy. The Festival had seemed the perfect cover for Moncur's trip. Maybe Billy had been executed to show the American just how ruthless SaS could be...

In hospital, recovering from his stab wounds, DCI Kilpatrick was smothered to death with his pillow. Two of his ribs had been cracked from the weight of his attacker pressing down on him.

'Must've been the size of a grizzly,' Dr Curt announced.

'Not many grizzlies about these days,' said Rebus.

He phoned the Procurator Fiscal's office, just to check on Caro Rattray. After all, Cafferty had spoken of her. He just wanted to know she was okay. Maybe Cafferty was out there tying up a lot of loose ends. But Caro had gone.

'What do you mean?'

'Some private practice in Glasgow offered her a partnership. It's a big step up, she grabbed it, anyone would.'

'Which office is it?'

Funny, it was the office of Cafferty's own lawyers. It might mean something or nothing. After all, Rebus *had* given Cafferty some names. Mairie Henderson had gone down to London to try to follow up the Moncur story. Abernethy phoned Rebus one night to say he thought she was terrific.

'Yes,' said Rebus, 'you'd make a lovely couple.'

'Except she hates my guts.' Abernethy paused. 'But she might listen to you.'

'Spit it out.'

'Just don't tell her too much, all right? Remember, Jump Cantona will take most of the credit anyway, and wee Mairie's been paid upfront. She doesn't *have* to bust a gut. Most of what she'd say wouldn't get past the libel lawyers and the Official Secrets Act anyway.'

Rebus had stopped listening. 'How do you know about Jump Cantona?' He could almost hear Abernethy easing his feet up onto the desk, leaning back in his chair.

'The FBI have used Cantona before to put out a story.'

'And you're in with the FBI?'

'I'll send them a report.'

'Don't cover yourself with too much glory, Abernethy.'

'You'll get a mention, Inspector.'

'But not star billing. That's how you knew about Mairie, isn't it? Cantona told the FBI? It's how you had all the stuff on Clyde Moncur to hand?'

'Does it matter?'

Probably not. Rebus broke the connection anyway.

He shopped for a coming home meal, pushing the trolley around a supermarket close to Fettes HQ. He wouldn't be going back to Fettes. He'd phoned his farewell to Ormiston and told him to tell Blackwood to cut off his remaining strands of hair and be done with it.

'He'd have a seizure if I told him that,' said Ormiston. 'Here, what about the Chief? You don't think...?'

But Rebus had rung off. He didn't want to talk about Ken Smylie, didn't want to think about it. He knew as much as he needed to. Kilpatrick had been on the fringe; he was more useful to The Shield that way. Bothwell was the executioner. He'd killed Billy Cunningham and he'd ordered the deaths of Millie Docherty and Calumn Smylie. Soutar had done his master's bidding in both cases, except Millie had proved messy, and Soutar had left her where he'd killed her. Bothwell must have been furious about that, but of course Davey Soutar had other things on his mind, other plans. Bigger things.

Rebus bought the makings for the meal and added bottles of rosé champagne, malt whisky and gin to the trolley. A mile and a half to the north, the shops on the Gar-B estate would be closing for the evening, pulling down heavy metal shutters, fixing padlocks, double-checking alarm systems. He paid with plastic at the check-out and drove back up the hill to Oxford Terrace. Curiously, the rust bucket was sounding healthier these days. Maybe that knock from Hay's van had put something back into alignment. Rebus had replaced the glass, but was still debating the door-frame.

At the flat, Patience was waiting for him, back from Perth earlier than expected.

'What's this?' she said.

'It was meant to be a surprise.' He put down the bags

319

and kissed her. She drew away from him slowly afterwards.

'You look an absolute mess,' she said.

He shrugged. It was true, he'd seen boxers in better shape after fifteen rounds. He'd seen punchbags in better shape.

'So it's over?' she said.

'Finishes today.'

'I don't mean the Festival.'

'I know you don't.' He pulled her to him again. 'It's over.'

'Did I hear a clink from one of those bags?'

Rebus smiled. 'Gin or champagne?'

'Gin and orange.'

They took the bags into the kitchen. Patience got ice and orange juice from the fridge, while Rebus rinsed two glasses. 'I missed you,' she said.

'I missed you, too.'

'Who else do I know who tells awful jokes?'

'Seems a while since I told a joke. It's a while since I heard one.'

'Well, my sister told me one. You'll love it.' She arched back her head, thinking. 'God, how does it go?'

Rebus unscrewed the top from the gin bottle and poured liberally.

'Whoah!' Patience said. 'You don't want us getting mortal.'

He splashed in some orange. 'Maybe I do.'

She kissed him again, then pulled away and clapped her hands. 'Yes, I've got it now. There's this octopus in a restaurant, and it's –'

'I've heard it,' said Rebus, dropping ice into her glass.

All Orion/Phoenix titles are available at your local bookshop or from the following address:

Mail Order Department
Littlehampton Book Services
FREEPOST BR535
Worthing, West Sussex, BN13 3BR
*telephone* 01903 828503, *facsimile* 01903 828802
*e-mail* MailOrders@lbsltd.co.uk
(Please ensure that you include full postal address details)

Payment can be made either by credit/debit card (Visa, Mastercard, Access and Switch accepted) or by sending a £ Sterling cheque or postal order made payable to *Littlehampton Book Services*.
DO NOT SEND CASH OR CURRENCY.

**Please add the following to cover postage and packing**

*UK and BFPO:*
£1.50 for the first book, and 50p for each additional book to a maximum of £3.50

*Overseas and Eire:*
£2.50 for the first book plus £1.00 for the second book and 50p for each additional book ordered

---

BLOCK CAPITALS PLEASE

*name of cardholder* .............................

*delivery address*
*(if different from cardholder)*

*address of cardholder* .............................

.............................

.............................

.............................

*postcode* .............................

*postcode* .............................

☐ I enclose my remittance for £.............................

☐ please debit my Mastercard/Visa/Access/Switch (delete as appropriate)

card number | | | | | | | | | | | | | | | | | |

expiry date | | | | |   Switch issue no. | | |

signature .............................

*prices and availability are subject to change without notice*